House of Commons, Moulvi S. M. Ali

Hyderabad Affairs

Volume 9

House of Commons, Moulvi S. M. Ali

Hyderabad Affairs
Volume 9

ISBN/EAN: 9783337403638

Printed in Europe, USA, Canada, Australia, Japan

Cover: Foto ©Andreas Hilbeck / pixelio.de

More available books at **www.hansebooks.com**

For Private Circulation.)

HYDERABAD AFFAIRS.

VOL. IX.

ENGLISH NEWSPAPER COMMENTS

ON THE

HYDERABAD (DECCAN) MINING COMPANY,

AND

OTHER MATTERS,

WITH

REPORT OF THE HOUSE OF COMMONS' COMMITTEE.

COMPILED BY

MOULVI SYED MAHDI ALI,

MOHSIN-UL-MULK, BAHADUR,

REVENUE AND FINANCIAL SECRETARY TO

H. H. THE NIZAM'S GOVERNMENT,

HYDERABAD (Deccan).

London:

TALBOT BROTHERS, 81, CARTER LANE, E.C.

1889.

300.—10-89.

TABLE OF CONTENTS.

BRITISH NEWSPAPERS.

DECCAN MINING CONCESSION INQUIRY

AND

HYDERABAD RAILWAY COMPANY.

HYDERABAD AFFAIRS.

EXTRACTS FROM ENGLISH NEWSPAPERS IN 1888

ON

THE HYDERABAD (DECCAN) MINES CONCESSION;

AND OTHER MATTERS.

THE HYDERABAD DEBT.—The arrival at Hyderabad of our minister at Athens, Sir Horace Rumbold, is announced in the Indian papers. It seems that a Commission was appointed some months ago by the Nizam's Government to inquire into the debts of the Hyderabad State. The object of Sir H. Rumbold's visit to the Nizam's capital is to lay before this Commission a claim for a sum of money variously reported as amounting to seven or eight lakhs of rupees. The amount is alleged to be due by the Hyderabad Government to the estate of the late Sir William Rumbold, one of the partners of a firm of bankers which, under the name of William Palmer & Co., was established at Hyderabad in the first quarter of the present century. The submission of Sir H. Rumbold's claim re-opens a disagreeable chapter in the history of our relations with the Hyderabad State. During the time that Sir Charles Metcalfe was resident at Hyderabad the difficulties he had to contend with in his endeavours to right the finances of that State were not lessened by this firm of English bankers. In the interests, as he believed, of the ruler to whose Court he was accredited, Sir Charles Metcalfe wished to limit the operations of Messrs. William Palmer & Co. These operations consisted principally in making advances to the Nizam's Government at high rates of interest. But the firm had powerful connections, and its interests were guarded by no less a person than Lord Hastings, the Governor-General of India. It is probable, therefore, that these interests did not suffer to any great extent from the disapprobation of the Resident, than whom, it is said, the East India Company never had a more able or disinterested servant. Amongst those who now besiege the Hyderabad Debt Commission Sir H. Rumbold appears, with a claim over which the dust of half a century must have gathered.—*Manchester Examiner*, January 13.

The Chief Justice of Hyderabad and the Situation in India.—A representative of a News Agency had an interview on Wednesday with his Honour the Mussulman Chief Justice of Hyderabad, the Nawab Fettah Newaz Jung Mehdi Hassan, who has just reached this country on a pleasure tour, accompanied by his wife. The Chief Justice visited the House of Commons on Friday, at the invitation of the First Lord of the Treasury, and heard the pensions debate, and subsequently the House of Lords, on the invitation of Viscount Cross, Secretary of State for India. He is well known to Indian jurists and scholars, and speaks English with rare purity of accent and diction. It was pointed out to the Nawab that in the newspapers of the 23rd inst. there was a telegram from Calcutta stating that an enthusiastic meeting had been held there by the natives to pass valedictory addresses to Lord Dufferin, and to vote other commemorative resolutions, in which meeting every resolution was carried by acclamation with great enthusiasm. It was stated moreover that some of the leading native organs at Bengal threatened to interrupt the meeting by organising a counter demonstration. The Nawab, having read the telegram, said: The entire native community is at one in its loyalty to the British Government. There is no real difference on this point between the different races of India. Educated people have very strong reason to be loyal, for they may easily see by studying Indian history that India has never been so prosperous and happy as she now is under the British rule. They realize fully the intellectual, social, and political benefits which the country is deriving from English rule. The uneducated classes, on the other hand, experience the more practical and tangible advantages which spring from that rule. In their daily life they are comparatively free from the oppression of the stronger and wealthier, and law, for the first time in the history of India, has given to them power to enjoy the benefits of liberty equally with their superiors. Security, liberty, and political equality are in the very atmosphere of India at present. As for Lord Dufferin, he has been one of the most popular of Indian viceroys; the demonstration of sympathy in Bengal to which the telegram alludes, is, I am convinced, entirely genuine, and I sincerely hope that before he leaves, all India, without exception, will unite in showing gratitude to him. The natives of India are by nature very warm-hearted, and are grateful for all kindnesses shown them. Lord Dufferin has done much for them during his short term of office, and they cannot forget this. With regard to what is said about 'counter demonstrations' and the like, it should be remembered that the class of persons which is responsible for these is not a numerous one. Our educated Bengali fellow-subjects, for whom I have otherwise a high esteem, are getting too radical. It is not Lord Dufferin in particular whom they object to. No viceroy will ever be able to satisfy them. Even if the Queen were pleased to appoint a Bengali viceroy, they would still find cause for dissatisfaction—if not on political, then all the more on personal or social grounds. On the other hand, Lord Dufferin has the admiration and esteem of the whole Mohammedan community, and millions of Hindus appreciate his services. As to the real public opinion in India concerning Lord Dufferin's action on the Central Asian question, continued the Nawab, Lord Dufferin averted an impending war, which would at least have retarded our progress and crippled our finances for many years. By his admirable tact and diplomacy he established close friendly relations with the ruler of the Afghans, and succeeded in setting up for him a boundary which will probably for a long time to come set a limit to Russian aggression. His Lordship devoted great attention to frontier defence—a thing of the utmost importance. In all this he has had our entire sympathy. Nothing can be more absurd than the cry of the native Press that the annexation of Burmah has had an injurious effect on the population of India, and that Lord Dufferin is reverting to Lord Dalhousie's policy. This simply misleads the English public. Burmah was an entirely independent State, as much out of India as Afghanistan is, and under an autocratic king, who behaved badly and tyrannically to his own people and insultingly to the Government of our Empress. From the Mohammedan point of view (we are not yet very Radical in our politics) this involved an insult to every one of us. Politically we are one nation with the English, and an affront offered to the Government of the Queen is felt by all of us. I may say that the troubles which we Mohammedans underwent after the death of the Prophet in attempting to adopt Republican principles of government, convinced us once for all that Royalty, with some sort of constitutional check on the king's power, is the best form of government. We do not in the least recognise the truth or the benefit of modern Radical principles. Our deepest feelings of affection and loyalty are centred in the persons of the Queen and her heirs. Any insult offered to the Throne on which she sits is a national insult. But besides this, it was a wise thing, on grounds of humanity, to annex the country of the barbaric Burmese. In a very short time the people themselves will recognise the blessings which England will bestow upon them. With reference to the feelings of the feudatory Princes in India towards the Government, and the offers of help alluded to in the press, and generally held to be spontaneous, and as to whether it would be wise of the British Government to accept them, the Chief Justice said that the feudatory Princes of India are completely loyal, and with good reason. They have no enemies to fight as formerly, and have time to devote to developing the resources they may expend on fostering the well-being of their countries. They avail themselves of the advices of British representatives, who are, as a rule, disinterested and experienced officials, and who have passed their lives in various branches of the Indian Administration. It is only natural, therefore, that they should make these offers, and it is impolite to doubt their spontaneity. As to the advisability of accepting them, in the Oriental way of looking at things, the Imperial Government should not accept them. No one who is thoroughly acquainted with the Oriental character and manners would advise the Government of India to accept these offers, however spontaneous they may be.—*Leeds Mercury*, March 31, [and many other papers].

When Parliament meets after the Recess, Mr. McLagan will bring before the House a question which will revive a controversy that created great excitement in Anglo-Indian circles a half-century ago. Mr. McLagan's action is to be taken in consequence of the reported settlement of a claim which Sir Horace Rumbold, British Minister at The Hague, preferred during his recent tour in India against the Government of the Nizam of Hyderabad, on the ground that a large sum of money due to his ancestor, Sir William Rumbold, had never been paid. The connection of Sir William Rumbold with the Hyderabad State is historical. He went out to India with Lord Hastings, whose ward he had married, and became a partner in the banking firm of William Palmer and Co., which did a lucrative business at Hyderabad in financing loans for the Nizam's Government at heavy interest. In 1820 a loan for sixty lakhs of rupees, or £600,000, to be paid within six years, was negotiated by Palmer and Co., in order to meet some pressing demands which the Nizam's Government had to meet. The rate of interest to be paid for the accommodation was 18 per cent., and it was further agreed that the partners of the firm should receive a bonus of eight lakhs of rupees. This arrangement was on the eve of being concluded when Sir Thomas (afterwards Lord) Metcalfe, who about this time became Resident of Hyderabad, interposed, acting under the belief that the system by which the Hyderabad Government became so largely indebted to a private firm was a pernicious one, and open to grave objection. In the place of the loan by Palmer and Co., he suggested to the Governor-

General (Lord Hastings) that the East India Company should guarantee a loan at 6 per cent., and that this should be substituted. The Palmer party were, perhaps naturally, highly incensed at Metcalfe's interferences, and their influence with Lord Hastings was strong enough to insure the unfavourable reception of the proposal. An acrimonious correspondence ensued between the Governor-General and the Resident, but the latter stuck to his guns, and eventually the question was settled, as he had suggested, by the raising of a loan under the guarantee of the Company's Government. The bonus to Palmer and Co. under this arrangement was disallowed, and it is believed that Sir Horace Rumbold's claim is based upon the non-payment to his ancestor of his share of this money.—*Yorkshire Post*, March 31.

Secunderabad, Deccan, East Indies.—(Communicated.)—It will be remembered by your readers that a few months ago the Nizam of Hyderabad offered the Indian Government a sum of £200,000 yearly for three years, such sum to be devoted to the national defences. It is in this territory that one of the most important and prospectively valuable mining concessions of modern times has been granted to an English syndicate. Under the powers of the concession the syndicate has the sole right to prospect, explore, examine, and develop any mineral property within the Nizam's dominions. The area to be explored contains over 80,000 square miles, and is known at various places to contain coal, iron, mica, antimony, silver, gold, and diamonds. Of these, coal, mica, and diamond mines are already in operation, and an important find of gold is reported in the vicinity of Raichore, near the southern boundary. The diamond fields are situate at Partial on the south-eastern limit, nearing the Masulipatam coast line. Coal has been found at several points, notably at Singareni, which lies about 120 miles east of Hyderabad. The coalfield at this place is of ten to twelve miles in area, and has two seams of commercial utility, one 6 ft. and the other 30 ft. in thickness. Mica is worked at about twenty miles from the coal-mines. Splendid iron ore is found in close proximity to the coal. A competent staff of Europeans has been engaged by Theo. W. H. Hughes, Esq., of the Geological Survey of India, to direct the coal operations, at the head of which is Mr. E. H. Phillips, late of Newstead Collieries, Notts. Mr. Lowensky, a mineralogist of note, has charge of the diamond mines, and is aided by several experienced men from the Kimberley diamond fields, South Africa. The latter gentleman has also charge of the mica mines, while the general prospecting operations are under the superintendence of Mr. Hughes. The concession runs to the close of 1891, during which time it will, no doubt, be the policy to locate the most promising districts for future working. In my next I purpose going into more practical detail.—*Colliery Guardian*, March 31.

The Mystery of the Nizam's Offer.—To the Editor of the *St. James's Gazette*.—Sir,—Every lover of justice must thank your journal for the persistent way in which it is endeavouring to draw the truth from the obscurity with which the Nizam's offer is still involved. Our prestige in India depends not a little upon our treatment of the Native States, and none deserves our sympathy more than Hyderabad. Everyone who is acquainted with the Nizam knows how warm-hearted and generous he is; hence the greater caution is needed lest his confidence should be abused. That the offer was made is undoubted, but the circumstances which induced it are still shrouded in mystery. It appears evident the Nizam's Prime Minister was only made acquainted with it after the fact, and then nobly supported his master. It is also certain that the Political and Financial Secretary (Mahdi Ali), whose knowledge of ways and means should have entitled him to an opinion, was never consulted. With whom, then, did it originate, and what were the motives? The name of a certain gentleman has been freely used by the Indian papers in connection therewith, and it has been inferred that in some way the shares purchased for his Highness's Government in the Hyderabad Mining Company were to be utilized for the first year's instalment (20 lakhs), the amount being about equivalent: a cover-point to enable this individual to get from the Hyderabad Treasury rupees in exchange for the shares which, it is suggested, came to him in consideration of having obtained the concession for his friends. It would be well for all interests that the matter should be investigated, and the writer of the letter to the *Times* made known. If the individual alluded to has really arrogated to himself such authority as to be able to hoodwink the Nizam, act in defiance of his Minister, bamboozle the Resident, and make a cat's-paw of the newly appointed secretary to his Highness, the sooner he is brought to book the better.—I am, Sir, your obedient servant,—VERITAS VINCIT. April 6th.

HYDERABAD, April 16.—The Nizam has suspended Abdulluk, the Home Secretary, on account of the nature of his connection with the Deccan Mining Company. The suspension has caused great sensation here.—*Times*, April 17.

SIRDAR ABDUL HUK, who, according to a Bombay telegram, has been suspended by his Highness the Nizam for alleged irregularities in connection with mining enterprises, is well known in the City and in London society. He has made several visits to this country on business connected with the Hyderabad Railway, and he was one of the notabilities who represented the Nizam at the Jubilee celebration last summer. When in London the Sirdar always occupied a suite of apartments in the Alexandra Hotel, where he entertained a great many persons of distinction in the social, the commercial, and the political world. One of his guests on the occasion of his last visit was the Duke of Teck, with whom he appeared to be on the most friendly, not to say intimate, terms. As showing the Sirdar's princely hospitality, we may mention that on the day of the Thanksgiving Service in Westminster Abbey, Abdul Huk hired the whole of a well-known hotel in Piccadilly for the reception of his friends, ladies and gentlemen, with their families, giving them a splendid luncheon when the Royal procession had passed. This little entertainment was said at the time to have cost the Sirdar some £2,000. Before his sudden and rapid rise in the favour of the Nizam he was at the head of the Hyderabad police, and upon the recommendation of the Viceroy was made a Companion of the Order of the Indian Empire for assisting Major Daniell, of the British service, in the capture of the notorious dacoit leader, Wassudeo Bulwunt Phadke. It is very possible now that Abdul Huk has been disgraced that we shall hear the true story about the sixty lakhs of rupees lately offered to the British Government by the Nizam. —*Pall Mall Gazette*, April 17.

THE HOME SECRETARY has been suspended—not Mr. Matthews, we hasten to observe, but the Home Secretary of Hyderabad, Abdulluk (or Abdul Huk, as the *Standard* calls him), who is suspected of shady practices in connection with a mining company. The disgraced Minister may thank his stars that he lives in modern times. Not so very long ago his suspension would have been of a different character.—*Globe*, April 17.

Hyderabad.—(From our correspondent.)—Secunderabad, Monday.—Very soon after the departure of Mr. Cordery and the arrival of the Acting Resident, Mr. Arthur Howell, an event has happened to openly disturb the harmony that had apparently existed in the administration of Hyderabad since the new Minister, Asman Jah, acceded to office twelve months ago. The Sirdar Diler Jung ul Mulk, C.I.E., one of the Chief Secretaries of the Nizam's Government, has just been suspended by order of the Minister. It is publicly given out that this step has been taken because the Sirdar had settled, on his own responsibility, the question of the Hyderabad Mines; but the true reason is believed to be the long-standing animosity of the Minister to the Sirdar Diler Jung, who is a man of marked character and ability, but not without powerful enemies both at the Nizam's Court and among the European community here.

(From our correspondent.)—Bombay, Monday.—Abdul Huk, the Hyderabad Home Secretary, has been suspended for suspicious connections with a Mining Company. He is charged with complicity in giving concessions to the value of eight hundred and fifty thousand pounds to London concessionnaires without an equivalent. His career has been a romantic one, and interesting revelations are expected. He was the Nizam's delegate in the recent Jubilee festivities.—*Standard*, April 17.

Hyderabad Affairs. -To the Editor of the *Standard*.—Sir,—In the name of the many friends made by the Sirdar Diler Jung during his two visits to England, I hope you will grant me a little space to ask your readers to suspend their judgment till all the facts are known in connection with the measure just taken against him by the Minister Asman Jah. I feel quite sure that, when the truth comes out, not merely will the Sirdar be cleared from the charge alleged against him, but that it will be found that his main offence in the eyes of the old party in power at Hyderabad consists in his having advocated with, and pressed upon, his young master, the Nizam, a policy of closer accord and more active participation with the English Government in Imperial matters.—I am, Sir, your obedient servant, Veritas.—April 17.

To the Editor of the *Standard*.—Sir,—I am directed by my Board to request you to give insertion to the following: Recent telegrams from India on the subject of the suspension of Abdul Huk Sirdar Diler Jung have given rise to a feeling that the interests of the Company are thereby affected. So far as my Board are aware, everything connected with the grant of the concession had the fullest cognizance of the Government of his Highness the Nizam, and the approval of the Government of India and of the Secretary of State for India. The proceedings connected with that concession are fully set forth in "The Return of Correspondence between the Government of India and the Secretary of State relating to the Concession of Mining Rights in the Deccan" (ordered by the House of Commons to be printed on the 16th September, 1887), and a reference to those papers will afford the best proof that the charge alleged to be brought against Abdul Huk Sirdar Diler Jung of having settled, on his own responsibility, the question of the Hyderabad Mines, is without foundation, and one that cannot affect the interests of the Hyderabad (Deccan) Company, Limited.—I am, Sir, your obedient servant, L. L. Hall, Secretary.

The Hyderabad (Deccan) Company, Limited, London, April 17.

[Mr. Hall's letter was sent to a large number of English papers, and was published by the majority of them.]

Hyderabad Curiosities.—To the Editor of the *St. James's Gazette*.—Sir,—Apropos of your letter signed "Y." respecting the Rumbolds' claim, which clearly states a case which must be answered by some one, there are other "reasons why" which might at the same time be answered. Why was Sir John Gorst paid a lakh of rupees out of the Treasury of Hyderabad in the year 1884, and for what services? Why was Abdul Huk, having been allowed by the late Sir Salar Jung £16,000 as a reward for his services in having floated the railway scheme, yet allowed to draw a cheque for £86,000 as commission thereon? Why was the same gentleman allowed to get the concession of the mining rights of the whole Deccan territory for ninety-nine years, which enabled him and his friends to divide £850,000 among them? Some other "reasons why" remain to be asked, but these may be enough for the present. —I am, Sir, your obedient servant,—WHY. April 17.—*St. James's Gazette*, April 17.

THE MYSTERY OF THE NIZAM'S OFFER.—Too much is heard at present of financial intrigues at Hyderabad—too much and too little. The mystery of the Nizam's offer of 60 lakhs has yet to be cleared up, and the sooner it is done the better; for as to that matter there are some very unpleasant rumours afloat. It is now said that the idea was started when Abdul Huk, a Hyderabad official, was in England last summer; and his account of the matter is, we hear, that it was suggested to him in London by "a Cabinet Minister," whose name is mentioned. This same Cabinet Minister even drafted a letter for the use of the Nizam in making the offer! The draft was taken to Hyderabad, on Abdul Huk's return, when the Nizam was pressed to carry out the suggestion, though he knew, as all his advisers must have known, that he had not the money for the purpose. Possibly he hoped, perhaps he was told, that the offer would not be accepted; the "Cabinet Minister" and his colleagues would be sufficiently pleased if it were made. However that may be, we know the offer was made; and we also know that when it was announced last autumn we were assured by the *Times* that the step taken by the Nizam was "entirely on his own initiative." "Spontaneous" was the term applied to it by a writer in that paper, who declared that he was the "only person in England" acquainted with the Nizam's motive. The story of the Cabinet Minister is not to be believed for a moment; but it is a most mischievous one to set afloat, and we are afraid it was invented to further, or cover, a very bad business.—*St. James's Gazette*, April 18.

THE SUSPENSION OF A HYDERABAD MINISTER.—THE STORY OF THE SIXTY LAKHS.—(FROM OUR OWN CORRESPONDENT.)—MADRAS, Tuesday.—The Sirdar Abdul Huk, who has been suspended from the office of Secretary to the Nizam of Hyderabad, at the instance of Mr. Howell, *locum tenens* of Mr. Cordery, the Resident, who is at present in Turkey, will be expected to give an account of his share in promoting, through alleged misrepresentations, the Nizam's singular offer of sixty lakh of rupees towards the defence of the north-western frontier. It is stated that while in London as Jubilee Commissioner Abdul Huk informed the Nizam's Government that an English Minister had recommended the making of such an offer by the Nizam. It was upon this supposed recommendation that Colonel Marshall, an officer near the Nizam's Court, went to the Viceroy at Simla to make the offer, with the assurance, it is said, that a cheque for twenty lakhs had been drawn upon Hyderabad funds in London, and was ready to be paid. The Viceroy, while civilly acknowledging the good intentions of the Nizam's Government, thought it best to withhold any acceptance of the gift until more mature consideration. It is now stated that subsequent investigations have thrown doubt upon the validity of the aforesaid cheque, and have given reason to believe that the Hyderabad Treasury was in no condition to bestow sixty lakhs on the frontier defence without seriously embarrassing the public resources and increasing the burdens of the people. The prudence of the Viceroy thus seems abundantly justified. It is further stated that unwise and unprofitable operations of the Nizam's Government in its own securities have been made by the advice and direction of the suspended Minister. Abdul Huk is not a native of Hyderabad, but a Moslem from another State. He was formerly employed in the police service of the Nizam, but is now believed to be immensely rich.—*Manchester Courier*, April 18.

[The above appeared in the *Western Morning News*, Plymouth, and a number of other provincial daily newspapers, the proprietors of which share the expense of foreign telegrams.]

Abdul Hakk, the "Indian dignitary" who has been suspended by the Nizam of Hyderabad for irregularities in connection with mining enterprises, is one of those clever intriguers who frequent the Courts of Oriental princes. He received his education at a missionary establishment, and at an early age entered the Nizam's police force. About nine years ago, in association with a British officer, he was instrumental in capturing a notorious Brahmin rebel who had given the British authorities much trouble, and threatened to foment a formidable rising against the Government. At a later period his undoubted talents and plausible address brought him to the notice of the then Prime Minister of Hyderabad, and he was sent to England to negotiate a loan for the Nizam's State Railway. He was successful in this mission, and on his return to India much scandal was created by an exposure of the extensive system of commissions which he had paid to obtain the loan. His own share in these irregular payments, it was officially stated, amounted to about £50,000. Abdul Hakk was in high favour with the Nizam at this time and subsequently, and though, considering his previous career, the cause assigned for his dismissal is very likely to have some foundation in fact, it is more probable that he has fallen into disgrace owing to intrigues such as he himself has often practised.—*Yorkshire Post*, April 18.

The news that the Nizam of Hyderabad has removed Abdul Huk, his Home Secretary, will not be pleasant reading for the shareholders of the Hyderabad Deccan Company. Abdul Huk, who is better known here by his title of Sirdar Diler Jung, was virtually the promoter of the Hyderabad Deccan Company, and it is because of the character of his connection with that enterprise that he has now been removed from office. According to statements sent over here from India, Abdul Huk, otherwise Sirdar Diler Jung, C.S.I., on a salary of 400 rupees, has grown to be worth several hundred thousand pounds. Last year this paid official of the Nizam came over here at the expense of the State, and made over to Messrs. Watson and Stewart a monopoly of all the mining rights in Hyderabad, in return for a royalty of about 8d. per ton on coal from the Singareni mines. The concessionnaires were also to have the right to work all the gold, copper, and other mines in the State for "a fair rent." This concession was subsequently sold to the Hyderabad Deccan Company, with a capital of £1,000,000 (£925,000 paid up), of which Mr. W. C. Watson and Mr. J. Stewart became directors. A large part of the shares issued are believed to have found their way into the hands of Abdul Huk and his friends, under circumstances which, in view of the present action of the Nizam and of the connection with the original scheme of the British Resident at Hyderabad, are now certain to be investigated by the India Office. The result will probably be the prompt cancellation of the Hyderabad-Deccan concession. The matter has already been brought to the attention of the Government, and we can promise our readers some interesting developments before many days.—*Financial News*, April 18.

THE HYDERABAD (DECCAN) SCANDAL.—We have received the following letter from the Hyderabad Deccan Company with reference to the dismissal of Abdul Huk, of which we treat in another column. The letter of the Company is very misleading. It is nowhere denied that the Company's concession was granted with "the full cognizance of the Nizam, the Government of India and the Secretary of State for India." What is alleged is that the approval of the concessions was improperly obtained by Abdul Huk in his official position for his private gain. The Nizam, being satisfied of this, has dismissed Abdul Huk, and as soon as the Government of India and the Secretary of State for India are satisfied of it the concessions of the Hyderabad Deccan Company are certain to be cancelled. This certainly will "affect the interests of the Hyderabad Deccan Company, Limited":—"The Hyderabad (Deccan) Company, Limited, 7, Great Winchester Street, London, April 17th, 1888. To the Editor of the *Financial News*.—Sir,—I am directed by my board to request you to give insertion to the following: 'Recent telegrams from India on the subject of the suspension of Abdul Huk Sirdar Diler Jung have given rise to a feeling that the interests of the company are thereby affected.' So far as my board are aware, everything connected with the grant of the concession had the fullest cognizance of the Government of H.H. the Nizam, and the approval of the Government of India and of the Secretary of State for India. The proceedings connected with that concession are fully set forth in 'The Return of Correspondence between the Government of India and the Secretary of State relating to the Concession of Mining Rights in the Deccan' (ordered by the House of Commons to be printed on September 16th, 1887), and a reference to those papers will afford the best proof that the charge alleged to be brought against Abdul Huk Sirdar Diler Jung of having settled on his own responsibility the question of the Hyderabad mines is without foundation, and one that cannot affect the interests of the Hyderabad (Deccan) Company, Limited.—I am, sir, your obedient servant, L. L. HALL, Secretary."—*Financial News*, April 18.

THE DECCAN MINING COMPANY.—To the Editor of the *Standard*.—Sir,—In order to dispose of the unfounded aspersions cast upon the validity and *bona fides* of the concession from the Nizam of Hyderabad, I am directed to set out the following extract from a letter dated the 17th December, 1884, addressed by his Excellency Nawab Salar Jung, then Prime Minister of Hyderabad, to the representative of the concessionnaires, who was asking some modifications in the concessions: "I have carefully read your letter of the 16th inst. and the draft you refer to. In reply, I beg to say that the draft has been prepared in England by a Committee of legal advisers of his Highness the Nizam's Government and Mining Engineers, with the knowledge of her Majesty's Secretary of State for India in Council, and contains necessary provisions to protect the interests of his Highness's Government." This disposes of the suggestion that the interests of the Nizam were not carefully guarded. If more proof is wanted, the following extract from a letter dated the 2nd February, 1886, addressed to the Secretary of State, and signed by Lord Dufferin, Sir Frederick Roberts, C. P. Ilbert, S. C. Bayley, T. C. Hope, A. Colvin, and T. E. Hughes, furnishes a complete answer. Referring to the concession, they say: "It may be sufficient to add that the agreement as now finally modified has been drawn up in accordance with our views, and should, in our opinion, be confirmed."—I am, Sir, your obedient servant, L. L. HALL, Secretary.—The Hyderabad Deccan Company (Limited), 7, Great Winchester Street, London, E.C., April 18.—*Standard*, April 19.

[The above letter was published in many papers.]

THE true story of the Nizam of Hyderabad's offer of £600,000 for the defence of the Indian frontier is bit by bit leaking out. Everybody who knows the Nizam knows that he is not a rich man, and that the sacrifice of so large a sum from his resources must affect an income which has served his turn only through the skilful husbandry of the late Sir Salar Jung. The suspicion is, indeed, that the Nizam's douceur to the British Government in India had its origin in a clever but sinister intrigue, which the disgrace of Sirdar Abdul Huk may bring to light, and in which certain of our own officials have had a hand. The clue to which we refer is as follows:—It may be remembered it was stated that the funds to back up the Nizam's offer were on deposit in London; and something was said about the cheque alleged as sent to Simla being drawn on these funds. It is still uncertain whether the said fund was in cash or only in securities, the latter being the most probable; but of what could these consist? It seems tolerably clear that neither cash nor securities could have been sent from Hyderabad. Hence the presumption arises that these shadowy funds or shady securities must have been part of the incidental results of certain "promoting" and stock-jobbing operations connected with the "financing" of the Nizam's railway purchase by a company here, and the promotion of the "Deccan Company," which was puffed to a premium a year or two ago. Now, what is known at the India Office of these money-market transactions? That is a question to be asked; but it would tax Sir John Gorst's ingenuity to give an adequate answer. It is said that the young Nizam has taken refuge in the seclusion of his harem palace. Is this because he begins to find that he has had too many counsellors, or that his "confidential" advisers have been too many for him? Probably we may soon hear, through demi-official channels, of his being denounced as a slothful and sensual monarch. Should this line be taken there is a corrective that ought to be applied by some competent authority—that is, a firm and impartial inquisition into the proceedings at the British Residency during the last four or five years. That might a "tale unfold."—*Star*, April 19.

The arrest of Abdul Huk, one of the leading officials in the State of Hyderabad, has caused much talk among Anglo-Indians here, for from very various reasons, the Sirdar Diler Jung, as he is otherwise entitled, is well-known to many of them. A friend of mine, who knows Hyderabad well, tells me that Abdul Huk, who was educated by the missionaries, and who is an exceedingly plausible personage, was the principal instrument in tempting Sir John Gorst, four years since (when, of course, the latter was out of office), to support the claim of the Peshcar, or deputy minister of Hyderabad, to be made chief minister upon the death of Sir Salar Jung; Sir John being paid fifty thousand rupees for his unsuccessful endeavour, which mainly consisted in drafting the claim in question. It was through this Peshcar that Abdul Huk, who was originally a police officer, has had a rapid rise in Hyderabad; and he was so trusted that he was allowed a sum of £50,000 in recognition of his success during a visit to England in financing a loan for the Nizam's State Railway. But a fall, at Indian Courts, is usually as rapid as the rise, and this fact Abdul Huk has now discovered for himself.—*Birmingham Daily Post*, April 19.

The Hyderabad (Deccan) Company.—The Hyderabad (Deccan) Company has been a child of mystery ever since it made its appearance on the Stock Exchange. Many questions were asked as to where it had come from, what it was, and who were in it; but none of them was ever satisfactorily answered. The strangest rumours have been afloat about the concession itself, and the way in which it was manipulated for the market. Its huge capital of a million sterling offered a striking contrast to the very vague and ambiguous character of its assets. To the ordinary commercial eye it had no visible means of support, and how it was to pay dividends on a million sterling was one of the secrets of financial jugglery. So easy is it, however, for the skilful promoter to conjure up visions of dividends, that this uncanny and impalpable stock was in the days of its infancy run up to 30 or 40 per cent. premium. So far the great expectations amid which it was launched have not been realised. Most of its early friends appear to have got tired of waiting for plums from the fabled gardens of Hyderabad to fall into their mouths. In the absence of dividends the premium has gradually and gently run off. Hyderabad-Deccans can now be very easily bought a couple of pounds under par, and if half-a-dozen sellers were to come into the market together they might soon find it very much lower. Worse things, however, are beginning to be said about Hyderabad-Deccan than that it has disappointed its too sanguine devotees. Ominous whispers of political scandal and financial jobbery are casting a blight over it. Countenance has, within the past few days, been given to these by the disgrace which has fallen on Abdul Huk, its native foster-parent. A leading Indian paper has been suggesting that not only this but various other incidents in the recent history of the Nizam's Court urgently demand to be inquired into. Our Indian contemporary hints cautiously at matters which we happen to have the means of speaking about openly and plainly. The Hyderabad (Deccan) Company has all through its short life been under suspicion of having been conceived in sin and born in iniquity. Facts collected on the spot and placed in our possession, give, to say the least, very strong colour to the suspicion. We take on ourselves the responsibility of their publication, for two reasons—first, that people may be put on their guard against a security of shady antecedents; secondly, that Parliament may be moved to investigate what appears to be a rank scandal in the administration of Hyderabad. A small band of speculators—partly English and partly native—have for some time past been systematically exploiting the State of Hyderabad. The Machiavelli is a Mahomedan, by name Abdul Huk, who, from a very subordinate office in the Nizam's police, rose to a position of singular influence, not only in Hyderabad itself, but with the Government of India, and even at the India Office. His oriental subtlety has taken a financial turn, and even a London promoter might envy him the success of his schemes. His first great *coup* was the promotion of the Nizam's Guaranteed State Railways Company. In working it he was too smart, not merely for the unsuspecting Prime Minister of Hyderabad, but for the cute people who acted as his fellow-promoters in London. After giving him a handsome slice of their profits, they were gratified to learn afterwards that he had obtained a second commission from the Nizam's Treasury. When this leaked out there was a great scandal at Hyderabad, and Abdul Huk was for a time in a very unpleasant corner. But it is in circumstances like these that clever men prove their mettle. Thanks to oriental diplomacy, in all the arts of which Abdul Huk is a master, he not only got off, but he arranged it so as he subsequently could pose as an ill-used man. His claim to the great mining concession which has furnished Hyderabad with a second scandal was deliberately based on the plea that he had made so little out of the railway! In his second scheme Abdul Huk treated with the Nizam's Government as a privileged person entitled to special consideration. He succeeded in impressing this view, not only on the Nizam's Ministers, but on the British Resident at Hyderabad, on the Indian Government at Calcutta, and on the India Office in London. The whole of these eminent and sharp-sighted authorities accepted Abdul Huk's version of himself, and even went out of their way to give him facilities for working as grandiose a rig as has ever been put on the British market. As the upshot of prolonged negotiations, carried on alternately at Hyderabad, Calcutta, and London, the Hyderabad (Deccan) Company made its appearance in January, 1886, with a capital of £1,000,000, the whole of which was represented to have been subscribed and fully paid. The promoters had put in of their own money only £25,000. The bewitching Abdul Huk had induced the Nizam's Government, after giving away a huge concession for literally nothing, to invest £125,000 in the undertaking thus highly favoured. The concessionnaires were pleased to accept the remaining £850,000 of shares as the price of the concession. The contrast between their treatment of themselves and of the Nizam's Government requires neither comment nor embellishment. Various attempts have been made to get at the inner history of this Indian Jonah's gourd. The Indian press has had occasional twinges of curiosity on the subject, and the Secretary for India has had his parliamentary repose disturbed now and then by sinister questions about it. It has even formed the theme of a small blue-book issued a few months ago. This purports to be a "Return of Correspondence between the Government of India and the Secretary of State relating to the Concession of Mining Rights in the Deccan." It might have been much more correctly styled a selection of correspondence, for the gaps in it are frequent and obvious. Despatches are referred to which cannot be found, and incidents crop up without any context. The best that can be said for such a return is that it appears to have been most carefully and cautiously edited. It tells as little of Abdul Huk's story as it possibly can, and puts forward secondary parties as masks to the real principals. Such a partial and one-sided disclosure of the facts could never have been accepted as complete, much less so now that Abdul Huk's own colleagues in the Government of Hyderabad have deemed it necessary to disown him. It is characteristic of the *Standard* to try to break his fall by attributing it to personal rivalry; but all the same, it may be wise to hear what his rivals have to say of him. As yet we have heard only the partial versions of his friends in the India Office and at Calcutta. The Government of India should, and no doubt will, in justice to itself, institute a searching investigation into Abdul Huk's financial career from the beginning, and unearth the secret history of both the railway and mining concessions. The Hyderabad-Deccan directors are not over anxious for an investigation. They met yesterday, but could do nothing better than issue a circular setting forth a few extracts from the letters in the blue-book above referred to, which have nothing at all to do with the matters now under discussion. The board, it must be remembered, includes the promoters of the scheme, and of them there will be more to say anon.—*Financial News*, April 19.

The shares of the Hyderabad Deccan Company had a further severe fall yesterday, and did not close much better than 7½ for the fully-paid £10 shares. After a careful perusal of a lengthy article on this company which appears in the *Financial News* this morning, we think it scarcely likely that any recovery will take place in these shares to-day. On the other hand, we venture to predict that Deccans will close to-night not much better than £6 a share. We advise all our readers who are interested in the Deccan Company to read the article to which we refer.—*Evening Post*, April 19.

This is a queer story that is going the rounds about the "munificent gift" of the Nizam of Hyderabad towards the cost of frontier defence in India. Your readers will probably recollect that in autumn last a sensation was caused in England by a pompous announcement in the leading columns of the *Times*, to the effect that the Nizam of Hyderabad, in order to show his deep friendship for the British Government, had offered the princely sum of six hundred thousand pounds to the Governor-General of India to help in defraying the cost of frontier defence in India. The *Times* was very eloquent over the affair, and said that no more magnificent proof of the devotion of the native Princes of India to British rule had ever been given. The chief merit of the offer was that it was said to be purely spontaneous, the Nizam having offered the money without the slightest previous consultation with any British official in India. The whole Tory Press of England rang with the Nizam's munificence, and

Russia was asked to take warning by this remarkable proof of the determination of the Indian Princes to help England at all hazards in repelling a Muscovite invasion of British India. Well, time rolled on, and nothing more was heard of the Nizam's offer. Now, horrible to relate, the whole thing is said to be a myth. One of the Tory journals this evening is grieved to have to confess that the affair is enshrouded in the most painful mystery. So far from the Nizam's offer having been spontaneous, it is said that the matter was suggested to his agent in England by a Cabinet Minister, and that when the agent forwarded the suggestion to Hyderabad, it afforded much merriment to the Nizam's friends, who knew the impossibility of his Highness making the gift, for the very good reason that he hadn't the money.—*Western Morning News*, April 19.

Hyderabad Curiosities.—To the Editor of the *St. James's Gazette*.—Sir,—The suspension of Abdul Huk, Home Secretary of the Hyderabad Government, may help to throw some light on more than one matter now obscure in regard to the affairs of the Nizam's State. The secretary of the Hyderabad (Deccan) Company says in the *Times* that the charge said to be brought against this person—namely, that he settled on his own responsibility the question of the mining rights of the Nizam's dominions—is without foundation, as everything connected with the grant of the concession had the fullest cognizance of the Nizam's Government and the approval of the Government of India. The secretary tells us that the proceedings connected with that concession are fully set forth in the parliamentary return of the 16th of September, 1887, relating to the mining rights in the Deccan. Now, it may be that the Nizam's Government had the "fullest cognizance" of the matter, as asserted; but if so, it does not exactly appear from the return in question. At the time the concession was granted, the Government of the Hyderabad State was vested in the Nizam and his Highness's Prime Minister with a council composed of the principal nobles of Hyderabad. Of this Council, which is a consultative body without executive functions, the Nizam is president and his Minister one of the members. In the parliamentary return referred to it does not appear that the concession of the mining rights, for ninety-nine years, of the entire State of Hyderabad, was ever brought before the Council. Though it was a question that must have deeply concerned the personal interests of one and all of the members, none of their opinions are recorded, and no mention of the Council is made. If that body was not allowed to have cognizance of the matter, the question arises, Why was it kept from them? A telegram from India states that Abdul Huk has been suspended for "suspicious connections" with the mining company. It is probable that the Nizam's Government has more than one charge to bring against him. The questions already asked by the *St. James's Gazette* with reference to the purchase by the Nizam last summer of a large number of unsold shares of this company, at a cost of £150,000—shares that a year before the Nizam had given away—remain unanswered; as also does your question whether the cheque for twenty lakhs tendered by a Hyderabad official, in part payment of the Nizam's offer of sixty lakhs, had anything to do with these shares.—I am, Sir, your obedient servant,—Y. April 18.—*St. James's Gazette*, April 20.

The following has been received in connection with the Hyderabad (Deccan) Company, Limited: To the City Editor of the *Daily Gazette*.—Sir, In order to dispose of the unfounded aspersions cast upon the validity and *bona fides* of the concession from the Nizam of Hyderabad, I am directed to set out the following extract from a letter dated the 17th December, 1884, addressed by his Excellency Nawab Salar Jung, then Prime Minister of Hyderabad, to the representatives of the concessionnaires, who was asking some modification in the concession:—

"I have carefully read your letter of the 16th inst. and the draft you refer to. In reply I beg to say that the draft has been prepared in England by a committee of legal advisers of his Highness the Nizam's Government and mining engineers, with the knowledge of her Majesty's Secretary of State for India in Council, and contains necessary provisions to protect the interests of his Highness's Government."

This disposes of the suggestion that the interests of the Nizam were not carefully guarded. If more proof is wanted, the following extract from a letter dated the 2nd February, 1886, addressed to the Secretary of State, and signed by Lord Dufferin, Sir Frederick Roberts, C. P Ilbert, F. C. Bayley, T. C. Hope, A. Colvin, and T. E. Hughes, furnishes a complete answer. Referring to the concession they say: "It may be sufficient to add that the agreement, as now finally modified, has been drawn up in accordance with our views, and should in our opinion be confirmed."—Yours faithfully, L. L. HALL, Secretary. —*Birmingham Gazette*, April 20.

THE Nizam of Hyderabad has suspended Abdulluk, the Home Secretary, on account of the nature of his connection with the Deccan Mining Company. The suspension has caused great sensation there. Various accounts are given as to the nature of the Minister's offence. The Bombay correspondent of the *Standard* says he is charged with complicity in giving concessions to the value of £850,000 to London concessionnaires without an equivalent. His career has been a romantic one, and interesting revelations are expected. He was the Nizam's delegate in the recent Jubilee festivities. The Secunderabad correspondent of the same paper says: "It is publicly given out that this step has been taken because the Sirdar had settled, on his own responsibility, the question of the Hyderabad mines; but the true reason is believed to be the long-standing animosity of the Minister to the Sirdar Diler Jung, who is a man of marked character and ability, but not without powerful enemies both at the Nizam's Court and amongst the European community here."—*Home News*, April 20.

THE HYDERABAD AND DECCAN MINING CONCESSION.—The Yellow-book issued at Hyderabad last month gives an account of the circumstances under which the Nizam of Hyderabad parted for 99 years with the monopoly of the mining rights in the rich territory of the Deccan, and how he was induced to repurchase a part equal to one-eighth of those rights by becoming a shareholder in the company organized to work the concession. It seems that after a protracted correspondence, in which the Government of India appear as the advisers of the Nizam, it was finally decided in January, 1886, to grant to Messrs. Watson and Stewart a concession for the mining rights in the Deccan. Among the conditions recommended by the Government of India was one to the effect that these gentlemen should be permitted to promote a company with a nominal capital of £1,000,000, but that not more than £150,000 should, at first, be issued, of which only £75,000 was to be called up. That this was the understanding was clearly shown in the correspondence of Mr. Cordery, the British Resident at Hyderabad, and of Mr. Durand, the Secretary of the Foreign Department in the Indian Government, with the parties to the concession. It must, however, be admitted that in the actual convention, which was finally drawn and signed in London on January 7, 1886, the terms above mentioned are not so clearly stated as in the correspondence of the Indian Government.

In July following the "Hyderabad (Deccan) Company, Limited," was incorporated. with a capital of £1,000,000, and £75,000 called up on £150,000 worth of shares, the remaining £850,000 being apparently retained by the promoters as consideration for their concession. The shares of the company were dealt in on the Stock Exchange, and after some time the number of shareholders became considerable.

The next important event in the history of this company took place in April, 1887, when the Sirdar Diler-ul-Mulk was in London to represent the Nizam at the Queen's Jubilee. It was then that his Highness was advised to acquire an interest in the company other than that which he had from the royalties to be paid to him from the mining operations which might be undertaken. It appears that he was induced, with the view of obtaining a "controlling interest" in the company, to give orders to purchase 12,500 of its shares, and the correspondence on this subject between his representative, the Sirdar Diler-ul-Mulk, and Mr. Watson, which we subjoin, is very instructive:—

"Sirdar Diler-ul-Mulk to Mr. W. C. Watson.

"Alexandra Hotel, June 2, 1887.

"Sir,—I am instructed by the Government of His Highness the Nizam to purchase 10,000 £10 shares of the Hyderabad (Deccan) Company, Limited. As you are the agent of the Government here, I write to ask you to be so good as to arrange for the purchase of these shares at the lowest possible price, not exceeding £12 per share, the Government having decided to invest only £120,000 in these shares.—I am, Sir, your obedient servant,

"Sirdar Diler-ul-Mulk."

"Mr. Watson to Sirdar Diler-ul-Mulk.

"Confidential.

"7, Great Winchester-street, E.C., June 3, 1887.

"Sir,—I beg to acknowledge receipt of your letter of yesterday's date, instructing me as agent of the Government of His Highness the Nizam to purchase 10,000 £10 fully-paid shares of the Hyderabad (Deccan) Company, Limited.

"I beg to point out to you that to purchase these shares at the price you name is a most difficult and almost impossible operation, and will require the greatest skill and circumspection. I would suggest that the Government should acquire a proportion of the £5 paid shares at the same *pro rata* price, say £7 per share, as the £5 paid shares carry the same dividend as the £10 paid, and by this the Government could acquire, say, 8,750 £10 paid shares and 3,750 £5 paid shares, thus having 12,500 shares for £131,250, being an addition of 2,500 shares at an extra cost of £11,250 only. Please be kind enough to send me your instructions on this point.—I have, &c.,

"W. C. Watson."

On receipt of this letter the Sirdar gave the following instructions:—

"June 3, 1887.

"Sir,—I am in receipt of your letter of to-day's date, and in reply beg to state that your suggestion appears to be a good one. The Government only intended to invest £120,000 and purchase 10,000 shares; but as the Government will obtain 12,500 shares and only have at present to pay £11,250 in addition to the £120,000, and have the contingent liability of £18,750—under these circumstances I authorise you to purchase 8,750 £10 fully paid and 3,750 £5 paid shares.

"Should the Government not wish to hold shares in excess of the £120,000, I understand from you that there will not be any difficulty in re-selling the additional shares at a profit.—I am, Sir, your obedient servant,

"Sirdar Diler-ul-Mulk."

The same day eight different firms of brokers were sent into the market to buy these shares for the Nizam. The whole of the shares were bought at one price, namely, 12, the highest figure at which the Nizam had said he was willing to purchase the shares. But what is more strange still is that when these shares were delivered they were handed in by these eight firms of brokers in two lots of 3,750 shares and 8.750 shares, all with consecutive numbers. Under these circumstances it is surprising that the Sirdar should have telegraphed to Colonel Marshal, the Nizam's private secretary, on the day in question—namely, June 3—as follows:—"Deccans firmly held by public, therefore with greatest difficulty succeeded in purchasing" the shares in question. It was added that the market closed at 12⅞, and that the shares thus bought were then worth £9,000 more than had been paid for them. The price has since fallen to 8.

It should be mentioned that only a month before the time the Nizam purchased these shares at a premium of 20 per cent. of their original nominal value, the actual sum which the company had spent in the Deccan was only £6,411. Of this only £2,780 had been spent in prospecting for new mines in the province, the remainder having gone in "establishment charges" and in the development of the Singareni coal mines, a part of the business on the importance of which the Indian Government had always laid stress. We understand that the whole case is now before the India Office, and it is to be hoped that a thorough investigation into all the circumstances attending the parting with the mining rights and the investment of the Nizam's money in the company will be held. The statement received in the City yesterday by telegraph that the Nizam's Government was "friendly and aiding the company" is probable enough, considering the financial interest which His Highness now has in the undertaking.—*Times*, April 21.

The Hyderabad and Deccan Mining Concession.—It is evident that a searching inquiry must be instituted into what is called the Hyderabad-Deccan mining concession scandal, in connection with which the Sirdar Diler-ul-Mulk was suspended the other day. A Yellow-book issued at Hyderabad gives an account of the circumstances under which the Nizam first parted for 99 years with the monopoly of the mining rights in the Deccan, and was afterwards induced to pay £131,000 for an eighth share of the rights which he had practically given away for nothing. The concession was granted to Messrs. Watson and Stewart on the condition that not more than £150,000 of the nominal capital of £1,000,000 was to be issued, and only £75,000 was to be called up. When the company was brought out, however, all the shares were issued at once, 85,000 £10 shares being taken as fully paid up by the promoters for their concession. On the other 15,000 shares £75,000 was called up, and this was the whole working capital of the company with a nominal capital of one million.

When the Sirdar Diler-ul-Mulk was in London as the Jubilee Commissioner he gave an order on behalf of the Nizam to purchase 12,500 shares in the company, and Mr. Watson, one of the concessionnaires, was instructed to buy. Eight different firms of brokers were sent into the market to buy the shares, which they did at £12, or a premium of 20 per cent., and although it was represented that the shares were held firmly by the public the shares when handed in by the eight firms of brokers had consecutive numbers. The price for Deccans rose thereupon to 12⅞, but they have since fallen to 8. At the time that the shares were bought only £6,411 had been spent by the company in the Deccan. For the credit of the Government of India, who sanctioned the concession, the whole of this questionable transaction must be investigated.—*Pall Mall Gazette*, April 21.

City Topics.—The Hyderabad-Deccan Disclosures.—The Deccan Company continues to attract unenviable attention. The *Financial News* to-day has a column and a half, and a special cablegram from Hyderabad, with regard to the affairs of this company. The *Times* follows in the wake of the *Financial News* by giving various extracts from a Yellow Book issued at Hyderabad last month. If we are any judges, after a perusal of these two articles we should say that the concession, if not obtained by fraud, was obtained by means very much like it, and we should not be at all surprised to see it cancelled. We would advise all those who hold shares to sell them without delay.

We recommend the shareholders of the Deccan Company to immediately call a meeting to consider their position.

We hear that it is likely Lord Randolph Churchill will in the House of Commons, next week, move an inquiry into the circumstances surrounding the concession of the Hyderabad Deccan Company, Limited.—*Evening Post*, April 21.

THE infamous Deccan plot is coming out as we anticipated. The story of the purchase of the shares in the puffed railway speaks for itself. The poor young Nizam was induced to purchase £131,250 worth of shares at 12, the price having since fallen to 8. Only a month before the Nizam made the purchase of shares at a premium of 20 per cent, and at the highest price that he was willing to pay of their nominal value, the actual sum which this wonderful company had spent in the Deccan was £6,411, the greater part of which was in "establishment charges." Meanwhile the Sirdar who drove the bargain has become an extremely wealthy man, owning huge blocks of houses in Calcutta, and rising from an absolute parvenu into a great magnate. The disgraceful part of the business is the mysterious connection between the Deccan job and the poor Nizam's Jubilee gift to the Indian Government. Of this more anon.—*Star*, April 21.

A GIGANTIC CITY INTRIGUE.—EXPLOITING THE NIZAM.—A STORY OF A JUBILEE NEGOTIATION.—A very interesting story of City intrigue is revealed in a long dispatch from Allahabad to the *Financial News*, being quoted from the *Pioneer* of yesterday. The Nizam of Hyderabad in January, 1886, granted to Messrs. Watson and Stewart a concession of the monopoly of the minerals in that State for 99 years, in return for moderate rents and royalties.

Mr. W. C. Watson and the Sirdar Diler Jung, who was, before he was ennobled, known to fame as plain Abdul Huk, had been collaborateurs in financing the Nizam's State Railway. These two had received in this connection more than £180,000, and the enormous promotion expenses incurred in floating that railway have more than once attracted the attention of Parliament. In July following the Hyderabad (Deccan) Company, Limited, was incorporated, with a capital of £1,000,000 and £75,000 called up on £150,000 worth of shares, the remaining £850,000 being apparently retained by the promoters as consideration for their concession. But what is to follow, says the dispatch, is infinitely worse. The public refuse to buy the shares. No one can be persuaded to give 30s. for them, for they are all in the hands of Messrs. Watson and Stewart. In order to mark up these shares, £1, £2, £10 a share, Watson must sell to Stewart and his bogus transferees. Stewart must sell to his; and Abdul Huk, the influential Hyderabad Minister, he, too, must be persuaded to play a part, and persuade his youthful Highness and the new English secretary to his Highness that the State ought to come into the London market, to spend £150,000 in buying and "booming" Mr. Watson's "fully paid" shares. The time is most opportune. The violent intrigues against Sir Salar Jung have brought about the result that the Minister has resigned, and the State is for an entire month without a responsible head. If once the announcement can be made in London that the shares of the Hyderabad (Deccan) Company are considered by the Government of Hyderabad worth buying at £12 each, then, indeed, the public can be trusted to flock into the market and buy readily. The Government of India are falsely assured that the Nizam is personally anxious that Abdul Huk should go over to London with the style, the title, the dignity of a Jubilee Commissioner. Incredible as it seems, this slight is put upon the Queen! The ex-policeman of Kallian is to be sent to London, in company with two great native nobles, to pose as a dignitary of the State of Hyderabad! With evident reluctance the Government of India is induced to sanction the appointment of Abdul Huk. The pretence upon which his Highness's signature is next obtained to the purchase of these shares is, that it is important—in the language of the Resident—that the Government of Hyderabad should obtain "a predominant interest in the concern." A predominant interest! It is only necessary to point out that a hundred thousand shares have been issued, that to each of these shares belongs an equal vote. The Government of the Nizam is therefore to obtain "a predominant interest" by purchasing at a premium one-tenth of the shares, and by controlling one-tenth of the votes! When next we hear of Abdul Huk, he is in London. He is now the Sirdar Diler-ul-Mulk Bahadur, C.I.E., Jubilee Commissioner, &c. From the Alexandra Hotel he pens a letter to Mr. W. C. Watson, who, with his partner, Mr. Stewart, is the owner of all, or nearly all, the 85,000 shares, and also of the remaining 15,000 shares. The concessionnaire is instructed to buy a mass of his own shares for the Government of Hyderabad. The whole of the shares were bought at one price, namely, 12, the highest figure at which the Nizam had said he was willing to purchase the shares. But what is more strange still is that when these shares were delivered they were handed in by eight firms of brokers in two lots of 3,750 shares and 8,750 shares, all with consecutive numbers. Under these circumstances it is surprising that the Sirdar should have telegraphed to Colonel Marshall, the Nizam's private secretary, on the day in question—namely, 3rd June—as follows:—"Deccans firmly held by public, therefore with greatest difficulty succeeded in purchasing" the shares in question. It was added that the market closed at 12¾, and that the shares thus bought were then worth £9,000 more than had been paid for them. The price has since fallen to 8. So the State of Hyderabad, having given away its mining rights for 99 years, forthwith comes to market to buy one-tenth of these same rights for the sum of £131,250 and a further liability, since incurred and paid, of £18,750. In fact, it comes to this, that the State of Hyderabad have given their mining rights for four generations to Messrs. Watson and Stewart, and also £75,000 to accept these rights. A more impudent, a more infamous, transaction has never been reported in these columns. The State of Hyderabad is on its trial, and, what is perhaps of more Imperial importance, the whole Residency system of India, and the obligations of the Supreme Power to the feudatory States must come under careful consideration and in open court. We know the general impolicy of such a course; but there are occasions when a storm clears the air. We believe this to be such an occasion. To deprecate a public inquiry by a competent Commission would, under the circumstances we detail to-day, weaken the moral influence of Great Britain in India. On that moral influence, and on that alone, our race must chiefly rely if we are to continue our tenancy of this immense dependency.—*Star*, April 21.

Rajahs and Promoters.—"Milking the Rajahs" is a phrase not altogether unknown on the Stock Exchange during recent years. It signifies, we believe, that the "milker" has succeeded in obtaining from some Indian nobleman or potentate something of a valuable nature without paying a fair price for it. Thus, a certain clever Company promoter received credit for having acquired for a few hundred rupees a gold mining concession which he afterwards sold in London for many thousands of pounds. Are native Princes so guileless, then, as to fall easy victims to sharp practitioners? In one way, many of them are as facile victims to Artful Dodgers as the veriest numbskull who was ever taken in by "confidence trick" swindlers. Let it only be breathed into their ears that the "milker" has influence with the powers that be, and let this pretence be supported by some show of intimacy with "authorities," and Rajah Ram Chunder trots to his fate as gaily as a doomed lamb.

It was possibly some affair of this sort which brought the disgrace and downfall of our late gorgeous visitor, Sirdar Diler Jung ul Mulk, of Hyderabad. Indian Society formed a rather favourable opinion of him when he was over here as the Nizam's representative during the Jubilee rejoicings. He bore the reputation of spending money freely, and any distinguished foreigner who couples that amiable trait with courtly manners and a picturesque costume at once wins John Bull's esteem. It is now alleged, however, that the open-handed Sirdar dabbled in matters not consonant with his august position as Home Secretary of Hyderabad. In a word, he lies under the imputation of having given concessions to the value of nearly a million sterling to some wily gentlemen in London without receiving anything in return. The property thus parted with belonged, it may be assumed, to the Hyderabad Government, as no objection would have been raised had Diler Jung merely made away with his own belongings. It may possibly come to light—in the interests of public morality we hope it may—who were the "milkers" in this instance.—*Graphic*, April 21.

The *Times* of this morning reveals the whole shameful story of the way in which the leading native prince in India, the Nizam of Hyderabad, was allowed by the Government of India, who are his guardians and should have been his protectors, to alienate for 99 years all the mineral rights in his dominions to a syndicate of Englishmen, who paid £150,000 for the concession, and immediately resold it in London for a million sterling. Subsequently the victimised Nizam was induced to invest £150,000 in the Company's shares in order to keep up their price in the English market. The question of public interest raised by this transaction is how the Government of India were persuaded to sanction it. Anglo-Indian civilians used to be above reproach, and even above suspicion, in regard to speculations of this character; but recent sales of gold-bearing land in Madras, and again the treatment of the Nizam, have a very ugly look, and ought to be inquired into by Parliament. Hyderabad has always been notorious for corruption and jobbery, and it is not pleasant to hear, in addition to the scandal about the Deccan Mining Company, that Sir Horace Rumbold recently went to the Nizam's Court armed with letters of introduction from the Prince of Wales and Lord Lytton, and obtained £30,000 in satisfaction of a claim 50 years old.—*Western Mail*, April 23.

Hyderabad-Deccan.—Abdul Huk, the ex-policeman of Kallian, who suddenly blossomed last year into a jubilee financier, is evidently proud of his new profession. Magnates of high finance are, as a rule, partial to secrecy. They do their finest work in subdued lights, and are by no means given to making proclamations on the housetops. That, however, does not seem to suit the character of Abdul Huk, *alias* Sirdar Diler-ul-Mulk Bahudur, C.I.E. He sees nothing to be ashamed of in being a very clever fellow and making good use of his opportunities. While his confederates in London were coyly keeping their thumb on the private history of the great Hyderabad-Deccan Concession, he, on his return home, submitted to his Government a long official report on the whole interesting operation. This has been published at Hyderabad in a Yellow Book entitled "Memorandum on the Budget Estimate of the Railway for Fasli, 1297." It is signed by the Sirdar himself as "Secretary Home Department (Railways)"—a fact of some significance in the Sirdar's short but brilliant career as a financier promoter.

The frankness with which Abdul Huk details in this Yellow Book his

Jubilee negotiations both with regard to the Nizam's State Railway and the mining concession is, from a public point of view, most commendable. From the point of view of Abdul Huk's English associates it is correspondingly awkward. Utterly unconscious of the fact that in this phlegmatic climate excessive cleverness is always suspected, and requires to have a veil of modesty thrown over it, he has described all the exceptionally smart things which he was privileged to take a hand in as if they were every-day incidents of City life. So pleased was he at his unexpected success that he complacently records every incident in the game, and every manœuvre that was resorted to for making a market in the shares. When he first came over in 1883, with the railway scheme, the mining concession was included in it, but the keen financiers to whom he addressed himself were not given to wasting two stones on one bird. They took out the mining concession and put it aside for subsequent use. It was only after the railway company had been successfully floated that they fell back on the mining scheme. This was the real reason for the delay, though Abdul Huk's explanation is put on other and more patriotic grounds. His own account of it is that, owing to the "vagueness of the first mining proposal and schedule he had a revised draft prepared by legal and mining experts." This draft agreement, he adds, "was fully and carefully considered in its minutest detail by H. E. the Minister and His Highness the Nizam, as well as by H. E. the Viceroy and Governor-General in Council, and after prolonged and mature deliberation was signed by the Minister at Hyderabad on the 7th January, 1885, in the presence of a representative of the Resident."

Abdul Huk has a great deal to explain regarding the wonderful constitution of the Company to which the concessionnaires transferred their rights. He disclaims any original responsibility for its one million sterling of capital, of which six-sevenths was to be water. At an early stage in the negotiations he says "he most strongly urged the fixing of the subscribed capital at £500,000, in order to secure the soundness of the undertaking, and prevent the concessionnaires from making the project a purely speculative one and reaping an unduly large profit." Considering that Abdul Huk himself is generally understood to have carried away a big slice of the proceeds of the 85,000 chromos issued as fully-paid shares, he must be a man of very fine moral sentiments. Even our own Joseph Surface might stand a poor chance against him in the moral line. For an ex-policeman, whose pay a few years ago was 150 rupees a month, and who now owns property in Bombay valued at half a million sterling, the Sirdar can be very careful indeed of the public interests. His original conviction that half a million sterling would amply suffice to exploit all the mineral wealth of Hyderabad, did not prevent his falling in readily with the proposal of his Capel Court allies to make it a million. The Sirdar was by no means an obstinate person. He paid due deference to his English advisers, and when they said it ought to be a million he amiably consented to take his share of the larger spoil.

All through his report Abdul Huk strives to convey the impression of having sacrificed his better convictions to the necessities of the situation. At every turn he met with some new surprise. When the £85,000 of watered capital was issued he did not expect that it would sell for more than thirty shillings a share, and it was a fresh delight to him to be able soon afterwards to buy them for the Nizam's Government at £12 per share. On this point the Sirdar has been most inconveniently communicative for his friends. He discloses the whole of the circumstances which led up to the now notorious rig in which eight brokers were sent into the market to buy Hyderabad-Deccans on a £12 limit. Oddly enough they all went straight to the same jobber, and with one exception they paid him the same price. The shares all came out of one shop, and they were numbered consecutively in two series, one from 5,055 to 8,804, and the other 91,251 to 100,000.

Those eight brokers and the one lucky dealer on whom they piled their large lines, will read with interest the following reflections which Abdul Huk makes *à propos* of the rig:—"Before the scheme had acquired its later reputation, the shares were so little valued in the market that they were offered at a lower figure than £1 10s., the average price above-mentioned, and even at that price no buyers were found, owing to the fact that the first call of £75,000 had to be paid forthwith for the agreed paid-up capital, leaving a further liability of £75,000 to be paid on such shares in future calls. With this view the market appears to have been forced by shareholders, and the result was the shares were found to be practically valueless. When, however, the actual value of the undertaking was proved by further prospecting operations, they became valuable securities, and therefore the *pros* and *cons.* of the case were submitted for the orders of his Highness." Joseph Surface again, larger than ever!

The "further prospecting operations" to which Abdul Huk refers, had taken place at the Court of Hyderabad, which has been the richest mine yet struck by him and his confederates. The Nizam had then a balance of £98,706 at the National Provincial Bank in London, which Abdul Huk coolly proposed to utilize for buying up shares, or, as professional promoters call it, "supporting the market." He even went so far as to suggest that it should be made up to £120,000 by obtaining an advance from the bank on securities it held belonging to the Nizam's Government. If this was a wonderful proposal to make, tenfold more wonderful was it that it should not only have been sanctioned by the Nizam's Ministers, but should have run the gauntlet of the British Resident at Hyderabad, the Indian Government at Calcutta, and the India Office in London. To give greater point to the joke, Abdul Huk was at this time being shepherded by a special committee of India Office officials, who must, indeed, have been very unsophisticated persons if they did not suspect the real drift of the proposed purchase of shares. In one of Sir Salar Jung's letters occurs this notable statement: "A special committee, composed of India Office officials, was subsequently appointed to watch Sirdar Diler Jung's proceedings, and give him advice during the course of his negotiations." It will be only fair to these officials that they should by-and-by have an opportunity of telling what they know about the gestation of the Hyderabad-Deccan Company, especially about the official rig, which, according to Sirdar Diler Jung, started the shares from 30s. to nearly £13.—*Financial News*, April 23.

THE Nizam of Hyderabad is, according to the agents of the Hyderabad-Deccan Company, "friendly, and aiding the Company." Probably the Nizam does not yet know the full extent to which he has been victimized, and, just as he been taken in twice already, he is no doubt being carefully nursed again. After what has been done in this connection in the name of the Nizam we shall not be very ready to give credence to stories of his wishes which come through interested sources.—*Financial News*, April 23.

THE HYDERABAD DECCAN COMPANY.—A great deal of interest is felt, not alone in the City, in the disclosures connected with the floating of the Hyderabad (Deccan) Company. Sirdar Abdul Huk, a member of the Nizam's Government, has been suspended from his functions, and is charged with some questionable dealings in the matter of a concession of the right to develop the mines in the territory of the Deccan. Whether or not the said mines are as productive as was represented is a minor question. Recent advices state that coal from the district has been sent for trial in the cotton mills of Bombay, that competent staffs have been sent out to deal with the coal mines, diamond fields, gold-fields, and portions of the company's concessions.

The shares of the company have lately fallen heavily in consequence partly of the fear that the concession may be cancelled. In that case the hopes of the shareholders of getting riches from the Deccan would vanish, and their only resource might then be an application to the representatives of the company in London. According to an official publication lately issued at Hyderabad the Nizam gave instructions for the purchase of a number of shares, stipulating that not more than £12 per share was to be paid. This price, it was said, was too low, or, at any rate, was a low one; but ultimately the shares were obtained at £12 each, and the surprising thing was that the shares bore consecutive numbers, tending to show that someone had sold in a block.

Who was it? and was the price a fair one? The Sirdar above mentioned is held responsible for the price given, which the Nizam's Government now consider unsatisfactory; but the question of the proper market price of shares is a most difficult one to settle. Another point arose in connection with the price for which the company's concession was sold to the general public; for out of a capital of one million sterling £850,000 apparently went to the promoters. It would at least be interesting to learn what the promoters did with this enormous sum. Thus there are two points to which the attention of Parliament might with advantage be directed. The Nizam is an independent Prince, but there is a British Resident at his Court, who probably exerts considerable influence over him.—*Daily News*, April 23.

THE *Times*, by way of enlightening us in regard to a matter about which a great deal more should be made known, speaks of "the Yellow Book issued at Hyderabad last month." This is presumably a publication of the Nizam's Government, giving a history of the Hyderabad Mining Concession. What the title of this book may be is not stated, but apparently in it is to be found a remarkable correspondence in reference to the purchase last summer by the Nizam of £150,000 worth of shares, which a few months before he had given away. Another Yellow Book, it may be remarked, has been recently issued by the Nizam's Government. It is styled "Budget Estimate for the year 1297 Fasli," which, being interpreted, means for the twelve months ending October, 1888. In this publication are also given the Budget Estimate and Revised Estimate of 1296—*i.e.*, for the year ending October, 1887. The purchase of the 12,500 shares "by the Nizam" was effected in June last year, to give him, as it was called, "a controlling interest" over a remainder of 87,500 shares; the total number of the company's shares being 100,000.

The remarkable thing about this book (which has eighty-six pages, and is of Blue Book size) is that there is no mention in it of any purchase of shares for which in June last £131,250 was authorised by the Nizam's Government to be paid. Why this sum is not given in the Revised Estimate for the year that ended last October nor in the Budget Estimate for the current year is a mystery: like the Nizam's offer of 60 lakhs, his "cheque on London" for 20, and some other matters. The story of the concession was published by the *Pioneer* at Allahabad, and the gist of it may be found in the *Financial News* of Saturday. It is not pleasant reading by any means; for, if what is stated is true, British officials have, consciously or unconsciously, been furthering the scheme of a mere adventurer, who has enriched himself at the expense of the Nizam's Treasury. In the East, where the power of the ruler is untrammelled, he does not usually contemplate with great concern the illicit gains of an official, even though they may be very great. Such misconduct affords a prospect of an easy way of replenishing the State Treasury; for, when the fitting time comes, the offender is made to disgorge, to the pleasure of everybody but the sufferer. In India, where the paramount power forbids so summary a process, it takes all the precautions it can to prevent the aggrandizement of an individual at the expense of a friendly and independent State.

Lord Dufferin may have felt assured that "the masterful hand of a Resident" would keep matters straight at Hyderabad. Whether it did so or not remains to be seen.—*St. James's Gazette*, April 24.

There was much excitement over the scandal about the Hyderabad-Deccan business, and shares have gone down 5 at one blow. For a long time past this Company has formed the subject of a number of rumours of a very serious character, and affecting several persons who have had to do with this Company and its inception. This Company was formed to take over a concession which had been granted by the Nizam over a tract of land said to contain coal. It was granted without any payment, and the concessionnaires formed a Company with a capital of £1,000,000, selling the concession for something like £900,000. It is reported that the shares were "rigged" on the Stock Exchange by the connivance of certain jobbers, the public being thereby induced to purchase them. No prospectus was ever issued, the process of saddling the public being undertaken by the jobbers in question in the Stock Exchange. It appears also that the Home Secretary to the Nizam, Abdul Huk, participated in the promotion money—in other words, shared the £900,000 profit; and, with a view of helping his co-partners, it is said, he induced the Nizam to purchase on the Stock Exchange £150,000 of share capital in the company owning the very concession which he had given away for nothing! It is believed that the Government of the Nizam is now going to take up the position that the concession was obtained from the Government by misrepresentation, and collusion with Huk's colleagues in the Ministry, and that its cancellation is contemplated. Of course, the unfortunate holders of the shares will protest at this; nor does it seem feasible that the concession should be cancelled, but whether there is no remedy against the persons who have taken £900,000 from the British public is another question, and that must be settled by the India Office authorities.—*Hawk*, April 24.

Hyderabad-Deccan.—Amongst the numbers of communications we have received concerning the Deccan Mining Company scandal, the following note is by an Anglo-Indian who has had many opportunities of studying the British Indian Residency system—from its good as well as its evil side; so that his observations, as bearing on the political aspect of this grave subject, may be of some value:—

"Having long known some of the leading facts about the 'financing' of this precious Deccan Company, and desired to see them brought to the light, I can only rejoice, along with many more, that you have been enabled to make the exposure so far thorough. It is possible that a somewhat plausible explanation may yet be offered as to the placing of the 85,000 shares; but, on the other hand, much more has yet to be said in censure of certain high-placed officials, both here and in India, without whose countenance and favour the glorified policeman would not have been able to exploit his master's treasury at all. You have not, nor is it needful, to accuse these persons of any sordid personal motives in the matter. They, like Cæsar's wife in another respect, are above suspicion of venality; but their weakness, their susceptibility to the skilful blandishments of a second-rate oriental Talleyrand, their political blindness in taking the wrong side with the reactionary intriguers of Hyderabad, are all indicative of peculiar dangers that beset our official dealings with the native States of India under modern conditions. But with reference to this part of the subject let me remark on the following passage towards the close of your special despatch in Saturday's issue:

"'The whole Residency system of India, and the obligations of the Supreme Power to the feudatory States must come under careful consideration in open court. We know the general impolicy of such a course; but there are occasions when a storm clears the air. We believe this to be such an occasion.'

"As a general proposition there is much to be said for this; but it is too large an order to fit this particular case. Under cover of it the culprits would escape, and nothing would be done. You, in your leader, are much nearer the mark in pointing out the Residency at Hyderabad as the focus of the intrigues, to which prompt and searching inquiry should be directed. You also point the moral in a more practical sense than the Allahabad writer when you remark:

"'It does not say much for the prescience of the Resident and of the Viceregal Government that such a palpable trickster should have thrown dust in their eyes so long, causing them to assent to and further the alienation of the rights of one of the most loyal of the fendatory Princes. . . . . . It is for the Government to thoroughly probe the whole of the disgraceful business, to punish the delinquents. . . . . . In doing this, too, the Government will have to inquire what strange influence has closed the eyes of the officials at the India Office to what has for months past been a scandal in business circles in India.'

"It is well to insist on enforcing the responsibility both of the Viceregal Government and the India Office; but, again, this is too wide a reference. With regard to the former of these two institutions, it is the Simla Foreign Office and its chief secretary that have to be called to account. As to the India Office, it is its Political Department, and the political committee of the Indian Council, that must be subjected to stern and impartial investigation. As to the Resident and the Secretary, whom we specially gave to His Highness the Nizam, they ought at once to be suspended, as the decorated policeman, in whom they believed, has been by his Government. It is easy to denounce parties and condemn departments, but to enforce responsibility it is needful to lay hands on the arch-offenders, and bring them before judicial tribunals."—*Financial News*, April 24.

THE HYDERABAD DECCAN COMPANY.—In view of the very inaccurate accounts that have been given, in various journals, of the mining concession granted two years ago to the Hyderabad Deccan Company by the Nizam's Government, it is worth while to place upon record an authentic account of the transaction. We have not to wait for the publication of a Yellow Book at Hyderabad to learn the facts connected with this concession, for they are all contained in a Parliamentary paper on the subject—East India (Deccan) Mines, Sept., 1887; and it is generally overlooked that the Government of India, both by the Viceroy in Council and through the Secretary of State, took the leading part in initiating and in concluding the agreement which assigned to this Company the mining monopoly of the Nizam's State. If the Yellow Book publishes for the first time the correspondence relating to the purchase of shares for the Nizam last June, it has to be noted that this publication would have appeared in the usual course; that the Sirdar himself was a party to its publication; that up to this moment the Nizam's Prime Minister has not formulated any definite charge against the Sirdar, and that we are in ignorance whether he has been suspended for this transaction or for something else. But if the denunciation of the concession is to be accepted as warranted by the facts, the chief culprits are not the concessionnaires or the Nizam's Ministers, but the Government of India.

The concession of exclusive mining rights to the syndicate represented by Messrs. Watson and Stewart arose out of the earlier financial operation conducted by those gentlemen in connection with the Nizam's State Railway. The railway which the late Sir Salar Jung had created, thirteen or fourteen years ago, had failed to confer the expected advantages on the State because, to use a phrase well known in railway enterprise, it "ended in air." To construct branch lines and extensions—to bring it, in short, into connection with the main Indian system—furnished the only sound way of making it financially successful and beneficial to the State. The Sirdar Diler Jung was sent from Hyderabad as the representative of that Government, and his mission was so successful that a new railway company was formed, with a capital of four and a-half millions. The first condition of the new undertaking was that the sum of £1,666,666 should be assigned to the Nizam's Government for the purpose of buying up the shares of the old company—an operation that cost about £850,000, leaving the residue as so much profit in the hands of the Nizam. The Sirdar had been promised by his Government before he started from India that he should be allowed a five per cent. commission on this amount, if his efforts were successful. They were successful, and he received his reward. There was no secrecy about it, and the matter was officially inquired into, with the result that the Sirdar was allowed to have received only his due.

It had been intended to link the mining and railway concessions together, but this plan was abandoned, and in January, 1884, the Sirdar decided that the consideration of the mines should be postponed until his return to Hyderabad. The years 1884 and 1885 were occupied with the discussion of the points arising out of the draft agreement, which was drawn up in the main, not by the business people anxious to get the concession, but by the solicitors to the India Office, Messrs. White, Borrett, and Co. That discussion was carried on at Hyderabad between Mr. C. A. Winter, representing the concessionnaires, and the Government in the person of the ex-Prime Minister, Sir Salar Jung. In a letter of 14th January, 1885, that Minister gives a brief sketch of the negotiations, and one of the most important passages in the document is the one admitting that Messrs. Watson and Stewart had received an assurance of priority in the concession of the mining rights. Moreover, this finds formal expression in the official letter (Feb. 2, 1886) of Lord Dufferin in Council: "It is possible, too, that a belief in the prospective grant of mining rights was not without its influence on Messrs. Watson and Co. when they undertook on favourable terms the financial arrangements for the formation of the Nizam's State Railway."

Notwithstanding this tacit understanding, the Minister, Sir Salar Jung, was negotiating with another group of financiers for the grant of the same concession, and it was this that induced Mr. Winter to write that he would accept the concession with Sir Salar Jung's modifications and limitations. The agreement would have been included then and there, but that the Government of India opposed the modifications Sir Salar Jung wished to introduce, and insisted on exercising a vigilant superintendence over the whole negotiation. As a consequence most of the modifications were withdrawn, and the arrangement in almost its original form became the deed of concession, signed at Hyderabad on 7th January, 1886, by Sir Salar Jung and the concessionnaires' attorney, in the presence of the official representative of the Government of India. In the covering despatch the Viceroy wrote that it "has been drawn up in accordance with our views, and should in our opinion be confirmed." After critical inspection by the India Council at home, it was confirmed by the Secretary of State, on the concessionnaires giving a guarantee, continued by the company, that all lands upon which mining operations had not really commenced in 1896 should be restored to the State.

From this narrative it will be seen that the mining concession was intended as a reward to Messrs. Watson and Co. for financing the railway on favourable terms; that the Government of India took official cognizance of it on this basis, and an active part in not making the terms too onerous for the concessionnaires. So far as appears, the Sirdar Diler Jung acted, to use Sir Salar Jung's own words, "with the caution that has marked all his proceedings," and was a person of secondary importance in the negotiation relating to the concession. It seems to us that the Indian Government is bound—for its own reputation is as much involved as that of any of the other parties—to insist on the Hyderabad Government promptly defining the exact charges it makes against the Sirdar Diler Jung, and to ensure an impartial consideration for them as well as for that official's defence.—*Standard*, April 24.

THE HYDERABAD DECCAN COMPANY.—What has been said in various journals with reference to the concession granted two years ago to the Hyderabad Deccan Company has led the *Standard* this morning to place upon record "an authentic account of the transaction," gathered from a Parliamentary paper issued in September of last year. The *Standard*, however, does not dispute the need for an inquiry, but only contends that "if the denunciation of the concession is to be accepted as warranted by the facts, the chief culprits are not the concessionnaires or the Nizam's Ministers, but the Government of India. . . . The mining concession was intended as a reward to Messrs. Watson and Co. for financing the railway on favourable terms; the Government of India took official cognizance of it on this basis, and an active part in not making the terms too onerous for the concessionnaires." We do not see that this mends the matter much from the public point of view. And then there is not a word said as to the subsequent sale of the shares of the company to the Nizam's Government, a transaction which throws some light upon the *bona fides* of the parties in the earlier transactions. Mr. Labouchere will put a question on the subject on Thursday next, and will ask for the appointment of a Select Committee.—*Pall Mall Gazette*, April 24.

THE SITUATION.—A prominent feature of the week has been the great Hyderabad (Deccan) scandal. The quarrel is a very pretty quarrel as it stands, and, with the very limited space at present at our disposal, we should only spoil it by attempting to explain it. In sober earnest, however, it is grave enough.—*World*, April 25.

THERE are some members on both sides of the House who are determined to get to the bottom of what seems to be the great scandal of the concession of mining rights in the Deccan. To-night Mr. Maclean, a faithful Conservative, sternly questioned the Under-Secretary for India on the matter, and was backed up on the other side by Mr. Labouchere. What was more important, Lord Randolph Churchill showed a disposition to throw himself into the fray, freezing his old associate, Sir John Gorst, with a question arising out of the earlier catechism. As a good deal will be heard of this case in the course of the next few days, it may be useful to summarise the facts as they were set forth by the members who are raising the storm. It is said that the consent of the Resident at Hyderabad and of the Indian Government was given in January, 1886, for 99 years to the concession by the Nizam of all mining rights in the Deccan to Messrs. Watson and Stewart, under the following conditions: That they would "promote a company with a nominal capital of £1,000,000, but that not more than £150,000 should be first issued, and £75,000 paid up, which sum was to be employed in working the coalfields of Singareni, and that the rest of the capital was only to be issued if it could be remuneratively employed in working other coalfields or mines, in building steel or iron works in the Deccan."

The concessionnaires promoted a company with a capital of £1,000,000, divided into 100,000 shares of £10, and they issued at once the entire capital, allotted to themselves, to a Mr. Sharp, and to Mr. Winter, the solicitor of the company, 85,000 shares, which were declared to be fully paid up, although nothing was paid on them. In June last one Abdul Huk, being in England as Jubilee Commissioner of the Nizam, purchased 10,000 shares for the Government of the Nizam at the price of £12 per share. It has been stated in the *Times* and other journals that the price of £12 per share was an artificial one, caused by fictitious dealings between the concessionnaires and their nominees, and by eight brokers being sent into the Stock Exchange by Abdul Huk simultaneously to compete for shares; that they were all, or almost all bought in two blocks, bearing consecutive numbers, from one jobber; that the Jubilee Commissioner telegraphed to Colonel Marshall, the British secretary of the Nizam, on June 3:—"Deccans firmly held by public; therefore with greatest difficulty succeeded in purchasing" the shares in question; and that Colonel Marshall replied that this arrangement was "eminently satisfactory."—*Bradford Observer*, April 25.

Mr. Labouchere will on Thursday move for the appointment of a Committee of Inquiry into the circumstances under which a concession of all the mining rights in the State of Hyderabad was recently granted to a syndicate for £150,000, and immediately resold in London to a company for £1,000,000. Should the Government refuse the inquiry Mr. Labouchere will move the adjournment on the subject, and will be supported by many Ministerialists, including Lord R. Churchill and Mr. James MacLean.—*North British Mail*, April 25.

The Hyderabad (Deccan) Company.—From time to time the business circles of the City of London have been startled by the exposure of some gigantic fraud, but these have been mostly perpetrated by men whose doings are more or less known, and their dupes have been the unsuspecting public. The story of the acquisition and floating of the Hyderabad (Deccan) Mine, which came to light last week, is startling, from the fact that the ruler of one of our largest Indian dependencies has been the victim, and the Government President and the Nizam's Secretary appear to have unwittingly aided the project, the prime mover in which has been Abdul Huk, formerly a policeman, but more recently the Prime Minister to the Ruler of Hyderabad, and now transformed into the Sirdar Diler ul Mulk. The London promoters, who appear to have pulled the strings, are Messrs. Watson and Stewart, together with the brother-in-law of one of them, Mr. Winter, a solicitor. The two first-named gentlemen are said to have made £180,000 out of the Hyderabad Railways, and, not content with this little plum, went for a coup of nearly one million sterling. In this they were completely successful, and had not these revelations come to light, would most probably have been left in undisturbed possession of their plunder. The history of the company is briefly this:—

The Nizam of Hyderabad was persuaded to sell the concession for working the minerals which are known to exist in the territory to Messrs. Watson and Stewart, who were to form a company with a capital of one million sterling, of which it was finally agreed that £150,000 should be issued, with £75,000 paid up, to commence operations. Instead of doing this, the promoters issued the whole capital, and allotted themselves 85,000 "fully-paid" £10 shares, for which they then endeavoured to find a market. To do this, heavy buying was necessary, and the brilliant idea was conceived of trying to induce the Nizam to obtain a controlling interest in the company by the purchase of its shares at 12. In this they were successful, and the unfortunate victim invested about £138,000 in the purchase of shares of the company at 12. It appears that the eight brokers sent in on the Stock Exchange to buy the shares bought them through the same jobber, and the shares delivered were numbered consecutively.

The public also probably came in and bought more. At present the Sirdar has been dismissed from his post in connection with the matter, and Parliament will be asked to look into all the circumstances of the deal, when it is highly probable that the concession will be annulled, and the promoters made to disgorge some of their plunder. Further details are awaited with interest; and the whole story reads more like a romance of the times of Clive and the East India Company, when vast sums were made out of the unfortunate Indian potentates, than a transaction in the sober City of London, and within a few hundred yards of Capel Court.—*Court and Society Review*, April 25.

CERTAIN quidnuncs have assumed to be very wise and learned concerning the affairs of the Hyderabad (Deccan) Company, and have even asserted that the panic which occurred last week in the market for the shares of the company was "unjustifiable." Information which has just come to hand in the form of an official publication—the Yellow-book issued at Hyderabad last month—fully confirms the rumours of a very serious character affecting the actual validity of the company which have for some time past been floating about.

The conduct of several persons is very gravely called into question who have had to do with the company, and been the prime movers from its inception. It appears that the present Nizam, the youthful Sir Salar Jung, was induced in 1886 to grant to Messrs. Watson and Stewart a concession for the mining rights in the Deccan. Among the conditions recommended by the Government of India was one to the effect that these gentlemen should be permitted to promote a company with a nominal capital of £1,000,000, but that not more than £150,000 should at first be issued, of which only £75,000 was to be called up. That this was the understanding was clearly shown in the correspondence of Mr. Cordery, the British Resident at Hyderabad, and of Mr. Durand, the Secretary of the Foreign Department in the Indian Government, with the parties to the concession. It must, however, be admitted that in the actual convention, which was finally drawn and signed in London on January 7, 1886, the terms above-mentioned are not so clearly stated as in the correspondence of the Indian Government.

Be that as it may, in July following the "Hyderabad (Deccan) Company, Limited," was incorporated, with a capital of £1,000,000, and £75,000 was called up on £150,000 worth of shares. Now comes the most astounding parts of the affair. The promoters of the scheme, Messrs. Watson and Stewart, according to the accounts received, coolly and unjustifiably, in direct contradiction to the terms of the concession, appropriated the whole of the remaining £850,000 of shares to themselves, "in consideration for their concession," which had been gratuitously obtained.

Time passed until we reach the summer of 1887, when a native, variously styled the Sirdar Diler-ul-Mulk and Sirdar Diler Jung, who at one period of his life was a policeman and private soldier, but who had been ennobled and raised to the rank of one of the Nizam's Ministers, came to London as the representative of the Nizam at the Queen's Jubilee. This man (who was formerly known as Abdul Huk, and was mainly instrumental to the granting of the "free" concession of the mining rights) has been suspended from his office pending the result of an inquiry instituted by the Indian Government.

Before coming to London last spring, Abdul Huk had succeeded in cajoling and persuading the Nizam to purchase shares to the amount of £150,000, in order to obtain a "controlling interest" in the company to which he had given a free concession!—these shares being part of the unauthorised issue which the promoters had allotted to themselves.

An important fact to be borne in mind is that only a month before the time the Nizam purchased these shares at a premium of 20 per cent. of their original nominal value, the actual sum which the company had spent in the

Deccan was only £6,411. Of this only £2,780 had been spent in prospecting for new mines in the province, the remainder having gone in "establishment charges" and in the development of the Singareni coal mines, a part of the business on the importance of which the Indian Government had always laid stress.—*Money*, April 25.

THE Under-Secretary for India explained yesterday that the Secretary of State had no knowledge of the purchase on behalf of the Nizam of shares in the Hyderabad (Deccan) Company. But seeing that the India Office was made aware of the proposal, it is difficult to see how it can clear itself of all responsibility. One thing Sir John Gorst has made clear. The Viceroy's telegram to the Secretary of State expressly mentions that the Resident recommended the purchase of the shares. It therefore devolves upon the Government to make inquiry at once into the conduct of Mr. Cordery in thus contributing to a transaction which he ought to have known was a gross misuse of the Nizam's money.—*Evening Post*, April 25.

MINING RIGHTS IN HYDERABAD.—In reply to Mr. J. Maclean,

Sir J. Gorst said: The contract of January 7, 1886, between the Government of the Nizam and Messrs. Watson and Stewart for the grant of mining rights in Hyderabad was described by me, in reply to a question in the House of Commons, on June 27, 1887. The contract itself, the negotiations which led to it, and the circumstances under which it was sanctioned by the Government of India and the Secretary of State, can be found in papers laid before Parliament in September, 1887. For the subsequent transactions of Messrs. Watson and Stewart, of the company formed, and of the Nizam's Government in relation thereto, the Secretary of State has no responsibility. A committee of the Council of India had in 1883 the question of a grant of mining rights in connexion with the proposed extension of the Nizam's State Railway under consideration. Their conclusions are to be found in the papers above mentioned, page 3, and were adverse to such grants. The matter was not again under the consideration of the Council or any committee thereof till after the contract of January 7, 1886, had been executed, with the approval of the Government of India. On May 16, 1887, the Secretary of State received a telegram from the Government of India in these words:—"Hyderabad mining operations promise well. Nizam's Government wishes to take shares in the company. The President thinks this desirable, and recommends our raising no objection; while accepting no responsibility, we have agreed." No action was taken on this telegram, and the Secretary of State was neither aware of the actual purchase of shares nor gave any assistance to Abdul Hak in relation thereto by appointment of a special committee or otherwise. If the hon. member will move for the Yellow-book it will be laid on the table.

Mr. J. Maclean asked whether it was considered that the Government of India had no responsibility for this transaction when it was consulted about the purchase of shares, and whether it had no responsibility for preventing an Indian Prince coming to London and being shamefully robbed.

Sir J. Gorst said the question was an argumentative one, and had better be put upon the paper.

Lord R. Churchill asked how it could be contended that the Secretary of State was not responsible for the action of the Government of India.

Mr. Labouchere asked whether a telegram sent by Colonel Marshall, the English private secretary to the Nizam, appointed by the Governor-General, sent to Abdul Hak did not affect the responsibility of the India Government.

Sir J. Gorst said he should like notice of the question.—*Times*, April 25.

The Hyderabad Mining Concession.—Sir John Gorst's reply to Mr. Maclean's interrogatories about the Nizam's concession of mining rights throughout his domains to an English company leaves not a little to be explained. Certainly, on the face of matters as they stand, there is more than an implication that the Indian Government took some part in the business. How far this part extended requires to be defined, and with that object we would suggest the institution of a searching investigation. The ugliest point is the large purchase of shares by the Nizam at a considerable premium, after almost giving away the concession which gave these securities their only value. So far as appears from the statements that have been published, the company had done little or nothing to enhance the value of its mining rights. It is highly desirable to ascertain, therefore, whether any official of the Indian Government, whether directly or indirectly, counselled our great feudatory to fling away his property with one hand, and to buy it back with the other at a fancy price. In matters of this sort it is of the first consequence that there should not be the least suspicion of official pressure or advice—the terms are practically synonymous at native courts. Every Indian prince has, of course, a perfect right to do as he pleases with his own property, provided he makes no use of it to embarrass or endanger the Suzerain's administration. But during recent years a certain process called "milking the rajahs" has come to be spoken of, and although this may be pure scandal, it behoves all officials to walk as warily as Cæsar's wife. It may be, of course, that it was for the advantage of the Deccan that its ruler should enlist British enterprise and capital for the development of the resources of his State. It may be, also, that he could not have obtained better terms for the concession even if he had submitted it to public tender. These are questions of comparatively small moment; the vital matter is whether any official connected with the Indian Government took part in the business.—*Globe*, April 25.

Our London Letter.—(from our own correspondent.)—House of Commons, Tuesday Night.—There are some members on both sides of the House who are determined to get to the bottom of what seems to be the great scandal of the concession of mining rights in the Deccan. To-night, Mr. Maclean, a faithful Conservative, sternly questioned the Under-Secretary for India on the matter, and was backed up on the other side by Mr. Labouchere. What was more important, Lord R. Churchill showed a disposition to throw himself into the fray, freezing his old associate, Sir John Gorst, with a question arising out of the earlier catechism. As a good deal will be heard of this case in the course of the next few days, it may be useful to summarise the facts as they are set forth by members who are raising the storm. It is said the consent of the Resident at Hyderabad and of the Indian Government was given in January, 1886, for 99 years, to the concession by the Nizam of all mining rights in the Deccan to Messrs. Watson and Stewart under the following conditions: That they would promote a company with a nominal capital of £1,000,000, but that not more than £150,000 should be first issued and £75,000 paid up, which sum was to be employed in working the coalfields of Singareni, and that the rest of the capital was only to be issued if it could be remuneratively employed in working other coalfields or mines, or in building steel or iron works in the Deccan. The concessionnaires promoted a company with a capital of £1,000,000, divided into 100,000 shares of £10, and having issued at once the entire capital, allotted to themselves, to a Mr. Sharp, and to Mr. Winter, the solicitor of the company, 85,000 shares, which were declared to be fully paid up, although nothing was paid on them. In June last, one Abdul Huk, being in England as Jubilee Commissioner of the Nizam, purchased 10,000 shares for the Government of the Nizam, at the price of £12 per share. It has been stated in the *Times* and other journals that the price of £12 per share was an artificial one, caused by fictitious dealings between the concessionnaires and their nominees, and by eight brokers being sent into the Stock Exchange by Abdul Huk simultaneously to compete for shares, and that they were all, or almost all, bought in two blocks bearing consecutive numbers from one jobber. That the Jubilee Commissioner telegraphed to Col. Marshall, the British Secretary of the Nizam, on June 3rd, "Deccans firmly held by public, therefore with greatest difficulty succeeded in purchasing" the shares in question, and Col. Marshall replied that this arrangement was "eminently satisfactory."

Sir John Gorst, who is very hard to catch, had his answers cut and dried to-night, and Mr. Maclean got very little out of him. But it is not intended that the matter shall rest where it is. Mr. Labouchere will on Thurday return to the hunt, asking whether, in view of the above facts, and with the object of protecting the subjects of the Nizam from the loss of £850,000, and British investors from the loss of their money by investing in the "paper" shares of this company under the impression that both its capital and the Stock Exchange operations connected with it were within the knowledge, and had the approval, of the Indian Government and Her Majesty's Secretary of State for India, the Government will agree to the appointment of a Select Committee to inquire into the formation of the company, the purchasers of shares by an agent of the Nizam, and the approval of the purchase by Colonel Marshall, and to report whether there is sufficient cause for the Nizam to be advised to abrogate or to be brought to justice. Lord Randolph Churchill has promised to back up the demand for a Select Committee, the appointment of which it will be difficult for Government to refuse.—*Sheffield Independent*, April 25.

WE are likely shortly to hear more about the already notorious Hyderabad concession, about which Mr. James Maclean asked a question in the House of Commons to-day. Mr. Labouchere will on Thursday request the Government to grant a Committee of Inquiry into the whole business, and should this be refused the hon. gentleman will later move the adjournment of the House, with the object of raising a debate on the subject. Mr. Labouchere is acting in this matter with the concurrence and support of many members of both sides, including Lord Randolph Churchill and the member for Oldham.—*Manchester Courier*, April 25.

THE affairs of the Hyderabad Mining Company have been brought into the fierce light of publicity by the dismissal of the Nizam's Home Secretary on the ground of his connection with the company. Mr. J. M. Maclean asked a question in the House of Commons last night on the subject, and Mr. Labouchere has a similar question on the notice paper for Thursday. The circumstances under which the company was floated are certainly suspicious, and demand inquiry. An English firm in 1886 obtained from the Nizam a concession of all mining rights in his territory for a period of 99 years, on the condition that they would promote a company with a nominal capital of £1,000,000, of which not more than £150,000 was to be first issued, and £75,000 paid up. When the company was started the entire capital was issued, the promoters allotting to themselves 85,000 of the £10 shares which were declared to be fully paid up, although nothing was paid on them. During the Jubilee celebrations last June, which Mr. Abdul Huk, or, to give him his recently acquired title, Sirdar Diler-ul-Mulk, attended as the Nizam's representative, he purchased on account of the Nizam, and apparently with his approval, 12,500 shares in the company at £12 per share, to which price, it is alleged, they had been artifically advanced by a clever manipulation of the market. Colonel Marshall, the British officer who was specially appointed some time since to advise the

Nizam in State affairs, expressed his approval of the arrangement, which he said was "eminently satisfactory." The investment might have appeared so at first, but it can scarcely be considered in that light now, as the shares which were bought at £12 have receded to £8, and are likely to fall still further. The company, however, has a valuable property in its concession, which, if properly worked, will in time yield profitable results. No part of India is richer in minerals of all descriptions than the Deccan, and capital is only needed to turn them to account.—*Yorkshire Post*, April 25.

HYDERABAD-DECCAN.—QUESTIONS ASKED IN PARLIAMENT—A SELECT COMMITTEE TO BE APPLIED FOR.—In the House of Commons yesterday, Mr. J. Maclean asked the Under Secretary of State for India whether it was true that the concession of all the mining rights in the State of Hyderabad, granted to a syndicate, with the sanction of the Government of India, for £150,000, was immediately resold in London to a company for £1,000,000. If, in order to force up the price of this company's shares, the Nizam was persuaded by his late Home Secretary, Abdul Huk, who had recommended the concession, to invest £150,000 in the purchase of shares at a premium; if it is the case, as stated by Sir Salar Jung, that "a special committee, composed of India Office officials, was appointed to watch Abdul Huk's proceedings, and give him advice during the course of his negotiation"; if the India Office was cognizant of and gave its sanction to such an investment of money belonging to a native prince under its protection; and if he would lay upon the table of the House a copy of the Yellow Book published at Hyderabad, in which Abdul Huk gives a full account of these transactions.

Sir J. Gorst: The contract of January 7, 1886, between the Government of the Nizam and Messrs. Watson and Stewart for the grant of mining rights in Hyderabad was described by me in reply to a question in the House of Commons on June 27, 1887. The contract itself, the negotiations which led to it, and the circumstances under which it was sanctioned by the Government of India and the Secretary of State, can be found in papers laid before Parliament in September, 1887. For the subsequent transactions of Messrs. Watson and Stewart, of the company formed, and of the Nizam's Government in relation thereto, the Secretary of State has no responsibility. A committee of the Council of India had in 1883 the question of a grant of mining rights in connection with the proposed extension of the Nizam's State Railway under consideration. Their conclusions are to be found in the papers abovementioned, page 3, and were adverse to such grant. The matter was not again under the consideration of the Council, or any Committee thereof, till after the contract of January 7, 1886, had been executed with the approval of the Government of India. On May 16th, 1887, the Secretary of State received a telegram from the Government of India in these words:—"Hyderabad Mining operations promise well. Nizam's Government wishes to take shares in the company. The President thinks this desirable, and recommends our raising no objection; while accepting no responsibility, we have agreed." No action was taken on this telegram, and the Secretary of State was neither aware of the actual purchase of shares, nor gave any assistance to Abdul Huk in relation thereto by appointment of a Special Committee or otherwise. If the hon. member will move for the Yellow Book it will be laid on the table.

Mr. Labouchere has given notice of a question to the Under-Secretary of State for India, in regard to the concession by the Nizam of Hyderabad of all mining rights in the Deccan to Watson and Stewart, under certain conditions, and in regard to the subsequent promotion of a company and the allocation of shares, which were declared to be fully paid up, although it is alleged nothing was paid upon them. The question, which is of altogether abnormal length, asks when the Government will agree to the appointment of a Select Committee to inquire into the formation of the company, the purchase of shares by an agent of the Nizam, and the approval of the purchase by Colonel Marshall, and to report whether there is sufficient cause for the Nizam to be advised to abrogate or modify, and for the guilty parties, if fraud be proved, to be brought to justice.—*Financial News*, April 25.

HYDERABAD-DECCAN.—The galled jades are beginning to wince over the Hyderabad-Deccan scandal. As we suspected, there must be some of them even in high quarters, otherwise it would be difficult to account for the remarkable statement which appeared in yesterday's *Standard* in all the dignity of large type. It professed to be an "authentic account of the transaction," called forth by the "very inaccurate accounts which had been given in various journals." When grave charges cannot be conveniently refuted, it is not unusual to indulge in sweeping declarations of inaccuracy. Such a method of defence is very elastic, and if performed with an air of authority it may impose on superficial readers. It has been very often tried against *The Financial News*; but never with much success. By this time we should have some experience in analysing subjects like the Hyderabad-Deccan scandal; we ought to know facts when we see them, and to be able to appreciate the value of evidence. If, as some people seem to suppose, we acted in matters of this sort from motives of morbid curiosity, we should, no doubt, occasionally get the wrong sow by the ear; but an instance of that kind has yet to be discovered, and it is not going to be found in the Hyderabad-Deccan scandal. Every word we have published regarding it was carefully weighed, and every statement can be supported by indisputable evidence.

As for the semi-official communication to the *Standard*, it can be very easily disposed of. Its manifest object is to bring together and to place in the most favourable light every extenuating circumstance that can be thought of for the concessionnaires. The whole style of it is inconsistent with the idea of its being the work of a well-informed and impartial person. The writer seems to have known either too much or too little: either he was unsophisticated, and wrote merely what he was told, or he was an interested party, and wrote what was most expedient. Whichever he was, he has known that he had a ticklish subject to handle, and he has handled it very gingerly. Our statements were specific enough, but he does not venture to lay hold of any one of them and contradict it. He merely suggests, in a fatuous, flabby way, that the facts referred to bear another interpretation. Doubtless they have already received any number of interpretations, and that of the *Standard* is only another addition to the crowd. But all the while the facts themselves remain exactly as we stated them, and they are "stubborn chiels," which even the *Standard* "winna ding."

Failing the power of direct contradiction, the *Standard* exercises all its skill to minimise our charges. It pooh-poohs the notion of any new discovery having been made, and refers to a Parliamentary paper issued in September last as containing all the facts of the case. That paper was, of course, one of the documents before us, and it was repeatedly referred to in our first article, but not always with commendation. It was distinctly declared to be an imperfect and unsatisfactory narrative, betraying in almost every page signs of discreet editing. When we add that it was prepared in the India Office, where Abdul Huk has always had friendly, if not still more intimate relations, sensible readers will be able to form their own opinion as to its impartiality. The "Yellow Book" published at Hyderabad tells the story much more fully and brings it down to a more interesting period. The India Office paper breaks off, like a serial novel, just where the plot begins to thicken. It ends practically with the signing of the agreement between the Nizam's Government and the concessionnaires, and conveys not the slightest hint of the dramatic incidents which followed a few months later: the manufacture of £850,000 of paper capital in the Hyderabad-Deccan Company, and the sale of 12,500 of these paper shares to the Nizam's Government at a premium of 20 per cent.

An Indian Office paper, issued in September, 1887, might, had it been deemed expedient, have very easily included in its narrative events which took place in June, 1886; but both the *papier mâché* shares and the subsequent rig in them at the Nizam's expense are severely ignored. The *Standard* itself follows the prudent example of the India Office. Its "authentic account of the transaction" has not a word to say, either about the *papier mâché* episode or about the eight little brokers who swooped down on the one little jobber and filled his pockets with £2 premiums. Our respect for age and dignity forbids us to speak of the *Standard* with anything but the most profound respect. We must point out, however, to our venerable contemporary that the world is full of people who lack the reverential faculty of *The Financial News.* There be cynical and sarcastic persons about only too ready to make fun of an elderly lady who rushes into the ring to explain everything and put everybody right, but misses the most important points of her mission.

All that rigmarole about the Nizam's State Railway and Abdul Huk's double commission is ancient history now. Neither is there much novelty in the story of how the mining concession was negotiated. Up to a certain point there was not much to say against the negotiations. On the face of it a mining monopoly of an entire State is a rather dubious kind of arrangement; but there can be no doubt that the Nizam's Government went into it with its eyes open, and that both the Government of India and the India Office countenanced the proceedings. The concession, as set forth in the published indenture of January 7, 1886, might quite conceivably have been negotiated in good faith on both sides. In itself it might have been legitimate enough as concessions go, though it is suspiciously vague and flexible in its terms. So far, we have made no charge as to the way in which the concession was obtained. It may have been honestly got or otherwise; that is still an open question. Our allegations bear distinctly and directly on the use subsequently made of the concession, to the serious prejudice, first, of the British public, and, secondly, of the Nizam's Government.

As the *Standard* appears to be boiling over with "authentic" information, will it be good enough to throw some light on the following points, which are the crux of the question at issue, though the "authentic account ' has very strangely overlooked them altogether?

First—Was it or was it not contemplated by the Nizam's Government, in fixing the capital of the proposed company at £1,000,000, that more than five-sixths of the amount was to be issued in paper shares and divided among the concessionnaires and their friends?

Second—Was it or was it not understood by the Government of India that such a gigantic stock-watering operation was intended to be carried out under its auspices and with its implied sanction?

Third—Were the responsible officials at the India Office aware or were they not of the elaborate conspiracy by which these paper shares were manufactured and palmed off on deluded investors, including the Nizam himself?

When the *Standard* has "authentic" information to give on these points, the public doubtless will be glad to receive it. Meanwhile, it is beside the question to fill the public ear with twaddle, telegraphic or otherwise, about the concession being valid and the Nizam still being friendly to the company in spite of his having been so egregiously fooled through it. In these respects we are prepared to be very liberal indeed with the promoters of the Hyderabad-Deccan Company. We shall grant them all that they ask and more as regards the concession itself, and their friendly relations at Hyderabad. What we desire to know in the public interest is how such a concession ever came to be got from the Nizam's Government for practically nothing, and to be immediately afterwards sold in this country for over a million sterling—many of the shares having been planted on the market at premiums of 20 to 30 per cent. The promoters are in a dilemma, which, put it as delicately as we may, convicts them of very sharp practice either in Hyderabad or London. Somebody has been badly used: either the Nizam in giving away the concession for nothing, or the shareholders of the Hyderabad-Deccan Company in having it foisted on them at a million' sterling. Will the *Standard*, in the plenitude of its "authentic" wisdom, decide for us which?—*Financial News*, April 25.

It is reported that Mr. Watson, the concessionnaire of the Hyderabad-Deccan Company and its chairman, is on his way back to London from Constantinople to the relief of the concern. It is not believed that he will be able to assure his proprietors that "he has not sold a share." The expected relief will have to come in some other form.—*Financial News*, April 25.

The Hyderabad (Deccan) Company.—The following telegram was received in London yesterday from Hyderabad: "The charge against the Sirdar Diler Jung does not relate to the purchase of the shares by His Highness the Nizam, but to the use of the term 'subscribed' in the second article of the deed. It seems to have been the intention of the Government of India to employ some such phrase as 'first issue of;' but in the face of the facts that the word 'subscribed' appears in the original draft of the arrangement drawn up by the solicitors of the Government in London, and that the Government of India had subsequent opportunities of amending the term, or of objecting to it, which was never done, there is considerable difficulty in adopting this view of the matter. In any case it remains to be proved how far the retention of this word was due to the Sirdar, while it must be considered doubtful whether the concessionnaires would have gone into the business at all if this view of the transaction had been enforced in 1885-6."—*Times*, April 25.

There are some members on both sides of the House who are determined to get to the bottom of what seems to be the great scandal of the concession of mining rights in the Deccan. To-night, Mr. Maclean, a faithful Conservative, sternly questioned the Under-Secretary for India on the matter, and was backed up on the other side by Mr. Labouchere. What was more important, Lord Randolph Churchill showed a disposition to throw himself into the fray, freezing his old associate, Sir John Gorst, with a question arising out of the earlier catechism. As a good deal will be heard of this case in the course of the next few days it may be useful to summarise the facts as they are set forth by members who are raising the storm. It is said the consent of the Resident at Hyderabad and of the Indian Government was given in January, 1886, for ninety-nine years, to a concession by the Nizam of all mining rights in the Deccan under the following conditions: That the concessionnaires would promote a company with a nominal capital of £1,000,000, but not more than £150,000 should be first issued, and £75,000 paid up, which sum was to be employed in working the coalfields of Singareni, and that the rest of the capital was only to be issued if it could be remuneratively employed in working other coalfields or mines, or in building steel or iron works in the Deccan. The concessionnaires promoted a company, with a capital of £1,000,000, and having issued at once the entire capital, allotted to themselves, to a Mr. Sharp, and to Mr. Winter, the solicitor of the company, 85,000 shares. In June last, one Abdul Huk, being in England as Jubilee Commissioner of the Nizam, purchased 10,000 shares for the Government of the Nizam at the price of £12 per share.

It has been stated in the *Times* and other journals that the price of £12 per share was an artificial price, caused by fictitious dealings, and that the shares were all, or almost all, bought in two blocks bearing consecutive numbers from one jobber; and that the Jubilee Commissioner telegraphed to Colonel Marshall, the British Secretary of the Nizam, in June—"Deccans firmly held by public, therefore with greatest difficulty succeeded in purchasing" the shares in question.—*Liverpool Post*, April 25.

We are likely to hear a great deal in the immediate future of the mining concession granted two years ago by the Goverment of the Nizam to the Hyderabad Deccan Company, for the arrest of Abdul Huk, otherwise known as the Sirdar Diler Jung, has brought the matter to a crisis; and as the Indian Government is involved in it, as well as many an English investor, the attention of the House of Commons is at once to be drawn to it. What may be regarded as a semi-official defence of Abdul Huk, who from a policeman reached last year the giddy height of a Jubilee Commissioner, and is now in prison, appeared in to-day's *Standard*, but a very different series of statements affecting that personage are contained in a long question which Mr. Labouchere intends to put to Sir John Gorst, the Under Indian Secretary, on Thursday. The practical request with which the question concludes is that a Select Committee shall be granted to inquire into the whole affair, and there is the best authority for stating that if the answer given is unsatisfactory the senior member for Northampton will move the adjournment of the House; but there is excellent reason for believing that a committee will be promised. Lord Randolph Churchill, I understand, is in sympathy with Mr. Labouchere's action in this matter, which, put at the mildest, is one that needs investigation. Some members well acquainted with Anglo-Indian affairs state that they do not impute fraud to the Government officials whose names have been mentioned in connection therewith, but they complain that these should have been mixed up in the business of concession granting. The concession itself, which was sold by the Hyderabad Government for little or nothing, is a good one, the Nizam's dominions being the richest in minerals of any in India.—*Birmingham Post*, April 25.

Nothing special occurred in the House of Commons with the questions except, perhaps, the tame answer given by Sir John Gorst on the subject of the Hyderabad concession, from which it appeared that Her Majesty's Government at home possesses very little influence over, and owe very little responsibility in respect of, the Executive in India.—*Birmingham Post*, April 25.

The Deccan Scandal.—A correspondent in the *Times* this morning puts in a plea for the Sirdar Diler Jung, but it only amounts to this, that there is no proof of any fraud on his part in connection with the concession to the Deccan Company. With respect to the purchasing of the shares, this writer simply passes the blame on to Mr. Watson, with whom he had all along been associated, for he says, "It is no evidence of bad faith that he should have unreservedly accepted the statement of the agent of the Government here." The scandal will not be cleared up until the following questions put by *Truth* are satisfactorily answered:—

"Why should the State of Hyderabad part with its mining rights to Messrs. Watson and Stewart for nothing? Why should £850,000 of the capital of the company go into the pockets of the promoters, in flat defiance of the terms of the concession? Why should the State of Hyderabad have bought back a quantity of shares, which represented nothing but the cost of printing them, from the promoters at £12 per share, thus making a present of above £100,000 to the concessionnaires for obtaining the concession? How possibly can it be supposed that the English investor can hope for a remunerative return on his capital, should he buy shares, when £150,000 of real capital has to earn a dividend upon a fictitious capital of £850,000, in addition to this £150,000?"

Owing to the rigging of the market, to the Nizam appearing on the scene as a purchaser, and to the semi-official sanction given to the scheme, four-fifths of the shares have been taken up by the public, mostly at a premium. Whether the Sirdar Diler Jung has benefited or not by this concession, he has been a mighty fortunate man, seeing that he has accumulated half a million sterling during the past six or seven years.—*Pall Mall Gazette*, April 26.

The scandal about the Deccan mines is going to be a big thing, and, I am told on the best authority, may result in a Ministerial crisis. The history of the affair is long and involved. But it is alleged by some people, though I do not say there is a word of truth in the accusation, that the exclusive right to work the mineral wealth of Hyderabad was secured from the Nizam on condition that a million sterling was sunk in his country. It is now asserted that the terms of the undertaking have not been strictly observed. There are numerous details which are too complicated to explain. But Mr. Labouchere is going to ask the Government to institute an inquiry into the reasons why the English Resident allowed the Nizam to sign away his rights in this fashion. If the Government refuses to allow the inquiry, I hear a coalition will be formed against it, which may be very dangerous.—*Leicester Post*, April 26.

[The above appeared in a number of provincial newspapers.]

Quite a panic occurred last week in the shares of the Deccan Company. They fell from £10 to £7 a share, although at the time of writing they have recovered somewhat. This effect was produced by the publication of a crude telegram of Reuter's agency, from Hyderabad, which announced that the Nizam has suspended Abdullak, the Home Secretary, on account of his connection with the Deccan Mining Company. The telegram further stated that the suspension created an immense sensation on the spot. The alarm has been aggravated by adverse criticisms on the validity of the concession and on the personal character of Abdullak, who was a foremost mover in the business.—*Life*, April 26.

The Indian Concession Scandal.—Attention has already been called in the Press to the Deccan Company, but it may be well to go into particulars in order distinctly to show how Indian public companies are launched in London, and how Indian Native Governments are fleeced. In 1883, it was suggested to the late Sir Salar Jung that it would be desirable that an English Company should be formed to develop the resources of the State of Hyderabad. Amongst those anxious to obtain the concession were Messrs. Watson and Stewart, and it was thought that they were in some special way entitled to it, because Mr. Watson, with a certain Abdul Huk as his associate, had financed the State Railway, and had received for this alone £180,000—a promotion amount which has more than once attracted the attention of Parliament.

The concession was finally given under the following conditions: It was for ninety-nine years, and covered all mining rights in Hyderabad. The capital of the Company was to be one million sterling. The first issue of shares was to be £150,000, of which 50 per cent. was to be called up at once.

There can be no ambiguity in regard to the conditions of the concession with respect to the issue of only a portion of the capital at first, and the expenditure of all moneys received from subsequent issues on remunerative works in the Deccan; for Mr. Cordery, the British Resident, in forwarding the revised draft of the concession to Sir Salar Jung (who had succeeded his father as Prime Minister), May 6, 1885, accompanied it by a memorandum from the Indian Government, in which the following passage occurs:—

"The first issue of shares has been reduced from £250,000 to £100,000, and the paid-up capital from £100,000 to £25,000. This has been done to meet the immediate requirements of the opening of the Singareni coal fields, which, judging from the circumstances of existing coal companies in Bengal, can be efficiently worked with a subscribed capital of the amount proposed in the altered clause. The nominal capital is left as originally drafted in Clause 1, as it is contemplated that further issues of shares will be made in the event of iron or steel works being started at Singareni, or the mineral wealth of the Province being developed at other sites."

This extract explains itself. The Indian Government were not prepared to allow one million sterling to be called up at once, and thrown away in prospecting, &c. A sufficient sum was to be subscribed to enable the coal-fields of Singareni to be worked, then more capital might be called up, and more shares might be issued to develop other mineral fields, or to construct iron or steel works. Hyderabad was to have eventually the million, or the greater part of the million, expended within her limits in remunerative developments, and the British investor was to be protected against the concessionnaires using bogus capital.

Equally clear is it that Sir Salar Jung gave the concession, rather because he was forced to do so, than because he himself deemed it an advantageous one to his country, and that the Government of India and the Secretary of State for India are responsible for it, as Sir Salar wrote, when announcing to the Government of India that the conditions had been arranged—

"I have been considerably influenced by Sirdar Diler Jung's (Abdul Huk) representations in granting the concession to Messrs. Watson and Stewart, when more favourable terms might have been secured. . . . . As the Resident, the Government of India, and the Secretary of State have approved of the proposal to grant the mining concession to Messrs. Watson and Stewart, I have accepted the revised draft as agreed to by Mr. Winter on behalf of Messrs. Watson and Stewart."

On January 7 the Deccan Mining Company was brought out in London. The entire share capital of one million was issued—viz., 100,000 shares of £10 each. Of these, 85,000 were described as fully paid-up shares, and went into the pockets of the promoters, not one farthing being paid on them; and on the remaining 15,000, which also were subscribed for by the promoters, £5 per share was called up at once, and the remaining £75,000 was paid up last November. The allotment of the 85,000 promoters' shares was as follows:—23,906 to Mr. Watson, 18,594 to Mr. Stewart, 7,969 to Mr. Sharp, and 34,531 to Mr. Winter, the solicitor of the company. The company therefore consists of 85,000 promoters' shares of £10, and 15,000 shares of £10 subscribed for by the promoters, of which less than £7,000 has been expended in the Deccan, except in salaries, &c., to highly-paid *employés* who have been sent out there.

So far, Messrs. Watson and Stewart had gained nothing. For them to do so, it became necessary to sell the promoters' shares to some one, or to sell the shares on which the face value had been paid up at a premium. The British public held aloof. The first step seems to have been to "make dealings" at a high price, by the promoters selling the shares backwards and forwards amongst themselves, and I find that the following transfers took place: Stewart to Watson, 3,966 shares; Watson to Stewart, 708 shares; Watson to Winter, 6,101 shares; Winter to Watson, 1,238 shares; Sharp to Watson, 4,052;

Messrs. Watson and Stewart to Watson, 23,906; to Stewart, 18,594; to Sharp, 7,969; to Winter, 31,541. These transfers were "backwards and forwards." Thus, 468 shares, Nos. 11,201 to 11,668, were allotted to Watson; he transferred them to Stewart, who transferred them back to Watson, who transferred them to Winter.

But this interchange of affairs did not lead to any profit. It was therefore suggested that the State of Hyderabad should come forward and buy shares, on the plea that it ought to hold a "predominant interest" in the concern. Abdul Huk, now converted into the Sirdar Diler-ul-Mulk, C.I.E., and Minister of Railroads, and Home Secretary for the Nizam's Government, therefore made his appearance in London as the "Jubilee Commissioner" from Hyderabad. On his arrival, he addressed the following letter to Mr. Watson (Messrs. Watson & Stewart):—

"I am instructed by the Government of H.H. the Nizam to purchase 10,000 shares of the Hyderabad Deccan Company, Limited. As you are the agent of the Government here, I write to ask you to be so good as to arrange for the purchase of these shares at the lowest possible price, not exceeding £12 per share, the Government having decided to invest only £120,000 in these shares."

To this Mr. Watson replied:—

[*Confidential.*]

"I beg to acknowledge receipt of your letter of yesterday's date, instructing me, as agent of the Government of his Highness the Nizam, to purchase 10,000 £10 fully-paid shares of the Hyderabad (Deccan) Company, Limited.

"I beg to point out to you that to purchase these shares at the price you name is a most difficult and almost impossible operation, and will require the greatest skill and circumspection. I would suggest that the Government should acquire a proportion of the £5 paid shares at the same *pro rata* price, say £7 per share, as the £5 paid shares carry the same dividend as the £10 paid, and by this the Government could acquire, say, 8,750 £10 paid shares, and 3,750 £5 paid shares, thus having 12,500 shares for £131,250, being an addition of 2,500 shares at an extra cost of £11,250 only. Please be kind enough to send me your instructions on this point."

On receipt of this letter, Abdul Huk telegraphed to Colonel Marshall, the Secretary of the Nizam:—

"Deccans firmly held by public; therefore with greatest difficulty succeeded in purchasing 8,750 fully-paid shares at twelve; 3,750 half-paid *pro rata* at seven, thus by chance securing 2,500 shares more at cost £11,250, and contingent liability £18,750, in excess sanctioned amount, £120,000. Market closes twelve three-quarters. Government shares now worth 9,000 more than paid. Signed, Sirdar Diler-el-Mulk."

In reply to this an answer was sent by Colonel Marshall that the arrangement was "most satisfactory."

On June 3, this "most satisfactory arrangement" was carried out. Mr. Watson sent eight of the leading London brokers simultaneously into the Stock Exchange to compete against each other for his own shares on behalf of the Government of Hyderabad. The brokers were Messrs. Cazenove & Ackroyds; Messrs. T. Ellis & Co.; Messrs. Borthwick, Wark, & Co.; Messrs. Anderson & Co.; Messrs. Hollebone; Messrs. T. & N. Oakley & Co.; Messrs. Stewart, Tily & Co.; and Messrs. Coates & Sons, and Mr. Watson charged the Government of Hyderabad a commission of £661 for his own services. It is a curious fact that these shares, bought in the open market, appear to have been mainly two blocks of shares, viz., those numbered from 5,055 to 8,804, and from 91,251 to 100,000, and they were all bought of the same jobber. And it is equally remarkable that these shares should have been converted before the sale into "shares to bearer," with the object, I presume, of concealing the fact that they were "promoters' shares"; the intelligent authors of this device having, apparently, not remembered that the ownership could be shown by the number marked on each share.

The transaction was closed with the following letter, addressed by Mr. Cordery, the Resident at Hyderabad, to Sir Asman Jah, who had succeeded Sir Salar Jung as Minister:—

"As you are aware, Sirdar Diler-ul-Mulk, C.I.E., has called on me and shown me all the papers connected with the performance of the three important duties for which he was directed to proceed to England. With regard to the purchase in the Deccan Mining Company, he seems to have effected a difficult transaction in a quiet manner, which prevented the purchase, large as it was, affecting the price at which your Government obtained a predominant interest in the concern. . . . I would now ask you to favour me with such a report of the transactions as I may be able to forward to His Excellency the Viceroy."

Since this deal, and influenced by this buying, the public has largely bought the shares at prices varying from £12 to £8, and there are now several hundred *bona fide* shareholders. Mr. Winter still holds a large number—indeed, so large a number that presumably they are held by him for some one who does not wish his name to appear.

It is not necessary to recapitulate. The details that I have given fully, I think, explain the "most satisfactory arrangement." Why should the State of Hyderabad part with its mining rights to Messrs. Watson and Stewart for nothing? Why should £850,000 of the capital of the Company go into the pockets of the promoters, in flat defiance of the terms of the concession? Why should the State of Hyderabad have bought back a quantity of shares, which represented nothing but the cost of printing them, from the promoters at £12 per share, thus making a present of above £100,000 to the concessionnaires for obtaining the concession? How possibly can it be supposed that the English investor can hope for a remunerative return on his capital, should he buy shares, when £150,000 of real capital has to earn a dividend upon a fictitious capital of £850,000, in addition to this £150,000? Are Mr. Cordery and Colonel Marshall absolute idiots, or what? Finally, what has the Government of India to allege for allowing itself to be hoodwinked and humbugged in so palpable a fashion? If an investigation be not instituted into "this most satisfactory arrangement," I can only say that the sooner we withdraw our advisers from native States in India the better it will be, not only for them, but for British investors, who fancy that we accept some sort of responsibility in regard to companies brought out with the approval of these advisers and of the Indian Government. Owing to all this financing, to the rigging of the market, to the Nizam appearing on the scene as a purchaser, and to the support given to this scandalous scheme by the Resident at Hyderabad, and the Indian Government, at present four-fifths of the shares have been bought by the public, mostly at a premium, and there are already 1,600 innocent victims of misplaced confidence in the Residency system of Indian Government. This investigation must be independent of the Indian Government, for it and its *employés* are amongst those whose action must be investigated.

Abdul Huk, I need hardly say, is still anxious to tap the British barrel. In 1884 three millions were obtained to take over and finish a State Railroad in Hyderabad, on a guarantee from the State of 5 per cent. for twenty years (inclusive of sinking fund). The net earnings of this State Railroad were in 1886 less than £50,000. But Abdul wants more money for self and partners. He has, therefore, elaborated a proposal to obtain an additional three millions to make further railroads. In order to get this sum, he had to show that the existing guarantee was practically extinguished (to use his own words) by the earnings of the existing State Railroad. This he has done by a juggling of figures that must make Mr. Goschen's mouth water. The ingenuous "native," with a smile, "childlike and bland," has issued a Railroad Budget for the year 1886. The actual earnings of the railroad during the year are set down at less than £50,000. Interest on large sums of money, which he has persuaded the Nizam to deposit with the National Provincial Bank to the amount of £150,000, is brought bodily in to swell the earnings of the railway, and in this fashion he conclusively shows that the net earnings of the railway "practically extinguish" the guarantee.

This Abdul Huk is a curious outcome of our Indian Government. He first entered the public service as a policeman. Sir R. Mead, then Resident at Hyderabad, imported him into a public office in some humble capacity, and with the modest salary of £30 a month. His rise has been rapid, and so intelligent is he that, in the course of six or seven years, he has been able not only to live luxuriously, but also to save above half-a-million sterling, the greater portion of which he has invested in real estate in Bombay. Who, after this, shall say that India is not a gold mine, and that intelligent activity in that country does not secure adequate reward?

When over here as "Jubilee Commissioner," Abdul Huk submitted an offer on the part of the Nizam to give the Indian Government about £500,000 to aid in the general defensive works for our Indian Empire. The Nizam himself is a wretched, whiskey-sodden lad, and it is understood that the offer was due to the suggestion of a Cabinet Minister. Be this as it may, it ought never to have been accepted. The State of Hyderabad has already surrendered several of its richest provinces, in return for which we are pledged to take on ourselves the defence of India. The people of the Deccan are already heavily taxed, and this gift could only be raised by borrowing of the native usurers at a heavy interest, and thus increasing the taxation.—*Truth*, April 26.

HYDERABAD-DECCAN.—THE STORY OF THE SCHEME BY WHICH ABDUL HUK MADE A MILLION FOR A FIRM OF ENGLISH PROMOTERS—THE NIZAM PAYS £130,000 FOR A TENTH INTEREST IN A CONCESSION THAT HE HAD GIVEN FOR NOTHING.—Special dispatch to *The Financial News*.—Allahabad, Friday, April 20.—The *Pioneer* prints to-day the full story of the Hyderabad-Deccan scandal, of which the following is the gist: So long ago as 1883 it was proposed to Sir Salar Jung that it would be to the interest of the Hyderabad if the mineral resources of that State could be developed by an English company. It was represented to Sir Salar Jung that a company could be formed which would agree to expend a million pounds sterling within the State, and would also pay moderate mining rents and royalties to the State; that in return for this expenditure the company should receive a monopoly of the minerals for ninety-nine years. The persons who were desirous of obtaining these concessions were Messrs. Watson and Stewart; the former of these gentlemen and the Sirdar Diler Jung, who was, before he was ennobled, known to fame as plain Abdul Huk, had been collaborateurs in financing the Nizam's State Railway. These two had received in this connection more than £180,000, and the enormous promotion expenses incurred in floating that railway have more than once attracted the attention of Parliament.

Mr. Winter, the attorney acting for Messrs. Watson and Stewart, took the view that his clients were especially entitled to apply for the mining concession because they had been so economical and so useful in financing the State Railway; and the younger Sir Salar Jung, who finally granted the concession, appears to have also been persuaded to acquiesce in that view, for, on January 14th, 1885, in announcing to the Government of India that the conditions of the concession had been arranged, Sir Salar writes:—

"I have been considerably influenced by Sirdar Diler Jung's representations in granting the concessions to Messrs. Watson and Stewart, when more favourable terms might have been secured."

What was the document—the revised draft of the concession? and what was it that the Resident, the Government of India and the Government of Hyderabad had agreed to concede? Mr. Cordery, writing from the Hyderabad Residency on the 6th May, 1885, forwards to Sir Salar Jung two memoranda from the Government of India, "one of which," in the words of the Resident, "describes the alterations suggested, while the other explains the grounds on which they are recommended." Mr. Cordery adds: "These are put so clearly that I have no need further to elucidate them."

The first clause states: "The concessionnaires will form a company with a capital of not less than £1,000,000, with the object of acquiring the rights of the concessionnaires."

The second clause states: "Before the 1st of January, 1886, a *First Issue* of shares to the amount of £100,000 shall have been taken up, and £25,000 actually paid up."

The memorandum on this clause recites: "The first issue of shares has been reduced from £250,000 to £100,000, and the paid-up capital from £100,000 to £25,000. This has been done to meet the immediate requirements of the opening of the Singareni Coal Fields, which, judging from the circumstances of existing coal companies in Bengal, can be sufficiently worked with a subscribed capital of the amount proposed in the altered clause. The nominal capital is left as originally drafted in Clause 1, as it is contemplated that further issues of shares will be made in the event of iron or steel works being started at Singareni, or the mineral wealth of the Province being developed at other sites."

. . . .

After some correspondence between Sir Salar Jung and the Government of India, the above project is finally sanctioned by both, subject to this modification, that while the capital is still to be a million sterling, the first issue of shares is to be increased to the amount of £150,000, and of this £150,000, the sum of £75,000 is to be called up. Subject to these conditions, Sir Sala Jung, with the sanction of the Supreme Government, signed the concession to Messrs. Watson and Stewart.

. . . . On the 7th of January, 1886, Messrs. Watson and Stewart bring out this company in London by issuing shares, not to the value of £150,000, but all the shares at once—one hundred thousand £10 shares—of which shares Messrs. Watson and Stewart pocket 85,000, which they describe as "fully paid," although not one penny piece has ever been paid for them by anyone! The remaining fifteen thousand shares Messrs. Watson and Stewart also subscribed for, paying up £5 on each of these shares! Instead of a First Issue of £150,000, as required by the direct terms of the concession, we have a first and also a final issue of a million sterling, and instead of £850,000 of unissued share capital remaining to be issued from time to time as required, we have the concessionnaires printing £10 shares to the number of 85,000, which are to rank as "fully paid," and which shares they pocket and make away with to re-sell! . . . .

But what is to follow is infinitely worse: £75,000 of working capital has been subscribed by the concessionnaires; every one of the hundred thousand shares is in their hands; the profit, if any, accruing on this £75,000 invested in a coal mine is to furnish the dividends upon the entire million pounds of "watered" share stock! That is to say, if there is a profit on this coal mining operation of even 20 per cent., the company will earn a dividend of only one and a half per cent. on its shares! . . . . The public refuse to buy the shares. No one can be persuaded to give thirty shillings for them, for they are all in the hands of Messrs. Watson and Stewart. In order to mark up these shares, one, two, ten pounds a share, Watson must sell to Stewart, and his bogus transferees. Stewart must sell to his; and Abdul Huk, the influential

Hyderabad Minister, he, too, must be persuaded to play a part, and persuade his youthful Highness and the new English secretary to his Highness that the State ought to come into the London market to spend £150,000 in buying and "booming" Mr. Watson's "fully paid" shares.

The time is most opportune. The violent intrigues against Sir Salar Jung—intrigues doubtless arranged for no other end than this—have brought about the result that the Minister has resigned, and the State is for an entire month without a responsible head. If once the announcement can be made in London that the shares of the Hyderabad (Deccan) Company are considered by the Government of Hyderabad worth buying at £12 each, then, indeed, the public can be trusted to flock into the market and buy readily. The Government of India are falsely assured that the Nizam is personally anxious that Abdul Huk should go over to London with the style, the title, the dignity of a Jubilee Commissioner! Incredible as it seems, this slight is put upon Her Majesty the Queen! The ex-policeman of Kallian is to be sent to London in company with two great native nobles, to pose as a dignitary of the State of Hyderabad! With evident reluctance, the Government of India is induced to sanction the appointment of Abdul Huk. The pretence upon which His Highness's signature is next obtained to the purchase of these shares is, that it is important—in the language of the Resident—that the Government of Hyderabad should obtain "a predominant interest in the concern." A predominant interest! It is only necessary to point out that a hundred thousand shares have been issued, that to each of these shares belongs an equal vote. The Government of the Nizam is therefore to obtain a predominant interest" by purchasing at a premium one-tenth of the shares, and by controlling one-tenth of the votes!

When next we hear of Abdul Huk, he is in London. He is now the Sirdar Diler-ul-Mulk Bahudur, C.I.E., Jubilee Commissioner, &c. From the Alexandra Hotel he pens a letter to Mr. W. C. Watson, who, with his partner, Mr. Stewart, is the owner of all, or nearly all, the 85,000 shares, and also of the remaining 15,000 shares. The concessionnaire is instructed to buy a mass of his own shares for the Government of Hyderabad. These shares he buys to the extent of £131,250, and this telegram is sent to the private secretary of the Nizam by the Sirdar Abdul Huk :—

"Deccans firmly held by public, therefore with greatest difficulty succeeded purchasing 8,750 fully-paid shares at 12, 3,750 half-paid *pro rata* at seven, thus by chance securing 2,500 shares more at cost £11,250, and contingent liability £18,750 in excess sanctioned amount £120,000. Market closes 12¾. Government shares now worth £9,000 more than paid.

"SIRDAR DILER-UL-MULK."

In reply to the above telegram, sent on June 6, 1887, came back the answer that the arrangement was "most satisfactory"!

On the 3rd of June last this deed was done. On the 3rd of June Mr. Watson, the joint owner of all the shares in this company, sent into the London market simultaneously eight of the leading brokers of the City of London to compete against one another for his own shares on behalf of the Government of Hyderabad. . . . . So the State of Hyderabad, having given away its mining rights for 99 years, forthwith comes to market to buy one-tenth of these same rights for the sum of £131,250 and a further liability, since incurred and paid, of £18,750. In fact, it comes to this, that the State of Hyderabad have given their mining rights for four generations to Messrs. Watson and Stewart, and also £75,000 to accept these rights. The man who owned these shares—shares never authorised to be issued—this man Watson is selected by Abdul Huk both to buy and to sell his own property at his own price! A more impudent, a more infamous transaction has never been reported in these columns.

. . . .

The State of Hyderabad is on its trial, and, what is perhaps of more Imperial importance, the whole Residency System of India, and the obligations of the Supreme Power to the feudatory States must come under careful consideration and in open court. We know the general impolicy of such a course; but there are occasions when a storm clears the air. We believe this to be such an occasion. To deprecate a public inquiry by a competent Commission would, under the circumstances we detail to-day, weaken the moral influence of Great Britain in India. On that moral influence, and on that alone, our race must chiefly rely if we are to continue our tenancy of this immense Dependency. As might have been expected, the notorious Abdul Huk is the central figure around which are made to revolve a British Resident, an official secretary deputed by Calcutta to assist the Nizam, together with certain so-called concessionnaires from London. We earnestly trust that the Resident and the secretary will demand an official inquiry, and without delay, to show that they are guiltless of all connection with the swindle perpetrated on the State of Hyderabad.

The Hyderabad Scandal.—The contribution we made two days ago to the inner history of the Hyderabad (Deccan) Company was a very small one as compared with that which we are enabled to print to-day. Even now the whole of the mysteries are not unveiled, but there is the skeleton of a most unsavoury story. Nor is the robbery itself the worst of the scandal, for the discreditable feature is, that this unblushing fraud upon the State of Hyderabad has been perpetrated under the very noses, and with the assistance, unconscious or intended, of a British Resident and a British secretary. We are unfortunately too familiar in the City with the crooked ways of some promoters, but never before, to our knowledge, has such an impudent scheme as this been carried out by the help of gentlemen high in official authority. The owners of the Hyderabad mining concession have made the Hyderabad Resident and the Nizam's secretary their tools.

It is almost impossible to believe that when Mr. Cordery was superintending the drawing-up of the concession, he was unaware that the uncalled capital was intended to be dormant, and was not meant to be vested in the concessionnaires. Yet he appears to have permitted Messrs. Watson and Stewart to violate at once the primary terms on which they received the mining rights in Hyderabad. If Mr. Cordery were conscious of the meaning of the words he wrote to the Indian Government at Calcutta, it certainly devolves upon him to demand an immediate inquiry to show that he should not be stigmatised as a partner in a gross trick on the potentate whose interests he was appointed to safeguard. The Nizam's secretary, Colonel Marshall, is not so directly implicated; but it was so plainly his duty to have seen through the tricks which were being practised on the Nizam, that he must bear his share of the obloquy of these transactions until he satisfies the public that he acted in ignorance. The alternatives between which these two officials have to choose are by no means pleasant.

Abdul Huk has already been found out and disgraced, and as he is no doubt simply an adventurer fighting for his own hand, he may be dismissed. But it does not say much for the prescience of the Resident and of the Viceregal Government that such a palpable trickster should have thrown dust in their eyes so long, causing them to assent to and further the alienation of the rights of one of the most loyal of the feudatory Princes. As to the concessionnaires, it is obvious that they cannot remain in the enjoyment of spoils obtained by such unscrupulous means. Their pockets have been well lined out of the Treasury of Hyderabad already, and the Indian Government cannot permit them to grow still fatter at the expense of the Nizam and his people. The probity of our Indian administration has never been called in question, and when occasional blots such as this have been discovered the central power has never been backward in undoing the wrong. In this instance valuable rights have first been juggled away, and then a youthful ruler, plastic in the hands of those whom a paternal Government has sent to direct him, has been cajoled into buying back, at an iniquitous price, a fraction of his own property. For one-half of the money paid for the watered shares of the Hyderabad (Deccan) Company the Nizam himself could have done far more for the mineral development of the country than this precious company has done. The concessionnaires have not even the excuse that they have done something for Hyderabad; they have simply diddled it. It is for the Government to thoroughly probe the whole of the disgraceful business, to punish the delinquents, and to restore to the Nizam as much of his property as can be rescued from the grabbers who have got hold of it. In doing this, too, the Government will have to inquire what strange influence has closed the eyes of the officials at the India Office to what has for months past been a scandal in business circles in India.

The Hyderabad (Deccan) Company reports that it has received the following telegram from its agent in Hyderabad: "The Government of His Highness the Nizam is friendly, and aiding the Company." We do not believe that there is a word of truth in this statement. We have, on the contrary, the best reasons for believing that the Government of the Nizam has determined to follow up the removal of Abdul Huk by the most stringent action against his English associates and the Company. We should advise the public to accept the agent's story with the utmost reserve.—*Financial News*, April 26.

Hyderabad-Deccan.—The Articles of Association, Agreements, and List of Shareholders.—So much interest has been excited in the affairs of the Hyderabad-Deccan Company, that we have obtained the following particulars of its formation from Somerset House. It will be observed that the agreement provides for the allotment to the concessionnaires of the 85,000 "fully-paid" shares. It must not be assumed that this authorisation destroys the objections which have been urged against the improper allocation of these shares, the point being that the concession was obtained from the Nizam upon the distinct understanding that of the million of the company's capital only £150,000 should be called up, the rest remaining as a reserve of capital for the future operations of the company. This understanding the concessionnaires set at defiance as soon as they reached London, transforming the uncalled capital into "fully-paid" shares, upon which nothing was paid. The following are the details given at Somerset House:—

Registered July 29, 1886, by Bircham and Co., 46, Parliament Street, Westminster. The capital of the company is £1,000,000, in 100,000 shares of £10 each. Any shares in the capital of the company may be issued as fully or in part paid up, in payment of the said concession or any property which the company is authorised to acquire, and the shares of which the capital shall from time to time consist may be divided into different classes, with such preferences, priorities, restrictions or special incidents as may from time to time be prescribed by the articles and special resolution of the company. The objects for which the company is established are: To acquire, undertake, work, carry on, deal with and turn to account wholly or in part the rights and obligations of the concessionnaires under a deed (called "the concession,") made January 7, 1886, between Nawab Mir Laik, Ali Khan, Bahadur Salur Jung, Nunir-ud-Daolah, Muktar-ul-Mulk, Imadas Sultana, Prime Minister of his Highness the Nizam, acting on behalf of the Government of his Highness the Nizam (in the articles of association called the Government), of the one part, and Wm. Clarence Watson and John Stewart (in the articles of association called the concessionnaires) of the other part, relating to certain lands and property, mining and other rights, adopting the said concession, and being liable thereunder as if it was the original concession. The first subscribers are :—

	Shares.
Wm. Clarence Watson, 7, Great Winchester Street, E.C., merchant...	1
John Stewart, 26, Throgmorton Street, E.C., banker........................	1
Chas. Albert Winter, 7, Great Winchester Street, E.C., solicitor.........	1
James Hemmerder, 26, Throgmorton Street, E.C., bank manager	1
Geo. Hy. Maxwell, barrister, 3, Ralston Street, Tedworth Square, S.W.	1
R. Pearce, Lanarth House, Holder's Hill, Hendon, secretary	1
John Martyn Milne, accountant, 13, Ravensbourne Road, Catford	1

An agreement made the 17th day of August, 1886, between the Hyderabad (Deccan) Company, Limited, of the one part, and William Clarence Watson, of 7, Great Winchester Street, E.C., and John Stewart, of 26, Throgmorton-street, of the other part. Whereas by an agreement dated the 16th of August, 1886, and made between the said William Clarence Watson and John Stewart, therein and thereafter called the concessionnaires, of the first part, the several persons specified in the schedule thereto of the second part, and the company of the third part, it was agreed that the concessionnaires should assign and transfer to the company certain rights conceded to the concessionnaires with reference to the lands, mines and property situate in the territories of His Highness the Nizam, and that in exchange therefor the company should allot the concessionnaires 85,000 shares of £10 each in the company, which shares should be deemed for all purposes to be fully paid up, and should do all things necessary for that purpose. And whereas the said agreement has been duly adopted by the company. Now these presents witness that it is hereby agreed as follows: —(1) The company shall forthwith cause their agreement to be registered with the Registrar of Joint Stock Companies. (2) On or before the 10th day of September next the company shall allot to the concessionnaires or their nominees 85,000 fully paid up shares in the company. The said shares shall be numbered 15,001 to 100,000, both inclusive, and shall be accepted by the concessionnaires in full satisfaction of all the claims and demands whatsoever of the concessionnaires in respect of the assignment and transfer as aforesaid, and otherwise as in the said agreement more particularly set forth.

Common seal of the Company.

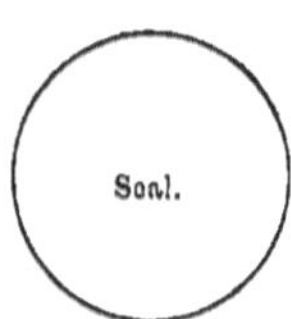

(Signed) G. H. M. Batten, Director.
E. S. Bernard Maurice, Secretary.
W. C. Watson.
J. Stewart.

The first return to Somerset House, dated December 9, 1886, contained the following interesting information :—

Nominal capital, £1,000,000, in £10 shares.
Number of shares taken up to December 9, 1886 ... 100,000
There has been called up on each of 15,000 shares ... £5
Total amount of calls received, including payments on application and allotment ... £75,000
Total amount agreed to be considered as paid on 85,000 ... £850,000
Total amount of calls unpaid ... nil
Total amount of money paid on shares forfeited... nil

The following is the latest return to Somerset House, dated August 10, 1887 :—

	Shares.
Allhusen, Christian, Stoke Court, Slough ...	640
" " " ...	140
" " " ...	20
" " " ...	20
(Transferred, and now no longer a member.)	
Ainsworth, Thomas, Park House, Waterford Ireland ...	10
" " " " "	10
(Transferred and now no longer a member.)	
Atkinson, Fredk. Wm., 140, Leadenhall St.	20
Allworth, Alfred, M.D., Peckham Road, S.E.	20
Adams, R. L., 10, Newton Grove, Leeds ...	55
Ashburner, Eliza, Torwood, Warlingham, Surrey ...	25
Anderson, Jas. Robert, 13, Parkside, S.W.	20
Akers, Hubert, The Oaks, Woodford... ...	10
Agutter, J. F., Lloyd's, E.C. ...	10
Alexander, Jas., 2, St. Helen's Place, E.C.	125
Anstruther, Sir W. C., Thankerton, N.B....	10
Armstrong, R. Y., Colonel, Junior United Service Club ...	16
Allen, Phœbe, Moffat, Dumfriesshire ...	15
Anderson, Charlotte Elizabeth, 32, Upper Phillimore Place, W. ...	5
Arnold, Harry, 114, North Street, Brighton	10
Ashburner, J. J. Charles, Torwood, Warlingham, Surrey ...	25
Aubrey, H. J., 56, St. George's Road, N. ...	50
Allinson, Wm., 77, Eaton Square, S.W. ...	15
(Transferred and now no longer a member.)	
Antill, A. L., 1, Gresham Buildings, E.C....	4
Averillo, J. S., 1, Florence Villas, Tottenham	750
Bretherton, Mrs. Maria, Tunbridge Wells...	100
Berkeley, R. W., 57, Amhurst Road, E. ...	20
Baker, A. J., Stock Exchange ...	25
" " " ...	23
" " " ...	2
Bryant, G. B., 16, Herne Hill, S.W. ...	10
Burstall, J. H., Bradford's Brough, Yorkshire ...	20
Baskerville, G., 17, Fitzwarren Street, Manchester ...	10
Bovill, W. D., 43, Grosvenor Road, S.W. ...	3
Arathoon, C. W., 50, Ladbroke Grove, W....	1
Allfrey, M., The Brewhouse, Clerkenwell Road, E.C. ...	35
Batten, G. H. M., 3, Ralston Street, Tedworth Square, S.W. ...	150
Bonner, Maurice Edward A., 46, Parliament Street, S.W. ...	150
Bishop, Wm. Hy., 1, Royal Exchange Buildings, E.C. ...	850
Brewin, Arthur, 6A, Austinfriars, E.C. ...	10
Blackburn, H. N., Great Barr, Walsall ...	10
Bush, H. J., Thornleigh, Sydenham Hill, S.E. ...	500
Barry, W. H., Major Rugby ...	10
Blackwell, Henry, jun, 3 and 4, Milk Street, E.C. ...	80
Brayley, Jas. Henry, 123, Chancery Lane, W.C. ...	10
Brown, Wm., Broxbourne, Croydon ...	100
Brooker, Edward, 4, Corbet Court, E.C. ...	10
Brown, Rd. Alexander, 23, Harp Lane, E.C.	100
Bird, Wm. Henry, 12, Christchurch Street, Folkestone ...	5
Barnes, Mary C., Horndean, Hants ...	3
Bauer, G. M., 16, Mark Lane, E.C. ...	100
Boycott, Elizabeth A. E. D., Pau, France...	7
Burn, C. M. P., Prestonfield House, Edinburgh ...	5
Barnes, J. Keith, St. Catherine's, Horndean, Hants ...	2
Braithwaite, J. B., jun., 27, Austinfriars, E.C. ...	50
Burland, Rev. C. J., St. Saviour's Vicarage, Shanklin ...	5
Bradley, William, Maidenhead ...	9
Boycott, H., Captain E. E. D., 26, Bruton Street, W....	50
Burt, P. J., 28 and 29, St. Swithin's Lane, E.C. ...	50
Brice, H. T., 20, Blessington Road, Blackheath...	5
Brown, T. P., 89, Wakehurst Road, S.W...	5
Beauclerck, W. A., 3, Bryanston Square, W.	50
Blake, J. H., Stock Exchange ...	333
Blythe, Major-General F. S., 3, Thornton Villas, St. Helier's ...	12
Bennett, William, Hampton Road, Teddington ...	20
Blandford, T. H., Belsoon, Navan, Ireland	10
Bartlett, P. R., 141A, Graham Road, Dalston	14
Butcher, W. D., Clydesdale Villa, Windsor.	25
Brown, H. G., Lansdown House, Shanklin.	20
Brett, H. A., 14, Holland Park Terrace, W.	30
Ball, J. B., 18, Leicester Road, Loughborough ...	200
Bennett, J., Salcombe, South Devon... ...	10
Borges, D., 12, Gloucester Place, W.... ...	2
Brownlow, W. V., care of Cox and Co., Craig's Court, S.W. ...	10
Barnes, K. H., St. Catherine's, Horndean, Hants ...	6
Bruxner, Henry, 14, Red Lion Square, W.C.	80
Baynes, A. H., 38, Spencer Park, S.W. ...	10
Barry, R. E., Major, Ryde ...	10
Burton, F. T., 24, Buckland Crescent, N.W.	25
Burra, T. F., Linton Vicarage, Maidstone..	30
Burman, W. H., 10, Throgmorton Avenue, E.C. ...	60
Brown, F. G., Gunleigh, Little Ealing ...	8
Burnand, L. W., 69, Lombard Street, E.C.	20
Bell, S. H. A., Woodberry House, Finsbury Park, N. ...	1
Bellew, P. G., Gratton Lodge, Queen's Co., Ireland ...	4
Bush, M. A., Thornlea, Sydenham, S.E. ...	2
Baker, C. M., 1, Copthall Chambers, E.C....	170
Barron, M., Stock Exchange ...	50
Bright, Rev. J. H., Clifton ...	10
(Transferred, and no longer a member.)	
Belfour, P. G., Stock Exchange ...	100
Balli, J., 20, Great Winchester Street ...	100
Buller, C. W., All Soul's College, Oxford ...	10
" " " " ...	10
Bryant, I. W., St. George's Club, Hanover Square ...	20
Brown, M. M., 3, Drapers' Gardens ...	500
Christie, R. C., Glenwood, Virginia Water	50
Carr, T., Tiverton Mills, Bath ...	50
Carr, J., Tiverton Mills, Bath ...	20
" " " " ...	30
Clapham-Reynell, J., Stock Exchange ...	10
Cornforth, W., 4, Queen Victoria Street, E.C. ...	10
Caldecott, J. B., 7, Finch Lane ...	10
(Transferred, and no longer a member.)	

Crawshaw, C. B., Bank Terrace, Dewsbury 20
Coppen, J. M., 18, Finch Lane, E.C.... ... 10
Craig, C. W., Birch Villa, Warlingham ... 5
Cotes, Chas., 3, Drapers' Gardens, E.C. ... 150
Crake, W. P., 2, Albion Street, W. 10
Churchward, F., Granville Park, Blackheath 50
Dennistoun, A., 123, Bishopsgate Street, E.C. 20
Eaton, J., Park View, Manchester 15
" " " 5
Eliott, G. A., 45, Anerley Park, S.E. ... 15
Furnivall, W. C., Deccan, India 250
" " 250
Franquerville, Comte de, care of Erard and Co., 18, Great Albemarle Street, W. .. 50
Baker, A. H., Stock Exchange 12
Brook, R. C., care of Cox and Co., Craig's court, S.W. 10
Burn, W. H., 74, Porchester Terrace, W.... 2
Brown, A. T. W., 6, Lothbury, E.C. 100
Barber, F., Elmfield, Norwood, S.E. 20
Bristow, H. J., 68, Cornhill, E.C. 100
Bevan, W. A., 54, Lombard Street, E.C. ... 50
Bushby, A. E., 3, South Eaton Place, S.W. 25
Budgett, J. S., Stoke Park, Guildford... ... 200
Brewer, J., Barnstaple 10
Bergue, A. M., 97, Church Road, Hove, Brighton 30
Boyce, J., Church End, Finchley, N.... ... 10
Butcher, G., Tring 20
Browne, J., Lieut.-Colonel, care of Cox and Co., Craig's Court, S.W... 50
Clarke, Ernest, 10, Addison-road, Chiswick 10
Clarke, Herbert, 20, Chatsworth Road, S.E. 10
Corlett, C. W., 34, Belvedere Road, S.E. ... 20
Cantrell, T. J., 11, Palace Gate, W. 40
Christie, A. H., 6A, Austinfriars, E.C... ... 25
Cleveland, F. W., 199, Maida Vale, W. ... 10
Craven, G. H., Bethune Road, Stamford Hill, N. 2
Clark, A. C., Queen's College, Oxford ... 5
Collyer, H. C., Beech Holm, Park Hill, Croydon 10
Cutler, S., 11, Vanbrugh Park, Blackheath 60
Cox, D., 20, Victoria Street, Bristol 40
Cox, J. C., Brockley, near Bristol 10
Colfer, J., Dingulph Mills, Waterford... ... 7
Caddon, B. D. S., Prudhoe-on-Tyne 10
Collyer, T. H., 7, Grove Hill, Dulwich ... 40
Carson, J., 75, Church Lane, Belfast... ... 25
Cundell, G. R., Brunswick House, Kew ... 25
Charlesworth, W. H., Stock Exchange, E.C. 50
Carter, A. A., Billiter House, E.C. 15
Carter, F., 6, Foyle Road, Blackheath ... 50
Cornish, H., 1, Chichester Place, Brighton 10
Collette, C. H., care of Twining and Co., 215, Strand 40
Campbell, H., 31, Threadneedle Street ... 30
Crawshay, T., Bonvilstone House, Cardiff... 50
Churton, A. B., 1, Cardington Villas, New Barnet 5
Cope, J. L., Wigginton Park, Tamworth ... 10
Crawford, A. E., 7, Beaufort East, Bath ... 10
Campbell, D. A. G. F., Padiham... 10
Corry, A. C., Old Lodge, Salisbury 10
Cutcliffe, Owen, J., 27, Cornhill, E.C.... ... 70
Custance, H. A. T., 33, Brompton Crescent, S.W. 50
Cure, M. M. C., care of Ransom, Bouverie and Co., 1, Pall Mall, S.W. 20
Chute, A. J. L., 3, Southwick Crescent, W. 6
Chave, W. F., The Moore, Hereford 15
Crosley, A. C., Brempton Vicarage, Hereford 10
Croysdale, Thos., Hawk House, Sunbury ... 10
Cross, T. R., High West Street, Dorchester 10
Crawley, Richard, 6, Lawrence Lane, E.C. 10
Crosley, F. E., 136, Buckingham Palace Road, S.W. 30
Charlesworth, J., Heaton, Bradford 20
Croft, J. A., Putney, S.W. 30

Clifton, William, 14, Waterloo Crescent, Dover 500
Chalk, A., 23, Throgmorton Street, E.C. ... 450
Cure, E. C., 8, Hereford Square, S.W. ... 50
Cousins, V., Hove, Brighton... 10
Cazenove, C., 183, Regent Street, W.... ... 460
Clark, W. H., Stock Exchange 65
Cohen, J. C., 4, Adam's Court, E.C. 25
Cox, H. F., 29, Threadneedle Street, E.C.... 50
Crofton, Rev. H. W., Wolverton Rectory, Bath 25
Crosley, J. C., Eynsford, Kent 50
Chick, A. Y., 58, Old Broad Street, E.C. ... 140
Commerell, Sir E., M.P., 45, Rutland Gate, S.W. 26
Drake, Sir W. R., 12, Prince's Gardens, S.W. 250
Denbigh, Earl, Lutterworth... 200
Dixon, W. E., 21, New Cavendish St., W. 50
Desmond, H. M. E., St. Vincent Lodge, Southsea 35
De la Rue, W., 73, Portland Place, W. ... 50
Debbie, R., St. James Road, Upper Tooting 10
Denshire, E., Ashstead House, Epsom ... 8
Dawnay, Hon. F. H., 8, Belgrave Square, W. 8
Donner, H. E., 23, Huntriss Row, Scarboro' 35
Dudgeon, W., 22, Great George Street, S.W. 10
Desborough, C. J., Hartford House, Huntingdon 35
Dawnay, Lieut.-Colonel, Beningbrough Hall, York 50
Dolphin, J., 8, Vanbrugh Terrace, Blackheath... 30
Downham, J., Chesham Field, Bury 50
Day, A. J., Northlands House, Southampton 10
Du Croz, C. J., 2, Moorgate Street Buildings, E.C.... 100
Davies, F. H., 18, Finch Lane, E.C. 10
Dod, C. W., Malpas, Chester 30
Darwall, R. C., 6, East Cliff, Dover 5
Donnison, F., Stock Exchange, E.C.... ... 5
Durham, R., St. Clair, Addiscombe 20
Dear, P. J., care of E. Ellis, Stock Exchange Buildings 5
Durlacher, F. H. K., Stock Exchange, E.C. 110
Darley, J. J., 26, John Street, Bedford Row 10
Daubeny, F. H., Dashwood House, E.C. ... 10
Denman, Hon. Mrs. J., 19, Eaton Terrace, S.W. 8
Dusgate, R., 3, Halkin Street, W. 50
Edmondson, T., 1, Royal Exchange Buildings, E.C.... 50
Evans, R. S., 30, Lowndes Street, S.W. ... 100
Ede, A., 43, The Avenue, Southampton ... 50
Ellis, E., 2, Royal Exchange Buildings, E.C. 100
Edgar, E., 3, Powis Place, W.C.... 5
Edis, Colonel A. W., 14, Fitzroy Square, W. 40
Eyre, E. J., Dorchester... 5
Evans, F. C., 54, Gresham Street, E.C. ... 5
Ellis, R. H., 2, Royal Exchange Buildings, E.C. 50
Edwardes, Lady B., care of Holt, Lawrie and Co., S.W. 1
Foster, M. H., Imperial Ottoman Bank, Constantinople... 100
Forbes, C. H. B., Bombay 2,231
Frost, D. T., Chudleigh, Devon 40
Frank, G., Kirbymoorside 20
Franklin, A. E., 21, Cornhill, E.C. 10
Franklin, H. A., 14, St. Quentin Avenue, W. 20
Francis, E. J., Bank of England, E.C. ... 10
Fox, J. A., Bailey's Hotel, W. 30
Fenner, H. J., Brookholme, St. John's Park 25
Fox, C. J., Spilsby 50
(Transferred, and no longer a member.)
Forrester, James, 87, Cannon Street, E.C. 5
Fraser, J. C., Bailey's Hotel, S.W. 20
Fairn, R., 85, Talfourd Road, S.E. 20
Funnell, A., 5, Alaska Street, S.W. 10
Fletcher, C., Stock Exchange 25
Guthrie, M., 2, Parkfield Road, Liverpool... 10 / 90

Goodall, F., Ascot 5
George, B. W. P., 47, Hatton Garden, E.C. 20
Goodyear, T. E., 64, Granville Park, S.E. 10
Govett, F. A., 4 and 6, Throgmorton Avenue, E.C. ... ... 50 / 50
Hunter, H., Tennyson Road, Worthing ... 20
Fitz-Hugh, A. J., 54, Old Steine, Brighton 1,000
Fox, T. P., 30, Mark Lane, E.C.... 100
Fraser, C. A., 10, Craven Hill, W. 90
Forrest, T. B., The Laurels, Anerley... ... 20
Fox, G., Stock Exchange, E.C. 300
Forbes, E. B., 5, Austinfriars, E.C. 145
Ferguson, G., Stock Exchange, E.C.... ... 80
Fitch, J., 5, Church Passage, E.C. 20
Ford, M. E., South Kensington Hotel ... 20
Fisher, T., 17, Temple-Row, Birmingham. . 10
Forrester, J. S., Naval and Military Club, W. 100
Foster, H. J., The Castle, Dublin 10
Flachfield, H., 36, Basinghall Street, E.C. . 25
Foster, H. D., 35, Circus Road, N.W. ... 200
Fergusson, W. S., North Villa, Dulwich ... 60
Forbes, R. W., 1, Argyll Road, W. 20
Fitzgerald, C. L. W., 29, Doughty Street, W.C.... 40
Fothergill, J. G., Sura, Wallington 5
Fothergill, J., Sura, Wallington 1
Forbes, W. F., Goodwood, Chichester ... 70
Fenwick, R. B., Merton 25
Field, A. A. J., 12, Queen Street, E.C. ... 100
Farmer, G., 10, Osbaldestone Road, N. ... 40
Gadban, P., 42, Old Broad Street, E.C. ... 400
Gaitskell, M. J., 52, Denmark Villas, West Brighton 20
Gray, J. W., Sandgate 10
Guy, J. P., Lendal, York 50
Gaitskell, C., 52, Denmark Villas, West Brighton 11
Green, H., Hayle Mill, Maidstone 40
Gilbert, T. H., 31, Selborne Road, Brighton 20
Goffin, R. E., 46, Clarendon Road, Norwich 7
Grumbridge, S. E., 12, East Street, Brighton 10
Grundon, J., 3, Threadneedle Street, E.C. 40
Giles, C. T., 2, Paper Buildings, E.C. ... 40
Guttmann, C., 21, Cornhill, E.C. 50
Gilling, T. G., Bunnerdown House, Bath ... 25
Grylls, W. M., Falmouth 10
Given, A., Colchester 10
Gunston, T. B., 38, Prince's Gardens, S.W. 50
Goldsmid, Sir Julian, M.P., 105, Piccadilly, W. 200
Grant, R. C., 32, Walbrook, E.C. 100
Gibbons, A. P., 111, Park Street, W. ... 10
Gribble, J. C., 12, Park Road, Richmond ... 100
Gascoyne, W. E., 10, Old Broad Street, E.C. 30
Green, T. J., Beckenham 30
Guilding, E. W., 19, Great Russell Street, W.C.... 300
Gigney, W., 40, Navarino Road, E. 10
Germaine, R. A., 1, Temple Gardens, E.C. 20
Gardner, A. G. H., care of Holt, Lawrie and Co. 5
Gray, H. R., Hove, Brighton 10
Gardner, S., 13, Copthall Court, E.C. ... 115
Gates, J., Adelaide Street, Hampstead ... 25
Gordon, J. A., 101, Bishopsgate Street, E.C. 200
Greenwood, E. W., Ripon 10
Gibson, B., 1, Upper Westbourne Terrace, W. 50
Groves, H. C. J., 6, Beverley Villas, Barnes 50
Gipps, Major-General, care of Holt, Lawrie and Co. 30
Gill-Russell, J. R. W., 16, Compton Terrace, N. 55
Gams, J., Alexandra Hotel, Knightsbridge 30
Hemmerde, J., 26, Throgmorton Street ... 1,500
Heenan, G. F. H., Hyderabad, India ... 50
Hogan, J. P. L., care of Grindlay and Co., Parliament Street 8
Hankey, Rev. M., Maiden Newton, Dorset 20
Hodges, J. E., Suffolk House, E.C. 25
Hart, J. L., 20, Pembridge Square, W. ... 100
Holroyd, T., Carlton Mills, Leeds 40

Hill, D. W., Woodbury Down, N. 50
Hughes Gibb, F., Bournemouth 120
Hutchinson, J. H., 15, Angel Court, E.C.... 10
Hill, H. D., 18, Billiter Street, E.C. 10
Heriot, R., 70, Old Broad Street, E.C. ... 40
Hunt, W. A., 15, New Broad Street 5
(Transferred, and no longer a member.)
Holt, T. R., 130, Tufnell Park Road, N. ... 10
Houston, W. C., 8, Grosvenor Mansions, S.W. 10
Hertslet, B. H., Richmond 5
Harris, R. C., 30, Throgmorton Street, E.C. 10
Haselden, E. B., Riverside, Woodberry Down 100
Harding, H. S., Harborne, near Birmingham 30
Hibbert, C. G., 6, Jewry Street, E.C.... ... 10
Herring, H. T., 40, Aldersgate Street, E. C. 5
Hall, G. W., Stock Exchange, E.C. 2
Harbord, Hon. A. E., 3, Drapers' Gardens, E.C. 100
Hampton, F. G., 7, Drapers' Garden's, E.C.—
May 27 4,212
June 17 1,277
June 29 75
June 30 40
July 4 160
July 8 1,651
Hedderwick, R. H. S., 2, Copthall Buildings, E.C.
(Transferred 20, June 28.)
Hawley, A., 38, Lime Street, E.C. 50
Hume, Major-General J. R., care of Cox and Co., S.W.... 5
Hubbard, A., Derwentwater House, Acton. 50
Hookins, J., Belmont, Dartford 10
Harper, J. P., 43, Hertford Street, W. ... 100
Hatherley, E., 45, Belgrave Road, S.W. ... 25
Hunter, P., 113, Belsize Road, N.W.... ... 10
Holt, B. W., 14, Savile Row, W.... 25
Hulton, R. E., 2, Copthall Buildings, E.C. 50
Harvey, T. N., 12, Gladstone Street, Waterford 10
Hurrell, A. S. J., 7, Finch Lane, E.C. ... 10
Hooper, J., St. Helier's, Jersey 10
Herbert, E. S., 6, Finch Lane 10
Hitchins, A. K., 11, Threadneedle Street ... 100
Hulton, F. C. L., 8, Hyde Park Mansions, W. 20
Hunter, B. W., Bull-and-Mouth Hotel, Leeds 10
Hooper, J., 31, Prince's Road, W. 5
Halford, C. A. D., 50, Prince's Gate 200
Hunter, C. P., Colonel, Oriental Club ... 40
Hughes, E. A., 1, Clement's Lane, W.C. ... 4
Harker, T. C., 9, Drapers' Gardens, E.C.... 100
Hibernian Bank, Limited, Dublin 10
Hume, E., 63, Dawson Street, Dublin ... 10
Hodgson, F. W., 4 and 5, Love Lane, E.C. 20
Hill, C. J., 43, Cambridge Street, Hyde Park 30
Harper, A., 175, Maida Vale, W. 30
Hilder, J. T., Stock Exchange 20
Hall, J., Newtown, Waterford 5
Hill, W., 1, The Circus, Greenwich 10
Hedderwick, J. D., 79, St. George's Place, Glasgow 200
Hurst, F., 7, Drapers' Gardens, E.C. ... 3,728
Hewlings, H. H., Boyne Lodge, Notting Hill 200
Hopkins, J. R. H., 2, Royal Exchange Buildings, E.C. 50
Hambro, E. A., 70, Old Broad Street, E.C. 100
Hurst, P., 4, Drapers' Gardens, E.C.... ... 20
Haines, General Sir F. P., care of Holt, Lawrie and Co. 30
Hamilton, J. A., Biarritz, France 81
Holden, Wm., 30, Throgmorton Street, E.C. 40
Harverson, J.... 25
Hunter, James Alexander, Lieut.-Col., care of Holt, Lawrie and Co. 40
Harvey, Mary Nunn, The Cliff, Shanklin, Isle of Wight 100

Hanson, J. Oliver, 112, Bishopsgate, E.C. . 20
Hughes, Wm. Theodore, 7, Great Winchester Street 200
Herbert, T. C., 75, Old Broad Street, E.C. . 100
Hodgson, H. J., Captain R.N. 5
Hunter, Charlotte } Foster, S. W. Hunter, J. A. Heman, J. A. 34
(Transferred 45 July 10th, 1887; 120 July 29th, 1887. Remarks say to S. W. O. Foster.)
Jupp, Chas., 1, Avenue Terrace, Eastbourne 30
Joel, Albert, 5, Queen's Gardens, Windsor 15
Johnston, Jane, Queen's Road, West Aberdeen 6
Johnston, R. B., 53, Botanic View, Belford 5
Jacobson, Francis A., 70, Grosvenor Road, Canonbury 5
Jacobson, Sarah Margaret, 70, Grosvenor Road, Canonbury 6
Jacobson, Susannah H., 70, Grosvenor Road, Canonbury 8
Jackson, Jos., 53, Shooter's Hill Road, S.E. —
(Transferred 10 shares May 27th, deceased.)
Jones, R. M., Woodstock House, Balham Hill 10
Johnson, Wm., 228, Blackfriars Road, S.E. 20
(Transferred, and now no longer a member.)
Packs, Alex. 10
(Transferred, and now no longer a member.)
Jennings, R. E. ... ... —
Jackson, A. E., 13, Westbourne Square, W. 15
Jackson, E. J., 13, Westbourne Square, W. 15
Johnston, Susan West, 53, Botanic View, Belford 10
Jackson, W. H., Lieut.-Colonel, 94, Piccadilly, W. 30
James, E. A. H., 48, Hargrave Park Road, N. 30
Jefferson, H. W., Stock Exchange, E.C. ... 50
(Transferred 50, July 8th, 1887.)
Jukes, Edward Clapham, Stock Exchange, E.C. 25
(Transferred 10, July 28th, 1887.)
Kay, F. H., Ely Grange, Frant, Sussex ... 165
(Transferred, and no longer a member.)
Kenna, P. A., 70, Ladbroke Grove, W. ... —
(Transferred 50, February 18th, 1887.)
Kent, H., jun., Kentore, Bromley, Kent ... —
(Transferred 40, July 8th, 1887.)
King, Thos., St. Clare, Madeira Road, Ventnor, Isle of Wight... 50
Kent, A. T., 5, Charles Street, Grosvenor Square 27
Kennedy, G. E. B., Bartholomew House, E.C. 10
Knight, H. J., Major, care of Cox and Co., S.W. 10
Knowles, H. C., 652, Holloway Road, N.... 5
Kraul, A. F. G., 12, Francis Terrace, Victoria Park 5
(Transferred, and now no longer a member.)
King, Thos., care of Mortlake and Co., Cambridge 50
Lander, W. W., 26, Throgmorton Street, E.C. 200
Lowensky, T. H., 31, Hatton Garden, E.C. 50
Law, A. R., Pall Mall Club, S.W. 10
(Transferred and no longer a member.)
Lee, H., 25, Highbury Quadrant... 20
Lloyd, Martha, Slepe Hall, St. Ives, Hunts } Lloyd, Anna, Slepe Hall, St. Ives, Hunts } 10
Landon, C. H., 2, Angel Court, E.C.... ... 1
Lacon, E. M., 40, Finsbury Circus, E.C. ... 10
Lacy, J. P., 414, Moseley Road, Birmingham 25
Lescher, F. H., 60, Bartholomew Close ... 10
(Transferred, and no longer a member.)
Lloyd, E. H., Neath, South Wales 10
Logg, Emily, 51, Freshfield Road, Brighton 10
Logg, S. R., 51, Freshfield Road, Brighton 5

Lewis, C. W. 5
(Transferred 10th, April 15.)
Lamb, J. B., White Street, Coventry... ... 10
McAdam, A. St. G., Rochdale, Sevenoaks... 10
Ledward, F., 30, Exchange Street East, Liverpool 30
Llewellyn, R. R., 153, Whitechapel-rd., E. 10
Haselwood, W. H., The Cedars, Nutfield, Surrey ... ... —
(Transferred 10, May 27th, 1887.)
Leven and Melville, Right Hon. Alexander, Earl of 8,250
Lawrence, W. C., 96, Elm Park Gardens, S.W. 25
Lawrence, J. M., 96, Elm Park Gardens, S.W. 15
Lennon, Rev. John Joseph, Wild Bank, Chorley, Lancashire 20
Lockwood, Colonel A. R. M., Bishop's Hall, Romford, Essex 19
(Transferred, and no longer a member.)
Leech, H. B., 49, Rutland Square, W. ... 10
(Transferred, and no longer a member.)
Lemaire, E. F., 3, Middleton Road, Wandsworth Common 5
(Transferred 5 shares July 8th, 1887.)
———, Lieut.-Colonel H. F. P., Junior United Service Club, S.W. 20
Lindo, Mortimer, Stock Exchange 50
(Transferred, 2 June 17th, 1887, and 1 July 8th, 1887.)
Loose, H. T., Magdalen Street, Norwich... 10
Lowe, F. J., 1, Elm Court, Temple, E.C.... 15
Lethbridge, G., 40, Threadneedle Street, E.C. 25
Lyon, A. O., Pall-Mall Club, S.W. 10
Lowry, Hy., Stock Exchange, E.C. 250
(Transferred, and no longer a member.)
Lewis, Walter, 1, Oak Villa, Honor Oak ... 200
(Transferred, and no longer a member.)
Law, Colonel Robert, Margate, Dunstable 5
Little, A. P. Little, 77½, Bishopsgate Street, E.C. 10
Lyster, C. D., 10, Throgmorton Street, E.C. 120
Lloyd, E.O., 7, Finch Lane, E.C. } Hardy, H. } 25
Lyon, Wm., care of A. Hughes and Co., 25, Old Jewry 20
Lawrence, Rt. Hon. John Hamilton, Lord, 66, Pont Street, S.W. 250
Lawrence, The Hon. Chas. Napier, 8, Chester Square, S.W. 100
Levita, E., Gresham House, E.C. 50
Moore, M. E., 19, Grafton Street, W. ... 150
(Transferred, and no longer a member.)
Millar, J., 13, King's Arms Yard, E.C. ... 150
(Transferred 10, July 8th, 1887.)
Murrieta, Mariano de, 7, Adam's Court, E.C. 25
Mace, Jane, Broduch Road, Upper Tooting, S.W. 20
Morgan, J. L., 4, Harcourt Buildings, Temple, E.C. 20
Mason, W. R., Hatton Court, Ipswich ... 5
Mathewson, J., 107, London Wall, E.C. ... 10
McCaul, J., 45, Frederick Street, Edinburgh 5
Mildred, F., jun., 62, Lombard Street, E.C. 5
Murray, Andrew Cleveland, Upper Maize Hill, St. Leonard's-on-Sea 10
(Transferred, and now no longer a member.)
Messum, Mrs., care of F. Cunningham, Esq. 3, Copthall Court, E.C. 2
(Transferred, and no longer a member.)
Mitchell, M., Peebles, N.B. 10
McKinskey, Col. A., Summer Hill, Bangor 5
Manning, H. L., Thames Bank, Staines ... —
(Transferred February 25th, 1887, and now no longer a member.)
Melbank, F. Henry, 22, Threadneedle Street, E.C. 40
Mogford, Geo. Davis, 49, Fernhead Road, St. Peter's Park, N. 1

Misa, M., 41, Crutchedfriars, E.C. 200
Middleton, Captain W. S., 32, Manchester Street, W.... ... ... —
(Transferred, and no longer a member.)
Makower, L., 40, Old Change, E.C. 60
Marten, F. W.... 10
(Transferred 10, January. 1887)
(" 20, May 27th ")
McLaggan, A., Bombay (clerk) 139
(Transferred 100, May 6th. 1887).
Mosley, T., Bangoiss, Iver Heath, Uxbridge 100
(Transferred, and now no longer a member).
Montagu, Hon. Elizabeth, 7, Stratford Place, W. 10
Marsh, J. J., 72, Wellington Street, Leeds 40
Munro, H., } 80, Lombard Street, E.C. ... —
Cragg, John }
Transferred 80, March 1st
" 30, March 25th
" 50, April 15th
Munday, Major R. E., Naval and Military Club, Piccadilly 10
Michael, W. A., 12, Tokenhouse Yard, E.C. 100
McFarlane, J.... 20
Mumford, L., 3, Threadneedle Street, E.C. —
(Transferred 10 May 27th, 1887.)
Montgomery, Major R. A., Naval and Military Club, Piccadilly, W. ... ... —
(Transferred 20, July 28th, 1887.)
Midlane, H., Stock Exchange, E.C. ... ... —
(Transferred 20, June 17th, 1887.)
McEwen, Lieut.-Colonel, Millfield, Prittlewell, Essex 5
Miller, J. S., } 2, Austinfriars, E.C. 20
Robinson, W. J. P., }
(Transferred, and now no longer members.)
Mitchell, R. W., Chester House, Wickham 356
Maguire, S. C. 10
McChlery, Wm., East India Club, St. James's Square, S.W. 100
Michiels, Leonie, 10, Croxteth Grove, Liverpool 20
McAdam, A. E., The News Rooms, Stamford Hill, N. 10
(Transferred, and no longer a member.)
Marr, W. M., 15, St. James's Square, S.W. 10
(Transferred, and no longer a member.)
Maryat, E. L., Oakfield, near Horley, Surrey —
(Transferred, and no longer a member.)
Mahoney, W. Short, Stock Exchange, E.C. 100
(Transferred, and no longer a member.)
Murray, Marion M., 5, Beach View Villas, Croydon Road, Anerley... 10
Mozley, H. W., Eton College, Windsor ... 40
Myers, N. S., 5, Drapers' Gardens, E.C. ... 10
Macdonald, J. J., 39, Threadneedle Street, E.C. 5
Mein, Captain Alexander S., care of Cox and Co., Craig's Court 20
Murrieta, Adriano de, 7, Adam's Court, E.C. 1,000
Martin, E. A., Cleveland, Sandown, Isle of Wight 1
May, P. W., 76, Mark Lane, E.C. 25
Mason, Mary A., 37, King Henry's Road, N.W.... 25
Mitchell, A. W., Phœnix Chemical Works, Hackney Wick, E.... 50
Newbery, George Jas., 26, Royal Exchange, E.C. ... ... —
Nelson, W. M., Wood Lea, Clifford., Leeds 50
Normand, W. J., Ivy Lodge, Dysart, Fifeshire 180
Nichols, —, 2, Dorno Villas, Cheltenham... 20
Noakes, F., 59, Church Road, Hove 20
Nicholson, F. G., 6, Warrington Crescent, W. 50
Nangle, H., 47, Rutland Gate, S.W. 10
(Transferred, and no longer a member.)
Noakes, H. W., Rockingham, Blessington Road, Lee... 50
New, Arthur T., London and Yorkshire Bank, Doncaster 10

Nalder, Francis, Chamber of London, Guildhall, E.C... 10
Nash, H. T., 8, Barlington Road, Clifton, Bristol 20
Nicol, J. G., Hallow, near Worcester... ... 5
Nicholson, Constance A., 6, Warrington Crescent, W. 50
Nevill, W. P., 4, Tokenhouse Buildings, E.C. 10
Norton, W., Stock Exchange, E.C. 2
(Transferred, and no longer a member.)
Northern, A., 19, Vernon Terrace, Brighton 60
Nye, Jesse, The Stock Exchange, E.C. ... 50
The Government of H.H. the Nizam, Hyderabad, India 3,750
National Provincial Bank of England ... 100
Novelli, L. W., the Oxford and Cambridge Club, Pall Mall 15
Oakley, Thos. N., 2, Copthall Buildings ... 136
(Transferred 10, February 18th, 1887.)
(" 154, March 1st, 1887.)
(" 110, May 6th, 1887.)
Oakley, F. J., The Stock Exchange, E.C.... 10
Oakley, W., 2, Copthall Buildings, E.C. ... 2
Ogilvie, F. D., Caledonian United Service Club, Edinburgh 30
Ochs, Sigmund, 83, Hatton Garden, E.C.... 5
Ochs, A. L., 83, Hatton Garden, E.C. .. 5
Oliver, W. H., Mothstone, Clifton Road, Wimbledon 5
Osmond, J., Clifton Road, Blackheath, S.E. 15
Osmond, W. R. } 416, Clapham Road, S.W. 10
Austin, Geo. }
Osmond, Henry, 416, Clapham Road, S.W. 6
Oakley, S. R., 2, Lombard Street, E.C. ... 1
Onions, J. H., Market Drayton 10
Oakley, Thos. Norris } 2, Copthall Buildings, E.C.... 110
Oakley, Wm. ... ... }
Pearce, R., Lanarth House, Holder's Hill, N.W.... ... ... —
(Transferred 50, April 5th, 1887.)
Postlethwaite, Geo. F., 22, Ryder Street, S.W.... 500
Postlethwaite, Jas. H., 22, Ryder Street, S.W.... 300
Payne, A., 37, Courtfield Garden, S.W. ... 60
(Tranferred and no longer a member.)
Pavy, Francis, 4 Bank Buildings 100
(Transferred 30 January 14th, 20 February 18th, 50 March 25th.)
Powles, A., 22, Royal Exchange, E.C. ... —
(Transferred 30 January 14th, 1887, and no longer a member.)
Porteous, D. S., Lawnstown Castle, Montrose 10
Phillips, S. E., 44, Warwick Road, W. ... 5
(Transferred 6, and no longer a member.)
Paine, H., jun. 15
(Transferred 10 June 17th, 40 July 8th, 50 July 14th, and 5 July 28th.)
Patterson, E. C., Wellesley House, Church Road, Upper Norwood 100
Powell, H. J., 4, Billiter Avenue, E.C. ... 5
Pound, H., 54, James Street, S.W. 10
Peacock, P. 10
(Transferred, and no longer a member).
Peacock, W., 153, Sandringham Road, Dalston, E. 7
Philips, J., Secretary's Office, General Post Office... 15
Puget, G. W. ... } 10
Puget, Mary L. }
Pratt, S. C., 14, Victoria Road, Old Charlton, S.E. 15
Phillips, R. K., 72, Mildmay Park, N. ... 20
Paynter, H. H., Lieutenant, care of Hallett and Co., 7, St. Martin's place, W.C. ... 5
Parsons, Amelia, Woodbine Terrace, Stroud 5
Pope, J. N. C., Shannon Court, Bristol ... 25
Robertson, W., 26, Throgmorton Street ... 105
(Transferred, and no longer a member.)

Name and Address	Amount
Rock, Joseph, 56, Friday Street, E.C. ...	800
Price, R. J. L., Rhilwas, Bala, N.W.	7
Pixley, S., 27, Old Broad Street, E.C. ...	100
Pain, R. T., 5, Victoria Street, Westminster	5
Powney, R. T., 14, Talfourd Road, Peckham, S.E.	15
Ponsonby, Hon. Mary Elizabeth, 9, Chapel Street, Belgrave Square	5
Ponsonby, The Hon. Frederick John William, Brooks' Club, St. James's ...	20
(Transferred, and no longer a member.)	
Raincock, H., 75, Old Broad Street, E.C. ...	20
Reeve, C., 214, High Holborn, W.C.	20
Richards, S., Turnerhall, Elton, N.B. ...	100
Reed, C. T., 13, Newman Street, Oxford Street, W.	10
Ray, J. F., 2, Copthall Buildings, E.C. ...	20
(Transferred February 18th, 1887.)	
Rishworth, T. R., 35, Talbot Street, Batley	7
Ryrie, R., St. Mildred's Court, E.C.	50
Rodman, W. H., 11, Royal Exchange, E.C.	10
Rowe, T. B., Glan Llyn, St. Kilda's Road, Stoke Newington	25
Redfern, W. L. M., 20, St. James's Square, S.W.	100
Robb, Isabella, 10, Woodbury Grove, Finsbury Park ... ... }	5
Robb, Edith, 10, Woodbury Grove, Finsbury Park ... ... }	
Robinson, J. Lewins, Edenbridge, Kent ...	60
(Transferred July 8th, 1887.)	
Reid, J., 39, Threadneedle Street, E.C. ...	20
Robinson, Sabina, Darley Dale, Farquhar Road, Upper Norwood	50
Rainer, H., National Bank of India and Madras	10
Ramsbottom, J., Stock Exchange	5
(Transferred July 14th, 1887.)	
Robinson, J. W., East End, Boxmoor, Herts.	10
Renny, W., St. Thomas Street, Portsmouth	5
Robinson, T. G., 112, Bishopsgate Street ...	200
Rowan, A. H., 24A, Earl's Court Gardens...	50
Rüffer, M., 39, Lombard Street, E.C.... ...	1,100
Relton, C. J., care of F. E. Wilson, 54, Lombard Street, E.C.	20
Raymond-Barker, A. B., Stock Exchange...	2
Rawlins, A. M., care of Cox and Co., Craig's Court, W....	10
Stewart, J., banker, 26, Throgmorton Street	11,704
(Transferred 9,000, January 14th, 1887.)	
,, 2,500, February 18th, 1887.)	
,, 100, January 17th, 1887.)	
Sharpe, H. P., 6, Curzon Street, Mayfair ...	500
Shaw, C. J., 84, Newhall Street, Birmingham	100
Sharp, J. H., Palmieri House, Western Road, Brighton ... ... }	15
Sharp, T. H., Palmieri House, Western Road, Brighton ... ... }	
Smythe, F. W., Imperial Bank, Constantinople	—
(8 transferred January 28th, 1887, and 2 transferred May 6th, 1887.)	
Searle, J., Stock Exchange	100
Sutton, W. R., 22, Golden Lane, Barbican, E.C.	25
Scott, D. M., 3, Drapers' Gardens	10
Stapylton, F. C., 24, Lombard Street, E.C.	20
Staley, T. P., 2, Fenchurch Avenue, E.C. ...	—
(10 transferred June 17th, 1887.)	
Sims, A. C., Harrow Weald Park, Stanmore	20
Stevens, R., 19, Wigmore Street, Cavendish Square	5
Stevens, R. M., 119, Chancery Lane, W.C....	35
Smith, F. G., 20, St. Leonard's-terrace, Chelsea	30
Speed, C., 81, South Hill Park, Hampstead, N.W.	—
(10 transferred February 18th, 1887.)	
Saunders, C. S., 40A, Springdale Road, Stoke Newington	4
Syrett, A., 45, Finsbury Pavement, E.C. ...	15
Stephenson, W., 42, Cheapside, E.C.... ...	5
Smithers, W. H., Baddow Court, Great Malvern, near Chelmsford	200
(100 transferred July 8th, 1888.)	
Smith, W. H., 28, Threadneedle Street, E.C.	2
Stokes, W., 16, Speedwell Road, Edgbaston	10
Sheppard, T., Laurie Park Gardens, Sydenham, S.E.	220
Scott, O. L., 25, Golden Square, W.	3
Spencer, T., 170, The Grove, Hammersmith, W....	10
Shorter, A., 20, Birchin Lane, E.C.	—
(75 transferred July 8th, 1887.)	
Stevens, W., jun., 421, Strand, W.C.	38
Stevens, G. N., 421, Strand, W.C.	50
Stern, J., 6, Angel Court, E.C.	50
(Transferred 40, July 18th, 1887.)	
(,, 10, July 21st, 1887.)	
Seaton, Eliza, 12, Westwick Gardens W., Kensington, W.	4
Street, Elizabeth, Marland Place, Southampton	—
(Transferred 5, July 8th, 1887.)	
Shaw, T. C. F. E., Oaklands, Wolverhampton	150
Slater, W. E., 16, Lancaster Road, South, Upper Tollington Park, N.	—
(Transferred 5, February 18th, 1887.)	
(,, 5, March 1st, 1887.)	
Schlesinger, L. B., 21, Cornhill, E.C.... ..	50
Spand, J. W. F. S., 17, Albyn Place, Aberdeen	—
(Transferred 10, March 25th, 1887.)	
Stearns, A. E., Stock Exchange	702
(Transferred 25, July 1st, 1887.)	
(,, 63, July 14th, 1887.)	
(,, 25, July 28th, 1887.)	
Scott, B. J., 7, Throgmorton Avenue, E.C.	35
(Transferred 25, May 6th, 1887.)	
Scholes, J. W., 19, Leadenhall Street, E.C.	50
Slimon-Macnair, J. B. T., 37, West Hill Street, Glasgow	20
Stern, H. de, 6, Angel Court, E.C.	—
(Transferred 50, April 15th, 1887.)	
(,, 50, May 6th, 1887.)	
Smith, Mary R., spinster; Jacobson, Sarah, spinster; Mellor, B. D., gentleman } 70, Grosvenor Road, Canonbury, N. ...	13
Stillingfleet, H. J. W., Hampton Bishop Rectory, Hereford	5
Sloop, F. C. S., 4, Hercules Passage, E.C.	—
(Transferred 20, January 28th, 1887.)	
Slaughter, F. A., 6, King's Road, Brownswood Park, N....	2
Smith, W. H. G., 46, Parliament Street, S.W.	5
Stanhope, Hon. E. T. S., 60th Rifles, care of Cox and Co., Craig's Court, S.W. ...	4
Sparrowe, Isabella, care of W. Bradley, Esq., Bourne End, Maidenhead	2
Scholtensack, G., Heathside, Blackheath, S.E.	100
(Transferred, and no longer a member.)	
Smythson, F. J., 1, Harper Street, Red Lion Square, W.C....	—
(20, transferred April 15th, 1887.)	
Strange, J. F., care of Pardorp and Co., 12, Mark Lane, E.C.	5
Swinton, A. A., Tregunter Lodge, Gilston Road, S.W.	50
Surgey, E., Cranford Bridge, Hounslow ...	100
Skinner, T. H., Tillington Hall, Petworth .	10
Smith, C. E., 61, Threadneedle Street, E.C.	20
Spence, J. W., 374, The Cliff, Higher Broughton, Manchester	10
Sutton, J. E., 33, Mechlenburgh Square, W.C.	10
Sellon, J. S., The Hall, Sydenham, S.E. ...	50
Stagg, R., Yardley Court, Tunbridge... ...	40
Stranaghen, A., Castle Street, Cardiff ...	50
Stephens, A. T., Castle Street, Cardiff ...	50

Spring, C., 55, St. George's Avenue, Tufnell Park, N. 20
Smith, Jane, Longford House, Buckhurst Hill, Essex 10
Schloesser, Ernest, 12, Dalcham Gardens, South Hampstead, N. 5
Sharp, J. H., 12, East Street, Brighton } Woodhams, E. W. } ... 25
Stewart, J., Ballywilliamroe, Ireland ... 20
Snoad, F., Stock Exchange, E.C. 4
(Transferred, and no longer a shareholder.)
Stevens, E., Springfield, Tulse Hill 100
(Transferred, and no longer a shareholder.)
Scholes, H. S., care of Cox and Co., Craig's Court, W. 20
(Transferred 60 May 6th, 1887.)
Smith, J. M., 6, Crosby Square, E.C. ... 5
(Transferred, and no longer a member.)
Sandison, R., Stock Exchange, E.C. 20
Stevens, J. P., Stock Exchange, E.C. ... 10
Smith, Helen E., 77, Trodescant Road, South Lambeth Road, S.W.... 7
Spielman, M. A., 31, Throgmorton Street, E.C. 10
(Transferred, and no longer a member.)
Sale, W. T., St. Botolph's Green, Leominster 50
Sharland, F., 31, Palace Road, Upper Norwood, S.E. 10
Smith, E. R., 11, Copthall Court, E.C. ... 60
Spelman, S., 27, Hanover Gardens, Kennington, S.E. 5
Scripps, C. T., 13, South Molton Street, W. —
(Transferred 10, July 27th, 1887.)
Stewart, C. J., 4, Adam's Court, E.C. 320
(Transferred 20, May 6th, 1887.)
(„ 50, May 27th, 1887.)
Stearn, T., Dalton House, Ipswich ... ... —
(Transferred 20, March 25th, 1887.)
——, Elizabeth Mary, The Avenue, Broudesbury, N.W. 2
Smith, A. H., 77, Trodescant Road, South Lambeth 5
Steele, A., Conservative Club, St. James' Street, S.W. 150
Stearns, H. M., Stock Exchange, E.C. ... 3
Seaver, H., 35, Royal Exchange, E.C. ... 5
Seed, G. A., 39, Spring Hill, Brooker Hill, Sheffield 5
Smith, W. M., and Smith, W. H. B., 1, Copthall Chambers, E.C.... 20
Sordina, A., care of Jackson and Till, 24 and 26, Commercial Sale Rooms, Mincing Lane, E.C. ... ... —
(Transferred 10, May 27th, 1887.)
(„ 10, June 17th, 1887.)
Searle, B. P., 31, Hilldrop Crescent, N. ... 10
(Transferred May 27th, 1887).
Snell, M. B., Ambleside, Tooting Bec-road, Streatham, S.W. 15
Sheppey, J. E., 5, Dale Street, Liverpool... 5
Scrivener, H.B., } March, E. } 38, Lombard Street, E.C. 1,225
(Transferred 50, July 14th, 1887.)
Swaffield, A. O., St. Ives, Worple Road, Wimbledon 25
Shatlock, T. F., Stock Exchange, E.C. ... 20
Schiff, A. G., Warnford Court, E.C. 200
Smith, Jonathan, Stock Exchange ... ... —
(10 transferred June 17th, 1887.)
Suttie, R. G., The Lodge, North Berwick, N.B. 11
Stonsby, C. J., The Strand, Derby 15
Syrett, Florence, 88, King Edward Road, Hackney 5
Stephen, J. Y., 16, Lennox Gardens, S.W. 100
Stern, H., 6, Angel Court, E.C. 60
St. Quinton, A. M. C., Lee Hall, Blackheath 10
Stevens, W., 421 Strand, W.C. ... ... }
Stevens, G. N., 421, Strand, W.C. ... ... } 100
Stevens, A. B., Springfield, Tulse Hill, S.W. }

Tottenham, L., The Murmurs, Exmouth ... 50
Tunley, G., 14, Clement's Lane, E.C... ... 30
(Transferred 30, March 25th, 1887.)
Thorp, W., Stock Exchange 5
Threlfal, R. P., 143, Church Street, Preston 30
Thorold, A. C. E., Hougham, Grantham ... 28
Tamer, G. D., 150, Norwood Road, S.E. ... 15
Tschop, J., Park Lodge, Sunningdale, Berks 5
Tenterden, Baroness Emma Mary, 17, Portland Place, W.... ... ... —
(20 transferred August 3rd, 1887.)
Thurburn, H., 43, Russell Road, Kensington 10
Tippinge, E., Longparish House, Whitchurch 15
Trower, H., 39, St. Mary-at-Hill, E.C. ... 300
Thomasson, J. S., 27, Ackers Street, Manchester 20
Taylor, E., 78, Blackman Street, Drury Lane, W.C. 5
Tiley, G. F., 4, Adam's Court, E.C. 40
Thorpe, T. W., Albion Brewery, Mile End, E. 60
(Transferred 40, July 28th, 1887.)
Thompson, J., 12, London Street, E.C. ... 10
Thorne, A., 21, Mincing Lane, E.C. 100
Thompson, J. S., Stock Exchange, E.C. ... —
(Transferred 30, July 15th, 1887.)
(„ 8, July 16th, 1887.)
(„ 10, July 21st, 1887.)
(„ 2, July 29th, 1887.)
Triggs, E. E., Westovers, Cuckfield, Sussex 6
Thompson, T. G., Heacham, Norfolk ... 10
Talbot, C., 33, Queen's Road, N.W. 10
Taylor, J. D., The Wergs, Wolverhampton 50
Thurburn, C. A., 16, Kensington Park Gardens, W. 10
Thackeray, Matilda, Montague House, Vanbrugh Park, Blackheath 45
Thackeray, Annie, Oaklands, Surbiton Hill, Kingston-on-Thames 20
Tedeschi, A., 29, Throgmorton Street, E.C. 50
Uzielli, T., 9, Gracechurch Street, E.C. ... 25
(Transferred, and ceased to be a member.)
Udall, J., 25, Townhead Road, Hertford 5
Vickerman, A., 6, Seymour Street, Portman Square 40
Vista, L. A. de la Boa, 32, Grosvenor Gardens, S.W. 10
(Transferred, and ceased to be a member.)
Varden, H. W., Stock Exchange, E.C. ... 10
Vyne, J. H., 7, Tokenhouse Yard, E.C. ... 50
Vanzeven, E., Higher Barrocks, Exeter ... 10
Vanzeven, J. N., 23, Lansdowne Crescent, Notting Hill, N.W. 4
Winter, Albert Charles, solicitor, 7, Great Winchester Street 3,875
(And transferred by power of attorney to W. C. Watson—
7,487, January 14th, 1887
3,750, June 17th, 1887.)
Watson, William Clarence, 7, Great Winchester Street, merchant 4,144
(And transferred 14,400 on January 14th, 1887
„ 9,072 on „ 28th, „
„ 1,798 February 18th, „
„ 3,330 March 1st, „
„ 1,254 „ 25th, „
„ 2,350 April 15th, „
„ 8,350 May 6th, „
„ 4,815 „ 27th, „
„ 2,060 June 17th, „
„ 50 „ 20th, „
„ 1,240 July 8th, „
„ 1,920 „ 14th, „
„ 400 „ 27th, „
„ 460 „ 28th, „
Watson, Reverend Edward John, 23, Woburn Square 100
(Transferred, and ceased to be a member.)
White, S., 1, Royal Exchange Buildings, E.C. 50
Wolff, F. A. C., Lower Tooting, S.W. ... 20

Name and Address	Shares
Whitmore, E. H., 4, Adam's Court, E.C. ...	115
(Transferred 215 on July 8th, 1887.)	
Warren, W., 346, King's Road, Chelsea, S.W. ...	—
(10 transferred on January 14th, 1887.)	
Wilton, G., Spring Gardens, Weybridge, S.W. ...	35
Whittlesea, J., 3, Buckingham Street, Brighton ...	50
Woods, A., Drapers' Gardens, E.C. ...	10
Williams, Cornhill, Bridgewater...	10
Wilson, J. H., 9 and 11, Fenchurch-avenue, E.C. ...	100
(Transferred, and ceased to be a member.)	
White, J., 36, Ditchley-rise, Brighton ...	10
Woodhorns, E. S., 12, East Street, Brighton	—
(Transferred 5, July 20th, 1887.)	
(" 10, " 28th, ")	
(" 10, " 30th, ")	
Weldon, W. H., 69, Gloucester Place, S.W.	30
(Transferred 10, July 8, 1887.)	
Wright, E., Fresh Wharf, London Bridge, E.C. ...	80
Webbe, G. A., care of Stewart, Pixley and Co., 4, Adam's-court, E.C. ...	170
Walton, Eliza J., 128, Inverness Terrace, Bayswater, W. ...	5
(Transferred, and ceased to be a member.)	
Whitfield, G. T., Spring Hill, Market Drayton ...	15
Watt, Mary Anne, 12a, Oxford and Cambridge Mansions, Hyde Park, N.W. ...	5
Witt, T., 40, Chancery Lane, W.C. ...	10
Warden, T., 5, Eton Gardens, Hillhead, Glasgow ...	30
Whitehead, B., 9, Stone Buildings, Lincoln's Inn, W.C. ...	60
Weston, M. B., St. Lawrence, Burstock-road, Putney, S.W....	5
Walker, H. T., 27, Throgmorton Street, E.C. ...	200
(Transferred 77, March 25th, 1887.)	
(" 66, April 15th, 1887.)	
(" 2, May 6th, 1887.)	
(" 5, July 8th, 1887.)	
Wollen, W. F., Codrington Villa, Central Hill, S.E. ...	20
White, T., Stondin Place, Brentwood, Essex	75
Watts, C. W., 62, Lombard Street, E.C. ...	10
Webbe, A. J., 9, Cambridge Square, N.W.	50
Wellington, C., 1, May Villas, Sutton, Surrey ...	10
Whatman, C. M. C., Breamore, Salisbury...	—
(Transferred 41, July 8th, 1887.)	
(" 25, July 9th, 1887.)	
Winch, W. R., 4, Fenchurch Street, E.C....	50
Wilson, T., Brockley Road, Beckenham ...	30
Wilson, G. F., Hether Bank, Weybridge ...	50
White, T., 293, Stratford Road, Birmingham ...	5
Watson, W., Seapoint Terrace, Monkstown, County Dublin...	20
Wigg, F., 62, Cleveland Square, N.W....	25
White, F. A., 2, Lime Street Square, E.C...	100
White, R. O., 180, Cromwell Road, S.W. ...	50
(Transferred, and ceased to be a member.)	
Ward, W., 31, Belsize Crescent, N.W. } Isaacson, W. W., 5, New Inn, W.C. ... } ...	50
Wontner, A. J., Stock Exchange, E.C. ...	70
Watt, H., 12, Oxford and Cambridge Mansions, S.W. ...	10
Ward, B. P., Junior Carlton Club, S.W. ...	15
Walsh, C. H., Army and Navy Club, St. James' ...	3
Waugh, A. T., St. Mary's Vicarage, Brighton ...	16
Western, Caroline, care of Ransom, Bouverie and Co., 1, Pall Mall East, W. ...	40
Walsh, W., } Hardy, Asa, } Little Lever Street, Manchester ...	200
Wainwright, G. E., 11, Copthall Court, E.C.	30
Welsted, B., 11, Charleville Grove, South Kensington ...	20
Wood, Emily, 11, Honeywill Road, S.W....	3
Waterer, M. E., 26, Fairfax Road, N.W. ...	40
Walker, F., 2, Chaple Street, Congleton ...	2
Wigram, W. A., 12, Westerby Place, South Kensington ...	20
Wood, S., 1, Crown Court, Threadneedle Street, E.C. ...	10
(Transferred on June 17th, 1887.)	
Wilson, G., Sedlescombe Road, St. Leonard's	10
Williams, F. H., 3, Drapers' Gardens, E.C...	50
Welton, W. W., Market Hill, Woodbridge	10
Wilson, W. J., Stock Exchange, E.C....	208
Whytt, E., Moss Hall Grove, Finchley, N.W.	5
Ward, C. B., 9, Abbey Road, St. John's Wood, N.W. ...	50
Woodroff, F. H., Stock Exchange, E.C. ...	100
Whitehead, T. S., 23, Leadenhall-st., E.C.	25
(Transferred, and ceased to be a member.)	
Wigram, R., 112, Bishopsgate Street, E.C.	130
Wade, R. B., 13, Seymour Street, Portman Square, W. ...	20
(Transferred, and ceased to be a member.)	
Whelan, J. L., 13, Old Broad Street, E.C... } Morris, O. A., 13, Old Broad Street, E.C.... }	75
Wood, J., 4, St. Enoch Square, Glasgow ...	20
Woollen, G., 26, White Horse Street, Radcliff, E. ...	20
Warter, J., 76, Mark Lane, E.C....	25
Wylie, J., West Cliff Hall, Hythe, Southampton ...	150
Walker, F. J., 24, Lennox Gardens, S.W....	40
Young, E. A., 41, Coleman Street, E.C. ...	10
Young, W. B., The Grove, St. Leonard's-on-Sea ...	10
Yakinthis, G., 8, Drapers' Gardens, E.C. ...	20
Yeates, J., 13, Colville Gardens, W. ...	10
(Transferred, and ceased to be a member.)	
Younger, M., 9, Pemberton Terrace, Junction Road, N. ...	50
Young, A. } Reid, J. } 39, Threadneedle Street, E.C...	100
Yates, M. S., Didsbury, Manchester ...	150
Young, G. H. B., 13, Moorgate Street, E.C.	10
Zarifi, M. J., 21, Great Winchester Street, E.C. ...	50
Winter, C. A., 7, Great Winchester Street, E.C. ...	21,250
(Share Warrants.)	

Deccans in Parliament.—A Committee of Inquiry Demanded—The Action of the Government.—In the House of Commons yesterday, Mr. Labouchere said: I beg to ask the Under Secretary of State for India whether the consent of the Resident at Hyderabad, and of the Indian Government, was given in January, 1886, for 99 years to the concession by the Nizam of all mining rights in the Deccan to Messrs. Watson and Stewart under the following conditions: That they would promote a company with a nominal capital of £1,000,000, but that not more than £150,000 should be first issued and £75,000 paid-up, which sum was to be employed in working the coalfields of

Singareni, and the rest of the capital was only to be issued if it could be remuneratively employed in working other coalfields or mines, or in building steel or iron works in the Deccan; and, if these were not the conditions, whether he can state what they were? Whether the concessionnaires promoted a company with a capital of £1,000,000, divided into 100,000 shares of £10, and, having issued at once the entire capital, allotted to themselves, to a Mr. Sharp, and to Mr. Winter, the solicitor of the company, 85,000 shares, which were declared to be fully paid up, although nothing was paid on them? Whether this was done with the approval of the British Resident at Hyderabad, or of the Indian Government: Whether, in June last, one Abdul Huk, being in England as Jubilee Commissioner of the Nizam, purchased 10,000 shares for the Government of the Nizam at the price of £12 per share: and whether he is aware that it has been stated in the *Times* and other journals that the price of £12 per share was an artificial one caused by fictitious dealings between the concessionnaires and their nominees, and by eight brokers being sent into the Stock Exchange by Abdul Huk simultaneously to compete for shares, and that they were all or almost all bought in two blocks bearing consecutive numbers from one jobber: Whether the Jubilee Commissioner telegraphed to Colonel Marshall, the British Secretary of the Nizam, on June 3, "Deccan firmly held by public, therefore with greatest difficulty succeeded in purchasing" the shares in question, and that Colonel Marshall replied that this arrangement was "eminently satisfactory": Whether this arrangement is deemed satisfactory by the Indian Government, or by the Secretary of State for India: And whether, in view of the above facts, and with the object of protecting the subjects of the Nizam from the loss of £850,000, and British investors from the loss of their money by investing in the "paper" shares of this company under the impression that both its capital and the Stock Exchange operations connected with it were within the knowledge and had the approval of the Indian Government and Her Majesty's Secretary of State for India, the Government will agree to the appointment of a Select Committee to inquire into the formation of the company, the purchase of the shares by an agent of the Nizam, and the approval of the purchase by Colonel Marshall; and to report whether there is sufficient cause for the Nizam to be advised to abrogate or modify the concession, and for the guilty parties, if fraud be proved, to be brought to justice.

Sir John Gorst replied: The company in question was formed under a concession granted by H.H. the Nizam, which was approved of by the Government of India, and no objection was raised to the wishes of the Nizam's Government to invest in the shares of the company. The Secretary of State for India has no knowledge of the other circumstances alleged by the hon. member. Colonel Marshall, whom he speaks of as a British Secretary, is not under the orders of the Government of India, and does not act as their agent in conducting the correspondence of the Nizam. Of course the Government has no objection to an inquiry into the action of Her Majesty's Government if, upon a motion made in the ordinary way, the hon. member can offer any *primâ facie* ground for believing that their conduct has been open to question. They do not think a parliamentary inquiry would be desirable into the conduct of a native sovereign or his ministers, for whose action in respect of matters of internal administration Her Majesty's Government are not responsible, and with which they are under a treaty obligation not to interfere. If any request for inquiry upon the matter should reach the Government of India from the Nizam, of course the fullest assistance in their power will be given to him.

Mr. Labouchere: May I ask the first Lord of the Treasury whether a committee of inquiry will be appointed to consider the Nizam's position in regard to the matter?

Lord R. Churchill: Before the right hon. gentleman replies, I may inform him that I have received a strong representation from a leading member of the

Government of Hyderabad, imploring me to use any influence I possess to protect the subjects of the Nizam from a fraud of the most remarkable kind, meaning the matter to which the hon. gentleman, the member for Northampton, has called attention. Under these circumstances I will add my appeal to that of the hon. member to the First Lord of the Treasury to allow a committee to be appointed to inquire into the matter without undue delay, because the loss threatened to the State of Hyderabad is stated by my official informant as one of great magnitude.

Mr. Labouchere: If the right hon. gentleman will give me facilities I will be perfectly able to lay before the House what I consider to be a *primâ facie* case.

Mr. W. H. Smith: The Government have already stated that if a *primâ facie* case can be made out for an inquiry, such as can properly be instituted by them, or any other inquiry which the Government can possibly accede to, they will be glad to afford all possible assistance in the matter; and if the hon. member will repeat the question to-morrow I will endeavour to see whether an arrangement can be made to enable him to bring on a motion.

Sir G. Campbell: Is the right hon. gentleman aware that there is a law forbidding financial transactions between European and native princes without the express sanction of the Government of India?

Sir J. Gorst: There is a law prohibiting the loan of money to native chiefs, but the transaction of a purchase of shares is one that is not restricted in any section of the Government of India.—*Financial News*, April 27.

THE MINING CONCESSION IN HYDERABAD.—(FROM OUR CORRESPONDENT.)—ALLAHABAD, THURSDAY.—The *Pioneer* publishes a long article which is a practical indictment of Mr. Cordery, the Resident at Hyderabad. Colonel Marshall's errors are described as errors of judgment, arising from too much zeal. The *Pioneer* holds that the Government of India is free from blame in the mining concession, saying: "The bargain to which they were a party was eminently practical and business-like. It only miscarried at the stage when their obligation to watch over its progress had ceased. True, they were parties to the purchase by the Nizam of a share in the company, but there was nothing particularly objectionable on the face of the proposal, and it was not consented to until the Resident wired a second time, and with impressive urgency, that the Nizam was anxious to hasten the completion of the business, or the tempting prospect would be lost. The Government of India previously telegraphed to the Secretary of State their serious objection, on principle, to large speculative dealings between native States and capitalists at home. Mr. Cordery is condemned for conveying to the Government of India his approval of Abdul Huk's proceedings."—*Daily News*, April 27.

A GOOD deal of interest has been evinced in the affairs of the Hyderabad-Deccan Company, whose shares have been pressed for sale at a heavy decline in prices. The company, it appears, was formed to take over a concession granted by the Nizam over a large area of land said to carry valuable coal deposits. The property, for which no payment had been made, was formed into a company with a capital of £1,000,000, the value placed upon it by the vendors being close upon £900,000. No prospectus was issued, but the shares were disposed of to the public through the agency of certain firms in London, and it is rumoured that the Government of the Nizam is now going to take some steps which will place the entire transaction clearly before the public, and show whether the company was or was not honestly floated by the promoters.—*Arrow*, April 27.

Abdul Huk.—Sirdar Diler Jung, *alias* Abdul Huk, the Mephistopheles of the Hyderabad-Deccan concession, is evidently no common-place Indian. It is not every man, even with brains and social position to help him, who can burst forth suddenly on the City as a grand financier. Companies with £1,000,000 sterling capital are the blue ribands of the speculative turf, which even old and experienced promoters aspire to in vain. Very seldom indeed are they caught at the first clutch, as happened to this wonderful Oriental —Abdul Huk. It may safely be taken for granted that our readers are dying with curiosity to learn something of Abdul Huk's antecedents. With the assistance of several Anglo-Indians who have known him for years, and have had opportunities of studying both his character and his methods, the following information regarding him has been collected.

Abdul Huk hails from a small town called Khallian, in the Presidency of Bombay. His first public position was in the native police, where he served for some time as a trooper. Thence he was transferred to the Berar Commission, where he held some minor appointment of a nondescript kind. Berar is a province of Hyderabad, which years ago was taken in pledge by the Government of India for claims of various kinds which it had against the Nizam. While in British hands it has always been governed by a so-called commission, in which there are not a few plums for Calcutta officials. While there Abdul Huk came under the notice of Sir Richard Meade, then British Resident at Hyderabad, and now chairman of the Nizam's Guaranteed State Railways Company, Limited. At Sir Richard's instance he was transferred to Hyderabad, where, as a hanger-on of the Residency, he found very congenial occupation for the diplomatic craft of which he is a master. His duties were of a kind for which no polite name can be found in our matter-of-fact language. Officially a mere nobody, he soon made himself practically a very important man.

Native States like Hyderabad are governed by an ingenious mixture of British dictation and native intrigue. The native ruler and his Ministers are mere puppets, whose wires are pulled from Simla through the local Resident. The only difficulty with them is, not to get them to do what they are told, but to see that they do nothing else. They have to be continually watched, and in this task agents of different degrees of respectability have to be employed. The Resident himself generally lives at a distance from the palace, and plays the part of a *Deus ex machina*. He sees nothing except through other people's eyes, and hears nothing save through other men's ears. His chief instrument is the native ruler's private secretary—an English official appointed by himself, and, as a rule, his personal friend. Through the private secretary he watches and controls the ruler. But every Minister and every official of the Court has also to be looked after. Hence the necessity for the Resident to keep about him sharp-eyed natives, initiated in all the secrets of oriental diplomacy. They fetch and carry for him, and act as his go-betweens with the palace.

A power such as theirs must be very great, even when honestly used. When abused, as it invariably is, it becomes a systematic tyranny to the native officials. These political spies—for they are nothing else—can go down to the palace and hector and bully to their heart's content in the name of the Resident; they can threaten or coax, as they find most convenient—all in the name of the Resident. The strongest native Minister and the highest nobles at Court bend the knee to them, all the while hating them at heart. It hardly requires to be said that they are continually being offered valuable presents—which they do not refuse. Sometimes, as in Abdul Huk's case, they not only make gigantic fortunes, but they get themselves promoted to high offices and dignities. This ex-trooper of police was, till disgraced the other day, Home Secretary for the State of Hyderabad. He had the impudence to pawn himself off last year on the British public during the Jubilee celebrations as a Hyderabadee noble. In the State he pretended to represent, he is as much a foreigner as his British masters. He is detested by the people, not only as an interloper, but as one who has enriched himself at their expense. His life would hardly be safe in the city of Hyderabad, and for politic reasons he prefers to live within the British cantonment of Secunderabad. There Abdul Huk poses as a grand seigneur, boasting with equal candour of his wealth and his political influence. To hear him speak it might be thought that he was in the habit of turning both Simla and the India Office round his little finger.

Nor does it appear that Abdul Huk is an empty braggart. Over and over again he has given tangible proof of possessing a powerful and mysterious influence in those quarters. Three successive Residents at Hyderabad—Sir Richard Meade, Mr. Jones and Mr. Cordery—seem to have allowed him to acquire a strange fascination over them. Notwithstanding all they must have known about his antecedents, and what they ought to have seen of his character, they gave him their official countenance, thereby enabling him to perpetrate the gigantic swindles with which he is now openly charged. Whatever his secret is, he has not allowed it to lose anything in the telling. As a boaster he leaves Baron Munchausen whole leagues behind. Latterly he has flown at much higher game than Residents or even India Office officials. When he returned from London last year he made very free with the names of British Cabinet Ministers. It was by that means he worked his crowning exploit—the famous "sixty lakh trick." By pretending to have got a confidential hint from his friend Mr. Goschen that offers of assistance on the frontier from the native States would have a good moral influence on Russia, he induced the Nizam—a youth of only one and twenty—to sign a letter to the Viceroy offering a gift of sixty lakhs of rupees. Then, in order to have his *coup* put beyond reach of accidents, and to lose no time in reaping the glory of it, he posted off to Simla and tendered a cheque on London for the first instalment of 20 lakhs.

What Abdul Huk's game really was in this peculiar transaction has not yet been fathomed, even by his friends. No special motive could be imagined at the time, save exuberant loyalty; but the Hyderabad-Deccan scandal had not then come to light. Abdul Huk, with his preternatural cuteness, may have scented trouble in the distance. At the close of the session a Member of the House of Commons had moved for information regarding the concession, and, by a coincidence which may not have been wholly accidental, this Parliamentary return appeared within a week or two of the announcement of the Nizam's offer of sixty lakhs. Various other odd circumstances attended the sixty lakh incident. At the end of September, before the Viceroy had had time to communicate it to the India Office, even by telegraph, a long letter appeared in the *Times* pronouncing a glowing panegyric on the Nizam and his illustrious Minister, Abdul Huk. Being printed in large type, written in an impressive semi-official strain, and signed "Political," it gave the impression of emanating from some very distinguished quarter. Very possibly it did! But whoever the writer was, there can be no doubt about his being a warm admirer of Abdul Huk. If we are not greatly mistaken, the same Roman hand has been at work again on the apology for Abdul Huk which figures in yesterday's *Times*, also with the distinction of large type and prominent position.

This Mahomedan adventurer, who, by his own account, has fleeced Hyderabad of half a million sterling, has cast his glamour over the press as well as over the India Office. The two professed leaders of British journalism—the *Times* and the *Standard*—have openly espoused his cause, whether from ignorance or for other motives does not lie with us to say, or even to guess. Our duty is simply to tell them and the British public what sort of man their *protégé* is, and to give them a few glimpses of his past career. Whether the training he has had was likely to make of him a philanthropist or financial hawk sensible men may judge for themselves. —*Financial News*, April 27.

THE DECCAN MINING COMPANY.—(FROM OUR CORRESPONDENT.)—SECUNDERABAD, April 26th.—The following information relative to the Deccan Mining Company's concession reaches me from an authoritative source:—

With reference to the use of the term "first issue," it is incorrect to suppose that the Nizam had anything to do with it. The draft—prepared by lawyers in England, and agreed to on January 8th, 1885—runs thus: "If such a company shall be formed before the said 1st day of January, 1889, and if before that day two hundred and fifty thousand pounds at least of its share capital shall have been subscribed for, and one hundred thousand pounds shall have been actually paid up in respect of the subscribed share capital."

To this draft both parties agreed in the following words:—"I agree to this draft as it now stands on behalf of William Clarence Watson and John Stewart.—Signed, C. WINTER, constituted Attorney, 7th January, 1885. I agree to this draft, with modifications shown in red, which bear my initials, on behalf of his Highness's Government.—Signed, SALAR JUNG, 8th January, 1885."

The concession finally signed is a verbatim transcript of the above agreed draft, excepting that the amount is reduced from two hundred and fifty thousand pounds to one hundred and fifty thousand pounds, and the date changed from the said 1st of January, 1889, to the expiration of the period fixed in Clause 1. This was signed by the Minister after reading, in presence of witnesses and representative of the English Resident, the deed of concession from beginning to end.

The reduction of the amount was due to the intervention of the Government of India. No such phrase as "first issue" was ever used by the Nizam's Government or the Government of India at any stage of the negotiations before January 8th, 1885, the day on which the final draft was concluded. The concessionnaires positively declined to accept the words first time, and the originally accepted wording was, therefore, allowed to stand, and was drafted, after prolonged discussion, by the First Assistant at the Minister's request. The whole negotiation in India was personally conducted between Mr. Winter, the Minister, and the Resident; all correspondence passed direct between them under the close supervision of the Government of India.—*Standard*, April 27.

SIR JOHN GORST returned an evasive answer when questioned to-night by Mr. Labouchere as to whether the Government would consent to the appointment of a Select Committee to inquire into the great scandal of the Hyderabad (Deccan) Mines, the history of which was related in this column the other day. But when Lord Randolph Churchill appeared upon the scene Sir John Gorst was thrust aside, and Mr. W. H. Smith tremblingly rose to reply to this twin arbiter of the destinies of the Ministry. He is to consider the matter and give a reply to-morrow. Should this not be satisfactory, the adjournment of the debate will be moved, and the whole thing forthwith thrashed out. But it is probable that the Government will capitulate, and make this step unnecessary. There are a great many more members on the Conservative side besides Lord Randolph Churchill who are determined to have the matter thoroughly inquired into. Lord Randolph Churchill has taken up the matter partly from his inherent distaste for anything like a job, but principally because a full investigation of the matter threatens to involve the Secretary of State for India in opprobrium. Lord Randolph Churchill, it is well known, "can't abear" poor Lord Cross, and means to make the most of this opportunity of paying off old scores.—*Liverpool Post*, April 27.

A FEATURE in the Mining Market during the past week has been the sudden and totally unexpected drop in the price of "Deccans," as the shares of the Hyderabad (Deccan) Co., Limited, are called in the market. Statements are made concerning this company which go to prove that the concession is not valid, and will be cancelled. On the other hand the company, and those who are not interested as "bears," say that the degradation of Abdul Huk cannot affect the position of the company to the slightest extent, inasmuch as the negotiations were conducted under the direct supervision of the India Office and the Indian Government. Time will prove. We certainly should not sell at present prices, although we must confess that the severe fall is enough to unnerve the strongest investor. Mysore Gold and the other classes of Indian mines are flat. With reference to Tintos, the dividend is unexpectedly good. These should improve. —*Piccadilly*, April 27.

INDIAN SCANDALS.—Whatever may be the secret history of the transactions in which the Sirdar Diler Jung—better known as Abdul Huk—is implicated, there is every reason to hope that it will soon be unravelled. A new British Resident has lately been appointed to Hyderabad—Mr. A. P. Howell—and he may be relied on to furnish Lord Dufferin with a thoroughly accurate and impartial account of all that has taken place. No doubt a part of the trouble may be ascribed to the remarkable division of authority at the Nizam's capital. The Viceroy is represented in the first place by the British Resident, a post held until lately by Mr. Cordery, an Indian civilian who may be known to English readers by the translation of Homer. But besides the Resident there is also the Nizam's English Secretary. Colonel Marshall was appointed to this office at the instance of Lord Dufferin, who seems to have hoped that a British officer renowned in Anglo-Indian circles for his social talents would find a way of smoothing the relations between the Nizam and his Ministers on the one hand, and between the Nizam's Government and the Indian Foreign Office on the other. Colonel Marshall, who had been transferred to the Deccan from a civil appointment in the Punjaub, rapidly made friends in his new position, and soon became to all appearances *bon camarade* with nearly all the notables of Hyderabad—Abdul Huk included. Whether it was wise on Lord Dufferin's part to have countenanced these novel relations between the Administration and a British officer who, although nominally acting as the Nizam's secretary, was known to be in the Viceroy's confidence, remains to be seen. There is just a suspicion that Colonel Marshall has been a trifle too enthusiastic in his endeavour to promote a pleasant feeling all round; but until we know how far he was concerned in the Nizam's offer, and how far he was, or might have been, acquainted with the game which Mr. Abdul Huk was playing, it would be rash to form any decided opinion.

The Nizam's famous cheque "on London" (for the defence of the frontier of India) is explained by a correspondent of the *Times*. It seems that when the Nizam's adviser, a British official, gave the Viceroy at Simla the Nizam's letter offering the Government of India a contribution of twenty lakhs for three years, the Hyderabad Government held shares and debentures of the Nizam's State Railway, the aggregate value of which at the time was £866,000. These shares and debentures were lodged in the National and Provincial Bank, and it was on these that the Nizam offered to draw, if required, a cheque for twenty lakhs, to meet the first year's instalment of his offer. This was "the fund in London of over a million sterling" on which, according to the Calcutta correspondent of the *Times*, the Nizam (at the same time that his letter was delivered) intimated to Lord Dufferin that he was prepared to give a cheque. The Government of Hyderabad had also at that time 12,500 shares of the Hyderabad Deccan Company, which it had purchased three months previously for £150,000, a sum about equal to twenty lakhs. Where these shares were lodged, and what was their worth, is not stated. The munificence of the Nizam is only equalled by the singularity of his conduct. Being a Nizam, and having made us a very handsome offer (under trying circumstances, if half what is now said about this offer is true), it might have been supposed that he would then wait to see whether his offer would be accepted. But that he did not do. He makes us an offer of cash, and before he knows whether it will be accepted or not he shows anxiety "to draw a cheque," which is rather remarkable. The correspondent of the *Times* states that the charges brought against an official of the Hyderabad State—charges of which the correspondent says he does not know the precise nature—should be "carefully sifted" and "calmly examined," as they may be susceptible of "an innocent explanation." No doubt; but the writer's attempted refutation of the charge brought against the Hyderabad official—which, as he says, can "only relate" to one of two recent transactions—appears to be somewhat premature. What, possibly, the Hyderabad Government is curious to know is how this official of theirs has been able in the course of some four years to amass a fortune said to amount to about a third of a million sterling. It seems that this person held a very obscure position in the British service till his services were lent to the Hyderabad State.

The modest fee of £83,000, which Abdul Huk pocketed as his reward for getting £1,660,000 out of the company purchasing the Hyderabad Railway seems to have been promised to him in writing by the late Sir Salar Jung. "The transaction," says a well-informed writer in the *Pioneer*, "has its shady side; especially as regards the secrecy observed towards the British Government. But the late Sir Salar Jung's pledges were respected by his son and by the Nizam; the Sirdar was in possession of the money; and it is not easy to see on what legal basis intervention would have been possible in a transaction entirely within the competence of a native Government's power over its own revenues." Far shadier on the face of it appears the mining transaction. The Sirdar Diler Jung has powerful friends in England, and perhaps they will help to explain the matter. The part played by the India Office undoubtedly requires to be elucidated. The information at present available tends to show that the usual course has been followed of interfering just sufficiently far in a business transaction to do no real good, and to incur the suspicion of being implicated in a mischievous intrigue.

Over and above the Hyderabad scandals, there are the Rumbold claims and some other affairs still unexplained. The moral of it all is not very satisfactory; but it might be as well to remember that because an Indian speculation is offered to English capitalists with the apparent approval both of the Indian Government and of the Secretary of State, we must by no means infer that it is blameless. The typical Anglo-Indian official, ever since the days of Colonel Newcome, has often been the tool of clever and scrupulous speculators. There are Colonel Newcomes in high position both under the Indian Government and in the India Office; and their connection, whether official or commercial, with a speculation does not always add to its safety.—*St. James's Gazette*, April 27.

The Deccan Mining Company.—The Secunderabad correspondent of the *Standard* says that the following information relative to the Deccan Mining Company's concession reaches him from an authoritative source:—

With reference to the use of the term "first issue," it is incorrect to suppose that the Nizam had anything to do with it. The draft prepared by lawyers in England, and agreed to on the 8th of January, 1885, runs thus: "If such a company shall be formed before the said day of January, 1889, and if before that day £250,000 at least of its share capital shall have been subscribed for, and £100,000 shall have been actually paid up in respect of the subscribed share capital." To this draft both parties agreed in the following words:

"I agree to this draft as it now stands, on behalf of William Clarence Watson and John Stewart.—Signed, C. A. Winter, constituted Attorney, 7th January, 1885. I agree to this draft, with modifications shown in red, which bear my initials, on behalf of His Highness's Government.—Signed, Salar Jung, 8th January, 1885."

The concession finally signed is a verbatim transcript of the above agreed draft, excepting that the amount is reduced from £250,000 to £150,000, and the date changed from the said 1st of January, 1889, to the expiration of the period fixed in Clause I. This was signed by the Minister after reading, in presence of witnesses and representative of the English Resident, the deed of concession from beginning to end. The reduction of the amount was due to the intervention of the Government of India. No such phrase as "first issue" was ever used by the Nizam's Government or the Government of India at any stage of the negotiations before the 8th of January, 1885, the day on which the final draft was concluded. The concessionnaires positively declined to accept the words first time, and the originally accepted wording was, therefore, allowed to stand, and was drafted, after prolonged discussion, by the First Assistant at the Minister's request. The whole negotiation in India was personally conducted between Mr. Winter, the Minister, and the Resident: all correspondence passed direct between them under the close supervision of the Government of India.

The Allahabad *Pioneer* publishes a long article which is a practical indictment of Mr. Cordery, the Resident at Hyderabad. Colonel Marshall's errors are described as errors of judgment, arising from too much zeal. The *Pioneer* holds that the Government of India is free from blame in the mining concession, saying:—

"The bargain to which they were a party was eminently practical and business-like. It only miscarried at the stage when their obligation to watch over its progress had ceased. True, they were parties to the purchase by the Nizam of a share in the company, but there was nothing particularly objectionable on the face of the proposal, and it was not consented to until the Resident wired a second time, and with impressive urgency, that the Nizam was anxious to hasten the completion of the business, or the tempting prospect would be lost The Government of India previously telegraphed to the Secretary of State their serious objection, on principle, to large speculative dealings between native States and capitalists at home. Mr. Cordery is condemned for conveying to the Government of India his approval of Abdul Huk's proceedings."—*St. James's Gazette*, April 27.

Some of the Anglo-Indian Members of Parliament, who happen to be members of the Carlton, have been troubled during the past few days by a representative of the Hyderabad Government, who has invaded even the sacred precincts of the latter institution, in the endeavour to secure support in regard to the affair of Abdul Huk. This matter grows more complicated daily, for Hyderabad is a perfect hotbed of intrigue, and strange revelations will be made if the Government grant an inquiry, as it is likely to do.—*Birmingham Post*, April 27.

The Deccan Scandal.—Mr. Labouchere secured a valuable ally last night in Lord Randolph Churchill in the matter of the Deccan scandal. Their combined influence obtained from the leader of the House a promise that if they can make out a *primâ facie* case for an inquiry, the Government will afford every possible assistance towards accomplishing the object in view. They will have little difficulty in doing so as soon as the facilities are afforded them, so that we may take it that an inquiry will be secured. The responsibility of the Government of India is denied, but Indian journals blame the British Resident at

Hyderabad for conveying to the Government of India his approval of Abdul Huk's proceedings.—*Pall Mall Gazette*, April 27.

It is understood that should there be any general expression of desire on the part of the House of Commons for the appointment of a Select Committee to inquire into the proceedings connected with the Hyderabad (Deccan) Mining Company, Mr. Labouchere's proposal will not be opposed. At the same time the Secretary of State for India, holding that his department has no responsibility for the transaction, will decline to take any initiative.—*Home News*, April 27.

Her Majesty's Government have shown a becoming willingness to give opportunities for proving that a case exists for inquiry into the purchase of Hyderabad-Deccan shares for the Nizam. This expression of willingness does not, of course, bring us very near an inquiry, but it is something gained. The Under-Secretary for India is disposed to tie up the subject in the bonds of red tape, as witness his disavowal of Governmental responsibility for the actions of Colonel Marshall. But as this officer was delegated to the service of the Nizam by the Viceroy, it is plain that if he was in any way guilty of carelessness or laxity in this matter, the Government should give facilities for inquiry into his conduct also. It is to be hoped above all that Mr. Cordery and Colonel Marshall will take steps to absolve themselves of complicity in the transactions which have created such scandal. They can easily secure inquiry by asking the Nizam to formally request the Indian Government to look into the subject, Sir John Gorst having undertaken that any request from the Nizam would be given effect to at once. Nothing can make the scandal less disreputable, but the public may at least hope that it will be proved that nothing more serious than over-confidence in Abdul Huk and the concessionnaires can be alleged against the British Resident.—*Evening Post*, April 27.

In the House of Commons there was a very long list of questions, foremost of which was one by Mr. Labouchere on the subject of the Nizam of Hyderabad's concession of mining rights in the Deccan to Messrs. Watson and Stewart. The facts, as set out in the question, are probably well-known, but briefly they may be stated as follows: The concessionnaires received authority to promote a company with a nominal capital of one million, of which not more than £150,000 should be first issued, and £75,000 paid up. As a matter of fact, the whole of the million was issued, and Mr. Labouchere wanted to know whether this was done with the approval of the British Government. He also wanted further particulars as to the purchase of shares, on behalf of the Nizam, of his Jubilee envoy, which created the report that the shares were being firmly held by the British public.

Sir John Gorst, in reply to the question, made the usual reply that the Government had no knowledge of the circumstance with regard to the purchase of the shares for the Nizam. The Government, however, would not refuse an inquiry into the conduct of the Government of India if a *prima facie* case were made out for believing that the conduct of the latter was open to question. Mr. Labouchere's emphatic demand for an inquiry into the occurrences which took place in England with regard to the company under a species of guarantee from the Indian Government, was backed up by Lord Randolph Churchill, and on Mr. Labouchere engaging to furnish materials for a *prima facie* case of inquiry, Mr. W. H. Smith undertook to find a day for the motion as soon as he could.—*Birmingham Post*, April 27.

The Hyderabad (Deccan) Company, Limited.—An Ugly Job.—His Highness the Nizam of Hyderabad is likely to become famous. His munificent offer to provide £600,000 towards the defence of India, of which sum £200,000 was to be paid by a draft on his agents in London immediately on the acceptance of the offer by the Imperial Government being notified, will not soon be forgotten—not so soon, perhaps, nor as completely, as in the interests of certain performers might be desired. But there was the offer, and it furnished the text for many a brilliant leading article. "Henceforth," we were told, "let all fears for the future of India disappear. When the great native rulers come forward with their coin to alleviate the strain on the Imperial Exchequer, the reign of love has begun in earnest. Troops may be withdrawn; Russia may be defied; scientific frontiers may be abandoned." The only flaw in the argument was that the great native ruler in question had not come forward with his coin. His munificent offer, which, strangely enough, was first made known throughout the unofficial columns of the *Times*, was not accompanied by a cheque to the Viceroy of India; who it is to be presumed might have been trusted to return the cheque if it could not be accepted. More than that, people who could be supposed to know stated that His Highness had no funds in London out of which any such cheque could have been met. This we admit was a low, material way of looking at such a transcendent matter, but the English are still in the main a hard-headed race. They are ready to take a great deal for granted about stars and angels, and such things, and they will swallow as much "flapdoodle" in the shape of gush about their fellow-creatures as the most guileless Yankee out; but when one of their fellow-creatures happens to talk to them about cheques or bills, they are all there at once, and names are discussed and means considered as carefully as if honour and sentiment were unknown terms. And so it came to pass that His Highness the Nizam's offer was received with mixed feelings, which gradually became concentrated in a form best expressed by the query, "What's the little game?" That brings us to the immediate subject of this article.

Everyone—everyone, that is, who follows Stock Exchange matters—has heard of "Deccans." Few, perhaps, even amongst those fortunate enough to possess the stock, know exactly what it is; fewer still know exactly how it was started, or how it has since been engineered; while the names of those who can see the end with clearness cannot even be guessed at, because they will not be found in the present list of shareholders. We will try, with the assistance of the *Times*, to throw some light on this subject, only remarking that there are people who suggest that there may be a connection between the Nizam's offer to assist the British Exchequer and the desire of some persons to assist their own exchequers by floating Deccan shares.

In 1886, according to the Hyderabad Yellow Book, the Nizam granted to Messrs. Watson and Stewart a concession for the mining rights of the Deccan. It does not appear that anything was paid for this concession, and, judged by the results, that part of the bargain would seem to have been equitable enough. Among the conditions recommended by the Government of India—the officials of which great department of State took a hand in the game—a game, it is to be hoped, some Truthful James of the future will be able to record "they did not understand"—was one to the effect that a company should be promoted with a nominal capital of £1,000,000, of which not more than £150,000 should at first be issued, £75,000 only of that to be called up. Accordingly in July, 1886, a company so constituted was launched and floated; the "tip" to buy Deccans became the order of the day with a certain class of writers, and the handful of stock issued was soon carried to a considerable premium.

This was mainly done by the influence of a section of the Press. One society paper, strong on the subject of amateur "Trusts," frequently advised the admixture of a certain proportion of Deccans to flavour such frivolous stocks as London and North-Western Railway and similar securities. The Deccans were to be to these stocks what the Orange Pekoe is to the humble Congou, or yeast to bread. They were to flavour the lump and to leaven it with the necessary vitality. The "rise" that was in them was to enliven the whole fund, and to cause it to swell and expand like the baker's dough. To buy Deccans became good business, but it was not good enough. The performers had £850,000 of unissued stock to turn into coin of the realm, not to mention the £75,000 uncalled on the actual issue. The British public, though appreciative, had become cool. The most ambitious lunatic generally confines his lunacy to one subject at a time. Diamonds had taken the place of Deccans with the gamblers, and at any rate there were no signs of the country going mad about the latter. Those who had them kept them, perhaps *pour cause*. Those who had not them felt they could get along without them. Something had to be done—something, or somebody—it does not matter much which term is used; it comes to the same thing.

So matters jogged on quietly enough until April, 1887, the blessed year of the Queen's Jubilee. At that glorious epoch, His Highness the Nizam, who loyally sent a representative to London, was induced, with a view to obtaining a "controlling interest" in the company, to give orders through the said representative to purchase 12,500 of its shares. What it was that required to be controlled we are not told; but as at that time only £6,411 out of the £75,000 subscribed had been spent altogether in the province it will be admitted that something required to be done to somebody, though why the Nizam should be the personage to do it, and why he should pay £120,000 for the privilege of looking after other people's business, is not so clear. Anyway, the following correspondence between the Nizam's representative and Mr. Watson took place:—

"Sirdar Diler-ul-Mulk to Mr. W. C. Watson.

"Alexandra Hotel, 2nd June, 1887.

"SIR,—I am instructed by the Government of His Highness the Nizam to purchase 10,000 £10 shares of the Hyderabad (Deccan) Company, Limited. As you are the agent of the Government here, I write to ask you to be so good as to arrange for the purchase of these shares at the lowest possible price, not exceeding £12 per share, the Government having decided to invest only £120,000 in these shares.—I am, Sir, your obedient servant,

"SIRDAR DILER-UL-MULK."

"Mr. Watson to Sirdar Diler-ul-Mulk.

"Confidential.

"7, Great Winchester Street, E.C., 3rd June, 1887.

"SIR,—I beg to acknowledge receipt of your letter of yesterday's date, instructing me as agent of the Government of His Highness the Nizam to purchase 10,000 £10 fully-paid shares of the Hyderabad (Deccan) Company, Limited.

"I beg to point out to you that to purchase these shares at the price you name is a most difficult and almost impossible operation, and will require the greatest skill and circumspection. I would suggest that the Government should acquire a proportion of the £5 paid shares at the same *pro rata* price, say £7 per share, as the £5 paid shares carry the same dividend as the £10 paid, and by this the Government could acquire, say, 8,750 £10 paid shares and 3,750 £5 paid shares, thus having 12,500 shares for £131,250, being an addition of 2,500 shares at an extra cost of £11,250 only. Please be kind enough to send me your instructions on this point.—I have, etc.,

"W. C. WATSON."

On receipt of this letter the Sirdar gave the following instructions:—

"3rd June, 1887.

"SIR,—I am in receipt of your letter of to-day's date, and in reply beg to state that your suggestion appears to be a good one. The Government only intended to invest £120,000 and purchase 10,000 shares; but as the Government will obtain 12,500 shares and only have at present to pay £11,250 in addition to the £120,000, and have the contingent liability of £18,750—under these circumstances I authorise you to purchase 8,750 £10 fully paid and 3,750 £5 paid shares.

"Should the Government not wish to hold shares in excess of the £120,000, I understand from you that there will not be any difficulty in re-selling the the additional shares at a profit.—I am, Sir, your obedient servant,

"SIRDAR DILER-UL-MULK."

Here the cloven foot becomes visible. "The same day," writes the *Times*, "eight different firms of brokers were sent into the market to buy these shares for the Nizam. The whole of the shares were bought at one price, namely, twelve, the highest figure at which the Nizam had said he was willing to purchase the shares. But what is more strange still is that when these shares were delivered they were handed in by these eight firms of brokers in two lots of 3,750 shares and 8,750 shares, all with consecutive numbers. Under these circumstances it is surprising that the Sirdar should have telegraphed to Colonel Marshall, the Nizam's private secretary, on the day in question—namely, 3rd June—as follows: 'Deccans firmly held by public, therefore with greatest difficulty succeeded in purchasing' the shares in question. It was added that the market closed at 12¾, and that the shares thus bought were then worth £9,000 more than had been paid for them."

Cannot anyone imagine the eight solemn winks with which the eight solemn brokers greeted each other as they proceeded to enter the House by as many different doors and windows as were available, in order to stalk the wily Deccans in a heap, a task which Mr. Watson astutely observed would require so much "skill and circumspection," and one which would even have made Buffalo Bill himself sit up? Cannot anyone imagine, also, the eight solemn winks with which the few jobbers on the "market" who deal in "rubbish," as stocks of the Deccan type are called, would be invited to make prices for £120,000 worth of a stock of which only £150,000 had been issued, the whole of which had passed out of their control?

For the information of country sisters, cousins, and aunts, it may be stated that stocks and shares are not exposed for sale in the Stock Exchange laid out on counters like flannel petticoats at a bazaar, neither are they, as a rule, the subject of private negotiation like Government contracts advertised "by public tender." The process is quite different. A dealer buys a stock which he does not want, or sells one which he has not got, in the hope of being able to balance his account at a profit by reselling what he has bought, or repurchasing what he has sold, in the current course of the day's business, and in this he generally succeeds. Apply that rule to Deccans and it will be seen that when Mr. Watson suggested that the instructions should be modified in order to facilitate the purchase, he must have known that, so far as the market was concerned, the modification would make no difference, because the stock could not be got there; while if it was to be acquired direct from the promoters, not to say by the promoters, the necessity for "the greatest skill and circumspection" in the purchase is not apparent.

At any rate the stock was bought, and as it could not have been bought in the market for the reasons given, we fail to share the astonishment of the *Times* that the whole of it should have been got at the same price, and that it should have been handed in by the eight solemn brokers in two lots of shares bearing consecutive numbers, because we do not see how otherwise the thing could have been done.

That part of the farce is played out, and it has apparently been about as unreal as the negotiations between the wirepullers of our two great Dock Companies. Whether any really useful investigation into the matter will take place or not we are unable to say, but we doubt it. The India Office is said to be inquiring into the matter, but the officials of that Department of State live in houses built of such very thin glass that to appoint them to inquire into a matter in which Indians or Anglo-Indians of rank may be implicated, is not consistent with a sincere desire on the part of the inquirer to know much. Still an inquiry ought to be held, and a strict one. Ugly rumours are about, and great names are freely mentioned in connection with the concession and the subsequent offer of the Nizam: which offer is even hinted to have been "put up" in London. It may be so, but it is certain that if it is so it will not be the India Office that will unearth the mystery. In the meanwhile the Committee of the Stock Exchange might throw a little light on the operations of the eight skilful and circumspect brokers. Their names, and the contracts showing the names of their dealers, would be interesting, and then the dealers' books showing where they got the stock they sold would complete the story, so far as Part I. is concerned. Parts II. and III. have yet to be written. They will come in time.—*Fair Play*, April 27.

THE MINING CONCESSION IN HYDERABAD.—ALLAHABAD, April 26.—The *Pioneer* publishes a long article which is a practical indictment of Mr. Cordery, the resident at Hyderabad. Colonel Marshall's errors are described as errors of judgment, arising from too much zeal. The *Pioneer* holds that the Government of India is free from blame in the mining concession, saying: "The bargain to which they were a party was eminently practical and business-like. It only miscarried at the stage when their obligation to watch over its progress had ceased. True, they were parties to the purchase by the Nizam of a share in the company, but there was nothing particularly objectionable on the face of the proposal, and it was not consented to until the Resident wired a second time and with impressive urgency that the Nizam was anxious to hasten the completion of the business, or the tempting prospect would be lost. The Government of India previously telegraphed to the Secretary of State their serious objection, on principle, to large speculative dealings between native States and capitalists at home. Mr. Cordery is condemned for conveying to the Government of India his approval of Abdul Huk's proceedings."—*Notts. Express*, April 28.

THE Hyderabad-Deccan scandal is to be investigated by a Parliamentary Committee, and we venture to predict that if this Committee does its duty thoroughly, as we have no doubt it will, such discoveries will be made as will rattle the dry bones of the India Office, and perchance lead to some important changes in that office.—*Financial News*, April 28.

THE DECCAN MINING COMPANY.—Mr. Labouchere asked the First Lord of the Treasury whether he would state what facilities he would give with a view to a motion being moved for the appointment of a Select Committee to inquire into the alleged malpractices connected with the Deccan Mining Company, Limited.

Mr. W. H. Smith: Perhaps the House will allow me to read a telegram received by the Secretary of State from the Viceroy of India upon this subject:—

"I consulted my Council to-day in reference to the Hyderabad Mining Concession. Government of India have no objection to the matter being fully investigated, either by Select Committee or by any other tribunal your lordship might approve of. Issues raised seem to lie between Abdul Huk and Hyderabad Government on one hand and concessionnaires and shareholders on the other.

Government of India expressly decline all responsibility with regard to purchase of the shares by Nizam's Government."

Under these circumstances the Government will certainly offer no objection whatever to the appointment of the committee which the hon. gentleman desires (hear, hear), and I will confer with him as to the method by which it shall be appointed and as to the day on which it shall be moved.—*Times*, April 28.

TO-NIGHT Mr. Labouchere is engaged in drawing up a list of the Select Committee which the Government this afternoon agreed to grant to inquire into the Hyderabad scandal. There is a fear in some of the best informed Anglo-Indian circles that unless this scandal can be stayed the difficulties in Hyderabad may so develop as to lead to serious internal commotions. The young Salar Jung, who was appointed Prime Minister by Lord Ripon on the death of his father, and who was dismissed from his post twelve months since because he could not work comfortably in harness with the Nizam, has some influential friends in this country, and it is more than hinted that the real explanation of the quarrel which led to his dismissal was no affair of State, but lay in the old phrase, *Cherchez la femme.* The Colonel Marshall who has been so much talked of in connection with the matter is not, as has been stated, private secretary, but personal adviser to the Nizam, a position in which he acts as a sort of connecting link between the Nizam and the British Resident. The whole affair is much complicated by individual considerations, and it is one which will fill the hands of Lord Cross for some time to come.—*Birmingham Post*, April 28.

THE Parliamentary Committee granted by Government to inquire into the Hyderabad mining transactions will probably consist of eleven members. It will include Mr. Labouchere, Mr. J. M. Maclean, Lord Randolph Churchill, Sir Richard Temple, and several other members interested in Indian affairs. Sir Richard Temple's presence on the Committee will be of great value, as among the numerous high posts he held during his service in India was that of Resident at Hyderabad. There is no man in the House of Commons who has a more thorough acquaintance with the subject to be investigated. and there is none more competent than he to unravel the network of intrigue which appears to surround this question.

A correspondent of the *Times*, who has evidently access to official sources of information, comes forward to defend the Hyderabad concessions. He argues that Abdul Huk's share in the transactions was confined to duties officially and publicly performed in accordance with instructions received from the Ministry at Hyderabad, and that the Nizam's Government was fully aware when it completed the purchase of shares in the company that only £75,000 of the capital was paid up and that 85,000 shares were founders' shares. As to the concession itself he contends that it was conferred upon Messrs. Watson and Stewart "as a reward for the successful negotiation of the great railway scheme, which has given Hyderabad several important lines, and which brought into the coffers of its ruler a sum of £800,000." The explanation is a very plausible one, but the writer entirely omits to mention several important facts which, to a great extent, nullify his argument. In the first place, Messrs. Watson and Stewart were rewarded for the part they took in floating the Nizam's State Railway Loan by the payment of commissions, which were so enormous that when they were made public an agitation was set on foot at Hyderabad for the repudiation of the whole transaction. This movement was eventually suppressed by the adoption of drastic measures by the Ministers in power who, at a moment's notice, deported several of the principal agitators and thus stifled inquiry.

The payment of the commissions, however, was subsequently officially admitted, and a record of the transactions may be found in the Hyderabad Yellow Books, which are the official publications of the Nizam's Government. Then as to the railway loan, the *Times* correspondent fails to state that the Nizam is compelled by the terms of the agreement with the company to guarantee a certain interest—we believe 4½ per cent.- on the entire capital of 4½ millions, and as the lines run through a sparsely populated country, there is sure to be a loss on the working, probably for many years to come. It is, therefore, incorrect to say that the Nizam has profited to the extent mentioned by the floating of the company. On one point the *communiqué* is in entire accordance with what we wrote a day or two ago on this subject, and that is with regard to the value of the mining concessions. Mineral wealth, the correspondent points out, exists in the Hyderabad State to a greater extent than in almost any part of India, and it is the more valuable as it has never before been worked to any serious extent. The company is actively prosecuting its operations, and it may prove after all that the Nizam's investment is not a bad one.—*Yorkshire Post*, April 28.

THE DECCAN SCANDAL.—As we anticipated yesterday, the Government has given Mr. Labouchere the Select Committee he asked for, and we may hope by-and-bye to get at the facts of this latest financial scandal. We see from the *Statist* this morning that some of the parties concerned in the Deccan coup are not unknown to fame, having had to do with the Honduras loan, the Peruvian Guano Company, and other concerns which have proved more profitable to the promoters than the shareholders.—*Pall Mall Gazette*, April 28.

HYDERABAD-DECCAN.—Things look bad in this direction. The *Standard* has the following from Secunderabad, under date 26th inst :—

With reference to the use of the term "first issue," it is incorrect to suppose that the Nizam had anything to do with it. The draft—prepared by lawyers in England, and agreed to on January 8, 1885—runs thus: "If such a Company shall be formed before the said 1st day of January, 1889, and if before that day two hundred and fifty thousand pounds at least of its share capital shall have been subscribed for, and one hundred thousand pounds shall have been actually paid up in respect of the subscribed share capital."

To this draft both parties agreed in the following words: "I agree to this draft as it now stands on behalf of William Clarence Watson and John Stewart. —Signed, C. WINTER, constituted Attorney, 7th January, 1885.—I agree to this draft, with modifications shown in red, which bear my initial, on behalf of his Highness's Government.—Signed, SALAR JUNG, 8th January, 1885."

The concession finally signed is a verbatim transcript of the above agreed draft, excepting that the amount is reduced from £250,000 to £150,000, and the date changed from the said January 1, 1889, to the expiration of the period fixed in Clause 1. This was signed by the Minister after reading, in presence of witnesses and representative of the English Resident, the deed of concession from beginning to end.

The reduction of the amount was due to the intervention of the Government of India. No such phrase as "first issue" was ever used by the Nizam's Government or the Government of India at any stage of the negotiations before January 8, 1885, the day on which the final draft was concluded. The concessionnaires positively declined to accept the words first time, and the originally accepted wording was, therefore, allowed to stand, and was drafted, after prolonged discussion, by the First Assistant at the Minister's request. The whole negotiation in India was personally conducted between Mr. Winter, the Minister, and the

Resident ; all correspondence passed direct between them under the close supervision of the Government of India.—*Weekly Bulletin*, April 28.

HYDERABAD-DECCAN.—The bursting of the financial storm on April 16th through the suspension of one of the chief secretaries of the Nizam's Government has been followed in this country with great interest, as, unhappily, a great many English investors have a direct pecuniary interest in the question. The demand put forward for an official investigation into the manner in which the concessions were allowed to be used for private ends, and the promotion of the Hyderabad-Deccan Company, is a very reasonable one, and as City rumours have taken great liberties with the names of prominent public personages, it would tend to clear the air if Parliament itself investigated the matter by means of a committee.

The Hyderabad-Deccan Company was formed in July, 1886, with a capital of £1,000,000 in £10 shares. What is sought to be ascertained is how and on what terms the concessionnaires secured rights which they disposed of to the company for £850,000, receiving fully-paid £10 shares in respect thereof. Amongst the promoters of the Company were William Clarence Watson, John Stewart, and C. A. Winter, who signed the Articles of Association. Watson and Stewart were the vendors of the concession. By the return of shareholders, filed in August, 1887, these three individuals and Henry Parkinson Sharp, described as of "no occupation," had disposed, out of the 85,000 shares they divided amongst them, of over 41,500 shares, which at the par value represented over £415,000, and they secured in a great many instances considerably over par value. The feature of the Nizam being induced to purchase shares at a considerable premium, and the manner in which the purchase was effected, has been referred to in detail in our daily contemporaries.

Some of the promoters of the Hyderabad-Deccan Company are not unknown to City fame. In 1875 Sir Henry James obtained the appointment of a Select Committee of the House of Commons to inquire into the manner in which foreign loans were introduced to the British public. Only four countries were dealt with, including Honduras and San Domingo. The gentleman who drew the agreements between the agents of the Honduras Government and the Government itself was Mr. Henry Parkinson Sharp. The San Domingo loan was for £700,000 odd, and all the Government received was less than £50,000 ; in this case also Mr. H. P. Sharp drew the agreements and was handsomely paid. The Select Committee were exceedingly anxious to have Mr. H. P. Sharp before them, but he did not attend.

In 1876 the Peruvian Guano Company, with a capital of a million, in shares of £5,000 each, obtained a contract from the Peruvian Government for two million tons of guano. Under this contract a trust was created by which the Peruvian Bondholders were to receive all the net proceeds, after the payment of an annuity of £700,000 to the Peruvian Government. Mr. Sharp had a part in the concerns of this company ; also the late Mr. John Stewart of Hyderabad-Deccan fame. Up to the breaking out of the war between Chili and Peru the Peruvian Company had received 1,130,000 tons of guano, all of the finest quality, but not one single shilling has ever gone into the pockets of the unfortunate Peruvian Bondholders.

Shareholders in other companies than the Hyderabad-Deccan have an interest in securing an inquiry as to the manner in which companies have been promoted by individuals. Mr. W. C. Watson was the vendor of concessions to the Borax Company, Limited, and received £900,000—£675,000 in Deferred Shares, £254,500 in Ordinary Shares, and the balance in cash. This was according to the agreement dated 5th January, 1888 ; but by the 22nd March, 1888, Mr. Watson had sold 2,060 Ordinary Shares, and stood on the register as holding 56,682 Deferred Shares of £10 each, having transferred 10,818.

The moral of the facts which have been disclosed is that the Limited Liability Acts require some drastic and immediate changes. The Government has been incubating a scheme for a long while, but it is moving very slowly in the matter; while the public is clamorous for a modification of the Acts, especially in respect of the disclosure in the prospectus of the material terms of contracts. So long as the system of filing only the ultimate contract is adhered to such scandals as those now brought to light are possible, and coteries of astute individuals are able to rake in coin without a check.—*Statist*, April 28th.

THE story of the Hyderabad (Deccan) Company is gradually being unfolded, but we have by no means heard the end of it.

The base treachery of the Indian ex-policeman appears to be a tale stranger than fiction, and one gasps for breath as the details of the great share transaction are disclosed.

The Indian Government are investigating the whole affair, and if some decided punishment is not inflicted upon somebody or other, it will be a scandal not only to the Indian but to the English Government also.—*Financial World*, April 28.

THE HYDERABAD-DECCAN CONCESSION SCANDAL.—£850,000 PROFIT ON RE-SALE.—This scandalous affair is attracting the attention of the City, and, it may be said, of London, and what are now called "revelations" continue to be made.

The revelations, however, are very stale; in the City every one knew that Messrs. Watson and Stewart, whoever they are, charged to themselves first, and the public afterwards, £850,000 for introducing a concession, which they had obtained for nothing, to the public notice.

How this could be done, and done with impunity, with so many members of the Indian Government looking on, who must have known of the facts, is one of the most extraordinary incidents that for a long time has been made public, and leads even friendly critics to impute reasons for their silence (not excepting men in very high authority) for which we can hardly believe there is any foundation, or otherwise a blow would be dealt at the Indian Government which would take a long time for it to recover from.

The facts of the case appear to be as follows: The said Watson and Stewart got a concession to negotiate the sale of a railway that had been constructed by the Nizam's Government, with a view to its extension, and accordingly an English company was formed to purchase the railway and find the additional funds for its extension to some coalfields.

The loan was issued, and out of the proceeds it is said that Watson and Stewart and Abdul Huk, a *ci-devant* policeman, since promoted to be Home Secretary, shared the sum of £180,000 promotion money. Subsequently a concession was granted to the same Watson and Stewart of the whole of the mineral lands of Hyderabad for ninety-nine years free of any payment, except a small royalty per ton on any minerals raised.

By the terms of the grant, they were empowered to form a company with a capital of £1,000,000 sterling, but it was stipulated that only £150,000 of the capital should at first be issued, and on that amount half, or £75,000, was to be paid up.

Messrs. Watson and Stewart registered the company, with a capital of £1,000,000, but instead of issuing £150,000 of shares, and making their profit on the shares, if it was a good thing, by any increased value of those shares, they sold to the company the concession for £850,000, receiving payment by allotment of 85,000 shares of £10 each, issued as fully paid-up.

This is evidently in contravention of the terms of the concession, which could never have contemplated any such action by them, since the terms sanctioned by the Indian Government distinctly stipulated that the money to be raised *at first* should be limited to £150,000, showing that the idea of the £1,000,000 capital was for issues from time to time as more capital was required, to be spent on the development of the enormous area of mineral lands in the state, instead of which Messrs. Watson and Stewart coolly took the £850,000 in shares and put them in their pockets. If they had done this, and kept them waiting for the development of the lands to give them value, the transaction would have been a monstrous one; but they did not do this but sold them as fast as they could; but this was not the limit to their extraordinary transactions, for a few months ago the same Abdul Huk, who came over to England to represent the Nizam at the time of the Jubilee as Commissioner, informed Messrs. Watson and Stewart that they were authorised by the Government of the Nizam to invest the sum of £120,000 in the purchase of shares of the company; and a correspondence which was very amusing took place between the native gentleman and the two concessionnaires as follows:—

On his arrival in London last June, Abdul Huk addressed the following letter to Mr. Watson (Messrs. Watson and Stewart):—

"I am instructed by the Government of H.H. the Nizam to purchase 10,000 shares of the Hyderabad-Deccan Company, Limited. As you are the agent of the Government here, I write to ask you to be so good as to arrange for the purchase of these shares at the lowest possible price, not exceeding £12 per share, the Government having decided to invest only £120,000 in these shares."

To this Mr. Watson replied:—

[*Confidential.*]

"I beg to acknowledge receipt of your letter of yesterday's date, instructing me, as agent of the Government of his Highness the Nizam, to purchase 10,000 £10 full-paid shares of the Hyderabad-Deccan Company, Limited.

"I beg to point out to you that to purchase these shares at the price you name is a most difficult and almost impossible operation, and will require the greatest skill and circumspection. I would suggest that the Government should acquire a proportion of the £5 paid shares at the same *pro rata* price, say £7 per share, as the £5 paid shares carry the same dividend as the £10 paid, and by this the Government could acquire, say, 8,750 £10 paid shares and 3,750 £5 paid shares, thus having 12,500 shares for £131,250, being an addition of 2,500 shares at an extra cost of £11,250 only. Please be kind enough to send me your instructions on this point."

On receiving the above letter, Abdul Huk telegraphed to Colonel Marshall, the Secretary of the Nizam:—

"Deccans firmly held up by public; therefore, with greatest difficulty succeeded in purchasing 8,750 fully-paid shares at twelve; 3,750 half-paid *pro rata* at seven, thus by chance securing 2,500 shares more at cost £11,250, and contingent liability £18,750 in excess sanctioned amount, £120,000. Market closes twelve three-quarters. Government shares now worth £9,000 more than paid.—Signed, Sirdar Diler-ul-Mulk."

Colonel Marshall replied to this that the arrangement was "most satisfactory."

It will be observed that the object of the purchase of the shares alleged was to get a "predominating" influence in the company, and seeing that they secured the purchase of about one-eighth only, it seems very difficult to understand how their object could be effected.

The shares, however, were purchased on the Stock Exchange through Messrs. William Morris, Hurst, Puckle & Co., a firm of jobbers well known in connection with the Deccan transactions, and who, from first to last, are said to have made over £80,000 out of the Deccan "deals."

The shares for the Nizam were, of course, supplied by Watson and Stewart, as at that time it is not believed the public held many shares. There had been simulated dealings in the shares on the Stock Exchange, but they would appear to have been between the parties themselves, apparently for the purpose of leading the public to believe that there were purchases and sales going on.

When, however, a paragraph was put forth in all the papers that the Nizam's Government were purchasing at 20 per cent. premium £150,000 of shares in the very concession that they had given away for nothing, the public apparently came to the conclusion that the shares were valuable, and accordingly it is believed that since then seven-eighths of the shares have been sold to the public at prices over £11 per share, thus, in fact, putting nearly £1,000,000 sterling in hard cash into the pockets of Messrs. Watson and Stewart.

We have shown that, according to the terms of the concession, there would appear to have been no authority for the issue of more than the amount of capital required to explore the lands; but what seems to demand inquiry is, how the Government of the Nizam, having stipulated that only £150,000 of share capital should be issued at first, and having since not authorised any further issue, should go into the market to buy a large amount of shares, unless they knew that the million had all been issued.

In that case, did they suppose that the million pounds of capital had been issued by the company, and the proceeds retained? If so, the thing was intelligible; but in that case did it not strike them as singular that such an amount should have been issued and so little done towards carrying out the objects of the concession? If, on the other hand, they knew that Watson and Stewart had taken £850,000 of shares for themselves out of the capital, how was it they did not remonstrate, and still more, how was it that they went and purchased for hard cash a large portion of the very shares held by them, and at 20 per cent. premium?

If the whole transaction had been done between Europeans we should have said that there was some influence at work that did not meet the eye; but when these transactions are done with Orientals and native princes, who cannot be supposed to be acquainted with company law and company proceedings, it becomes doubly apparent that some subterranean influence has been at work, the character of which will have to be gone into when the Committee which has been asked for by Mr. Labouchere in the House of Commons (supported by by Lord Randolph Churchill) is granted by the Government.

The suspension of Abdul Huk, which has taken place, is not sufficient, and does not meet the case. There are certain English *attachés* to every native prince's court who are supposed to watch over the monetary transactions of the prince to whom they are delegated, and in this case the fullest explanation will be required from those resident at Hyderabad as to how it came about that they did not draw the attention, first of the Nizam's Government, and next of the Indian Government, to the extraordinary transaction which had taken place in London, by which a concession granted for nothing was next week sold for £850,000 profit, and, subsequently, that £150,000 worth of the very shares appropriated by the concessionnaires should be foisted on the Nizam's Government, and that at a premium of 20 per cent.!

We must go back to the time of Warren Hastings for a transaction to equal that of the Hyderabad-Deccan Company.

Why the duty of prospecting the mineral lands of the Nizam should have been given to two obscure Englishmen and for a period of ninety-nine years, seems to require explanation. The Nizam had evidently abundant funds, since he had a surplus of £800,000 from the sale of the railway, after repaying the loan that he had raised on the railway; and seeing that up to the present period only £50,000 or £60,000 has been spent by the Deccan Company, it is quite clear that the operation was well within the power of the Nizam's Government to have carried out without the intervention or help of any capitalist.

Englishmen are a small body in India as compared with the vast native population, and their rule is by *prestige*. Take that away, and you have the conditions of the period of the Indian mutiny. Nothing could be so likely to remove the *prestige* we enjoy in India as the publicity in the native newspapers afforded to a transaction such as this, and we trust that the Government, however much they may appear to be desirous of screening certain officials, will see it to their interest, as it is unquestionably their duty, to grant immediately a Select Committee of the House of Commons to inquire into the whole of the transactions connected with the concession and the appropriation of its capital, with a view to fixing the blame where it is due, and to place the legality or illegality of the company's issue clearly before the public, who are asked at this moment to purchase the shares on the Stock Exchange.—*Stock Exchange*, April 28.

WHAT a fuss is being made about the Hyderabad-Deccan Company, and what a flood of light it throws upon the way in which the price of shares can be manipulated by a clever promoter. I will, one of these days, give a list of the companies which have emanated from the same source as this, and you will all open your eyes—and possibly never believe in premiums again. There is nothing so ridiculous as this premium business; in ninety-nine cases out of a hundred it is purely fictitious, and newspapers are much to blame in circulating about what practically amounts to a falsehood. If ever there was a bubble price, it was that at which Deccan shares were quoted month after month.—*Modern Truth*, April 28.

HYDERABAD-DECCAN COMPANY.—To the Editor of *The Financial News.*—SIR,—I am one of the unfortunate shareholders in the above who bought at 11⅝ and sold in the last fortnight. On receiving transfer deed, I found that the purchaser is the notorious W. C. Watson, so he at least has not done badly. It would be interesting to know how many shares he has recently picked up, and with what purpose in view.—I am, sir, yours, etc., BOUGHT AND SOLD. April 27, 1888.—*Financial News*, April 28.

THE Hyderabad scandal can be treated from innumerable points of view. The *Statist* points out one or two significant incidents in the history of the associates of the concessionnaires. It recalls that Mr. Henry Parkinson Sharp, who was actively concerned in the operation of unloading the 85,000 "fully-paid" shares upon the public, was connected with the notorious San Domingo Loan of £700,000, of which only £50,000 went to the borrowing Government. Other equally interesting side lights are thrown by our contemporary on the Hyderabad concession coterie.—*Financial News*, April 30.

THE story of the Hyderabad Concession, in so far as yet revealed, promises to be one of the most interesting of recent date in our Indian relations. It seems to have about it all the elements of a "scandal," and the pity is that it should occur so soon after South India has been disturbed by the land-owning jobbery and intrigues of the Madras Presidency. The memorable "Review Minute" of Sir M. E. Grant-Duff was very far from throwing full light upon the shady transactions which took place there in the beginning of the gold fever. And yet the shadiest of these would be wholesome and honest in comparison with the Deccan "job," if all that Mr. Labouchere insinuates be true. As to that, however, it were well to suspend judgment, for many reasons.

In the first place, it is eminently undesirable to create obstacles in the way of the immense work of development in Hyderabad, of which the Deccan Company only represents a part. The territory of the Nizam is exceedingly rich in mineral resources. The coalfields of Singareni are reported by competent authorities to be the richest and most accessible for mining of any in India; there are known deposits of diamonds, and the gold veins are believed to outrival those of Mysore. What the locality lacked was railway communication between the Nizam's coalfields and the great ports on the east and west coasts. When this is provided it is expected that Hyderabad coal will stock all the coaling stations of India.

At present the railway is in course of construction—the last of the material for it is in process of being shipped—and in the course of a few months Hyderabad will be bound with iron links to the ports of the Coromandel Coast, as it is already to Bombay. But, more than that, the waters of the Godaveri River and of the allied system of canals will be available for the cheap and ready transport in all directions of the produce of the Singareni coal-fields.

A great work is, in fact, in progress, in the greatest native State of India, and it was doubtless in consequence of the prospective increase of revenue that the Nizam made his magnificent offer to the Viceroy for frontier defence. At any rate, it seems pretty certain that the Treasury of the State could not at present bear the charge which the generous Sovereign proposed to lay upon it in the effusiveness of his loyalty to the Imperial Government. But, unfortunately, the Nizam's Government seems to have committed a great commercial blunder. We put aside in the meantime, because as yet unproved, the allegations as to malpractices on the part of Hyderabad and British officials. The blunder consisted in the Nizam's Government having granted to a single firm for a very long term of years the concession of the sole mining rights in the territory.

This is a very large order, for the Nizam's dominions are very extensive, and monopolies are good neither for young nor for old States. Still, the concession was granted with the approval of so astute a man as Sir Salar Jung, ex—and probably future—Prime Minister of the Nizam, with the approval of the rest of the Nizam's Ministers, and with the approval, or, at any rate, the countenance, of the Viceroy in Council. There does not seem to be any room for doubt that the negotiations were open and free, that the terms were fully discussed and understood both at Hyderabad and at Calcutta, and that the concession finally signed in favour of Messrs. Watson and Stewart was completed with the concurrence of the British Resident at the Nizam's Court.

So far, good; for however injudicious it may have been for the Nizam's Government to grant such a large monopoly to a private firm, while also engaged on its own account in extensive railway building, which can only be made remunerative on the development of the mines, it was a definite business transaction. But now begins the "scandal." It is alleged that the concession which was obtained in Hyderabad for £150,000 was sold in London to a company, promoted for the purpose in July, 1886, for £1,000,000. From this operation only two conclusions can be drawn: either the concessionnaires obtained a marvellously good bargain, or the British shareholders have been induced to enter into a marvellously bad one. A capital of one million, however, is not by any means too large for the development and working of the Hyderabad mines, so that it is apparently the Nizam who is the real sufferer.

According to Mr. Labouchere, or rather according to the allegations upon which he based a series of questions to Sir John Gorst the other night, one of the conditions of the concession for 99 years was that the concessionnaires should form a company with a nominal capital of £1,000,000, but that not more than £150,000 should be at first issued, which sum was to be employed on the coal-fields at Singareni. The company was formed, but it is alleged that the whole capital was issued, including 85,000 shares at £10 each, declared to be fully-paid up, allotted to the promoters. The shares were sent up to £12 in the market, and the Nizam was induced by one of his own Ministers, who was in England for the Jubilee celebrations last year, to buy 10,000 of these shares at £12 per share.

Now it is asserted that this was a purely fictitious price made by a little knot of brokers acting in concert with the holders, and that as soon as the transfer to the Nizam had been completed the price fell away to a discount. It is openly asserted that the price of £12, indeed, was only "made" by Abdul Huk himself sending eight brokers simultaneously into the Stock Exchange to compete for the shares. Meanwhile he reported to the Nizam that the shares were "firmly held by the British public," and that there was the "greatest difficulty in purchasing." The allegation is that the shares he did purchase were not held by the public, and the brokers had not the slightest real difficulty in getting them—if matters stood as is reported.

That there was something wrong the Nizam now seems to believe, for he has suspended Abdul Huk, and also his Sirdar, Diler Jung, for being concerned in the transaction. That transaction, in plain English, is alleged to be the making of a fictitious "market" for the purpose of defrauding the Nizam—in violation also, it would seem, of the understanding on which the Stock Exchange Committee grant a "settlement" in new issues of stock or shares. But in India the allegations go further. The *Pioneer* of Allahabad asserts that the colleague of Abdul Huk in the affair was the Nizam's British Secretary. This gentleman has no sort of official connection with the British Government, but, unfortunately, the name of the British Resident at Hyderabad has also been brought into the affair. The *Pioneer*, indeed, brings very grave charges against that official which cannot be passed over.

Sir John Gorst explained the other night that the India Office has no knowledge of the circumstances related by Mr. Labouchere, and does not recognise the agency of Colonel Marshall, the Nizam's secretary, in any way. Moreover, the Imperial Government is not called upon to inquire into the conduct of native Sovereigns, or the Ministers of native Sovereigns. There are, moreover, large questions of public morality involved. There is, for instance, what Lord Randolph Churchill called the moral duty "to protect the State of Hyderabad from a fraud of the most remarkable kind," and there is the conduct of a high British official in question. In these circumstances it is gratifying to learn that the Government have, with the ready assent of the Viceroy, agreed to the appointment of a Select Committee to inquire into the whole circumstances, and of the alleged transaction in shares.

That the inquiry will be impartial and thorough is before all things desirable; and that, if malpractices have been committed, both punishment and restitution should be swift all who know India will admit. Our very existence there depends upon the maintenance of the unsullied purity of the British name. The jobbery, bribery and trickery, which are in the native mind a part of ordinary native life, have never been associated with British administration. Absolute justice and absolute integrity are the means by which, far more than by the sword, we have held India, and by which alone we can continue to rule her. Thus it is that anything in the form of official venality in India assumes an Imperial importance and must be judged from the Imperial standpoint.—*Glasgow Herald*, April 30.

The so-called Deccan scandal is the subject of a great deal of comment in different circles. In bringing the matter to an issue Mr. Labouchere is displaying that truly Brutus-like virtue to which he has so sedulously schooled himself during recent years, for some of the people who are likely to be disagreeably affected by the coming disclosures are those whom he meets day by day in private society. Anglo-Indian circles are considerably excited about the affair. One of the gentlemen most prominently connected with the peccant company belongs to the old hereditary Bengal clique, was very prominent at Simla a few years ago, and has near relatives high up in the India Office itself.

It has been commonly rumoured on the Stock Exchange for some time past "that there was a good deal of squaring going on" in India, with a view to facilitating the operations of those over here who wished to obtain a sale for their shares in the concern. The proceedings of the Select Committee will drag on for a long time, and the incidental revelations which some people hope will result may be more interesting politically than the mere details of the transaction connected with the shares themselves. These revelations will probably be used for years to come as stock arguments in depreciating the supposed excellence of Indian administration. Of the merits of Indian administration it may be remarked that we can know little except what Indian administrators themselves have to say. The Indian opposition or "vernacular" press is scarcely a trustworthy source of information, and it is as well occasionally to bring the actual working of the Indian machine to the test of a Parliamentary examination.—*Glasgow Herald*, April 30.

It would be interesting to know, in view of the prominent part that he may have to take in the Hyderabad (Deccan) inquiry, if Sir John Gorst, Under-Secretary of State for India, is related by marriage (or otherwise) to Mr. W. C. Watson, the chairman and concessionnaire of the Hyderabad (Deccan) Company.—*Financial News*, May 1.

The Hyderabad-Deccan Scandal.—Official Statement by the Nizam's Prime Minister: Important Revelations.—A telegram from Calcutta says that the following statement has been made by the Nizam's Prime Minister, Sir Asman Jah, on the Hyderabad mining scandal. It is anticipated that the Sirdar's explanation will shortly be published:—

"On the 7th of November, 1882, Messrs. Watson and Stewart submitted a proposal to the Nizam's Government for the acquisition of a monopoly of mining rights in his Highness's dominions. On the 10th of January, 1883, the late Sir Salar Jung minuted on this proposal, and decided to sanction the concession on the terms, *inter alia*, that the concessionnaires should raise a limited liability company, with a capital of £1,000,000, and expend at least £100,000 in the development of the mines. On the 15th of March, 1883, the Government of India approved generally the terms of the concession. On the 30th of March, 1883, the Council of Regency authorised the Sirdar Diler-ul-Mulk to proceed to England (*a*) to carry out the suggestions made by the Government of India enumerated, and (*b*) to act on all instructions received from the late Minister. On the 5th of July, 1883, the Secretary of State for India authorised the Sirdar to open negotiations.

"A revised draft, differing in some details from the terms of the original proposal, was prepared in England, under the directions of the Sirdar, by a committee of legal and mining experts, though nothing was said as to who the gentlemen were. The Sirdar telegraphed to the Senior Administrator in Hyderabad that he had arranged the mining scheme on the basis of his instructions. That draft I have not seen.

"Writing on the 16th of December, 1884, on behalf of Messrs. Watson and Stewart, their solicitor (Mr. Winter) asked the Minister that the stipulation of the draft of the concession, providing that the proposed company should subscribe £500,000, of which £100,000 should be actually paid up, should be waived in favour of the stipulation contained in his clients' original proposal that the nominal capital of the company should be £1,000,000, of which £100,000 should be expended.

"'I would submit,' writes Mr. Winter, 'that the first issue of shares be for £100,000, of which a proportion—say, £25,000—shall be paid up at once, and the balance in calls at short notice as and when required.'

"This is a most important statement. It fixes the concessionnaires with the knowledge and acceptance of the stipulation of a first issue. On the 17th of December, 1884, Sir Salar Jung informed Mr. Winter that he could not accede to any departure from the agreement as drafted in England, which he professed his readiness to accept if signed by the concessionnaires. To this Mr. Winter agreed by a letter dated the 7th of January, 1885. In a long letter to the Resident, dated the 14th of January, 1885, Sir Salar Jung, reviewing the situation, says, 'I have consented that the amount to be subscribed shall be reduced from £500,000 to £250,000; but he insisted upon £100,000 being paid up on the formation of the company. On the 6th of May, 1885, the Resident informed the Minister that the Government of India had had the draft agreement under consideration, and enclosed in his letter two memoranda from the Supreme Government in connection therewith. 'These memoranda,' the Resident added, 'are put so clearly that I have no need further to elucidate them.' The memoranda in question embody the following recommendations: The capital of the company to be not less than £1,000,000, the first issue of shares to amount to £100,000, of which £25,000 should be actually paid; and the concessionnaires to be released, and the caution-money of £100,000 to be returned on the company agreeing to the terms of the concession as drafted. The reasons for these recommendations are thus explained:—'Clause 2—the first issue of shares to be reduced from £250,000 to £100,000, and the paid-up capital from £100,000 to £25,000. This is done to meet the immediate requirement for the opening of the Singareni coalfields, which, judging from the circumstances of the existing coal companies in Bengal, can be efficiently worked with the subscribed capital. The amount of the proposed nominal capital is left as originally drafted in Clause 1, as that contemplated a further issue of shares to be made in the event of iron or steel works being started in Singareni, or the mineral wealth of the province being developed in other sites.'

"In recapitulating the various proposals Sir Salar Jung points out, in a letter written to the Resident and dated the 10th of August, 1885, that the Government does not feel justified in reducing the first issue of shares to less than £150,000, or the paid-up capital to less than £75,000. The Resident supported in the main the modifications suggested by the Minister, and the Government of India ultimately accepted them.

"On the 7th of January, 1886, a formal agreement for the concession was signed between the Government of Hyderabad, by the ex-Minister on their behalf, and by the concessionnaires. This was subsequently ratified by the Secretary of State for India. It is not clear who drew up this agreement, nor does anything show that Sir Salar Jung had, before accepting it, the benefit of any legal advice, nor is it clear on what instructions and by whom given the agreement took shape. Some inkling as to the true state of the circumstances may be gathered, however, from the following facts. The Sirdar was sent to England in 1883 to negotiate a mining concession. The late Sir Salar Jung had stipulated merely that a company should be formed with a capital of £1,000,000, but apparently had not stipulated for a first issue. The Sirdar had an agreement drawn up by a committee of legal and mining experts, which may possibly be the concession of January 7, 1886, or the basis of that concession. In 1883 the Sirdar telegraphed from England to the Senior Administrator in Hyderabad that he had arranged a mining scheme on the basis of his instructions. It may be that the concession of January 7, 1886, is silent as to any first issue, because it was drafted to meet the instructions of 1883, which said nothing about a first issue; but, if this be so, the Sirdar should certainly have taken greater care to see the terms of the agreement of 1883 altered to meet the changed requirements of 1886. The omission to do so is, in my opinion, extremely reprehensible, if nothing worse. If the omission was intentional, the Sirdar's conduct was fraudulent; if accidental—which I cannot believe—the Sirdar was guilty of most culpable negligence and *laches*.

"By the concession agreed to between the parties, the concessionnaires should form a company within six months, with a capital of not less than £1,000,000, £150,000 to be subscribed, and £75,000 to be paid. In the event of such terms being complied with it was lawful for the concessionnaires to transfer to such company the benefit of the concession. It is clear that before the concessionnaires could legally transfer any interest in the concession the following were the conditions precedent: (*a*) A company with a capital of not less than £1,000,000; (*b*) a subscription share capital of £150,000; (*c*) actual paid-up capital of £75,000. Until and unless these conditions were complied with, the concessionnaires could not transfer the right to any intended company."—*Financial News*, May 1.

The Hyderabad (Deccan) Scandal.—It is curious to see the vigour and persistence with which certain people are trying to make the Sirdar the scapegoat. Those who did not hesitate to accept his lavish hospitalities when he was here, in the heyday of success, are now unable to find a civil word for him, and are altogether oblivious of the time-honoured maxim which holds that every man ought to be regarded as innocent till he has been proved guilty. It is positively indecent to prejudge the case in the absence of the Sirdar and of Mr. Watson. Perhaps the Sirdar may, with fatalistic resignation, turn the other cheek to his smiters.

But it will be a very different reception they will get from Mr. Watson, who has returned in hot haste from Constantinople. He is now back in London, and his first act on arriving was to ask the Government to examine him before the Select Committee—a course which plainly indicates the *mens conscia sibi recti*. Before that Committee he will be sure to have fair play, and we are bound to believe him when he says he will put a very different complexion on the case, and show the utter groundlessness of many of the statements which have been made respecting his share in the transaction.

The matter has reached a grave point now at which a full and complete inquiry is absolutely indispensable to all concerned, and not less to the India Office than to the confidential advisers of the Nizam, or to Mr. Watson and the Sirdar. A grossly unfair and malignant attempt has been made to prejudice the case against the two last-mentioned, and as the affair is very complicated, only those who have been behind the scenes can fully and satisfactorily unravel the mystery.

Mr. Watson will not long remain silent, and we shall also hear now what the Sirdar has to say about the matter. Surely those who are so very uncharitable can afford to hear both sides before they are so very positive. For our own parts we are, as yet, no more prepared to tak e one side than the other. But we do say, let the accused all have fair play. We are always bragging about fair play being an Englishman's motto.

But, unfortunately, there are many, and more especially in the financial world, who may make it their motto, but who do not make any other use of it —who do not for an instant feel it incumbent to apply it to themselves, as a rule of conduct in dealing with accused persons. They no sooner get the facts —or some friend's version of them—than they at once proceed to constitute themselves judge, jury, and (as far as they can do so) executioner as well.

Yet no one knows better than an average Englishman how common it is to be quite convinced one way, after hearing the case for that side, and yet, with the most perfect fairness and justification, to take the other side after hearing both. We fancy the Deccan case will give us another illustration of this way of changing front.—*Financial Times*, May 1.

The Deccan Company.—To the Editor of the *Standard*.—Sir,—There is a point in connection with the Deccan Company which has been singularly misrepresented. So far from the Nizam, or the Nizam's subjects, losing eight hundred and fifty thousand pounds by the concession, as stated by Mr. Labouchere in the House of Commons, they do not lose one single farthing. The Nizam retains the right to levy royalties on all the minerals worked, and it is from the development of the mineral wealth of the Deccan, and the revenue which will consequently come in from royalties, that he will benefit. If the eight hundred and fifty thousand pounds, instead of being issued as paid-up shares, were in hand in cash for the purpose of working the mines—and this, it is said, is what was intended under the concession—the only benefit arising to the Nizam would be the royalties on the minerals produced at the mines.

If, on the other hand, the eight hundred and fifty thousand pounds necessary to work the mines is raised by the Deccan Company, either by borrowing or by means of subsidiary companies (both of which courses are contemplated in the deed of concession), the Nizam is in exactly the same position, neither better nor worse, for he still gets the royalties on the minerals produced. So far as he is concerned, while there may be a question between himself and his agent, it does not matter to him to what extent the concession is "watered," so long as the mines are developed.

While it does not matter to the Nizam, it does matter to the British public, and if any have been induced to buy shares upon the representation that the whole capital was available for working the concession, they would have grave cause of complaint.—I am, Sir, your obedient servant, R. April 28.—*Standard*, May 1.

When the Hyderabad-Deccan Company comes to be investigated, it will be just as well to have the investigation conducted by officials who are not related to the promoters of the enterprise. If, as is now alleged, Sir John Gorst is related to one of them, he will doubtless see the propriety of refraining from official activity in the matter.—*Financial News*, May 2.

There is no ostensible connection between the affairs of the Smyrna and Cassaba Railway and those of the Hyderabad (Deccan) Company. Nevertheless it is scarcely surprising that at the meeting of the former company, held a day or two ago, the business of the latter should have been incidentally mentioned. In both of these undertakings the redoubtable Mr. Watson is prominently interested. Having moulded the Nizam's advisers to his views, he is now trying his hand upon the unspeakable Turk. The results, in this instance, remain to be shown. It may be that there will be a slip 'twixt cup and lip. At present everyone is in the dark. Too much light (or, indeed, any) appears to be considered undesirable for the shareholders of the Smyrna and Cassaba Company. They were adjured at the recent meeting to sit still and let Mr. Watson have a free hand. Some few of them appeared indisposed to take the advice thus given. Mr. Hutchinson, one of the number, suggested an adjournment of the meeting, in order that Mr. Watson (who is said to be on his way home from Constantinople) might take his co-proprietors into his confidence before committing them to any new bargains with the Turk. To that end Mr. Hutchinson proposed an amendment, which was duly seconded, but the majority of those present meekly followed the bidding of the chairman *pro. tem.*, and Mr. Watson is to do with them as may seem good in his own eyes.—*Financial News*, May 2.

The Hyderabad (Deccan) Company.—The reported doings, or rather the reported mis-doings, of the Hyderabad (Deccan) Company have attracted such an amount of attention during the past fortnight that it may be expedient for us, as the first financial journal which dealt with the subject, to again revert to its affairs. The Hyderabad (Deccan) "scandal," as it is now termed, has figured as a heading in all the important papers from the *Times* downward; but we ask our readers whether it has not been somewhat a case of locking the stable door and raising the cry of thief after the mare has been stolen. Never until last month—with the exception of a few days about a year ago—has the price of these shares fallen as low as par; but it is only since this grevious decline that the subject has challenged such an amount of attention. Now we do not profess to any special knowledge which is denied to other journals, but, in common fairness, we wish to insist upon the fact that the company and the company's conduct was subjected in our article of the 28th of March to an amount of criticism which we venture to think would have been amply sufficient to deter most reasonable readers from buying the shares at their then price; or, to go further, may have been the means of causing some who were shareholders then to part with their holding and take the advice we offered, which was to the effect that they had better wait and see what transpired. Even months before this attention was repeatedly drawn in our columns to the extraordinary delays which took place about the raising of the coal from the Singareni Coalfield, and to the still more extraordinary silence of the board of directors upon the subject. To substantiate these statements a few quotations may aptly be made from our article of the 28th of March. "It is matter of surprise," we wrote, "how soon the prosperous-sounding speeches delivered by chairmen at statutory meetings are allowed to drop into oblivion. Indeed, it seems almost a recognised thing that chairmen should be allowed to expatiate upon golden prospects and panegyrise the company's officials without much notice being taken of it. Nevertheless, it is a great mistake. Persons connected with mining companies may know how to take these speeches—in fact, are well aware that one-half of them are rubbish—but country people have no such means of knowledge, and therefore are virtually bound to accept the airy-founded data presented to them." Now we contend that this is not exactly the kind of preamble which precedes an article written for the purpose of praising up a company or advocating a purchase of its shares. Somewhat the reverse. And yet at the time when these lines appeared in print not a whisper was current about that which a week or so later was deemed of such disagreeable importance as to occupy the criticism of the House of Commons, and to cause certain leading members to request a special committee of investigation. It is not necessary to recapitulate the charges now made, which, if true, will expose one of the most barefaced company-promoting scandals of the past ten years. It is our desire to emulate the moderation which was satirically termed the speciality of the Hyderabad Company's officials, therefore no conclusions must be hastily jumped at. Everything depends upon the defence. The case for the prosecution has been made out—in fact has been already somewhat overdone—and it now remains for a thorough explanation to be given, which will not only satisfy the House of Commons and the Government of India, but also the shareholders who so eagerly sought the shares they now hold, and in almost every instance paid a premium for them. We say still, as we said in our previous article, "the chairman's speech at the statutory meeting of the Hyderabad-Deccan Company was a mistake. In fact it literally bristles with magnificent prospects. Is the future of the company entirely dependent upon coal? Then coal in itself will be more than sufficient to carry everyone connected with the company to the summit of affluence. Should coal prove a failure, and only the gold mining industry be attended to, then gold by itself exists in such quantities over so many square miles that no fear need be apprehended about exorbitant dividends!" And so on. Nothing, in fact, short of impoliteness and personality, could have more strongly expressed the scepticism with which his absurd speech was viewed. Quotations were also made from the report framed by Mr. Theodore W. Hughes-Hughes, Deputy-Superintendent of the Geological Survey of the Government of India, and exception was taken to what was termed "a careful and moderate estimate." As Lord Clive, when accused of peculation in India, announced that he stood astounded at his own moderation, so Mr. Hughes-Hughes may well now stand astounded at his own extravagance of estimate. But, as we said, "even halve Mr. Hughes' estimate, and sufficient coal remains to carry the company to certain prosperity." The public were also reminded of the non fulfilment of part of these unfounded and impossible promises, most of which, the chairman inferred, erred only on the side of moderation. "The company's agent in India was at that date—namely, the date of the report—spoken of as expecting to ensure a daily output of a thousand tons of coal by October. October has passed six months ago, and still there is no news to hand of this daily output having been reached yet." October has now passed seven months ago, and the position is so far changed that the public to-day seem very uncertain in their minds whether the company have sufficient capital to carry on works which have merely been commenced at Singareni. They have issued all their capital in paper shares, and chiefly to themselves. These paper shares, which, unfortunately for the working of the company, are fully paid, the promoters have since assiduously and most cleverly sacrificed to the too credulous public at a premium varying from a few shillings to £4 and upwards. The concern was not unduly or unwisely "puffed." On the contrary, it was always looked upon as a quiet but steady going concern, and largely taken up by Anglo-Indians. So far so good. The share list did contain a good many names of Anglo-Indians, but where are those names now? Echo may well answer where? Their names are replaced by those of many deluded persons who were quietly advised to buy into the company as one whose property might easily double or treble in value, just as the property sold by Messrs. Arthur Guinness and Company did. We looked upon the Hyderabad (Deccan) Company quite in this light about a year ago, but as detailed last month, the temporisings, the excuses, and, above all, the significant silence of the board began very naturally to undermine this faith, and caused us to make remarks which must have appeared at the time to be merely due to malice, or else to ignorance. Another quotation will exemplify this. Upon the subject of the delays and excuses, we wrote, on the 28th of March: "If questioned regarding the delay of opening the railway to the coalfield any member of the board would at once reply that the monsoon rains in themselves were ample reasons for any delay, and would proceed to detail accounts of damage done and temporary bridges carried away. This is all very true, we should reply, but does the south-west monsoon not do much the same damage every year, and necessitate a partial or entire suspension of many industries? If so, could not the member of the board have taken this important factor into account from the beginning and allowed for this not uncommon freak of nature by including some modicum of necessary delay in one of their careful and moderate estimates? The member of the board might perhaps think that we meant to be nasty upon the matter, but after all to make allowance for the usual tropical rainy season is not unreasonable." We did mean to be nasty, and moreover denounced it as "puerile in the first instance to fix dates in the easy way which the chairman did at the first meeting," and said that it was "perhaps equally foolish of the public to believe them." No journalistic writing can go much further than this, if it wishes, like the Hyderabad (Deccan) board, to make a speciality of moderation. All that we did profess to know was that the names on the register of shareholders were gradually changing. This was certainly a straw which showed which way the wind blew, especially when added to the network of excuses which had to be woven round every statement of the board's in order to keep them above the salt water of open disbelief at the hands of the investing public. Now that the crash has come everyone is, of course, equally wise and prudent. It was while the sea was calm that we hinted that the company did not exactly show "mastership in floating." "How long are thousands of pounds to be lying in the form of certificates which do not yield a penny of interest? The general form of advice is to hold on to shares, and they may be worth a hundred per cent. more than their present value. This advice has one drawback. It is not new." These kind of questions were asked while the sea was calm. How easy it is to give answers now, the value of the shares being just about fifty per cent. less than the price they once stood at! Time and a committee of inquiry instituted by the House of Commons, and aided by information from the Government of India, may throw much light upon all that which is now little better than conjecture. Sirdar Abdul Huk doubtless has a defence, probably a very specious one, and possibly an incontrovertible one, which may cause his character to shine out as brightly as the sun did upon the Jubilee Day, when he appeared with such satisfaction to—himself. Regarding the recent disclosures, no one could have dreamed of their magnitude. All we can say upon this subject is that we were not surprised. To pretend that everything which is known now was known to us a month ago would be incorrect. Suspicions are, however, often as cogent as actual facts. The unknown is proverbially terrible, and this feeling was adequately expressed by the concluding advice that intending buyers should "wait and see" before sinking any substantial sum of money in the Hyderabad (Deccan) pit. "We would ourselves far sooner pay a higher price when we had more data to go upon than make any purchase in the dark. Besides, who might the sellers be? If Anglo-Indians, then the outlook would not be encouraging, and no one could desire to buy shares at five or ten shillings above the price at which some Bangalore civilian is willing to sell his present holding." A good deal of these quotations must sound like blowing our own trumpet, but in the present case it is but fair; and, moreover, it is but expedient in the public interest to draw attention to advice which might most assuredly have saved hundreds of thousands of pounds to anyone who acted upon the gist of the article in question. We claim justly that we bayed the lion while he was alive. Now that he shows signs of crumbling to pieces, of course every jackal in the land can have a bite at him. Neither is he killed yet. The company may arise and gird its defence around it, and prove that the promoters have been men of that guileless calibre who only seek the public good and sink all personal acquisition of filthy lucre. They may have transferred their shares into the names of widows and country parsons from the philanthropic motives which obtain so commonly in this City of London, especially in that portion of it who go down into the earth in mines and occupy their business in floating companies; men who prefer to sell at a loss rather than wait for certain dividends, which must be distributed a few months later. These appear to be the class of gentlemen connected with the Hyderabad Deccan Company. The young Nizam will have cause to remember them if Government cannot take steps to restore anything that he may have signed away in ignorance. Our native States are always supposed to be under British protection. The unfortunate Nizam of Hyderabad appears to have been subjected to it in a manner rather calculated to bleed him to death. A little balance of £98,000 of his, which was lying at his bankers, was invested for him by some of his protectors in the Hyderabad Deccan Company. We fear it will be some time before either he or the public, who have been made co-martyrs with him, will see the light of much return upon their capital. And so we take our leave of a company whose affairs just at present have the possibility of being more discussed in a court of justice than in a newspaper.—*Barker's Trade Journal*, May 2.

THE NIZAM'S RESERVE FUND.—To the Editor of the *Times*.—SIR,—Your correspondent in his communication of Thursday under-estimates the amount of the funds standing to the Nizam's credit at the bank in London. In addition to the stock he mentions there is also the sum of £100,000 deposited many years ago in the name of trustees as a guarantee for the old railway. There has been some delay in transferring this from a special to the general account, but it is entirely released from liability, and the Government of the Nizam last September were not aware of the technical reasons which entailed the subsequent delay. This £100,000 must, therefore, be added to the £860,000 railway stock, bringing up the total to nearly a million, exclusive of any accrued interest.

An explanation of the Nizam's offer to pay the amount of his contribution by cheque in London is to be found in the very general criticism since made in the native press and elsewhere that his State was overburdened, and could not afford this fresh outlay. He showed great delicacy in the endeavour to remove the doubts of the Viceroy on this point by offering to draw the amount from a reserve fund, which would demonstrate that he had no intention of resorting to fresh taxation.

Some of his English critics who have impeached his motives and questioned the genuineness of his proposal might take a lesson from his Highness. Apparently they would have believed more in his sincerity if he had presented the Viceroy with the surplus reserve of the Berars, which is almost identically the same amount; but if the Nizam had done this what should we not have heard of his indelicacy and rudeness! We can hardly expect the other princes of India to be encouraged to imitate the example of the Nizam by the manner in which his offer has been received, and by the imputation of interested motives which are said to have dictated it.—Yours faithfully, SIGMA.—*Times*, May 8.

SIR H. RUMBOLD'S CLAIM ON THE NIZAM.—In the House of Commons last night, Mr. M'Lagan asked the Under-Secretary of State for India whether the claim for 11 lakhs of rupees submitted to the Nizam's Government by Sir Horace Rumbold, British Minister at the Hague, which had been settled by the payment to him of three lakhs, was the same claim as that referred to in the extract from the Hyderabad report for 1294, Fasli (1884-5); and whether that claim was settled with the knowledge and under the advice of the Resident, whose guest Sir Horace Rumbold was last winter, when he went to Hyderabad armed with letters from Lord Lytton and other influential persons, as stated in the Indian papers; if so, upon what grounds the Resident advised the admission of a claim which had been rejected a few years before "under the advice of the Government of India."

Sir J. Gorst: I must refer the hon. member to my answer to his question on April 9, when I stated that the Secretary of State had no official information on this subject. Both the Secretary of State and the Viceroy expressly refused to interfere in the matter of this claim.—*Times*, May 2.

WHAT a show up this Hyderabad (Deccan) business is, and how unexpected! Many journals now give the company's affairs a prominent place who have never previously done more than quote the current price of the shares. The most exasperating thing is that one and all lead the public to suppose that all has been patent to the respective editors for the past six months.

All I can say upon this point is that attention has been drawn intermittently to the non-fulfilment of the company's promises, such as the raising of the 1,000 tons of coal per day by the end of November last.

Many of the current charges against the company are irrelevant, such as the rise of Abdul Huk from a policeman to his present position. The question resolves itself thus—What has he *done?*—not—what was he originally? The Parliamentary inquiry may settle this, but in the meantime it is not of much value to trace his antecedents, unless it can be found that he has been guilty of any previous dishonesty.

The dilatoriness and silence of the Board has been remarked on in these Notes constantly—at a time, too, when the affairs of the company attracted but little attention at the hands of the financial Press.—*Barker's Trade Journal*, May 2.

SIR JOHN GORST AND THE HYDERABAD-DECCAN COMPANY.—To the Editor of the *Financial News.*—SIR,—Your query in to-day's issue is most pertinent. I will answer it. Sir John Gorst is connected by marriage with Mr. W. C. Watson, chairman of the Hyderabad-Deccan Company.—I am, sir, yours, etc., SMYRNA.—*Financial News*, May 2.

THE Government have promised a Select Committee to inquire into the Hyderabad (Deccan) scandal; but if, as is alleged, Sir John Gorst is connected by marriage with Mr. W. C. Watson, the chairman of the Hyderabad (Deccan) Company, and a gentleman who has a good deal to explain in connection with this business, it is to be expected that Sir John Gorst will not be a member of the committee. It is necessary to draw attention to this matter since, as Under-Secretary for India, Sir John Gorst's nomination as a member of the committee would be taken as a matter of course by the outside public.—*Star*, May 2.

THE HYDERABAD (DECCAN) SCANDAL.—In the examination of candidates for honours in reaping profit from the public, it has been for some time past the fashion to place Mr. Jay Gould as *facile princeps*, at the head of the list; but we venture confidently to say that no such scandalous transaction can be proved, or even be alleged, against that great Transatlantic financial juggler as that recently run to earth in connection with the Hyderabad (Deccan) mining concession. As a scandal it assuredly beats the record. The Imperial Land Company of Marseilles, the San Domingo Loan, the Emma Mine, and many others, must now be relegated to a back seat. It is probable that we have not yet heard the worst, but the matter has been promptly brought before Parliament, and it is certain that a strong Select Committee will be forthwith appointed to examine into it most thoroughly. It is almost beyond belief that hundreds of investors—many of them shrewd City men—could have been induced to buy, at a premium even, shares which were seventeen-twentieths "water," and three-twentieths working capital, with nothing in sight wherewith to earn dividends except the profits of a coal mine not yet developed.

There promises to be much ado about the scandal in the Commons, since Lord Randolph Churchill—who was the guest of the Nizam some three years ago—has responded to that prince's appeal to recover for him his abstracted minerals. Lord Randolph is, consequently, likely to have his hands full for some time to come, for even the jobbery and scandals in the great spending departments which he brought to light seem small by the side of this scandal, in which the India Office appears to be involved. There was, by the way, a very official and red-tape complexion in that anonymous contribution which appeared with all the dignity of large type in the *Times* of Thursday last, and a defence of the concessionnaires on the evidently officially-inspired lines laid down by the *Standard* on the 24th inst. will scarcely weigh much with the Select Committee. As to the shares themselves, we counsel the public to let them severely alone. The concession as it now stands is certain to be modified, and the company, to say the least, will be reconstructed: investors who may be anxious to become shareholders in the company will be wise to postpone any action to this end till the capital has shrunk to a reasonable bulk through the evaporation of its superfluous moisture. Meanwhile the action of the India Office, whatever it be, will be severely criticised; if it should turn out that the honest investor has been fleeced because the Resident at Hyderabad and the permanent officials in London have been, so to speak, blindfolded by the ingenious Huk, what are we to think? By the way, the strange disguises of Doctor Hyde and Mr. Jekyll are not half so puzzling as those of this India police-officer, whose name is Abdul Huk, when it is not Sirdar or Diler Jung, or Diler-ul-Mulk Bahadur. The law of England provides that every share in a company shall have a distinguishing number so that it may be traced. In some similar fashion Hyderabad promoters—even though policemen—should be numbered or ticketed when, as in this remarkable history, they play, with more than London assurance, the Heathen Chinee in Capel Court.

From the Viceroy's telegram it appears that the Indian Government divide the issues to be submitted to the Select Committee into two categories—those which lie between the Nizam's Government and the irrepressible Huk, and those between the concessionnaires and the shareholders of the Hyderabad (Deccan) Company. With the former we have at present no disposition to meddle; politicians must be left to decide them; and it is very questionable, moreover, whether a State which can produce a financial genius like Abdul Huk stands in need of any assistance from us. But concerning the issues between the conncessionnaires and the shareholders it is obviously our bounden duty to say a word or two, since there is a universal feeling in the City that an immediate inquiry by the Committee of the Stock Exchange is necessary into the manner in which the company was introduced on the Stock Exchange, and into the character of the subsequent dealings in the shares. It is not too much to say that the introduction of the company to the "House," and, through it, to the public, was in itself mysterious. There was no issue of a prospectus setting forth the nature and capital of the company, the names of the directors, officials, and solicitors, the terms of the concession, or the enormous amount to be paid for it to the vendors by the shareholders.

The company was formally registered at Somerset House on the 29th July, 1886, and in August of that year a "memorandum" (a copy of which is here before us) farcically or designedly marked "private," was circulated by quires, together with a pamphlet commending the richness of the Nizam's dominions, among the members of the Stock Exchange. This memorandum set forth that the capital of the Company was £1,000,000, "in 100,000 shares of £10 each; 85,000 being fully paid, and 15,000 on which £5 per share is paid;" that it has acquired a concession from the Nizam's government, with the approval of the Secretary of State for India, to work eight specified coal and iron mines, and to "prospect, test, and select for development" apparently every mineral and precious thing contained in the 82,700 square miles which constitute the Nizam's territory. "The famous Golconda diamond mines are included in the concession. The value of diamonds exported from the Cape during the last ten years exceeds £40,000,000, and there are no reasons why the Golconda mines, when effectively worked, should not be equally prolific." "Gold will be prospected for during the cold season, and in order to obtain the most reliable data on this and other matters the services of an Indian Government official of the Geological Survey are in course of being obtained." "Garnets are found;" "hematite iron ore, superior to the best Swedish, exists;"

"talc exists, and can be obtained in large quantities;" "petroleum is said to exist, and to have been used by the natives for years past;" and so on, and so on.

Such, without any allusion to directors, contracts, purchase money, vendors' shares, etc., is the underground wealth of the company detailed in the "private memorandum," which appears to fulfil all the duties of an attractive prospectus without any of its responsibilities. No one could imagine for one moment that the 85,000 fully paid £10 shares had been issued as fully paid to the concessionnaires, and that, together with the 15,000 half-paid shares, they were about to be foisted, at a substantial premium, on the public by the machinery of a private memorandum, an organized staff of efficient and zealous brokers, and the granting of an official settlement. It can scarcely be questioned that in purchasing his shares (at 20 per cent. premium) the Nizam was led to believe that he had acquired a controlling interest in the company, which, as he thought, had issued only £150,000 of its capital. All these matters will, no doubt, be fully investigated by the Select Committee; but we suggest that in the meantime the Stock Exchange Committee should be beforehand in the work of disentangling the subject, so far as regards the Stock Exchange, from the mystery which seems to surround it. They will do well to include within the scope of their inquiry the circumstances attendant upon the orders for the purchase of some 12,000 shares, executed by eight Stock Exchange firms at the same price and on the same day. These shares appear all to have come out of a single name; every share can be traced; and we may safely predict that if the true facts of the case were carefully elucidated, a flood of light would be poured on the whole transaction, and we should then know the names of the persons really responsible in the matter. The Stock Exchange Committee are, as it were, once more on their trial at the bar of public opinion. If they fail now to do their duty promptly and efficiently they may rest assured that the attention of the Government will be forcibly directed to their shortcomings, and themselves, their laws, and the institution they represent be speedily subjected to the active supervision of the State.—*The World*, May 2.

A CORRESPONDENT wants to know if the Abdul Huk, who figures so prominently in the Hyderabad-Deccan scandal, is the Abdul who was some years ago manager of the *Sultan Divan* at Manchester. Perhaps Mr. W. C. Watson can enlighten us upon this point.—*Financial News*, May 3.

THE HYDERABAD (DECCAN) SCANDAL.—It has been pointed out to us that there are many misrepresentations in the current statements with regard to this matter, the majority of which may, however, safely remain unexplained until the Select Committee reports. That body will give, probably, a more minute explanation than some of the people concerned will care about. In the meanwhile, it seems clear that, so far from the Nizam, or the Nizam's subjects, losing £850,000, as stated by Mr. Labouchere in the House of Commons, they will not lose anything. On the contrary, the Nizam, in the exercise of his right to levy royalties on all the minerals worked, will, if the company is active and prosperous—and, in fact, in any event—derive a considerable income from that source.

If the £850,000, instead of being issued as paid-up shares, had been kept as cash in hand, for the purpose of working the mines (which is now alleged to have been the original intention) the Nizam would have been no better off than he is now, since he would still have had only the royalties agreed upon. If the Company, after all their large capital, have still not funds sufficient to work the mines, they have ample means of securing them either by borrowing, or by forming subsidiary companies, both of which are contingencies contemplated in the deed of concession. Should the company altogether fail to work the mines, which is not at all a probable contingency, since, in that case, they would have to sacrifice the valuable position they have secured at a heavy outlay, no doubt it will be found that provision has been made for carrying on the work in some other way, so that the Nizam shall, after all, not be the loser. If this has not been done, it ought to have been done by the Nizam's advisers.

Although the affair is so complicated, the general points seem simple enough —the Nizam in any event is protected; because, if from any cause whatever the company should forfeit their concession, he is then in a position to sell the rights to someone who really could carry out the undertaking. If they do not forfeit their position, but really carry on the work, he is then as right as he could be under any other possible circumstances.

It is not the Nizam, therefore, but the shareholders whose immediate future wears a somewhat uncomfortable aspect, but whose position so far as we can see at present is by no means so desperate as the "bears" for purposes of their own, which are sufficiently obvious, would have us believe.

The position of the concessionnaires and promoters is not at all an enviable one, since if it should be shown, as the result of the Select Committee inquiry, that the subscribers were given to believe that, after the payment of promotion and other preliminaries, there would be ample capital left to work the concession, and if just the opposite should prove to be the case, then there will have to be a considerable amount of disgorging, so that there will be one more illustration of the adage that ill-gotten gains are difficult to hold.—*Financial Times*, May 3.

In the City.—The Hyderabad Deccan Company.—Mr. Labouchere will to-night nominate the members of the Select Committee to inquire into the formation and promotion of the Hyderabad Deccan Mining Company (Limited), the circumstances under which the concession held by that company was obtained from the Government of Hyderabad, and the subsequent operations on the London Stock Exchange by persons interested in the company. The Committee will consist of seven members—Sir Henry James, Sir Richard Temple, Mr. Slagg, the Solicitor-General for Scotland, Mr. McLagan, Mr. Bristowe, and Mr. Labouchere. The Committee will have power to send for persons, papers, and records. It is telegraphed from Simla that the Nawab Mehdiali, Financial Secretary of the Hyderabad Government, will leave Bombay on Friday to give evidence. He is said to be a man of high character and ability.—*Pall Mall Gazette*, May 3.

Mr. Cordery, the Resident at Hyderabad, recently entered on a furlough of four months. He will thus have leisure to throw much wanted light upon the relations of the Indian Governments and British officials to the Deccan Concession. Recent Indian papers mention that the Nizam was beginning to waken up and take an active interest in the affairs of his State, and no doubt the suspension of Abdul Huk, who had another big railway scheme on hand, was due to the more direct personal intervention of the Nizam in the administration of Hyderabad.—*Financial News*, May 3.

The Hyderabad-Deccan Property.—(*Deccan Times*, April 7, 1888).—On Tuesday morning Sir Charles Elliott, K.C.S.I., accompanied by Mr. Furnivall and Colonel Conway-Gordon, the director-general of railways in India, and several European and native gentlemen belonging to His Highness's Government, proceeded by special train to Yelindalapad, the coal mines' station. The visit, we may remark, was not an official one in the strict acceptation of the term; on the other hand, it was no doubt prompted to give the member of council who holds the D. P. W. portfolio an opportunity of judging for himself the railway work recently carried out in this State. The party reached Kazipett at 11 o'clock a.m., where they breakfasted.

At Warungal, Sir Charles was received by Mr. Framjee, the first Taluqdar, whose quiet but graceful decoration of the station elicited general praise. A guard of honour, composed of a strong company of the regular police and a few of the irregular troops, was drawn up on the platform. The latter presented the most ludicrous appearance, and the sooner these undoubtedly respectable but useless gentlemen are struck off the rolls of His Highness's army the better for the coffers of his State. It is a crying shame to allow such men to travesty a military parade. At 3 o'clock p.m. Yelindalapad was reached, and without a moment's delay Sir Charles Elliott went down the mines, accompanied by Mr. Phillips and a small party of gentlemen.

Mr. Phillips explained everything to the distinguished guest, who appeared to thoroughly enjoy his journey into the bowels of the earth. Some of those who went down to the coal mine seemed when emerging from it as if they had come out of a shower bath. We believe the galleries are sufficiently high to allow of an ordinary man to walk upright through them, so the fatigue of a visit should not be as great as many try to make out. We are not in a position to say what opinion the Public Works Member formed of the working of the mines, but the output of 25 tons a day, considering the time the mine has been open, or rather work resumed, and the fact of 50 tons per diem being the figure some six months ago, appears remarkably small. In the event of the company not finding gold or diamonds, will the coalfields ever pay them is the question that naturally suggests itself.

We understand the want of activity and life struck those who went to observe; matters seem as they were months back, which should not be, and point to something being wrong. What is the cause? Is it want of proper management? If so, that can be easily remedied. It is want of sympathy between employers and employed? If such be the case, that, too, could without difficulty be set right. Anyhow there is something amiss, and the sooner affairs are put on a proper footing the better for those shareholders who may be looking out to sell.

In the evening some twenty-two sat down to Mr. Furnivall's hospitable table, and by 10.30 p.m. the special was wending its way back to Warungal. The night was delightfully cool, so those who can sleep in a train must have had a most enjoyable night's slumber. Before dawn the train drew up at Warungal Station, where the Bombastes Furiosa army again appeared on the scene and treated the visitors to a tune (?) on the drums. After partaking of early tea Sir Charles, accompanied by Colonel Conway-Gordon, Mr. White, and Mr. Chirag Ali, visited the Warungal Fort and the Famous Mutwada temples. Colonel Ludlow, Messrs. Moosktak Hossain and Framjee joined the party at the temples, and the two last-named showed Sir Charles over the district offices and schools.

A pleasant hour's drive brought them all to Kazipett, where an excellent breakfast was laid out in the waiting-room. The distance of 80 miles from Kazipett to Hyderabad was accomplished in three hours and ten minutes. In the evening Sir Charles Elliott and Colonel Gordon left for Wadi. Mr. Forbes, the first Assistant-Resident, and the gentlemen who had visited the mines the previous day, with the exception of Sirdar Diler Jung, were on the platform to say good-bye to Sir Charles, who, by his courteous and impressive manner, has won golden opinions here. Mr. Dunlop, the engineer in charge of the open line; Mr. Crawford, the judicial superintendent; and Mr. Martin, the engineering superintendent, accompanied the special carriages to Wadhi.—*Financial News*, May 3.

THE *Times* and the *Standard* seem to be using every effort to whitewash Abdul Huk. I think they will have their work fairly well cut out, as what is now known as the "Deccan" scandal is one of the blackest bits of company promoting on record. There is no doubt that Abdul Huk cajoled the Nizam to part with the mining rights of Hyderabad to Messrs. Watson and Stewart for *nothing!* There is no doubt that £850,000 of the capital of the company went into the pockets of the promoters in direct defiance of the terms of the concession; and there is no doubt that the State of Hyderabad was induced to buy back a quantity of the shares at £12 per share, shares which represented nothing but the cost of printing and paper. All these questions will have to be explained before Sirdar Diler Jung, *alias* Abdul Huk, can pass cleanly through his whitewash baptism. It will take a great deal of explanation to prove that he has been nothing more than fortunate in contriving to accumulate a fortune of half a million sterling in six years.

The history of Abdul Huk is a very interesting one. He hails from Khallian, a small town in the Presidence of Bombay. His first public appointment was as a *trooper* in the Native Police. He then held some minor, probably menial post in the Berar Commission, Berar being a small province in Hyderabad, which was taken in pledge by the Government of India for claims which it had against the Nizam. From this position he gradually worked his way up, until by sheer impudence he was enabled to pose at the Jubilee celebrations last year as an Indian noble. At Hyderabad he is cordially detested, inasmuch as he has enriched himself at that city's expense. And as his life would not be particularly safe in the city of his adoption, he is at present domiciled at Secunderabad.—*Society Herald*, May 5.

Some time ago we called attention to the holding of Mexican Railway Ordinary stock by the National Provincial Bank as a most peculiar feature in banking investments. The register of the Hyderabad (Deccan) Company now reveals that the same bank holds one hundred shares in that company. It may be, of course, that the shares have fallen accidentally into the hands of the bank, but in view of the circumstances that the chairman, Mr. Wade, was at one time a shareholder in the Deccan Company, and that the same remark applies to Mr. Hanson and Mr. R. Wigram, we are not surprised that one of the proprietors of the bank should have written to us suggesting that the investment was deliberately made. At any rate the directors owe the shareholders some explanation of the circumstances under which the bank's money was invested in a mining concern, surely not the most perfect security which could have been chosen.—*Financial News*, May 7.

The Hyderabad-Deccan Scandal.—Since we last referred to the Hyderabad-Deccan scandal considerable progress has been made in its exposure. The Calcutta and Bombay papers received by last mail furnish full particulars of the suspension of Abdul Huk, including the text of the order of the Nizam's Government under which it took place. This we reprint in another column, and as a corollary to it we reproduce a very significant telegram published yesterday by the *Times* from its Calcutta correspondent:—

"It is stated that a telegram has been handed to the Hyderabad Government from Mr. Watson, alleging that Abdul Huk received a quarter of the company's shares under a letter of permission from the Regent, and that the shares sold to the Nizam were purchased from Abdul Huk. The history of this letter is being investigated."

Mr. Watson is at present in London, and if the above statement had been incorrect it would no doubt have been promptly contradicted. Standing as it does it may be accepted as an indication of the tactics which are going to be adopted by Abdul Huk's English confederates. At first they tried to pooh-pooh the whole affair, and professed to be confident that their Indian friend would come out with flying colours. They got the *Times* and the *Standard* to publish pathetic appeals on his behalf for fair play. The British public were implored not to act rashly; but to reserve their judgment until Abdul Huk had been heard in his defence. Apparently that line of policy has not answered their expectations. Injured innocence has not produced the impression it was expected to do, and the Sirdar's English friends are going on a new tack. When he hears of the telegram said to have been sent to the Hyderabad Government, he will conclude that they have thrown him over and mean to let him sink or swim as he best can. Whatever may be thought of their courage, it will soon be seen that their second thoughts are more politic than their first. He would be a very sanguine man who hoped to save Abdul Huk after the strong and explicit charges made against him in the Order of Suspension.

One of the telegrams to the *Standard*, which betrayed such a peculiar tenderness for Abdul Huk, impudently represented his suspension to be due to the personal ill-will of the Minister, Sir Asman Jah. That was promptly denied both at Hyderabad and at Bombay; but the *Standard* correspondent was either too great or too soft-hearted a man to take any notice of the contradiction. Sir Asman Jah, however, can afford to let the insinuation pass for what it is worth. In the Order of Suspension he presents an array of charges which speak for themselves without requiring any assistance from personal motives. The Sirdar is asked for explanations on ten separate points in the history of the Hyderabad-Deccan concession. First: Why does it contain no stipulation limiting the concessionnaires to a *first issue* of shares of the intended company, as arranged in writing by the Nizam's Government and the Government of India? It is obvious that all the official references to the 15,000 shares which the concessionnaires were required to issue and pay up to the extent of £5 per share contemplated holding the rest of the company's nominal capital in reserve. The idea clearly was that the £75,000 to be raised at once was to be applied to the development of the Singareni coal-fields and to prospecting for mines. When a mineral discovery was made there was to be a mining lease taken, and fresh capital raised for working it. Nowhere in all the voluminous correspondence is there the slightest hint given either to the Hyderabad Government or the Government of India that the £850,000 might be thrown in the market at the will of the concessionnaires.

The second question put to the Sirdar is: If, as requested, he showed the draft concession to Mr. Fitzgerald, the First Assistant-Resident, and pointed out to him the necessity of a clearer stipulation with regard to the first issue of shares. This leads to a third and pointed inquiry as to what authority the Sirdar had to consent to a gift of £850,000 of fully paid-up shares by the directors of the company to the concessionnaires? In the light of the statement now attributed by the *Times* to Mr. Watson, that Abdul Huk himself received a quarter of these shares, namely, £210,000 worth, this may be a very awkward question indeed. If, as now appears, Abdul Huk had no authority to sanction a gift of 85,000 shares to Messrs. Watson and Stewart, still less authority had he to share the spoil himself. The fourth explanation he is asked for reminds him that he had given no information whatever to his Government as to how the Hyderabad-Deccan Company and the concessionnaires intended dealing with the unsubscribed capital. The fifth question is another home thrust, for it asks him to explain how the balance between subscribed and nominal capital has been disposed of?

These first five questions relate, it will be observed, entirely to the issue of the £850,000 of watered stock. The next four deal with the purchase of 12,500 shares for the Nizam's Government. As to that, the Sirdar is requested to show where the difficulty was which he pretended to have found in buying those shares. If, as is now alleged, he himself was the vendor, through some convenient nominee, he ought to have a good deal more information than he has yet thought it advisable to disclose.

Another touch of invisible green in the transaction about which the Prime Minister feels curious is the employment of Mr. Watson, a concessionnaire and director of the company, as purchasing agent for the Nizam's Government. The trifling commission of £660, which he was paid for his services, would be a bagatelle beneath the notice of a man who had lately made a quarter of a million sterling off his own bat. Moreover, Mr. Watson is not a commission agent, much less is he a stockbroker's jackal. His intervention in the purchase must have been due to more recondite motives, which the Prime Minister of Hyderabad is fully justified in trying to find out.

The eighth and ninth queries are of secondary importance; but the series winds up with a poser: Has the Sirdar himself, directly or indirectly, received any remuneration in shares, money or otherwise? That is a very straight question, which Abdul Huk, with all his craft, will hardly be able to squirm out of answering. Evidence exists as to the issue of the 85,000 shares and their distribution among the insiders, which will effectually checkmate any attempt to put a new face on facts. The contracts required in such cases by the law of joint stock companies will enable every share to be traced. The Hyderabad Government evidently have their finger on the right spot so far as Abdul Huk is concerned. They also seem to be determined to get at the truth and the whole truth. Can we count on the Government of India to be equally resolute and single-minded in dealing with their officials? Explanations are as badly wanted from some of them as from the disgraced Sirdar; but there will be desperate efforts made in high places to put the public off the scent. Our intention is to keep them on it and to make it too warm a scent to be disguised by any quantity of official rose water.—*Financial News*, May 8.

Abdul Huk's Disgrace.—The Official Decree Removing Him from Office, and Reasons for Taking that Step.—The following is the full text of the order of the Nizam's Government suspending the Sirdar Diler-ul-Mulk:

Proceedings of his Highness the Nizam's Government with reference to the concession of Mining rights, and to the purchase of shares by Government in the Hyderabad-Deccan Mining Company, as dealt with in the Home Secretary's Memorandum on the Railway Budget for 1297 Fasli.

1. His Highness's Government, having carefully read the memorandum by the Sirdar Diler Jung Diler-ul-Mulk, Home Secretary, on the Budget Estimate of the railway for Fasli 1297, and contenting themselves for the present with that portion of the memorandum which deals with the concession of mining rights to Messrs. Watson and Stewart, and the Sirdar's concession with the negotiations which terminated ultimately in the formation of the Hyderabad-Deccan Company, Limited, and with the purchase by the Sirdar on behalf of the Government of 12,500 shares in the said company, are pleased to pass the following interlocutory order.

2. In the first place, the Government desire the Sirdar to explain how, and by whose authority, he trangressed their distinct order prohibiting the printing and issuing of any official paper without first submitting a draft thereof for the Minister's perusual and approval. The first and only intimation which the Government received of any intention on the Sirdar's part to issue a report was the infringement by him of the Government order.

3. The Government, in regretting, cannot too severely censure a departure from their distinct orders, which were formulated expressly for the purpose of securing official decorum and the executive and administrative efficiency of State affairs.

4. The Government are unable to understand much of the contents of the Sirdar's memorandum by reason of an absence therein of a sufficient statement of facts, although they consider there is enough upon record to arouse painful apprehension that the Sirdar, in his dealings with the concessionnaires and the company, has not been actuated by that honest devotion to the interests of the Government which they have a right to expect generally from all their subordinates, and more particularly from one who, like the Sirdar, was especially entrusted by them with the conduct and completion of negotiations, on the successful issue of which they had a large and important stake.

5. The Government direct the Sirdar to furnish them with a full and detailed explanation on the following points:

(*a*) Why the concession, dated the 7th of January, 1886, to Messrs. Watson and Stewart contains no stipulation that the concessionnaires shall limit the issue of shares by the intended company, to a first issue, seeing that the Government of India and of Hyderabad had repeatedly and expressly laid down in writing that the issue of shares was to be a first issue, with the specific intention that the company should have a reserve fund in the shape of uncalled-up capital, wherewith to meet either possible contingencies or to enlarge the company's operations in other directions; and seeing that Mr. C. A. Winter, the company's solicitor, had in a letter, dated the 16th December, 1884, and published on page 1 of Appendix K of the Sirdar's memorandum, accepted on behalf of his principals, the proposition that the issue of shares was to be a first issue.

(*b*) Did the Sirdar call upon Mr. Fitzgerald, the First Assistant Resident, as desired in that officer's letter, dated September 22, 1885, with the draft concession, and did he go over that concession clause by clause with Mr. Fitzgerald? If so, did the Sirdar, as the Government's agent, and as such familiar with their views and intentions, point out to Mr. Fitzgerald the necessity for introducing into that draft that stipulation with reference to the "first issue" upon which the Supreme and the Hyderabad Governments had so frequently insisted, and if not, why not?

(*c*) By what authority the Sirdar consented or did not object to the gift by the directors of the mining company of 85,000 fully paid-up shares to the concessionnaires, seeing that the Sirdar was fully aware of the intention of the Supreme and Hyderabad Goverments to the contrary, referred to in the paragraph immediately preceding.

(*d*) Why the Sirdar, on becoming acquainted with the intention of the mining company thus to deal with their unsubscribed capital, did not at once inform his Government thereof?

(*e*) What the Sirdar means by the following statement in paragraph 99 of his memorandum: Thus the fixing of the fully-paid shares at £850,000 was the result of limiting the subscribed capital to £150,000. The Sirdar will be good enough to explain how the balance between the subscribed and nominal capital could thus be disposed of, in direct contravention of the expressed injunctions of the Supreme and Hyderabad Government that there was to be only a first issue of 15,000 shares, and a reserve capital to which the company could have recourse as time and circumstances might necessitate?

(*f*) What was the difficulty which the Sirdar experienced in the purchase of the shares, to effect which he had been sent to England as the Government's trusted agent, seeing that he became the possessor of 12,500 shares within 24 hours of his requesting Mr. Watson, the Government's agent in London, to acquire them for him?

(*g*) Why did the Sirdar employ Mr. Watson to purchase the shares on behalf of the Government, seeing that Mr. Watson was (1) one of the two concessionnaires, (2) a director of the Hyderabad-Deccan Company, and (3) had in each capacity a direct personal interest in the sale of the said shares? If he was the agent of the Government in England, how, when, and by whom was he so appointed?

(*h*) What was the foundation for the Sirdar's statement in his telegram (printed as Appendix I. 4 in his memorandum) that the mining shares were "firmly held by the public"? What step, if any, did the Sirdar take to verify that statement? At the time of that statement by how many people were the company's shares held?

(*i*) What steps did the Sirdar take to test the truth of the necessity for the exercise of that "greatest skill and circumspection" set forth in Appendix L. 2 of the memorandum, without which it would appear the shares in question could not be obtained? In what did that exercise consist?

(*j*) To whom did the 1,000 fully paid shares, endorsed to bearer, and purchased through Messrs. Borthwick, Walk and Co., belong?

(*k*) Did the Sirdar himself receive, directly or indirectly, through the concessionnaires, or any other person, any remuneration in the shape of shares, money, or any other consideration? If so, what, when, where, why, and from whom?

6. So gravely do his Highness's Government view the conduct of the Sirdar as disclosed by the contents of his own memorandum, the omissions in which seem to be even more serious and suspicious than its statements, that pending the receipt of the Sirdar's explanation, and subject to any action which the Government may feel called upon to take upon its receipt, His Highness's Government have decided to suspend Sirdar Diler Jung Diler-ul-Mulk from his offices of Home Secretary and Government Director of His Highness the Nizam's Guaranteed Railway and the Hyderabad-Deccan Company.

7. The Sirdar will accordingly hand over charge to-morrow morning at 9 o'clock to the Private Secretary to the Minister, at the Minister's Palace in the City, and will, at the place and hour named, entrust to that official all documents in connection with the Railway and Mining Department.

Notice of the Sirdar's suspension from office will be communicated to the Political and Financial Secretary, to the Accountant-General, and to the Agent and Chief Engineer of His Highness the Nizam's Guaranteed Railway Company and the Deccan Mining Company; the National Provincial Bank of England will also be informed of the Sirdar's suspension by telegram.—Asman Jah, Minister to His Highness the Nizam. Hyderabad, April 14, 1888.—*Financial News*, May 8.

Abdul Huk should not require the services of "his solicitors in London" when he is so well represented by the *Times*. The ex-policeman's champion now explains that he has not published his defence because difficulties are thrown in the way of his obtaining the necessary documents. It is, apart altogether from what is known and proved regarding Abdul Huk, a little strange that the *Times* should take up the cudgels on behalf of a discredited adventurer against the Minister of a loyal Indian potentate. —*Financial News*, May 10.

There is no reason now why we should be astonished at anything we may hear about the Nizam's offer. Were it otherwise, some surprise might have been felt that no despatches have been as yet received from India in regard to the contemplated gift of the Nizam. This is what Sir John Gorst is reported to have said in the House a few days ago in reply to Mr. Labouchere. As the offer of 60 lakhs of rupees by a Nizam to help us in defending the Indian frontier is not exactly an every-day affair, it might have been supposed that the Government of India would have communicated the offer to the Secretary of State. But that does not seem to have been done. Therefore we may infer that, for some reason or other, the Indian Government did not consider it worth while to do so, or to submit any opinion as to whether the proffered cash should be accepted or refused. The Nizam's offer was made known in England at the end of last September. A month later the correspondence between the Viceroy and the Nizam was published. Lord Dufferin informed the Nizam that he had the greatest satisfaction in acquainting the Queen-Empress with the contents of his Highness's letter containing his offer. A few days after her Majesty the Queen sent the following telegram :—"I warmly appreciate the fresh proof of your Highness's friendship for the British Crown, which is fully reciprocated." All this happened more than six months ago, and yet no despatches from India on the subject!—*St. James's Gazette*, May 12.

A SPECIAL meeting of the Viceroy's Council took place at Simla before the mail left to consider a communication on the subject of the Hyderabad (Deccan) scandal, received from the Secretary of State for India. The *Pioneer* says that the telegram from India lately published in the *Standard* is "a deliberate suggestion of untruth," and shows how easily a journal of high character may be misled when without the means of checking the information supplied to it by correspondents in distant countries.—*Allen's Indian Mail*, May 14.

NAWAB MAHDI ALI.—Nawab Mahdi Ali, Mohsin-ul-Moolk, Bahadur, Political and Financial Secretary, Hyderabad, the representative of H. H. the Nizam in the Hyderabad-Deccan business, will reach England on Whit Sunday. As we have already informed our readers, the Nawab comes upon a double errand. First, he is to testify as to Abdul Huk's singular proceedings, and to show what His Highness's Government really meant in sanctioning a share capital of one million sterling, with a first issue of £150,000. Next, he is armed with powers to arrange with the company and the *boná fide* shareholders as to future proceedings, so as to save them as much as possible from loss. As to the first point, so clear are the allegations, so ominous is Abdul Huk's prolonged silence, that probably all is over save the shouting and—the disgorging. As to the next, that point is of much importance to a great many very estimable individuals, some of whom are most deeply involved. A few words, showing the manner of man Sir Asman Jah, the Minister, has sent to England, may bring some comfort to souls that at this moment must be anything but happy.

Imprimis, Mahdi Ali is an upright and highly honourable man, one who may be thoroughly depended upon, and who is capable withal. A gentleman, well qualified to judge, who was recently in Hyderabad, has stated that Mahdi Ali was really the main-spring of the Government. The present Minister—he who exhibited what, considering the exact condition of affairs, is really rare courage in suspending Abdul Huk—after declaring Madhi Ali's services, in a recent communication, "simply invaluable," goes on to say, "I bear willing testimony to his exceptional abilities, his high integrity, and his devotion to his duties." Again, "I have . . . a very high opinion of his character and qualifications." "High integrity," "High opinion of his character"; these are features of conduct and character which will make Mahdi Ali's presence in this country at this juncture most acceptable. Sir Stewart Bayley, the Lieut.-Governor of Bengal, when he was Resident in Hyderabad—for far too brief a period—found Mahdi Ali one of the most responsible officials and most trusted adviser of the late Sir Salar Jung.

The late Minister, whose great services through over thirty years to the British Government in India can never be overrated, was wont to say of Mahdi Ali that there was no one who at times gave him more unpalatable advice, but, at the same time, there was no man on whose honesty of purpose and soundness of judgment he could better rely. There is no doubt that, through all the troublous times which have followed in Hyderabad since the untimely death of the late Sir Salar Jung, the Nawab Mahdi Ali has been the mainstay of the State. Mahdi Ali's career is a most interesting one, and serves to show what great opportunities there are for men of character and ability in Native India as compared with British India. In 1855 Mahdi Ali commenced service in the office of Mr. A. O. Hume, collector of Etawah, on 20s. per month. At the end of six years, when he had become a Tahsildar at just twenty times the salary he started with, Mr. Hume said of him: "He is beyond measure industrious and withal ambitious. . . He is a very good Arabic scholar. . . . As regards revenue work, he is probably one of the very best revenue officers in the North-West Provinces. As to his character, it is due to him to state that I have never heard one single complaint against him of any kind since he was appointed Sherishtadar." Two years later Mr. Hume wrote: "As far as many years' experience enables me to judge, his integrity is utterly unimpeachable." There was no chance—on the principle on which British India is administered—of such a man finding a worthy sphere of labour under the Viceroy, and he resigned his position. In what is known as the Official Character Book an entry appears concerning him, from which two extracts may be made: (1) "Energy, industry, talent, and integrity are all to be found combined in him to an extent very seldom equalled." (2) "It is simply absurd that with his abilities and experience, he, a man who would rule a province far better than most provinces are nowadays ruled, is allowed to continue in the comparatively humble post of Tahsildar and deputy magistrate." The late Sir Salar Jung had heard of Moulvi Mahdi Ali, and offered him a post. The Moulvi accepted it, and since 1874, when he took up the duties of Inspector-General of the Revenue Department, the signs of his beneficent statesmanship are to be found writ large in every part of Hyderabad administration. So successful was he in revenue work that a competent authority (Sir Stewart Bayley) has declared that in this respect Hyderabad is better off than the permanently-settled Province of Bengal. This praise does less than justice to the completeness of this Mohammedan statesman's work. In addition he overhauled the mode of presenting the State's finances, introducing, at the same time, the system of preparing annual budget estimates and of issuing financial statements. During the famine of 1876-77 there was only one part of Southern India in which that terrible disaster was met and conquered; everywhere else Famine was master. In Hyderabad the disaster was faced, was fought, was conquered, and Mahdi Ali was the conqueror. He has undertaken nothing that he has not successfully performed.

We have placed the above facts before our readers to enable them to take some measure of the man in whose hands, more than in those of any other person or persons, depends largely the fate of the future of the Hyderabad-Deccan Company. We congratulate all interested in the circumstance that his Highness the Nizam has sent so upright and so able an envoy at a time when uprightness and ability are so greatly needed to unravel the tangled web of trickery and fraud, and to place the large interests involved on a sound footing.—*Financial News*, May 15.

THE very interesting letter which appears elsewhere in our pages, written by a Mahommedan gentleman who has held a high office in one of the greater native States of India, deserves close attention. Speaking of what he knows, our correspondent is above all desirous to bring home to Englishmen the dangers, not to the Mahommedans alone, but to all India, of the premature spread of Radical principles. He points out that his co-religionists are by nature worshippers of royalty and aristocracy, haters of officials of low extraction, and still rather distrustful of education. It is a little startling to learn that twenty years back it was a mark of Mahommedan respectability not to know English, and that our correspondent had to learn it secretly. Things are no doubt changed; but the Mahommedans of the upper class are still too uneducated for official work, and they will not be ruled by their inferiors. Then they are over uncivilized, as yet, not to feel gratitude for the benefits English rule has given them, and they have in addition a radical contempt for their loquacious and clever friends the Hindoos. Last of all, the Mohammedan neither understands nor longs for those elective forms of rule which seem to English Radicals the *summum bonum* of human possibility. If the Indian Mussulman had to work an elective system he would work it badly. At the same time he appreciates the strong rule and the masterly administration of the English; and he is alive to the fact that his own youth are not trained in an atmosphere likely to produce the energy and political purity of his British governors.—*St. James's Gazette*, May 16.

Political Views of the Indian Muslims.—To the Editor of the *St. James's Gazette*.—"Sir,—Some time ago I had occasion, in the columns of the *Times*, to give the English public what information I could concerning the political and social attitude of the Mahommedans of India towards the British Government and the English race respectively, and thus, I believe, incurred a good deal of hostile and angry criticism from the native press in India. In asking your favour to allow me to reopen the subject, I must premise that I do so because I firmly believe, with the Indian 'Grand Old Man,' Sir Syed Ahmed, that great dangers attend the premature spread of Radical principles in India—dangers not to the Mahommedan community alone but to the whole people. If the English people at home, who are determined heart and soul to do justice to India, once take up with the idea that India is discontented, and that British rule in India is despotic and partial, they will move heaven and earth with the sincere intention of improving it; and in the wake of such premature improvement there will follow ruin. This must be my sufficient excuse for once more risking the displeasure of the more Radical of my fellow-countrymen.

"Let me first repeat that I do not for one moment mean to inspire doubt as to the loyalty of my Bengalee friends. I respect and admire them; they are intellectually the pick of the country, and the educational system of India rests mainly on them. But in matters of grave national importance, like the present, we should seek, it may be, to express our differences of opinion without endangering our mutual friendly relations. If they find themselves in unfortunate disagreement with our views, the heaviest charge that they can bring against us is that our opinions take their rise from selfish and self-regarding motives. Now, so many actions in this world spring from selfish motives (even a mother's love of her child may be said to be largely selfish in its origin) that I think we lie under no very terrible indictment when we are accused of being moved to differ from our Hindoo brethren by a keen desire to protect our own interests. We are quite aware that our difference splits 'United India' into hostile camps, and so weakens our general cause; but even so we are acting from a deep sense of duty to our country, and are doing no more than your 'Grand Old Man' found himself compelled to do with sorrow from a similar sense of duty. At the same time I should be guilty of injustice if I did not fully and publicly acknowledge our gratitude to those Englishmen whose generosity has led them to identify themselves in the most disinterested way with the National Congress movement. We lament their political views, yet we cannot help admiring such men as Mr. Norton, Mr. Hume, and Mr. Digby.

"And now I come to the causes which keep us aloof, however painful the severance may be, from the National Congress movement. And foremost among these I will touch on those causes which might be called 'sentimental;' a statement of which will perhaps be liable to excite further ridicule from the Indian press, but which nevertheless are hard undeniable facts.

"First: we Mahommedans are by nature the worshippers of Royalty and Aristocracy—a most barbarous feeling, you will say, but there it is: we feel it. We talk a great deal of high birth, and make much of it, although all such talk is, perhaps, utter nonsense. Many a poor man in India who obtains a precarious livelihood by knocking about the streets may be found to boast of high birth, and to expect the deference and respect which is commonly paid to men in high position. To some extent, no doubt, he submits to the hardship of circumstances; yet nothing can induce him to abate one jot of his pretensions, or prevent him from looking with sovereign contempt on self-made men and upstarts. It is an open secret that until very lately we regarded with horror and disgust our native Government officials—a class of men for the most part of low extraction. Many an extra Assistant-Commissioner in Oudh was spoken of habitually as 'bunya' or 'teli' (grain-seller or oil-seller), because then the higher class of people was not sufficiently educated even for these petty appointments. No doubt education has now made considerable progress among us; yet even to-day it is a common saying in the North-West Provinces that a Mahommedan of forty years of age or upwards, if he is perfectly versed in English, is in ninety-nine cases out of a hundred a man of low birth. Twenty years ago it was a mark of respectability among Mahommedans not to know English. I well remember how I began the study of English surreptitiously, with the primer concealed in my pocket, as we used to do in our childhood with romances. It was only after the death of my guardians that General Barrow, the then Chief Commissioner of Oudh, sent me to the Wards' Institution, a place for educating the sons of noblemen, to learn English.

"Now, in view of these circumstances, it seems to me simply unbearable that the Mahommedans should be submitted to the rule of persons whom, rightly or wrongly, they regard as second-rate, in spite of their education, or that they should have boys fresh from school and destitute of administrative experience placed over their heads. The objection may be sentimental; but existing sentiments are often giant political forces, and while they exist must be respected. The education of the upper classes has really made very little progress in India. Go to the Talukdars of Oudh, or the great landed aristocracy of Bengal, and you will find they much prefer to be under a man of alien race, whose birth and social position in England they have no means of knowing, than to be subjected to a countryman of their own whose intellectual qualities may perhaps entitle him to respect, but who will never command respect among a people given over to this old-fashioned and unappreciative method of thinking.

"The second cause, founded also on sentiment, is that we have not yet become sufficiently civilized to look with contempt on the institutions of our country or the natural feelings of our nation. Sense of gratitude for benefits, extreme politeness, and an obliging and forgiving disposition, have long been characteristics of the Indian people—Hindoos or Mahommedans. The abuse levelled at successive Viceroys by the native press is so marked a piece of ingratitude to those who spend labourious years in the attempt to better our condition, that we cannot be induced to identify ourselves with those who employ these political methods. I admit that these methods are not unusual in politics, and that some of the papers in England abuse even the Queen herself, but I say that we are not yet advanced enough to be able to appreciate the beauty of these things.

"The third sentimental cause of our alienation from the purposes of the National Congress is what I must admit to be a narrow-minded feeling. We are aware that the Hindoos are far superior to us in intellectual education, while we are decidedly superior to them in those other qualities which are requisite in a nation of rulers. Thus it is impossible for either to rule the other; and we fear that, were any system of representation introduced, however earnestly our intellectual superiors might endeavour to obtain for us an equal share in the administration, our intellectual inferiority would be too much for them and would send us to the bottom. I do not wish to throw mistrust on my Hindoo fellow-subjects. I am sure they will not withhold a helping hand; but in our present state an angel from heaven would find it difficult to help us.

"These are all potent and substantial reasons, and, although I have classed them as sentimental, yet the sentiments they spring from are general, and so carry force with them.

"Now I come to reasons which are not sentimental in their origin or character. The political constitution of every country is the outcome of its social constitution; in other words, social institutions are made political by receiving legal sanction. Thus, if you transplant the political institutions which have grown up in one country to another where the social institutions and circumstances are widely different, they are pretty sure to prove failures. Now, I will analyze the demands of the most advanced section of my fellow-countrymen. I will take only a few of their more moderate demands—as, for instance, the demand for an elective method of choosing the Legislative Councils. Now, election is a purely European institution; so we must have regard to the social circumstances of England, where the system prospers, as well as to our own present condition. In England primary education is so general that even a porter or a coachman can read the papers and form opinions on the politics of the day. In India, on the other hand, the majority of even upper-class people, great landlords and bankers, are completely ignorant of all that goes on outside the narrow circle of their own private affairs. To them politics is an unintelligible term; they do not know what representation or election means. Yet these men are the backbone of the Indian Empire, and must have a vote to determine what they do not understand. Their constitutional duties would be most perplexing to them. In England long-established usage and civilization have made the English people patriotic and keenly interested in the public welfare. They are taught to sacrifice their convenience and their time for the good of their country. In India the bulk of those who, on account of their position in society, must be given a voice in the proposed new orders of things, are purely selfish. I do not blame them for their selfishness, for it arises from their circumstances and education. Politics are strange to them; they do not care to be bothered with public affairs; even small municipalities, into which they are occasionally dragged, are a burden to them, and we all know how they behave there. Except in the Presidency towns, the municipal committees, educational boards, and local funds committees are everywhere ridiculous institutions. The members do not take the least interest in them, avoid attending as much as possible, and, when coaxed by the district officer to put in an appearance, go there to yawn. Once there, their main object is to terminate the meeting; and when any question arises for settlement they vote Yes or No, according as this purpose is best served by an affirmative or negative decision. In England public affairs take the first place. Members of Parliament devote themselves entirely to the public good; and in the establishment of a club or in any other business the same perseverance and public spirit are evident. The result is that the English achieve great works and establish lasting institutions. But in India every one puts his private affairs first and considers public business a burden; he hates sitting long at a meeting, and is disgusted if he has to attend regularly. He establishes clubs in imitation of the English, and these fail after the lapse of a few months: the books get dusty, the members neglect the payment of their subscriptions, and the club-house ultimately becomes a paradise for sparrows and bats. In England patriotism is so strong that we never hear of anyone selling the interests of his country for anything. In India, setting aside the people of education or high birth, by the rest this would be done with little scruple. The English are independent in their mode of thinking, while Indians are brought up in a society where politeness is carried to the point of weakness; the influences of society, of friendship, and of private sympathy have a preponderant effect on their minds. Now, suppose the elective system were introduced: to whom is the suffrage to be given? To young university students? Certainly not; but to the class of landowners and others of high position. Now, these men have had no systematic education, and have not the character necessary for this privilege. They will be harassed on every side, and all sorts of undesirable influences will be brought to bear on them. It would be dangerous to entrust such a power to them; it would be tenfold more dangerous to entrust it to anyone else; and thus the system that works so admirably in England would lead to no good or safe result in India.

"Next let me take the demand for a Civil Service examination to be held in India. This is a very rash and premature demand. A disinterested consideration of the matter will show how fine a service the covenanted service in India has been. The members of this service are, in fact, the ruling body of India, and on the healthy tone of the service depends the welfare of the country. Now, it is not intellectual education alone that fits a man for so commanding a position; it is the sum total of many moral and mental qualities that forms the character of an administrator. In England, children are brought up in a healthy and pure atmosphere, and so have their characters naturally formed in way to fit them for such a position. Indians are brought up, until the age of fifteen or sixteen, in the most unhealthy domestic circumstances, under a depraved female influence, and educated only on a system which is rotten to the core. In the absence of that early systematic training which forms the character, they cannot be expected to possess the qualities necessary in that important service. Those who admit the advantage of English administration must also admit the necessity of the predominance of the English element in the service. And this does not necessarily mean the predominance of Englishmen, but the predominance of men of English education and of English modes of thinking.

"So much for the political views of the Mahommedans. In another letter I hope, by your permission, to treat the social questions which arise in the country—a subject which you have always been foremost in bringing before the English public.—I am, Sir, your obedient servant,—MEHDI HASAN, FATHAH NAWAZ JUNG."—*St. James's Gazette*, May 16.

WE understand that Abdul Huk has been served with a notice on behalf of the Government of Hyderabad to refund the sum of £151,631, the amount realised by the sale of his shares to the Nizam through Mr. W. C. Watson, as agent for the Government of Hyderabad, on June 3 last. The work of retribution has begun.—*Financial News*, May 16.

POLITICAL VIEWS OF THE INDIAN MUSLIMS.—To the Editor of the *St. James's Gazette*.—Sir,—My friend Mehdi Hasan really ought not to condemn the action of those Anglo-Indians who support the National Congress. Why do we support the Congress and its proposals? Largely because we are envious of Hyderabad and other Native States. Those States take away from the British provinces the best of their Mahommedan and Hindoo sons. Without begrudging him to the Nizam, we want Mehdi Hasan in the chief justiceship of the North West Provinces, not in that of Hyderabad. We should be sorry to put his Highness of Hyderabad to inconvenience, but we wish to have Mehdi Ali's incomparable statesmanlike and administrative abilities busied in solving the problems of government in one or other of our Presidencies and provinces. We are jealous of Mysore, Baroda, Indore, Travancore, and other States getting the services of men like Sir Dinkar Rao, Sir Madhava Rao, Mr. Dadabhai Naoroji, Mr. Raghunath Rao, and the late Mr. Runga Charlu—statesmen for whom there is no room in our scheme of rule. We want British India to receive some of the many benefits which follow from the judicial and administrative efforts of such men. That is why we support the Congress. We believe it will be a means to that end. "India"—in that sense—"for the Indians" would also mean India for England in a more powerful sense than is now possible.—I am, Sir, your obedient servant, WM. DIGBY. May 16.—*St. James's Gazette*, May 17.

THE HYDERABAD-DECCAN INQUIRY.—The Parliamentary Committee appointed to inquire into the circumstances attending the formation of the Hyderabad-Deccan Mining Company, Limited, the circumstances under which the concession was obtained, and the subsequent operations on the Stock Exchange, met yesterday in the House of Commons, the period within which the Committee would receive applications for parties to be represented by counsel having expired.

The proceedings were private, and the Committee will report to the House of Commons to-day.—*Financial News*, May 17.

ACCORDING to information which I have received from India, the Deccan "scandal" is causing great excitement there, and particularly in Bombay, where the accused, Sirdar Dilar Jung or Abdul Huq, as he is generally designated, is well known. His suspension from the office of Minister of the Interior in the Hyderabad Government pending the clearing up of his connection in the mining company caused the utmost sensation throughout India, but I understand that nothing effectual can be done till the House of Commons Committee has reported on the precise position and responsibilities of the Government of India in the whole matter of the company's contracts with the Nizam's Government.—*Glasgow Herald*, May 18.

THE terms which Abdul Huk offers by way of reparation in connection with the mining concession include the refunding of £150,000, on the condition of the Nizam stopping the action against him, and continuing the concession. This, however, the Nizam declines to do, and will move the High Court to attach Abdul Huk's property at Bombay, which is valued at twenty lakhs of rupees.—*Financial Times*, May 18.

IN THE CITY.—THE DECCAN MINING SCANDAL.—It must be somewhat annoying to the influential journals which stood up for Abdul Huk to hear that he has made an offer of reparation on the condition that the Nizam stops the action against him and continues the concession. He is willing, it appears, to refund £150,000, which was the sum paid by the Nizam for the shares bought ostensibly from English shareholders, although really from Abdul Huk himself. The Nizam, however, is not to be bought off, more especially as the Sirdar's property in Bombay is said to be worth £200,000, and that can be attached. Now that the Select Committee will soon begin its inquiries, it would be a pity if the whole pretty story were not unfolded.—*Pall Mall Gazette*, May 18.

IT appears that Abdul Huk has offered by way of reparation to refund £150,000 on condition that the Nizam will stop all proceedings against him. That the Nizam has properly declined to do. He prefers to move the High

Court to attach Abdul Huk's property at Bombay, which is worth a good deal more than £150,000. Efforts to burke inquiry are not confined to the Nizam's ex-Secretary. Others nearer home, and nearer Downing-street, are having an anxious time of it. They know what must follow if not only the truth, but the whole truth, comes out.—*Star*, May 18.

The Deccan Scandal.—The Bombay correspondent of the *Standard* states that the Sirdar Abdul Huk has made an offer to repay the whole of the Nizam's investment in the Deccan Mining Company's shares, on condition that no proceedings are taken against him, and that the concession is not cancelled. The Nizam's Government deline to accept these conditions, and contemplate moving the Bombay Courts for the attachment of the Sirdar's property here, which is said to be worth twenty lakhs (£200,000).—*Echo*, May 18.

The Deccan Company.—(from our correspondent.)—Bombay, Thursday.—The Sirdar Abdul Huk has made an offer to repay the whole of the Nizam's investment in the Deccan Mining Company's shares on condition that no proceedings are taken against him, and that the concession is not cancelled. The Nizam's Government decline to accept these conditions, and contemplate moving the Bombay Courts for the attachment of the Sirdar's property here, which is said to be worth twenty lakhs (£200,000).—*Standard*, May 18.

City Topics.—With regard to the Deccan Company, a very important telegram has been received from Bombay, stating that Abdul Huk offers terms by way of reparation in connection with the mining concession, which include the refunding of £150,000, on the condition of the Nizam stopping the action against him and continuing the concession. This, however, the Nizam declines to do, and will move the High Court to attach Abdul Huk's property at Bombay, which is valued at twenty lakhs of rupees. We are also given to understand that the concessionnaires on this side, Messrs. W. C. Watson and Charles Winter, would also be willing to refund a considerable portion of the profits they have made out of this undertaking for the purpose of placing the company on a sound financial footing. We consider both these propositions to be of the greatest importance to the shareholders, whose position is evidently far stronger than they had lately thought. Under the circumstances, we think Deccans are certainly cheap at 6¼.—*Evening Post*, May 18.

The Nizam of Hyderabad has refused Abdul Huk's offer of £150,000 to compromise the action against the latter in connection with the mining concession. The Nizam has resolved to attach Abdul Huk's property at Bombay.—*Liverpool Post*, May 18.

A Central News telegram from Bombay states that the terms which Abdul Huk offers by way of reparation in connection with the mining concession include the refunding of £150,000, on the condition of the Nizam stopping the action against him and continuing the concession. This, however, the Nizam declines to do, and will move the High Court to attach Abdul Huk's property at Bombay, which is valued at 20 lakhs of rupees. Abdul Huk is evidently beginning to take fright, and he may yet be induced to tell the truth about the English end of the Hyderabad deal. If he would do this, and at the same time explain the circumstances under which he received £80,000 from Mr. Watson as his share of the Hyderabad

Railway scheme, he would be performing a real service to the State which he has so greedily plucked.—*Financial News*, May 18.

The Deccan Scandals.—The Persons Concerned to be Represented before the Committee by Counsel.—In the House of Commons, yesterday, the clerk at the table read the resolution adopted by the Committee on the Hyderabad Mining Concessions. It stated that applications had been received from the Nizam of Hyderabad, the Hyderabad-Deccan Mining Company, and a number of other persons concerned, asking to be represented before the Committee by counsel. The Committee, it further stated, were of opinion that it would be advisable "to allow counsel to represent the said applicants for the purpose of assisting the Committee, subject to such restrictions as the Committee may from time to time direct."

Sir Henry James moved: "That the Select Committee on the East India (Hyderabad-Deccan) Mining Company have leave to hear counsel to such extent as they think fit on the matter referred to them."

Sir Edward Watkin inquired whether the words "to such extent as the Committee might think fit" were words of limitation which would in any way prevent the inquiry being of the most searching character.

Sir Henry James replied that the object was to obtain the fullest inquiry, and the words alluded to had been introduced to give the Committee control over counsel. To prevent them from introducing irrelevant matter counsel did require to be controlled.

The motion was agreed to.

A telegram from Bombay states that the terms which Abdul Huk offers by way of reparation in connection with the mining concession include the refunding of £150,000, on the condition of the Nizam stopping the action against him, and continuing the concession. This, however, the Nizam declines to do, and will move the High Court to attach Abdul Huk's property at Bombay, which is valued at 20 lakhs of rupees.—*Financial News*, May 18.

In the House of Commons, on Thursday, the clerk at the table read the resolution adopted by the Committee on the Hyderabad Mining Concessions. It stated that applications had been received from the Nizam of Hyderabad, the Hyderabad-Deccan Mining Company, and a number of other persons concerned, asking to be represented before the Committee by counsel. The Committee, it is further stated, were of opinion that it would be advisable "to allow counsel to represent the said applicants for the purpose of assisting the Committee, subject to such restrictions as the Committee may from time to time direct." Sir Henry James moved: "That the Select Committee on the East India (Hyderabad-Deccan) Mining Company have leave to hear counsel to such extent as they think fit on the matter referred to them." Sir Edward Watkin inquired whether the words "to such extent as the Committee might think fit," were words of limitation which would in any way prevent the inquiry being of the most searching character. Sir Henry James replied that the object was to obtain the fullest inquiry, and the words alluded to had been introduced to give the Committee control over counsel. To prevent them from introducing irrelevant matter counsel did require to be controlled. The motion was agreed to. A telegram from Bombay states that the terms which Abdul Huk offers by way of reparation in connection with the mining concession include the refunding of £150,000, on the condition of the Nizam stopping the action against him, and continuing the concession. This, however, the Nizam declines to do, and will move the High Court to attach Abdul Huk's property at Bombay, which is valued at 20 lakhs of rupees.—*Mining Journal*, May 19.

The Parliamentary inquiry into the circumstances surrounding the promotion of the Deccan Company will examine witnesses on June 1 next. The first witness will be the secretary of the company, following upon whom will be Mr. W. C. Watson.—*Evening Post*, May 19.

The Deccan Mining Scandals.—Further developments in the so-called "mining scandal" are reported from Hyderabad. The Calcutta correspondent of the *Times* says: The Nizam's Government has served notice on Abdul Huk of its repudiation of the purchase of shares made by him last year, demanding repayment of £158,631 paid for 12,500 shares. This includes £18,750, the balance of the call due on 3,750 half-paid shares, drawn by Abdul Huk after his return to India. The repudiation was made on the ground that Abdul Huk had concealed from the Nizam's Government the fact that he was interested in the company, and that the shares actually purchased were his own property.—*St. James's Gazette*, May 21.

When Abdul Huk was in England in 1882 he was one of a party who went down to Trentham in a special car, at the invitation of the Duke of Sutherland. Among the party was George Sheppard Page, a gentleman well known in New York for his devotion to fish culture and practical jokes. Abdul Huk, in leaving the car, wished some assistance in carrying or putting on his cloak. He said to Page, "Take my cloak," in much the same manner that he would have ordered a servant. Page determined to take a little of the swagger and conceit out of the Indian swell, assumed that Abdul Huk had made him a present of the cloak, and thanked him most extravagantly and profusely for the splendid gift. Abdul Huk, in order to get back his cloak, was compelled to apologise and explain, much to the delight and amusement of the rest of the party.—*Star*, May 22.

The Hyderabad (Deccan) Company.—As many hundreds of people must be interested in the shares of this Company, we hasten to lay before our readers the following account of an interview which a representative of ours has recently had with a gentleman who knows every in and out of the whole matter. We are not at all deterred from this by the fact that much of the information accorded differs somewhat from that which was to hand a month or so ago, and which we animadverted upon more or less severely. The public will doubtless be able to judge for themselves whether our informant is well posted or not in the matter by his replies to our questions, and also as to whether his more favourable view of the matter is likely to turn out correct.

"How do you view this Hyderabad Deccan business, and what is to be the probable course of the shares?" asked our representative.

"Well, I think the public have jumped too hurriedly to a conclusion, and upon many points it will be found that the charges brought against the concessionnaires will be fairly answered. The only point where I myself own that there has been underhand practice indulged in, is the Sirdar selling his own shares to the Nizam; until this came out my opinion of his conduct was favourable, but this was a wrong thing to do, and there is no doubt that he will be disgraced for doing it, and deservedly so."

"But what about his having the shares given him in the first instance? Was not this a bribe?"

"Certainly not—that is just where public opinion has overstepped the mark. Sirdar Abdul Huk produced a letter from the late Regent of Hyderabad, who was acting for the Nizam during his minority, authorising him to make anything out of the business which he honestly could by helping Mr. Watson in the matter. Perhaps you are not aware that the mining right for ninety-nine years was offered to a good many people upon the condition that they took the railway, and refused before Mr. Watson took it up. Abdul Huk himself was commissioned to come over here to England to try and get some big London house to take over the railway. This, as you can see by a glance at the map, was cut straight through a wild tract of country to strike the nearest point of the Bombay and Madras line. Had a more circuitous route been taken, which would have tapped some towns and villages, all might have been well, but the line was not earning *one per cent.*, and yet the Nizam's Government had to pay away the guaranteed interest year after year. They got tired of this, and hence the Sirdar's mission. I believe the concession and the railway was offered to the Rothschilds, and also that Sir Evelyn Baring, who was then in India, recommended them to try Baring Brothers in London, but naturally they said, We do not want to burden ourselves with such a white elephant as a railway which will not yield 1 per cent. That which both Rothschilds and Barings refused, Mr. Watson's syndicate took up. They relieved the Nizam's Government of an incubus, and paid the money demanded. *For this* they received the concession, namely, a lease for 99 years of the Singareni Coalfield, and any other mines which they opened within five years."

"Then you think the concession will hold good?"

"Undoubtedly I do, although I have read every line which has been written about how the Nizam had been swindled; but it is my fixed belief that the concession will hold good, and that Abdul Huk's dealing *here* was fair and above board. The Sirdar was accused before of receiving a commission upon some matter, a railway scheme, I think, and he at once produced a letter from Sir Salar Jung showing that he had *obtained authority for what he had done.* He was at once exonerated, and will be again regarding the bringing about of the concession, as I say he can, or has produced an official letter, showing that he had done nothing underhand."

"But you own he behaved badly in the matter of selling his own shares."

"Yes, there he did, and as I say, his reputation will be blasted altogether; but I am merely arguing that *this* is a separate matter only affecting the Nizam personally, and one which cannot in any way annul the concession to Mr. Watson's syndicate."

"Is Mr. Watson to blame in the matter?"

"I cannot see that he is. Here, again, some journals appear to have run off with the idea that a big swindle has been perpetrated. The concessionnaires appear to me to have had a perfect right to ask what they liked for the concession. It is merely what vendors of gold mines have done hundreds of times. They estimated that the money derivable yearly from the Singareni Coal Field would more than meet interest upon a million sterling. They had taken over that which other people had refused. The Nizam's Government were quite as anxious to get rid of their railway and its guaranteed interest as the syndicate were to buy it. The syndicate may have got the best of the bargain, or they may not. It would be premature to say yet which has."

"What about the Parliamentary inquiry?"

"Well, I think some of the men chosen are not altogether unbiassed men, but still I believe they can only ratify the concession. I am not at all saying that there has not been some very dirty work done. I own it, I deplore it, I condemn it, and we trust that the Parliamentary enquiry will find out the real people to be shown up, but everything to do with the concession has been in legal order, and Parliament will have no grounds for cancelling the agreement."

"And about the Nizam's purchase of 12,000 shares?"

"Yes, that is where the word scandal will be applied, in my opinion. The Nizam ordered Messrs. Watson and syndicate to purchase this amount of shares for him at 12 during the month of June. Now, this could not have been done, as the attempt to buy such a quantity of Shares in the Stock Exchange would have run the price up to 15 or 16. The price *was* about 12, and the Sirdar quietly transferred the requisite amount of shares out of his own name and took the money. Had they honestly said 'We cannot buy the shares at 12, but Sirdar Abdul Huk offers all his at this price,' everything would have been straight enough, but this was not done. Hence the scandal."

"Then about the concession, you think that everything was as it should have been?"

"I cannot go quite so far as *that.* It does seem to me that some sharpish practice was indulged in. All I contend is, that this was strictly kept within the limits of the law, so that there is no chance of the actual concession being cancelled; and, moreover, I think that when this is given out the shares will recover quickly in price. It is quite evident that most people now are afraid that Parliament will annul the contract, and say that it was obtained fraudulently. This is the opinion I am told in the Stock Exchange. Do not for a moment set me down as a champion for the misdeeds of Sirdar Abdul Huk, all I can say is that his dealings were square enough—*legally*, until he sold the Nizam his own shares. I say that, in my opinion, he had a perfect right to those shares, and will, moreover, be able to substantiate that right. This, I take it, is all that affects the *Company*, and I should strongly counsel all my fellow shareholders to stand the brunt of the Parliamentary Commission before they sell out."

"What about the coalfield?"

"*That*, again, I feel sure enough about. Of course the working will take time, but already a contract *has* been entered into for the supply of 500 tons a week, to commence in June. This is something, although very much less than was promised."

"Then you are satisfied with the course of the concern?"

"Not at all. I am disgusted. All I say is, that things are not exactly as they are made out by influential papers, who would lead one to suppose, in fact say, that the whole concern is one gigantic swindle from beginning to end. *This* it is not. It was begun fairly enough, and might have been carried out fairly. Mr. Watson is, I believe, in London, and will doubtless answer all the questions put to him when the time comes. It is useless for him to say now, although he must be very much troubled in his mind over the whole matter. If he has acted dishonourably, I see little chance of its not being commented upon pretty severely. If he has acted fraudulently, I make no doubt he will be punished; but I think you will find that he has a better defence than the public know of or expect."

"Is the Sirdar a popular man in Hyderabad?"

"No. Extremely unpopular, which he has brought upon himself more or less by his *début* but of honesty. Now, all that will be changed, for those whom he has offended by refusing their bribes, small or great, will now leave no stone unturned until they have hounded him to ruin. Unfortunately, he had his price, and was far too eager to obtain cash by unwise means for the shares which he had received official sanction to accept, considering that he had given his time and his services to bring about the sale of the unprofitable railway. Much that has been said of his origin is perfectly true. He was formerly a policeman, but surely his having risen reflected all the more credit on him."

"What is your view of anyone buying shares to-day?"

"That they could do no harm provided they bought them from substantial people. If the present Parliamentary inquiry ratify and uphold the concession then the price must rise immediately, whereas in the possible case of their deciding it to be null and void, then I take it every bargain would have to be undone, and the money paid for the shares to-day would have to be returned. I am, of course, no legal authority, but this has been done before in a similar case, so that any buyer ought to be exceedingly careful from whom he makes his purchase. I know, as a fact, that some of the biggest men in the market are keeping a perfectly 'even' book in Hyderabad Deccans until some result is known; in fact, as I say, their view tends towards the belief that the 'whole affair is a swindle.'"

"What about Mr. Watson's connivance at Abdul's selling his own shares to the Nizam?"

"That is a poser, and a matter upon which I am no value as an authority. Of course, one might say that Mr. Watson received orders to buy this large amount of shares at the price of 12, and that it was not stipulated where or how the purchase was to be effected. Please understand that I am not satisfied with this defence at all, and trust that some better explanation may be forthcoming. One thing I will say. The detractors of the Deccan business have stated, I think, that no market existed for the shares prior to the Nizam's purchase. This anyone knows to be erroneous, for the shares stood at their *highest*, about 14, *before* the Nizam's purchase. No one could possibly have bought twelve thousand shares without raising the price; in fact, the order was impossible to execute, and so the purchase of the Sirdar's shares can be legally defended upon that score. But all this transaction I look upon as a low caste deal, and one which most men would be ashamed to be mixed up in. It will naturally cause hundreds of people to imagine that everything connected with the Company is dishonest, and years of good dividends from the coal will be required to eradicate this feeling from the public mind. For that reason, I believe, the price of the shares is unduly depressed; but I tell you plainly that lots of men, who know quite as much about all the negotiations as I do, say the shares will fall to thirty shillings, and that the capital should never have been more than £150,000. It's a nasty business altogether, but it is no good for people to attack everyone blindly and spitefully. The Parliamentary Commission will decide, and, *I* say, will not fail to ratify the concession."—*Barker's Trade and Finance*, May 23.

I hear that Abdul Huk, who was the chief person involved in what is known as the Hyderabad scandal, has "climbed down," as the Americans say, and has offered to accede in every way to the wishes of the Nizam, if the proceedings which are being carried on are dropped. Mr. Moreton Frewen has been mainly instrumental in unearthing this scandal. He was for some time secretary to Sir Salar Jung, and in that capacity became acquainted with the manner in which the Nizam had been taken in. Mr. Frewen has had a varied experience, from cattle ranching to Indian finance; and he is a shrewd man with great determination. Any abuse he may make up his mind to investigate runs a small chance of remaining concealed. Mr. Frewen is a brother-in-law of Lord Randolph Churchill's.

Talking of Indian matters reminds me that the Guicowar of Baroda, who is one of the most popular of the Eastern potentates, is about to make another visit to England. Brighton is looking forward to his going down there again, as the inhabitants of that fashionable watering-place have not forgotten the lavish way in which he spent his money there last autumn. I hear, though, that he intends to make London his headquarters, as he missed a good deal of the Jubilee festivities last year, and is anxious to see what a "London season" really means. It is not surprising that these Indian princes find London an agreeable sojourning place. They are universally feted and made much of, and great ladies divide their admiration between the priceless jewels and the handsome features of their dusky guests. Looked down upon in their own country, they are courted to an absurd extent over here. No wonder they like England.—*Western Daily Mercury*, Plymouth, May 23.

Mehdi Ali, the distinguished official who has been appointed by the Nizam to represent the State of Hyderabad at the coming Parliamentary inquiry into the alleged Deccan mining frauds, has arrived in Europe, and has been spending the Whitsuntide holidays in Paris with his friends. He is expected in London to-morrow. He is accompanied by an intelligent Parsee functionary of the State, Furdoonjee Jamsetjee, who has been for many years a member of the Cobden Club, and who is well known for his kindnesss to English visitors to India.—*Manchester Guardian*, May 24

THE HYDERABAD (DECCAN) COMPANY.—A correspondent asks us the very pertinent question, "Was Mr. Thomas Lynn Bristowe, M.P., who has been selected as one of the Parliamentary Committee to inquire into the Hyderabad Deccan Stock Exchange dealings, a partner in the firm of Bristowe Brothers referred to in the evidence of Mr. Lawrence Baker at page 197 in the Blue Book of the minutes of evidence before the Commission on the London Stock Exchange?" We answer, "Yes; Mr. Thomas Lynn Bristowe, M.P., is a partner in the firm of Bristowe Brothers. He is also the identical person referred to in Mr. Lawrence Baker's evidence (page 197) as a partner in the Costa Rica Syndicate, on the committee for the quotation of which loan he sat and voted in the interest of himself, his firm, and all his co-partners, of whom Mr. Lawrence Baker was one; and as our correspondent suggests, they 'saw their way to grant that quotation.'" Mr. Lawrence Baker, when before the Royal Commission, had resigned his membership of the Committee of the Stock Exchange, and was unwillingly compelled to defend the honour of himself and sturdy partner from a decision of his own committee, which he considered unjust, and upon which his Costa Rica partner, Bristowe, had sat and voted, when Messrs. Baker and Sturdy were arraigned before and punished by the only tribunal they recognise or fear. By a singular coincidence, both Mr. Baker and Mr. Bristowe find themselves members of another "House," and more singular still Mr. Bristowe has now been selected to sit upon a Parliamentary Committee to judge of the acts of the Hyderabad Deccan party, some prominent members of which were actually Mr. Bristowe's co-partners in the Costa Rica deal. Mr. Bristowe then gave himself and his co-partners the benefit of his vote; will he be able to help them again on his present committee? Our correspondent says:—"The quality of mercy is not strained; it droppeth as the gentle dew from heaven." On referring to the Blue Book ("Mr. Baker's evidence, 6th December, 1887, page 197") we find that the Costa Rica Syndicate, which both Mr. Baker and Mr. Bristowe so substantially supported by their vote in committee, was composed of Messrs. Erlanger and Co., Messrs. Baker and Sturdy (£40,000 stock), Mr. William Morris, Mr. Joseph Tucker, Mr. T. Morris, Mr. Norman Morris (since deceased), Messrs. Cawston and Co., Messrs. Bristowe Brothers, Messrs. Hilder and Moens, Messrs. Hichens and Harrison, Messrs. Ionides and Barker, Louis Cohen, Messrs. Murietta and Co., and Mr. F. Vilmet (forty-one persons in all guaranteed the placing of £800,000 stock). Shall we add that Messrs. Baker and Bristowe, as members of the Syndicate, and also as members of the Committee of the Stock Exchange, not only guaranteed the placing of £800,000 stock on a too confiding and subsequently defrauded public, but also guaranteed that a quotation should be granted by the committee of the Stock Exchange, and Mr. Bristowe now sits in judgment upon the Parliamentary Committee selected to inquire into the acts of the Hyderabad Deccan offenders, some of the most prominent of whom were his fellow-workers in the Costa Rica business? Can Mr. Bristowe judge these men fairly without fear or favour, and if he can, will he and dare he do so? How will Mr. William Morris like to be judged by his late co-partner, and do the other members of the Commission know the past or present relations of Mr. William Morris and Mr. Thomas Lynn Bristowe?—*Financial Times*, May 26.

THE HYDERABAD DECCAN COMPANY.—To the Editor of the *Financial Times*.—Sir,—Can you inform me if Mr. Thomas Lynn Bristowe, M.P., who has been selected as one of the Parliamentary Committee to inquire into the dealings on the Stock Exchange, was at any time a partner of, or connected with, the firm of Bristowe Brothers, referred to in the evidence of Mr. Lawrence Baker at page 197 in the Blue Book of the minutes of evidence before the Commission on the London Stock Exchange? Mr. Lawrence Baker there admitted he was a member of the Stock Exchange Committee, and, at the same time, in conjunction with Bristowe Brothers, member of a syndicate for *underwriting* a Costa Rica Loan. It was subsequently proved by the production of the minute book of the Stock Exchange Committee that Mr. Lawrence Baker and one of the partners of Bristowe Brothers sat on the Committee and voted on the question of settlement and quotation for the Costa Rica loan referred to. If I am correct in my surmise it is certain that both Mr. Bristowe and Mr. Baker sat on the committee to decide a quotation question, in which they were personally and financially interested, and that they saw their way to grant that quotation. Mr. Bristowe is now, in his Parliamentary capacity, sitting upon a commission to judge the Hyderabad Deccan delinquents, some of whom were formerly his partners in the Costa Rica Syndicate. "The quality of mercy is not strained."—Yours obediently,—A Witness before the Royal Commission.—*Financial Times*, May 26.

The Parliamentary inquiry into the Deccan scandal will commence examining witnesses on June 1st. The secretary of the company and Mr. W. C. Watson are to be the first witnesses called. I expect a good deal of excitement in the course of the inquiry.—*Society Herald*, May 28.

The officials of the India Office have been collecting documents to lay before the House of Commons Committee of Inquiry into the Hyderabad-Deccan contract. I have reasons to believe that extraordinary evidence will be forthcoming, before the committee, as to the manner in which the capital intended to work the contract was appropriated.—*Morning News*, May 28.

When the work of the session is resumed on Thursday a number of new commissions and committees will get to work. The committee appointed to inquire into the circumstances of the Deccan concession are likely to make some sensational discoveries. A representative of the Nizam, who has just arrived in this country to watch the progress of the inquiry, has the fullest power to act at his own discretion in the matter. He may either annul the concession, modify it, or make a new one.—*Manchester Courier*, May 29.

Abdul Huk, caught with his hand in the till of the State of Hyderabad, has offered to make restitution. His offer has been accepted; but the Nizam makes no promises as to his future action in the matter. He may still bring his faithless servant to account in the courts; he may still proceed against his confederates. So far the net result of the exposures in *The Financial News* of the Hyderabad-Deccan scandal is that the State is £151,000 the richer, and that Abdul Huk is minus just that amount of plunder.—*Financial News*, May 30.

Abdul Huk has abandoned all defence, and has arranged to pay the full value of the Nizam of Hyderabad's shares, seven lakhs (seventy thousand pounds), in cash, and the balance by mortgage of his Bombay properties. The Nizam is also free to take further action against Abdul Huk, and may also cancel the concession, though that is not probable.—*Financial News*, May 30.

The Deccan Company.—Simla, May 29.—An agreement has been signed by which Abdul Huk returns £151,631 to the Hyderabad Government in respect of the mining shares sold to the Nizam last year. Abdul Huk pays 11 lakhs in cash, and assigns three properties in Bombay as a security for the balance. He is to pay 5 per cent. interest up to the date of the signing of the agreement and 6 per cent afterwards, and he gets back his 12,500 shares. This arrangement does not affect the future action of Abdul Huk personally or as regards the concession.—*Times*, May 30.

The feeling on the Stock Exchange yesterday was much improved, mainly by a second consideration of M. Tisza's speech. The matter is no longer expected to lead to the least serious results. At the same time a turn came in the much down-trodden and, of late, neglected American department, New York no longer pressing sales, but showing a disposition to cover its "shorts" by purchasing stock which operators on that side had sold in advance. News also arrived that something like a satisfactory end to the Hyderabad Deccan Mining Concessions scandal was in view, and Guinness's Brewery Stock has risen to the highest point on record. It is rather unusual to find the Stock Exchange at all cheerful on the eve of the Derby Day, a period when a good deal of the speculative nature which almost perennially impels the British public into some sort of gambling is let loose on Epsom Downs, and leaves the vicinity of Capel Court. It is proverbially proper on the Stock Exchange to "buy before the Derby and sell before Goodwood," these two races marking the beginning and the close of the fullest period of the London season. On the Stock Exchange, as on the racecourse, English people have ceased to take their pleasures sadly, whatever may be the after-effect of excessive gambling.—*Daily News*, May 30.

That interesting Oriental, Abdul Huk, has come to the conclusion that it will be best for him not to defend his connection with the Hyderabad Company, and has offered to disgorge the proceeds of the venture. This is satisfactory news, and it will lighten the labours of the committee which is to meet on Friday to inquire into the circumstances attending the formation of the Company. But what do the *Standard* and the other London newspapers which defended Abdul Huk when the matter was first brought to light think of the surrender? They no doubt received their information from what they considered reliable sources, but they were misled. There is no place in the world where it is more difficult to discover the truth than Hyderabad. The place is a hot-bed of intrigue, and when important issues are at stake no effort is spared to advance the cause of a certain faction. Agents are despatched hither and thither in hot haste, and the controversy which may have cropped up is directed with a skill that would not discredit a caucus wire-puller. All this is well understood in India; but in England people are less acquainted with the ways of the Hyderabadis, and are apt to bestow confidence where confidence is not deserved. Hence the blunder of our London contemporaries in defending what was indefensible.—*Yorkshire Post*, May 30.

City Topics.—Now that Abdul Huk has refunded to the Nizam's Government the plunder he made out of the sale of his shares thereto, the necessity of the Royal Commission pursuing the inquiry into the subject appears somewhat limited. In any case there is no danger of what is hinted at in the *Standard* of yesterday, as to the concession held by the Deccan Company, Limited, being cancelled.—*Evening Post*, May 30.

The Hyderabad Deccan Scandal.—(Special despatch to the *Financial News*.)—Simla, May 29.—Abdul Huk has agreed to return to the Nizam of Hyderabad £151,000, being the price he received from his Highness for his shares in the Hyderabad-Deccan Company. Abdul Huk pays seven lakhs of of rupees at once, and gives a mortgage on his property in Bombay to secure the payment of the balance, with interest at the rate of 6 per cent. This arrangement does not in any way prejudice any future action against Huk or in respect to the Deccan Company's concession.—*Financial News*, May 31.

It is difficult, however, to cast the horoscope of the Stock Markets, and under present conditions we do not care to advise our readers to do anything for a week or two. We are not pessimistic, but we think that there will not be a very big rise this side of the autumn. Miscellaneous securities are steady, and we are pleased to see that those who did not get out of their Hyderabad Deccans have now an opportunity of selling out at a higher price. We do not advise the sale of Deccans, however, as we hear news favourable to the shareholders. The result of the Parliamentary inquiry will soon reveal much which is at present dark, and we advise Hyderabad Deccan shareholders to wait for the explanations which are sure to be elicited. The Mining Market is "off colour," to use a sporting term. The copper "boom" seems on the break, and we should not be surprised to see Tintos much lower before long. When the fall does come, it will be sharp and decisive. After having been down as low as 17¾, they have recovered to 18⅛. Mysores and De Beers and most others, too, are flat, and look like being flatter still.—*Piccadilly*, May 31.

The Select Committee appointed to inquire into the circumstances attending the floating of the Hyderabad (Deccan) Mining Company will meet to-day, under the presidency of Sir Henry James, and will open the investigation. The first witnesses called will be the officials connected with the London office of the company.—*Daily News*, June 1.

Hyderabad Deccan Mining Scandal.—Parliamentary Inquiry.—The Select Committee of the House of Commons appointed to inquire into the conditions under which the East India Hyderabad Deccan Mining Company was floated met to-day for the first time in Committee Room 17, for the reception of evidence.

Sir H. James, M.P., presided, the other members of the Committee present being Mr. Labouchere, Mr. Bristowe, Mr. M'Lagan, Mr. Slagg, Sir R. Temple, and the Solicitor General for Scotland.

The terms of the reference were to inquire into the circumstances attending the promotion of the company, and the subsequent operations on the Stock Exchange.

Sir H. Davey, Q.C., Mr. Trevor White, and Mr. J. D. Inverarity represented Sirdar Diler Jung; Mr. Pember, Q.C., and Mr. Lewis Coward appeared for the Hyderabad Mining Company; and Mr. Littler, Q.C., represented Mr. Watson.

The Committee met at twelve o'clock, when, at the request of the Chairman, the room was cleared.

Upon re-admission to the room,

Sir H. James said it might be convenient that he should state that the evidence would be taken upon oath. The Committee had come to a conclusion with regard to the hearing of counsel. The Committee proposed to retain the inquiry entirely in their own hands, but while so doing would accept the assistance of counsel when necessary. Thus all witnesses would be examined by the Committee, but in the case of any evidence affecting anyone being given, the person affected would be at liberty to apply to the Committee to cross-examine.

The inquiry then proceeded.

Mr. Levien, Secretary to the Stock Exchange, was the first witness called. Having been sworn, the Witness, in answer to Mr. Labouchere, said that he knew nothing of the company except what he had heard and read in the newspapers, and what was common gossip about it. The rules and regulations of the Stock Exchange had been entirely disregarded in the respect that no application had been made either for a settlement or official quotation, and none of the conditions and rules with regard to special settlement or quotation had been obeyed.—Witness here read the rules of the Stock Exchange with regard to this.

Continuing his evidence, he said that Rules 131 and 132 of the Stock Exchange, which he also read, had been disregarded.

Mr. Pember, Q.C., said he should like to put a question to the Witness.

The Chairman: Perhaps you will kindly state for whom you appear.

Mr. Pember: The Company. (To Witness): Is it not a common practice on the Stock Exchange for members to deal in shares for which no application had been made or settlement?

Witness: Yes.

Mr. Pember: As a matter of fact, there is no rule to prevent them from so doing?

Witness: No.

Mr. Pember: So that when you said that the rules of the Stock Exchange had been entirely disregarded, these rules did not apply to this company until they chose to apply for a settlement?

Witness: No.

The Chairman: What is the time that generally elapses between the issuing of a prospectus of a company and asking for a settlement?

Witness: As a rule application for a settlement follows very promptly. I have known it to be applied for within a week.

Further questioned by the Chairman, Witness said that if no settlement was asked for there was nothing to prevent brokers dealing with the shares, but those dealings would not be under the control of the Stock Exchange.

Mr. Hall, the Secretary of the Hyderabad Deccan Mining Company was next called and sworn. In reply to Mr. Labouchere, he stated that he had held his position as secretary since October, 1887. The company was registered in July, 1886. Mr. Milne was his predecessor in the office. The remuneration to the directors of the company was about £1,500 a year. The chairman had the same sum, and the managing directors did not get any more. The company had in cash now about £85,000. Nothing was paid for the promotion of the company by the company.

Mr. Labouchere: Who paid for the printing of the shares and the articles of association?

Witness: I don't know exactly, but I believe the company did.

Further questioned, Witness said he could not give the total of what the company paid for the cost of bringing out the company.

Witness was then questioned as to the expenses at the company's mines, and gave particulars of money spent in machinery, &c. The latest report from the coal mines was that about 150 tons of stuff a week had been raised. That had been the average since the commencement of this year.

Questioned as to the latest report about the diamonds, Witness stated that there had been a difficulty in securing labour.

Mr. Labouchere: What particular reason had the company for suppesing that diamonds would be found in the company's mines?

Witness: I cannot say.

Questioned with reference to the shares and transfers, Witness said that he did not know anything whatever about the dealings with these, nor was he acquainted with a list of transactions which Mr. Labouchere had read to him, from which it seemed that in October, 1886, Mr. Watson was acquiring several lots of shares, and was at the same time selling.

Witness was then questioned with reference to the agreement entered into by which 85,000 shares of £10 each were transferred to Mr. Watson and Mr. Stewart, the concessionnaires, and stated that that agreement was approved by three gentlemen—Batten, Hemmerdy, and Milne—holding one share each.

Witness, in reply to further questions, stated that he had no record of how those three gentlemen, acting directors, with £1 shares each, arrived at the estimate value of the concession for which they agreed to give 85,000 shares. He had searched, but failed to find any trace of the manner in which they arrived at the value of the mines.

The Chairman here read the agreement, which set forth that the concessionnaires should assign and transfer to the company certain rights conceded to them in the kingdom of the Nizam.

Asked whether any transfer of such rights had been made, Witness replied that there had been a transfer of such rights. Such transfer was made by document, which he handed in to the Committee. He could not recollect how many of the 85,000 shares had been re-transferred to the public. Upwards of £40,000 had been sent over to Hyderabad for the purpose of working the mines. There had been, he said, so far as he knew, no return from the mines, and no profit. He had not received any communication from the Nizam's Government as to what had become of the 85,000 shares. He was not aware that any notification of the handing over of 85,000 shares was sent to the Nizam or the Indian Government.

In answer to Mr. Slagg, Witness said although there had been no return of profits from Hyderabad some gold had been sold. The proceeds thereof had, however, been spent in India.

In answer to a question by Sir R. Temple, Witness said that the 85,000 shares stated in the agreement to be fully paid up, had nothing paid on them. They were taken "as paid up," but as a matter of fact nothing was paid on them.

Witness, replying to the Chairman, described the locality of the mines, and stated that an expert, Mr. Levinsky, was now in Hyderabad further testing the ground.

In reply to questions put by Mr. Pember, Q.C., Witness stated that the country that required prospecting was about 550 square miles in extent. The company had sent out machinery for diamonds to the value of £15,000 or £16,000. The machinery was shipped in November and December of last year. According to the last report the machinery was not at work. The railway to the coal mine was opened on the 1st of January of the present year. The company were sinking shafts and sending out new machinery. Until the railway to the mine was opened it was practically impossible for them to get the machinery to the mines at all. Their operations have been checked by the outbreak of cholera.

Mr. Pember, Q.C.: At what date did Lord Lawrence join the Board?

Witness: In July, 1887.

Replying to further questions by Mr. Pember, Q.C., Witness said he could not give the Committee the total number of shareholders, but he thought the learned Counsel was correct in suggesting that they numbered about 730. A balance-sheet was sent to the Nizam's Government.

By Sir R. Temple: I don't know whether any diamonds or any other precious stones were found at Deccan.

By a Counsel: I believe no prospectus was issued before or after the shares were allotted.

The Witness was frequently asked to raise his voice, but he continued to speak in such a low tone that the remainder of his evidence was inaudible.

Mr. Batten, chairman of the Hyderabad Deccan Mining Company was next examined by Mr. Labouchere as to the financing of the Nizam's State Railway by Mr. Watson, to whom £100,000 was given to cover expenses prior to the railway going to allotment. With regard to the coal fields, they had received excellent reports. Diamonds, however, had not been discovered.

Mr. Labouchere: Do you consider, as chairman of the company, that £60,000 would be sufficent to open up a gold field and a diamond field?

Witness: Yes, quite sufficient to prove its value.

In reply to the Chairman, Witness said he was Chairman of the Hyderabad Company. He was introduced to the company by Messrs. Watson and Stewart. He had no hesitation in saying that with reference to the Deccan company they were doing their best to develop the mining property, and had received excellent reports from the officials abroad. He was aware that the company was to be started long before it really was.

The Chairman: You knew that these 85,000 shares would reach the public?

Witness: I thought they would probably reach the public.

The Chairman: Who was to look after the interests of the public?

Witness: I supposed that the public would look after their own interests.

The Chairman: I see that you are a member of the Bar?

Witness: I am, but I do not practise.

The Chairman: When you became chairman of the company did you consider that you owed any duty towards those who were intended to be shareholders hereafter?

Witness: I did not consider that I owed any duty to anybody except to my company.

The Chairman: So you were careless of the interest of those whom you intended to become shareholders?

Witness: I did not regard myself as the protector of the public.

The Chairman: Then you, as chairman of the company, were careless whether they had valuable or worthless shares in their possession?

Witness: I considered the property well worth a million.

The Chairman: Ah, that is not what I asked. I see that the subscribers to the articles of association were Watson, Winter, Stewart, and Peace. Winter was Watson's solicitor. The only independent person is Pearce. Who is Pearce?

Witness: Pearce is Watson's clerk.

The Chairman: At that time the subscribers held one share each?

Witness: Yes; nominally for the formation of the company.

The Chairman: They were actually concessionnaires anxious to do the best they could for themselves?

Witness: Yes.

Referring to the agreement of the 16th of August, the Chairman asked who checked it, and the Witness replied that the lawyers of the company checked it.

What steps did you take to see if they were giving value for it?—They were giving concessions.

What else?—Nothing else.

How did you come to the conclusion that the value was £850,000?—There were 81,000 square miles of country. The company had reports from engineers as to the value of the coal.

Did they make an estimate of money value?—They made an estimate of the quantity of coal. To qualify as a director I took a hundred £10 shares. When they were transferred Mr. Watson paid the money.

If the shares were par value he was giving you £500. Why should he do that?—I don't know.

What premium did the shares reach?—I believe they went up to 84. I have never sold a share or received one farthing of profit, except my director's fees, more than which I have invested in shares.

By Mr. Bristow: There never was a prospectus issued of this company. A private circular was drawn up by Mr. Watson, and shown to a few persons.

Would you consider that a fraudulent circular?—No, certainly not.

Do you know who issued it?—Well, Mr. Watson showed it to me. I believe it was drawn up by Mr. Watson for the use of his friends.

By Mr. Littler, Q.C.: I have never received a letter from a single shareholder complaining that he was not aware of what he was doing.

By Mr. Pember: There have never been any relations between the company and the public. Mr. Watson paid the expenses of getting up the company.

At this stage the Committee adjourned till Tuesday next, at twelve o'clock. —*Standard*, June 1.

The Deccan Mining Scandal.—Parliamentary Inquiry this Day—Disregard of Stock Exchange Rules.—The Select Committee of the House of Commons, appointed to enquire into matters relating to the Hyderabad Deccan Mining Company, met in Committee-room No. 17, at the Houses of Parliament, at noon to-day. The Committee consists of Sir Henry James (chairman), Mr. Bristowe, Mr. Labouchere, Mr. McLagan, Mr. Slagg, the Solicitor-General for Scotland, and Sir Richard Temple.

Sir Horace Davey, Q.C., Mr. T. D. Inverarity, of the Bombay Bar, and Mr. Trevor White appeared for Sirdar Diler Jung. Mr. Pember, Q.C., appeared for the company.

The room was cleared for some time. When the doors were opened, the Chairman said the Committee had come to a resolution with regard to the hearing of counsel. The Committee proposed to retain the inquiry entirely in their own hands, but while so doing would accept the assistance of counsel when necessary. Thus all witnesses would be examined by the Committee, but in the case of any evidence affecting anyone being given, the person affected was at liberty to apply to the Committee to be allowed to cross-examine.

Mr. Levien, secretary to the Stock Exchange, was the first witness called. Examined by Mr. Labouchere, he said he knew nothing of the company except what he had read in the papers and common gossip about it. The rules and regulations of the Stock Exchange had been entirely disregarded in the respect that no application had been made either for a settlement or official quotation, and none of the conditions of the rules with regard to special settlement of quotation had been obeyed. Rules 131 and 132, which he read, had been broken. In regard to these rules any dealings done on the Stock Exchange had been done in violation of the rules. No action had been taken; no action ever was taken unless application was made on the ground of fraud.

Cross-examined by Mr. Pember, witness said it was a common practice on the Stock Exchange to deal in shares for which no special quotation had been made. There was no rule to prevent it. There was no rule to prevent members of the Stock Exchange entering into any contract. When he said the shares were dealt in in disregard to the rules, the rules did not apply to this company until it asked for a settlement.

Mr. Hall, the secretary to the Deccan Mining Company, was the next witness.—*Evening Post*, June 1.

There was the other day a very interesting party at Pope's Villa, Twickenham, an historic house, now the country residence of Mr. Labouchere. The principal guest was the Financial Secretary and Chancellor of the Exchequer of the Nizam of Hyderabad, who has come over here to give evidence before the Select Committee on the Deccan mining scandal. This emissary of an Indian potentate is profoundly impressed with the dignity and autocracy of the Secretary of State for India, the Under Secretary, the Viceroy, and all the principal officials who rule India. I hear that he left Pope's Villa with quite new and more wholesome views of the situation. He learned that the Secretary of State for India, the Viceroy, and all the rest of these dignitaries are subordinate to the House of Commons as represented by a Select Committee. Members of such a Committee are, the dusky emissary learned, even as the Brahmins compared with natives—of no caste. If the India Office and the Viceroy are to be feared, much more is a Select Committee of the House of Commons, and the best thing for any one concerned to do is to make a clean breast of all he knows. The Nizam's agent will presently appear before the Committee to give evidence, and will make an interesting figure. He does not speak English, and is accompanied by an interpreter, who, it is hoped, translated with due graphicness the lessons conveyed.—*Liverpool Post*, June 1.

There is no truth in the rumour mentioned by an Anglo-Indian paper that Mr. Cordery, the late British resident at the Court of the Nizam, has been suspended from office in connection with the Hyderabad scandals. I understand that there is a disposition to assail Sir John Gorst for having received a heavy fee—I believe £7,000—for visiting India to advise the Peishcar a few years ago. But in justice to Sir John it should be stated that when he accepted a commission from the Hyderabad functionary to go out to India he was not in office—indeed, the Conservative party were not at the time in power. There is perhaps this to be said, that although Sir John Gorst was so munificently recompensed for his journey, he was not called upon to do a stroke of work, as the treaty in connection with which his services were retained never got beyond the stage of talk. With reference to the Deccan mining transaction, I may mention that the deputation from the Nizam's Government—Nawab Mahdi Ali and Furdonjee Jamsetjee—arrived in London from Paris on Friday, and have since been busily engaged in preparing for the Parliamentary inquiry which commences to-morrow. They have taken up their quarters at the Alexandra Hotel, where the notorious Abdul Huk lived *en Prince* last summer and entertained half the big people of London. It is not expected that the Special Committee will sit more than twice a week.—*Manchester Guardian*, June 1.

The Hyderabad Scandal.—The Parliamentary Committee appointed to inquire into the circumstances attending the formation and promotion of the Hyderabad Deccan Mining Company, Limited, the circumstances under which the concession was obtained, and the subsequent operations by parties interested on the London Stock Exchange, met in the House of Commons yesterday, Sir Henry James presiding. Mr. Labouchere was among the members present. The Committee allow the Nizam of Hyderabad, the Hyderabad Deccan Company, the Sirdar Diler Jung, Mr. William Clarence Watson, Mr. Henry Parkinson Sharp, and Mr. James Graham Stewart to appear by counsel. The most intense interest in the proceedings was manifested, the room and corridors being crowded, extra accommodation having to be improvised for the convenience of counsel, of whom over a dozen appear, the decorous dulness of an ordinary inquiry before a select committee being quite absent. Native witnesses are expected to be examined. The Chairman intimated that the committee had determined to keep the conduct of the case in their own hands. The witnesses would be examined by members of the committee, and if the evidence should affect any parties represented by counsel, they would be permitted to cross-examine. If it was desired that other witnesses should be called, application must be made. The extent to which counsel should be permitted to address the committee would be determined at a later stage. Copies of the evidence would be supplied to parties willing to pay for the same. Mr. Levien, Secretary to the Stock Exchange, stated that no application for a settlement was ever made by this company. He understood that it consisted of £150,000 public shares and £850,000 concessionary shares. Until special settlement had been granted for the public shares a settlement would not be granted for the concessionary shares. The rules and regulations of the Stock Exchange had been entirely disregarded by this company. No application had been made either for a settlement or quotation. There were often dealings in shares before a settlement was granted, but in the majority of substantial companies settlement was asked for, and as a rule within a fortnight or a month. If no settlement was asked for, there was nothing to prevent brokers dealing quite irrespective of a settlement by the Stock Exchange. The witness was cross-examined by Mr. Littler, Q.C., on behalf of the company, by Mr. Pember, Q.C., and other counsel. Mr. Hall, secretary of the Hyderabad Deccan Company, said he became secretary on the 10th October, 1887. His predecessor was Mr. Milne; the first directors were Mr. Batten, Mr. Hemmerdy, and Mr. Milne. They were elected by the first shareholders, who were Mr. John Stewart, Mr. H. P. Sharpe, Mr. W. C. Watson, Mr. Winter, Mr. Batten, Mr. Hemmerdy, Mr. Milne, and Mr. Pearce. There was an agreement to pay the concessionnaires £850,000 in fully paid-up shares. The present directors were Mr. Batten, Mr. Watson, Mr. McColvin, Lord Lawrence, and Mr. Sharpe. Mr. Hemmerdy, Mr. Pearce, and Mr. Milne had resigned. Mr. Winter was elected on the 19th August, 1886, Mr. Sharpe in November 1886, Lord Lawrence in July 1887. The remuneration of the directors was £300 a year. The first call of £75,000 was paid at once, and the second call of £75,000 on the 1st November, 1887. The company had at present in cash £85,000. Nothing was paid for promoting the company; the concessionnaires paid everything. About £25,000 had been spent in machinery, and about £13,000 or £14,000 in dynamite machines; £5,200 in rent and salaries at the London office. There was £3,200 in the agent's hands, and other sums with other agents. They had been raising from 150 to 180 tons of coal a week. They had not been working the diamond mines owing to cholera. They were in Golconda. They had not been worked for 200 years. The company knew nothing of the flowery description of the Golconda mines in the first prospectus. He did not know anything about Mr. Watson buying and selling shares about the same days.

By the Chairman: The first directors had only one share each. They were Messrs. Batten, Hemmerdy, and Milne. They agreed at their first meeting that £850,000 in shares be paid to Messrs. Watson and Stewart in August, 1886. He did not know how they satisfied themselves of the value of £850,000. Mr. Batten and Mr. Hemmerdy resigned almost immediately afterwards, and Messrs. Watson and Stewart were appointed additional directors. Not a penny of the £850,000 ever reached the coffers of the company. More than £40,000 had been sent over to Hyderabad for working the mine. The £150,000 shares had all been paid up. There had been no profitable working of the mine. They had had no representations from the Nizam's Government as to what had become of 85,000 shares.

By Sir Richard Temple: He did not know that any exploiting had been made since February 18, 1887, when Mr. Lewinski reported that he could not speak positively that he could find diamonds in payable quantities, but he had confidence in the mines, though he did not like to be too sanguine.

By Mr. Pember: Lord Lawrence joined the board in July, 1887. On the 14th June in that year it was reported to the board that the Government of the Nizam had purchased 12,500 shares, and the board agreed that the Government should have two representatives on the board of directors, and subsequently the Sirdar and Lord Lawrence were appointed on condition that they should resign if the Government ceased to hold 12,500 shares. The company was now busy prospecting for gold, but it had been checked by the outbreak of cholera. They were still sinking shafts in the coal mine, so that the present output was no guide to what would be the ultimate output. Until the railway was made they could not get the machinery there at all. There were now about 730 shareholders.

Mr. Batten gave evidence as to the construction of the railway to the mines, and said its capital was £2,000,000 in shares and £2,500,000 in debentures. The Nizam was to receive £350,000. He did actually get £100,000 in cash, and £241,000 in debentures. There was a guarantee by the Nizam of 5 per cent. on the shares, and 4 per cent. on the debentures for 20 years. He did not think the railway ever earned more than £15,000. The Nizam had therefore to pay £40,000 a year. Subsequently he had to pay £100,000 a year, less the earnings of the company.

Mr. Labouchere: And this was such a bargain for the Nizam that he, out of absolute gratitude, gave Mr. Watson the concession for the Deccan mines.

Examination continued: He subscribed for 100 £5 shares. Mr. Watson relieved him of them, gave him the £500 back, and then transferred to him 100 of his fully paid-up shares to qualify him as a director. He had not paid for them, but he would have to pay for them when the company began to pay a dividend, or to give them up.

By the Chairman: He assented to the payment of the £850,000 in paid-up shares. He had never received a halfpenny from the company except his director's fees, which he had invested in shares. He did not, as chairman, take any steps for the protection of the public who subscribed. They would know the terms of the purchase. The concessionnaires would have been losers if the the thing had proved a failure. No doubt £850,000 of the million capital would go into the pockets of the concessionnaires if they were able to sell their shares, but they had deposited £150,000.

By Mr. Slagg: The prospectus was not issued by the company, but by Mr. Watson for the information of his friends, and was never sent out to the public.

Examined by Mr. Littler and Mr. Pember, Mr. Batten gave particulars of the working of the railway, and stated that its prospects were in the highest degree satisfactory.

The committee adjourned at 4 o'clock until Tuesday next at 12 o'clock.—*Globe*, June 2.

The Hyderabad (Deccan) Company.—The Select Committee of the House of Commons appointed to inquire into the circumstances attending the formation and promotion of the Hyderabad (Deccan) Mining Company, Limited, the circumstances in which the concession was obtained, and the subsequent dealings in the shares on the London Stock Exchange, met yesterday at the House of Commons, Sir Henry James presiding.

Mr. Pember, Q.C., and Mr. Lewis Coward appeared for the Hyderabad (Deccan) Mining Company; Mr. Littler, Q.C., and Mr. Cripps for Mr. William Clarence Watson; Mr. Reginald Brown for Mr. James Graham Stewart; Mr. Myburgh, Q.C., for Mr. H. Parkinson Sharp; Sir Horace Davey, Q.C., Mr. Inverarity, of the Bombay Bar, and Mr. Trevor White appeared for Abdul Huk, the Sirdar Diler Jung; and Mr. J. D. Mayne, Mr. Eardley Norton, and the Hon. A Lyttelton appeared for the Nizam of Hyderabad.

The Chairman said that, in accordance with the resolution of the House of Commons, the evidence of the witnesses would be taken upon oath, and the Committee would accept the assistance of counsel when necessary. The witnesses would be examined by the members of the Committee, and if any of the evidence affected any of the parties represented by counsel, application could be made to put questions to the witnesses.

Mr. Francis Levien, the secretary of the Stock Exchange, was the first witness examined by Mr. Labouchere. He said dealings in connexion with the concern had taken place not in violation, but in disregard of the rules of the Stock Exchange.

Mr. L. Hall, secretary of the Hyderabad Company, said it was registered in August, 1886. The first directors were Messrs. Batten, Hemmerdy, and Milne. The capital of the company was £1,000,000, 85,000 fully-paid shares of £10 each being paid for the concession. The remuneration of the directors was £300 per annum each. The company had now in cash about £83,000. About £40,000 worth of machinery had been sent out. The London office had spent about £5,400 in salaries, &c. A private memorandum was produced which set forth the objects of the company.

The agreement to give 85,000 fully-paid shares for the concession was approved by three gentlemen holding one share each?—Yes.

Was any inquiry made by anyone as to £850,000 being a fair price to pay for the concession?—Witness did not know. Messrs. Watson and Stewart were the concessionnaires. He undertook to hand in to the Committee a statement of how many of the 85,000 shares had been re-transferred to the general public, showing the prices paid.

How much money has been sent to Hyderabad for working the mines? I think you said £40,000?—More than that altogether.

Have there been any returns from Hyderabad; any profitable working? —No.

Has there been any communication on the part of the directors of the company and the Nizam's Government as to what has become of the 85,000 shares?—No.

Mr. Bristowe asked to be shown a copy of any notification about the 85,000 shares that had been sent to the Nizam's Government.—Witness said no notice had been given.

Sir Richard Temple pressed the Witness as to whether the expert who reported had seen a single diamond. The Witness.—I do not think so. I was not secretary at the time.

At the date of the report had the ground been thoroughly tested, or partially, or not at all?—They are on the spot now.

Who?—Mr. Levinski, the expert who drew up the report.

Mr. Labouchere: Have any of the shares for £850,000 been converted into shares to bearer?—£21,250.

In whose names were they when they were converted?—Mr. Winter.

Mr. Littler, Q.C., asked to reserve his examination of the witness.

Mr. Pember: Were all the shareholders aware, as a matter of fact, of the contents of the agreement of 1886?—Yes.

There was no need to put the agreement before a meeting of shareholders, because all the shareholders were parties to the agreement?—That is so.

Sir Henry James intimated that the Committee understood that point.

Mr. Pember drew attention to an extract from the proceedings of the Nizam's Government, Home Department, Mines, No. 165, dated Hyderabad, the 9th of March, 1887, which, he said, contained an admission that the notification had been received.

Sir Henry James said that the Committee had it, and drew attention to the fact of there being a provision in the agreement of the 16th of August for the Nizam's Government to be notified.

At what date did Lord Lawrence join the Board?—July, 1887. At a meeting on the 14th of June, 1887, a resolution was passed by the company that it was desirable for two nominees of the Nizam's Government to be on the Board, and ultimately Lord Lawrence and Abdul Huk, the Sirdar Diler Jung, joined. The Sirdar is no longer the representative of the Nizam's Government on the Board. Futteh Newaz Jung, the Chief Justice of Hyderabad, now is, and has been appointed since this inquiry was instituted. Continuing, the witness said that the machinery and shafts at the mine were still in course of construction. There were now 730 shareholders in the company, and he would give the Committee details of the considerations paid for the shares. As to the alteration of the shares to bearer, that was done to avoid the necessity of their being sent to England for registration. The balance-sheet of the company had been sent to the Nizam's Government.

Mr. Batten, replying to Mr. Labouchere, said he was the chairman of the company.

You have not discovered diamonds?—We are prospecting.

With regard to a memorandum setting forth the prospects of the company, marked private, and of which counsel subsequently stated that only 30 copies were given out,

Sir Henry James questioned witness as to whether it would not lead an ordinary reader to imagine that £850,000 had been paid up?—The witness replied that a perfect stranger reading it should make further inquiries.

Did you not take any steps to give the public information that the £850,000 would go into the pockets of Watson and Stewart, and not into the coffers of the company?—The public were informed that the £850,000 was given for the concession. The witness added that he had never sold a single share or received anything beyond his director's salary from the company.

By Mr. Littler.—The value of the £10 shares was now about £7, notwithstanding this inquiry. There was no distinction between the shares, which were all £10. No individual shareholder that witness was aware of had complained of being misled or taken in.—*Times*, June 2.

The opening event of the Parliamentary inquiry into the affairs of the Hyderabad Deccan Company, Limited, which was commenced yesterday at the House of Commons, was signalised by the entry of the most unpopular man on the London Stock Exchange, viz., Mr. Frank Levien. To commence with, this gentleman was questioned as to the peculiar method in which a settlement in the shares of the Deccan Company was obtained. In the first place Mr. Levien attempted a distinct wriggle. He said that it was not usual for a settlement in any business or company, the shares of which are dealt in on the London Stock Exchange, to be granted without the sanction of the Committee, of which stupid body he has been the assiduous servant for the last twenty years. Being further questioned, however, he made the admission that lately certain transactions, such as dealing for the coming out, had been entered into, and a settlement for the same executed in due course. Mr. Levien, like the committee, has lived far too long.—*Evening Post*, June 2.

The Hyderabad Scandal.—The Parliamentary Committee appointed to inquire into the circumstances attending the formation and promotion of the Hyderabad Deccan Mining Company, Limited, the circumstances under which the concession was obtained, and the subsequent operations by parties interested on the London Stock Exchange, met at the House of Commons yesterday, Sir Henry James presiding.

Mr. Levien, secretary to the Stock Exchange, stated that no application or a settlement was ever made by this company, and he understood that it consisted of £150,000 public shares and £850,000 concessionary shares. The rules and regulations of the Stock Exchange had been entirely disregarded by this company.

Mr. Hall, the secretary of the Deccan Company, said the present directors were Lord Lawrence, Messrs. Batten, Watson, Winter, Colvin, and Sharp. The articles of agreement were not subscribed to at a meeting of shareholders The remuneration of the directors was £300 each. The first call was £75,000 in July, and in November, 1887, a second call was made for a second sum of £75,000. The company had now in cash £85,000. The cost of the company was borne by the concessionaires.

About £25,000 had been spent, chiefly in machinery for the Sangarene coal mines; £13,000 to £14,000 had been spent in diamond mine machinery. They were raising about 150 tons of coal a week from the mine. The diamond mine was not being worked, as cholera prevented them obtaining labour. The mine was at Golconda. It had not been worked for 200 years. They had not found any diamonds since the company was floated. An agreement was made to pay the concessionnaires £850,000 in fully paid-up shares. Not a penny of the £850,000 ever reached the coffers of the company. The witness could not state how many of these shares had been unloaded upon the public.

Mr. Batten, one of the directors of the company, was next examined at great length by Mr. Labouchere as to the terms of the concession and the stake of the Nizam in the State Railway. Most of the facts elicited have already been published in a Parliamentary paper. The railway was now making about £50,000. The Nizam had to pay, roughly, about £150,000 a year for twenty years as a guarantee for the railway, less its receipts. The witness said he subscribed for one hundred £5 shares. He had since exchanged these shares for fully paid-up shares given to him by Mr. Watson. He had not paid for the shares. The agreement was that they should be paid for when the company paid a dividend. They had received excellent reports from their prospecting officers in India. The £850,000 of shares were allotted to Messrs. Watson and Stewart with the full concurrence of all concerned. Only three persons and the two concessionnaires were concerned. He certainly did anticipate that these shares would eventually be offered to the public. In reply to the chairman, the witness said he did not think when he became a director that his duty was to protect the public. The public had nothing to do with the matter, no shares having been issued. He did not assume the *rôle* of general protector of the public. He did take steps to ascertain the value of the concession. He read the Government reports and all possible statistics. Their engineer (Mr. Furnival) had sent home a most satisfactory report.

Sir Henry James: Did you take any steps to acquaint the public with the fact that £850,000 worth of shares out of a nominal capital of a million were held by two men?—The witness said the future buyers could easily ascertain the stake of Messrs. Watson and Stewart. For himself he would say he had never received a farthing of profit out of the company. In reply to Sir Richard Temple the witness said the open railway was about 300 miles in length, and would be finished next year. He thought this was an enormous benefit to the Nizam's dominions, and would be cheaply purchased for the guarantee of £150,000 a year. But for the aspersions made upon the company they would probably have disposed of their valuable property, and the shareholders would have received a million for it.

The Committee adjourned until Tuesday next at twelve o'clock.—*Pall Mall Gazette*, June 2.

The Deccan Mining Inquiry.—Yesterday, at noon, the Parliamentary Committee appointed to inquire into the circumstances attending the formation and promotion of the Hyderabad Deccan Mining Company (Limited), the circumstances under which the concession was obtained, and the subsequent operations by parties interested, on the London Stock Exchange, sat in one of the committee rooms of the House of Commons. Sir Henry James presided, and the other members of the committee present were: Mr. Labouchere, Sir Richard Temple, the Solicitor-General for Scotland, Mr. Bristowe, Mr. M'Lagan, and Mr. Slagg.

Sir Horace Davey, Q.C., Mr. T. D. Inverarity (of the Bombay Bar), and Mr. Trevor White appeared for the Sirdar Diler Jung; Mr. Pember, Q.C., for the Company; and Mr. Littler, Q.C., for Mr. William Clarence

Watson, one of the promoters. The Nizam of Hyderabad, Mr. Henry Parkinson Sharp, and Mr. James Graham Stewart were also represented by counsel.

The Chairman stated at the outset that the committee had determined to keep the conduct of the case in their own hands. The evidence of all the witnesses, apart from special resolution, would be taken upon oath by members of the committee, but if the evidence affected any parties represented by counsel, cross-examination would be permitted. If it was desired that other witnesses should be called, application must be made. The extent to which counsel would be permitted to address the committee would be determined at a later stage, and copies of the evidence could be had by persons willing to pay for the same.

Mr. Levien, secretary to the Stock Exchange, examined by Mr. Labouchere, said he knew nothing of the company except through the papers and common gossip. The company had never made any application to the Stock Exchange for a settlement or quotation, but he understood that it was started with a nominal capital of £1,000,000, made up of 100,000 shares of £10 each, of which £150,000 were public, and £850,000 concessionary. Until special settlement was granted for the public shares no concession would be granted for the concessionary shares. The rules and regulations of the Stock Exchange had been entirely disregarded, and especially Rules 131 and 132. No action had been taken by the Stock Exchange, because it was not the custom to do so unless application was made on the ground of fraud.

By Mr. Pember, Q.C.: It was a common practice on the Stock Exchange to deal in shares for which no special settlement and quotation were made. There was no rule to prevent it. Brokers and jobbers were at liberty to make what contracts they pleased. The rules which he had said were entirely disregarded did not apply to the company unless it asked for a settlement.

Mr. Hall, secretary to the Hyderabad Deccan Mining Company (Limited), stated that he had held office since October, 1887. The present directors were Lord Lawrence, Mr. Batten, Mr. Watson, Mr. Winter, Mr. Colvin, and Mr. Sharp, and their remuneration was £300 a year each. In July, 1887, a first call was made of £75,000, and in the following November a second call was made for the same amount. The company's cash in hand amounted now to about £85,000. Of the money already expended about £25,000 went for machinery, chiefly for the Sangarene Coal Mines, while between £13,000 and £14,000 was paid for diamond mining machinery. They were raising about 150 tons of coal per week from the mine. The diamond mine was not being worked, as an outbreak of cholera had prevented the company obtaining the necessary labour. He did not know what particular reason there was for supposing that diamonds would be found at Golconda. It had not been worked for 200 years. No diamonds had been found there since the company was floated. At the formation of the company the concessionnaires were to receive, under an agreement, £850,000 in fully paid shares, and these were allotted to Messrs. Watson and Stewart. The first directors held one share each. He could not say upon what basis the value of the concession was fixed at £850,000. Messrs. Watson and Stewart were subsequently appointed directors. Not one penny of the £850,000 ever reached the coffers of the company. So far as he knew there were no reports of the value of the mine before the allotment, but there was a formal transfer of the rights of the concessionnaires. Some of the 85,000 shares were transferred to the public by Messrs. Watson and Stewart. The present number of shareholders was 730. At the present time the company were prospecting for gold on a large scale. The railway to the coal mines was only opened on January 1 of the present year, and the company were still sinking shafts and sending out machinery. The present output was no criterion as to what the mines would yield when in full working order. There were 550 square miles of country to be still prospected.

Mr. Batten, chairman of the company, went in detail into the terms of the concession, and the stake of the Nizam of Hyderabad in the State Railway. The railway was now making about £50,000. The Nizam had to pay roughly about £150,000 a year for twenty years, less receipts, as a guarantee. With regard to the mining company, he had subscribed for 100 £5 shares, which he had since exchanged for fully-paid shares given him by Mr. Watson. He had not paid for them, as he took them upon an agreement to pay for them when the company paid a dividend. Excellent reports had been received from their prospecting officers in India. The £850,000 of shares were allotted to Messrs. Watson and Stewart with the full concurrence of all concerned; only three persons and the two concessionnaires were concerned. He was asked to become a director by Messrs. Stewart and Watson.

The Chairman: You knew eventually that these 85,000 shares would reach the public—that the object was that they would come into the hands of the public?

Witness: I thought they would probably reach the public.

Who was to look after the interests of the public?—I suppose the public would look after their own interests when they received the shares.

You are a member of the bar?—Yes, but I have never practised.

When you became chairman of the company did you consider you owed any duty towards those who were intended to be shareholders hereafter?—None, except to the company.

So you were careless of the interests of those whom you intended to become shareholders?—I did not think I was their protector.

You, as chairman of the company, were careless whether they had valuable or worthless shares in their hands?—I considered the property well worth a million.

The subscribers to the articles of association were Watson, Winter, Stewart and Pearce. Winter was Watson's solicitor, and the only independent person is Pearce.

Who is Pearce?—Pearce is Watson's clerk.

The subscribers held at that time one share each?—Yes; nominally, for the formation of the company.

Actually they were concessionnaires anxious to do the best they could for themselves?—Yes.

Who drew up the agreement?—The solicitors to the Company.

Who are they?—Bircham and Drake.

On whose instructions?—The concessionnaires', I suppose.

Well, the concessionnaires went to Bircham and Drake and told them to draw up an agreement by which they were to get 85,000 shares. Who checked that agreement?—I suppose the Company. There was no outside public concerned in it.

But you knew that the shares would go to the public? Here is £850,000 given to these two gentlemen. I ask you now what steps did you take to see that they gave value for that?—They gave the concession for it.

What steps did you take to see that they gave value for it?—I had the deed by which the concessions were transferred to the company.

Did you take any professional estimate of the value?—I myself thought the concessions very valuable.

But what steps did you take to ascertain their real value?—I had two volumes on the Nizam's dominions, and I got all the reports and statistics I could find.

How did you come to the conclusion that the value was £850,000?—

There were 81,000 square miles of country. The company had reports from engineers as to the value of the coal.

Did they make an estimate of money value?—They made an estimate of the quantity of coal.

Did you, as chairman of the company, make any estimate of the capital that ought to be expended to develop the coal mine?—We only intended to spend enough to prospect the value of the property, and find other companies to work it.

You knew the public were to be told that the capital of the company was £1,000,000?—I knew nothing of the kind.

Did you take any steps to give the public information that £850,000 of that capital would not go into the coffers of the company at all, but into the pockets of Stewart and Watson?—The same process by which the public would know the capital was £1,000,000 would have informed them that the vendors would have £850,000.

In reply to further questions, the witness stated that for his own part he had never received a farthing of profit out of the company. But for the aspersions cast upon the undertaking the company would probably have disposed of their valuable undertaking, and the shareholders would have received a million for it. No prospectus was ever issued by the company, but before its formation Mr. Watson issued a private memorandum to his friends.

The committee adjourned until Tuesday next.—*Daily Telegraph*, June 2.

Mr. Batten, chairman of the Deccan Mining Company, who was rather severely handled by Sir Henry James yesterday, is a retired Anglo-Indian "Civilian." His sister is married to Sir John Strachey, of the Secretary of State's Council. Mr. Batten, we believe, acted for a time as private secretary to Lord Lytton when he was Viceroy of India. With his interest—and interest counts for a great deal in our Eastern Empire—Mr. Batten might have looked forward to occupying the highest posts in the service, had not his health broken down and rendered his retirement necessary. Mr. Hall, another witness at yesterday's sitting of the Special Committee, though not an ex-official, is also an Anglo-Indian. He was a partner in the once famous Bombay mercantile house of Nicol and Co., which ceased to exist after the Glasgow Bank failure a few years ago.

Mr. Winter, the solicitor whose name has been mentioned so prominently in connection with the affairs of the Deccan Company, has for some years been a partner in the firm with which the late Right Hon. A. S. Ayrton was associated before he gave up law and came home to take up politics. Mr. Ayrton happened to be in Bombay at a time when the inhabitants of the Western capital were more than usually litigious, and he amassed a considerable fortune from legal business. He was popular with the natives, a large number of whom assembled to bid him farewell on his departure for England. After decorating him with flowers in the approved Oriental fashion, they induced him to make a short parting speech. "My friends," he said, in the gravest possible manner, "my last words to you before I leave the shores of India shall be these: 'Whatever you do, always strive to avoid litigation!'" Although, owing largely to native competition, English lawyers in India do not make, at any rate so rapidly, the large fortunes that their predecessors made in the good old days, still, as the legal gentlemen who have come from Bombay and Madras to assist in the investigation of the Hyderabad scandals could say, Mr. Ayrton's good good advice has not hitherto borne much fruit. It is even now better to be a barrister or solicitor in India than an uncovenanted civilian whose pensions are paid in a debased currency.—*Pall Mall Gazette*, June 2.

THE HYDERABAD SCANDAL.—The Parliamentary Committee appointed to inquire into the circumstances attending the formation and promotion of the Hyderabad Deccan Mining Company, Limited, the circumstances under which the concession was obtained, and the subsequent operations by parties interested on the London Stock Exchange, met at the House of Commons yesterday, Sir Henry James presiding. Mr. Labouchere was among the members present. The committee allow the Nizam of Hyderabad, the Hyderabad Deccan Company, the Sirdar Diler Jung, Mr. Witliam Clarence Watson, Mr. Henry Parkinson Sharp, and Mr. James Graham Stewart to appear by counsel. Intense interest was manifested in the proceedings, the room and corridors being crowded, and extra accommodation having to be improvised for the counsel.

The Chairman intimated that the committee had determined to keep the conduct of the case in their own hands. The witnesses would be examined by members of the committee, and if the evidence should affect any parties represented by counsel, they would be permitted to cross-examine. If it was desired that other witnesses should be called application must be made. The extent to which counsel should be permitted to address the committee would be determined at a later stage. Copies of the evidence would be supplied to persons willing to pay for the same.

Mr. Levien, secretary to the Stock Exchange, stated that no application for a settlement was ever made by the company, but he understood that it consisted of £150,000 public shares, and £850,000 concessionary shares. Until special settlement had been granted for the public shares a settlement would not be granted for the concessionary shares. The rules and regulations of the Stock Exchange had been disregarded by the company.

Mr. Hall, the secretary of the Deccan Company, said that he had held that position since October, 1887. He was examined at great length as to the formation of the company. The minute-book and bankers' pass-books were handed in, and the members of the committee were supplied with copies of the articles of association. The present directors, witness said, were Lord Lawrence, Messrs. Batten, Watson, Winter, Colvin, and Sharp. The articles of agreement were not subscribed to at a meeting of shareholders. The remuneration of the directors was £300 each. The first call was £75,000 in July, and in November, 1887, a second call was made for a second sum of £75,000. The Company had now in cash £85,000. The cost of the Company was borne by the concessionnaires. About £25,000 had been spent, chiefly in machinery for the Sangarene coal mines; £13,000 to £14,000 had been spent in diamond-mine machinery. They were raising about 150 tons of coal a-week from the mine. The diamond mine was not being worked, as cholera prevented their obtaining labour. The mine was at Golconda. It had not been worked for 200 years. They had not found any diamonds since the company was floated. An agreement was made to pay the concessionnaires £850,000 in fully paid-up shares. The first directors had only one share each. They were Messrs. Batten, Hemmerdy, and Milne. They agreed at their first meeting that £850,000 in shares should be paid to Messrs. Watson and Stewart in August, 1886. The witness did not know how they satisfied themselves of the value of £850,000. Mr. Batten and Mr. Hammedy resigned almost immediately afterwards, and Messrs. Watson and Stewart were appointed additional directors. Not a penny of the £850,000 ever reached the coffers of the company. There were no reports of the value of the mine before the allotment of shares, so far as he knew. There had been a formal transfer of the rights of the concessionnaires. Some of the 85,000 shares had been transferred to the public by Messrs. Watson and Stewart. They were allotted on the 16th of August to those gentlemen jointly, and on the 30th of August 23,906 were transferred to Mr. Watson separately, 18,594 to Mr. Stewart separately, and

7,567 were transferred to Mr. Sharpe, and 34,531 to Mr. Winter. The consideration of the transfer to Mr. Sharpe and Mr. Winter was nominal, 5s. per £10 share. The witness could not state how many of these shares had been unloaded upon the public. The present number of shareholders was 730, and he would give the committee a list of those who had bought and paid for their shares in the market. The witness explained the circumstances under which Lord Lawrence had become a director of the Company in July, 1887, and under which the Nizam's Government had purchased 12,500 shares of the Company. At the present time the Company were prospecting for gold on a large scale. The railway to the coal mines was only opened on the 1st of January of the present year, and the Company were still sinking shafts and sending out machinery. The present output was no criterion as to what the mines would yield when they were in full working order.

Mr. Batten, one of the directors of the company, was next examined at great length by Mr. Labouchere as to the terms of the concession and the stake of the Nizam in the State railway. Most of the facts elicited have already been published in a Parliamentary paper. The railway was now making about £50,000. The Nizam had to pay, roughly, about £150,000 a year for twenty years as a guarantee for the railway, less its receipts. The witness said he was secretary to the railroad and chairman of the mining company. He subscribed for one hundred £5 shares. He had since exchanged these shares for fully paid-up shares given to him by Mr. Watson. He had not paid for the shares. The agreement was that they should be paid for when the company paid a dividend. They had received excellent reports from their prospecting officers in India. The £850,000 of shares were allotted to Messrs. Watson and Stewart with the full concurrence of all concerned. Only three persons and the two concessionnaires were concerned. He certainly did anticipate that these shares would eventually be offered to the public. In reply to the chairman, the witness said he was asked to become a director by Messrs. Stewart and Watson. He was a barrister, but had never practised. He did not think when he became a director that his duty was to protect the public. The public had nothing to do with the matter, no shares having been issued. He did not assume the *rôle* of general protector of the public. He did take steps to ascertain the value of the concession. He read the Government reports and all possible statistics. Their engineer (Mr. Furnivall) had sent home a most satisfactory report.

Sir Henry James: Did you take any steps to acquaint the public with the fact that £850,000 worth of shares out of a nominal capital of a million were held by two men?—The witness said the future buyers could easily ascertain the stake of Messrs. Watson and Stewart. For himself he would say he had never received a farthing of profit out of the company. In reply to Sir Richard Temple, the witness said the open railway was about 300 miles in length, and would be finished next year. He thought this was an enormous benefit to the Nizam's dominions, and would be cheaply purchased for the guarantee of £150,000 a year. But for the aspersions made upon the company they would probably have disposed of their valuable property, and the shareholders would have received a million for it. There was never a prospectus issued by the company. Examined by Mr. Littler and Mr. Pember, the witness gave particulars of the working of the railway, and stated that its prospects were in the highest degree satisfactory.

The committee adjourned at four o'clock until Tuesday next at twelve o'clock.—*Morning Advertiser*, June 2.

The Hyderabad Scandal.—The Parliamentary Committee appointed to inquire into the circumstances attending the formation and promotion of the Hyderabad-Deccan Mining Company, Limited, the circumstances under which the concession was obtained, and the subsequent operations by parties interested on the London Stock Exchange, met at the House of Commons yesterday, Sir Henry James presiding. Mr. Labouchere was among the members present. The committee allow the Nizam of Hyderabad, the Hyderabad-Deccan Company, the Sirdar Diler Jung, Mr. William Clarence Watson, Mr. Henry Parkinson Sharp, and Mr. James Graham Stewart to appear by counsel. Intense interest is manifested in the proceedings, the room and corridors being crowded, and extra accommodation having to be improvised for the counsel, of whom over a dozen appear.

The Chairman intimated that the committee had determined to keep the conduct of the case in their own hands. The witnesses would be examined by members of the committee, and if the evidence should affect any parties represented by counsel they would be permitted to cross-examine. If it was desired that other witnesses should be called, application must be made. The extent to which counsel should be permitted to address the committee would be determined at a later stage. Copies of the evidence would be supplied to persons willing to pay for the same.

Mr. Levien, secretary to the Stock Exchange, stated that no application for a settlement was ever made by this company, and he understood that it consisted of £150,000 public shares and £850,000 concessionary shares. Until special settlement had been granted for the public shares a settlement would not be granted for the concessionary shares. The rules and regulations of the Stock Exchange had been entirely disregarded by this company.

Mr. Hall, the secretary of the Deccan Company, said that he had held that position since October, 1887. He was examined at great length as to the formation of the company. The minute-book and bankers' pass-books were handed in, and the members of the committee were supplied with copies of the articles of association. The present directors, witness said, were Lord Lawrence, Messrs. Batten, Watson, Winter, Colvin, and Sharp. The articles of agreement were not subscribed to at a meeting of shareholders. The remuneration of the directors was £300 each. The first call was £75,000 in July, and in November, 1887, a second call was made for a second sum of £75,000. The company had now in cash £85,000. The cost of the company was borne by the concessionnaires. About £25,000 had been spent, chiefly in machinery for the Sangarene coal mines; £13,000 to £14,000 had been spent in diamond mine machinery. They were raising about 150 tons of coal a week from the mine. The diamond mine was not being worked, as cholera prevented them obtaining labour. The mine was at Golconda. It had not been worked for 200 years. They had not found any diamonds since the company was floated. An agreement was made to pay the concessionnaires £850,000 in fully paid-up shares. The first directors had only one share each. They were Messrs. Batten, Hemmerdy, and Milne. They agreed at their first meeting that £850,000 in shares should be paid to Messrs. Watson and Stewart in August, 1886. The witness did not know how they satisfied themselves of the value of £850,000. Mr. Batten and Mr. Hammedy resigned almost immediately afterwards, and Messrs. Watson and Stewart were appointed additional directors. Not a penny of the £850,000 ever reached the coffers of the company. There were no reports of the value of the mine before the allotment of shares, so far as he knew. There had been a formal transfer of the rights of the concessionnaires. Some of the 85,000 shares had been transferred to the public by Messrs. Watson and Stewart. They were allotted on the 16th of August to those gentlemen jointly, and on the 30th of August 23,906 were transferred to Mr. Watson separately, 18,594 to Mr. Stewart separately, and 7,567 were transferred to Mr. Sharpe, and 34,531 to

Mr. Winter. The consideration of the transfer to Mr. Sharpe and Mr. Winter was nominal, 5s. per £10 share. The witness could not state how many of these shares had been unloaded upon the public. The present number of shareholders was 730, and he would give the committee a list of those who had bought and paid for their shares in the public market. The witness explained the circumstances under which Lord Lawrence had become a director of the company in July, 1887, and under which the Nizam's Government had purchased 12,500 shares of the company. At the present time the company were prospecting for gold on a large scale. The railway to the coal mines was only opened on the 1st of January of the present year, and the company were still sinking shafts and sending out machinery. The present output was no criterion as to what the mines would yield when they were in full working order.

Mr. Batten, one of the directors of the company, was next examined at great length by Mr. Labouchere as to the terms of the concession and the stake of the Nizam in the State Railway. Most of the facts elicited have already been published in a Parliamentary paper. The railway was now making about £50,000. The Nizam had to pay, roughly, about £150,000 a year for twenty years as a guarantee for the railway, less its receipts. The witness said he was secretary to the railroad and chairman of the mining company. He subscribed for one hundred £5 shares. He had since exchanged these shares for fully paid-up shares given to him by Mr. Watson. He had not paid for the shares. The agreement was that they should be paid for when the company paid a dividend. They had received excellent reports from their prospecting officers in India. The £850,000 of shares were allotted to Messrs. Watson and Stewart with the full concurrence of all concerned. Only three persons and the two concessionnaires were concerned. He certainly did anticipate that these shares would eventually be offered to the public. In reply to the chairman the witness said he was asked to become a director by Messrs. Stewart and Watson. He was a barrister, but had never practised. He did not think when he became a director that his duty was to protect the public. The public had nothing to do with the matter, no shares having been issued. He did not assume the *rôle* of general protector of the public. He did take steps to ascertain the value of the concession. He read the Government reports and all possible statistics. Their engineer (Mr. Furnival) had sent home a most satisfactory report.

Sir Henry James (warmly): Did you take any steps to acquaint the public with the fact that £850,000 worth of shares out of a nominal capital of a million were held by two men? The witness said the future buyers could easily ascertain the stake of Messrs. Watson and Stewart. For himself he would say he had never received a farthing of profit out of the company. In reply to Sir Richard Temple the witness said the open railway was about 300 miles in length, and would be finished next year. He thought this was an enormous benefit to the Nizam's dominions, and would be cheaply purchased for the guarantee of £150,000 a year. But for the aspersions made upon the company, they would probably have disposed of their valuable property, and the shareholders would have received a million for it. There was never a prospectus issued by the company. Examined by Mr. Littler and Mr. Pember, the witness gave particulars of the working of the railway, and stated that its prospects were in the highest degree satisfactory.

The committee adjourned at four o'clock until Tuesday next at twelve o'clock.—*Daily News*, June 2.

The Hyderabad (Deccan) Company Inquiry.—The Select Committee appointed to inquire into the circumstances attending the floating of the

Hyderabad (Deccan) Mining Company met yesterday, under the presidency of Sir Henry James. The chairman intimated that the committee had determined to keep the conduct of the case in their own hands. The witnesses would be examined by members of the committee, and if the evidence should affect any parties represented by counsel, they would be permitted to cross-examine. If it was desired that other witnesses should be called, application must be made. The first witness called was Mr. Levien, secretary to the Stock Exchange. He said no application for a settlement had been ever made by the company. He understood that it consisted of £150,000 public shares and £850,000 concessionary shares. The rules of the Stock Exchange had been entirely disregarded by this company. Mr. Hall, secretary to the company, then gave evidence at great length as to the constitution of the company, the remuneration of the directors, etc. Mr. Batten, chairman, also gave evidence, and the committee adjourned till Tuesday.—*Morning Post*, June 2.

Hyderabad Deccan Mining Scandal.—Yesterday the Parliamentary Committee appointed to inquire into the circumstances attending the formation and promotion of the Hyderabad Deccan Mining Company, Limited, the circumstances under which the concession was obtained, and the subsequent operations by parties interested on the London Stock Exchange, met in the House of Commons yesterday, Sir Henry James, M.P., presiding. Mr. Labouchere, Mr. Bristowe, Mr. M'Lagan, Mr. Slagg, Sir R. Temple, and the Solicitor-General for Scotland were among the members present. The most intense interest was manifested in the proceedings, and the room and corridors were crowded.

Sir H. Davey, Q.C., Mr. Trevor White, and Mr. J. D. Inverarity represented Sirdar Diler Jung; Mr. Pembroke, Q.C., and Mr. Lewis Coward appeared for the Hyderabad-Deccan Mining Company; and Mr. Littler, Q.C., represented Mr. Watson.

The Chairman intimated that the committee had determined to keep the conduct of the case in their own hands. The witnesses would be examined by members of the committee, and if the evidence should affect any parties represented by counsel, they would be permitted to cross-examine. If it was desired that other witnesses should be called, application must be made. The extent to which counsel should be permitted to address the committee would be determined at a later stage. Copies of the evidence would be supplied to parties willing to pay for the same.

Mr. Levien, secretary to the Stock Exchange, stated that no application for a settlement was ever made by this company. He understood that it consisted of £150,000 public shares and £850,000 concessionary shares. Until special settlement had been granted for the public shares a settlement would not be granted for the concessionary shares. The rules and regulations of the Stock Exchange had been entirely disregarded by this company. No application had been made either for a settlement or quotation. There were often dealings in shares before a settlement was granted, but in the majority of substantial companies settlement was asked for, and as a rule within a fortnight or a month. If no settlement was asked for there was nothing to prevent brokers dealing quite irrespective of a settlement by the Stock Exchange.

The witness was cross-examined by Mr. Littler, Q.C., Mr. Pember, Q.C., and other counsel.

Mr. Hall, secretary of the Hyderabad-Deccan Company, said he became secretary on October 10th, 1887. His predecessor was Mr. Milne; the first directors were Mr. Batten, Mr. Hemmerdy, and Mr. Milne. They were elected by the first shareholders, who were John Stewart, Mr. H. P. Sharpe, Mr.

W. C. Watson, Mr. Winter, Mr. Batten, Mr. Hemmerdy, Mr. Milne, and Mr. Pearce. There was an agreement to pay the concessionnaires £850,000 in fully paid-up shares. The present directors were Mr. Batten, Mr. Watson, Mr. M'Colvin, Lord Lawrence, and Mr. Sharpe. Mr. Hemmerdy, Mr. Pearce, and Mr. Milne had resigned. Mr. Winter was elected on August 19, 1886, Mr. Sharpe in November, 1886, and Lord Lawrence in July, 1887. The remuneration of the directors was £300 a year. The first call of £75,000 was paid at once, and the second call of £75,000 on November 1, 1887. The Company had at present in cash £85,000. Nothing was paid for promoting the Company; the concessionnaires paid everything. About £25,000 had been spent in machinery, and about £13,000 or £14,000 in dynamite machines; £5,200 in rent and salaries at the London office. There was £3,200 in the agent's hands, and other sums with other agents. They had been raising from 150 to 180 tons of coal a week. They had not been working the diamond mines owing to cholera. They were in Golconda. They had not been worked for 200 years. The Company knew nothing of the flowery description of the Golconda mines in the first prospectus. He did not know anything about Mr. Watson buying and selling shares about the same days.

By the Chairman: The first directors had only one share each. They were Messrs. Batten, Hemmerdy, and Milne. They agreed at their first meeting that £850,000 in shares be paid to Messrs. Watson and Stewart in August, 1886. He did not know how they satisfied themselves of the value of £850,000. Mr. Batten and Mr. Hemmerdy resigned almost immediately afterwards, and Messrs. Watson and Stewart were appointed additional directors. Not a penny of the £850,000 ever reached the coffers of the company. More than £40,000 had been sent over to Hyderabad for working the mine. The £150,000 shares had been all paid up. There had been no profitable working of the mine. They had had no representations from the Nizam's Government as to what had become of 85,000 shares.

By Sir Richard Temple: He did not know that any exploiting had been made since February 18th, 1887, when Mr. Lewinski reported that he could not speak positively that he could find diamonds in payable quantities, but he had confidence in the mines, though he did not like to be too sanguine.

By Mr. Pember: Lord Lawrence joined the board in July, 1887. On June 14th in that year it was reported to the board that the Government of the Nizam had purchased 12,500 shares, and the board agreed that the Government should have two representatives on the board of directors, and subsequently the Sirdar and Lord Lawrence were appointed, on condition that they should resign if the Government ceased to hold 12,500 shares. The company were now busy prospecting for gold, but it had been checked by the outbreak of cholera. They were still sinking shafts in the coal mine, so that the present output was no guide to what would be the ultimate output. Until the railway was made they could not get machinery there at all. There were now about 730 shareholders.

Mr. Batten gave evidence as to the construction of the railway to the mines, and said its capital was £2,000,000 in shares and £2,500,000 in debentures. The Nizam was to receive £350,000. He did actually get £100,000 in cash and £241,000 in debentures. There was a guarantee by the Nizam of 5 per cent. on the shares and 4 per cent. on the debentures for twenty years. He did not think the railway ever earned more than £15,000. The Nizam had therefore to pay £40,000 a year. Subsequently he had to pay £100,000 a year, less the earnings of the company.

Mr. Labouchere: And this was such a bargain for the Nizam that he, out of absolute gratitude, gave Mr. Watson the concession for the Deccan mines.

Examination continued: He subscribed for one hundred £5 shares.

Mr. Watson relieved him of them, gave him the £500 back, and then transferred to him one hundred of his fully paid-up shares, to qualify him as a director. He had not paid for them, but he would have to pay for them when the company began to pay a dividend, or to give them up.

By the Chairman: He assented to the payment of the £850,000 in paid-up shares. He had never received a halfpenny from the company except his directors' fees, which he had invested in shares. He did not as chairman take any steps for the protection of the public who subscribed. They would know the terms of the purchase. The concessionaires would have been losers if the thing had proved a failure. No doubt £850,000 of the million capital would go into the pockets of the concessionnaires if they were able to sell their shares, but they had deposited £150,000.

By Mr. Slagg: The prospectus was not issued by the company, but by Mr. Watson for the information of his friends, and was never sent out to the public.

Examined by Mr. Littler and Mr. Pember, Mr. Batten gave particulars of the working of the railway, and stated that its prospects were in the highest degree satisfactory.

The committee adjourned at four o'clock until Tuesday next.—*Daily Chronicle*, June 2.

Moulvie Mahdi Ali, the official deputed to represent the Hyderabad Government in the inquiry relating to the Deccan Mining Company's business, arrived here last Friday from India. He is staying with his suite at the Alexandra Hotel, which used to be patronised on his visits to England by the enterprising Abdul Huk. Moulvie Mahdi Ali was invited to go to Epsom on Wednesday in the Royal train, and he must have been amused to see the way he was described in the evening papers.—*Vanity Fair*, June 2.

The silver lining to the cloud which at present lowers over Hyderabad politics comes in the form of huge fees, which the lawyers from Bombay are pocketing. When the last mail left India, five barristers, only one of whom is a lawyer of any real merit, were engaged at Hyderabad on fees varying from 1,000 to 2,000 rupees per diem. The daily legal expenses of Abdul Huk alone were put down at 5,000 rupees. What an El Dorado for the profession still exists in the far east. And yet the good folk of Bombay complain that the local bar is almost absolutely devoid of talent, and that the public not only have to pay the usual exorbitant price for legal aid, but get nothing but the most absolute mediocrity for it.—*Court and Society Review*, June 2.

The Deccan Mining Scandal.—Parliamentary Inquiry.—The Select Committee of the House of Commons appointed to inquire into the conditions under which the East India Hyderabad Deccan Mining Company was floated met yesterday for the first time in Committee Room 17 for the reception of evidence.

Sir H. James, M.P., presided, the other members of the committee present being Mr. Labouchere, Mr. Bristow, Mr. M'Lagan, Mr. Slagg, Sir R. Temple, and the Solicitor-General for Scotland.

The terms of the reference were to inquire into the circumstances attending the promotion of the company and the subsequent operations on the Stock Exchange.

Sir H. Davey, Q.C., Mr. Trevor White, and Mr. J. D. Inverarity represented Sirdar Diler Jung.

Sir H. James said it might be convenient that he should state that the evidence would be taken upon oath. The committee had come to a conclusion with regard to the hearing of counsel. The committee proposed to retain the inquiry entirely in their own hands, but while so doing would accept the assistance of counsel when necessary. Thus all witnesses would be examined by the committee, but in the case of any evidence affecting anyone being given the person affected would be at liberty to apply to the Committee to cross-examine.

Mr. Levien, secretary to the Stock Exchange, was the first witness called. Having been sworn, the witness, in answer to Mr. Labouchere, said that he knew nothing of the company except what he had heard and read in the newspapers, and what was common gossip about it. The rules and regulations of the Stock Exchange had been entirely disregarded in the respect that no application had been made either for a settlement or official quotation, and none of the conditions and rules with regard to special settlement or quotation had been obeyed.

Mr. Pember, Q.C., said he should like to put a question to the witness.

The Chairman: Perhaps you will kindly state for whom you appear.

Mr. Pember: The Company. (To witness:) Is it not a common practice on the Stock Exchange for members to deal in shares for which no application had been made for settlement?

Witness: Yes.

Mr. Pember: So that when you said that the rules of the Stock Exchange had been entirely disregarded, these rules did not apply to this company until they chose to apply for a settlement.

Witness: No.

The Chairman: What is the time that generally elapses between the issuing of a prospectus of a company and asking for a settlement?

Witness: As a rule application for a settlement follows very promptly. I have known it to be applied for within a week.

Further questioned by the Chairman, witness said that if no settlement was asked for there was nothing to prevent brokers dealing with the shares, but those dealings would not be under the control of the Stock Exchange.

Mr. Hall, the Secretary of the Hyderabad Deccan Mining Company, was next called and sworn. In reply to Mr. Labouchere, he stated that he had held his position as secretary since October, 1887. The Company was registered in July, 1886. Mr. Milne was his predecessor in the office. The remuneration to the directors of the company was about £1,500 a year. The chairman had the same sum, and the managing directors did not get any more. The company had in cash now about £85,000. Nothing was paid for the promotion of the company by the company.

Mr. Labouchere: Who paid for the printing of the shares and the articles of association?

Witness: I don't know exactly, but I believe the company did.

Further questioned, witness said he could not give the total of what the company paid for the cost of bringing out the company.

Witness was then questioned as to the expenses at the company's mines, and gave particulars of money spent in machinery. The latest report from the gold mines was that about 150 tons of stuff a week had been raised. That was about the average since the commencement of this year.

Questioned as to the latest report about the diamonds, witness stated that there had been a difficulty in securing labour.

Mr. Labouchere: What particular reason had the company for supposing that diamonds would be found in the company's mines?

Witness: I cannot say.

Questioned with reference to the shares and transfers, witness said that he did not know anything whatever about the dealings with these, nor was he acquainted with a list of transactions which Mr. Labouchere had read to him, from which it seemed that in October, 1886, Mr. Watson was acquiring several lots of shares, and was at the same time selling.

Witness was then questioned with reference to the agreement entered into, by which 85,000 shares of £10 each were transferred to Mr. Watson and Mr. Stewart, the concessionnaires, and stated that that agreement was approved by three gentlemen—Batten, Hemmerdy and Milne—holding one share each.

Witness, in reply to further questions, stated that he had no record of how those three gentlemen, acting directors, with £1 shares each, arrived at the estimate of the value of the concession for which they agreed to give 85,000 shares. He had searched, but failed to find any trace of the manner in which they arrived at the value of the mines.

The Chairman here read the agreement, which set forth that the concessionnaires should assign and transfer to the company certain rights conceded to them in the kingdom of the Nizam.

Asked whether any transfer of such rights had been made, witness replied that there had been a transfer of such rights. Such transfer was made by document, which he handed in to the committee. He could not recollect how many of the 85,000 shares had been re-transferred to the public. Upwards of £40,000 had been sent over to Hyderabad for the purpose of working the mines. There had been, he said, so far as he knew, no return from the mines and no profit. He had not received any communication from the Nizam's Government as to what had become of the 85,000 shares. He was not aware that any notification of the handing over of 85,000 shares was sent to the Nizam or the Indian Government.

In answer to Mr. Slagg, witness said although there had been no return of profits from Hyderabad some gold had been sold. The proceeds thereof had, however, been spent in India.

In answer to a question by Sir R. Temple, witness said that the 85,000 shares stated in the agreement to be fully paid-up had nothing paid on them. They were taken as paid up, but, as a matter of fact, nothing was paid on them.

Witness, replying to the chairman, described the locality of the mines, and stated that an expert, Mr. Levinsky, was now in Hyderabad testing the ground.

In reply to questions put by Mr. Pember, Q.C., witness stated that the country that required prospecting was about 550 square miles in extent. The company had sent out machinery for diamonds to the value of £15,000 or £16,000. The machinery was shipped in November and December of last year. According to the last report the machinery was not at work. The railway to the coal mine was opened on the 1st of January of the present year. The company were sinking shafts and sending out new machinery. Until the railway to the mine was opened it was practically impossible for them to get the machinery to the mines at all. Their operations had been checked by the outbreak of cholera.

Mr. Pember, Q.C.: At what date did Lord Lawrence join the Board?

Witness: In July, 1887.

Replying to further questions by Mr. Pember, Q.C., witness said he could not give the committee the total number of shareholders, but he thought the learned counsel was correct in suggesting that they numbered about 730. A balance sheet was sent to the Nizam's Government.

By Sir R. Temple: I don't know whether any diamonds or any other precious stones were found at Deccan.

By a Counsel: I believe no prospectus was issued before or after the shares were allotted.

Mr. Batten, chairman of the Hyderabad Deccan Mining Company, was next examined by Mr. Labouchere as to the financing of the Nizam's State Railway by Mr. Watson, to whom £100,000 was given to cover expenses prior to the railway going to allotment. With regard to the coalfields, they had received excellent reports. Diamonds, however, had not been discovered.

Mr. Labouchere: Do you consider, as chairman of the company, that £60,000 would be sufficient to open up a gold field and a diamond field?

Witness: Yes, quite sufficient to prove its value.

In reply to the Chairman, witness said he was chairman of the Hyderabad Company. He was introduced to the company by Messrs. Watson and Stewart. He had no hesitation in saying that, with reference to the Deccan Company, they were doing their best to develop the mining property, and had received excellent reports from the officials abroad. He was aware that the company was to be started long before it really was.

The Chairman: You knew that these 85,000 shares would reach the public?

Witness: I thought they would probably reach the public.

The Chairman: Who was to look after the interests of the public?

Witness: I supposed the public would look after their own interests.

The Chairman: I see that you are a member of the bar?

Witness: I am, but I do not practise.

The Chairman: When you became chairman of the company did you consider you owed any duty towards those who were intended to be shareholders hereafter?

Witness: I did not consider that I owed any duty to anybody except to my company.

The Chairman: So you were careless of the interests of those whom you intended to become shareholders?

Witness: I did not regard myself as the protector of the public.

The Chairman: Then you, as chairman of the company, were careless whether they had valuable or worthless shares in their possession?

Witness: I considered the property well worth a million.

The Chairman: Ah! that is not what I asked. I see that the subscribers to the articles of association were Watson, Winter, Stewart, and Pearce. Winter was Watson's solicitor. The only independent person is Pearce. Who is Pearce?

Witness: Pearce is Watson's clerk.

The Chairman: At that time the subscribers held one share each?

Witness: Yes; nominally for the formation of the Company.

The Chairman: They were actually concessionnaires anxious to do the best they could for themselves?

Witness: Yes.

Referring to the agreement of the 16th of August, the Chairman asked who checked it, and the Witness replied that the lawyers of the company checked it.—*Manchester Guardian*, June 2.

Light on the Deccan Scandal.—Mr. Labouchere Investigating.—The investigation into the Deccan financial scandal commenced to-day, when the Special Committee of the House of Commons appointed to look into the matter had its first sitting. The members present were Sir Richard Temple, the Solicitor-General for Scotland, Messrs. Labouchere, M'Lagan, Slagg, and Bristow, M.P.'s. There was a very large attendance of counsel, witnesses, and others interested in the inquiry. Before calling upon the witnesses Sir Henry James announced that the Committee had resolved that all the evidence should be taken on oath.

The first witness called was Mr. Levien, secretary of the Stock Exchange. Mr. Levien, in reply to Mr. Labouchere, said he understood that the capital was composed of £150,000 floated capital and £850,000 concessionary shares. The rules of the Stock Exchange had been totally disregarded by the company. No application had been made for a settlement or a quotation.

In reply to Mr. Pember, Q.C., representing the company, the witness said that the rules of the Stock Exchange had not been broken but disregarded. The Exchange had no power to enforce the rules until an application had been made for a settlement.

Mr. Hall, the Secretary of the Deccan Company, said that he had held that position since October, 1887. He was examined at length as to the formation of the company. The minute and bankers' pass books were handed in, and the members of the committee were supplied with copies of the articles of association. The present directors, witness said, were Lord Lawrence, Messrs. Batten, Watson, Winter, Colvin, and Sharp. The articles of agreement were not subscribed to by a meeting of shareholders. The remuneration of the directors was £300. The first call was £75,000 in July, and in November, 1887, a second call was made for a second sum of £75,000. The company had now in cash £85,000. The cost of the company was borne by the concessionnaires. About £25,000 had been spent, chiefly in machinery for the Sangaree coal mines. £13,000 to £14,000 had been spent in diamond mine machinery.

Mr. Pember, Q.C., undertook on behalf of the company to produce an account of the expenditure of the company.

They were, continued the witness, raising about 150 tons of coal a week from the mine. The diamond mine was not being worked as cholera prevented them obtaining labour. The mine was at Golconda. They had not found any diamonds since the company was floated.

Mr. Hall, in reply to Sir Henry James, said he was unable to say how the £850,000 allotted to Messrs. Stewart and Watson was arrived at as the value of the mines. There were only three directors present when this allotment was made. They were Messrs. Batten, Hemmerdy and Milne. Nobody else was consulted. He could not say that a single penny had ever found its way into the coffers of the company in return for this allotment of £850,000 in 85,000 shares of £10 each. All the rights of the concessionnaires had been transferred to the company. The document was handed in, and Mr. Hall undertook on the next hearing to produce particulars of the transfers made from the £850,000 worth of shares. Witness said there had been no profitable working of the mines, and no return of profit. In reply to Mr. Slagg, he said there had been no mining for metal, and no prospecting. The only operation had been at the coal mine.

In reply to Mr. Pember, Mr. Hall said that at the present time the company were prospecting for gold on a large scale over 560 square miles of country. The railway to the coal mines was only opened on 1st January last, and the company were still sinking shafts and sending out machinery. The present output was no criterion as to what the mines would yield when they were in full working order. The number of shareholders was over 730, and many of them had given valuable consideration for their shares.

The Committee subsequently adjourned.—*Star*, June 2.

The Hyderabad Scandal.—The Parliamentary Committee appointed to inquire into the circumstances attending the formation and promotion of the Hyderabad Deccan Mining Company (Limited), the circumstances under which the concession was obtained, and the subsequent operations by parties interested on the London Stock Exchange, met at the House of Commons yesterday, Sir Henry James presiding. Mr. Labouchere was among the members present. The Committee allow the Nizam of Hyderabad, the Hyderabad Deccan Company, the Sirdar Diler Jung, Mr. William Clarence Watson, Mr. Henry Parkinson Sharp, and Mr. James Graham Stewart to appear by Counsel. Intense interest was manifested in the proceedings, the room and corridors being crowded and extra accommodation having to be improvised for the counsel, of whom over a dozen appeared. The chairman intimated that the Committee had determined to keep the conduct of the case in their own hands. The witnesses would be examined by members of the Committee, and if the evidence should affect any parties represented by counsel, they would be permitted to cross-examine. If it was desired that other witnesses should be called, application must be made. The extent to which counsel should be permitted to address the Committee would be determined at a later stage. Copies of the evidence would be supplied to persons willing to pay for the same.

Mr. Levien, secretary of the Stock Exchange, stated that no application for a settlement was ever made by this company, and he understood that it consisted of £150,000 public shares and £850,000 concessionary shares. Until special settlement had been granted for the public shares a settlement would not be granted for the concessionary shares. The rules and regulations of the Stock Exchange had been entirely disregarded by this company.

Mr. Hall, the secretary of the Deccan Company, said that he had held that position since October, 1887. He was examined at great length as to the formation of the company. The minute book and bankers' pass-books were handed in, and the members of the committee were supplied with copies of the articles of association. The present directors, the witness said, were Lord Lawrence, Messrs. Batten, Watson, Winter, Colvin, and Sharp. The articles of agreement were not subscribed to at a meeting of shareholders. The remuneration of the directors was £300 each. The first call was £75,000 in July, and in November, 1887, a second call was made for a second sum of £75,000. The company had now in cash £85,000. The cost of the company was borne by the concessionnaires. About £25,000 had been spent, chiefly in machinery for the Sangarene coal mines; £13,000 to £14,000 had been spent in diamond-mining machinery. They were raising about 150 tons of coal a week from the mine. The diamond-mine was not being worked as cholera prevented them obtainining labour. The mine was at Golconda. It had not been worked for 200 years. They had not found any diamonds since the company was floated. An agreement was made to pay the concessionnaires £850,000 in fully paid-up shares. The first directors had only one share each. They were Messrs. Batten, Hemmerdy, and Milne. They agreed at their first meeting that £850,000 in shares should be paid to Messrs. Watson and Stewart in August, 1886. The witness did not know how they satisfied themselves of the value of £850,000. Mr. Batten and Mr. Hemmerdy resigned almost immediately afterwards, and Messrs Watson and Stewart were appointed additional directors. Not a penny of the £850,000 ever reached the coffers of the company. There were no reports of the value of the mine before the allotment of shares, so far as he knew. There had been a formal transfer of the rights of the concessionnaires. Some of the 85,000 shares had been transferred to the public by Messrs. Watson and Stewart. They were allotted on the 16th of August to those gentlemen jointly, and on the 30th of August 23,906 were transferred to Mr. Watson separately, 18,594 to Mr. Stewart separately, and 7,567 were transferred to Mr. Sharp, and 34,531 to Mr. Winter. The consideration of the transfer to Mr. Sharp and Mr. Winter was nominal, 5s. per £10 share. The witness could not state how many of these shares had been unloaded upon the public. The present number of shareholders was 730, and he would give the Committee a list of those who had bought and paid for their shares in the public market. The witness explained the circumstances under which Lord Lawrence had become a director of the company in July, 1887, and under which the Nizam's Government had purchased 12,500 shares of the company. At the present time the company were prospecting for gold on a large scale. The railway to the coal mines was only opened on the 1st of January of the present year, and the company were still sinking shafts and sending out machinery. The present output was no criterion as to what the mines would yield when they were in full working order.

Mr. Batten, one of the directors of the company, was next examined at great length by Mr. Labouchere as to the terms of the concession and the stake of the Nizam in the State Railway. Most of the facts elicited have already been published in a parliamentary paper. The railway was now making about £50,000. The Nizam had to pay, roughly, about £150,000 a year for twenty years as a guarantee for the railway, less its receipts. The witness said he was secretary to the railroad, and chairman of the mining company. He subscribed for one hundred £5 shares. He had since exchanged these shares for fully paid-up shares given to him by Mr. Watson. He had not paid for the shares. The agreement was that they should be paid for when the company paid a dividend. They had received excellent reports from their prospecting officers in India. The £850,000 of shares were allotted to Messrs. Watson and Stewart with the full concurrence of all concerned. Only three persons and two concessionnaires were concerned. He certainly did anticipate that these shares would eventually be offered to the public. In reply to the chairman witness said he was asked to become a director by Messrs. Stewart and Watson. He was a barrister but had never practised. He did not think when he became a director that his duty was to protect the public. The public had nothing to do with the matter, no shares having been issued. He did not assume the role of general protector to the public. He did take steps to ascertain the value of the concession. He read the Government reports, and all possible statistics. Their engineer (Mr. Furnival) had sent home a most satisfactory report.

Sir Henry James (warmly): Did you take any steps to acquaint the public with the fact that £850,000 worth of shares out of a nominal capital of a million were held by two men? The witness said the future buyers could easily ascertain the stake of Messrs. Watson and Stewart. For himself he would say he had never received a farthing of profit out of the company. In reply to Sir Richard Temple, the witness said the open railway was about 300 miles in length, and would be finished next year. He thought this was an enormous benefit to the Nizam's dominions, and would be cheaply purchased for the guarantee of £150,000 a year. But for the aspersions made upon the company, they would probably have disposed of their valuable property, and the shareholders would have received a million for it. There was never a prospectus issued by the company. Examined by Mr. Littler and Mr. Pember, the witness gave particulars of the working of the railway, and stated that its prospects were in the highest degree satisfactory.

The Committee adjourned at four o'clock until Tuesday next at twelve o'clock.—*St. James's Gazette*, June 2.

Social Antipathies in India.—In dealing with the people of Asia, Lady Hester Stanhope observed, a downright manner amounting even to brusqueness is more effective than any other; and amongst the English of all ranks and classes there is no man so attractive to Orientals as an honest, open-hearted, and positive naval officer of the old school. Mr. Eastlake, to whom her ladyship's opinion was imparted, considers it well worth recording; and hardly any one who has seen in India the influence enjoyed by just such Englishmen as Lady Hester described would doubt the truth of the proposition. What the French regard as an altogether unamiable trait in our national character is really one of the secrets of our success in the East.

It must be admitted, however, that the self-confidence of the Englishman tends at times not merely to brusqueness but to a supercilious and almost aggressive disregard of other people's feelings; and this inurbanity is by no means enjoyed by Orientals. The Chief Justice of Hyderabad, in a very interesting letter printed elsewhere, laments the exclusiveness of Anglo-Indian society; and he not without reason maintains that it is a source of political danger. Even though the reluctance of the English in India to meet native gentlemen at a club, or to play lawn tennis with Parsee ladies, may not actually threaten to undermine the foundations of the empire, we certainly lose much by holding ourselves so entirely aloof; and it is lamentable to find natives of high position, character, and attainments, like our correspondent the Fathah Nawaz Jung, labouring under the conviction that Englishmen do not treat them with the civility which they have a right to expect.

Besides stating the grievance, Mr. Mehdi Hasan endeavours to find the true explanation of it. He dismisses the idea that the position of woman in the East accounts for the exclusiveness of Anglo-Indian society. Nor will he admit that a divergency of etiquette in regard to eating and drinking keeps the races apart. The real obstacle to a closer intercourse must, he thinks, be sought for elsewhere. His own view of the matter is that our earlier experiences with barbarian races in other parts of the world have given rise to an uncontrollable instinctive feeling of contempt for any people with a dark complexion. According to this theory we class the natives of India—more or less unconsciously—with Africans and Maories. Naturally enough, a Mahommedan gentleman bitterly resents what he can only look on as an impertinence. But we may venture to hope that Mr. Mehdi Hasan is mistaken in this respect. It is not the antipathy of the white man for "the nigger" that has fixed what seems a social barrier between the English and Moors, as old travellers were accustomed to call the natives of India. The true explanation, whatever it may be, is certainly not this.

Most likely the sentiments and prejudices that stand in the way of a freer intercourse between the races are so complex that any simple explanation would be impossible. We are partly to blame, or rather to be pitied, for a certain stiffness of demeanour which always makes a foreigner ill at ease in our company. The average Englishman behaves no worse to the native of India than he often does to a German or an Italian. As a nation we are seldom happy in our intercouse with strangers of another race; and Indian gentlemen are apt to mistake the *gaucherie* of our national manners for contemptuous intolerance. Then again, the conditions under which most Englishmen live in India have helped to make it difficult for the two races to join in social amusements. The hard-worked Anglo-Indian has little time to cultivate the amenities of society, save those which conduce most directly to his own health and comfort. He has little leisure to fulfil the rather exacting requirements of Oriental etiquette. A tropical sun leaves only a few hours in the day for the pleasures of life, and these are more easily pursued in the company of his own countrymen.

Nevertheless we need not despair of a means being found whereby to bridge the social gulf now existing. All decent Englishmen see that the grosser incivility of which Mr. Mehdi Hassan complains is "bad form," to say the least of it. On a campaign in the excitement of commercial speculation, in the calmer researches of study, Englishmen and Asiatics become warm friends; and nothing is needed to promote the same feeling in every-day intercourse than slight compromises and advances on both sides. Our correspondent would do well to caution his countrymen against being over-sensitive; while Englishmen, we may hope, will learn to cultivate more just and generous sentiments.—*St. James's Gazette*, June 2.

Race Estrangements in India.—To the Editor of the *St. James's Gazette*.—Sir,—Having dealt in my previous letter at some length with the political attitude of the Indian Muslims towards the Government of India, I should like to say something concerning their social relations with members of the ruling race. I venture to assure you that the whole subject of the intercourse of Europeans and natives in India, however trifling it may appear to the nonchalant or satirical, is of the first importance; indeed, I am convinced that the future success of British rule in India depends on a successful solution of this problem. All the clamour of the native newspapers, all the public demonstrations of discontent, and all the private heart-burnings with which we are familiar, point to an estrangement taking its rise generally from circumstances purely personal or social, but unhappily tending to infect the political atmosphere.

The Government of India is, from its position, incapable of doing anything to remedy matters; it is the generous open-hearted English people who alone, with the co-operation of natives of India, can lead the way to a better state of things. You in England have societies for the cultivation of the arts and sciences, societies for the study of Asiatic literature, societies for the total suppression of vice, societies for the prevention of cruelty—in short, you have erected an altar to every god in the Pantheon of the virtues. You reached us a helping hand when we were sinking in the depths of anarchy, ignorance, and misery. Will you now allow the best of the nations of India, your pride as well as ours, who are willing to fight side by side with you against any foe in the name of English honour, to become gradually alienated, until you see the good work, of which your noblest sons have laid the foundations in attempting to raise India to the level of European civilization, vanish in smoke? These nations are becoming more enlightened daily, and what was a suitable policy twenty years ago is often merely injurious now.

Let me first dismiss one ancient fallacy, which never fails to make its appearance when the social conditions of India are discussed in England: namely, that it is the seclusion of their women by natives of India that is answerable for all that is unhappy in social inter-relations; that the Purdah system is the sad instrument of all our woes. I do not deny that this system is a grave obstacle to social intercourse; but when it is put forward as a main obstacle it always seems to me to be as an excuse rather than as a reason. The Parsees bring out their ladies, who are as well educated as English ladies, without the least benefit to the mutual relations of the races: hence much deplorable ill-feeling in Bombay. Again, among the peoples of India there are some who bring out their wives and others who do not; but this difference in custom has never prejudiced their mutual social relations, as it is alleged to have done in the case of the English.

It goes to the root of the matter at once to take instances where there is no possible question of reciprocal exhibitions of the fairer sex, but where mutual relations are still of the worst. The rule of the Bombay Yacht Club and other Indian clubs, forbidding the introduction of natives under any circumstances, is a case in point. An English gentleman who is in London to-day was lately staying in the Byculla Club, and a native gentleman, a member of the Governor's Council, who went to see him, was shown in by the back door. The Englishman was much annoyed at this incivility, and on making inquiry was told that natives were not allowed in the club on any pretext. His Royal Highness the Duke of Connaught, I am told, found himself in a difficulty when he graciously invited the members of the Hyderabad polo team to the same club. As a final instance I may give that of the Gymkhana which was built in the Bombay Presidency, the cost being contributed mainly by wealthy Parsees. Last year a rule was passed prohibiting the use of it to natives, and the Parsee ladies were consequently prevented from playing lawn tennis there. Is the cause of this to be found in the Purdah system?

All these instances are taken from Bombay, where civilization and education are much advanced, and where ill-feeling vents itself by way of the tongue and the pen; but the same exclusive attitude may in Upper India become the source of graver political dangers.

In truth, the Purdah system in India has not in the past, any more than any other specific national or tribal custom, been an obstacle in the way of friendly relations between the peoples of India. The *Pioneer*, the best-informed paper in India, in combating some of my arguments on this question, admits as much. "Sometimes," it says, "people argue that the lack of friendly social intercourse in India has to do with the different notions English and Indians entertain about the place of women in creation. But difference of opinion need not always be an impediment to friendship. No native gentleman would ever be otherwise than perfectly respectful in social intercourse to English ladies. . . . . It would be nonsense to contend that you could not be friends with a man without also being on intimate terms with his wife."

These are perfectly sound remarks, and will be endorsed by all who know India well. I go farther, and say we have no right to question each other's customs. The Mahommedans and Hindoos have been for centuries together with the greatest difference in customs and manners; but this difference has always been respected by both parties, even when the delicate question of the position of women was concerned. The Hindoos are most particular about the birth and family of their women; if a Brahmin marries a Kshatriya woman, both of them are socially excommunicated. The Mahommedan law, on the other hand, is diametrically opposed to this. Marriage into our community places a woman of any position in life on a level with us, and she takes the rank of her husband. Yet this vast difference on an important social question has never made any breach between the Mahommedans and Hindoos, who have always received each other according to their respective customs.

No greater weight can be attached to prejudices in the matter of eating and drinking. The *Pioneer* says: "The wretched difficulties about eating and drinking are at the root of the whole trouble. Perhaps European social intercourse is made to revolve round eating and drinking a great deal too much." Yet the last few years' progress has shown us that even community of eating and drinking, which some pedants call "commensality," does not serve to bring the different races of India closer together. Many Parsees, Mahommedans, and educated Hindoos have got rid of their exclusive prejudices in this matter, and yet seem to feel still more bitter towards one another. A friend of mine, English educated, and quite free from all these prejudices, who has deservedly won the high esteem of the Government of India, and who has in recognition of his abilities been promoted by Government to the highest honours, tells me that the higher the position he reached, and the greater the formal recognition he consequently received in society, the more keenly he felt his real social estrangement from the English.

It is sometimes alleged that a truer cause is to be found in the fact that in India everything is official. The official class are kept employed by their duties, and, being in authority, are bound, it is said, to keep aloof. There is something in this; but it is not the cause of the general estrangement. Nor is there any real need that the English official class should treat their native colleagues with so marked an indifference, in which, I should add, they are imitated by the non-official class who have not the same excuse. "If we associate with natives," these are apt to urge, "it is difficult to fix a limit; if we admit one of them to membership in our clubs, why not another? And yet some natives of importance are not fit persons to associate with." I confess I do not see the force of this. Such social questions in every race ought to be decided separately on considerations of individual merit, as they are decided even among ourselves. If an unfit person becomes a candidate for election to a club, let him be blackballed; it is easy to avoid the comradeship of a man of bad character without offending thereby many men of good character by making the question a national one.

A truer cause of the wrong relations which we all regret is to be found in the fact that the English have long been a nation of pioneers and colonists, and having acquired land in America, Africa, Australia, and New Zealand, where the natives are barbarian peoples and have died out or been absorbed by the English. They regard the natives of India in the same light, and overlook the fact that we have ourselves been a great nation, with our own history, our own literature, and our own Government, which once stood high among the Governments of the world. We are no aborigines; we are born to live, not to dwindle away or be absorbed in another nation. And now since we have become the children of England by adoption the English have become our brothers, and we ought to attempt to bridge the social gulf, to co-operate in the work of government, and together to raise the English Empire high in fame.

As this is my last letter, let me explain how great political evils may result from social estrangement between the two races, and thus cause detriment to British rule and British honour. I am aware that I am touching on a delicate subject, and will only indicate in general what might be more fully set forth in particular. The members of the two races mix so little on a common social platform that they are entirely unacquainted with each other's real feelings and motives, which are expressed only at the dinner table or in other private ways, and which, in many cases, furnish the clue to important political movements. There is no real general interchange of opinion between the two races, save by means of the violent newspapers, which succeed only in widening the gulf every day. The result is a mutual misunderstanding, removable only by more complete knowledge.

Now, scientific navigation and railways have brought England very near to India; and it is no longer out of the reach of all save members of the civil and military services and adventurous traders, but is resorted to by Englishmen of every class, high and low, noble and ignoble, many of whom go to India to seek their fortunes. Englishmen of the baser sort take advantage of the estrangement between the races, and, playing on the ignorance prevalent among natives of the real character of their rulers, represent themselves as persons of influence with those who are in power; to whose company the native only knows that they have a facility and frequency of access that is impossible for a native gentleman, who will be treated with much formal courtesy, but who finds anything in the way of informal intimacy with the English exceedingly difficult of attainment. By the leverage of social intimacy with the rulers of the country, acting on the general ignorance of the wholly unpolitical and uninfluential nature of that intimacy, many a noble name has been used as a tool for scandalous designs.

The *Pioneer* itself admits all this in a recent article on the subject of Hyderabad. "Of all the denizens of the capital," it says, "the low-class Englishman and quasi-European, 'with his loins girt up to run with speed be the errand what it may,' is the most notorious and the worst." Again it says, "It is only necessary to examine the history of every prominent scandal which has occurred in Hyderabad during the past five years, in all of which some more or less sordid object has been the mainspring, in almost all of which an Englishman, in some capacity, has been mixed up to understand the dislike, the disrespect—we might almost say the contempt—with which in that State the very name of Englishman has come to be regarded."

All this is too true, and if we go to the root of the matter we shall find that it is the want of social intercourse and mutual acquaintance between the races that makes it possible for a low-class or unprincipled Englishman to raise himself to power by playing on this mutual ignorance. It is a noble characteristic of the Indian races to suffer in silence, and many mysterious things which happen every day in India, especially in the Native States, will be exposed only by future historians of India. There is, as it were, a high wall between the two nations, built by prejudice; and it is only by hearsay that each can know what is going on on the other side. In the every-day business of Native States some English people are entire masters of the situation. Their personal friendship with the British representatives, their apparent influence with the Englishmen in power at headquarters (an influence which is wrongly inferred from the politeness shown by these officials), is always turned to their private advantage. They can thus bring the master whom they professedly serve down on his knees before them. The mouth of every native gentleman is shut; for he believes, and sometimes with reason, that these men could bring him into disgrace if they liked. But all these things would be rendered impossible by a free and friendly social intercourse between the two races.—I am, Sir, your obedient servant, Mehdi Hasan, Fathah Nawaz Jung. May 29.—*St. James's Gazette*, June 2.

There were some very piquant revelations before the Hyderabad Concession Committee to-day. The report is well worth reading in full as a specimen of what promoters of "companies" can do under the present Limited Liability Acts. Mr. Labouchere is evidently of opinion that at last his chance of unearthing financial grievances has come, and he certainly made the running heavily to-day. There was a large array of counsel present, Mr. Horace Davey being conspicuous among them.—*Manchester Examiner*, June 2.

In a letter to the *Statist*, a correspondent calls for a Parliamentary inquiry into the affairs of the Peruvian Guano Company, Limited, with which two of the promoters of the Hyderabad (Deccan) Company were intimately connected, but we think it is rather late now to go into the Peruvian question.—*Financial Critic*, June 2.

Hyderabad-Deccan.—To the Editor.—Dear Sir,—I bought some shares in the above at a little over 12 at the recommendation of an influential member of the London Stock Exchange, and have read with some interest the remarks you have made with reference to this concern and those connected therewith. What would you advise me to do now, and when does the investigation take place?—Yours obediently, Deceived.—Maldon, May 31st, 1884.

The first meeting of the Committee took place yesterday, and the revelations are likely to be as lively as they are interesting, especially as the Committee have power to examine on oath any witnesses they may choose to call, including those jobbers who assisted in the rigging of these shares (unless they are on the continent), and when the evidence is made known, the shares of this undertaking will fall to their intrinsic value, which, in our opinion, is very difficult to define. At the last account some brokers made them up at 7, but it would be impossible for anybody to get anything like this price. We should advise all interested to sell while they can.—*Financial Critic*, June 2.

I hear that the Minister of Finance of the Nizam's Government is now on his way to London to give evidence before the House of Commons Committee on the Hyderabad mining scandal. At one time Abdul Huk himself expressed his intention of doing the same thing, and actually left Hyderabad, it was believed, for the purpose. It appears, however, that he only went away to consult his counsel at Secunderabad. The *Pioneer* of Allahabad, which was the first journal to expose the scandal, complains that Mr. Cordery, the resident at the Nizam's Court, did not exercise as much vigilance in the matter as he ought to have done.—*Glasgow Herald*, June 2.

I am not quite certain whether the most important of to-day's proceedings at Westminster did not take place at the Sessions-house opposite Parliament-green some time before Mr. Speaker took the chair. I am not alluding to the select committee on what is called the Hyderabad scandal, but to the revelations before the Royal Commission respecting the Metropolitan Board of Works. Of course, the matter is *sub judice*, and decisions must be suspended, but a member of the Board admitted receiving £2,000 with respect to plans for a music-hall which could not be erected before the Board of Works had approved of the plans; while another witness admitted having made £15,000 over the site for the Colonial Institute, and making costly presents, or "fees," to several members of the board, and a year's salary to one of the surveyors. This evidence has created profound sensation in London, for the operations of the Board of Works are of the most gigantic character. This Royal Commission was appointed on the motion of Lord R. Churchill, and it was high time that an inquiry was instituted. It is quite clear that only the mildest of revelations has yet seen the light.—*Liverpool Courier*, June 2.

THE HYDERABAD SCANDAL.—There are two points in the evidence before the Hyderabad Deccan Commission which strike us as being ridiculous, yet perfectly natural. One is in the evidence of Mr. Levien and the other is in that of Mr. Batten. The one shows a delightfully innocent egotistical foolishness, the other a thoroughly practical cynicism. In answer to Mr. Labouchere, Mr. Levien is reported to have said that the rules and regulations of the Stock Exchange had been entirely disregarded in the respect that no application had been made for either a settlement or an official quotation. Continuing his evidence, he said that Rules 131 and 132 had been disregarded, and he kindly read these two rules.

Mr. Pember, however, quickly pricked this little bubble of self-importance, and he had to execute what he might call a retrograde movement, and admit that no rule had been broken, as no application had been made for a special settlement: that there was no occasion for a company to apply for one if they did not want it, and that shares of a company could be, and were dealt in, by members of the Stock Exchange, which had not had a special settlement. In fact, he admitted that his previous statements were all magniloquent rubbish.

Turning from this spectacle of misdirected energy, it is quite refreshing to read the evidence of Mr. Batten, the chairman of the company. In answer to a question, he replied that he supposed the public would look after their own interests, and further that he did not consider that he owed any duty to anybody except to the company.

Of course the public, until they became shareholders, were no concern of his. Once brought into the fold, of course they would receive his tender care, but until then they were as heathens, and outside the pale.

We are pleased to meet a man who not only knows what his duty is, but does it, even in the face of unkind criticism.—*Financial Times*, June 4.

ACCORDING to the news which comes to hand to-day in the Indian papers by the overland mail the Nizam's Government appears to have thrown Abdul Huk completely over. One paper says that the Sirdar is surrounded by astrologers and professors of the occult sciences, but it thinks that the poor man is likely to need all the help that these can give him, with the help of the lawyers who have been retained in the case thrown in too.—*Allen's Indian Mail*, June 4.

A HYDERABAD telegram to the Bombay papers states that Mr. Inverarity has gone to England in Abdul Huk's interests on a fee of Rs. 60,000 for three months. The Nizam's Government have served notice on Abdul Huk of their repudiation of the purchase of shares in the Deccan Mining Company made by him last year, and demanding of him repayment of £158,631, the price paid for 12,500 shares. This sum includes £18,750, the balance of the call due on 3,750 half-paid shares, which amount was drawn by Huk after his return to India. The repudiation is made on the ground that Abdul Huk concealed from the Nizam's Government the fact that he was interested in the company, and that the shares partially purchased were Abdul Huk's own property. The Minister's proposed visit to Simla has been abandoned for the present, owing to Nawab Mehdi Ali's absence.—*Allen's Indian Mail*, June 4.

THE HYDERABAD MINING SCANDAL.—The Nizam's Government have served notice on Sirdar Diler Jung of their repudiation of the purchase of shares in the Deccan Mining Company made by him last year. They demand of him repayment of £158,631, the price paid for 12,500 shares. This sum includes £18,750, the balance of the call due on 3,750 half-paid shares, which amount was drawn by Huk after his return to India. The repudiation is made on the ground that Abdul Huk concealed from the Nizam's Government the fact that he was interested in the company, and that the shares actually purchased were Abdul Huk's own property. The Sirdar is represented as being surrounded by astrologers and other professors of the occult.

The *Statesman* publishes a long article giving a history of the Hyderabad mining scandal, which represents an Englishman named Charles Hawes, in concert with Mr. Winter and a man named Barnet, negotiating with Abdul Huk to obtain a concession for a railway which he undertook to do in consideration of a commission paid to himself of 1½ per cent. on a capital of four millions, subsequently raised to 2½ per cent. or £120,000, Mr. Hawes stipulating in return that Abdul Huk should also secure a concession of the mining rights of the State for them for thirty years, at a nominal annual royalty of £1,000. The value of this concession was estimated at £1,500,000. Finally, it was arranged amongst them that Mr. Hawes should have a three-anna share, Mr. Barnet three annas, Mr. Winter two annas, Mr. Forbes, of Bombay, two annas, and Abdul Huk six annas. Huk obtained £100,000 out of the £120,000 paid for the railway concession, but what became of the remaining £20,000 the *Statesman* does not know.

Mr. Hawes, who is now living at Rajkote, and who was the originator of the idea of a mining concession, seems to have been dropped out of the confederacy when he could not get English financiers to take it up, and Mr. Winter got Mr. Watson to work it, assuring him it was worth £400,000 to him. The *Statesman* says it was to no purpose that it exposed the true character of the railway scheme again and again. Mr. Cordery was all-powerful as Resident, and Abdul Huk had secured such support in London that it seemed hopeless to contend against the influence leagued against the young Nizam. The retirement of Mr. Cordery and the advent of Mr. Howell changed matters. The Viceroy, it is said, was incensed at being deceived about the offer of sixty lakhs and the successful prosecution of the Rumbold claims when he had absolutely prohibited assistance being given from the Residency.—*Allen's Indian Mail*, June 4.

So far the evidence given before the Hyderabad Committee has fully realised the expectations of those who believed that a great scandal would be brought to light. But it is extremely doubtful (our London Correspondent says) whether the Radical members who have sought to make political capital out of the affair will be satisfied with the outcome of the inquiry. They proceeded originally on the assumption that a Conservative Ministry was responsible for the arrangements under review, but speedily found that the principal negotiations were conducted when Mr. Gladstone's Government was in power, and that blame, if blame there was, attached to them. Before the inquiry closes some revelations are likely to be made which will further undeceive them on this point. Facts will, I believe, be adduced which will show that a complete statement of the incubation of the mining scheme was placed before Lord Ripon so far back as 1884, and that he entirely ignored it, the result being the establishment of the company on its present footing. By neglecting the plain duty imposed upon him of taking effectual measures to prevent the young Nizam from being induced to give his consent to the formation of the company, Lord Ripon, therefore, is mainly chargeable with responsibility for the irregularities which have since been exposed. He cannot shelter himself behind the plea of want of power to interfere, as the Nizam at that time was a minor, and the Government of the Deccan was to a great extent under Lord Ripon's charge. The matter is almost sure to come before Parliament sooner or later, and it will be interesting to see what explanation is offered of Lord Ripon's action.—*Yorkshire Post*, June 6.

The Hyderabad (Deccan) Scandal.—We do not care to make more than a passing allusion of pure scorn to the eloquent silence of most of our contemporaries on this subject. Without doubt they are all actuated by the same delicate sense of reserve which restrains them from commenting upon, or even referring to, a matter that is still *sub judice*. Our own perceptions, we grieve to think, are not so preternatually fine. We take leave to imagine that the Select Committee of the House of Commons will seek to arrive at the whole truth of this business, and they can be assisted in their search in no better way than by that concentration of public interest which the press alone can evoke. A great scandal has arisen; grave political complications have occurred, involving the relations of our Indian Government with their most powerful feudatory vassal; many hundreds of innocent and unsuspecting investors have been fleeced of large sums of money; and all this to enrich a small gang of unscrupulous speculators, some of whom were already more than sufficiently enriched by the previous practice of their predatory principles.

In view of this state of things, the London press maintains a discreet silence; we, however, do not propose to do anything of the kind, and in this we humbly believe we are but doing our duty to our readers, the public. A year or so ago the *Times* thought fit to make almost daily allusion to "Deccans." Every advance of 2s. 6d. a share was duly chronicled in its City columns, although it must have been well aware that the company had no official quotation on the Stock Exchange, and therefore had no position as a *bonâ fide* investment. We say, without the smallest hesitation, that it was entirely owing to the recognition accorded to the company by the *Times* and at least one other morning paper, that it became possible for the concessionnaires to foist their rubbish upon English investors. Without the hearty co-operation of certain newspapers the fraud could not have been perpetrated, and we are more sorry than surprised to see that the journals which made dealing in Deccan shares easy now decline to insert a single word which might reflect upon the character and conduct of their quondam *protégés*.

On this point we cannot refrain from asking two questions, in the hope that the investigations of the Select Committee will supply the answers: Who was "Political," who wrote to the *Times*—last September, if we mistake not—about the Nizam's offer of money and troops for the defence of the frontier? and who was the correspondent of the same journal, whose communication appeared about the 20th April in all the dignity of large type, for the purpose, seemingly, of whitewashing the suspended Sirdar at the expense of the Nizam's Prime Minister, Sir Asman Jah, whose energy and decision have promptly brought the culprit to bay, and are above praise?

It will be seen that we by no means share the opinion that because the eminent Sirdar, once known as Abdul Huk, has been made to disgorge a portion of his plunder, we ought to consider the matter as settled, and cease on that account to regard it as a topic of general interest. From the very first we have maintained that the relations existing between Abdul Huk and his master the Nizam were not alone in question. The Nizam, we thought, could probably take care of himself in the matter, and events have shown that we were right. He can make abundant political capital out of the incident, which is greatly to be regretted; but in a pecuniary sense it would have been strange indeed if an Eastern potentate could not compel an erring subject to "do him reason." We write in the interest of the public who have been induced to buy Abdul Huk's rubbish at high prices. The mere fact that this Oriental financier and his European confederates have been compelled to refund the money paid for 12,500 shares would seem to indicate that Abdul Huk and Company have now that number of shares to sell, and if they get no more than, say, ten shillings a share for them, the amount will represent so much clear profit. We claim that Abdul Huk should be made to take back every share that he has sold, not only to his master the Nizam, but to English investors; that thereafter this precious concession should be cancelled, and the Nizam be left to explore his mining properties with his own money in future.

The evidence already taken by the Select Committee of the Commons is instructive reading, and would be more so were the public to read it from the official verbatim report, instead of contenting themselves with the condensed and garbled version of it presented by the press. We do not propose, however, to comment upon it at this early stage of the proceedings, preferring to reserve our remarks until the "startling revelations" in store, and the drastic exposure imminent, leave us a freer hand to deal with names and incidents. With the political features of the subject it is, as we have before said, scarcely our province to interfere; our duty is obviously more concerned with the "City" aspect of the matter—with the introduction of the company to the Stock Exchange, and the nature of the transactions which enabled the concessionnaires and their agents to float so successfully the shares on the public.

We still maintain that in the desire of the Committee to arrive at the true inwardness of this portion of the subject under inquiry, they will find in their easiest, and indeed their only, course to thoroughly probe and investigate the circumstances which attended the now famous, and the now cancelled, Nizam "deal." The names of the brokers' clients for whom the shares were bought, the manner in which they were bought, the names of the jobbers—or jobber—who sold them, and the persons or person for whom the dealers—or dealer—were acting, ought all to come out; and if this is done as it ought to be done we shall be in no manner of doubt as to the whole nature of this transaction. We cannot too earnestly repeat our strong conviction that the key to the whole mystery—if mystery it can be called—will be found most readily upon the investigation of the circumstances which surrounded the purchase of the Nizam's shares.—*World*, June 6.

THE HYDERABAD INQUIRY.—The Select Committee of the House of Commons appointed to inquire into matters relating to the Hyderabad Deccan Mining Company resumed yesterday, Sir H. James presiding.—Mr. Hall, secretary to the company, recalled, produced a number of documents which were asked for at the last sitting, including a report furnished by Mr. Molesworth, the company's engineer in Hyderabad. It was arranged that the secretary should be recalled on the next hearing, and cross-examined. Particulars of the company's shares were next furnished, after which Mr. Evans, stockbroker, was examined at great length as to the sale of the company's shares on the Stock Exchange. He could have sold the whole capital of the company at the time, and would have been glad to have had the opportunity. He presumed that Abdul Huk was the owner of shares when he first saw him, but he did not know how he came by them. He got about £360 commission. It was desired that it should be made known that the Hyderabad Government was buying the company's stock.

Sir Henry James: Do you mean to say that it was a *bona fide* transaction for Abdul Huk to buy his own shares for his Government and to employ six brokers to sell to himself as representing his Government?

Mr. Evans would rather not express an opinion. Pressed, he admitted that his object in employing six brokers was to improve the price of the shares. He did this in the interest of himself, his friends, and the public. He would rather not say what his commission was before the 1st of June.

The Committee decided that the question must be answered.

Mr. Evans said he was paid 10s. a share, and if he had known what was likely to follow he would have asked for a pound. (Laughter.)

Mr. Littler proved that the public had every opportunity of satisfying themselves as to the constitution of the company.

Mr. Winter, brother-in-law of Mr. Watson, and a solicitor, gave evidence. He had an interview with Abdul Huk, who wished the promoters to pay him £120,000 in cash. The witness considered it was a bribe, as Abdul Huk was acting for the Nizam's Government, and he asked him what authority he had for asking this money. In January, 1882, Abdul Huk showed him a letter from Sir Salar Jung, which stated that his Highness's Government appreciated the services rendered by Abdul Huk, and had no objection to his receiving any remuneration with which the promoters chose to reward his services.

In reply to Mr. Labouchere, the witness detailed at great length the course of the negotiations.

In further cross-examination, Mr. Winter said he was remunerated for his efforts with one-eighth of the shares received by the concessionnaires. He promised Abdul Huk one-fourth share. On the 14th of January, 1882, Abdul Huk told him that his Government were aware of this. When Abdul Huk received the money for the payment of the railway and paid it into the National Provincial Bank less £83,000 his commission, he stuck to this—in spite of the objections of Sir Salar Jung, who appealed to the Viceroy; but the Government of Calcutta declined to interfere. He considered that he was justified in taking the money under the letter of Sir Salar Jung the elder.

Mr. Labouchere asked if it were not a singular coincidence that Abdul Huk, the owner of so many shares, had not his name on the register.

The witness said he transferred the shares in blank; in fact, lodged them with the Sirdar's banker.

Sir Horace Davey, as representing Abdul Huk, read a telegram he had received from Secunderabad, stating that an agreement had been signed between Abdul Huk and the Nizam. The Sirdar Abdul Huk had repurchased the shares which he had sold to the Nizam for £151,631, with interest.

Mr. Mayne, representing the Nizam, confirmed this.

After some discussion, it was arranged that the original letter shown to Mr. Winter should be produced, and the inquiry was adjourned until Friday.
—*Daily News*, June 6.

The Deccan Mining Scandal.—A few of the trade secrets of the City were disclosed yesterday at the adjourned inquiry into the Deccan Mining scandal. The euphemisms were dropped under the examination of Mr. Labouchere and Sir Henry James, and a spade was called a spade. For "introducing the business" Abdul Huk obtained a fourth of the 85,000 shares which were allotted to the concessionnaires, but every precaution was taken to conceal the fact that any shares were ever held by him. How the oracle was worked on the Stock Exchange was also explained. The concessionnaires kept peddling out these shares to the public, but they evidently did not go fast enough, and so the Nizam's Government were induced to come in as buyers.

Abdul Huk with all solemnity ordered the purchase of 12,000 shares on behalf of the Nizam, and Mr. Watson keeping up the farce as solemnly pointed out that there would be great difficulty in obtaining the shares, although they were held largely by themselves. Simultaneously they instructed an agent to sell the required number of shares to a broker, and to send into the Stock Exchange half a dozen other brokers to buy them back, thus concealing the source from whence they came, and at the same time reckoning upon the good effect upon the market of purchases by the Nizam at a premium. All this was supposed to be perfectly *bonâ fide* business, but the restitution by Abdul Huk to the Nizam's Government of £151,631, with interest at 5 per cent., of which, the committee has been informed by telegraph, shows that even the parties concerned have now changed their mind on the subject.—*Pall Mall Gazette*, June 6.

The Inquiry into the Deccan Mining Company.—The Select Committee of the House of Commons appointed to inquire into the circumstances of the formation of the East India (Hyderabad) Deccan Mining Company met yesterday under the presidency of Sir Henry James. The different parties concerned in the inquiry were represented by counsel as before.

Mr. Hall, secretary to the company, was recalled, and put in a number of documents relating to its business. One document, read by the chairman, showed that 85,000 shares were divided as follows:—Mr. Stewart, 8,868; Mr. Sharp, 3,781; Mr. Winter, 460; Mr. Watson, 4,249; warrants to bearer, 21,250; other people, 46,392. Fifteen thousand shares were held, half by Watson, Winter, Sharp, and Stewart, and half by other persons.

Mr. Pember promised that a statement of the consideration paid by the public for the 54,000 shares should be placed before the Committee.

Mr. Richard Stanton Evans, who was examined by Mr. Labouchere, gave evidence as to the part he had taken in selling shares for Mr. Watson. He said that after the statutory meeting of the company he received an intimation that there was a spontaneous inquiry on the Stock Exchange for Deccan shares. He went to Mr. Watson and offered to sell shares for him. There were 20 people at the statutory meeting. There was nothing printed or published. He sold several thousand shares for Mr. Watson from time to time. He sold them to the broker, and this went on for some months. He should say he sold 20,000 or 30,000 shares. He dealt with shares on the 3rd of June, but he could not say that Abdul Huk personally told him to sell. He should say Mr. Watson did. He told him to sell as many shares to the best buyers as he possibly could. He did not remember whether they were Abdul Huk's shares. Mr. Watson had a written sketch with regard to the Golconda diamond mines, and he was not sure whether it was on his suggestion that it had been printed for the information of the private shareholders.

By the Chairman: I could not say positively that I knew that on the 3rd of June Abdul Huk was interested in the shares.

You got 8,750 fully-paid and 3,750 on which £5 were paid from Abdul Huk, and I suppose either Abdul Huk or Watson told you that they had those shares to sell?—Some one told me.

Therefore, you went to a broker?—I went to a broker and told him to sell to a jobber. The broker was Mr. Hurst, and I told him to sell 12,000 shares at my price, 12, and not the market price. He would have sold at 10 or 15 had I told him, and he could have got the purchasers.

You gave a commission to Hurst to sell to a jobber, and you gave the commission to somebody else to buy, so that you found the seller and the buyer?—Yes; I thought it would be a good thing for the company if it became known on the Stock Exchange that the Government were buying. I had a commission of £360.

May I suggest that you went to six firms instead of one firm to make the transaction look genuine, and lead the public to believe that it was an absolutely *bona-fide* transaction?—Certainly, and I consider that it was a *bona fide* transaction.

There were six persons buying from one broker, and one person selling to himself as representing his Government. Do you consider that a *bona fide* transaction?—I was anxious in my own interest that as many people as possible should know that the shares were being bought by the Government.

You thought it would improve the market value of the shares?—Certainly.

Watson had shares in his possession?—Certainly, but he did not want to sell them.

Witness, in further examination, said he had sold shares for Watson before the 3rd of June, and, after being pressed, admitted that he had received 10s. for each share sold, and added that he was sorry he had not asked a sovereign. The company could not have obtained, and was not able now to obtain, a quotation on the Stock Exchange, owing to the rule which prevented a quotation where the vendors held more than one-third of the shares.

Mr. Winter, retired solicitor, in the course of his testimony, said Abdul Huk had originally stipulated to be paid £120,000 in cash for introducing railway business to whoever got the railway. Witness said he could not consent to anything of the kind. Abdul Huk then stated that he had the permission of the Hyderabad Government to make any terms he could with the company; but being told that a verbal statement of that character was insufficient, he afterwards produced a written one from the Government, and the money was paid.

Sir Horace Davey stated that a telegram had been received from Abdul Huk in which he stated that an arrangement had been come to between himself and the Nizam's Government for the repurchase of the shares of which he had become possessed, for £151,630, with interest. An agreement for that purpose had been signed.

The Chairman: That seems to be a restoration of the money which he has received.

Sir H. Davey: Yes, I understand that is so.

The Committee adjourned until Friday.—*Times*, June 6.

THE DECCAN INQUIRY.—EVIDENCE BEFORE THE ROYAL COMMISSION.—HOW THE SHARES WERE WORKED OFF.—THE FIRST ISSUE OF £100,000.—THE SOLICITOR'S REMUNERATION.—The Select Committee of the House of Commons appointed to inquire into the circumstances attending the promotion of the East India (Hyderabad) Deccan Mining Company, and subsequent operations on the Stock Exchange, met again yesterday, Sir Henry James presiding. The various parties concerned were represented by counsel as before. The members of the committee present were Mr. Labouchere, Mr. M'Lagan, Mr. P. J. Robertson, Mr. Bristowe.

Mr. Hall, secretary to the company, produced a large number of documents (many of which had been ordered by the committee) relating to the company, and including reports from officials as to the mines.

The Chairman: The 85,000 shares were divided as follows:—Mr. Stewart, 8,868; Mr. Sharp, 3,781; Mr. Winter, 460; Mr. Watson, 4,249; warrants to bearer, 21,250; other people, 46,392. The 15,000 shares were held half by Watson, Winter, Sharp and Stewart, and half by other persons. (To witness.) Can you give the consideration for the transfer?

The Witness: I can do so, but it will take some time.

The Chairman: The Committee would like that information. Did these gentlemen, Messrs. Watson, Winter, Sharp and Stewart, get rid of their shares and buy them back before March 26, 1888?—I cannot give that information.

A Shareholder: The repurchases, if they existed, would appear on your books?—Yes.

Mr. Pember, Q.C. (for the company), produced a return, dated August 10, 1887, showing that Watson at that time held 4,744 shares; Winter, 3,875; Sharp, 4,977; Stewart's executors, 11,704; warrants to bearers, 21,250; and 689 of the public, 53,450.

The Chairman: Then there has been some buying back?—No doubt, sir. In May, 1888, the public held 54,000 shares.

Mr. Pember: Yes.

The Chairman: Please to understand that we want the consideration given for these shares.

Mr. Pember: It will take some time; but I understand you want the consideration paid by the public for 53,000 or 54,000 shares.

The Chairman: Yes; give us the highest price and the lowest price during each month from the formation of the company.

Mr. R. Evans, the next witness, examined by Mr. Labouchere, said: I am engaged in financial operations, and have been connected with the placing of the shares of the Deccan Company.

You were in communication with Mr. Watson?—Yes.

When?—I could not say. It was after the formation of the company.

The first regular meeting was held on August 10, 1886?—I was in communication with Mr. Watson regarding that, but not in connection with the Deccan Company.

When were you in communication with him respecting the sale of shares? —On the afternoon of the statutory meeting.

A Spontaneous Inquiry for Shares!!

What was the nature of Mr. Watson's communication to you?—After the meeting I went into my office and I read an intimation that there was a spontaneous inquiry on the Stock Exchange for Deccan shares. I made myself acquainted with the fact. I then went to Mr. Watson and said to him, "Now these shares are being talked about, and I think I could sell a lot of them for you at a premium; may I do so?" He took some little time to consider, and I communicated, therefore, with some friends, and made Mr. Watson an offer, which he accepted, for the sale of the shares.

Do you mean there was an inquiry for Deccan shares on the part of the public?—On the part of the public.

You have just said that you spoke to private friends?—Yes; after the statutory meeting.

I gather that the statement at the statutory meeting was so favourable that there wasa considerable demand for Deccan shares?—Certainly.

How many people were at the statutory meeting?—Twenty or thirty shareholders.

There was nothing printed or published?—Nothing.

The inquiry arose among people who wanted more shares?—Yes; as an evidence, one man who had got some of these shares, asked whether he should buy more. I said I should not advise him.

The inquiry was, some twenty people asked whether they had better buy a few more shares themselves. Was it stated at that statutory meeting that Mr. Watson had acquired for nothing £850,000 worth?—I do not know. I think I was only present a little late. I think Mr. Batten was in the chair.

He made a speech, of course, stating that this company was a very valuable one?—I do not remember that.

What was the nature of your offer to Mr. Watson? Did you make him a bid?—I did, but I forget its nature now.

The price?—There were several thousand shares. I sold them for Mr. Watson in my own name. I knew I could sell them; I had got buyers.

All between the statutory meeting and the afternoon?—Oh, yes; the shares were afterwards sold from time to time. Whenever I could sell any on the Stock

Exchange, I went to Mr. Watson, who gave me shares to sell. I sold them to the brokers, and this went on some months.

30,000 Shares Sold for Mr. Watson.

How many did you sell altogether?—I should say between 20,000 and 30,000 shares.

Can you account for the fact that while Mr. Watson was registering shares out of his name, he was at the same time registering shares into his name?—I should say that he was selling shares on behalf of himself, Mr. Sharp and Mr. Stewart. Each time he wanted to effect a settlement, he took shares out of his own name, as he was always on the spot. I should think they were perpetually regulating their accounts.

You dealt with a considerable number of shares on June 3. Did you see Abdul Huk, and did he tell you to sell?—I cannot say he personally told me to do so.

Who did?—Mr. Watson, I should say.

With Huk's knowledge, of course? Wilson sent for you and asked you to buy a large number of shares?—He told me to sell so many shares to the best buyers I possibly could. He did not tell me whether they were for Abdul Huk. I could not remember whether they were Abdul Huk's shares.

Did you give this advice to Mr. Watson, that he could not buy 10,000 shares, and that, therefore, he had better buy 8,750 fully-paid shares and 2,750 on which £5 was paid?—I think I did not give that advice. It was perfectly impossible to buy 500 or 1,000. I saw Mr. Watson on June 3, the day of the sale, several times. I could have sold the whole of the capital of the company at that time within a very short period; indeed, there was a mania then for mining securities.

Look at that, please. [Producing a printed document of the diamond mines.] Do you know anything about it?—I suppose Mr. Watson ordered it to be printed. I do not know it was not distributed at all. I had one copy one evening, and I had to return it next morning. The object of it was to give some information to the people who had subscribed. It was suggested that something should be printed instead of talking about the company so much.

The suggestion came from you?—I think so: I am not sure.

That was to inform the existing shareholders of the position of the company?—Something of that nature. All the printed documents were returned, so far as I know.

The Golconda Mine! One Victim!

Mr. Labouchere: That is to say, the information was given to the shareholders without the slightest idea of getting more shareholders. The hon. gentleman then proceeded to read the document, which set forth that for many centuries no other than the diamonds of the mines of Golconda were known. They had not been worked for two centuries, but that if the system pursued in South Africa were adopted, diamonds in paying quantities could be obtained. A reliable expert considered that these mines would prove of immense value, and probably exceed any yet found in South Africa. (To witness): Do you know that?—I know that the Indian diamond is more expensive than any other in the world. It is of finer quality.

Mr. Labouchere continued to read the document, which set forth that the value of the diamonds exported from the Cape during the last ten years exceeded £40,000,000, and added that surely there were no reasons why the Golconda mines, when effectively worked, should not be equally prolific. (To witness): You are the author of that?—I am not. It was sketched out in Mr. Watson's office.

For his own private reading about this £40,000,000, eh?—No; he could not talk to everyone, and the sketch was there.

He said: "Just read that, and then go to Evans and he will tell you how to get the shares"?—(Laughter)—No, nothing of the sort.

Is not this an extraordinary document if it is not to induce anybody to buy shares, but simply for the benefit of those who have already bought shares?—I am not sure that he was not selling shares at that time.

Then this was what was called then "generally salted public opinion" (Laughter.) This was before he had sold a single share to the public, and he handed you and other people this prospectus to read?—I asked for it, and said I would like to read it. The document was on his desk. It was printed and given to private shareholders.

It induced you to buy some?—Yes.

And they got one victim?—One victim. (Laughter.)

BUYING SHARES FOR THE NIZAM.

The Chairman: I do not understand this transaction at present. Come to June 3rd. You saw Abdul Huk and Mr. Watson?—On the 2nd or 3rd.

Did you know Abdul Huk was interested in the shares at all at that time?—I could not say positively; I presume so.

Do you know whether he had acquired them by allotment or purchase?—I do not.

You wanted, as I understand, to buy shares—18,750 fully paid-up, 23,750 on which £5 had been paid—and you could not get those in the market?—Certainly not.

You got those shares into your possession from Abdul Huk and Watson, and you wanted to buy shares as for an agent of the Government?—Mr. Watson was buying shares.

Was he instructed by Abdul Huk?—I do not know.

You wanted to get the shares for the Government?—Certainly.

I suppose Watson told you that either he or Huk had got those shares to sell?—Someone told me.

Therefore you went to a broker?—I went to a broker and told him to sell to a jobber. The broker was Mr. Hurst, and I told him to sell 12,000 shares, giving him the price.

Your price, and not the market price?—Certainly; I told him to sell at 12.

If you had told him to sell at 10 or 15 he would have done it, provided he could have found the purchasers?—Yes.

You told him the price that had been agreed upon by Huk and Watson?—I assume so; it must have been so.

You gave a commission to Hurst to sell to a jobber 12,000 shares, which you provided? You then gave a commission to somebody else to buy at the same price, so that you found the seller and you found the buyer?—Yes.

What was the object of going through this form?—Because it would become known on the Stock Exchange, and be a good thing for the company, that the Government were buying.

What did you get for this?—I forget now.

I think you must try to recollect?—I think I had a commission. I do not know exactly what it amounts to; I think about £360.

For taking two messages, or rather twelve messages?—A genuine *bona fide* transaction.

You went to different brokers. Why did you separate these matters? In dealing with large sums like these I went to responsible firms.

May I suggest to you that it was to make the transaction look genuine?—No.

Was it to make it appear to the public that the transaction was genuine?—The public would not know.

Was it not to obtain publicity?—Certainly.

That really was the reason?—In my mind, sir.

Did you not think that the public would believe that it was an absolutely *bona fide* transaction?—Certainly. I consider it was a *bona fide* transaction.

Abdul Huk, buying his own shares on the part of the Government?—What do you mean?

Would you call it a *bona fide* transaction to buy them from himself on the part of the Government, and then, instead of transferring them to his own hand, to go and get these brokers to come and buy? Do you represent that as a *bona fide* transaction?—I would rather not express an opinion upon it.

Why not?—I understand that Abdul Huk telegraphed to his Government what he was doing.

There were six persons buying from one broker, and one person selling to himself as representing his Government. What do you say to it, now you look back on it, Mr. Evans?—I was anxious in my own interest that as many people as possible should know that these shares were being bought by the Government.

You were anxious that everybody should know that these shares were being bought by responsible agents of the Government in order that people would be induced to buy the shares?—No.

You thought that it would be injurious to the market value of the shares, and that those who wished to sell would get a higher price?—Certainly.

Watson had shares in his possession?—Yes; but he did not want to sell them.

You had sold shares for Watson before June 3rd?—Yes.

What did you get?—An agreed commission.

What was it?—I would rather not state it?

Why not?—Because it is simply filling the mouths of other people. I should be pleased to give it you privately.

I am afraid the Committee cannot take it privately. (After a consultation.) You must answer the question, Mr. Evans. What was the commission you obtained for placing those shares with the brokers and jobbers? I am speaking of the commission on Watson's shares, independently of June 3?—Allow me to explain. When I went to Mr. Watson on the afternoon of the statutory meeting about the sale of the shares, I naturally wanted to make as much as possible, and offered to sell the shares over par and at a premium if he gave me 10s. a share, and after consideration he said "Yes." That was the bargain made before any dealings. If I had known as much as I know now I would have asked him for a £1 a share. (Laughter.) No prospectus was issued to the public, and the company did not obtain a quotation on the Stock Exchange, and could not now obtain one, owing to the rule which prevents a quotation being given where the vendors take more than one-third of the shares.

By Mr. Littler, Q.C.: All the particulars about the company were printed in Mr. Burdett's list, and therefore were accessible to the public. The facts were also, I believe, printed in the City article of the *Standard* of December 13, 1886.

In answer to the Chairman, Mr. Littler said his object in eliciting these facts was to prove the publicity that was given to the transactions of the company.

£120,000 FOR ABDUL HUK.

Mr. Winter, examined by Mr. Labouchere, said: I am a solicitor, but have retired from practice. When in practice I was for a time a member of the firm of Prescott and Winter. My first connection with these Hyderabad matters was in 1874, when my firm acted for the Nizam's Government, in regard to the first railroad. We were instructed by Mr. Seymour Kaye. My first connection with the mining concession was in 1881, and there was associated with the mining concession the purchase of the railroad. The scheme was in the hands at the time of a gentleman named Hawes, who had a partner named Moetz; but, so far as I know, the latter had nothing to do with it. The first intimation I had of any project was at an interview with Abdul Huk at which Mr. Hawes was present.

In what capacity were you acting?—I should say that in starting I was acting as Mr. Hawes's solicitor.

What was the nature of the scheme?—The nature of the scheme was to make an extension of the existing railway, and in consideration of doing that the promoters of the railway were to be entitled to a mining concession in the form of an absolute monopoly for 99 years covering the mines of the whole State.

Did not the scheme also include the purchasing of the then existing railway?—Yes.

What were to be the terms of the purchase?—The purchase-money was to be two crores of rupees—in round figures, two millions sterling—and the Nizam's Government was to guarantee interest at 5 per cent. for five years.

Who were the partners forming the company to carry out that scheme?—When it really got into form the partners were myself, Mr. Forbes, a Bombay merchant, and a Major Strutt.

Who was Major Strutt?—He was in Bombay connected with some companies.

Was Mr. Barrett in it?—No; not at that time. He had dropped out. He had been in the scheme originally.

And so had Abdul Huk, had he not?—His name never appeared in it. The scheme underwent several changes.

There was an arrangement, I believe, by which Abdul Huk was to be a partner, or to receive moneys?—Yes; what he stipulated for was that he should be paid £120,000 in cash for himself for introducing the railway business.

What do you mean by introducing it?—He was acting on the part of the Government of the Nizam.

To whom do you consider that he introduced the business?—He made his proposal to the promoters.

That is, he made terms as to the conditions on which he would recommend Sir Salar Jung to grant the concession?

Then there was an agreement to give him £120,000?—Yes.

It was known to you that he had been sent down to represent Sir Salar Jung?—Yes.

No Railway, no Mining Concession.

Did you not consider the transaction a bribe?—Certainly I did. When the terms were first stated to me I said, "I shall do nothing of the kind. I am not going to prepare all these deeds, and put my clients to a lot of expense, and then to have the whole thing knocked on the head because you have been bribed." Huk then said that he had authority from the Nizam's Government to make the best terms he could for himself. I said I could not be satisfied with a personal assurance of that kind. He then undertook to produce me a written document from his Government to say that he was free to make the best terms for himself. That was towards the end of 1881, and early in 1882 he did produce a letter from Sir Salar Jung intimating that as he was doing service to the promoters as well as to the Nizam's Government, he was at liberty to take any remuneration they might be willing to give him. That letter was dated January 5, 1882. In the same month Abdul Huk was sent to Calcutta to lay the project before the Government of India. The Government said the promoters did not appear to be of sufficient financial standing to justify them in approving the scheme. Therefore, so far as those particular promoters were concerned the scheme dropped, but it was kept alive by other names. Abdul Huk was then sent to England to consult the Nizam's London agents, Messrs. Rothschild. I don't know what Abdul Huk did in England, as I was in India at the time. I don't remember the exact date when Mr. Watson became connected with the scheme, but I should imagine it was about the end of 1882.

Was not Mr. Watson already in the first proposal?—Only through me.

He is my brother-in-law. I telegraphed him from Bombay, saying I should come home, and Mr. Barnett sent a telegram through me to Mr. Watson, the purport of which was to offer him a share in the promotion. I did not come on the scene in London until after Mr. Watson had made his proposal. His original proposal was only in connection with the mining scheme, which was then entirely separated from the railway scheme. In the early part of 1883 Mr. Watson told me that he had received a telegram from the late Sir Salar Jung saying that his proposal would meet with his full consideration, and that Abdul Huk was authorised to communicate with him. Abdul Huk arrived shortly afterwards, and he met Mr. Watson. I don't know what passed between them; but later on Abdul Huk informed me that Norton, Rose and Co. had failed to go on with the railway scheme.

Mr. Watson was present and Abdul Huk said: "If you don't put the railway scheme through you shall not have the mines." Mr. Watson demurred, not wishing to undertake the additional burden of pushing through a railway which everybody else had given up; but Abdul Huk was very determined about it, that unless we put the railway through, we should not have the mines. Mr. Watson eventually gave way, and the money for the purchase of the railway was duly subscribed. Mr. Watson then began to press Abdul Huk about the mines. The latter said he had been discussing the subject with the India Office, that they disapproved of the vagueness of the proposal, and that he had been sent to a firm of solicitors, Messrs. White and Co., in order that they should prepare a proper scheme. I believe the draft deed was settled by Lord MacNaghten and others.

Messrs. White and Co.'s Deed.

On examining it I found it was totally different from Mr. Watson's proposal. Instead of containing a mining monopoly for 99 years, it was only a prospecting license for five years, with a large prospecting fee to be paid. It differed in various other details. As to the subscribed capital, our proposal was to form a company with £1,000,000 of nominal capital, of which £100,000 should be the first subscription, with £25,000 paid up. Messrs. White and Co.'s deed stipulated for a first subscription of £500,000, with £100,000 paid up. We did not like Messrs. White and Co.'s deed, and we did our best to get Abdul Huk to modify it. He said he was entirely in the hands of the India Office, and that we must send our objections to the solicitors. We did so, but our objections were unheeded. Abdul Huk then returned to India, and it was arranged that I should go out and try to arrange the matter with the Nizam's Government.

You are aware that the Sirdar, even if he had wished, could not have concluded any agreement with you, owing to the Secretary for India insisting on any agreement being first submitted to the Government?—That is not quite the case. The Sirdar, as I understood, had full power to negotiate with us on the lines of the draft.

But he could not complete any engagement unless he first informed the Secretary of State of what he intended?—I cannot undertake to interpret official language; but, as a matter of fact, the agreement was not concluded without the Secretary of State being first informed of it. I arrived in Hyderabad in September, 1884. I had power at that time to act as Mr. Watson's representative. My object in going to Hyderabad was to get an appointment with Sir Salar Jung to discuss with him the points of difference respecting the deed. Sir Salar Jung, on my applying through the Resident for an interview, sent me a message asking me to put in writing the chief points I wished to discuss with him. I did so in a letter dated December 16, 1884. (Letter read.) Messrs. White and Co.'s deed fixed the minimum first subscription at £500,000, with £100,000 paid up. I wanted to cut that down as much as possible—to cut down the subscription, in fact, to £100,000, with only £25,000 paid up.

The "First Issue" of £100,000.

In your letter to Sir Salar Jung you speak of the "first issue" of £100,000. What was to become of the other £900,000?—That is a point I had not considered. Perhaps I should not have used the phrase "first issue."

Had not Sir Salar Jung the right to assume if you used the words "first issue," there would be a first issue and a second issue? Had he not a reasonable right to assume that when you said first issue, you meant first issue?—I don't know.

Do you mean to say that he knew you so well that he knew when you said first issue you did not mean first issue?—(Laughter.)—The words were put in without consideration. I never thought that they would be discussed at any future time—certainly not that they would be discussed in the way they are being discussed to-day.

When you wanted a reduction of from £5000,000 to £250,000 or £100,000, what was your object?—To enable the company to be started with the smallest amount of money.

You say you are not a financier?—No.

You were a partner?—No.

You received payment for your services?—Yes.

You own no shares?—Oh, yes; I have been paid for my services by shares.

You are aware that the Lord Chancellor has framed rules for the payment of solicitors, but I assume that your rate of remuneration was quite above those rules?—I am not aware that I have been overpaid. (A laugh.)

You observed that the Government of India used precisely the same words as yourself, "first issue"?—They took them out of my letter.

The second modification is that the first issue of shares has been reduced from £250,000 to £100,000, and the paid-up capital from £100,000 to £25,000, and the Government of India explained that that was done to meet the immediate requirements of the opening of the Singareni Coalfields, and the nominal capital was less as originally drafted in order that a fuller issue of shares might be made if iron, steel, or other minerals were found worthy of being developed. You read that, you say, at the Resident's, and yet you say you did not discuss any of these memoranda?—Yes; because I had already signed the draft. There had been a certain amount of bad feeling between myself and Salar Jung, and I declined to discuss them. I said to Mr. Caudrey that I was perfectly prepared to leave the matter to be settled between the two Governments.

Do you mean to tell me that you had in your mind the desirability of making the first issue as small as possible, in order that you and your confederates might pocket the rest?—I am not aware that I had any confederates.

You were partners?—I was a solicitor acting for my clients.

Well, what did you receive?—I received one-eighth.

Of £850,000! Then you were a partner to all intents and purposes, and it was your interest to get as much as possible, in order that your one-eighth might be increased?—I tell you I did not consider that point; but if you put it in that way there is no answer to your question but yes.

You were a partner?—I was to be paid by result.

You were an absolute partner?—That is for you to form your own opinion.

Would you contest it?—I did not consider I was a partner. I considered I had been paid by results, although my payment was a portion of the results. My idea was that we should form a company, paying up as small an amount as we could; and we should develop the company's property, find out what we had got, and then sell it to other people.

Allow me to ask this: Did you pay up your one-eighth of the shares?—Yes.

That makes an absolute partnership. You as a partner paid a certain sum into the partnership, and received a certain number of shares *pro rata*?—Whatever it is, that is what I got.

Yet you didn't think it worth your while to express an opinion on these negotiations coming from the Indian Government?—No, I could not; I left it entirely to be settled between themselves. If the first issue had remained as it was I should not have objected.

When they reduced the figure of the first issue it was not with the slightest intention of benefiting the concessionnaires?—I think you will find that it was with the object of benefiting the concessionnaires. They thought the terms too onerous.

The Usual Solicitor's Remuneration.

Have you seen a letter from Salar Jung to Mr. Cordery, dated August 18? [The hon. member read the letter, which stated that the Government of India suggested the reduction of the capital, because they thought that the coalfield could be efficiently worked with the smaller sum, and in order to ensure the soundness of the company, so that the mineral resources of His Highness's territories should not be locked up by any failure on the part of the company, who would have the monopoly of all the mines in the country.]—I never saw the letter until it was printed. The Indian Government seems to think that £100,000 is a sufficient amount to secure the stability of the undertaking.

I beg your pardon; to start the undertaking. They are thoroughly penetrated with the idea that this is to be the first issue?—You have the letter before you. I cannot interpret another man's reading of it.

I ask you first to interpret your own. I am only using your own words all through. Now we have the letter from Mr. Cordery to Mr. Durant, in which he states he has shown you these memoranda. "I submitted," he says, "the two memoranda to Mr. Winter, who concurred generally in the proposal with the exception of one point." So it appears you read the memoranda?—I have told you that I glanced over it. That is the way Mr. Cordery is pleased to put it.

It is hardly the same as your account that you just glanced over it?—Mr. Cordery said, "I think the Government of India has done more for you than you have done for yourselves."

Had you stated to Mr. Cordery your position in regard to this?—I don't see I have had any reason to take Mr. Cordery into my private confidences.

You were supposed to be an agent receiving usual solicitor's remuneration?—I don't know what you mean by usual solicitor's remuneration. I left India on August 18, 1885, and did not return to Bombay till December 21. I went to Hyderabad at the end of December, and on arrival there I met Abdul Huk, who told me that the draft had been completed between the Nizam's Government and the Indian Government. He handed me a copy of the draft, and on examination I found there had been a further alteration. A clause had been inserted making the Singareni Coalfields the first work, and reducing the subscribed capital from £250,000 to £150,000. These were the only alterations since I had approved of the draft in the previous year. Mr. Fitzgerald, in the absence of Mr. Cordery, was the representative of the Indian Government and Abdul Huk of the Nizam's Government.

Abdul Huk takes £83,000.

Did you know that Abdul Huk was to receive a four-anna share (meaning a quarter) of the amount to be paid to the Nizam's Government?—Yes: I had seen a letter authorising this, signed by the late Sir Salar Jung, who died in 1883.

Did the Nizam's Government know of this?—I presume so.

Are you aware that Abdul Huk took the money from the bank without the knowledge of his Government?—No; he did not do that. What he did when he received the first money for the Nizam's Government was to pay it in to their account less £83,000. It is not quite true to say that Salar Jung, the younger, contested this. He wrote a letter asking Abdul Huk whether he had kept the whole of this £83,000 himself, or whether he had divided it with anybody else. The Sirdar replied that he had kept it all to himself. Salar Jung then wrote to the English Government, asking if they approved of the Sirdar taking so large a commission. That went before the Government of India, and I understand that they declined to interfere, so that the Sirdar stuck to his £83,000.

You have only heard this?—I saw the letters.

Was any communication made by you to anybody else that Abdul Huk was to receive this four-anna share?—No; I never mentioned it. I regarded it as a State secret.

It was a State secret from the then Prime Minister?—I believe he knew it.

Then nobody knew it except you and Abdul Huk, and a dead man?—I don't know.

Was the letter from the late Sir Salar Jung true or false?—It was certainly a true one, for I know Sir Salar Jung's handwriting.

He was the representative of the Nizam's Government? The more you got the more he got? —I suppose that would follow.

Then that was a bribe?—Supposing it be represented as a bribe, I still submit that the Sirdar is justified in receiving anything he could get under that letter.

A letter written in 1882 referring to proposals which had fallen to the ground?—The proposals never fell to the ground. They never fell into other people's hands.

Well, but if a proposal gets into other hands it falls to the ground. If the people disappear, the proposals disappear. Besides, the proposals were entirely different. The first were really a great bargain for the Nizam's Government? —No; I don't think there is any alteration except in the names of the parties.

The first proposal was that in consideration of getting money at 5 per cent., the parties should have the mining concessions; but the second proposal had nothing to do with the railway. You say you were shown the letter of the dead man, and you did not say anything to Mr. Cordery, to Salar Jung the younger, or to anybody?—I believe he knew that I had always understood that the letter was written for the late Sir Salar Jung by one of the officials, who is still an official of the Court, and who would have knowledge of that letter. I didn't allude to it in the least to Mr. Cordery, although he was the channel of communication between the Government of India and that of the Nizam.

A State Secret.

So you did not think fit to tell Mr. Cordery that this man, who was being put forward as the negotiator of the Nizam, was to be bribed by you? You paid over his £200,000 odd without taking the trouble to ask whether they knew anything about the letter or what it was worth with respect to the concession?—I knew it was written by Sir Salar Jung.

You are not an expert in handwriting?—No.

You kept it, as you say, a State secret from the State?—The State ought to have known it for themselves. It was not for me to commence a discussion about it.

Who were your partners?—Messrs. Watson and Stewart were the concessionnaires. I received one-eighth and Abdul Huk one-fourth. Mr. Sharp was to pay up some of the caution money, but I cannot tell the exact amount. I was not in England at the time. I took my proportion of the £5 paid shares, and the shares which were to go to Abdul Huk were allotted in my name. There was no one here to sign on his behalf. I was going back to India in the autumn, and it was thought desirable that the shares should be in my name, so that I should hand them over to Abdul Huk and get from him his proportion of the £75,000. In December, 1886, I received a telegram from the Sirdar referring us to a banker in London who was instructed to pay me his portion of the £75,000 in exchange for the transfer of the £5 paid shares. The other shares were altered to shares to bearer.

Then you have the fact, the coincidence if you like, that Abdul Huk's name is nowhere disclosed as a holder of shares?—Yes.

By the Chairman: It appears to me that the Hyderabad Government did at that time and afterwards always intend that there should be a first issue of £150,000 in shares. I think you take that view?—I meant it in my letter.

Have you any reason to believe that they ever altered that intention?—Well, I must explain. The negotiations between the Resident and the Nizam's Government took place between August and December, 1885. During that time I was in England, and knew nothing of what took place between the two Governments. I did not continue to ask for modifications after January 7.

I have come to the conclusion that in 1885 the first issue of shares was contemplated to amount to £150,000. Do you think the Hyderabad Government ever deviated from their intention that that should be so?—No; I have said I never had any further negotiations with the Nizam's Government.

Can you suggest any fact, or any words spoken or written by the Hyderabad Government's representative, to cause you to come to the conclusion that they ever changed their opinion that £150,000 should represent the first issue of shares?—Of course, I don't know. I had no means of ascertaining the views of the Government, because I never saw the correspondence.

Can you point to anything to lead you to think that the Hyderabad Government changed its intention?—Well, sir, the only thing I can point to is that the first use of the words "first issue" was made by myself, and I used the words inadvertently. They took my words up.

Did you at that time intend that there should be the first issue, or that there should be absolutely no more issues of shares, and that that would be a first issue; or was your mind in doubt upon the point?—No, certainly. I was pointing to £100,000 being paid up, and nothing else. I intended that the concessionnaires should not be liable to pay £100,000. That is certainly what I meant.

Did you ever discover the inadvertence?—No.

A Telegram from Huk.

Sir Horace Davey, Q.C.: I appear for Abdul Huk, and I think that I ought to say that we have received a telegram from Hyderabad from him, in which he states that an arrangement has been come to between himself and the Nizam's Government for the repurchase of the shares in question for £151,631, with interest, and that the agreement for that purpose between the Nizam's Government and himself has been signed.

The Chairman: That is a restoration of the money he has received.

Sir Horace Davey: Yes; he has taken back the shares. That is all we know. Whether the money has been actually paid I can't say.

Mr. J. T. Mayne: As representing the Nizam's Government, I may say that that telegram is authentic.

Cross-examined by Sir H. Davey: Witness produced a copy of Sir Salar Jung's letter to Abdul Huk, with a declaration, signed by the present Home Secretary, of the Nizam's Government, and stamped with the Government's seal, that the copy is a faithful one.

In reply to Mr. Labouchere, witness stated that his eighth share gave him about 11,000 shares. Of these he had still about 3,000 or 4,000; the rest had been sold from the pool which was formed by the holders of these fully-paid shares.

The Committee adjourned at a quarter past four until 12 o'clock on Friday next.—*Financial News*, June 6.

Apropos of "The Deccan Company," we hear that Abdul Huk has abandoned all defence, and has arranged to pay the full value of the Nizam of

Hyderabad's shares, seven lakhs (seventy thousand pounds) in cash, and the balance by mortgage of his Bombay properties. The Nizam is also free to take further action against Abdul Huk, and may even cancel the concession.—*Barker's Trade and Finance*, June 6.

So far, the evidence given before the Hyderabad Committee has fully realised the expectations of those who believed that a great scandal would be brought to light. But it is extremely doubtful (our London correspondent says) whether the Radical members who have sought to make political capital out of the affair will be satisfied with the outcome of the inquiry. They proceeded originally on the assumption that a Conservative Ministry was responsible for the arrangements under review, but speedily found that the principal negotiations were conducted when Mr. Gladstone's Government was in power, and that blame, if blame there was, attached to them.

Before the inquiry closes some revelations are likely to be made which will further undeceive them on this point. Facts will, I believe, be adduced which will show that a complete statement of the incubation of the mining scheme was placed before Lord Ripon so far back as 1884, and that he entirely ignored it, the result being the establishment of the company on its present footing. By neglecting the plain duty imposed upon him of taking effectual measures to prevent the young Nizam from being induced to give his consent to the formation of the Company, Lord Ripon, therefore, is mainly chargeable with responsibility for the irregularities which have since been exposed. He cannot shelter himself behind the plea of want of power to interfere, as the Nizam at that time was a minor, and the Government of the Deccan was to a great extent under Lord Ripon's charge. The matter is almost sure to come before Parliament sooner or later, and it will be interesting to see what explanation is offered of Lord Ripon's action.—*Yorkshire Post*, June 6.

Sirdar Diler Jung and the Hyderabad (Deccan) Company.—A return, moved for by Mr. James Maclean, has just been presented to the House of Commons, containing a copy of a memorandum of Sirdar Diler Jung, Secretary to His Majesty the Nizam's Government (Home Department), on the Budget Estimate of the Railway for Fasli 1297. The document in question, which, though not dated, appears to have been written towards the close of last year, chiefly deals with matters connected with the administration of the railway department, but it contains several allusions to the Hyderabad (Deccan) Company, owing to the relations of that undertaking with the Nizam's State Railway, as defined in Clauses 3 and 13 of the Company's agreement which relates to the working of the Singareni coalfields. Reference is also made to the purchase of shares in the Hyderabad Company by the Nizam's Government, the circumstances connected with which are now being investigated by a Select Committee of the House of Commons. The Sirdar's account of this transaction is given in the memorandum, from which we take the following extracts:—

"Reference has been made in this memorandum to the purchase by Government of certain shares in the Hyderabad (Deccan) Company. The mining concession, it will be remembered, was at one time part and parcel of the railway scheme, but was subsequently separated. When I proceeded to England in 1883, full authority was conferred upon me to sign all necessary documents, and transact business of whatever nature connected with the mining and railway projects. Owing to the vagueness of the first mining proposal and schedule, I had a revised draft prepared by a committee of legal and mining experts; but since the installation of His Highness was approaching, I considered it advisable to postpone the definite conclusion of the contract, and gave the concessionnaires merely a verbal promise that I would do my best to bring about a satisfactory settlement. Sir Salar Jung, writing to the First Assistant Resident on the subject on the 14th of January, 1885, observed as follows :—

"'The orders of the Council of Regency no doubt invested Sirdar Diler Jung with full power to conclude the mining agreement, and he would doubtless have done so had he considered it prudent ; but, with the caution which has marked all his proceedings, he did not communicate the orders of the Council of Regency officially to Messrs. Watson and Stewart, nor did he give any general acceptance, or even assurance, based on the original proposal. His Highness's Government could not, in its own interests, let the opinion of professional experts pass unheeded and conclude such an important agreement on the terms of the original proposal in the face of repeated and authoritative assertion that it was vague and would lead to complications.'

"The draft agreement drawn up by the experts was fully and carefully considered in its minutest detail by H. E. the Minister and His Highness the Nizam, as well as by H. E. the Viceroy and Governor-General in Council, and after prolonged and mature deliberation was signed by the Minister at Hyderabad on the 7th of January, 1885, in the presence of a representative of the Resident. The agreement was subsequently considered and ratified by Her Majesty's Secretary of State for India.

"Up to this point the Government interest in the undertaking was confined to the ownership of the land on which the company is carrying on its operations and the income derived from prospecting fees and royalty. Limited though the assets of the Company were, with fully paid shares amounting only to 17-20ths of the capital of one million pounds, it was deemed of importance that a sufficient number of shares should be acquired to give the Government, as in the case of the railway, a predominant interest in the concern, with a certain amount of control over the operations of the mining company.

"I would here mention the circumstances which made it possible for the concessionnaires to dispose of their rights to the company at the high price of £850,000 in fully paid £10 shares, out of a capital of one million. At an early stage in the negotiations, and acting on the advice of the legal advisers of His Highness's Government, I most strongly urged the fixing of the subscribed capital at £500,000, in order to secure the soundness of the undertaking and prevent the concessionnaires from making the project a purely speculative one and reaping an unduly large profit, a tendency towards which had been indicated by the original proposal of the concessionnaires to raise only £100,000 by debentures, and not to provide any subscribed capital at all. On the pressing representation, however, of Mr. Winter, the company's attorney, the late Minister reluctantly agreed to reduce the subscribed capital to £250,000, but it was subsequently further reduced, because the Government of India had, in the interim, in their printed memorandum A. and B., forwarded with Resident's letter dated the 6th of May, 1885, suggested that £100,000 was a sufficient capital with which to work the Singareni coal-fields. Although Sir Salar Jung did not agree with the Government of India, the subscribed capital was, in deference to their wishes, fixed at £150,000; but Sir Salar Jung, in his letter to the Resident dated the 10th of August, 1885, pointed out that the Government of India proposed to modify the revised draft, and thus actually made the concession more favourable to the promoters than was contemplated in the draft agreed to by their constituted attorney ; as, however, the object of the Government of India was to bring about the floating of a practical scheme, His Highness's Government had assented, as far as possible, to the suggestions made. Copies of the correspondence referred to are appended, marked

K. Thus the fixing of the fully-paid shares at £850,000 was the result of limiting the subscribed capital to £150,000 (notwithstanding my oft-repeated representations to fix it at £500,000), with the result that the value of each share practically amounted to only £1 10s., instead of £10; that is to say, £150,000 divided by the total number of shares, 100,000. Had the amount of subscribed capital been fixed, as I had strongly urged, at £500,000, the concessionnaires would have been deprived of the opportunity of profiting in the way they did. Of course, this reduction of the subscribed capital does not directly affect the Government of His Highness in any way; but the carrying out of my proposal would have resulted in the Company having £500,000 to expend in mining operations instead of only £150,000."

After describing at some length the reasons which justified the expectation that the prospects of the company were favourable, Sirdar Diler Jung goes on to say:—

"His Highness having called upon the Political and Financial Secretary, the Nawab Mohsin-ul-Mulk (Moulvi Mehdi Ali) for an expression of his opinion, that officer stated that, after careful consideration of the proposal in both its aspects—viz., the pecuniary benefit to Government and the control that it would be able to exercise over the operations of the company—he had arrived at the conclusion that it was desirable that the investment in the shares of the company should be made. 'The Sirdar,' said the Political and Financial Secretary, 'had been very cautious in exhibiting every possible unfavourable feature, and had pointed out that possibly neither gold nor diamonds might be found;' but he was nevertheless of opinion that the investment would be profitable, and that it would confer upon the Government the right to control the transactions of the company. Moulvi Mehdi Ali also stated that there was a balance of £80,867 in the special account with the National Provincial Bank and £17,839 in the general account, making a total of £98,706, and that the difference of £21,294 between this amount and £120,000, the sum required to purchase the shares, might be advanced by the National Provincial Bank, the advance being refunded in due course.

"The proposal was also laid before the Resident for submission to the Government of India, from whom, however, no reply was received to the telegrams sent by the Resident at the urgent request of Sirdar Diler-ul-Mulk, as will be seen from the following telegrams from the Resident to His Highness's Government:—

"'Mahbleshwar, May 10, 1887.

"'No reply yet received from Foreign.'

"'Mahbleshwar, May 11, 1887.

"'About investment, I do not think India will interfere one way or the other, but no reply has yet arrived.'

"The reason for the silence of the Government of India was that the matter had been referred to the Secretary of State. It was considered in committee, and laid before the Council and passed, the proposal having been considered by the whole Council, including the Secretary of State, who has the best means of judging of its value, as sound and desirable, both from a political and financial point of view. The approval of the Government of India was also subsequently signified. The following order was passed by His Highness in the case:—

"'His Highness is pleased to accord his warm approval of the investment, and directs that it be carried out. The Resident's consent has also been obtained. His Highness orders 10,000 shares to be purchased at the most favourable rates, up to £12 per share. The money is to be paid out of the special and general accounts of the railway at the National Provincial Bank.'

"On my arrival in England, however, I found the purchase of the shares a more difficult matter than I had expected, as they were firmly held by the public as a sound investment. After discussing the matter with experts and brokers in committee, I addressed Mr. Watson, the Government agent, who regarded the contemplated purchase as a most difficult negotiation, and suggested that the Government should acquire a proportion of the £5-paid shares—that is, to purchase, say, 3,750 £5-paid shares at £7 each, and 8,750 full-paid shares at £12 each, or 12,500 shares for £131,250, leaving a sum of £18,750 to be paid on future calls.

"By this arrangement 2,500 shares in excess of the number authorized would be purchased at an additional cost of £11,250 in cash, *plus* £18,750, to be paid in future. This proposal was telegraphed to India on June 3rd, 1887, eliciting a reply from His Highness on the 6th idem that the arragement was 'most satisfactory.'

"Copies of the accounts and documents relating to the transaction, showing in minutest detail the amount paid for the shares, the sources from and the manner in which purchased by several leading brokers through the Stock Exchange, together with a copy of the Resident's letter dated August 19th, 1887, to the address of His Excellency the Minister, in which that gentleman expresses an opinion of the value of the investment and of the manner in which the negotiations connected with it were conducted, are attached to this memorandum as Appendix L, 1 to 8. I believe that the latest quotation of the shares is £12-5, so that the Government investment is already worth considerably more than the amount paid. Owing to the purchase of these shares the Government have acquired the right, so long as they hold them, to nominate two directors on the board. The Right Hon. Lord Lawrence and Sirdar Diler-ul-Mulk have been so appointed, the former to attend the meetings of the board in England and keep the Government fully informed of its proceedings, and the latter to control the operations of the company in India."—*Times*, June 7.

THE DECCAN MINING SCANDAL.—Yesterday the Parliamentary Committee appointed to inquire into the circumstances attending the formation and promotion of the Hyderabad Deccan Mining Company, Limited, resumed its sittings in No. 9 Committee Room of the House of Commons.

Mr. Pember, Q.C., and Mr. Lewis Coward were counsel for the company; Sir Horace Davey, Q.C., and Mr. J. D. Inverarity, of the Bombay Bar, and Mr. Trevor White appeared for Sirdar Diler Jung; and Mr. Mayne was for the Nizam's Government.

Mr. Watson, examined by Mr. Labouchere, said that the first negotiations with regard to the concessions for opening the railway and mines were, he believed in 1881. Mr. Winter telegraphed to him from Bombay, and witness asked for further particulars. The proposal was for a five years' concession guaranteed by the Nizam, with the mining concession thrown in, in consideration of a short guarantee asked for by the Nizam. The thing, however, fell through, owing to the Bombay Government saying that they should not advise the Nizam to engage to give a concession. Witness's impression was that his name was not entered. It was after this that Abdul Huk came to England for the purpose of negotiating with Rothschild, Baring, and others. The capital of the new company was to be two millions sterling, with power to raise two and a half millions in Four per Cent. Debentures, with a guarantee of 5 per cent. upon the two millions, and a guarantee of 5 per cent. upon the Debentures—1 per cent. of which was to be taken as a sinking fund—£1,666,000 was to be paid to the Nizam's Government; £500,000 being in Debentures, £650,000 in cash, to be given to the English Guaranteed Six per Cent. shareholders, and £200,000 was to be deposited with trustees to secure the interest to be repaid to the Nizam's Government. Before the old railroad a perpetual guarantee of £30,000 was given. Witness was paid a commission of 5 per cent. on £740,000. The debentures were placed at 90. The company got 85, and now they stood at 105. The actual expenditure out of pocket was £93,000. Witness did not underwrite anything himself. Witness took £70,000 of shares, and lost 15 per cent. owing to the shares going down. Sir Salar Jung died in 1883. The sending of Abdul Huk to England was approved of by the Regency. On his arrival he communicated with the India Office. During the negotiations the Sirdar thought that the India Office should consider the proposal, and it was said that they had instructed him to get an agreement drawn up by Wright, Goddard, and Co. Winter sent witness a draft contract to sign in 1885. Witness knew nothing of the negotiations between the Nizam's Government and the India Office until he saw them stated in the Parliamentary Blue-books. The agreement was finally signed on the 7th January, 1886, in India, and then it was submitted to witness as a casual contract to be accepted by him or not as he thought proper. So long as the concessionnaires provided £150,000 wherewith to work the business, to meet the royalties, and other things, which were very heavy, they were to be at liberty to make what they could out of it. The Government afterwards acknowledged the good services they had performed. The concession in the mines was given on account of their having been so useful in the matter of the railway scheme. He derived that from the Nizam's agent, and from letters sent by Lord Dufferin. Abdul Huk confirmed the terms before witness's proposal went in. He was not to be a partner, but was to offer to buy 2,000 shares, stating that a great demand for them had sprung up. Ten shillings was paid for each, conditionally that witness should not sell any under par. The prospectus was not a little flowery. It was printed after the Company was formed and the shares allotted. The value of diamonds exported from the Cape, it was said, exceeded forty millions, and there was no reason why the Golconda Mines should not be equally prolific. Witness arrived at the conclusion from people who were connected with the Cape diamond business. He sold shares notwithstanding, though he was not anxious to do so. Abdul Huk was to receive one quarter of the mining concession. Witness knew that he was acting as the representative of the Nizam, with the authority of the Indian Government. Abdul Huk was to have a quarter of the first issue of £150,000, but his name did not appear on the register. Witness informed the India Office of the formation of the Company. The India Office became aware of the sale of the concession for £850,000 in the April following. Mr. Sharp was brought in by Mr. Stewart, and they found £100,000 deposited between them. Mr. Sharp was to have one-sixteenth. With respect to Mr. Evans, the witness said that he came to him and told him a piece of good news that the Nizam's Government had decided to buy 10,000 £10 shares of the Company, giving £12 for them.

By Mr. Labouchere: He could not say that Abdul Huk did not wish the public to know that he was selling his shares, but certainly he might seek to conceal the fact from his own Government.

How did the public know that he had shares?—They were deposited in the Chartered Bank of India in his own name.

Then if a person deposited shares in a bank the general public knew of it?—He did not tell the public at large that he had the shares.

You had no reason to suppose that his Government knew that he had the shares? He had every reason to suppose that they knew of it.

Did you tell the Government?—No; why should he? Abdul Huk told him so.

By Sir Henry James (the Chairman): The capital of the Company was fixed at a million by witness and Mr. Stewart. The concession was given in consideration of their services in respect to the railway and their providing the capital. The mining concession was given as a reward. At the first meeting in England, in August, 1886, he did not tell the shareholders as to their exercising any discretion as to witness and Stewart taking the £850,000 profit. The concession he considered to be worth the money, and the gold alone was very valuable. Mr. Stewart and witness selected the directors, who were to protect the interest of the shareholders in this country. Mr. Batten had had a large experience in India.

Sir H. James: And in other companies?—No, he should not say that. The solicitors explained the agreement. The allotment was made in the names of Watson, Sharp, and Stewart. Abdul Huk had not paid then, but had agreed with Mr. Winter to do so. The company was formed privately. Messrs. Batten, Hamedy, and Milne exercised judgment and discretion as shareholders, although they were qualified and selected by witness and Messrs. Stewart and Sharp. Witness and Stewart afterwards became directors.

What shares were originally allotted to you?—23,000 personally.

Then you proceeded to buy shares?—No. I sold them. The document of August, 1886, was not framed for the purpose of selling shares; it was printed to give information to his friends who had shares and who wished to have them. It was not given to certain Stock Exchange brokers as brokers, but as friends of his. They were anxious to see what the company was, and some may have thought that they would like to take shares.

You state that 85,000 shares had been fully paid-up. Would that show that they had been given as a concession?—Witness thought so. He should read it as being the vendor's shares.

How many shareholders are now on the register?—About 700.

How did the public know the value of the concession?—Such a thing soon got talked about in the City. It passed from mouth to mouth, and spread far more rapidly than if it had been in print. People said, "Oh, you have made a lot of money;" and they talked about it, about there being 83,000 square miles of mining land, in which diamonds, coals, and other minerals were to be found. The shareholders were protected by having the concession. He considered, when he gave the advice contained in the letter referred to, that it would be a good thing for the Government to have as many shares as they could. The letter was written at the request of Abdul Huk as a means of justifying the sales of his own shares and the price asked for.

By Mr. Slagg: Did you consider that £150,000 capital was sufficient?—It was sufficient for prospecting and developing the mines. When they could prove they had the capital they could raise as much more money as they liked. They could form separate companies. There were 550 square miles of gold-bearing land, and in that case a million capital would be a mere bagatelle. They had a prospecting right of five years, and at the present they had got the gold and the coal, on which a royalty would have to be paid.

By Mr. M'Lagan: The putting in of the 5,000 shares, as having been fully paid up, was no unusual thing.

Mr. Littler, Q.C. (for Mr. Watson), said he would defy any of the public to come forward and say they had been misled by the document referred to.

By Sir Richard Temple: A sample of the gold had been sent to this country. The existence of about 40 miles of diamond-yielding strata had been proved. It had been stated that some of the native washers had found small diamonds, and that portions of the ground was identical in its formation to that at Kimberley. If some of the men had not bolted, it is probable that diamonds would have been placed before the Committee. There was no doubt about diamonds being there. The blue clay had been excavated by M. Levinsky and others. The result of the work so far, he considered, justified the statement he had made. The coal far exceeded their expectations. Witness had sold upwards of 52,000 of his own shares for £550,000. The share list would disclose the names of the holders.

Sir R. Temple: What had the shareholders got for their money?—They had one of the finest coal mines in India. It contained an unlimited supply of coal, sufficient to supply the Southern and other railways, the steamers, and mills, as well as 550 square miles of gold-bearing strata, worth at least one million or a million and a half. There would be no difficulty in the company issuing £550,000 preference shares, and so working it out themselves. There was no limit in the capital that was originally fixed, but it was not to be less than £150,000. If new companies were formed, they would, of course, have shareholders of their own. They would have to pay royalties, or something tantamount, to the parent company, and from that source dividends would be paid according to its net earnings. Witness expected to share in the profits to the extent of his holding. The £850,000 in the balance-sheet represented money paid. When the company's works were developed, an immense amount of good would be done to the population of the Deccan. The position in July, 1887, was absolutely in accordance with the agreement as laid down between the company and the Government of the Nizam.

The Committee adjourned till Tuesday next, when Mr. Watson will be further examined. Other witnesses, including Mr. Cordery and Mr. Fitzgerald, are then expected to attend.—*Financial Times*, June 9.

Looking into the Deccan Deal.—The adjourned inquiry about the Hyderabad Deccan Mining and Railroad Company was resumed before the Parliamentary Select Committee at the House of Commons at noon yesterday.

Mr. Watson, one of the concessionnaires, after a long examination by Mr. Labouchere, on permission being given, handed in a written statement. He had never underwritten anything himself. He took up about £70,000 of shares, and lost about £15,000 by the transaction, owing to the vicious attacks on the railway. He sold 2,000 shares at par, and Mr. Evans received 10s. per share as his commission. The circular produced he had printed for his friends and not for the public. He could not understand how Mr. Labouchere succeeded in obtaining a copy.

Mr. Labouchere: Never mind, I've got it. (Laughter.)

Mr. Watson, continuing, said Abdul Huk sent for him and informed him that he had a piece of good news to communicate—the Nizam's Government wanted to purchase 10,000 £10 shares. The shares could not have been got in the market, and that being so, Abdul Huk decided to sell them his own shares at £12. This was much below their value, and he could have sold them in the market for considerably more. He was certain of this, any evidence would be immediately forthcoming to prove it. Abdul Huk told him that he would inform his Government that he had sold them his own shares, but he did not do so.

The Committee meet again on Tuesday.—*Star*, June 9.

The Deccan Mines Inquiry.—The Select Committee of the House of Commons appointed to inquire into the circumstances attending the promotion of the East India (Hyderabad) Deccan Mining Company and subsequent operations on the Stock Exchange met again yesterday, Sir Henry James presiding.

Mr. Watson, identified with the promotion of the company, examined by

Mr. Labouchere, said he became one of the promoters in the year 1882, and gave an account of the manner in which the old railroad company had been bought at a cost of £625,000 and the new company formed.

The amount that you agreed to pay the Nizam was £1,666,000?—Yes.

It was paid in this fashion—£500,000 of shares; £625,000 of cash, to be given to the English debenture-holders or Guaranteed Six per Cent. shareholders; £200,000 as security for the first payments of the guarantee—£200,000 to be deposited with trustees to secure the interest under the guarantee, the interest on the £200,000 to be paid to the Nizam's Government; £100,000 in cash, and £241,000 in debentures?—Yes.

The £100,000 paid to the Nizam was reduced by £83,000 given to Abdul Huk?—They paid him that; it was their own money, and their own business.

Making these deductions, the Nizam has only £12,000 in cash?—That would be so, but the Government £1,666,000 for a railway bringing them in something like £12,500 a year, which was over 100 years' purchase. They got £500,000 in a security which is to-day worth £570,000, and they got £241,000 in a security which is also greater in value, making probably another £270,000 odd, and they have £200,000 invested to their benefit.

The Nizam gives a guarantee of £88,000 for 20 years, and a perpetual guarantee of £18,000?—That is splitting up the business. He guarantees 5 per cent. on the total capital of the railway company. And he has a responsible company who have constructed a magnificent system of railways. At present the Nizam may not be very much of a gainer, but prospectively he will be.

We may take it that you made about £7,000 over the transaction?—I lost about £15,000.

The Witness, continuing, said he had raised £1,500,000 capital for the railway and had received £100,000, of which £93,000 went in expenses. For working the Singarene coal-fields another £20,000 would be required, and for that they would have an output of 1,000 tons a day.

The mining concession was granted to you in consequence of your services in raising capital for the railroad?—Yes.

You considered yourself perfectly safe when Abdul Huk told you that he was to be allowed to receive a present, and when you were told he had seen the letter to that effect?—Perfectly; especially when the authority came from Sir Salar Jung, who was practically Regent. I first agreed to give Abdul Huk a share in the mining concession before November 1882, when my proposal was sent in. He received a quarter of the first issue of £150,000, though his name did not appear on the register. The shares were in the name of Winter. The transaction was very officially communicated to the Government in April following, and a copy of the document could be produced from the India Office. His friends had applied for shares, and he had never offered them to the public for sale until after the statutory meeting.

The Witness was requested to look at a prospectus which he had issued about the Golconda Diamond Mines, and he explained that he had caused it to be printed for private circulation, and so that he might not be called upon to answer repeated questions about the mines. Only thirty copies had been struck off, and he did not know how Mr. Labouchere had become possessed of one.

Is it not flowery for a prospectus?—It is a private memorandum drawn up after the formation of the company.

Referring to the purchase of shares by Abdul Huk, Mr. Watson stated that Abdul Huk said the Nizam's Government wanted to buy 10,000 shares at 12. He had pointed out the difficulty of such an operation, as the shares were at 12½, and suggested that he should buy 8,750 fully-paid shares, and 3,750 £5 paid shares. The latter was the precise number of shares held by Abdul Huk, who did not wish the public at large to know that he held shares, though the witness did not understand that he desired to conceal the fact from his Government. Indeed, Abdul Huk told the witness that he had informed his Government. Abdul Huk said he would sell his shares rather than that his Government should be disappointed.

By Sir H. James: The directors of the company protected the interests of the shares, and the directors were selected by the concessionnaires. There were now about 700 shareholders on the register.

The Committee adjourned.—*Times*, June 9.

THE adjourned inquiry into the circumstances attending the promotion and conduct of the Hyderabad Deccan Mining and Railroad Company, Limited, was yesterday resumed before the Parliamentary Select Committee of the House of Commons. Sir Henry James, Q.C., M.P., presided. The examination of Mr. Watson occupied the entire sitting, and the proceedings were adjourned till Tuesday.—*Chronicle*, June 9.

IN another column we have dealt with some aspects of the recently-published memorandum of Sirdar Diler Jung on the Hyderabad (Deccan) Company. It may be well to supplement those remarks by a few further observations on the purchase by His Highness the Nizam of a considerable stake in the Company. All through this business we find the negotiations have been conducted with the utmost frankness, candour, and regularity. Sirdar Diler Jung says: "His Highness having called upon the Political and Financial Secretary, Moulvi Mehdi Ali, for an expression of his opinion, that officer stated that after careful consideration of the proposal in both its aspects, viz. (1) The pecuniary benefit to Government, and (2) the control it would be able to exercise over the operations of the Company—he had arrived at the conclusion it was desirable the investment in shares should be made." The Political and Financial Secretary urged on His Highness that the Sirdar had been very cautious in exhibiting every possible feature, and had pointed out that possibly neither gold nor diamonds might be found; but he was nevertheless of the opinion that the investment would be profitable, and that it would confer upon the Government the right to control the transactions of the Company. A more natural and legitimate desire could not have been entertained; neither could there have been devised a more business-like method of attaining the end proposed, and his Highness ordered the purchase of 10,000 shares on the most favourable terms up to £12 per share. Even a special fund was laid under contribution to the object in view. The money is to be paid out of the special and general accounts of the railway at the National Provincial Bank."

An arrangement for the purchase of certain shares was made accordingly, viz., 3,750 £5 shares at £7 each, and 8,750 fully-paid shares at £12 each, or altogether of 12,500 shares for £131,250, leaving a sum of £18,750 to be paid in future. By this arrangement 2,500 shares in excess of the number authorised would be purchased at an additional cost of £11,250 cash, plus £18,750 to be paid in future, or in excess in money to the amount of £30,000. The proposal was telegraphed to His Highness on 6th June, 1887, and the Nizam's reply was "most satisfactory."

The market operations may have been somewhat 'cute, but with a buyer of the Nizam's status could scarcely expect to buy within its own margin. The operators were sharp as well as fortunate men, but we know one in the City who, under the circumstances, would have his scruples in acting in the same way.

In further proof of the regularity of this transaction, and of the approval which it met with in official quarters, we may observe. Copies of the accounts and documents relating to the transaction show in the minutest detail the amount paid for the shares, the sources from and the manner in which they were purchased by the several leading brokers through the Stock Exchange, together with a copy of the Resident's letter, in which that gentleman expresses an opinion of the value of the investment, and the manner in which the negotiations connected with it were conducted.—*The Bullionist*, June 9.

SIRDAR DILER JUNG AND THE HYDERABAD (DECCAN) COMPANY.—A return, moved for by Mr. James Maclean, has just been presented to the House of Commons, containing a copy of a memorandum of Sirdar Diler Jung, Secretary to His Majesty the Nizam's Government (Home Department) on the Budget Estimate of the Railway for Fasli 1297. The document in question, which, though not dated, appears to have been written towards the close of last year, chiefly deals with matters connected with the administration of the railway department, but it contains several allusions to the Hyderabad (Deccan) Company, owing to the relations of that undertaking with the Nizam's State Railway, as defined in Clauses 3 and 13 of the Company's agreement which relates to the working of the Singareni coalfields. Reference is also made to the purchase of shares in the Hyderabad Company by the Nizam's Government, the circumstances connected with which are now being investigated by a Select Committee of the House of Commons. The Sirdar's account of this transaction is given in the memorandum, from which we take the following extracts :—

Reference has been made in this memorandum to the purchase by Government of certain shares in the Hyderabad (Deccan) Company. The mining concession, it will be remembered, was at one time part and parcel of the railway scheme, but was subsequently separated. When I proceeded to England in 1883, full authority was conferred upon me to sign all necessary documents, and transact business of whatever nature connected with the mining and railway projects. Owing to the vagueness of the first mining proposal and schedule, I had a revised draft prepared by a committee of legal and mining experts; but since the installation of His Highness was approaching, I considered it advisable to postpone the definite conclusion of the contract, and gave the concessionnaires merely a verbal promise that I would do my best to bring about a satisfactory settlement. Sir Salar Jung, writing to the First Assistant Resident on the subject on the 14th of January, 1885, observes as follows :—

"The orders of the Council of Regency no doubt invested Sirdar Diler Jung with full power to conclude the mining agreement, and he would doubtless have done so had he considered it prudent; but, with the caution which has marked all his proceedings, he did not communicate the orders of the Council of Regency officially to Messrs. Watson and Stewart, nor did he give any general acceptance, or even assurance, based on the original proposal. His Highness's Government could not, in its own interests, let the opinion of professional experts pass unheeded, and conclude such an important agreement on the terms of the original proposal in the face of repeated and authoritative assertion that it was vague, and would lead to complications."

The draft agreement drawn up by the experts was fully and carefully considered in its minutest detail by H. E. the Minister and His Highness the Nizam, as well as by H. E. the Viceroy and Governor-General in Council, and after prolonged and mature deliberation was signed by the Minister at Hyderabad on the 7th of January, 1885, in the presence of the representative of the Resident. The agreement was subsequently considered and ratified by Her Majesty's Secretary of State for India.

Up to this point the Government interest in the undertaking was confined to the ownership of the land on which the Company is carrying on its operations, and the income derived from prospecting fees and royalty. Limited though the assets of the Company were, with fully-paid shares amounting only to 17-20ths of the capital of one million pounds, it was deemed of importance that a sufficient number of shares should be acquired to give the Government, as in the case of the railway, a predominant interest in the concern, with a certain amount of control over the operations of the Mining Company.

"I would here mention the circumstances which made it possible for the concessionnaires to dispose of their rights to the Company at the high price of £850,000 in fully-paid £10 shares, out of a capital of one million. At an early stage in the negotiations, and acting on the advice of the legal advisers of His Highness's Government, I most strongly urged the fixing of the subscribed capital at £500,000, in order to secure the soundness of the undertaking, and prevent the concessionnaires from making the project a purely speculative one, and reaping an unduly large profit, a tendency towards which had been indicated by the original proposal of the concessionnaires to raise only £100,000 by debentures, and not to provide any subscribed capital at all. On the pressing representation, however, of Mr. Winter, the Company's attorney, the late Minister reluctantly agreed to reduce the subscribed capital to £250,000, but it was subsequently further reduced, because the Government of India had, in the interim, in their printed memorandum A. and B., forwarded with Resident's letter dated the 6th of May, 1885, suggested that £100,000 was a sufficient capital with which to work the Singareni Coal-fields. Although Sir Salar Jung did not agree with the Government of India, the subscribed capital was, in deference to their wishes, fixed at £150,000; but Sir Salar Jung, in his letter to the Resident, dated the 10th of August, 1885, pointed out that the Government of India proposed to modify the revised draft, and thus actually made the concession more favourable to the promoters than was contemplated in the draft agreed to by their constituted attorney; as, however, the object of the Government of India was to bring about the floating of a practical scheme, His Highness's Government had assented, as far as possible, to the suggestions made. Copies of the correspondence referred to are appended marked K. Thus the fixing of the fully-paid shares at £850,000 was the result of limiting the subscribed capital to £150,000 (notwithstanding my oft-repeated representations to fix it at £500,000), with the result that the value of each share practically amounted to only £1 10s., instead of £10; that is to say, £150,000 divided by the total number of shares, 100,000. Had the amount of subscribed capital been fixed, as I had strongly urged, at £500,000, the concessionnaires would have been deprived of the opportunity of profiting in the way they did. Of course, this reduction of the subscribed capital does not directly affect the Government of His Highness in any way; but the carrying out of my proposal would have resulted in the company having £500,000 to expend in mining operations instead of only £150,000."

After describing at some length the reasons which justified the expectation that the prospects of the Company were favourable, Sirdar Diler Jung goes on to say:—

"His Highness having called upon the Political and Financial Secretary, the Nawab Mohsin-ul-Mulk (Moulvi Mehdi Ali) for an expression of his opinion, that officer stated that, after careful consideration of the proposal in both its aspects—viz., the pecuniary benefit to Government and the control that it would be able to exercise over the operations of the Company—he had arrived at the conclusion that it was desirable that the investment in the shares of the Company should be made. "The Sirdar," said the Political and Financial Secretary, "had been very cautious in exhibiting every possible unfavourable feature, and had pointed out that possibly neither gold nor diamonds might be found;" but he was nevertheless of opinion that the investment would be profitable, and that it would confer upon the Government the right to control the transactions of the Company. Moulvi Mehdi Ali also stated that there was a balance of £80,867 in the special account with the National Provincial Bank, and £17,839 in the general account, making a total of £98,706, and that the difference of £21,294 between this amount and £120,000, the sum required to purchase the shares, might be advanced by the National Provincial Bank, the advance being refunded in due course."

The proposal was also laid before the Resident for submission to the Government of India, from whom, however, no reply was received to the telegrams sent by the Resident at the urgent request of Sirdar Diler-ul-Mulk, as will be seen from the following telegrams from the Resident to His Highness's Government:—

"Mahbleshwar, May 10, 1887.

"No reply yet received from Foreign."

"Mahbleshwar, May 11, 1887.

"About investment, I do not think India will interfere one way or the other, but no reply has yet arrived."

The reason for the silence of the Government of India was that the matter had been referred to the Secretary of State. It was considered in committee, and laid before the Council and passed, the proposal having been considered by the whole Council, including the Secretary of State, who has the best means of judging of its value, as sound and desirable, both from a political and financial point of view. The approval of the Government of India was also subsequently signified. The following order was passed by His Highness in the case:—

"His Highness is pleased to accord his warm approval of the investment, and directs that it be carried out. The Resident's consent has also been obtained. His Highness orders 10,000 shares to be purchased at the most favourable rates, up to £12 per share. The money is to be paid out of the special and general accounts of the railway at the National Provincial Bank."

On my arrival in England, however, I found the purchase of the shares a more difficult matter than I had expected, as they were firmly held by the public as a sound investment. After discussing the matter with experts and brokers in committee I addressed Mr. Watson, the Government agent, who regarded the contemplated purchase as a most difficult negotiation, and suggested that the Government should acquire a proportion of the £5-paid shares—that is, to purchase, say, 3,750 £5-paid shares at £7 each, and 8,750 fully-paid shares at £12 each, or 12,500 shares for £131,250, leaving a sum of £18,750 to be paid on future calls.

By this arrangement 2,500 shares in excess of the number authorised would be purchased at an additional cost of £11,250 in cash, *plus* £18,750, to be paid in future. This proposal was telegraphed to India on June 3, 1887, eliciting a reply from His Highness on the 6th idem that the arrangement was most satisfactory.

Copies of the accounts and documents relating to the transaction, showing in minutest detail the amount paid for the shares, the sources from and the manner in which purchased by several leading brokers through the Stock Exchange, together with a copy of the Resident's letter, dated August 19, 1887, to the address of his Excellency the Minister, in which that gentleman expresses an opinion of the value of the investment and of the manner in which the negotiations connected with it were conducted, are attached to this memorandum as appendix L 1 to 8. I believe that the latest quotation of the shares is £12 5s., so that the Government investment is already worth considerably more than the amount paid. Owing to the purchase of these shares the Government have acquired the right, so long as they hold them, to nominate two directors on the board. The Right Hon. Lord Lawrence and Sirdar Diler-ul-Mulk have been so appointed, the former to attend the meetings of the board in England and keep the Government fully informed of its proceedings, and the latter to control the operations of the Company in India.—*Bullionist*, June 9.

The Hyderabad (Deccan) Company.—Never was there a more ridiculous storm in the tea-pot than the little tempest of virtuous indignation which has been raised about the concessions granted to this Company. A return, moved for by Mr. James Maclean, has just been presented to the House of Commons, containing a copy of a memorandum of Sirdar Diler-Jung, Secretary (Home Department) to the Government of His Majesty the Nizam. Here is an authoritative document to guide those who wish to form a fair and impartial judgment on the controversy which for several weeks past has raged with unwonted and unjustifiable bitterness. One chief merit of this document is that it has an authority and value altogether apart from the specific issues that have now been raised. It deals chiefly with matters connected with the administration of the railway department, and with a larger subject, of which mining is a part. The allusions to the Hyderabad (Deccan) Company fall naturally into this comprehensive document, owing to the relations of the undertaking with the Nizam's State Railway, as defined in certain clauses of the Company's agreement, which relates to the working of the Singareni coalfields. Fortunately for the vindication of the parties, copious reference is made to the purchase of the shares by the Nizam's Government, which are at present the subject of inquiry by a Select Committee of the House of Commons.

Up to a certain date the interest of the Government in the Company was confined to the ownership of the land on which the Company is carrying on its operations, and to the income derivable from prospecting fees and royalties. The mining concession, which subsequently fell into the hands of the Company, was part of the railway scheme, but it was found desirable to separate the mining from the railway enterprise. In the resolution for the separation was created a new situation, in which the concession became necessary, and in which the concessionnaires found their opportunity. That they have made the most of their opportunity is evidence of their intelligence, their enterprise, and their *savoire faire*, rather than of a cupidity bordering on fraud, which has been so unjustly alleged against them. The mineral wealth of the area assigned to the concessionnaires is indisputable, and, we believe, undisputed. Of its extraordinary value the Nizam's Government was well aware, but, for all that, it needed European intelligence, business aptitude, and capital to secure a development of that wealth at all commensurate with its well-known capabilities. There was no undue haste in framing the terms of the concession, as they were finally offered to concessionnaires. The following is the account of the transaction as given in the memorandum in question by Sirdar Diler Jung:—"When I proceeded to England in 1883 full authority was conferred upon me to sign all necessary documents and transact business of whatever nature connected with the mining and railway projects. Owing to the vagueness of the first mining proposal and schedule, I had a revised draft prepared by a committee of legal and mining experts; but since the installation of His Highness was approaching I considered it advisable to postpone the definite conclusion of the contract, and gave the concessionnaires merely a verbal promise that I would do my best to bring about a satisfactory settlement." So far the proceedings of the Sirdar were marked with great caution and propriety. The draft agreement of the experts was at length drawn up, and was afterwards "fully and carefully considered in its minutest details by H. E. the Minister, and His Royal Highness the Nizam, as well as by H. E. the Viceroy and Governor-General in Council, and after prolonged and mature deliberation, it was signed by the Minister at Hyderabad on the 7th January, 1885, in the presence of a representative of the Resident. The agreement was subsequently considered and ratified by Her Majesty's Secretary of State for India.

The Sirdar further remarks: "The fixing of the fully paid-up shares at £850,000 was the result of limiting the subscribed capital to £150,000. Had the amount of subscribed capital been fixed, as I strongly urged, at £500,000, the concessionnaires would have been deprived of the opportunity of profiting in the way they did. . . . The carrying out of my proposal would have resulted in the Company having £500,000 instead of only £150,000 to expend in mining operations." For this modification of the terms on which the Sirdar insisted the Government of India is responsible. It is a surrender made to the views and wishes of that Government. From this account it is plain that the Indian authorities, in a mood of over-caution, created the facilities for the making of large profits by the concessionnaires. They availed themselves of those conditions as other business men would have done in the same situation. And that is all that can be said on the subject. Fraud, indirection, corruption, are out of the question altogether.—*Bullionist*, June 9.

THE HYDERABAD DECCAN COMPANY.—The Hyderabad Deccan Committee met to-day, Sir Henry James presiding.

Mr. Watson, one of the concessionnaires, was examined at great length by Mr. Labouchere. Witness said he first heard of the proposal to obtain a concession from the railroad in 1881. Abdul Huk subsequently negotiated with him in London, and insisted that the railroad should be taken in hand before the mining concession could be entertained. He maintained that the Nizam's Government would greatly benefit by the construction of the railroad. He got 4 per cent. on £748,000 of debentures for guaranteeing to place them at ninety. He took up £70,000 of shares, and lost £15,000 by the transaction. Abdul Huk told him he was to be allowed to receive a present from him.

Replying to Sir H. James, witness said that he and Mr. Stewart selected the directors. They also fixed the capital at one million, £150,000 of which was to be paid up, and £850,000 in shares to be received by the concessionnaires for their services. When Abdul Huk came to him and said the Nizam's Government wanted to purchase ten thousand shares, it was subsequently decided that Abdul Huk's own shares should be sold to the Government. Abdul Huk had told his Government that it was his own shares they were buying. He did not believe it now. He wrote a letter to Abdul Huk saying it would be almost impossible to buy the shares in the market. He did so at Abdul Huk's request. It had already been arranged that Abdul Huk's shares should be bought. In reply to Sir Richard Temple, witness said that if money were required to develop the concessions it could be raised by issuing fresh shares, or by forming new companies.—The room was cleared, and on the public being re-admitted the Chairman said that any witnesses who wished to be examined must send in a statement and the committee would decide.—The committee then adjourned until Tuesday.—*Portsmouth Times*, June 9.

THE HYDERABAD DECCAN MINING SCANDAL.—The Hyderabad Deccan Committee met yesterday, Sir Henry James presiding.

Mr. Watson, one of the concessionnaires, was examined at great length by Mr. Labouchere. Witness said he first heard of the proposal to obtain a concession for the railroad in 1881. Abdul Huk subsequently negotiated with him in London, and insisted that the railroad should be taken in hand before the mining concession could be entertained. He maintained that the Nizam's Government would greatly benefit by the construction of the railroad. He got 4 per cent. on £748,000 of the debentures for guaranteeing to place them at 90. He took up £70,000 of the shares, and lost £15,000 by the transaction. Abdul Huk told him he was to be allowed to receive a present from him.

Replying to Sir Henry James, witness said that he and Mr. Stewart selected the directors. They also fixed the capital at £1,000,000—£150,000 of which were to be paid up, and £850,000 in shares to be received by the concessionnaires for their services. When Abdul Huk came to him, and said the Nizam's Government wanted to purchase 10,000 shares, and it was subsequently decided that Abdul Huk's own shares should be sold to the Government, he believed that Abdul Huk had told his Government that it was his own shares they were buying. He did not believe it now. He wrote a letter to Abdul Huk, saying it would be almost impossible to buy the shares in the market. He did so at Abdul Huk's request. It had already been arranged that Abdul Huk's shares should be bought.

In reply to Sir Richard Temple, witness said that if money were required to develop the concessions, it could be raised by issuing fresh shares, or by forming new companies.

The room was then cleared, and on the public being re-admitted, the Chairman said that any witnesses who wished to be examined must send in a statement, and the Committee would then decide.

The committee adjourned until Tuesday.—*Aberdeen Free Press*, June 9.

The Hyderabad Scandal.—The Select Committee of the House of Commons appointed to inquire into the formation and promotion of the Hyderabad Deccan Mining Company, the circumstances under which the concession held by the company was obtained from the Government of the Nizan, and the subsequent Stock Exchange transaction, was resumed on Tuesday. Mr. Richard Evans, who stated that he was engaged in financial matters in the City, said that Abdul Huk, the owner of 8,000 shares, nominally bought this number up for the Hyderabad Government, employing six brokers in order that it should be known the Government were purchasing.

The Committee adjourned till Friday, when the first witness called was Mr. Watson, one of the concessionnaires. He maintained that the company had a large available capital at the present moment. He called £88,000 a large available capital for the purposes the company had in view. He did not tell the Government here that 85,000 shares were held by the concessionnaires. Sir Henry James announced that the Committee would meet again on Tuesday, when Mr. Watson will be recalled, and Mr. Cordery and Mr. Fitzgerald will be examined.—*Lloyd's Weekly News*, June 10.

We begin to doubt whether much will come of the inquiry which Mr. Labouchere's Committee is holding into what is called the Deccan scandal. A great many rascally practices are being exposed, and that alone may do good if the public will learn wisdom by them, but anything like punishment to the guilty seems improbable. In the "City," moreover, blackguardism is so much a matter of course in high places that the moralisings of the committee will only be laughed at. Morals, with too many financial geniuses and powers, consist in doing anything and everything which the law is not likely to catch you for.

Men often go to the City, like the Yankee to the San Francisco mining market, to try "how much they can get away with," and the bigger the haul the greater the admiration they excite. Envy is often stronger in the hearts of the fleeced than wrath. "If I had only been half as sharp as that fellow I should not have lost my money," is the common reflection, and there are hundreds of fellows, we will wager, in this very Deccan business, who look up to Watson and Stewart—poor defunct Stewart!—with a sort of awe. To them the dealings in the shares are all right and proper, and it will beat Mr. Labouchere to convince them to the contrary.—*Weekly Dispatch*, June 10.

The Hyderabad (Deccan) Company, Limited.—To the Editor of the *Financial News*.—Sir,—As one of the unfortunates (who holds 50 shares of this company, and who paid more for them than His Highness the Nizam at £12) I I trust to your acknowledged sense of fairness to allow me space to make some remarks, so that prejudicial action by the Imperial Government may be prevented by the formation of a wholesome public opinion through your important and widely-circulated journal. I shall, as briefly as I can, try to give some reasons why Imperial interference should not be attempted, viz. :—

(1) Because full particulars of the company were known by the report of it in *The Financial News* of November 26, 1886; the *Bullionist* of December 4, 1886; the *Standard* of December 13, 1886; as well as in Burdett's List; and from the British Government taking no notice, it led the British public reasonably to infer that there was nothing wrong.

(2) Because the Government of India, the India House, and His Highness the Nizam, were all parties to, or in the knowledge of the agreement, and either directly or indirectly approved of it.

(3) Because, however improperly Abdul Huk may have acted (and I do not seek to exonerate him in the least) in regard to the concession, the British public held him to be the duly accredited representative of His Highness the Nizam. In point of fact, therefore, his actions became actually those of His Highness, who cannot, in honour, equity, or law, repudiate them.

(4) Because if Abdul Huk's actions could be set aside now, it would be equally competent for His Highness at some future time to ignore and nullify the doings of his political and financial secretary before the sitting committee.

(5) Because the Nizam's Government have apparently been deceived and outwitted by one of their duly-appointed officials, it would be a much greater injustice that his (duly authorised) actions should entail serious loss on shareholders than that the Government of His Highness should suffer for his delinquency.

(6) Because the act of His Highness and his Government in coming into the open market and buying a large number of the shares of the company homologated his Minister's actions as to the concession, and also the formation of the company, and thus tended to mislead the British public by placing himself on the level of a shareholder.

(7) Because were such an inequitable course as the cancelling of the concession attempted, it would have a far-reaching depreciatory effect upon all other Indian and colonial obligations and undertakings.

Apologising for occupying so much of your valuable space,—I am, sir, yours, &c., A British Subject.—June 9.—*Financial News*, June 12.

The disclosures before the Hyderabad Committee are sufficiently scandalous, but I hear that the zeal of the Separatist members for "a thorough investigation" has manifestly abated since it became clear that Lord Salisbury's Administration is in no way responsible for the arrangements which have been challenged. Mr. Gladstone, in fact, was in office when the original negotiations took place, and the person principally responsible is Lord Ripon, who plainly neglected his duty in 1884, when he ought to have taken measures to prevent the Nizam, who was then a minor, from allowing the company to be formed. How Lord Ripon is to excuse his culpable apathy in the matter it is difficult to conjecture, and I shall await his explanations with much interest.—"*Atlas*" *in the World*, June 13.

Yesterday before a Select Committee on the Hyderabad Mining Scandal, the Nawab Mohsin Ul Mulk, accredited representative of the Nizam in England, was examined. He produced all the documents in the possession of the Nizam's Government bearing on the question. Witness was present at Hyderabad when Abdul Huk stated emphatically that he had no shares whatever in the company, had no connection with it, and had made no profit out of it. This was in October, 1886, and again in February, 1887. A document was produced in which Abdul Huk strongly advises the Nizam's Government to purchase 10,000 shares in the company, and quotes Lord Beaconsfield's purchase of the Suez Canal shares as a precedent. Upon this advice, the Nizam's Government ordered the purchase of the shares. Huk telegraphed to Watson, but the latter denies that he received the telegram, though a reply was produced.—*York Herald*, June 13.

The disclosures before the Hyderabad Committee are sufficiently scandalous, but I hear that the zeal of the Separatist members for a thorough "investigation" has manifestly abated since it became clear that Lord Salisbury's Administration is in no way responsible for the arrangements which have been challenged. Mr. Gladstone, in fact, was in office when the original negotiations took place, and the person principally responsible is Lord Ripon, who plainly neglected his duty in 1884, when he ought to have taken measures to prevent the Nizam, who was then a minor, from allowing the company to be formed. How Lord Ripon is to excuse his culpable apathy in the matter it is difficult to conjecture, and I shall await his explanations with much interest.—*World*, June 13.

The Deccan Inquiry.—Abdul Huk's Commission for "Valuable Services."—Mr. W. C. Watson thinks the public have got full value for their money.—The Select Committee of the House of Commons appointed to inquire into matters relating to the Hyderabad (Deccan) Mining Company resumed its sittings yesterday at the Houses of Parliament. The Committee consists of Sir Henry James (Chairman), Mr. Bristowe, Mr. Labouchere, Mr. McLagan, Mr. Slagg, the Solicitor-General for Scotland, and Sir Richard Temple.

The Nawab Mohsin-ul-Muk was the first witness examined, and the oath was in his case dispensed with. The evidence was taken through the Secretary of the Prime Minister of Hyderabad, who acted as interpreter. He said he attended at the request of the Nizam's Government to give evidence and to submit certain documents and answer any questions put to him. He himself knew very little about the subject of the concession. As regards the concession, the present Sir Salar Jung, the ex-minister, knew the facts, for it was in his time the concession was granted. He handed in a document to the Chairman, and it was read *sotto voce* to the members of the Committee. After consultation, the Chairman said the letter was one from the late Prime Minister of Hyderabad to the present Prime Minister, defending his action in the matter of the concession; but the Chairman said that it seemed to be too purely a personal matter for the attention of the committee to be engaged upon it.

The witness was then examined by Mr. Mayne for the Nizam's Government. He said he did not know Mr. Hughes, one of the officials of the Resident in Hyderabad. He did not know his writing.

In 1887 he was financial secretary to the Nizam's Government. Abdul Huk placed before Colonel Marshall in his presence a memorandum relating to the purchase of 10,000 shares. Colonel Marshall was secretary and confidential adviser to His Highness the Nizam. He identified the memorandum now put in. He read it, but first had a conversation with Abdul Huk about it. A translation done in Hyderabad was attached to it. The memorandum was signed by Abdul Huk. Orders were written upon it by His Highness the Nizam and Col. Marshall, and he (witness) also wrote his opinion upon it. Previous to this time he was not consulted about the concession, and had no personal knowledge of the matter.

As to Abdul Huk's memorandum advising the investment, he (witness) wrote a memorandum also advising it. He would have invested his own money in it, and he said at the time, though no diamonds had been found, he believed that the shares would go up to 30 or 50. He had been told by Mr.

J. Rock that Abdul Huk held many shares. He mentioned this to Abdul Huk, and Abdul Huk indignantly denied that he had any shares whatever in the concern. At the time of Abdul Huk's suspension he denied that he had any shares, and he implied that he had no sort of profit in the matter. On one occasion Abdul Huk had described it as a most advantageous investment, and had induced others to buy shares. He was personally cognisant of Abdul Huk's claim for £83,000, arising out of the railway. He knew that Abdul Huk had sent in a letter of December 28, 1881, purporting to be from Sir Salar Jung, relating to them. He (witness) identified the letter. It was signed by Sir Salar Jung. Abdul Huk was suspended on April 14 this year.

The Chairman here read a translation of what appeared to be the whole or part of certain marginal notes, or of a distinct document, by Sir Salar Jung to Abdul Huk. It was to the effect that the writer felt it incumbent upon him to express his entire satisfaction at the faithfulness and zeal Abdul Huk had shown. It urged Abdul Huk to "continue to persevere," and promised that he "should reap from time to time" the fruits which are "the reward of faithfulness and integrity." "You can yourself appropriate," the translation continued, "the full commission agreed upon as remuneration for your valuable services; this is secret."

Examination by Mr. Mayne continued: In February, 1885, Abdul Huk's claim to £83,000 with regard to the railway was under the consideration of the Government. He identified a copy of an order appointing Abdul Huk to act in London to negotiate for the mining concession.

Sir Horace Davey, for Abdul Huk, asked for a translation to be made of the witness's endorsation of Abdul Huk's memorandum, and the interpreter said it was as follows:—"May 7, 1886. I have carefully considered this proposal, and have considered slowly and cautiously the advantages and disadvantages. The Sirdar has shown the disadvantages that may hereafter accrue, and that if gold and diamonds are not found probably it would result in a loss. I am of opinion that the Government should buy 10,000 shares, which promise hereafter to be profitable, and then the Government will have the right to control the affairs of the company." A telegram was sent by the Government ordering the purchase of the shares, addressed to W. C. Watson, 7, Great Winchester Street. This was on May 10.

The Chairman asked Mr. Watson, who was in the room, whether he had received the telegram, and Mr. Watson said he had not. He used the A B C code with Abdul Huk.

Examination of witness continued by Sir Horace Davy: He produced a printed copy of the original proposal made by Watson and Stewart on November 7, 1882, for the mining concession, and also a letter from Mr. Watson to Abdul Huk, dated February 8, 1884.

Mr. Pember, Q.C., was about to ask a question when the Chairman asked by whom he was instructed. He replied that he was instructed by a committee of directors, not including the concessionnaires. Their names were Lord Lawrence, Mr. Colvin, and Mr. Batten.

The Chairman: The Committee must know whether this appearance is at the expense of the company generally, or at the expense of those three gentlemen?

Mr. Pember: The solicitor who instructs me says he assumes it will be at the expense of the company generally. There has been a meeting of the shareholders. I take it that the committee of directors have instructed me to represent the shareholders who have bought their shares in the open market, and the company would be interpreted, so far as I am concerned, by the shareholders and directors, not including the concessionnaire.

Mr. Pember then asked his questions, which related to various documents. The witness said he did not know whether the memorandum of the articles of association and the agreement of August 17, 1886, were sent over to the Nizam's Government.

Mr Watson was then recalled, and asked by Mr. Mayne whether he had a document, being an agreement between himself and the Nizam's Government, for ensuring 1½ millions of capital for the railway. He replied that he had. He did not recollect receiving a telegram from Abdul Huk on May 10, asking him to purchase, and stating that he was authorised to purchase, 10,000 shares. He would look up the matter. He did not remember replying to the telegram. Throughout this matter from first to last, he had never had a complaint from the Nizam's Government, or from any present shareholder or purchaser of shares. There was not the slightest pretence for saying that he had ever bought or sold shares for the purpose of rigging the market.

Mr. Labouchere: The Nizam guaranteed £150,000 in the railways, and owing to this has to pay £100,000?—Yes.

Coal is now produced at the rate of 150 tons per week?—Yes.

The diamondeferous zone has produced one diamond worth 30s.?—The new ground has produced nothing, for the reason that they have not been able to work it, owing to the cholera. Five stones were found by some natives among the refuse heaps, which simply indicate that diamonds exist. We have now about 900 men working, and any day we may receive reports that diamonds have been found.

What is the actuality as to the auriferous process?—The actuality is that gold has been discovered. We know the gold is there.

You derive your ideas from reports?—Yes.

The reports of Mr. Levinky and Mr. Hughes?—Yes, and the general prospecting staff there.

Paid by the company?—Certainly.

So that these reports are by the paid officials of the company?—Yes, all respectable men.

By Sir R. Temple: In reference to your answers in the concluding part of last sitting, I would like to ask you this: Is it right that out of a nominal capital of one million, three-quarters of a million should go as promotion money to the private and separate use of the promoters of the company?—I think it is quite right that the concessionnaires should have that concession, and I think the public have got full value for their money. The concessionnaires sell at the price they have fixed; they are entitled to do so, and to get the money, and the property is worth the money. The Singareni Coalfield is worth half a million.

What is its present annual income?—Very little. It must be developed, for the company is in its infancy. We have got the machinery and everything ready for working the coal.

The experts are all in the pay of the company, and are therefore the servants of the company?—Yes.

Have you any independent witness of any kind whatever to strengthen the evidence as to the value and productiveness of these mines?—I have handed in some reports.

As regards the diamonds and coal, I ask you whether there is any beyond the paid servants of the company?—We rely entirely on our own men. Mr. Hughes is the geological surveyor to the Government of India. He has the whole of the district from being an officer of the highest standing. He is now in the pay of the company, but the Government can claim his services at any time.

By Mr. M'Lagan: When you say that the public have got value for their money, you looked upon this as a speculation?—Certainly; we paid the money and might have lost it.

What profit do you make per ton of coal?—About three shillings.

You hoped to make 6 per cent. on the million of money?—Yes.

And what output would be necessary?

Mr. Pember: 360,000 tons.

Witness: We are informed that we shall be able to get 1,000 tons a day.

Mr. Fitzgerald, examined by Mr. Labouchere, said: I was acting Resident in Hyderabad in 1885, when Mr. Cordery was away at Simla. I sent the draft concession on to Mr. Cordery.

Did an interview take place between you and Abdul Huk?—I don't remember.

You were left in charge ot the residency at Hyderabad; you receive this important concession and letters from the Government of Calcutta, and yet you do not know anything about it?—I don't remember whether there was an interview.

What do you remember about the whole transaction?—I don't remember that.

But what do you remember? You must remember something?—I don't remember that.

What do you remember about the concession. You remember certain documents sent you by Mr. Durand?—Yes.

Did you see them?—Yes.

Did you form the conclusion that there was to be a first issue, and that then further issues of shares were to be made?—Yes.

That is the conclusion you formed?—Yes.

You had a letter from Mr. Durand, in which he says: "The first issue of shares may be for £150,000, £75,000 paid-up"?—Yes.

You have no recollection whether you had to go through the concession with anyone?—No.

You sent a letter. Mr. Cordery came back, and you handed the whole matter over to him?—Yes.

You did not discuss the matter with him?—Not at that time.

With Mr. Watson?—No.

With Sir Salar Jung?—No.

You really never had any official correspondence about it?—No.

When the letter was sent you nothing took place on it until Mr. Cordery returned almost immediately?—That is my recollection.

Mr. Slagg: You had nothing to do with the drawing up of the concession in any way?—No.

Mr. Bristowe: Did you understand that £850,000 was to go to the concessionnaires?—Oh, no, certainly not.

You did not know what was to take place?—No.

Sir Richard Temple: Have you a general knowledge ot the concession?—Yes, but not a special knowledge.

Which you acquired in your capacity as first assistant to the Resident?—Yes.

Mr. Slagg: Did you hear anything which would lead you to suppose that £850,000 would go to the concessionnaires?—No.

Then this was quite new to you? You have only heard it lately?—I have only heard it lately.

Sir Richard Temple: Would you regard such an arrangement as consistent or inconsistent with your understanding of the matter?—Inconsistent.

Absolutely inconsistent?—Yes.

Mr. Slagg: Have you had any experience of other concessions of the same nature?—No.

Can you form an opinion as to the payment to the concessionnaires?—If it was to be granted, I should think some mention of it should be made in the concession.

That payment is inconsistent with your interpretation of the agreement?—I think so.

You say that such a payment was not mentioned?—No.

Nor indicated?—No.

Mr. Littler, Q.C.: How did you expect the concessionnaires were to be paid?—I did not know.

But you thought they would get something?—If the company was good they would get something in that way.

How could they be paid except either in shares, or money, or something?—I have no experience in such matters.

You did not know how they were to be paid?—No.

Sir Richard Temple: Was this a part of the concession?—I really do not know that I thought much about it.

Is it not set forth in the papers that the capital of the company is one million?—Yes.

Did you understand that £850,000 was part of it?—I certainly understood that the whole of the million was to be *bona fide* capital.

If the concessionnaires sold the concession, would they not ordinarily obtain a price for it?—I suppose so. I do not know how it would be done.

Would the price be represented by £850,000 in shares?—I do not know at all.

Mr. Littler, Q C.: Were you present on May 5, 1882, when a letter from Sir Salar Jung was shown to the Resident?

The Chairman: The one marked "secret and private."

Mr. Littler: In which Sir Salar Jung approves of Abdul Huk receiving all he can get.

The Chairman: Do you recollect the letter?—I do not know what it is about.

Mr. Littler: It is a letter from Sir Salar Jung to Abdul Huk, and we believe it was sent to the Resident.

The Chairman: But that has nothing to do with Mr. Fitzgerald.

Mr. Littler: We want to show that the Resident knew. [Letter handed to witness.]—I have never seen it before.

Mr. Mayne: Did you, as a matter of fact, go through the old draft with reference to the new instructions which came from the Government of India to Sir Salar Jung, and frame a new draft with reference to those instructions?—I think I did.

Do you remember drawing up a sort of comparative statement of all the different forms this concession had taken, and the different instructions of the Government of India, and of Sir Salar Jung, in reference to his concession?—Yes.

Mr. Mayne: I submit, for the use of the counsel, Mr. Fitzgerald's statement drawn up by him in the preparation of the draft, and a letter from Mr. Fitzgerald forwarding it to Abdul Huk.

The Chairman stated that the committee proposed continuing its inquiry on Friday next, and they trusted that the investigation would conclude on that day. The remaining witnesses having been examined, counsel would be permitted briefly to address the committee within the limits already prescribed.

The Committee then adjourned until Friday next, at noon.—*Evening Post*, June 18.

The Deccan inquiry obtains a piquant interest foreign to the *technique* of that remarkable transaction, from the many-sided performances of Sir Richard Temple, one of the members of the commission. There has been, I am afraid, a tendency amongst certain irreverent minds to laugh at Sir Richard, but to-day he distinctly scored when he advanced to the front as a successful student of Hindostanee. He corrected the interpreter more than once, and himself set about examining Indian witnesses in their native tongue. Sir Henry James was charmed, and Sir Richard triumphed. His rebuke of the counsel also, and his appeal for the succour of the Chairman against the intimidation of those learned gentlemen were very fine bits of moving scenery.—*Western Press*, June 13.

THE DECCAN MINES INQUIRY.—The Select Committee of the House of Commons appointed to inquire into the circumstances attending the formation of the East India Hyderabad (Deccan) Mining Company, and the transactions on the Stock Exchange subsequent to its establishment, met again yesterday in Room 9, House of Commons, Sir H. James presiding. The members present were Mr. Labouchere, Sir Richard Temple, Mr. M'Lagan, Mr. J. P. Robertson, Mr. Bristowe, and Mr. Slagg.

The Nawab Mohsin-ul-Mulk, the accredited representative of the Nizam's Government in this country for the purpose of the inquiry, was examined by Mr. Maine, counsel for the Nizam. He was accompanied by Faridoongi Jamsetji, Secretary to the Prime Minister of the Nizam's Government, who acted as interpreter. In reply to counsel, the witness stated that he was political and financial secretary to the Nizam's Government, and had been requested to appear before the Committee on behalf of that Government. He had been sent for two reasons—to communicate any papers or documents that might be required and which he possessed, and to answer any questions on matters within his knowledge. He was financial secretary in 1887, and in May of that year Abdul Huk was at Hyderabad. He showed the witness, in the presence of Colonel Marshall, who was private secretary and confidential adviser to His Highness, a memorandum relating to the purchase of 10,000 shares in the mining company. The witness recognised the signature to the memorandum as that of Abdul Huk. The witness wrote on the document some observations approving the investment by the Government in those shares. Abdul Huk had told him, in the presence of Colonel Marshall, that it would be very advantageous to the Nizam's Government, and that if there had been no objection he would have invested in them himself. As he was connected with the Deccan Mining Company officially, Abdul Huk stated that he could not take any shares himself. He also said that, although gold and diamonds had not yet been discovered, the shares were already at par, and whenever they found diamonds or gold the shares would go up 30, 40, or 50 per cent. All this was told in the previous October to Mr. Rock, an agent in England of the Nizam's Government, and then in India, and that gentleman was informed that Abdul Huk held a great many shares in the Deccan Mining Company. The witness spoke to Abdul Huk about it, and he angrily and indignantly denied the statement that he had any shares whatever in the concern. A committee meeting was held at Hyderabad at which were present the Nawab Vicar-ul-Umrah, Sir Salar Jung, and the witness. In the presence of those persons Abdul Huk was asked whether he had any shares in the Deccan Mining Company, and he replied, "No."

Sir Richard Temple: The literal translation is, "No sort or part."

The witness, continuing, said he was conversant with the transactions connected with Abdul Huk's claim for £83,000 arising out of the railway. He knew that Abdul Huk sent to the Nizam's Government a document purporting to be an agreement between the late Sir Salar Jung and himself, authorizing him to receive the money in connexion with the transaction. (The letter was produced.) Abdul Huk was suspended on the 13th or 14th of April of this year by the Nizam's Government.

The Chairman read a translation of the letter, which eulogized the services of Abdul Huk, and informed him that he could appropriate the whole of the commission "as a reward for his good and faithful services." It concluded, "And this a secret."

The witness, resuming, said this document had been put in to support Abdul Huk's claim to the £83,000 under the railway concession. That claim was still under the consideration of the Nizam's Council of State.

The Chairman pointed out that it was not the duty of the Committee to inquire into any question now arising between the Hyderabad Government and the Minister of that Government. They were only concerned with the Minister and the Government so far as regarded transactions in this country.

At this stage of the inquiry a long memorandum to the Nizam's Government by Abdul Huk was put in. It traced the formation of the company; gave reasons for and against the acquisition by the Nizam's Government of shares in the Deccan Company, and concluded by advising the purchase of 10,000 shares, so that the Government would have a voice in the affairs and management of the company, just as it had a voice in the affairs and management of the railway. The memorandum further stated that the Resident fully approved the investment. He telegraphed to the Government of India on the subject, and thought the Government would have no objection to the investment being made. The memorandum was dated May 7, 1887.

By Sir H. Davey: The witness had made observations in this memorandum which he translated in the sense of advising the investment. Colonel Marshall also advised in the same sense. On the 10th of May, 1887, the Nizam ordered that 10,000 shares were to be purchased "by wire" at the most favourable rates up to £12 per share.

The Chairman pointed out that in the "buff" book, containing Abdul Huk's defence, the words "by wire" were left out, and as a matter of fact no order had been given until Abdul Huk came home on the 4th of June.

Mr. Pember, in reply to the Chairman, stated that he represented the committee of directors—Lord Lawrence, Mr. Colvin, and the chairman of the company, and the shareholders who had purchased in the open market.

The Chairman: At the expense of the directors?

Mr. Pember: The solicitor who instructed him, assumed at the expense of the company.

The witness (continuing) said the work done at the Singareni coalfields was less now than before.

By Mr. Labouchere: Abdul Huk was Secretary of the Nizam's Home Department, and Chief Director of the Railways and Mines, and was qualified to act on his own initiative. When the mining concession was granted by Sir Salar Jung, he was about 22 or 23 years of age. Down to May last, four or five small diamonds had been found in the company's mines. There had been no discovery of gold: though hope was held out that eventually it would be forthcoming.

Mr. Watson, re-called, submitted various printed documents in regard to the resources of the mines, and said he considered that £150,000 was amply sufficient for prospecting purposes. While he thought it would be a good thing to have the Nizam as a partner, he had had nothing to do with advising him. There had been no complaint from either the Nizam's Government or from any shareholders or purchasers of shares.

By Mr. Labouchere: The Nizam had guaranteed £150,000 on the railroad, and now had to pay £100,000. From the Singareni coalfields a yield of 150 tons was being obtained. Owing to the visitation of cholera the diamond mines had not been worked, but now 900 men were being employed, and good reports might be received at any moment. The auriferous mines, only lately prospected, had not yet yielded anything.

By Sir R. Temple: The reports as to the mines were from the company's paid experts—one of whom was Mr. Hughes, Chief of the Geological Survey of the Government of India.

By Mr. M'Lagan: The company made a profit of about 3s. per ton.

Mr. Fitzgerald, Resident at Hyderabad in 1885, examined by Mr. Labouchere, said he never understood that by the terms of the concession the £850,000 worth of shares was to go to the concessionnaire.

The Committee adjourned.—*Times*, June 13.

An additional element of interest was given to the proceedings of the Hyderabad Committee at the House of Commons yesterday by the examination of Nawab Mohsin-ul-Mulk, better known as Moulire Mahdi Ali, the Nizam's special representative. The Nawab is a fine specimen of the best type of Mahommedan official in India. In early life he was in the service of the British Government, on small pay, and at the request of the late Sir Salar Jung, ever quick to recognise merit, was transferred to the Nizam's Civil Service, to assist in the introduction into the Hyderabad State of the system of administration which is followed in British India. He quickly rose, step by step, to all but the highest post in the Government, and now fills the office of Revenue and Financial Secretary. He has come to England with very extensive powers, extending even to the cancellation of the mining concession granted to the Hyderabad Company should he think fit. The evidence he gave yesterday was of a very important character, referring as it did to the official connection of the Nizam's Government with the Company. The Committee is expected to conclude its deliberations next Tuesday, when the various counsel engaged will deliver addresses on behalf of their respective clients.—*Yorkshire Post*, June 13.

THE DECCAN INQUIRY.—ABDUL HUK'S "VALUABLE SERVICES."—MR. W. C. WATSON THINKS THE PUBLIC HAVE GOT FULL VALUE FOR THEIR MONEY.—The Select Committee of the House of Commons appointed to inquire into matters relating to the Hyderabad (Deccan) Mining Company resumed its sittings yesterday at the Houses of Parliament. The Committee consists of Sir Henry James (chairman), Mr. Bristowe, Mr. Labouchere, Mr. M'Lagan, Mr. Slagg, the Solicitor-General for Scotland, and Sir Richard Temple.

The Nawab Mohsin-ul-Mulk was the first witness examined, and the oath was in his case dispensed with. The evidence was taken through the Secretary of the Prime Minister, who acted as interpreter. He said he attended at the request of the Nizam's Government to give evidence and to submit certain documents and answer any questions put to him. He himself knew very little about the subject of the concession. As regards the concession, the present Sir Salar Jung, the ex-minister, knew the facts, for it was in his time the concession was granted. He handed in a document to the Chairman, and it was read *sotto voce* to the members of the Committee. After consultation the Chairman said the letter was one from the late Prime Minister of Hyderabad to the present Prime Minister, defending his action in the matter of the concession; but the Chairman said that it seemed to be too purely a personal matter for the attention of the committee to be engaged upon it.

The witness was then examined by Mr. Mayne for the Nizam's Government. He said he did not know Mr. Hughes, one of the officials of the Resident in Hyderabad. He did not know his writing. In 1887 he (the Nawab) was financial secretary to the Nizam's Government. Abdul Huk placed before Colonel Marshall in his presence a memorandum relating to the purchase of 10,000 shares. Colonel Marshall was secretary and confidential adviser to his Highness the Nizam. He identified the memorandum now put in. He read it, but first had a conversation with Abdul Huk about it. A translation done in Hyderabad was attached to it. The memorandum was signed by Abdul Huk. Orders were written upon it by his Highness the Nizam and Colonel Marshall, and he (witness) also wrote his opinion upon it. Previous to this time he was not consulted about the concession, and had no personal knowledge of the matter. As to Abdul Huk's memorandum advising the investment, he (witness) wrote a memorandum also advising it. He would have invested his own money in it, and he said at the time that although no diamonds had been found, he believed that the shares would go up to 30 or 50. He had been told by Mr. J. Rock that Abdul Huk held many shares. He mentioned this to Abdul Huk, and Abdul Huk indignantly denied that he had any shares whatever in the concern. At the time of Abdul Huk's suspension he denied that he had any shares, and he implied that he had no sort of profit in the matter. On one occasion Abdul Huk had described it as a most advantageous investment, and had induced others to buy shares. He was personally cognisant of Abdul Huk's claim for £83,000, arising out of the railway. He knew that Abdul Huk had sent in a letter of December 28, 1881, purporting to be from Sir Salar Jung, relating to to them. He (witness) identified the letter. It was signed by Sir Salar Jung. Abdul Huk was suspended on April 14 this year.

The Chairman here read a translation of what appeared to be the whole or part of these marginal notes, or of a distinct document from Sir Salar Jung to Abdul Huk. It was to the effect that the writer felt it incumbent upon him to express his entire satisfaction at the faithfulness and zeal Abdul Huk had shown. It urged Abdul Huk to "continue to persevere," and promised that he "should reap from time to time" the fruits which are "the reward of faithfulness and integrity." "You can yourself appropriate," the translation continued, "the full commission agreed upon as remuneration for your valuable services; this is secret."

Examination by Mr. Mayne continued: In February, 1885, Abdul Huk's claim to £83,000 with regard to the railway was under the consideration of the Government. He identified a copy of an order appointing Abdul Huk to act in London to negotiate for the mining concession.

Sir Horace Davey, for Abdul Huk, asked for a translation to be made of the witness's endorsation of Abdul Huk's memorandum, and the interpreter said it was as follows:—"May 7, 1886. I have carefully considered this proposal, and have considered slowly and cautiously the advantages and disadvantages. The Sirdar has shown the disadvantages that may hereafter accrue, and that if gold and diamonds are not found, probably it would result in a loss. I am of opinion that the Government should buy 10,000 shares, which promise hereafter to be profitable, and then the Government will have the right to control the affairs of the company." A telegram was sent by the Government ordering the purchase of the shares, addressed to W. C. Watson, 7, Great Winchester Street. This was on May 10.

The Chairman asked Mr. Watson, who was in the room, whether he had the telegram, and Mr. Watson said that he did not. He used the A B C code with Abdul Huk.

Examination of witness continued by Sir Horace Davey: He produced a printed copy of the original proposal made by Watson and Stewart on November 7, 1882, for the mining concession, and also a letter from Mr. Watson to Abdul Huk, dated February 8, 1884.

Mr. Pember, Q.C., was about to ask some questions, when the Chairman asked by whom he was instructed. He replied that he was instructed by a committee of directors, not including the concessionnaires. Their names were Lord Lawrence, Mr. Colvin, and Mr. Batten.

The Chairman: The Committee must know whether this appearance is at the expense of the company generally, or at the expense of those three gentlemen.

Mr. Pember: The solicitor who has instructed me says he assumes it will be at the expense of the company generally. There has been a meeting of the shareholders. I take it that the committee of directors have instructed me to represent the shareholders who have bought their shares in the open market, and the company would be interpreted, so far as I am concerned, by the shareholders and directors, not including the concessionnaires.

Mr. Pember then asked his questions, which related to various documents. The witness said he did not know whether the memorandum of the articles of association and the agreement of August 17, 1886, were sent over to the Nizam's Government.

Mr. Watson was then recalled and asked by Mr. Mayne whether he had a document being an agreement between himself and the Nizam's Government for ensuring $1\frac{1}{2}$ millions of capital for the railway. He replied that he had. He did not recollect receiving a telegram from Abdul Huk on May 10, asking him to purchase, and stating that he was authorised to purchase 10,000 shares. He would look up the matter. He did not remember replying to the telegram. Throughout this matter from first to last he had never had a complaint from the Nizam's Government, or from any present shareholder or purchaser of shares. There was not the slightest pretence for saying that he had ever bought or sold shares for the purpose of rigging the market.

Mr. Labouchere: The Nizam guaranteed £150,000 on the railways, and owing to this has to pay £100,000?—Yes.

Coal is now produced at the rate of 150 tons per week?—Yes.

The diamondiferous zone has produced one diamond worth 30s.?—The new ground has produced nothing, for the reason that they have not been able to work it owing to the cholera. Five stones were found by some natives among the refuse heaps, which simply indicate that diamonds exist. We have now about 900 men working, and any day we may receive reports that diamonds have been found.

What is the actuality as to the auriferous process?—The actuality is that gold has been discovered. We know the gold is there.

You derive your ideas from reports?—Yes.

The reports of Mr. Levinsky and Mr. Hughes?—Yes, and the general prospecting staff there.

Paid by the company?—Certainly.

So that these reports are by the paid officials of the company?—Yes, all respectable men.

By Sir R. Temple: In reference to your answers in the concluding part of last sitting, I would like to ask you this. Is it right that out of a nominal capital of one million, three quarters of a million should go as promotion money to the private and separate use of the promoters of the company?—I think it is quite right that the concessionnaires should have that concession, and I think the public have got full value for their money. The concessionnaires sell at the price they have fixed; they are entitled to do so, and to get the money, and the property is worth the money. The Singareni Coalfield is worth half a million.

What is its present annual income?—Very little. It must be developed, for the company is in its infancy. We have got the machinery and everything ready for working the coal.

The experts are all in the pay of the company, and are therefore the servants of the company?—Yes.

Have you any independent witness of any kind whatever to strengthen the evidence as to the value and productiveness of these mines?—I have handed in some reports.

As regards the diamonds and coal, I ask you whether there is any beyond the paid servants of the company?—We rely entirely on our own men. Mr. Hughes is the geological surveyor to the Government of India. He has the whole of the district from being an officer of the highest standing. He is now in the pay of the company, but the Government can claim his services at any time.

By Mr. M'Lagan: When you say that the public have got value for their money, you looked upon this as a speculation?—Certainly: we paid the money, and might have lost it.

What profit do you make per ton of coal?—About three shillings.

You hoped to make 6 per cent. on the million of money?—Yes.

And what output would be necessary?

Mr. Pember: 360,000 tons.

Witness: We are informed that we shall be able to get 1,000 tons a day.

Mr. Fitzgerald, examined by Mr. Labouchere, said: I was acting Resident in Hyderabad in 1885, when Mr. Cordery was away at Simla. I sent the draft concession on to Mr. Cordery.

Did an interview take place between you and Abdul Huk?—I don't remember.

You were left in charge of the Residency at Hyderabad; you received this important concession and letters from the Government of Calcutta, and yet you do not know anything about it?—I don't remember whether there was an interview.

What do you remember about the whole transaction?—I don't remember that.

But what do you remember? You must remember something.—I don't remember that.

What do you remember about the concession? You remember certain documents sent you by Mr. Durand?—Yes.

Did you see them?—Yes.

Did you form the conclusion that there was to be a first issue, and that then further issues of shares were to be made?—Yes.

That is the conclusion you formed?—Yes.

You had a letter from Mr. Durand, in which he says: "The first issue of shares may be for £150,000, £75,000 paid up"?—Yes.

You have no recollection whether you had to go through the concession with anyone?—No.

You sent a letter, Mr. Cordery came back, and you handed the whole matter over to him?—Yes.

You did not discuss the matter with him?—Not at that time.

With Mr. Watson?—No.

With Sir Salar Jung?—No.

You really never had any official correspondence about it?—No.

When the letter was sent you nothing took place on it until Mr. Cordery returned almost immediately?—That is my recollection.

Mr. Slagg: You had nothing to do with the drawing up of the concession in any way?—No.

Mr. Bristowe: Did you understand that £850,000 was to go to the concessionnaires?—Oh, no, certainly not.

You did not know what was to take place?—No.

Sir Richard Temple: Have you a general knowledge of the concession?—Yes, but not a special knowledge.

Which you acquired in your capacity as first assistant to the Resident?—Yes.

Mr. Slagg: Did you hear anything which would lead you to suppose that £850,000 would go to the concessionaires?—No.

Then this was quite new to you? You have only heard it lately?—I have only heard it lately.

Sir Richard Temple: Would you regard such an arrangement as consistent or inconsistent with your understanding of the matter?—Inconsistent.

Absolutely inconsistent?—Yes.

Mr. Slagg: Have you had any experience of other concessions of the same nature?—No.

Can you form an opinion as to the payment to the concessionnaires?—If it was to be granted, I should think some mention of it should be made in the concession.

That payment is inconsistent with your interpretation of the agreement?—I think so.

You say that such a payment was not mentioned?—No.

Nor indicated?—No.

Mr. Littler, Q.C.: How did you expect the concessionnaires were to be paid?—I did not know.

But you thought they would get something?—If the company was good they would get something in that way.

How could they be paid except either in shares, or money, or something? —I have no experience in such matters.

You did not know how they were to be paid?—No.

Sir Richard Temple: Was this a part of the concession?—I really do not know that I thought much about it.

Is it not set forth in the papers that the capital of the company is one million?—Yes.

Did you understand that £850,000 was part of it?—I certainly understood that the whole of the million was to be *bonâ fide* capital.

If the concessionnaires sold the concession would they not ordinarily obtain a price for it?—I suppose so. I do not know how it would be done.

Would the price be represented by £850,000 in shares?—I do not know at all.

Mr. Littler, Q.C.: Were you present on May 5, 1882, when a letter from Sir Salar Jung was shown to the Resident?

The Chairman: The one marked "secret and private."

Mr. Littler: In which Sir Salar Jung approves of Abdul Huk receiving all he can get.

The Chairman: Do you recollect the letter?—I do not know what it is about.

Mr. Littler: It is a letter from Sir Salar Jung to Abdul Huk, and we believe it was sent to the Resident.

The Chairman: But that has nothing to do with Mr. Fitzgerald.

Mr. Littler: We want to show that the Resident knew. [Letter handed to witness.] I have never seen it before.

Mr. Mayne: Did you as a matter of fact go through the old draft with reference to the new instructions which came from the Government of India to Sir Salar Jung and frame a new draft with reference to those instructions?—I think I did.

Do you remember drawing up a sort of comparative statement of all the different forms this concession had taken and the different instructions of the Government of India and of Sir Salar Jung in reference to his concession?—Yes.

Mr. Mayne: I submit, for the use of the counsel, Mr. Fitzgerald's statement drawn up by him in the preparation of the draft, and a letter from Mr. Fitzgerald forwarding it to Abdul Huk.

The chairman stated that the committee proposed continuing its inquiry on Friday next, and they trusted that the investigation would conclude on that day. The remaining witnesses having been examined, counsel would be permitted briefly to address the committee within the limits already prescribed.

The committee then adjourned until Friday next, at noon.—*Financial News*, June 13.

THE Deccan inquiry obtains a piquant interest, foreign to the *technique* of that remarkable transaction from the many-sided performances of Sir Richard Temple, one of the members of the Commission. There has been, I am afraid, a tendency amongst certain irreverent minds to laugh at Sir Richard, but to-day he distinctly scored when he advanced to the front as a successful student of Hindostance. He corrected the interpreter more than once, and himself set about examining Indian witnesses in their native tongue. Sir Henry James was charmed, and Sir Richard triumphed. His rebuke of the counsel also and his appeal for the succour of the Chairman against the intimidation of those learned gentlemen, were very fine bits of moving scenery.—*East Anglian Times*, June 13.

THE inquiry into the Deccan scandal should be carefully followed by all who take an interest in public men, and particularly in England's dealings with the important friendly native States. Mr. Watson's evidence on Friday has seriously implicated our Indian officials. Government will have to go into the witness box, and, though it will now of course clear itself of suspicions which are inspired by Mr. Watson, it will probably not escape without censure for the carelessness which permitted the manœuvres of Abdul Huk and Mr. Watson. It is important that all official Englishmen should be trusted as officials by those who are supposed to benefit by the retention of our Residents among them.—*Piccadilly*, June 14.

WHAT is known as the Deccan inquiry is still proceeding. It is alleged that Abdul Huk induced the Nizam of Hyderabad to invest very largely in a bogus mining enterprise, of which Huk was himself the principal proprietor, though he represented himself as having no interest in it whatever. Huk was the head of the Nizam's Home Department and the chief director of railways and mines. The proceedings at the last sitting were remarkable for the valuable aid which one of the committee, Sir Richard Temple, an ex-Indian administrator, was able to render in checking the errors of the interpreter, thanks to his knowledge of Hindustanee. He examined several of the witnesses in their native tongue, and altogether rendered considerable service in the elucidation of the facts.—*York Evening Press*, June 14.

YOUNG ladies are, or used to be, fond of asking their male acquaintances to plead guilty to their special preferences in a neatly illuminated volume entitled "Confessions." It is a pleasing pastime, this form of confession, affording the opening for candid sentiment tempered with facetiousness. Amongst the points upon which the male acquaintance aforesaid finds himself interrogated is one relating to his favourite hero in fiction. When you know the man to whom the question is put you know the hero he will hit upon.

Thus, we are convinced that if Abdul Huk, the coloured hero (as distinquished from Mr. Watson, the pale-faced hero) of the Deccan exploit, has read English novels, he, the hero of real life, would put his fingers on those pages in "The Newcombes" which tell of the celebrated Rummun Loll. Probably he has formed himself upon the type of that dusky plotter. In fact, if for Rummum Loll you read Abdul Huk, and for the great Bundelcund Banking Company you substitue the Hyderabad-Deccan Company, a remarkable parallel is at once established. Verily, Thackeray was a prophet.—*Evening Post*, June 15.

RESPONSIBILITY FOR THE HYDERABAD SCANDAL.—(*Deccan Times.*)—We have already, for instance, stated that the mining concession was not signed until some time after His Highness's installation, a period when, it was well known, the gravest differences subsisted between His Highness and his Minister. In this divided state of the counsels of the Government the Residency influence was, of course, paramount, and it is difficult to see how the Government of India can escape responsibility in this matter, when it is admitted that Mr. Cordery's assistant checked the deed, clause by clause, and that it was in the same officer's presence and on his assurance that Sir Salar Jung signed the document. But here it becomes very material to ask, Did Sir Salar Jung in a matter of such exceeding importance take his Master's pleasure before signing this document?

Considering the nature of the relations which then existed between him and the Sovereign, he could have had little assurance that he had it virtually by reason of any perfect familiarity with his wishes and intentions. Even if he considered the act covered by the powers of the Dewanship, one would suppose that ordinary prudence and caution, if not courtesy, would have recognised the value with which the Sovereign's sanction would have invested the whole proceedings. Moreover it must not be forgotten that there was at the time a Council of State in existence, and if any question, then surely this, involving a a million sterling of money, was a question fit to be debated therein. When the members of the Council heard that the agreement had been completed without any consultation with them on the matter, some of them resented the slight. Had the papers indeed been presented to the Council, the parties interested full well knew that they would have been thrown out, as terms much more favourable had in the meantime been offered. But as a matter of fact the question was not settled before his Highness's installation.

Long after this event mining rights over a portion of His Highness's dominions were actually granted to certain other parties, and orders were issued in due course thereof through the Revenue Board, which was then in existence, intimating that such a concession was in fact made. When, however, the Residency heard of the matter, the affair was reported to the Government of India, and several communications passed between the Resident and the ex-Minister on the subject. It was, we believe, strongly rumoured at the time that a Russian syndicate had agreed to find the working capital, and this was popularly assigned as the reason for the explanation which the ex-Minister was called upon to make upon the subject. The contract was thereupon cancelled and annulled, too, it is believed, at the instance of the Resident. Surely all this was a further reason, if one were at all necessary, for laying the deal, brought up by Mr. Winter before the Council of State for debate and approved before final signature. For this omission the Residency is wholly responsible and it is, as we have said before, very difficult to see how the Government of India can now evade responsibility in the matter.—*Allen's Indian Mail*, June 15.

The papers to hand by the present Overland Mail bring little news of importance to comment upon. The Hyderabad (Deccan) scandal continues to be widely discussed, and the tone of the remarks generally is not complimentary of the honesty of Abdud Huq, or the wisdom of Mr. Cordery, who, it is said, might have prevented all the scandal had he but exercised some discretion and judgment, especially as he could hardly be ignorant of Abdul Huq's character and antecedents. But Mr. Cordery has now been examined before the London Commission, and until their report is published comment on our part would be not only in bad taste, but unfair.

The fact that Abdul Huk has made restoration of the gains which he is supposed to have made by the sale of his shares to the Nizam, ought to assist the Royal Commission in forming their opinion as to the whole transaction. The astute Native is still a very rich man, if the reports in the Bombay papers be true. One of these papers states that he has property in that city to the amount of two lacs of rupees, but it hints at something very like a local "scandal" as to the way he obtained it:—The Sirdar's first purchase was the Government Central Press, in the heart of the Fort, a building which, as former Government House and subsequently as the Secretariat, possesses much historical interest. By many the sale of this building was considered as a piece of vandalism; but what was considered to be most objectionable was the fact that this building, which occupies one of the best sites in the Fort, was sold by private treaty by the Collector. No one knew that the old Secretariat was in the market until the purchase had been made by Abdul Huk." If this be so, it would seem that London brokers and "promoters" have not all the "crooked wisdom" of the world to themselves.—*Allen's Indian Mail*, June 15.

Mr. Cordery, the Resident at Hyderabad when the Deccan Company's concession was approved, has vindicated himself of all knowledge of the extraordinary pranks played by Abdul Huk and his friends. Mr. Cordery understood that a "first issue" of £150,000 meant a first and not an only issue to the public, and was quite in the dark as to Abdul Huk's private transactions with the promoters, and as to the appropriation of the balance of the shares as fully paid by the vendors. The Select Committee has thus been instrumental, though that was not part of its ostensible work, in establishing the integrity of the British officials associated with the original project.—*Evening Post*, June 16.

Hyderabad-Deccan.—By degrees we are getting to the bottom of his innocent deal, and no longer wonder at Mr. Watson's perfect dinner-parties, or Mr. H. P. Sharp's reckless expenditure in horseflesh. New York would have lynched the gang six months ago: but London will forget the entire business directly, and kiss the boots of those who have gorged the plunder.—*Weekly Bulletin*, June 16.

The Deccan Scandals.—Four arrests, according to the Bombay correspondent of the *Standard*, have been made at Hyderabad of persons who are charged with having intercepted telegrams to the Resident. One of the prisoners is the clerk to Abdul Huk, and another is a relative of his. Several documents of importance in connection with the inquiry into the Deccan scandals have been abstracted from the British Post Office.—*Evening Post*, June 16.

The Deccan Inquiry.—The inquiry into the Deccan concession brought out this fact yesterday that Mr. Cordery, the late British Resident at Hyderabad, had no idea that the sum of £850,000 was to be taken by the concessionnaires. He was under the full belief that the million of capital was to be spent in developing the mines of the country, and he considered it was contrary to the spirit of the concession to dispose of the £850,000 of shares in London in the manner that had been done. Of course the partnership of Abdul Huk in the speculation was carefully concealed from him. General Richard Strachey, who looked into the concession before it was granted on behalf of the Indian Government, never heard of the arrangement with regard to the 85,000 shares until July last, but he does not appear to have regarded it as the business of his department to limit the amount to be paid to the concessionnaires, and so he repudiates all responsibility. In that case, why the Indian Government should have troubeld itself about the matter does not appear.—*Pall Mall Gazette*, June 16.

The Deccan Mining Company.—The inquiry into the formation and operations of the East India (Hyderabad) Mining Company (Limited) was resumed yesterday, befor a Select Committee of the House of Commons.

Mr. Cordery, Resident at Hyderabad in 1883, examined by Mr. Labouchere, gave evidence with respect to the negotiations for the sale of the railway He clearly understood that the £150,000 was to be the first call, and that the balance was to be available for the purposes of the enterprise. Had he known that Abdul Huk was a partner in the company he would not have allowed the negotiations to go on. He had not the remotest idea, nor did he believe that the Ministers of the Nizam knew, that Abdul Huk was a partner, or that he was to receive a commission from Mr. Watson. With regard to the mining concessions, Witness said he had heard of no other diamond mines than the old Golconda mine. There was a report of auriferous strata by Mr. Hughes, who occupied a high position in the Geological Survey of India. The coal and iron mines were in Singarene. He should say that over £150,000 would be required to work them, although on that point he had no positive knowledge.

Mr. Watson, recalled and examined by the Chairman, explained his transactions in the shares of the Company. He said that of the £5 shares making £150,000, he possessed altogether 5,000. He had sold shares of the Company for himself and others on the Stock Exchange.

The Chairman: What would you get for them?—The prices varied, averaging about £10 each for the £10 paid.

The net result of this statement is that you disposed of 64,015, including 3,325 transfers, and have the balance of shares, 5,559?—Yes. Those are all I hold now. The fully-paid shares I retain are 2,600. There were allotted to me in round numbers 24,000.

If you thought the Company so prosperous, why did you sell?—One wants to realise. It is a merchant's business to sell and go into something else.

I want to know how much you received for your allotted shares, of which you have 2,600 remaining?—£188,000; that is, under an average of £10 a share. The £5 shares are blended in the statement.

What was your share from the public?—£209,300.

And you have still a total of 5,559 shares?—Yes.

And if they sold at the same price that would mean £60,000 more?—Yes.

And for all this you gave nothing except transferring the concession?—No.

The Committee adjourned till Tuesday.—*Standard*, June 16.

THE DECCAN SCANDALS.—(FROM OUR CORRESPONDENT.)—BOMBAY, Friday Night.—Four arrests have been made at Hyderabad of persons who are charged with having intercepted telegrams to the Resident. One of the prisoners is the clerk to Abdul Huk, and another is a relative of his. Several documents of importance in connection with the inquiry into the Deccan Scandals have been abstracted from the British Post-office.—*Standard*, June 16.

THE HYDERABAD MINES INQUIRY.—The Select Committee of the House of Commons appointed to inquire into the circumstances attending the formation of the East India (Hyderabad) Deccan Mining Company met again yesterday, Sir Henry James presiding. The other members present were Mr. P. J. Robertson, Mr. Slagg, Mr. Bristowe, Mr. Labouchere, and Sir R. Temple. The parties were represented as before, Mr. Pember, Q.C., with Mr. Lewis Coward, appearing for the company; Mr. Mayne, with Mr. Eardley Norton and the Hon. Alfred Lyttleton, for the Nizam; Sir Horace Davey, Q.C., with Mr. Inverarity and Mr. Trevor White (of the Bombay Bar), for Abdul Huk; and Mr. Littler, Q.C., with Mr. Cripps, for Mr. Watson.

The Chairman called upon Mr. Seymour Keay to explain a letter which he had sent him, expressing a desire to put in an official document of Abdul Huk's defence, which communication, the chairman added, practically pronounced a document written in pencil, put in on Tuesday last, to be a forgery, Abdul Huk having admitted substantially that it was a forgery.

Mr. Seymour Keay: Hardly that.

A copy of the printed document was put in.

Mr. Seymour Keay said the production of the document practically proved that the allegation that the pencil writing was by Sir Salar Jung was an afterthought, because the document just put in was Abdul Huk's official defence.

The Chairman inquired whether Mr. Keay had anything to support the allegation of forgery.

Mr. Keay: Yes, Sir, this document. May I mention the way——

The Chairman: No; the Committee will not hear you.

Mr. Mayne: Have you got before you, Sir, what the document is?

The Chairman: We have nothing before us.

Mr. Cordery, Resident at Hyderabad in 1883, examined by Mr. Labouchere, gave an account of the negotiations in respect of the sale of the railway, and stated that he clearly understood that the £150,000 was to be the first call, and that the balance was to be available for the purpose of the enterprise. Had he known that Abdul Huk was a partner he would have declined to allow the negotiation. He had not the remotest idea, nor, he believed, did the Ministers of the Nizam know, that Abdul Huk was a partner, or that he was to receive a commission from Mr. Watson.

Referring to the mining concession, Witness, in reply to Sir R. Temple, said from his experience he had not heard of any other diamond mine than the old Golconda Mine. There was a report of auriferous strata by Mr. Hughes, who occupied a high position in the Geological Survey of India, though he was not at the head of it. Mr. Hughes stated what was his opinion. The coal and iron mines were in Singarene. Iron had been discovered. He should say that capital over and above the £150,000 would be required to work them, though he could not speak positively.

Did you think it prudent to concede the whole of the mining right in the Deccan to a private party or corporation of Europeans?—There was the expectation of a million of capital being spent in the country, and that was laid stress upon by everybody as one of the principal reasons of the concession being a good thing. There was a general desire to spend capital in India, and it was felt that the Nizam should not fall behind, He should have thought the terms of the concession, considering its spirit and intention, were sufficient to preclude such operations as had taken place in London; but, seeing how the concession had been made use of, he supposed the terms were not sufficient. Had he thought at the time there could have been any such loophole as had been experienced, he would have taken steps to prevent it.

By Mr. M'Lagan: The company was formed with a capital of a million, which was to be spent in the Deccan.

Do you think that Messrs. Stewart and Watson, or any sane men, having an eye to their own interests, would undertake all that risk and trouble without remuneration?—I should have thought that the placing of the shares would have brought them a very large sum. The shares were not to be placed out and not to be called for unless there was a discovery of more mines, which would have led to a running up of the shares to a premium.

But supposing there was no discovery of mines?—Then there would have been no harm done. The £150,000 was a speculation.

They were to take all the risk of the speculation without getting any remuneration or seeing their way to getting it?—It was so, if you put it in that way; but nobody raised any objection to the concession.

Could you find fault with Messrs. Stewart and Watson legally for acting as they have done?—It depends whether they understood the spirit and intention of the concession.

By Mr. Slagg: In the opinion of the Government of India the railway concession and the mining concession were not linked together at all. Mr. Watson's association with the railway had not weighed with witness in the least. He gave his consent to the purchase of the shares without really knowing anything whatever about the formation of the company.

Mr. Watson, re-called, explained the transactions connected with the acquirement and sale of shares. Of the £5 shares, making £150,000, he possessed 5,000. He had sold fully-paid shares for himself and others, the average price being £10. He had disposed of 64,015 shares, and held now a balance of 5,559. The fully-paid shares he had now numbered 2,600. In round numbers there had been allotted to him 24,000 shares. He had sold, though the company was so prosperous, because it was a merchant's business to realize his money and undertake something fresh. He had received £188,000 for his shares, which was under an average of £10 a share. He paid Evans £21,300 commission for the shares he sold for him, and his share for the public was £209,000, and he had still 5,539 shares, which at the same price as the others represented about £60,000 more. For all this he gave nothing except the transfer of the concession to the company. He had never bought or sold shares on the same day.

General Richard Strachey was next examined as to the position taken by the Government of India in reference to the negotiations for the concession.

The Committee adjourned.—*Times*, June 16.

With reference to the so-called Deccan scandal, which is causing Mr. Henry Labouchere, M.P., and Sir Henry James and his colleagues such an infinity of trouble, and which, so far as we can see, without any practical result, the subjoined native opinion, taken from the *Statesman and Friend*, of India, under date May 19th, is worth perusal :—

"It was inevitable, of course, that the Hyderabad Mining Company should suffer heavily from the depreciation of its shares, during the Parliamentary inquiry into the circumstances under which the concession was obtained from the Nizam; but we cannot say how *bona fide* shareholders in the Company—the men who have honestly invested money therein—should be affected thereby. The shareholders have bought the mining rights of the Nizam, and honestly paid the concessionnaires for them. The way in which the concession was obtained is a matter between the concessionnaires and the Nizam, and not between the shareholders and the Prince. The Nizam has been swindled out of his mining rights, and the sole question at present is—Who are the men that swindled him? That question determined, we shall be able to say whether it is the Nizam who should sustain the loss, or the Government of India, a question that cannot be decided until the Select Committee has made its report, nor even then probably until the question has been brought before the Law Courts."

It will be seen from the above that our original opinion, that the concession was perfectly valid, and that those in high places at the Nizam's court were perfectly aware even if they pretended to be ignorant of the facts, that the concession was granted legally, and consequently cannot be invalid, is borne out to the fullest extent by our contemporary.—*Bullionist*, June 16.

To the Editor of *Vanity Fair*.—Brixton, 6th June, 1888.—Dear Sir,—May I ask for your advice on the following?—viz.:

1. A month or six weeks ago I bought some Deccans at £7 10s., and have carried them over twice at a loss; they are now about £5 10s. Would you advise buying more to average, or cut my loss?

2. I also hold some Masons, bought at 13¼, now 9 to 10. Shall I close my account and cut my loss or buy some more to average?

3. About two years ago I bought Day Dawns at 2¼, and although the crushings have been very good, the price has gradually given way, and lately tumbled down to 14s., 15s. Can you tell me what is the cause of it? I hear all sorts of dismal rumours about the Mine.

4. Do you think Delagoa Bay Railway are likely to improve during the next three months?

I have much pleasure in saying I consider your "Advice Gratis" a great boon to many readers of your paper, as it is so difficult to get reliable advice on Stock and Mining matters.

Thanking you in anticipation, I remain, yours truly, Mines.

[In reply to "Mines," if he can afford it, he should certainly average his Deccans. We believe, and we have always expressed our belief to this effect, that the concession of the property is valid, and that the result of the present Parliamentary inquiry will prove it to be so. With regard to Mason and Barry, we do not care to advise, the Copper Market being in such a critical condition.

As regards Day Dawns, we should not sell during the present depression of the Mining Market; and, with reference to No. 4, we consider them to be a good speculative investment.]—*Vanity Fair*, June 16.

THE DECCAN INQUIRY.—THE RESIDENT AT HYDERABAD HAD NO IDEA THE CONCESSIONNAIRES WOULD TAKE £850,000 OUT OF THE CAPITAL.—THE INDIA OFFICE IS NOT THE NIZAM'S DRY NURSE.—The Select Committee of the House of Commons appointed to inquire into matters relating to the Hyderabad (Deccan) Mining Company resumed its sittings yesterday, at the Houses of Parliament. The Committee consists of Sir Henry James (Chairman), Mr. Bristowe, Mr. Labouchere, Mr. McLagan, Mr. Slagg, the Solicitor-General for Scotland, and Sir Richard Temple.

Sir Horace Davey, Q.C., Mr. T. D. Inverarity, of the Bombay Bar, and Mr. Trevor White appeared for Sirdar Dilar Jung. Mr. Pember, Q.C., and Mr. J. C. Lewis Coward appeared for the company. Mr. Mayne appeared for the Nizam's Government; and Mr. Littler, Q.C., appeared for Mr. Watson.

The Chairman called for Mr. Seymour Keay, and upon that gentleman answering to his name, said that he had written to the committee stating that he desired to hand in a printed copy which went to prove that the marginal notes said to have been written by Sir Salar Jung were an after-thought by Abdul Huk.

Mr. Keay handed in the document, and said it practically proved that the allegation that the pencilled writing on a document before sent in to the Committee was by Sir Salar Jung was an after-thought by Abdul Huk. He desired to explain how the document he handed in supported his statement, but the Chairman would not permit him, and for the present he would simply receive the document.

Mr. Cordery, late British Resident at Hyderabad, was the first witness. Examined by Mr. Labouchere, he said: I went to Hyderabad in April 1883. At the time I first heard of these mining and railway proposals there was a provisional Government at Hyderabad. Sir Salar Jung had died two months before and the provisional Government was prepared to sign a convention which had been before the Secretary of State. They so far consulted me about it as to ask whether it should be signed then and there. I said I thought a new Government might be better to sign it. These negotiations had to do solely with the mining concessions. There was no question of reward because of what Mr. Watson had done with regard to the railways. The question was allowed to drop until the provisional proceedings had ceased, and Sir Salar Jung the younger had been made Prime Minister. At that time Abdul Huk was Home Secretary, his principal work, apart from internal administration, being connected with the railway. Mr. Winter came to Hyderabad as the representative of Mr. Watson. He stayed at my house two days. At that moment I had the draft contract which had been drawn up in England, and had been sent to Hyderabad, and came from the Government of India. Mr. Winter asked for an interview with Sir Salar Jung, and I procured him that, and then he entered into negotiations with Sir Salar Jung. There was subsequently a despatch from the Calcutta Government saying that all negotiations ought to go through me. I read the memorandum from the Calcutta Government, and I understood from it that £150,000 was to be the first call, and the balance was to be available for the purposes of the enterprise.

In your conversation with Mr. Winter, was any reference made to this?—Very likely. Undoubtedly, he said the memorandum. I can't remember the words of the conversation.

Then he fully understood it?—Yes.

Did you know at that time that Abdul Huk was a partner?—I had not the remotest conception of it. Up to that time I thought he was antagonistic to it.

Then you had no sort of notion that Abdul Huk was to receive a commission from Mr. Watson?—Not the slightest; such a thing never occurred to me. I never saw the letter dated January 5, 1882, which has been put in, from the late Sir Salar Jung, in which he said he had no objection to Abdul Huk receiving any remuneration in connection with the mining scheme with which the concessionnaires might reward his services. I never saw that letter until the question had been raised in London. Mr. Winter never in any way suggested that Abdul Huk was a partner.

Is it in your knowledge whether Sir Salar Jung the younger knew anything about the matter?—I should say he knew nothing about the partnership. He would not have trusted him if he had. I regarded Abdul Huk as an honest, independent representative of the Nizam's Government.

If it had come to your knowledge Abdul Huk was a partner in the matter, I presume you would not have allowed the negotiations to go on?—Certainly I should have thrown it up at once.

When did you first know that £850,000 was to be given to the promoter?—I did not really know it until quite lately; when I heard it I was amazed. Abdul Huk would have known that, of course, but the rest of the Ministers did not know it, I believe.

Can you tell us anything about the purchase of the shares?—I remember that in May, 1887, acting on the analogy of the railway, I thought it would be a good thing that His Highness should have a share in the mining company. I thought so at the time.

The Witness was examined at some length with respect to a telegram which was produced at the last meeting of the committee, stating that a letter from Sir Salar Jung to Abdul Huk, dated January 5, 1882, had been found at the British Residency at Hyderabad. Witness could not conceive how it got there, and was positive he had never seen it. It might have been put there during his absence at Calcutta; but it had never been submitted to him. If it had he could not have forgotten it, because he had to go up to Calcutta to explain the whole matter. Questioned about clause 11 of the concession, which states that leases may be granted of mines from the concessionnaires or their nominees; that the amount of royalty shall be reserved, but that that royalty shall form a fair rent, witness said he could not explain why this definition of a royalty got into the concession. He thought it meant a "fair rate" rather.

You actually signed it with the definition in it "fair rent," and you thought it meant "fair rate." Why on earth did you not say fair rate?—I really don't quite understand.

When you advised the Government of the Nizam to sign an agreement, saying that a royalty meant a fair rent, you say that you meant it to mean a fair rate?—I meant that the royalty should be fixed in the manner proposed by the mining engineers. I alone did not accept it. It was accepted by the Government of India and the Secretary of State in London. I really don't understand the point.

By Sir R. Temple: I am generally acquainted with the policy of the concession. I intended the concession to mean the coal mines and any future mines which might be discovered. I included all mines; but what I had expressly in my mind was iron mines and the manufacture of steel. I had heard of diamond mines being possible—or rather, it was suggested that in the old workings diamonds might well have been left behind, which improved machinery and appliances would bring to light. Besides the old Golconda Mines I have never heard of any diamond mines in the Deccan. It was in the heads of the concessionnaires, so to speak, that there was gold also. The coal mines are not of themselves sufficient to justify a capital of a million sterling, and it was always understood that the £150,000 would be employed in the Singareni coal mines, not including the iron mines. Excellent iron has been discovered.

Do you consider it safe or prudent to concede the whole of the mining rights of the Deccan to a private party or company of Europeans?—Yes, I do. I thought this an excellent project in itself. The expenditure of a million within the country was laid stress upon by everybody, and was one of the principal reasons why this should be done.

Looking at the past experience of Hyderabad, you do not see any political objection to such extensive and comprehensive concession?—The times have changed. The desire to employ capital in India has become much stronger, and there was no reason, I though, why the Nizam should fall behind the rest.

Have I understood rightly that you regard the manner in which the £850,000 of shares were disposed of in London to be contrary to the spirit and intention of the concession?—Yes; I do.

Knowing, then, what you know, do you still consider the terms of the concession were sufficiently explicit?—Now I see how they have been made use of, and therefore I suppose they were not. But I, myself, should have thought they were.

You thought at the time there was not a loophole for any such transaction?—And I got good reason for thinking so, as the agreement was drawn up by the lawyer to the Nizam. If I had thought there was any such loophole I would have interfered to stop it.

It did not occur to you that concessions of this kind granted to European capitalists might lead to some embarrassing speculations, or speculations embarrassing to the Nizam's Government?—I cannot say there was no risk attending it, but I thought that the risk was worth running for the development of the Nizam's country. The scheme itself appeared so thoroughly sound, that if it had been carried out as intended, it would, I think, have been a great success.

By Mr. McLagan: My view is that a million has to be spent in working the mines. I thought the remuneration of the promoters would be what they would make in starting the company. The rest of the shares I understood would not be put up unless more mines were discovered, which discovery would lead to the running up of the shares to a very large sum. The shares were originally placed on the market at par. If there had been no mines, then the £150,000 would have been lost as a speculation.

Then the promoters were to run all risk and have nothing but chances of a bad speculation?—If you put it that way I suppose it is so.

Don't you think this is a very loosely drawn document?—It has been made such use of that I think it must be.

Could you find fault legally with Watson and Stewart for acting as they have done?—It depends on whether they knew of the spirit of the concession.

I know the Government of India puts a different interpretation upon it than they do. Don't you think they were entitled to do as they have done?—I have given my reasons for thinking the contrary.

By Mr. Slagg: I went through the deed myself, clause by clause. Sir Salar Jung did not sign it my presence, and I don't know whether he consulted the Nizam before he signed it. The Nizam took an interest in the amount of his royalties. He understood that part of it, but he did not devote himself much to public matters at that time. The Council of State very rarely met after Sir Salar Jung's accession to the Ministry. It is only a consultative body, and has no power. I never heard of the concession coming to the knowledge of the Council, and the Council resenting the concession. I never heard of more favourable terms having been offered. From the point of view of the Government of India the railway concession and the mining concession were not linked together at all. Watson's association with the railway did not weigh with me at all. When I say that in my opinion the scheme is sound, of course I mean that a million of capital is spent in the development of the country.

By Mr. Bristowe: I never saw the memorandum of Abdul Huk advising the purchase of shares by the Nizam's Government. I consented to the purchase, but I never saw the memorandum. I believe it came before Colonel Marshall.

You might have known that more than 15,000 shares had been issued, or it would not have been possible for the board to acquire 10,000. Did you make any inquiries?—No.

You gave your consent to the purchase of the shares really knowing nothing about the formation of the company?—Nothing.

By Sir H. James: In February, 1885, I was in communication with Mr. Winter, who at that time was the agent of Messrs. Watson and Stewart.

You saw him frequently about the concession?—I saw him during his stay, which was not very long. I was also in communication with Abdul Huk. I do not remember that Abdul Huk took any part in arranging the terms of the concession. Abdul Huk was supposed to be the adviser of Sir Salar Jung.

Witness (continuing), in reply to Mr. Mayne, stated that Abdul Huk feared he would be blamed because shares had not been reserved for the Nizam in the same way as they had been reserved for Messrs. Watson, and he had replied that he did not think it would make much difference, as the price would not be very much above par. He was under the delusion that Messrs. Watson were responsible for the £850,000.

By Mr. Littler: The Singareni coalfields were very valuable, and the Government were very anxious to get them opened as soon as possible. It depended on the discoveries of minerals whether there was a field for new capital.

In reply to Sir Horace Davey, Q.C., the witness said he had seen a despatch from the Government of India to his predecessor in the Residency, approving of a concession being granted to Messrs. Watson and Stewart, in accordance with the original proposal. Asked by the Chairman if he could identify the handwriting of certain letters which had been produced, the witness said he thought they were in the handwriting of Sir Salar Jung's private secretary. As to the actual signature, he would not like to swear to it, as Sir Salar Jung and his son wrote exactly alike.

Mr. Watson, re-called, placed before the committee a written statement, as to his transactions in Deccan Mine shares. Replying to the Chairman, who perused the list, the witness said that he originally possessed 5,000 £5 shares. He subsequently acquired more by transfers from Sharp, Stewart, and others, until eventually he possessed 12,194 of the £5 shares. They had since been converted into £10 shares. Of the 12,194 he had disposed on the Stock Exchange of 8,869.

What did you get for them?—The price varied, but the average was £10 for every fully paid-up share.

How many of what are called fully paid-up shares of £10 have you acquired or possessed? Have you altogether had in your possession 64,015? And, if so, how did you obtain them?—By various transfers to me and by purchase. Certain shares were transferred to me by Watson, Stewart and Winter in the way of adjustments on sales. I used to sell for all, and the others would pay me any balance due by transferring shares. It was a pooling transaction.

At present you hold only 2,600 fully paid-up shares?—That is so.

There were originally allotted to you in round numbers 24,000 shares? —Yes.

Is it fair to ask you, if you took such a favourable view as you represent you did of the prospects of the company, why you sold those shares?—It was in the ordinary course of business to realise ready money with the view of going in for fresh things.

How much money have you received from the sale of your shares?—£188,000 in all.

That was your profit in addition to the shares you still hold?—Yes.

You also had transactions in the market in the way of buying and selling?—Not much in the way of buying, but I acquired a number by transfers from Stewart, Sharp and Winter. Those transfers have to be counted as against the sales.

What did you buy shares for?—To make money.

What was the financial result of your purchases in the market?—It is impossible for me to tell. Mr. Anderson acted as my broker. He sold shares in the market, and then I placed a sufficient number at his disposal to enable him to supply the persons to whom he had sold.

In order to get rid of your shares how much did you pay in the form of broker's commission?—Upwards of £27,000.

Then we must add that £27,000 to the £188,000 you have received from the sale of shares? And you still hold 5,259 shares?—Yes.

That would mean about £60,000 more?—Yes.

And for all that you have given nothing except what you have done by getting the concession and transferring it to the company?—That is all that has taken place.

Mr. Labouchere: You paid nothing for the concession.

In further examination the witness said that on May 10, 1887, he received a telegram from Abdul Huk, saying, "Government wish to purchase 10,000 shares Deccan. What price can you buy at?" He, as he found by reference to his papers, although he had quite forgotten the circumstance, telegraphed back, "Yours to hand. To buy 10,000 shares without exciting market requires time and cautious dealing. Price about £12."

Why did you not sell your own shares upon the receipt of that telegram?—I did not want to sell them.

Why not?—I had sold as many as I wanted to sell. Besides, the telegram from Abdul Huk was only an inquiry as to the price; it was not an absolute authority to purchase. Moreover, I had no £10 shares at the time.

Mr. Labouchere: How about the pool?

Witness: The pool had been broken up. It had finished in the January before.

Examination by Mr. Labouchere continued: It is true that in my original evidence I said that Abdul Huk came to me at the Alexandra Hotel, Hyde Park, and said: "I have got some good news for you. The Nizam's Government has decided to buy 10,000 £10 shares at £12." I do not consider that inconsistent with the fact of my having previously received the telegram. The telegram, as I have said, was only an inquiry as to price.

In reply to Mr. Mayne, witness said that he could, if necessary, produce the original agreement between himself, the Nizam's Government, and the railway company, in regard to the construction of the railway. The copy which had already been produced, however, was, he believed, correct.

Mr. Littler, Q.C., wished to ask the witness as to whether a telegram had been received as to the present condition of the mines.

The Chairman: I don't think we should attach much importance to any telegram sent after the commencement of this inquiry.

Mr. Littler: But this telegram shows what is being done.

The Chairman: But the fact that something is stated in a telegram does not prove that it is true. From whom does the telegram come?

Mr. Littler: It is from the agent for the mines, and it says that sixty tons of coal per day are now being raised.

The Chairman: After Mr. Cordery's evidence, the Committee will probably believe that there is coal there, and that it is not unlikely that you are getting sixty tons a day.

General Richard Strachey deposed that he was an officer of the Indian Government, and had held the same position throughout the negotiations respecting concessions. He produced copies of despatches recording the part taken by the India Office in these matters. Although the Government of India assented to Abdul Huk conducting negotiations in regard to the railway and mining concessions, it did so on the distinct understanding that he should not conclude any engagement without first informing the Government of its nature. The Government felt, as representing the paramount power, that they were bound to satisfy themselves that, in entering into any agreement, the Nizam's Government fully understood its responsibilities and obligations, and that due precautions had been taken to safeguard its interests. The railway concession was given on the distinct understanding that it was altogether without prejudice to the ulterior object of the mining concession.

Is it a fact that when Abdul Huk was negotiating the railway business at the India Office, he most distinctly affirmed that he had no personal interest in the matter whatever?—He said that to myself. The discussion about the concession began in 1882, and assumed definite shape in 1883—the mines being separated from the railway. Abdul Huk was advised to go to a firm of respectable solicitors, so that he might be advised whether or not he was going beyond the instructions of his own Government, and it was suggested further, with regard to the contemplated mining concession, that he should also consult solicitors who were conversant with that sort of business. He did so, and the assistance of the India Office was invited. They were so dissatisfied with the scheme brought from India that they would have nothing to do with it. The matter took a fresh shape, and the India Office was informed of the concession having been granted. He never heard of the arrangement with regard to the 85,000 shares given to the concessionnaires until the first accounts of the company were received in July, 1887. The Public Works Committee of the India Office had a telegram from the Viceroy about the intention of the Nizam's Government to purchase shares on May 16th, but no opinion was expressed on the matter.

By Mr. Slagg: Colonel Marshall was not in any way connected with the Government of India; he was a servant of the Nizam's Government. The interpretation put upon the concession was not suspected. If it had been, possibly a different view would have been taken of its merits. Mr. Hughes was a superintendent of the geological survey. It was the custom to lend the services of officers of the Government of India.

By Mr. Labouchere: This concession was ultimately sent home to the India Office as it is drawn up. Did anybody look into it?—I did personally.

Was consent given to it?—Yes.

Did you look into the terms?—I did.

Are we to understand that the India Office consented to a concession, which they understood was to enable the concessionnaires to take £850,000 out of the capital, £1,000,000?—It was not their business. ("Oh," and laughter).

Do I understand that this was the intention of the sixteen gentlemen who sat round the Council table?—They did not sit.

Did they form any opinion from reading it as to what was to be done?—No.

They did not think it worth while?—They did not think it their business.

Whose business was it?—Nobody's, of course. The India Office is not the dry nurse of the Nizam. (Laughter.)

The Calcutta Government sent the agreement home to the India Office?—Yes.

And the India Office looked over the contract?—Yes.

Did you see that the contract carried out the intention of the Calcutta Government?—So far as I examined it, yes.

What was the intention? Was it that the nominal capital should be as originally contemplated, and that a further issue of shares should be made?—The company was to be formed with a capital of not less than £1,000,000. There was nothing to prevent a further issue of shares.

You consider it perfectly legitimate and proper that the concessionnaires should receive £850,000?– Have I said it? (Laughter.)

Well, you have implied it?—I have not only not implied it, but I have expressed no opinion upon it.

Would it not have been wise on the part of the committee to have looked into the concession in order to see that this transaction was impossible?—They did look into it. If you could tell me how I could have foreseen it, I think you would be very clever. (Laughter.) I had no conception that the concessionnaires would take any more for the concession than what reasonable people would call fair. As there was to be a concession to the company it is obvious that there would be some consideration. It would not be transferred for nothing.

Then you, as the guardian of these Nizams and people, consider it perfectly legitimate to encourage A and B, who are mere financiers, to sell such a concession for what they can to the company?—That was the intention of it.

Of what?—Of the contract. It was the intention that somebody should be paid.

Might not the Nizam, the Calcutta Government, and the Government of India have come to the conclusion that Watson was going to do the same thing in the case of the mining company as he did in the case of the railway—that he was merely going to made a profit upon the raising of the capital?—Yes.

There is not one word in the concession limiting the amount to be paid to the concessionnaires. Don't you think it would have been desirable to limit it?—Yes, we know now.

Then the committee were remiss?—No, they were not remiss. They were not all-wise. I should say that if this honourable committee had had before them at that time this very document, it does not follow that they would have done differently. (Laughter.)

Don't you think it would be possible to find six sane men in the India Office who would have thought it desirable to take precautions, knowing what the promoters are?—It is very easy to be wise after the event.

Mr. Labouchere: But we want our officials to be wise before the event.

Witness: But you don't always get them. (Laughter.)

Mr. Labouchere: No, we don't.

The Chairman stated that the Committee hoped to conclude its investigation on Tuesday next, when the examination of General Strachey would be resumed.—*Financial News*, June 16.

The Committee which is inquiring into the Deccan Company continues to yield food for entertainment and reflection. Mr. Henry Labouchere and General Strachey had a neat sparring match yesterday, in the course of which the hon. gentleman adroitly "got in" with the remark that he had never accused the General and his colleagues at the India Office of the crime of being wise men. It is a curious feature of this inquiry that the members of the Committee sternly refute the bullying of witnesses on the part of the counsel. That is a privilege which Sir Henry James and his colleagues reserve to themselves. They certainly protect the witnesses from their natural enemies.—*Hull News*, June 16.

H.H. The Nizam's Guaranteed State Railways.—This company was incorporated in virtue of a concession granted on 27th December, 1883, by the Government of the Nizam, with the consent of the Secretary of State for India, to acquire and work the existing Nizam's State Railway, 121 miles in length, from Wadi on the Great Indian Peninsula Railway to Hyderabad and Secunderabad, and also to construct and work new lines of railway from Hyderabad, *via* Warangul, to the southern frontier of the Hyderabad State, and to the northern frontier. The consideration paid by the company for the existing railway, lands for the new lines, and for other concessions and obligations undertaken by the Nizam's Government was £500,000 in fully paid-up shares, and £1,166,666 in cash to be applied as follows—viz., £625,000 to acquiring the interest of the English shareholders in the existing line, £200,000 to form the first payment to the guarantee fund, and £341,666 to the Government. Subsequently, in March, 1885, the Government took £241,600 in debentures, instead of cash, at the then current price, the company agreeing to pay £39,000 in cash in July, 1890.

From the report just issued for the second half of 1887, it appears that the mileage worked, 208 miles, was the same as in the corresponding period of 1886, but that the results were not so favourable. The coaching receipts, owing to the fact that fewer troops and horses for military purposes were carried, and fewer special trains run, were Rs.16,459 lower, and the receipts from goods and sundries also show a net decrease of Rs.17,885. The working expenses, mainly on account of the charge for maintaining the Secunderabad-Warangul section, falling on revenue instead of capital, and heavier locomotive charges, were Rs.163,037 higher. The rate of working, owing to these unfavourable charges, rose from 46 per cent. to 69·95 per cent., the main results of the half-year's working being, in sterling, as under :—

	1887.		1886.		Inc. or dec.
Earnings	£50,758	....	£55,838	....	– £5,080
Expenses	35,506	....	25,688	...	+ 9,818
Per cent. of earnings	69·95	....	46·00	....	+ 23·95
Net	15,252	....	30,150	....	– 14,898

The total of the debentures at the end of the year was £1,000,000, and the amount required to cover the 4 per cent. interest on this total is £20,000 for the half-year, so that, for the past six months, the net earnings were £4,748 short of the sum required to meet this charge. Under the concession, the Government of the Nizam guarantee for twenty years an annuity equal to interest at the rate of 5 per cent. on the total amount of the share and debenture capital up to £4,500,000—the capital now stands at £2,000,000 capital stock, and £1,000,000 debentures. The residue of that annuity, after paying the 4 per cent. on the debentures and 5 per cent. on the capital stock, is to be invested to form a sinking fund, now amounting to £15,178, primarily for the redemption of the debentures. As security for the due payment of the annuity, the Government are bound to maintain a guarantee fund of £200,000 in the hands of two trustees. The concession further provides that the amounts paid to the company in respect of the annuity are to be repaid with simple interest at 5 per cent. out of the net earnings of the road, 5 per cent. per annum being secured in the first instance to the shareholders, with one moiety of the surplus profit over 5 per cent. On the 1st January, 1914, and at certain subsequent dates, the Nizam's Government can purchase the undertaking on payment of a sum equal to the then share and debenture capital, plus a bonus of 25 per cent. on the share capital; but if not so purchased, the line will vest in the Government at the end of 99 years.—*Railway News*, June 16.

YESTERDAY, at a meeting of the committee on the Deccan Mining Company, Mr. Cordery, British Resident at Hyderabad, was examined, and asserted most emphatically that he had no idea at the time the negotiations were going on that Abdul Huk and his partner were the concessionnaires or he would have stopped the whole affair. He also considered that giving 85,000 shares to the concessionnaires was contrary to the spirit and intention of the agreement. He had never seen the letter—said to have been found among the Residency papers—and did not believe that it could have got there by fair means.—*Journal of Commerce*, June 16.

THE DECCAN MINING SCANDAL.—A conspiracy has been discovered at Secunderabad, says a Bombay telegram of Saturday, to procure telegrams passing through the local telegraph office from the Resident and the Nizam's Government regarding the mining scandal. Several persons are implicated, amongst whom is Ahmed Ali, the son-in-law of Abdul Huk's brother, the Subadar. The telegraph signaller and another person have already confessed before a magistrate their share in the conspiracy, and are now under arrest. Three others, including Ahmed Ali, have been admitted to bail. The object of the conspiracy appears to be to keep Abdul Huk informed of passing events.—*Evening Post*, June 18.

ANOTHER ABDUL HUK CONSPIRACY.—HIS CONFEDERATES MILK THE TELEGRAPH WIRES, BUT ARE DISCOVERED AND ARRESTED.—(Special Telegram.)—Hyderabad, June 18, 1888.—A conspiracy has been discovered at Secunderabad to procure copies of the telegrams passing through the local telegraph office, from the Resident and the Government of the Nizam, regarding the Deccan mining scandal. Several persons are implicated, among whom is Ahmed Ali, son-in-law of Abdul Huk's brother, the Subadar. The signaller at the telegraph office and another person confessed before a magistrate, and are now under arrest. Three others, including Huk's relative, have been admitted to bail. The object of the conspiracy was to keep Abdul Huk informed of passing events.—*Financial News*, June 19.

ABDUL HUK has little to learn in the trickery department of civilization. A special telegram from Hyderabad, which we publish to-day, shows that his friends have been carrying on a conspiracy to milk the telegraph wires at Secunderabad, and so to keep the wily Sirdar informed of all that was taking place in connection with the mining scandal, regarding which he has a natural curiosity. But this, like the original tricks of Abdul Huk, has been discovered, and his confederates are now under arrest like himself. There seems to be no end to the ingenuity of this enterprising ex-policeman.—*Financial News*, June 19.

THE Deccan Select Committee will sit again to-day, when the examination of General Richard Strachey will be continued. General Strachey's evidence is well worthy of attention. It proves that there was nobody in the India Office who understood what the concession was really giving to Mr. Watson and his friends, and further, that nobody considered it his business to take any trouble to find out. General Strachey's one excuse, is that "it is easy to be wise after the event;" but it would be infinitely more satisfactory if the country could feel that India Office officials—and not them alone—were able to discover when a thing is wrong, and not require to wait till the newspapers tell them so. Then, of course, it is too late. After General Strachey's humiliating admissions, surely the India Office will take care that if a document of which it cannot make head or tail comes before it again, the papers will be submitted to some competent person. The India Office may not be "dry nurse to the Nizam;" but when they undertake to see the Nizam safely through a piece of business the officials ought to have some idea of what they are about.—*Financial News*, June 19.

THE Financial Secretary of the Government of Hyderabad is now on his way to England to give evidence before the Select Committee of the House of Commons in regard to the Deccan scandal; and I also hear that several leading members of the Bombay Bar were engaged by the Nizam and Abdul Huk in connection with the investigation; but so far as these two parties are concerned, the whole matter is settled by Abdul Huk paying to the Nizam £150,000 in respect of all claims against him. The Select Committee of the House of Commons has, however, to proceed with its work, which is to examine, not the relations between a native prince and his minister, but the conduct of the Government of India and the India Office in reference to this mining scandal. By the way, the *Pioneer* of Allahabad, which was the journal to expose the whole affair, censures severely the negligence of Mr. Cordery, the British resident at the Nizam's Court; but, as the intrigue was carried on in England, it is not quite easy to see what Mr. Cordery could do to prevent it.

Mr. Inverarity, of the Bombay Bar, who has come to England to look after the interests of Abdul Huk before the House of Commons Committee, has been retained for three months from the time he leaves Bombay, and his fee is sixty thousand rupees; so that he gets a visit home and a princely fee out of the Deccan business—by no means the only man who has made a little money out of it. A stockbroker employed told the Committee that he charged ten shillings a share for the sale of the 12,000 shares, and added that if he knew as much as he does now he would have charged £1.—*Hawk*, June 19.

General Strachey, who was yesterday examined by the Deccan Mines Committee, says that the India Office accepted no responsibility, and the Government of India did nothing in the matter to which exception could be taken. That, we venture to say, will not be the opinion of the Committee. The fact that the Government of India had sanctioned the concession, and that Abdul Huk was sponsored, so to say, by the India Office, went far to induce the public to take shares in the company. It was the plain duty of the Government of India to make searching inquiries before approving the concession, and, failing to make these inquiries, much of the responsibility for what afterwards happened must rest upon the Viceroy and his advisers.—*Star*, June 20.

Light on the Deccan Deal.—General Strachey is Severely Cross-Examined by Mr. Labouchere.—The Select Committee of the House of Commons appointed to inquire into the circumstances attending the formation and subsequent proceedings of the Hyderabad Deccan Mining Company resumed its sittings yesterday. In the absence of Sir Henry James, who was pleading in the case of Wood v. Cox, the Solicitor-General for Scotland presided.

General Strachey, recalled, stated in reply to Mr. Labouchere, that the concession never came before the Secretary of State in a complete state until after it had been executed by the Nizam's Government. In October, 1885, Lord Randolph Churchill, when Indian Secretary, wrote to Lord Dufferin pointing out the desirability of the sanction of the India Office being obtained in connection with concessions of this character. Lord Dufferin asked that in the case under discussion the sanction of the India Office might be telegraphed. This was done.

Mr. Labouchere: And yet you say the Secretary of State was not responsible?—I did not understand you.

Was the Secretary of State responsible or not for this concession?—He was in a certain sense.

In what sense?—In the sense of acting in a friendly way for the Nizam's Government.

Witness further said it was rather a difficult thing to say whether or not the Nizam's Government had any right to make a concession to a British subject without the authority of the Secretary of State. He knew something, more or less, of the practical working and the law of a limited liability company. He did not think the Nizam's Government, who gave the concession for nothing, was in any way defrauded by anything which Watson afterwards got for it. Abdul Huk had received power from the Nizam's Government, and could do as he pleased. He would throw the matter entirely on the Nizam's Government, notwithstanding all the correspondence and the fact that the matter had been referred to their legal advisers. Abdul Huk was practically the Nizam's Government, so far as the agreement was made.

Mr. Labouchere: But you interfered in this agreement?—We interfered so far as we considered the interest of the Nizam's Government required it.

And would you not think that the interest of the Nizam's Government required that he should get all it was worth? Did not the interference of the Government of Calcutta put £250,000 in Watson's pocket?—I suppose so.

You sent to Lord Dufferin to send over these contracts for your mere formal amusement?—Not at all. He held the Nizam's Government did not act honestly with them. He did not accept the responsibility of leaving it to Watson to decide whether he was to get £250,000 or £500,000 for it. His (witness's) brother's name was on the directorate before a single share was subscribed. Mr. Batten, chairman of the mining company, was his brother-in-law.

To Mr. Slagg: If he had to do the same thing again, and he was deceived by the Government with which he dealt, he could do nothing differently. If they were made responsible for what was done by Indian States it would be putting a burden on the Government, and prevent the working of English capital.

Mr. Watson, one of the concessionnaires, was examined by the Chairman, and, in reply to numerous questions, admitted that in the course of his transactions he had been making practically free gifts of the moneys. To one man, a Mr. Hemmerdy, after he had ceased to be a director, he presented £10,000 merely because the gentleman was an old friend, and other gentlemen who happened to purchase some shares found themselves benefited by sums of upwards of £200,000.

After further evidence the inquiry was adjourned.—*Star*, June 20.

NO CONNECTION WITH THE DECCAN COMPANY.—Sir Richard John Meade, chairman of the general meeting of the members of the Nizam's Guaranteed State Railways Company yesterday, said the Nizam's Railway had no concern with the Deccan Company, and he trusted that that would be thoroughly understood. They had been assured of the continued and friendly interest which would be taken in the railway by the Nizam's Government.—*Star*, June 20.

YESTERDAY, at the Deccan inquiry, General Strachey was examined at length by Mr. Labouchere as to the responsibility of the Indian Government for the mining concessions. He contended that his responsibility was limited to advising the Nizam on information before them, and as the Nizam's Government, represented by Huk, did not act honestly in stating its intentions, the Indian Government could not do otherwise than it did. Witness's brother, Sir John Strachey, was chairman of the Nizam's Railway Company, and Mr. Batten, chairman of the Mining Company, was brother-in-law to Sir John. Mr. Watson, recalled, answering the chairman, said he gave Mr. Hemmerdy, an old friend, one of the first directors who voted the agreement giving the concessionnaires 85,000 shares, a thousand shares worth £10,000, but it was not as a reward for voting. He sold Hughes, who reported on the prospects of the company, £3,300 worth of shares for £1,000; gave Furnival, another engineer who reported, 500 shares, value £5,000, for nothing. These were not bribes to get favourable reports.—*Journal of Commerce*, June 20.

Some more interesting evidence was given to-day before the Committee of the House of Commons engaged in considering the Deccan scandal. Sir Henry James, fresh from the case of "Wood *v.* Cox," did not arrive until the proceedings were far advanced. General Strachey was being examined at the time by Mr. Labouchere, but subsequently Mr. Slagg took him in hand and examined him very close with a view of fixing the responsibility of granting the concession upon the Indian Government and the Council of India, but the witness persisted, as he had done during a lengthy examination by Mr. Labouchere, that the Nizam's Government was alone responsible. General Strachey broke down completely under this examination. It is quite clear from the course of to-day's proceedings that the Committee will make a strong report, if one may anticipate their decision, as to the carelessness of the India Office in dealing with important questions of this character.—*Manchester Examiner*, June 20.

Everyone ought to read the full account of the Hyderabad Deccan inquiry which has been carried on before the Parliamentary Committee. In spite of all the jobbery, all the unfair profits, and all the playing into each other's hands, on the part of the promoters, I still am of opinion that no cancellation of the concession will be made. That the most awful and unscrupulous profits have been made cannot be denied; but, unfortunately for the company, nearly everything has been done in a legal form. The Nizam alone was *done* fraudulently, and the money obtained from him has been duly restored by Abdul Huk.

Before me is a photograph of the gorgeous Yacht Club Chambers at Bombay, recently built by Abdul Huk, and upon which a mortgage has been handed over to the Nizam as security for the balance outstanding.

Whatever further unworthy facts the next and final sitting of the Parliamentary inquiry may elicit, it is certain that the coal raising is being hurried on with at Singareni, if only to show up the value of the coalfield, and to modify disappointed and bitter shareholders by the hopes of a speedy dividend. This it is useless to expect for another eighteen months at least, and many more contracts will have to be entered into with the Indian railway companies before profits can be made even on paper.—*Barker's Trade and Finance*, June 20.

The Deccan Inquiry.—The Part taken by the India Office in the Negotiations—Evidence of Members of the Stock Exchange.—The Select Committee of the House of Commons, appointed to inquire into the circumstances attending the concession to this company of the mining rights of the State of Hyderabad, resumed its sittings yesterday morning. During the earlier part of the proceedings the Solicitor-General for Scotland presided, Sir Henry James not arriving until about one o'clock. There were also present Sir R. Temple, Mr. Labouchere, Mr. McLagan, Mr. Bristowe, and Mr. Slagg. The attendance of the general public was again very considerable.

Sir Horace Davey, Q.C., Mr. T. D. Inverarity, of the Bombay Bar, and Mr. Trevor White appeared for Sirdar Diler Jung. Mr. Pember, Q.C., and Mr. Lewis Coward appeared for the company. Mr. Mayne appeared for the Nizam's Government; and Mr. Littler, Q.C., appeared for Mr. Watson.

General Strachey, recalled and examined by Mr. Labouchere, said: Before the draft concession, and when he first came to London, Abdul Huk, as I understand it, came as the representative of his Government. The Secretary of State was satisfied on this point, and advised Abdul Huk to go to a respectable solicitor to see that everything that was being done was right. It was also suggested that as this mining business was peculiar and technical, he had better go to a solicitor who was conversant with this sort of business, and who would be competent to advise. So far as I understand, we—the Government of India—accepted no responsibility at all. The Secretary of State was in the position of a friendly adviser to the agent of the Nizam's Government in the matter of this mining concession. He had nothing further to do with it.

Was not Lord Dufferin told to send home the final concession to the Secretary of State?—I have no recollection of anything of the sort. There was some little misconception as to that. The fact is that when Lord Randolph Churchill was Secretary of State a letter was sent to him informing him of the £83,000 which Abdul Huk received, in respect to the railway by permission of the late Sir Salar Jung. That was considered entirely objectionable, and in order that the possibility of such an arrangement should be guarded against in future the Secretary of State wrote the letter (produced) which ordered that such concessions were to be submitted to him. But it was a general instruction, not given with regard to that particular concession. This, in the opinion of the Governor-General, is one of the concessions to which the general instructions applied. My impression is that a reply or telegram was sent from the Secretary of State assenting to the agreement after certain alterations had been made.

Yet you say the Secretary of State was not responsible?—I don't understand it. He was responsible in a certain sense—in the sense of acting in a friendly way for the Nizam's Government. And let me say that I think the whole of this discussion has assumed a shape I am not responsible for. It was stated in the agreement between the Nizam's Government and Mr. Winter—it was stated specifically, and apparently with some intention, that Abdul Huk was authorised by the Nizam's Government to enter into this agreement. Therefore, the Secretary of State had a perfect right to assume that what Abdul Huk had done was really the act of the Nizam's Government. It appears to be unreasonable and an improbability that the Secretary of State should assume that the act of the agent of the Nizam's Government was an act against his own Government. Of course, if the Secretary of State had had the smallest suspicion that Abdul Huk was making an arrangement with the view of his own personal profit, the agreement would have been set aside.

Had Abdul Huk a right to make a financial agreement with a British subject without the sanction of the Governor-General in Council or the Secretary of State?—That is a moot point, and I don't feel competent to decide it.

But the statute of George III. forbids, without the consent of the British Government, any person entering into a financial transaction with the native princes?—I think not. The question of the proper construction of that statute is a difficult one, and I am not in a position to give any opinion upon it. I think no good can come from asking my personal opinion upon it. You must not suppose the concession came merely before me. It was laid in the regular way before the office, and we took the advice of the legal officers. This particular point to which you are referring is a difficult one, and it is a question whether the statute does apply.

About this £150,000 of first issue?—Yes; the intention of the Government of India was that £150,000 should be paid up, and immediately applied to the working of the mines, and that the difference between this £150,000 and the million should, in the future, be available as required for extending the operations of the company. The question is whether, under the circumstances, it would have been possible to have framed a contract which would have prevented that being done which is done, and what I say is this: that what Abdul Huk, acting on behalf of the Nizam's Government did, was to make an arrangement which was diametrically opposed to the avowed intentions of the Indian Government and of his own Government.

That arrangement was sent home to England?—Yes; but we had no knowledge of it. What I say is, that if the Nizam's Government and his agents had been asked, they would have said that this which has happened could not have happened. I put it in this way broadly. I look upon Abdul Huk, so far as this concession is concerned, as the Nizam's Government. He was the special agent of that Government, and from that point of view the Nizam's Government made an agreement with the concessionnaires with the intention of applying the difference between £150,000 and a million pounds to their own personal ends. The only thing the Government of India could do was to look at the surface of the thing. It is quite easy now to see what Abdul Huk's intention was then. I quite admit if it could have been seen then it would have been desirable in some way or other to guard against it. I am quite unable, though, to say how it could be done. If the Nizam's Government and its officers had been honest, that which has occurred could not have occurred, and they could perfectly well have controlled the amount of remuneration that was to be ultimately given to the concessionnaires.

But did not Mr. Durand write that the negotiations were to go on, not between Sir Salar Jung and Mr. Winter, but through Mr. Cordery?—Yes.

And you say there was no responsibility?—I don't say there was no responsibility; I say there was responsibility according to their lights.

Was what the Nizam gave away worth to anybody £850,000?—I should say it was worth what it would fetch, but I don't understand that the Nizam gave anything away.

Then what was the concession?—Ah, that is another thing. It is true that Mr. Watson sold it to the company for £850,000. All I can say is that I should be very sorry to give £850,000 for it.

Do you consider it is worth anything?—I should not say it is not.

Was not the Nizam's Government plundered of anything—say £850,000, say a million—anything for which Mr. Watson could sell the concession?—There you go into deep water. It is alleged, as I understand, that the Nizam's Government gave Abdul Huk plenary powers to do what he liked and to get what he could.

I am asking this question—this concession was given for nothing by the Nizam's Government, and Watson sold it to the company. Was not the Nizam's Government, who had given it for nothing, defrauded—plundered of any amount that Mr. Watson may have received from the company?—I think not, because it appears to me that the agreement, on the face of it, implied that something should pass as between the concessionnaires and the company. I say the Nizam's Government itself made the arrangement. I throw it entirely on the Nizam's Government.

Which is ordered to negotiate, through Mr. Cordery, to send the agreement home and submit it to your committee and the legal advisers? You actually say that the Nizam's Government is responsible?—Certainly. The Nizam's Government had made the contract with the knowledge that this was going to be done. They didn't inform us that the Nizam's Government had given Mr. Watson power to sell his concession for £850,000. If they had we wouldn't have consented to it. Abdul Huk was the Nizam's Government. We interfered as far as we thought that on the face of it the interests of the Nizam's Government required. We considered it for the advantage of the Nizam's Government that they should get the mines worked.

If the original proposal for an issue of £500,000 had been adhered to, Mr. Watson could not have obtained his £850,000?—No.

Is it not a fact that the suggestion of the Calcutta Government put £350,000 in Watson's pocket?—It was the means of putting it in.

You don't consider that the Nizam's Government depended on the English Government in any sort of way?— No; I say that the Nizam's Government is Abdul Huk.

Then, you say this contract was sent to you merely as a sort of form or amusement?—Not at all. I say that, as far as reasonable men could act, we did act in the interests of the Nizam's Government. I said our responsibility is limited. That it was our business to advise the Nizam's Government, supposing that that Government was treating us honestly, but I say it was not treating us honestly. We did not recommend that the concession should be carried through. What we did say was that we had no objection to it.

Would it have gone on if you had stated you had an objection?—I don't know. I can't say what the power of the Secretary of State may be.

Witness here produced a letter from the Nizam's State Railway Company to his department dated 1885, stating that Abdul Huk was authorised by Sir Salar Jung to receive £83,000 on account of the railway transactions which had been so often mentioned in the course of the inquiry. Answering further questions by Mr. Labouchere, he said: Mr. Hughes is a servant of the Government of India in the Geological Department. The mining company wanted somebody they could trust to report on the value of the concession, and they asked the Secretary of State that Mr. Hughes, who was in England on leave at the time, should be allowed to make a geological examination. He had previously surveyed districts contiguous to the Nizam's territory. The Secretary of State assented. Mr. Hughes would be allowed to receive payment for the company.

Would you call it a bribe giving Mr. Hughes a large number of shares? —I should think it was an objectionable transaction.

Would you be surprised to hear that that objectionable transaction had taken place?—I should be surprised at nothing.

Mr. Watson appointed your brother, Sir John Strachey, as chairman of the railway?—Yes.

Are you aware that your brother's name appeared on the prospectus as director, and I believe subsequently as chairman, before any of the shares were subscribed?—I suppose that would be so.

Mr. Batten was secretary of the mining company?—Yes.

He is your brother's brother-in-law?—Yes. As you put it in that way, I think it right I should add that Sir John Strachey was asked to become chairman of the railway company. It had been arranged that Sir Bartle Frere was to be the chairman. Sir Bartle Frere said it was extremely desirable, in the interests of the Nizam, that some responsible person should be chairman. When he left the country Sir R. Meade, who had been Resident at Hyderabad, took the place.

By Sir R. Temple: Both Sir J. Strachey and Sir R. Meade occupied that position with the knowledge and approval of the Secretary of State. Their object was to see that the thing was started with justice, and to protect the public interest.

By Mr. Slagg: As I understand it, the Hyderabad State is an independent State, and the relations of the Nizam's Government and the British Government are regulated by treaty?—There is no doubt that the Government at Hyderabad is greatly under the influence of our Resident, but it is an influence merely. We have no power to give orders; we have the power of interfering with the action of a British subject, but that is a limited power. I did not form any opinion on the point as to how Mr. Watson's concession was to be paid for. As I have stated more than once, the precise manner in which the transfer was to be made from the concessionnaires to the company did not arise.

If you had the same thing to do again I suppose you would do it in a different manner ?—If I had the same thing to do over again, and I was again deceived by the Government I was treating with, I think it quite possible that I should do it in the same manner.

Don't you think in future the Government will be well advised to take precautions against the possibility of being deceived ?—If you throw upon us the responsibility of seeing that nothing whatever is done wrong in the transaction of the affairs of the native States of India, all I can say is that you put a tremendous burden upon the Government, and that it is an impossibility for us to undertake it.

By Mr. Littler, Q.C. : Undoubtedly there is a capital supply of coal at Singareni, which will be of very great value to the Indian railways themselves.

Mr. Watson, recalled and examined by Sir Henry James : One of the original directors, Mr. Hemmerdy, was a friend of mine. On October 3, I gave him 1,000 shares, worth at par £10,000. I did that because he was an old friend of mine, and had rendered me many services for twenty years previously. He was not then a director.

Do you suggest that it had nothing whatever to do with his acts as a director ?—Nothing whatever.

Why, didn't that form part of the consideration ? Have you given any other old friend of yours £10,000 worth of shares besides this director ? —He was ill ; that was the reason I gave them.

He voted with the other directors these 85,000 shares, and then you gave him £10,000 of shares. Did you buy any of them ?—No ; he holds them still. They have been at a price at which he might have sold them for £12 each.

We have heard a great deal of Mr. T. W. H. Hughes. Did you know him before the formation of the company ?—I have had no communication with him about any subject except the company. He was lent to the company and paid by the company to survey and report to the company.

On May 9 you sold to him 200 £5 paid shares and 200 fully-paid shares for £1,000. Was that the market price in May, 1887 ?—No ; the price was about £11.

Why did you let him have 200 fully-paid shares, worth £2,200, for nothing ?—To give him an interest in the company.

He was the man who used to make the reports. Did you wish him to keep these shares ?—He was free to keep them or not.

How could he have an interest in the company if he sold them and bought them back on July 4—200 shares for £2,390 ?—I sold them for him in the market.

Was not that a profit to the gentleman you were borrowing from the Government of India to make reports ?—I gave him these shares so that he might have an interest in the company, and throw his whole soul into it.

How did you carry out that object when you bought back the shares ?— I have no doubt at that time he had a reason for selling ; whether he intended to buy them back I don't know.

Did you regard this £2,200 as a gift ?—Scarcely that. It was a bonus to him, if you like. I never gave them to him in order that he might send unfair reports.

Why should Mr. Hughes not send perfectly fair reports without these 200 shares ?—He would ; but he was very hard at work in the jungles, and I thought he ought to have some compensation.

But he was to be paid ?—Still I thought he ought to have some compensation.

By Mr. Bristowe : A great deal has been heard to-day of the question how you were to be remunerated. Is there not another way, by taking a share of the profits when earned ? I mention this because many people have asked in what way you were to be remunerated—That would not have been a realisable security. (Laughter.)

But it would have secured to you as much as you were entitled to take?—There are many ways of being remunerated.

Mr. Cordery, recalled at his request, made two or three unimportant alterations in his evidence of Friday last.

Sir Theodore Hope, examined by Sir R. Temple: I was a member of the Council of the Governor-General of India, responsible for the Department of Public Works at the time of this concession. Our object was to ensure a sufficient capital being provided for the thoroughly efficient working of the Singareni Coal Mine, and as far as possible to provide no more capital than was necessary to carry out that object, and to do a reasonable amount of prospecting in the other portions of the concession. Further, the object of the agreement was to provide that capital should be forthcoming in a regular way to carry out any of the other undertakings which the concession contemplated, providing the prospecting should show it was practicable and likely to prove remunerative. I have only been a month in London since I came from India, and I had paid no general attention to these proceedings until Thursday last, when I was informed that the Committee wished to examine me. I am aware that £150,000 has been raised for what I may call the primary purposes, as contemplated in the agreement, and that the concessionnaires received £850,000 as the price of the concession.

According to your knowledge and belief, are these transactions in accordance with the intentions of the Government of India when they sanctioned this contract?—I believe that so much of the transaction as relates to the £150,000 is in accordance with the intention of the agreement which the Government of India advised the Nizam's Government to accept, and that the transactions relating to the £850,000 are not in accordance with that intention.

Had the Council, when you were a member of it, any idea that such a transaction would have happened?—As regards the transaction as a whole, certainly not. The Government of India undoubtedly contemplated that the concessionnaires should receive something when they formed the company in some form or other; but no member of the Government, I believe, contemplated that the remuneration would take the form it has.

The Chairman: Having now the knowledge you have, if their attention had been called to the exact words, would they, do you think, have allowed this £850,000 to be paid for the concession?—I should suppose that if it had been pointed out to them that the wording of the contract was such as to admit of a transaction of this kind taking place, they would probably have pointed it out to the Nizam's Government, and suggested that the Nizam's Government and their advisers should look into the point.

Or, in other words, could they have foreseen that the wording of the contract would have covered or permitted any transaction of this kind, they would have caused the wording to be amended?—They would have pointed out that there was a hole in the draft which certain persons had left for themselves.

The room was then cleared, in order that the Committee might deliberate on the course counsel might be permitted to pursue. On re-admission,

The Chairman asked Mr. Littler, Q.C., who appeared for Mr. Watson, what witnesses he wished to call.

Mr. Littler replied that he desired to call Mr. Morgans, a member of the firm of Messrs. Morgans, consulting mining engineers.

The Chairman: Has he ever been to Hyderabad?

Mr. Littler: No, he has not; but he has read the reports put before the Committee.

After some discussion,

The Chairman decided that the Committee could not hear Mr. Morgans' opinion upon the reports. The Committee would form their own opinion. If Mr. Morgans would give the Committee any new facts they would hear him.

Mr. Morris (member of the firm of Messrs. Morris, Hurst and Buckle), examined by Mr. Littler, said: I have been 53 years on the Stock Exchange. We were the largest dealers in Deccan shares, as jobbers. We knew when we began to deal with the shares that the 85,000 shares belonging to the concessionnaires did not in any way represent cash. I do not think I knew Mr. Watson at the time. I think we got our information from Mr. Evans. It did not surprise us at all that the 85,000 shares did not represent cash. We were very anxious to deal. I think the shares had pretty nearly a continuous rise.

So far as you know, during the whole time was there any fictitious dealing?—None whatever; it was all *boná fide* dealing.

Did you ever find any trace in the market of Mr. Watson pressing sales or making a market?—No. I knew Mr. Watson was selling.

Mr. Labouchere: And buying?—I have only heard that twice. I do not know of his buying, except 2,000 shares that he had oversold, or that he had sold and wanted to buy back.

What do you say is the effect on shares which are not officially quoted?—It does not make the slightest difference. In fact, there is at the present moment a most gigantic speculation going on, and has been for the last six months—I speak of the De Beer's Mining Company; and the shares have never obtained a settlement or a quotation.

Is it unusual, Mr. Morris, in mining matters, for a large sum in shares to be given to the promoters?—It is very usual.

The Chairman: You say you are not surprised that the concessionnaires have taken £850,000 worth of shares. Have you the slightest knowledge of the value of the concession?—Not myself. But I suppose if Mr. Watson put £150,000 into a mining venture he expected to make £750,000 profit. If he did not, he would lose his £150,000, and his 85,000 shares would not be worth 5s.

Supposing the company got nothing—no diamonds, no coal, and supposing Mr. Watson had 85,000 shares, which through your exertions he got the public to buy, what would the public get in return for those shares?—I tell you the public are very much in the habit of buying what they know nothing whatever about. We only deal with brokers, who, we assume, buy for the public.

Do you think the company should have inquired what was being got in return when Mr. Watson was given £850,000 worth of shares?—I know nothing at all about what the company ought to do.

Before the company gave him that amount, should they not have inquired the value of the concession?—Probably; I should have assumed that somebody connected with the company would have done so. I suppose the directors.

Who introduced those shares to you first as a matter of business?—We bought the shares of Mr. Evans. I have no doubt that three-fourths or four-fifths of the shares sold by Watson came to us.

What did you make by the transaction?—I could not tell. I make as much as I can; that is my business. (Laughter.)

How much did you gain upon the transaction?—I really could not say, but I should like to give £10,000 to have it over again—(laughter)—so that will give you the best idea.

More than £10,000?—I will not say; I must be cautious after saying that.

As you wanted these shares, Evans got them, as he told us, from the concessionnaires, from Watson?—Yes.

You said you were not aware that Watson was buying and selling?—I said I was not aware he was buying, with the exception of the 2,000 shares which he had oversold.

Mr. Slagg: Your purchasers were the brokers?—Yes.

Mr. Wm. Henry Bishop, examined by Mr. Littler, deposed: I have been a stockbroker on the Stock Exchange for 38 years. I telegraphed when away for £20,000 worth of Deccan shares, and on my return I got £19,000 worth. I remember a memorandum stating various facts with regard to the undertaking, and I ascertained to the best of my ability what was the character of the undertaking.

What meaning do you attach to the words on the memorandum, "fully paid up"?—That would mean that the company had not received any money in respect of the 85,000 shares. "Fully paid" I should take to mean issued fully paid; though I am not all sure my definition is correct. I never had any doubt in my own mind that it was intended to work this company by subsidiary companies.

Do you say, as a stockbroker, anything unfair or improper was occurring on the Stock Exchange in respect of the dealing with these shares?—Nothing of the kind came under my observation.

The Chairman: Who gave you this memorandum?—Mr. Watson.

For what purpose?—In order that I might ascertain the character of the undertaking to which I subscribed.

To whom were the £19,000 worth of shares transferred?—I cannot tell you without referring to my books. I recollect Charles James Shaw.

You bought the shares at £9?—Yes, I bought them for my clients.

You hold some yourself?—Yes.

Witness (continuing) explained that it was commonly understood, on the formation of a company, that fully-paid shares meant shares given by the company in consideration of something or other; and I should think it is the opinion of the general public. The company ought to get the value for those shares, and no wise man would put himself in the position of a director if he could not justify this action.

The Chairman: Was it not the duty of the company to see when they gave 85,000 shares to the concessionnaires what value they were to get back?—I rather assume that their minds were satisfied on that point; but I agree with you that their minds should have been satisfied. I thought the shares I bought were worth the money. I relied on Mr. Watson's integrity and position. I gave £9, and handed them to my clients at the same price.

By Mr. Slagg: I should think my clients took the shares, not for a speculative purpose, but as an investment. They acted on my judgment in the matter.

Sir R. Temple: What were the statements before you that induced you to invest?—One was about the Singareni Coalfields, which were ascertained to contain a very large amount of coal.

Then you risked this £20,000 mainly on the statement in the memorandum which referred to the coal?—I had seen some other reports and statements. Mr. Watson did not hold me to my telegram, and I might have taken a less number of shares had I chosen.

By Mr. Labouchere: I did not take the shares on my own account, but for my clients. If you want to know how I was remunerated, however, I may state that I received 2s. per share from Mr. Watson.

Mr. Slagg: So far as you know, were your clients influenced by the fact that the Secretary of State for India had sanctioned this contract? Do you think a fact of that sort would give greater value to the shares?—

Value is a question which would depend on the prospects of a remunerative return, but if you mean security, I should think it would give greater security.

It would give a certain endorsement ?—Yes.

Mr. Littler proposed to call Mr. Rock, but as that gentleman was not present,

Lord Lawrence was the next witness called, examined by the leading counsel.

You are a director of the Deccan Mining Company ?—Yes.

How did you become a director ?—I wrote to ask some of my friends, and I made some inquiries, and some of them thought it right I should become a director.

Until that time you had no connection with the company whatever? —None at all.

Did you afterwards buy shares in the company ?—Yes. My brother and myself bought about 1,000 shares each through our own brokers; we gave 12¼ for them. I think that I hold about 500. I may say that I bought them on the strength of the Nizam being a shareholder, and hearing that he had bought shares about the same price, I thought that I could not be very far wrong. I imagined also that every detail of the business had been before the Government of India, and passed through the India Office. There was nothing to lead me to suppose that the position of the company or the concession was impugned. If any charge was to be brought against anybody connected with the company, particularly the Nizam, I should have thought that, as representing the Nizam on the board, I was the proper channel through which the grievance should have been communicated.

The Chairman: When did you hear first that there was anything not quite straightforward ?—In the *Standard*. I met Abdul Huk in society. He called upon me. I forget who introduced him to me; at all events, he was introduced.

Was he representing the Nizam at that time ?—I was told so.

At the time of the Jubilee ?—Yes.

By Mr. Labouchere: A considerable number have invested in shares from the fact of your being a director ?—A considerable number I am told.

When you became aware that the company had only £150,000 worth of capital, what action did you take ?—I do not know that I took any action.

If you had known that the capital was £150,000 you would not have taken these shares ?—If I had known the company was worth £1,000,000 perhaps I might.

Anyhow, you did not convey this fact to shareholders who might be ignorant of the matter ?—I was about the last shareholder myself.

You were on the board with Abdul Huk as the representative of the Nizam ?—Yes. I was invited by the board to be a director. The Nizam had the power to increase the number of directors, I fancy, so I was asked to become one.

Are you aware the Nizam is no longer a shareholder ?—Yes; and I am no longer a director, strictly speaking. I am rather in a curious position, and I do not know whether I am a director or not.

Is Abdul Huk still a director ?—No; he is not. He is suspended.

By Mr. Slagg: I believed the investment to be a good one at the time.

If it had not been for a sort of Government guarantee, you would not have invested ?—No. I think I spoke to Sir Ashley Eden about this. I know I have to several.

Has the Nizam's Government, while you have been on the board, conveyed to you in any way as its representative on the board, any complaint as to the formation of the company ?—No.

Mr. Morgans (mining engineer), at the request of Mr. Pember, was then examined as to the question of fair rent, which he defined as a rent to be fixed by the rents which ruled in the district.

Mr. Labouchere: Are you a shareholder?—I am not; I am perfectly independent.

Have you been to Hyderabad?—I have not.

Are there any mines in Hyderabad except this?—No; but there are some in Mysore adjoining.

Mysore is some way off?—It is to the south.

Did you report on the Mysore mines?—No.

Do you know anything about them?—Yes; I do.

Are you aware that the public lost a good deal of money over them? —And gained.

Are you aware the mining experts put in very flowery statements about the mines?—Well, that is very commonly done. (Laughter.)

The Chairman, replying to a question by Sir H. Davey, said: Though incidentally Abdul Huk's conduct has been touched upon here, I do not think this is the tribunal to try him.

This was the whole of the evidence.

The Chairman: The course the committee propose to take is to adjourn until two o'clock on Friday, when a further witness will be called by the committee in consequence of the evidence given to-day. His evidence will be short, and the counsel will then proceed at once to make such observations as the committee point out to counsel they desire to have made. The committee do not wish elaborate arguments in this case, and will hear concise statements from them as to the facts they wish to have considered. Of course, the importance of these facts will have to be pointed out by the counsel in order to show their material bearing on the evidence. The addresses of the counsel cannot be at all long. They must be confined to a narrow space, while setting forth the material facts that bear on this inquiry.

The committee then adjourned until Friday, at two o'clock.—*Financial News*, June 20.

The Hyderabad (Deccan) Inquiry is advancing slowly but satisfactorily. The main interest of the piece, so far as the City is concerned, at all events, has not yet been reached. The tale is gradually unfolding itself, and the evidence already gathered is instructive and damning enough. It would serve no useful purpose to enlarge upon it at this incomplete stage of the inquiry, but after the stockbrokers who were employed in the Nizam "deal" have been examined, we shall doubtless have something to say on the whole subject.—*The World*, June 20.

The Hyderabad Inquiry.—The Select Committee of the House of Commons charged with this inquiry met again yesterday, the Solicitor-General for Scotland (Mr. P. J. Robertson), in the absence of Sir H. James, occupying the chair.

General H. Strachey, of the India Office (recalled), was examined at considerable length by Mr. Labouchere. He stated that the Secretary of State had acted in the way of a friendly adviser to Abdul Huk, and the India Office were not aware of the arrangement which the agent of the Nizam's Government was making, or they would have set the whole thing aside. On the face of it Abdul Huk was the accredited agent of the Nizam's Government, and in that way he was treated. The agreement with regard to the concession was actually made between the concessionnaires and the Nizam's Government.

Mr. Watson (recalled) said, in reply to the Chairman, that he gave Hemmerdy, one of the original directors, and who resigned shortly after voting the agreement allotting the 85,000 shares to the concessionnaires, 1,000 fully-paid shares, the market value of which was at the time £10,000. On May 9, 1887, the witness sold Hughes 200 £5 paid shares and 200 fully-paid shares for £1,000; the market value of those shares was about £3,500. He sold them cheaply to give Hughes an interest in the company, but bought back the shares from Hughes on July 4. The witness also gave Furnival, who had also reported on the mines, 500 fully-paid shares for nothing. This was also to give him an interest in the company. He denied that his object in these transactions was to reward Hemmerdy for voting the agreement, or to bribe Hughes and Furnival to report favourably as to the prospects of the company, so as to assist in selling the shares.

Sir Theodore Hope, a member of the Indian Council, was examined; and, on the resumption of the inquiry after luncheon, Mr. Morris (of Morris, Hurst, and Buckle), a stockjobber, gave evidence that there was no fictitious dealing, all was *bona fide*. His firm dealt only with the brokers, and it was impossible to know whether the shares were bought for speculation or investment.

Lord Lawrence, called by Mr. Pember, said he was a director of the Deccan Company. He became a director about the end of July last, at the request of the board. His brother and himself bought about 1,000 shares at 12¼ in the open market. He bought on the strength of the Nizam being a shareholder, the concession having been approved by the Home Government. He certainly never thought there had been any irregularity in the doings of the company. He met Abdul Huk in society, at the Queen's Jubilee garden party among other places. He would not have joined the company or invested in it but for the statement that the Government had sanctioned the agreement.

The committee adjourned until Friday at two o'clock, when counsel will be heard.—*Morning Post*, June 20.

The Deccan Mining Scandal.—The Select Committee of the House of Commons charged with this inquiry met again yesterday, the Solicitor-General for Scotland (Mr. P. J. Robertson), in the absence of Sir H. James, occupying the chair.

General R. Strachey, of the India Office (recalled), was examined at considerable length by Mr. Labouchere, and he stated that the Secretary of State had acted in the way of a friendly adviser to Abdul Huk, and the India Office were not aware of the arrangements which the agent of the Nizam's Government was making, or they would have set the whole thing aside. On the face of it Abdul Huk was the accredited agent of the Nizam's Government, and in that way he was treated. The agreement with regard to the concession was actually made between the concessionnaires and the Nizam's Government.

Mr. Watson, recalled, said, in reply to the Chairman, that he gave Hemmerdy, one of the original directors, and who resigned shortly after voting the agreement alloting the 85,000 shares to the concessionnaires, 1,000 fully-paid shares, the market value of which was at the time £10,000. On May 9, 1887, the witness sold Hughes 200 £5 paid shares, and 200 fully paid shares for £1,000; the market value of those shares was about £3,500. He sold them cheaply to give Hughes an interest in the company, but bought back the shares from Hughes on July 4. The witness also gave Furnival, who had also reported on the mines, 500 fully-paid shares for nothing. This was also to give him an interest in the company. He denied that his object in these transactions was to reward Hemmerdy for voting the agreement, or to bribe Hughes and Furnivall to report favourably as to the prospects of the company, so as to assist in selling the shares.

Mr. W. T. Hooper, a member of the Indian Council, was examined; and, on the resumption of the inquiry after luncheon, Mr. Morris (of Morris, Hurst, and Buckle), a stockjobber, gave evidence that there was no fictitious dealing, all was *bonâ fide*. His firm dealt only with the brokers, and it was impossible to know whether the shares were bought for speculation or investment.

Lord Lawrence, called by Mr. Pember, said he was a director of the Deccan Company. He became a director about the end of July last, at the request of the board. His brother and himself bought about 1,000 shares at 12¼ in the open market. He bought on the strength of the Nizam being a shareholder, the concession having been approved by the Home Government. He certainly never thought there had been any irregularity in the doings of the company. He met Abdul Huk in society, at the Queen's Jubilee garden party among other places. He would not have joined the company or invested in it but for the statement that the Government had sanctioned the agreement.

The Committee adjourned until Friday at two o'clock, when counsel will be heard.—*Daily Chronicle*, June 20.

The Select Committee of the House of Commons appointed to inquire into the circumstances attending the formation of the East India (Hyderabad) Deccan Mining Company, and into subsequent operations on the Stock Exchange, met again yesterday. General Strachey said the Secretary of State was in the place of a friendly adviser to the agent of the Nizam's Government, who had been authorised to enter into a mining concession. The Secretary of State was deceived by the responsible agent of the Nizam's Government. If he had had the smallest suspicion that Abdul Huk was making an arrangement of the sort he did make, the whole thing would have been set aside.

Lord Lawrence, called by Mr. Pember, said he was a director of the Deccan Company. He became a director about the end of July last at the request of the Board. His brother and himself bought about 1,000 shares at 12¼ in the open market, on the strength of the Nizam being a shareholder. He met Abdul Huk in society—at the Queen's jubilee garden party among other places. He had heard that several of his friends had bought shares since he joined the Board. He was the representative of the Nizam on the Board. Practically, he had not decided what to do in the matter, but he would do all possible to protect the interests of the shareholders. He would not have joined the Company or invested in it but for the statement that the Government had sanctioned the agreement. The Committee again adjourned.—*Standard*, June 20.

The Hyderabad Inquiry.—The Solicitor-General for Scotland first, and subsequently Sir Henry James, presided yesterday over a meeting of the Select Committee of the House of Commons appointed to inquire into the circumstances attending the formation of and subsequent operations connected with the East India (Hyderabad) Deccan Mining Company.

General Strachey was recalled, and examined at length by Mr. Labouchere as to the part taken by the India Office in the negotiations which led to the granting of the mining concession. As far as he could recollect, he said, the heads of an agreement were laid before them, which they thought were unsatisfactory, and the Secretary of State advised Abdul Huk to go to a respectable solicitor and see that he was doing nothing beyond that which he was authorised to do. At the same time it was also suggested that, as mining business was of a peculiar and technical description, it would be advisable to consult a solicitor who was conversant with that sort of business.

Mr. Labouchere: As I understand it, Abdul Huk was told by the India Office that he was not to sign under the powers of the Nizam, but that negotiations were to be continued in Hyderabad?—General Strachey: That was in 1883.

So that the India Office accepted the responsibility of desiring Abdul Huk not to act on the instructions of the Nizam's Government, but to take the question back for further discussion to Hyderabad?—As I understand it we accepted no responsibility. The Secretary of State took no initiative at all; he acted merely as a friendly adviser to the Nizam's Government.

Then might Abdul have signed without a protest from the Secretary of State?—The concession did not come before the Secretary of State at all; only the draft came before him.

Wasn't Lord Dufferin told to send home the concession as agreed upon—the final concession—to the Home Government?—I have no recollection of anything of the sort.

Mr. Labouchere, having drawn General Strachey's attention to certain correspondence of February, 1886, said: Lord Dufferin asks in a letter here for the sanction to the agreement, to be sent by telegram. Was that sanction given?—I cannot say off-hand. My impression is that there was a telegram sent eventually.

Giving sanction?—Yes, after certain modifications had been agreed to.

And yet you say the Secretary of State was not responsible for this concession?—I don't understand you.

Was he responsible or not?—He was responsible in a certain sense.

What sense?—Merely in this: in the sense that he was acting in a friendly way for the Nizam's Government. And let me say that the position in which the Secretary of State was, was apparent on the face of it. He was deceived by the Nizam's Government—that is to say, the agent of the Nizam's Government. On the face of the agreement between the Nizam's Government and Mr. Winter, it was stated specifically that Abdul Huk was authorised by the Nizam's Government to enter into a mining concession. The Secretary of State had a perfect right to assume that Abdul Huk was authorised to do what he did. It would be altogether unreasonable to expect the Secretary of State to defend the Nizam's Government against its own acts and the acts of its accredited representative. Of course if the Secretary of State had had the smallest suspicion that Abdul Huk was making an arrangement with a view to his own personal profit, the subsequent questions would not have arisen.

Had the Nizam's Government the right to make any financial contract with a British subject without the consent of the Governor-General of India sitting in Council or the Secretary of State?—That is a moot question, and I am not the person to decide it.

But is there not a statute governing the point?—The question of the proper construction of 37 George III., chap. 147, sec. 28, is a difficult one. No good can be served by asking me my personal opinion about it. Although I have said nothing about the particular way in which this concession was dealt with at the India Office, you must not suppose it merely came before me and that I looked at it. It was looked at in the regular way in the office. We took what advice we thought advisable from the legal officers.

Is there any special treaty with the Nizam's Government with regard to this?—I don't know at all.

Then you are not prepared to say whether the right to enter into an agreement without the consent of the Secretary of State for India exists or not?—Personally I am not. It was perfectly true the intention of the

Government of India was that £150,000 should be paid up and immediately applied to the working of the mine, and that the difference between that sum and the million should in future be available in extending the operations of the company. There never had been any doubt about that. The real question was whether it would have been possible to frame a contract which would have prevented what had since been done. I looked upon Abdul Huk so far as this affair was concerned, as the Nizam's Government. From that point of view the Nizam's Government made an agreement for the difference between the £150,000 and a million to work to their own personal advantage. If the Nizam's officers had been honest what has occurred would never have occurred, and they could perfectly well have controlled the remuneration ultimately to be paid to the concessionnaires.

Do you hold that the concession was worth the price of £850,000 put upon it?—You must be more explicit.

Was what the Nizam was giving away worth £850,000 to anyone?—In the ordinary expression of things it was worth what it would fetch. Watson sold it after.

Do you consider it worth £850,000?—All I can say is I should be sorry to give that for it.

Do you consider it was worth anything?—I am not prepared to say it was.

Wasn't the Nizam's Government plundered of anything Watson could sell the concession for?—There you get into deep water. That is really what I cannot say. The Nizam's Government gave Abdul Huk plenary power to do what he liked.

Then you throw all responsibility on the Nizam's Government?—Yes.

With all this correspondence and the agreement being sent home?—Certainly. Abdul Huk was authorised to make the agreement.

But the Government interfered in the agreement?—Not at all. We interfered so far as we thought, on the face of it, the interests of the Nizam's Government required it.

Did the interests of the Nizam's Government require that he should give a contract that was worth £850,000, more or less, for nothing?—It was not worth £850,000.

More or less, I say?—There was an idea that the Nizam's Government would get the benefit of the development of gold on other mines.

Did you advise the Nizam's Government that the concession ought to be carried out?—No; what we did say was that we had no objection. We authorised his going on.

You think this concession would have been carried out if the Secretary of State had written that he entirely disapproved of it?—It is possible.

But not probable?—I should say not. All ultimate arrangements were left to be settled between the concessionnaires and the Nizam's Government. After the negotiations the India Office wrote to Abdul Huk complimenting him upon the way he had carried them out, but when they learned that Abdul Huk had received a commission, notwithstanding he had told the India Office he was in no way personally interested, it was not, as the whole thing was done and Sir Salar Jung was dead, thought expedient to take any notice about it. Mr. Hughes, who was a servant of the Government of India, was asked to survey the concessions.

Then would Mr. Hughes be allowed to receive a bribe from Watson? Should you call it a bribe if Mr. Hughes received a large number of shares?—I should call it an objectionable transaction.

Should you be surprised if you heard that that objectionable transaction had taken place?—I should be surprised at nothing.

Are you aware that your brother's name appears on the prospectus of the railway company, of which he was chairman, before any of the shares were subscribed?—I suppose it was so.

Was it there through the influence of Watson ?—I cannot tell you.

Isn't Mr. Batten chairman of the mining company ?—Yes.

Isn't he your brother's brother-in-law ?—Yes.

Mr. Labouchere : I have nothing more to ask you.

General Strachey : As you put it that way I should explain that before Sir John Strachey became chairman of the railway company it was felt that a responsible gentleman should be secured for the position, and Sir Bartle Frere was asked to assume it. When he left the Resident at Hyderabad took the position.

By Mr. Slagg : To throw upon the India Office the responsibility of seeing that nothing wrong is done in any native State would be to throw a tremendous burden upon them, and more than we could undertake.

Replying to a question by Mr. Littler, the witness said he had every reason to think that the Singarene coalfields were of great value.

Mr. Watson (re-called), examined by Sir H. James, said Hemmerdy, one of the directors, was a friend of his, and he gave him 1,000 shares. He gave the shares to him because he was an old friend of his, and in return for the many services he had rendered him for twenty years previously. That gift of shares, that might have become worth £10,000, had nothing whatever to do with Hemmerdy's work as a director. He sold Mr. T. W. H. Hughes, an official of the Indian Government and the superintendent of the geological reports to the company, 200 £5 shares and 200 fully-paid up shares for £1,000. At the market price then the 200 fully-paid shares would have been worth £2,200. He sold these shares for £1,000 in order to give Hughes an interest in the company. Subsequently he bought back the shares, and gave £2,300 for them. Mr. Furnivall got 500 shares.

The Chairman: So Hemmerdy, a director who voted these shares to you, had £11,000 ; Hughes, who reported on the mines, made £1,390 and also 200 £5 shares ; and Furnivall made £5,500 ?—Yes.

Mr. Theodore Hooper, member of the Council of the Government of India, stated that if it had been contemplated that the wording of the concession would have permitted £850,000 to go to the concessionnaires they would have advised the Nizam's Government to seek legal advice.

Mr. Littler, on behalf of Mr. Watson, called Mr. Morris, stockbroker, who stated that he knew from the first that the 85,000 shares dealt in did not represent cash. He did not find traces of Mr. Watson making a market.

Mr. W. H. Bishop stated that he bought £19,000 worth of shares. He regarded the sale of shares as *bona fide*. The words in the prospectus, "fully-paid," relating to the 85,000 shares, conveyed to his mind that the company did not receive money for them.

Lord Lawrence spoke of purchases of shares made by himself and friends. He was influenced in the purchases he made by the fact that the agreement for concession had passed through the India Office.

After formal evidence as to documents and the interpretation of the phrase "fair rent," as applied to leases, the Committee adjourned until Friday at two, when counsel will be heard.—*Daily News*, June 20.

THE DECCAN MINES INQUIRY.—The Select Committee of the House of Commons resumed the inquiry into the circumstances attending the formation of the East India (Hyderabad) Deccan Mining Company, Sir Henry James presiding.

General Strachey, of the India Office, who was again examined by Mr. Labouchere, said he understood that Abdul Huk came with instructions from his Government to enter into negotiations about the concession. The Secretary of State was satisfied that he was acting as the agent of the Nizam's Government, and acted with regard to him in the quality of a friendly adviser, recommending Abdul Huk to go to a respectable firm of solicitors, who were, moreover, conversant with the matters which he was sent to negotiate. The India Office accepted no responsibility at all, nor had the Secretary of State for India taken any initiative in these measures. Before Abdul Huk returned to Hyderabad the Secretary of State dropped the subject, and informed the Government of India that he had nothing further to do with the matter. The position of the Secretary of State was that he had been deceived by the responsible agent of the Nizam's Government, and it was not to be assumed that the Secretary of State should have defended the Nizam's Government against the action of their own accredited agent.

Of course, had the Secretary of State entertained the smallest suspicion that Abdul Huk was making an arrangement such as he had made he would have put the whole thing aside. It was a moot question, on which he could not give a decisive opinion, whether the Nizam's Government had power to make a financial contract with a British subject without either the consent of the Governor-General of India in Council or the Secretary of State under 37 George III., cap. 147, sec. 28. He was not aware of any special treaty with the Nizam's Government. The real question was whether under the circumstances it would have been possible to have framed a contract which would have prevented Abdul Huk from doing that which was done. Abdul Huk was the avowed agent of the Nizam's Government, and therefore, so far as the contract was concerned, the India Office was entitled to look at it from that point of view. They had no knowledge of Abdul Huk's intentions. Now they did know them, of course, it was quite easy to see what might have been done. Ultimately all arrangements were left between the concessionnaires and the Nizam's Government. He should think the giving of shares to Mr. Hughes in return for his services an objectionable transaction.

Would you be surprised to learn that such a transaction has taken place? —I should not be surprised at anything.

Witness (continuing): Sir John Strachey, his brother, was brother-in-law to Mr. Batten, but he should explain that before Sir John Strachey became chairman of the railway company it was felt that a gentleman of responsibility should be asked to assume the office, and with that view Sir Bartle Frere was asked to take it.

By Mr. Slagg: As Hyderabad was an independent State, our relations with it were regulated by treaty, though no doubt our Government greatly influenced that of the Nizam, an influence which, however, did not extend to the giving of orders. In reference to the concession, if the India Office had the same thing to do over again, they would act in exactly a similar manner, not knowing they had been deceived. It was a question of deception, and it would be to throw a burden greater than they could bear to ask the India Office to undertake the responsibility of seeing that nothing wrong was done in any of the native States. They had, on the other hand, to be careful that they did nothing which would prevent the flow into the native States of capital required for their development.

By Mr. Littler: He believed that the Singarene coal-fields were very valuable.

Mr. Watson was then recalled and examined by the Chairman as to certain Deccan share transactions. Witness stated that Mr. Hemmerdy was one of the five directors of the company, and to him he had given 1,000 £10 shares, which at the then price were worth £11,000. He gave Hemmerdy these shares for the services which he had rendered him during the previous 20 years. Hemmerdy ceased to be a director for the reason that he became ill. To Mr. Hughes, the geological surveyor, he gave 200 £5 paid shares and 200 fully paid shares. For the latter 200 Hughes paid £1,000 and subsequently those shares were rebought by the company for £2,390. This was not a gift to Hughes for his reports, but to give him an interest in the company. Besides, it was felt that some of the profits should go to a man who was working hard in the jungle. To Mr. Furnivall he had given 500 shares, which were worth £5,500. So that Hemmerdy got £11,000, Hughes £1,390 and 200 £5 paid shares, and Furnivall £5,500.

Mr. Theodore Hooper, a member of the Council of the Government of India for Public Works Purposes, in the course of his testimony, said had it been thought that the concession would have allowed £850,000 to go to the concessionnaires, the Government of India would have recommended the Nizam's Government to take legal advice on the point.

The room was cleared that the Committee might deliberate with regard to the course counsel could be permitted to take. On re-admission,

Mr. Littler, Q.C., on behalf of Mr. Watson, sought to adduce the evidence of an expert to give his opinion of the value of the mines from the reports before the Committee.

The Chairman: Has the expert been to Hyderabad?

Mr. Littler: No, sir.

The Committee declined to admit the evidence, stating, through the Chairman, that they would form their own opinion from the reports.

Mr. Morris, a stock-dealer, and acquainted with the Stock Exchange for 50 years, said he had dealt with brokers in nearly the whole of the 85,000 shares belonging to the concessionnaires, which he knew did not in any way represent cash. That did not surprise them at all. There was a continuous rise in the shares. He saw no sign of Watson pressing sales or making the market.

Mr. W. H. Bishop, stock-broker, spoke to buying £19,000 worth of stock on behalf of client, at £9, receiving 2s. per share from Mr. Watson. He held a part of the £19,000 worth of shares himself.

Lord Lawrence, the last witness, said he had bought shares because of the Nizam being a shareholder, and hearing that he had bought shares at about the same price as himself. 12¼. He thought he could not be very far wrong, especially when he further considered that every detail of the whole thing had been before the Government of India, and had passed through the India Office. With Abdul Huk, he represented the Nizam on the Board. He was among the last of the shareholders.

The Chairman stated that on Tuesday next, at 2 o'clock, another witness called by the Committee will be examined and counsel will be permitted to make short and concise statements showing what facts they consider to be material on the case. He pointed out, in reply to Sir H. Davey, that though Abdul Huk's conduct might have been incidentally touched upon in the course of the inquiry, it could hardly be considered that the Committee were trying his case.

The Committee adjourned.—*Times*, June 20.

The Nizam's Guaranteed State Railways.—The sixth ordinary general meeting of the shareholders in His Highness the Nizam's Guaranteed State Railways Company (Limited) was held yesterday at Winchester-house. Lieutenant-General Sir R. J. Meade presided, and in moving the adoption of the report stated that the difficulties experienced in completing the section from Warangal to Dornakul, and the mineral branch thence on to the coalfields, had prevented the opening of those lines for public traffic until after the close of the half-year, but they were formally opened on the 1st January last. Since then a regular service had been maintained on those portions of the line. The progress of the Dornakul frontier section, and also of the British (Bezwada) section, had been seriously retarded by outbreaks of sickness, including cholera, among the labourers employed on the works; but a recent telegram from their chief agent and engineer, Mr. Furnivall, reported that the cholera having ceased all was now progressing favourably on both sections, and he hoped to open thirty-two miles from Dornakul towards the frontier about the 20th prox., leaving only twenty-two and a half miles of that section still unfinished. They hoped that the large bridge across the Wyra River and the other remaining works would be finished so as to admit of the opening of the whole line throughout to Bezwada by or before the close of the present year.

The gross earnings for the half-year had been 746,783 rupees, and the working expenses had been 69·95 per cent. There had been a reduction of 34,344 rupees in the gross earnings as compared with those for the corresponding period of 1886. The board had hoped that the commencement of the coal traffic would have had an important influence on the receipts for the half-year, but that had not been the case. The output of coal had been as yet not even sufficient for the requirements of their own line. That had no doubt been chiefly, if not altogether, due to the delay in the arrival of the machinery and plant required for the working of the mine. Cholera also broke out at the coal-field. A recent message from their agent informed them that the deliveries of coal had now increased to 60 tons daily. Having explained the causes which had led to the heavy working expenses in the half-year, he assured them that the board and their agent were fully alive to the importance of economy. The traffic receipts up to the 19th ult. gave promise of the gross earnings reaching nearly 8¾ lakhs of rupees for the current half-year, or nearly one lakh more than the estimate of their agent. From Wadi up to the frontier was 310 miles, and they would, they hoped, have completed that part of their system at a cost of £9,500 per mile, including the sum they paid the Nizam's Government for the old line.

The line which they had themselves constructed under their own management was admitted to be the cheapest in India, and all the reports they had received as to its condition were very favourable. He could not refrain from referring to the course which had been taken by the Nizam's Government as to the Hyderabad Deccan Company, but he trusted that the shareholders would thoroughly understand that they had nothing to do with that company, except in so far as they were interested in the efficient working of the coal mines, in view of the speedy commencement of the coal traffic, to which they had been looking forward, and for which they were still waiting. As, however, some anxiety might be felt by the proprietors on the matter, he thought he might inform them that on the suspension of the Sirdar Diler-ul-Mulk, the Prime Minister of Hyderabad assured the directors, through Mr. Furnivall, of his cordial support being given to the railways, and that the Sirdar's suspension and removal from office would in no way affect the interests of the company.

Similar assurances had been repeated by the present official director, the Nawab Fathah Nawaz Jung Bahadur, whose appointment had been in every way gratifying to the directors; and also by the Prime Minister, from whom he (the Chairman) had received a letter dated the 16th ult., his Excellency adding that he would continue to protect the interest of the company most carefully. He concluded by acknowledging the services of Mr. Furnivall and his staff.

The Nawab Fathah Nawaz Jung Bahadur seconded the motion.

Mr. Austin said he doubted the propriety of the payment which had been made to Mr. Watson, and he felt sure that the shares would not have been subscribed for had it been stated in the prospectus that Mr. Watson was to receive £100,000 for floating the company.

The Chairman, in reply, stated that the fact of the payment in question having been made had appeared in the accounts from the first. It had been approved by the shareholders, and the payment had been made with the sanction and approval of the Secretary of State. It was a payment regarding which the directors of the company had no concern, and the subject, moreover, had nothing to do with the business before the meeting.

In answer to Mr. Martin Wood, the Chairman added that they were tied down by their contract to adopt the same rates as were in force on the Great Indian Peninsula Railway. The sinking fund was being properly looked after, 1 per cent. being handed over every half-year to the trustees to invest. The Nawab Mohsin-ul-Mulk Bahadur, the representative of the Nizam's Government in England, afterwards addressed the meeting, and assured them that his Highness's Government would continue to afford every support to the company, in which they were by far the largest shareholders. The suspension of the Sirdar was a matter of no concern to the railway company, nor was his suspension in any way connected with his duties as the State Railway official. The report was then adopted, and the payment of interest for the half-year ending the 30th inst., at the rate of 5 per cent. per annum on the capital stock of the company, was agreed to. On the motion for re-electing the retiring directors, exception was taken to the re-appointment of Mr. Winter. The chairman stated that Mr. Winter was originally proposed by the Nizam's Government, and he had rendered the company valuable assistance. Mr. Winter said that a garbled statement had been made to the meeting. The only position he had occupied in regard to the Deccan mining business was that of solicitor for the concessionnaires. He "worked the business" for them and was paid by results. Nothing had been alleged against him by the Nizam's Government, the Deccan Company, or by the railway company. Should any stigma be attached to him as the result of the Parliamentary inquiry he would place himself in the hands of the directors. The chairman put the motion, and declared it carried by nine to seven. The auditors were afterwards re-elected. —*Times*, June 20.

Yesterday General Strachey, examined at length by Mr. Labouchere as to the responsibility of the Indian Government for the mining concession, contended that the responsibility was limited to advising the Nizam on information before them, and as the Nizam's Government represented by Huk did not act honestly in stating their intentions, the Indian Government could not do otherwise than it did. The witness's brother, Sir John Strachey, was chairman of the Nizam Railway Company. Batten, chairman of the Mining Company, was brother-in-law to Sir John Watson. Recalled, answering the Chairman, he said he gave Hemmerdy, an old friend, one of the first directors, who voted for the agreement giving the concessionnaires 85,000 shares, a thousand shares worth £10,000, but not as a reward for voting. He also sold to Hughes, who reported on the prospects of the company, £3,300 worth of shares for £1,000. He gave Furnivall, another engineer who reported, 500 shares, value £5,000, for nothing. These were not bribes to get favourable reports.—*Sheffield Daily Telegraph*, June 20.

Abdul Huk's Speculation.—The Calcutta correspondent of the *Times* states that the Nizam's Government has called on Abdul Huk to give full explanation as to certain large sums of money received by him while floating the Hyderabad State Railway in London in 1883. It would seem from the light now thrown on Hyderabad affairs in general that there is ample justification for this measure. When the State Railway was sold to an English company by Abdul Huk, at the end of the year 1883, for a sum of £1,666,666 (the promoters being Messrs. Watson and Stewart, who subsequently became the concessionnaires of the Mining Company), one of the inducements held out to the Nizam's Government to sanction the project was the large amount of ready money that the sale of the railway would bring in to the Treasury. For among the obligations devolving on the company was one to pay down, out of the purchase-money of £1,666,666, the sum of £341,666 in cash within six months from the date of first general allotment of shares.

But when the time came for the company to pay this sum the Hyderabad State got no such amount in cash nor anything like it; and it was cash that the State wanted. What it got was debentures of the company—which, not having been issued, had no marketable value—and a sum nominally of £100,000. But as Abdul Huk, the Nizam's "Home Secretary," took from this sum within a month after the railway had been sold, the sum of £83,666, it was not the State but its servant that got cash down. After other payments had been made out of the £100,000, the balance left to the State amounted to £7,636; rather more than one-twelfth of the modest little fee which the Home Secretary had promptly credited himself with. He had taken this sum on the strength of a promise which he said had been made to him by the Regent, the late Salar Jung. Now that a new Resident has gone to Hyderabad, and the Government of the Nizam has been for the first time allowed some freedom to deal with a shady official, it will probably endeavour to find out how a promise of the late Salar Jung, with reference to a railway project under consideration at the time of his death (or more probably to a previous one, which had been rejected under the advice of the Government of India), can be considered valid in reference to another project not entered upon at the time of his demise, and not accepted till some months after.—*St. James's Gazette*, June 20.

Deccan Mining Inquiry.—The Parliamentary inquiry into the circumstances attending the formation and subsequent operations of the East India Hyderabad Deccan Mining Company (Limited) was resumed on Tuesday in one of the committee rooms of the House of Commons. Sir Henry James presided, and the other members of the committee were the Solicitor-General for Scotland, Mr. Labouchere, Sir R. Temple, Mr. McLagan, Mr. Bristowe, and Mr. Slagg. The various parties concerned were again represented by counsel.

General Strachey, recalled and examined as to the action of the India Office in regard to the concession, stated generally that if they had the duty to perform over again they would act in exactly a similar way, not knowing that they had been deceived. The whole question turned upon the deception which had been practised. Abdul Huk had been treated by the Secretary of State as the accredited agent of the Nizam's Government, and the Secretary of State had assumed towards him the position of a friendly adviser. When Abdul Huk returned to Hyderabad the Secretary of State informed the Government of India that he had nothing more to do with the matter.

Mr. Watson, who was also recalled, was questioned by the chairman as to certain share transactions. He stated that to Mr. Hemmerdy, one of the five directors of the company, he had given 10,000 shares, which at the then price were worth £11,000. This gift was for services rendered during the previous twenty years. To Mr. Hughes, the geological surveyor, he gave 200 shares, £5 paid, and sold 200 fully-paid shares for £1,000. Subsequently these were rebought by the company for £2,390. These gifts were not for Mr. Hughes's reports, but in order to give him an interest in the company so that he might throw his whole energies into it, besides which he thought a man should enjoy some profit for working hard in the jungle. To Mr. Furnivall he gave 500 shares, which were worth £5,500.

Sir Theodore Hope, a member of the Council of India for Public Works Purposes, said that had it been contemplated that the concession would have permitted £850,000 to be given to concessionnaires the transactions would have been set aside.

Mr. Morris, stockdealer, and Mr. Bishop, stockbroker, were called by Mr. Littler and examined on behalf of Mr. Watson, after which Mr. Morgans, a mining engineer, gave evidence for the company on the question of "fair rent."

The committee adjourned until Friday next.—*Telegraph*, June 21.

THE Select Committee of the House of Commons appointed to inquire into the circumstances attending the formation of the Hyderabad-Deccan Company will conclude its labours to-day. From the facts so far made public, and which led to the appointment of the committee, it seemed that a very huge financial job had been perpetrated. However, the committee has not succeeded in elucidating anything very unusual or startling so far. The chief facts brought to light are that the Nizam of Hyderabad gave a certain Mr. Watson, in return for services rendered in connection with the Hyderabad Railway, certain concessions of mining territory which have been proved to be rich in coal, and in which diamond mines were worked some two hundred years ago. This concession was a pure gift to Mr. Watson, who, like a shrewd business man, at once came to London and formed a company, of which five of his personal friends were made directors, with a capital of a million sterling.

These five friends of Watson's voted £850,000 to him and a person named Stewart, associated in the concession. These shares were fully-paid up, and in course of time the concessionnaires unloaded the shares upon the public. The point of the inquiry was as to whether the concession was worth this sum, and the committee has not done much to prove anything one way or the other as to this. Mr. Watson naturally declares that he was entitled to get as much for the concession as he possibly could, and affirms that it is well worth the money paid for it. The real question is as to whether the public have been protected by any precautions being taken to ascertain the value of the concession, or as to whether it is really worth the amount paid for it. Sir Henry James, the chairman, has ruled that counsel can only interfere to elucidate new facts, but will not allow argument. The question raised is one of vast importance in connection with such companies.—*Evening Telegraph*, June 22.

THE DECCAN SCANDAL.—To the Editor of the *Financial News*.—Sir,—As the appearance during the inquiry into the above of names the same as my own has been the source of much personal annoyance to me, permit me through your columns (where the evidence has been fully reported) to say that I am not, and never have been, in any way whatever, directly or indirectly, connected with or interested in the above, and have, indeed, no knowledge on the subject.

Pardon my thus intruding on your space, and believe me to remain, Sir, yours, etc., JOSEPH HURST, Lamb Building, Temple, E.C., June 21, 1888.—*Financial News*, June 22.

THE evidence given by General Strachey before the Deccan Mines Committee is not calculated to impress ordinary minds favourably. He says that the India Office accepted no responsibility, and the Government of India did nothing in the matter to which exception could be taken. Some people, at least, thought that the Government of India sanctioned the concession, and thus practically sponsored Abdul Huk. It was owing to the supposed semi-official sponsorship on the part of the Indian Government that the public were induced to subscribe.

The Government of India, it was assumed, ought to have made inquiries, both in the interests of the Nizam and the investing public. This cool disavowal of all responsibility reveals the real state of things. People at home have, perhaps rashly, expected too much from the Indian Government. It is not the business of Indian officialism to protect the interests of Indian potentates, nor has it either the time or the inclination to trouble itself with the delusions of investors who should pay more heed to the principle of *caveat emptor*. It is not the business, apparently, of the Indian Government to pry into the doings of financiers, even when native States are concerned.—*Home and Colonial Mail*, June 22.

The Deccan Inquiry.—The India Office and the Government of India, as represented by General Strachey, have peculiar notions about responsibility. The General was examined on Tuesday by the Select Committee which is inquiring into the Deccan business, and he started by saying in very emphatic language that the Government of India accepted no responsibility at all. According to General Strachey, " the Secretary of State was in the position of a friendly adviser to the agent of the Nizam's Government in the matter of this mining concession. He had nothing further to do with it." Let us see how that is borne out by the facts.

In the first place it may be pointed out that though General Strachey professes to be in doubt as to its interpretation, a statute of George III. forbids, without the consent of the British Government, any person entering into a financial transaction with the native princes. There are high reasons of State, which will be obvious to everyone, which make it very necessary that this statute should be observed. And, as a matter of fact, the concession was in due course put before the India Office. "Of course," says General Strachey, " if the Secretary of State had had the smallest suspicion that Abdul Huk was making an arrangement with a view of his own personal profit, the agreement would have been set aside." But the India Office had no such suspicion, and therefore, according to General Strachey, it incurred no responsibility.

That is a curious theory. The India Office ought to have had suspicion, and much more than suspicion. It was its duty to get at the facts, and it could have done so had it tried. Abdul Huk was already a suspect, or ought to have been. General Strachey admits that they were aware of the £83,000 this person had received on account of the railway, and considered the acceptance of it "entirely objectionable." It was owing to this transaction that the Secretary of State ordered that in future concessions should be submitted to him. But when Abdul Huk next appeared upon the scene, under circumstances that invited suspicion, he was received with childlike confidence, and far from pulling him up General Strachey and his colleagues furthered his plans in every possible way!

The Nizam's Government was ordered to negotiate, through the British Resident, Mr. Cordery; the agreement was sent home and submitted to the Indian Council and its legal advisers, and yet there was never a suspicion as to Mr. Watson's right to sell his concession for £850,000! And as the India Office is blameless, so, if we are to accept General Strachey's view of the matter, the Government of India are in no way to blame. "The only thing the Government of India could do," says the General, "was to look at the surface of the thing." If it could not do more than that it would have been much better if it had done nothing at all.

The intention of the Government of India was that £150,000 should be paid up and immediately applied to the working of the mines, and that the difference between this £150,000 and the £1,000,000 should in the future be available, as required, for extending the operations of the company. As a matter of fact, the terms of the concession made it possible for Mr. Watson to put £850,000 of the £1,000,000 into his own pocket. And we are asked to believe that the Government of India, and the India Office, could not be expected to know anything about this arrangement!

We have said that it would be much better that the Government of India and the India Office should have nothing to do with the financial dealings of British subjects with native princes, with mining concessions, and the like, unless it institutes a real examination into proposed arrangements. There can be no question that many of the public who put their money into this Deccan Mining Company did so because the Secretary of State for India had approved the contract, and it was understood that the Government of India had examined and sanctioned it. If this opinion had not been general the shares would never have got up to £12. How entirely misleading it was is shown very conclusively by General Strachey's admissions.—*Stock Exchange*, June 23.

THE Hyderabad Deccan inquiry goes slowly on its way, and the methods by which the public are imposed upon are gradually being unravelled. It is some comfort to know that when the new Companies' Act comes into force in September next, it will not be so easy for unscrupulous promoters to make such enormous hauls at the expense of confiding investors. I observe that one weekly organ still thinks Deccans are a good investment. The point which I have endeavoured to make clear since the exposure first took place is that granting it is impossible to cancel the concession, the working capital of the company has never, and can never be, more than £150,000.

The capital on which dividends have to be paid is £1,000,000. So far, nothing has resulted from the Golconda diamond mines, which have not even been opened up, and no sort of returns have been obtained from the Singareni coalfields. How much of this £150,000 remains now? If the properties are so vast as is stated, will the unspent portion of the £150,000 be sufficient to develop them up to the point of paying dividends on the £1,000,000 of capital? These are the questions for shareholders to consider. Pending the decision of the Royal Commission it would not be right to comment on the evidence given by the simple-minded Mr. Watson, or his friend Mr. Richard Evans. Later on I shall have perhaps a few remarks to make on it.—*Topical Times*, June 23.

THE HYDERABAD DECCAN INQUIRY.—The holders of Deccan shares will feel so far relieved by the announcement that the Nizam's Government will under no circumstances adopt any course which would have the effect of infringing the just rights of those shareholders who have advanced their money to the company *bona fide* in reliance upon the concession granted. It remains, however, to be seen whether they have got value for their money, for it is also the opinion of the Nizam's Government that the amount paid to the concessionnaires was unfair and unreasonable, "so unreasonable as to amount to a fraud upon the concession." Will the concessionnaires follow the example of Abdul Huk and make restitution?—*Pall Mall Gazette*, June 23.

THE Hyderabad Deccan Committee met again yesterday. Sir E. Bradford, secretary in the Solicitor's Department of the India Office, gave evidence to the effect that no special treaty existed with the Nizam which prohibited British subjects from making financial contracts with the Nizam. Mr. Mayne addressed the committee on behalf of the Nizam's Government. Mr. Littler followed on behalf of Mr. Watson, and maintained that Mr. Watson and those associated with him had acted with *bona fides* throughout.—*Morning Advertiser*, June 23.

ABDUL HUK AND SIR SALAR JUNG.—THE GREAT MINISTER'S SON DOUBTS THE EXISTENCE OF THE ALLEGED LETTER.—(From our own Correspondent.)—Allahabad. June 22, 1888.—Sir Salar Jung has addressed the following letter to the Indian papers to-day: "I find from a telegraphic report of the evidence given by Nawab Mohsin-ul-Muhl, before the Parliamentary Committee of Inquiry into the Hyderabad-Deccan Mining Company, that the Nawab observed that he did not believe Sir Salar Jung, junior, or the present Prime Minister had any knowledge of the late Sir Salar Jung's letter authorising Abdul Huk to receive remuneration.

"I am ready, so far as I can, to confirm the evidence which the Nawab gave on this important point. The letter in which Diler Jung alleges that my father expressed his willingness that the Sirdar should receive any remuneration for his services that the promoters might think he was entitled to was never shown to me, and I can hardly think that if it had been in existence at that time the Sirdar would have omitted bringing it under my notice or the notice of his Highness for confirmation.

"How greatly his claim would have been strengthened if the letter which he alleges had been sent him by my father had been confirmed is too obvious to need pointing out."—*Financial News*, June 23.

THE DECCAN MINING SCANDAL.—The Select Committee of the House of Commons appointed to consider the circumstances attending the formation of the Hyderabad (Deccan) Mining Company resumed their investigations yesterday afternoon, for the purpose of concluding the evidence and hearing counsel.

Colonel Sir Edward Bradford, Secretary to the Political Department of the India Office, was examined, and said there was a statute, but no special treaty, prohibiting British subjects from entering into financial relations with the Government of the Nizam without the sanction of the Government of India.

Mr. Mayne, on behalf of the Nizam's Government, then addressed the Committee, and stated that the Nizam, when he had the whole facts before him, would give them his most anxious consideration, with such advice as he might be able to obtain, and he would then adopt a course determined by honesty and good faith. He submitted that the conduct of the concessionnaires in diverting £850,000 of the entire nominal capital to their own pockets from the coffers of the company was a fraud upon the concession.

Sir H. Davey argued that Abdul Huk was not responsible for the drawing up of the concession.

Mr. Littler then proceeded at much length to address the committee on behalf of Mr. Watson.

The Chairman: You have got to show what Mr. Watson did to earn £850,000.

Mr. Littler: He has done this: To the Nizam these mines were absolutely worthless. He has floated the mines on the English market, which the Nizam could not have done for himself.

The Chairman: But Hyderabad did not get the money?

Mr. Littler: Hyderabad has got (if we are right in our valuation) an enormous income in royalties.

The Chairman: Let the thing stand as it is. All that it has got at present is £150,000 for working the mines.

Mr. Littler: If the mines are worthless Hyderabad has lost nothing; if the mines are good, Hyderabad has got an enormous consideration. What was given to us was that which was worthless to the Nizam until it was developed.

The Chairman: Was £150,000 sufficient to develop?

Mr. Littler: Certainly.

The Chairman: And when it did develop these mines were worth a million?

Mr. Littler: If our expenditure of £88,000 is successful in prospecting, then the concession is worth £850,000.

Mr. Labouchere: Can you state any Government in Europe that has given £8500,000 for floating a railway?

Mr. Littler: They have not given it, but in the case of the Manchester Ship

Canal they had to pay 5 per cent. for floating the company, and that is in England, where there is no risk whatever.

Mr. Pember, for certain shareholders in the company, said he wished to address the committee upon the possible effect of their report upon the concession—it might induce the Nizam to revoke the concession.

The Chairman: You heard the statement of Mr. Mayne that you would not be affected by any action the Nizam might take. We cannot enter into any legal question as to whether the concession was a good one.

Mr. Eardley Norton assured the Committee that the Nizam's Government had no intention of interfering with the title of the Company; the interests of *bona fide* shareholders would certainly be protected.

The Committee then adjourned, the Chairman intimating that at their next meeting they would consider their report.—*Daily Chronicle*, June 23.

The Hyderabad Inquiry.—The Select Committee of the House of Commons appointed to consider the circumstances attending the formation of the Hyderabad (Deccan) Mining Company resumed their investigations yesterday afternoon, for the purpose of concluding the evidence and hearing counsel.

General Sir Edward Bradford, Secretary to the Political Department of the Government of India, examined by Mr. Labouchere, said there was a statute, but no special treaty, prohibiting British subjects from entering into financial relations with the Government of the Nizam without the sanction of the Government of India.

In answer to Mr. Slagg, the witness said that the position of the Nizam towards the British Government did not differ so far as he knew from the position of the other native States. All of them were in a manner under the protection of the British Government.

Mr. Mayne then addressed the committee on behalf of the Nizam's Government He stated that under no circumstances whatever resulting from that inquiry could the Nizam consider himself justified in adopting any course which would have the effect of infringing the just rights of the shareholders, who had advanced their money honestly and *bona fide*, in reliance upon the genuineness of the concession.

Mr. Mayne went on to submit that Abdul Huk was not authorised to receive what he did from the concessionnaires, that he knew himself that he was not so authorised, and that Mr. Watson also never believed that he was so authorised, and that he therefore knew that he was corruptly bribing Abdul Huk. He maintained that the letters of Sir Salar Jung permitting Abdul Huk to receive remuneration related entirely to a railway scheme that fell through, and had no relation whatever to the mining concession; but he maintained that the most complete proof that both Abdul Huk and Mr. Watson knew they were acting corruptly was to be found in the secrecy and concealment with which the reward was paid. His next proposition was that it was the understanding of all parties to one side of the contract that the balance of the capital was to be reserved for the working of the company, and that the concessionnaires themselves accepted this meaning. Consequently the transfer of £350,000 to their own pockets was a fraud on the concession. It was intended that the concessionnaires should be handsomely rewarded of course, but not by the sale of the concession to other people. Even if they had a right to sell it, they had no right to appropriate such an extravagant and unreasonable amount.

Mr. Littler followed on behalf of Mr. Watson. He maintained that Mr. Watson and those with him had acted with *bona fides* throughout. They risked £150,000, and were entitled to make what they could out of the speculation. They were never informed what the view of the Government of India was as to the way in which the capital was to be dealt with.

The Chairman asked if counsel would show what Mr. Watson did to entitle him to £850,000.

Mr. Littler pointed out that at the time what was called £850,000 was only 85,000 bits of paper.

The Chairman: But your contention all along is that the property was worth £850,000, and in that case what Mr. Watson got was worth £850,000. What did he do to entitle him to that?

Mr. Littler: He risked £150,000, and if the mines are successful the Nizam's Government will receive enormous sums in royalties, and the company will reap large dividends.—*Daily News*, June 23.

The Hyderabad Mines Inquiry.—The Select Committee of the House of Commons appointed to inquire into the circumstances attending the formation of the East India (Hyderabad) Deccan Mining Company met again yesterday, Sir Henry James presiding.

Colonel Sir E. Bradford, K.C.S.I., secretary to the political department of the India Office, examined by Mr. Labouchere, said there was a statute forbidding British subjects from entering into financial relations with the Government of the Nizam. There was no special treaty with that object. He thought the permission of the Government of India should have been obtained to the concession. He thought the Government of India or the Secretary of State responsible for any orders or advice given under the statute, undoubtedly. There was nothing in the statute about the sale of concessions. It referred to loans. There was a treaty of 1798, providing that no European should be employed in or remain in the Nizam's territory without the consent of the Indian Government.

Mr. Littler then put in a printed copy of the letter of Sir Salar Jung to Abdul Huk, witness stating that it had been received from India last Friday.

Mr. Pember put in a report of an analysis of the quality of the Singareni coal.

Mr. Mayne, Q.C., on behalf of the Nizam's Government, said that when the evidence had been laid before the Nizam's Government they would take the matter into their most anxious consideration. They would then adopt a course determined not merely by technical considerations of law, but of honesty and good faith. Under no circumstances would the Nizam consider that he was justified in adopting any course which would have the effect of infringing the just rights of those shareholders who had advanced their money to this company *bona fide*, in reliance upon the concession granted. He submitted that the diversion by the concessionnaires of £850,000 of the entire nominal capital of the company into their own pockets from the coffers of the company was a fraud upon the concession—a fraud carried out with the assistance of and in collusion with Abdul Huk, who was not authorised by the Nizam's Government to accept a bribe from the concessionnaires; neither did Abdul Huk himself believe that he had been authorised; nor did Mr. Watson and Mr. Stewart, in dealing with him, believe that he was authorised to accept a bribe. The evidence and correspondence bore out that view. When dealing with the shares, Abdul Huk was in the same room with Watson, and Abdul Huk, having the shares to dispose of, got Watson to write him a letter about the difficulty of selling them at the price demanded. All the circumstances clearly showed that Watson did not *bona fide* believe that in giving a large sum of money to Abdul Huk he was doing an act which was open, above-board, and authorised by the Nizam's Government. They further showed that the difference between the nominal capital and the subscribed capital was to be reserved honestly and *bona fide* for the purpose of meeting the future wants of the company. He admitted that the concession in respect of this point had an ambiguous meaning, but the document must be read in connection with all that took place between the parties. The amount paid to the concessionnaires was unfair and unreasonable, and so unreasonable as to amount to a fraud upon the concession.

Sir Horace Davey, Q.C., on behalf of Abdul Huk, contended that the argument that the letter from the late Sir Salar Jung, under which Abdul Huk was to receive remuneration from the concessionnaires, applied only to the proposal of the Bombay Syndicate would not bear a moment's investigation. The form which the concession finally took was a form in regard to which Abdul Huk was absolutely free from responsibility. The Committee would not expect him (Sir Horace Davey) to defend the conduct of Abdul Huk in secretly selling to his own Government the shares of which he himself was possessed. Neither from a moral nor a legal point of view was he there to defend it. Abdul Huk, acting on the wise advice of learned counsel in India, had returned this money with 5 per cent. interest to the Nizam's Government, which, indeed, had made a profit of £10,000 out of the transaction, through the differences of exchange, because the exchange had been made in stirling and not in rupees.

The Chairman: Some good comes out of evil.

Sir Horace Davey, continuing, reminded the committee that the original proposal made in November, 1882, by Watson and Stewart was that they should undertake to expend only £100,000; but when Abdul Huk came to London and was referred by the India Office to Messrs. White and Borrett, they proposed a company with a capital nominally of one million, a subscribed capital of half a million, and £100,000 paid up. It was Mr. Winter who induced Sir Salar Jung to reduce the subscribed capital to £250,000, and Abdul Huk had nothing to do with it. In fact, the evidence showed that his advice to his Government was to keep the subscribed capital at half a million. It was the ignorant and mischievous action of the Indian Government—which showed itself as ignorant as a body on questions affecting the law of companies—which was responsible for reducing the subscribed capital still further to £150,000. Undoubtedly the £150,000, in their belief, was to be a first call, but if they had had the slightest knowledge of the law on the subject they would have seen what was the real purport of the concession. For that reduction Abdul Huk was in no way responsible.

Mr. Littler, Q.C., representing Mr. Watson, argued that, in regard to the payment of a quarter share to Abdul Huk, Watson had every reason to suppose that the Nizam's Government knew of the arrangement, for the solicitor (Winter) was informed of it on his first visit to Hyderabad. He was told it was a State secret, and therefore he mentioned it only to those immediately concerned. Mr. Littler read extracts from the documents and evidence to prove that the royalties to be paid to the Nizam were to be fixed after the prospecting, and not after the mines had begun to be worked, as some of the Committee seemed to suppose, and contended that Watson had all along looked at the mining and the railway transactions as a whole. As to the railway company, Mr. Watson had succeeded where Messrs. Rothschild and Messrs. Morton, Rose, and Co. had failed. Moreover, if they were successful in their prospecting, as they expected to be, they would have conferred incalculable advantages upon the Nizam's Government, whose mineral wealth was valueless in the face of their want of capital or credit to obtain it. Counsel referred to the evidence of Mr. Bishop and Mr. Morris, to the market price of the shares, and to the fact that Watson himself still held largely as all proving that, in the judgment of experienced and careful City men, the speculation was likely to prove a good one; for it was essentially a speculation—as one witness put it, "a rich man's business and not a poor man's"—and if it turned out badly the concessionnaires would lose every penny of the £150,000 they had paid themselves. In any case the Nizam could lose nothing, and his State would in all probability be an enormous gainer. He repudiated the suggestion that Watson had obtained the concession by bribes.

The Chairman asked how it was that the reports of the engineers on the value of the property were not obtained before the £850,000 worth of shares were allotted to the concessionnaires.

Mr. Littler replied that it was necessary to fix some definite price for the concession before the company was floated. The £850,000 worth of shares would have been allotted, inasmuch as the subsequent reports showed that the property was worth that amount.

Mr. Pember, on behalf of the company, feared that the only thing that could possibly be done upon the report of the Committee would be that the concession should be tampered with in some way or another.

The Chairman pointed out that the Nizam's counsel had already undertaken that the *bonâ fide* shareholders should not be affected by the Nizam's action. The Committee could not go into the legal question whether the concession was good or not.

Mr. Pember then submitted that no essential fraud had been shown in obtaining the concession, and that, therefore, the title of the *bonâ fide* shareholders was good.

Mr. Norton repeated the assurance given by Mr. Mayne that the Nizam's Government had no intention whatever of interfering with the title of the *bonâ fide* shareholders.

The Committee adjourned at ten minutes to six o'clock.—*Times*, June 23.

The Hyderabad Deccan inquiry is drawing to a close, and but little result need be expected therefrom, except to show what jobbery has frequently to be resorted to before the public can be induced to subscribe to a new company. The opinion of the market is that the concession must stand good for what it is worth.

How many companies would come out the better for such an exhaustive inquiry as the Deccan Company has been subjected to? Is it likely that all the transactions of the many vendors of gold mining properties would bear the broad light of day? In how many cases have "presents" of shares been given to intimate friends who have taken some trouble over the promotion? We are careful not to use the term "bribe" for fear of shocking Messrs. Watson and Stewart.—*Citizen*, June 23.

The Hyderabad Committee held its last sitting for the taking of evidence to-day, and will meet next week to prepare its report. This, I understand, will strongly condemn certain of the practices which have been revealed, but will not seek to interfere with the concession granted by the Nizam.—*Birmingham Post*, June 23.

The Deccan Inquiry. — What Counsel Say on Behalf of their Respective Clients.—The Indictment of Abdul Huk and the Concessionnaires.—The Select Committee of the House of Commons appointed to inquire into the circumstances attending the formation of the East India (Hyderabad) Deccan Mining Company met again yesterday—Sir Henry James presiding. The members present were Mr. Labouchere, Mr. P. J. Robertson (Solicitor-General for Scotland), Mr. Slagg, Mr. Bristowe, Sir R. Temple, and Mr. M'Lagan. The proceedings were not commenced until two o'clock, and the Committee did not rise until ten minutes to six. In anticipation of hearing the speeches of the learned counsel appearing for the different parties concerned, there was a large attendance of city men, and not a few of the general public. There was no opportunity for forensic display, the chairman, in accordance with the stipulation he had made at the previous sitting, limiting the learned counsel to a concise statement of their view of the facts, and to showing how they had a material bearing as affecting their clients.

Sir Edward Bradford, Secretary of the Political Department of the India Office, was called by the committee and examined by Mr. Labouchere.

Is there any special treaty forbidding British subjects from entering into financial relations with the Government of the Nizam?—There is a statute.

No special treaty?—No.

Would the statute in a case such as this render the permission of Her Majesty's Government necessary?—There would be no direct necessity for that, but I think it certainly should have been asked.

And it should not have been carried into effect if permission were not given?—I think certainly not.

Mr. Slagg: Does not the treaty with Hyderabad endow the Government of India with greater powers in respect of internal affairs than exists with regard to other States?—I should say not than all other States.

Than most?—I think it does.

The Hyderabad Treaty places the Nizam especially under the protection of the Government of India, and the Government of India itself holds, or professes to hold, a sort of position of guardianship over the Nizam. Is that so in other States?—I am not aware of any.

In that respect the Government of India does act as a protector to the Nizam. It is the case, is it not, that no financial transactions of any importance can be arranged between the Nizam's Government and the concessionnaire or any person without the approval of the Government of India under the statute, and with regard to the general practice?—Certainly, with regard to the general practice.

Would you not argue from that state of facts that the Government of India is practically responsible for anything of this nature that is really done?—I think the Government of India or the Secretary of State are responsible for any order or advice they give under the statute.

Mr. M'Lagan: The Act to which you refer says nothing about concessions; it refers to loans. The question arises how far it affects this concession. The words of the Act are: "No British subject by himself or any other person shall directly or indirectly for his use and benefit, take, receive, hold charge of, or be concerned in any bond or loan or security . . . . granted by any such native princes." There is nothing said about concessions there?—No.

Therefore no offence is given to the Act; it does not refer to this case at all?—Not at all.

This is a very serious matter to the concessionnaires. The Act says: "That any British subject, etc., shall be punished as if incurring a misdemeanour," and anybody connected with a loan with any native State renders himself liable to a prosecution. We are speaking of this concession, and "if it is contrary to the intended meaning of this Act it shall be declared null and void for all purposes." Do you think the concessionnaire has acted contrary to this statute?—It is, in my opinion, a disputed point how far he would be liable.

Mr. Slagg: I think there is a treaty of 1798 which provides that no European shall be employed in or remain in the Nizam's territory without the consent of the Government of India?—Yes, that is so.

Sir R. Temple: Is it not a fact that the Nizam is prohibited from employing any European in his service without the consent of the Government of India? —I do not think there is any prohibition, but it has become the practice and usage.

Is not that specified?—No. The words read by the hon. member (Mr. Slagg) I know are in the treaty.

Mr. Littler (producing a document containing copies of letters from Sir Salar Jung to Abdul Huk): Is not that an official print of the Government of India?—Yes; that came from India last Friday.

Mr. Littler: Those are the letters to which Mr. Cordery referred as sent to him in a covering letter, and as having been communicated to the Government of India.

Mr. Pember put in a report by an eminent chemist of an analysis of the quality of the Singareni coal.

Mr. Mayne (addressing the committee on behalf of the Nizam's Government) said: Sir, I think I should be exceeding my functions, as representing the Nizam's Government, if I were to attempt to lay before this committee any argument or any views as to what their rights or what their remedies may be on the state of facts disclosed by this inquiry. When all the evidence and facts are before the Nizam's Government, coupled with the report of this committee, of course the Nizam will take the matter into his most anxious consideration, with such advice as he may be able to obtain, and he will then adopt a course which will be determined, not merely by technical considerations of law, but by questions of policy, and of honesty and good faith. But, sir, I am authorised to state, and I think, perhaps, it may be of assistance to my learned friend who represents the company, that under no circumstances would the Nizam consider that he was justified in adopting any course which would have the effect of infringing upon the just rights of those shareholders who have advanced their money to this company honestly and *bona fide* in reliance upon the concession he granted. With that preliminary observation, the first view I intend to submit to the Committee is shortly this —that the conduct of the concessionnaires in diverting £850,000 of the entire nominal capital of the company into their own pockets from the coffers of the company was a fraud upon them. The proposition I submit with reference to the evidence is that Abdul Huk was not, in fact, authorised by the Nizam's Government to accept the bribe which he has received from the concessionnaires, that he did not himself believe he was authorised, and that Mr. Watson and Mr. Stewart in dealing with him did not believe that he was authorised to accept that bribe. The point rests on three letters which are now admitted to be genuine, and emanating from Sir Salar Jung. The first letter is dated December 28, 1881, in which Abdul Huk was authorised to appropriate the 5 per cent. commission "in any manner you think proper in rewarding the services of those who have been mainly instrumental in starting this (railway) scheme, and in carrying it through." The second letter of January 5, 1882, said there was no objection to Abdul Huk receiving remuneration for the railway and mining schemes, for in being rewarded for his services he was only receiving his due. That letter had reference to the negotiations with the Bombay syndicate, which fell through. The third letter, dated 10th January, 1883, on which was the pencilled memorandum of Sir Salar Jung to Abdul Huk, concluded with these words: "You can yourself appropriate the whole of the commission agreed upon as remuneration to your good and valuable services, but this is secret." Now, the "commission agreed upon," it is quite clear, I submit, was the commission mentioned in the first letter of December 28, 1881, and the words "agreed upon" refer to that communication. That is the proposition I put before you. You will find that Abdul Huk in his defence, which is before the Committee, gives in full the letters of 1881 and 1882, but omits from that of 1883 the words—"You can yourself appropriate the whole commission," etc.

Sir Horace Davey objected that, according to the announcement of the Chairman, the Committee was not the tribunal to try Abdul Huk.

The Chairman said the Committee adhered to that decision, and requested Mr. Mayne to confine his observations to the salient facts on which he relied, giving them simply a narrative of the transaction for their assistance. He asked what the learned counsel suggested by Abdul Huk's omission of the words "commission as agreed upon," etc.

Mr. Mayne: The only thing I can suggest is that he might have thought that the words "but this is secret" would cast a reflection upon Sir Salar Jung, as doing an act in his capacity of Prime Minister which should have been public and above-board. On account of that circumstance perhaps it was that he left out all reference to the passage in the letter in putting the document containing it before Sir Salar Jung's son.

The Chairman: Do you suggest that Sir Salar Jung did something wrong? This was a communication to the Government, and why did not he set out the whole of the facts?

Mr. Mayne: I merely call attention to the fact. My next proposition on the evidence is that Watson and Stewart did not themselves believe that Abdul Huk had the authority that he professed to have to take a quarter. My proposition is that they believed they were bribing him corruptly, and not merely doing something which the Government had authorised him to attend to. When Abdul Huk came back to England, in 1883, Watson could hardly have supposed that a very exceptional authority of this character, given by the Prime Minister, in reference to one state of things, could continue to apply *ipso facto* to another state of things under another Prime Minister. Again, when the money is ultimately given, we find it is given with every circumstance of secrecy and concealment. The shares were first of all allotted in the name of Winter, and not of Abdul Huk. Then from Winter's name they are changed into shares to bearer, so that no trace is left behind which would be evidence that Abdul Huk had ever been in possession of the shares at all. Then we find an extraordinary communication going on between Abdul Huk and Watson. Being together in the same room, and Abdul Huk having shares which he was prepared to dispose of, Abdul Huk gets Watson to write him a letter about the difficulty of getting the price of the shares. Abdul Huk then writes a letter back to Watson, who is before him, accepting Watson's proposal, which they carried out in such a manner as to leave no trace behind that Abdul Huk had anything to do with the shares. All these circumstances go to show that in giving the large sum of money which he did to Abdul Huk he was acting above-board and under the authorization of the Nizam's Government. Another proposition I put before you is that it was understood by all parties to the concession that the difference between the nominal capital and the subscribed capital was to be renewed for the legitimate purposes of the company. The evidence is so fresh in the recollection of the committee that I do not propose to go into it.

The Chairman: Do you say, on the part of the Nizam's Government, that is the proper legal reading of the concession?

Mr. Mayne: I do not say the terms support that conclusion, save to this extent, that it excludes a different meaning. I cannot go further than that. Upon the document as it stands, and without any evidence whatever of the meaning put upon it by one side or the other, I should say that it was an ambiguous document.

The Chairman: Your contention is that for all that had taken place before certainly the Government, and probably the concessionnaires, anticipated that no other construction could be put upon it than that the £850,000 was for the purposes of the company.

Mr. Mayne: I limit myself to saying that the document was ambiguous; but from all that had taken place, both sides had a knowledge of the meaning to be put upon it. What is the position of the Nizam's Government? If the company continues in its present position the effect is this, that whereas the Nizam's Government intended to have a company with a million of money, which would start on the framework of the scheme with a capital of £150,000, and as the scheme developed would bring in the rest of the money, now they have got a company with £150,000 and nothing else. If the company remains in its present position no doubt the Nizam's Government will be greatly injured; but it is said that it will not be injured, because further capital will be raised either by the issue of the debentures or by constituting new companies.

As regards the first course, I venture to point out that there is a difficulty because the dividend will have to be spread over a still further surface. Already they have to give up 17-20ths of the profits to pay the dividend on the £850,000 of concessionnaires' shares, and it is not human nature to suppose that they will be willing to bring in another 3-20ths to sweep away the remaining profits into their pockets. Then as to the new companies. Mr. Watson says, "Oh, if we find gold we shall be able to sell a gold mine for a million." But then he has not even got the mine; all he has got is the right under the concession to prospect and find out that there is a mine, then to plot out the particular piece of land, then to take a lease of it, and after that to work it at a fair rent. This fair rent would be calculated thus—on the one side you would put on the cost of working, plus a liberal and an ample profit for the risk run and capital invested; on the other hand you would put the result of the working of the mine, and the balance would be a fair rent.

The Chairman: This is detail with which the Committee is thoroughly conversant.

Mr. Mayne: Then, Sir, there is just one other point. The suggestion will probably be made that the Nizam's Government have acquiesced expressly or implicitly, by way of laches, with these transactions.

The Chairman: That may affect the legal position of parties, but it cannot affect the moral position either in relation to us here or the Indian Government. The question of laches cannot affect our report for a moment.

Mr. Mayne: Up to May, 1877, everything that passed between the Nizam's Government and Abdul Huk was put forward or kept back much as he wished, and, as I say, in the interest of Mr. Watson; but in May, 1887, he did, no doubt, put forward this memorandum in which the £850,000 transaction was mentioned, but he put it forward when the Minister who knew everything about the matter was absent, and when it was to be submitted to the Nizam, a boy of twenty, and to Colonel Marshall, neither of whom knew anything about it. And in the memorandum he makes a mis-statement as to the effect of this concession, which would have the effect of stopping inquiry.

Sir Horace Davey, Q.C. (for Abdul Huk): I will confine my observations to Abdul Huk's part in that which is undoubtedly before the Committee—circumstances under which the concession was made, and its present shape. I will only make this one observation on the allegation of Mr. Mayne, that the letter authorising Abdul Huk to receive remuneration from the concessionnaires referred only to the proposals made by the Bombay syndicate—that that allegation won't stand a moment's investigation in the light of the facts which have been brought ought in the course of this inquiry. As regards Abdul Huk's transaction, with regard to what took place in this country, I assert that he was absolutely free from responsibility as to the form the concession took. Whether the concession justified what Mr. Watson and his friends did or not, this at least is plain and conclusively proved by the evidence—that whatever the form of concession was, Abdul Huk had no responsibility in that matter. With regard to the other subject, you would not expect me to defend the transaction in which Abdul Huk sold his own Government secretly the shares which were his own property. It may be that he considered that the officers of his Government were informed as to his position in the matter, but at any rate he has been advised, and well advised, by counsel of distinction in India, and taking that advice, he has returned the money, with 5 per cent. interest. He takes back the shares, and the Nizam's Government make a handsome profit of £10,000 through the difference in exchange, because the change is made in sterling, and not in rupees.

The Chairman: Some good comes out of evil.

Sir Horace Davey: Yes. I will therefore confine the few observations I am going to make to the purpose of showing how the draft received its present form, and how, so far as that is concerned, Abdul Huk is perfectly free from blame. I would remind you that the original proposal, made on November 7,

1882, was that Messrs. Watson and Stewart were to form a company for the working of the mines, and should undertake to spend £100,000. That was all. Nothing was said about what the subscribed capital should be or the paid up capital; and yet that proposal was approved by the Government of India in a despatch of March 15, 1883. Accordingly, shortly after the death of the great Sir Salar Jung, Abdul Huk was sent to England to negotiate a concession on the terms of that proposal. The India Office wisely advised him to procure the services of a solicitor of respectability and distinction, and accordingly he went to Messrs. White and Borrett, who prepared a draft providing that a company should be formed with a nominal capital of £1,000,000, a subscribed capital of £500,000, and a paid-up capital of £100,000. There is nothing in the draft limiting the amount which was to be paid to the concessionnaires, either in the form of fully-paid shares or otherwise.

The Chairman: That would scarcely affect the case of Abdul Huk.

Sir Horace Davey: Yes; if it was said he was in collusion for the purpose of procuring the concession under which the concessionnaires obtained £850,000. I say he had nothing to do with that. Now, I go to India. Abdul Huk accepted that draft, notwithstanding the profit of Watson. Mr. Winter, however, goes to India, negotiates personally with Sir Salar Jung, and secures the reduction of the £500,000 to £250,000. The evidence, so far as it goes, is that Abdul Huk protested against it and did his best to keep the subscribed capital at £500,000. But what was the action of the Government of India? I do not hesitate to say that it was entirely through the ignorance and mischievous action of the Government of India that the concession got into the form it now is. What I want to point out is that the only practical alteration between the draft as prepared by White and Borrett, and the clause in the concession finally agreed upon, is in the figures. As to whether the draft meant when it left the workshop of Messrs. White and Borrett what it meant when it was finally completed in the concessions, we have several versions of what was in the mind of the Indian Government. Mr. Cordery, a gentleman whose services have been of the greatest value to the Government of India, but who does not know anything about law of companies, says he thought the £150,000 was to be a first call.

The Chairman: Is your argument that in the draft as originally drawn by Messrs. White and Borrett, the difference between the nominal and the subscribed capital—£500,000—was to go to the concessionnaires?

Sir Horace Davey: Not to go necessarily, but to be dealt with. The company might buy the concession for a certain number of paid-up shares. The company could make its own contract. I don't see what this is all about; either this was a contract with the company, or it was not. If it was not, it was made under the circumstances which Mr. Watson stated, and if other shareholders come in (whether by purchase or otherwise) and don't like the bargain, they would have a right to say, "This is no contract binding on the company, because you made it yourselves."

The Chairman: You must confine yourself to Abdul Huk's case, please.

Sir Horace Davey: I only want to say this, that the company is formed for the purpose of engineering mines. Did the Committee ever hear of a company formed for the purpose of acquiring a concession which was not paid for?

The Chairman: You are not arguing Abdul Huk's case. Do you mean to say Abdul Huk is responsible for the terms of the concession?

Sir Horace Davey: I say he is not; he acted on the advice of the solicitors. So far as the evidence goes he urged that the concession should remain in the form it originally was.

The Chairman: If that is so it is not a part of your case to discuss the effect of the concession as it was drawn. If he is not responsible for it, why discuss that for which he is not responsible.

Sir Horace Davey: I do not think I should be justified in proceeding further. I would only point out that the commission, in its present form, is signed by the legal solicitor of the council.

The Chairman: Still, if Abdul Huk is not responsible, how does that assist you?

Sir Horace Davey: It does, indirectly, Sir. All I have to say in regard to the quarter share is, that if Abdul Huk is wrong, the law courts are open to the Nizam's Government; and I am instructed that the Nizam's Government are entering into possible litigation on the subject.

The Chairman: But it is paid back.

Sir Horace Davy: And they are taking the shares. Now they say they will have the money and the shares.

The Chairman: The Committee will not consider that point.

Sir Horace Davey: I regret that imputations have been thrown out in the witness chair and elsewhere, as to documents having been forged or surreptitiously inserted into the Residency archives.

The Chairman: Mr. Cordery has set that right. He corrected his evidence on that point.

Sir Horace Davey: I can only express my regret that such a charge has been made.

Mr. Littler, Q.C. (for Mr. Watson): I may say at once that I am going to defend our conduct in believing that Abdul Huk had a right to become what I may call a speculator with the concessionnaires. Mr. Winter, you will remember, when he went to India to discuss the subject with Abdul Huk, at the very beginning, was informed about this letter of the late Sir Salar Jung. Believing —as Mr. Watson has believed all along—that the railway and the mining transactions were a whole, and that his limited reward on the former was to be compensated for by obtaining the concesssion, Mr. Winter was justified in accepting Abdul Huk's word. It was a State secret, and accordingly Mr. Winter did not publish it to the world, but when he came home communicated it to Mr. Watson.

At the request of the Committee the learned counsel referred to several documents proving this, and also that the royalty on the discovered mines was to be ascertained by the results of the prospecting.

Mr. Labouchere: How can you find the value of the mine until it is worked?

Mr. Littler: You always ascertain that beforehand. That is the reason for prospecting. An hon. member to the right of the chairman (the Solicitor-General for Scotland) knows a good deal about Scotch mines. I know a good deal about English mines. No man would spend £50,000 or £60,000 in starting a mine until he knew what he had to pay for royalty.

Mr. Labouchere: I have put into mines very often without knowing, and I have lost my money. (Laughter.)

Mr. Littler: But no man would spend £50,000 on another man's land until he had found out what royalty he had to pay, otherwise he would be entirely at the landlord's mercy.

Mr. Labouchere: But it is referred to arbitration.

Mr. Littler: But the royalty is reserved in the lease. That is not a postponement.

Mr. Labouchere: But they were not lawyers who looked into this. They were only simple-minded people. (Laughter.)

The Chairman: The purpose of the clause the committee take to be this—that the Government undertook to give the lease, and arbitrators should be appointed if necessary to agree on a fair rent.

Mr. Littler: But the fair rent is to be in the lease. To go on where I was before. In 1884, Mr. Winter came home. We were going to spend £100,000 of our money in a country for which nothing had been done before. We might not have found anything worth having. But we have found something. What we originally promised to do was to spend £100,000, and nothing was said about capital. But Messrs. White and Borrett say: "Oh, these are mere founders' shares; nobody will be responsible," and so they drew up the draft, which was modified until it got to the terms in the concession. Then the concessionnaires paid up their £150,000 and spent it as required. £88,000 being now in the bank to be expended. If it had been a failure all this would have been lost, and no one would have taken over their shares. But people of experience and knowledge in the City of London were of opinion that this was a good investment. Look at Mr. Bishop. He is no fool. He has been 38 years in business, and he buys these shares, to hold some and to recommend others. It was, as one of the witnesses put it, "A rich man's business, and not a poor man's." The men who bought these shares were prepared to put them in their strong boxes and wait until they turned out worth either a great deal more or nothing at all. They relied, as Mr. Bishop said, upon "the standing and position and integrity of Mr. Watson." And what have we done for the Nizam? We did that which Rothschilds demanded 10 per cent. for doing, and failed. We did what Moreton, Rose and Co. demanded $7\frac{1}{2}$ per cent. for doing, and failed. We succeeded in bringing out the railway company, and in the words of the Government of India, thereby immensely raised the credit of the Government of Hyderabad. He had done something which deserved some sort of compensation. You may say £850,000 is an enormous compensation. But it was not £850,000. It was 85,000 pieces of paper, which he was obliged to take in this way—a quarter of which went to Abdul Huk.

The Chairman: Is it not your case that the concession was worth £850,000?

Mr. Littler: That it has turned out worth it.

The Chairman: That it was worth £850,000, as a fact. I mean, not for market operations, but in material value.

Mr. Littler: Not to the Government of Hyderabad.

The Chairman: To the company which took it.

Mr. Littler: I say the shareholders got the value for their money.

The Chairman: Therefore Watson had £850,000 worth to give. You have got to show what he had done to earn that £850,000.

Mr. Littler: My answer is, to the Nizam these mines were absolutely worthless. We have floated the mines in the English market. The Hyderabad Government had not the capital to work them with, nor the credit to raise it. It is only worth £850,000 on the assumption that the mines are good; if they are worthless the Nizam Government has lost nothing, whilst if they are good they have got an immense income in royalties.

The Chairman: Will you turn your attention to telling us what Mr. Watson had done either in service or money to entitle him to this £850,000?

Mr. Littler: The State gets somebody else to do the prospecting. They get out of the Singareni coalfields a royalty of 8 annas a ton. We floated his railway, and besides spending money to develop Singareni we undertake to spend another £70,000 in prospecting, and the Nizam gets £7,000 a year all the time we are prospecting whatever happens. Singareni was worth nothing without the railway.

The Chairman: Yes, but the railway is settled. They settled that for £100,000.

Mr. Littler: Legally it was. Legally we have no claim, and if the Nizam chose to say "We shall not give you the concession," we couldn't say anything.

Mr. Labouchere: Can you point to a case in Europe in which a country has given a promoter £850,000 for making a railway?

Mr. Littler: I should like to ask how much Rothschilds got for floating the Ship Canal.

The Chairman: They raised £10,000,000, and got 5 per cent. This is £850,000 for £150,000.

Mr. Littler: I say that what has happened has distinctly proved that the directors were justified in what they did.

The Chairman: You say that if the property was there it was worth £850,000.

Mr. Littler: Certainly; you have before you the reports of some of the ablest engineers in the world.

The Chairman: Why were not those reports obtained before the £850,000 was paid?

Mr. Littler: Because we were bound to bring out the company within six months.

The Chairman: But you were not bound to take £850,000 for the concession.

In reply to the Chairman,

Mr. Pember, who represented the company, said he presumed that the only consequence which could possibly happen upon the report of the Committee, was that the concession might be tampered with in some way or other. The result of any report the Committee might make might be to induce the Nizam, for instance, to revoke the concession, or to deal with it in some way disadvantageous to the shareholders.

The Chairman: I must remind you that the grantors of the concession are represented here, and that Mr. Mayne has communicated his intention that the *bona fide* shareholders whom you represented shall be protected.

Mr. Pember: I submit that this committee, as representing the English Parliament, should take care in their report to express their opinion as to whether this concession was obtained by fraud by Abdul Huk. Upon the documents before you, I should say that Abdul Huk had nothing to do with obtaining the concession.

The Chairman: If it was obtained by fraud, then by whom do you say it was perpetrated?

Mr. Pember: I cannot tell you. I say it was not obtained by fraud. There is no fraud, so far as I can see, in any of the negotiations.

The Chairman: You must know that these shares would be passed over to the public. Ought not some one to have seen that the £850,000 worth of shares represented the real value of the concession?

Mr. Pember: I can't say I think so.

Mr. Labouchere: Why was Mr. Batten wanted at all?

Mr. Pember: To do administrative work—to make allotments of shares, and subsequently to administer the affairs of the company. All I wish is that you should take care of the title of the *bona fide* shareholders.

The Chairman: I am sure the Committee will do everything they can to protect the interests of the present shareholders; but when I say shareholders, of course there are shareholders and shareholders.

Mr. Pember: I desire to add that Lord Lawrence, who was asked to become a director of the Company, does deserve the sympathy, not only of this Committee, but of all right-thinking people. It must be very galling and very irritating to a man of his position and honour to be told, without the slightest warning, that he is the director of a bubble company, when he has been asked to fill that position by a person whom he met in the highest circles of English political society, and I hope that at least he may have some substantial proof of the consideration of this Committee.

Mr. Eardley Norton (of Madras): I wish to say that the Nizam's Government has never at any time, not even before this Committee, contemplated any intention of interfering with the title of this Company. The Nizam's Government would desire me to repeat the assurance that whatever may be the report of this Committee, the interests of the *bona fide* shareholders will certainly be protected.

The Chairman having thanked learned counsel for their assistance, the Committee adjourned at ten minutes to six o'clock.—*Financial News*, June 23.

OUR correspondent at Allahabad telegraphs us the full text of an important letter which Sir Salar Jung has addressed to the Indian papers, confirming the recent statement of the Nawab before the Hyderabad-Deccan Committee, that neither Sir Salar Jung, junior, or the present Prime Minister, had ever seen the letter of the late Sir Salar Jung to Abdul Huk authorising him to accept remuneration for his services from the promoters of the railway company. Evidently, if the Hyderabad-Deccan Committee do not make thorough work of Abdul Huk and his confederates it will not be the fault of the Nizam and his Ministers. They are taking a great deal more trouble to clear themselves of this unsavoury scandal than is thought necessary by some distinguished officials nearer home. The contrast which the energy of the Hyderabad Court presents to the lukewarmness of the India Office can hardly escape notice. Abdul Huk's doom is fixed, so far as it can be at Hyderabad. By the way, what is to be done with his 12,000 shares which he has been compelled to take back from the Nizam? They will, of course, have to come on the market, and it may find them rather difficult of digestion.—*Financial News*, June 23.

THE Hyderabad Committee held their last public sitting yesterday, the whole of the day being occupied with the addresses of the various counsel. Two or three private meetings will (our London Correspondent says) be held for the purpose of considering and drafting the reports, which may be expected in about a fortnight. I hear on good authority that the committee are likely to make some severe comments on the irregularities—to give them a mild title—which have been brought to light in connection with the formation of the company. The evidence which has been given has created a strong impression that between Abdul Huk and his associates the Nizam and the public has come very badly off. Abdul Huk has admitted his error by making restitution, and placing himself entirely at the mercy of the Nizam. The course the concessionnaire will take will probably depend in a great measure upon the tenour of the Committee's report. I have reason to believe that the concession of mining rights will not be withdrawn, but it is possible that the conditions upon which it is granted may be materially modified.—*Yorkshire Post*, June 23.

THE TWO FINANCIAL SCANDALS.—The power of the financial press has never been better demonstrated than in the case of the two Commissions which are at present inquiring into the corrupt practices of certain officials connected with the Metropolitan Board of Works and the Hyderabad (Deccan) Mining Company. It is not too much to say that the disgusting revelations in the first case would never have seen the light of day had it not been for the action taken by our daily contemporary, the *Financial News*, on this subject, while the outcry raised by the press on the cool appropriation of £850,000 in shares in the latter led to the appointment of two Commissions. As these two bodies have not yet finished their labours, it would be premature to give an opinion, but enough has already come to light in the two cases to show to what extent plunder is made in the City of London under the very noses of unsuspecting persons.

We venture to think that if the press will combine to keep their weather eye open, and to denounce those schemes which are calculated to enrich the individual at the expense of the public, it will prevent investors from becoming the prey of unscrupulous parties as much as the new Companies Act which we have discussed above. It may perhaps seem hard to blame men in responsible positions, and of undoubted honesty, for not looking closer into what was happening under their very eyes, but it says volumes for their inattention to details that officials should have been hoodwinked in the way they appear to have been. The fierce light of day which has been shed on the proceedings of the parties concerned in these two instances should warn others from following their example, and the dread of publicity will doubtless act as a wholesome deterrent from similar practices. With many the motto appears to be that the sin lies, not in committing the offence, but in being found out, and as the danger of this has now been made apparent through the recent action of the press, we think that fewer of these scandals will be perpetrated in the future.—*Sunday Times*, June 24.

THE HYDERABAD (DECCAN) MINES INQUIRY.—Captain Sutherland, personal secretary to his Excellency Sir Asman Jah, reached London yesterday morning. He brings important papers for Nawab Mohsin-ul-Mulk from the Hyderabad Government, and is fully conversant with the latest proceedings at Hyderabad in connexion with this case. Captain Sutherland is staying at the Alexandra Hotel.—*Times*, June 25.

I AM delighted to hear from India that that genial and kindly gentleman, Sir Salar Jung, is likely soon to be restored to favour by his sovereign, the Nizam, and that as a first step he will return from his exile to Hyderabad. On his return from England, lately, he was sent away from the capital, with orders not to approach it without permission. He will soon, if all I hear be true, be not only back in Hyderabad, but resume the place he held, until lately, as Prime Minister, and which his illustrious father held for so long.—*Hawk*, June 26.

THE DECCAN MINING SCANDALS.—The inquiry into the Deccan mining scandals has come to an end. The report of the committee has still to be printed, but certain broad facts have come out in the course of the investigation which are deserving of special note. For example, we maintain at every native Court, upon a gigantic salary (paid, it must be observed, not by ourselves, but by the native State), a Resident and staff, whose special duty it is to keep the Indian Government acquainted with all that is going on in the State to which they are accredited. These political appointments, as they are called, are the great prizes of the Indian service. Only officers of exceptional ability and exceptional knowledge of the native character are supposed to be eligible for them. The post of Resident at the Court of the Nizam is considered the highest and most important of them all. And yet what is apparent from the evidence taken by the Deccan Committee of Inquiry? Simply this, that the Resident and his staff, the Calcutta Foreign Office, and the India Office at home were all hoodwinked and outrageously duped by one native policeman whom a former Resident had innocently imported into the State from British India.

For it is worth remembering that until Abdul Huk, under the benign protection of the British Residency, developed into a Hyderabad nobleman of ancient family, and, in that character, represented the Nizam on the occasion of the Queen's Jubilee here in London, he had been the son of a Bombay cultivator, with nothing but his pay as a policeman to live on. From first to last there have not been two opinions regarding this man in either the Court or the population of Hyderabad. He was known to high and low as a greedy and unscrupulous patron. The only quarter in which this notorious fact was not known was in the British Residency. We see from this the ease with which conspiracies may be hatched in India of which the so-called rulers of the country know absolutely nothing until they have exploded under their feet. We can learn from this how a district may be seething with bitterness and discontent, and yet the responsible officials be reporting to Government in perfect good faith that it is loyal and perfectly tranquil.

These revelations disclose another aspect of our rule which is worth noting. In all these native States, what we understand by the feudal feeling is as strong to-day as it was in Europe during the Middle Ages. High birth, ancient descent, are still considered to give their possessors a sort of divine right to rule. The feeling of clanship which binds in ties of loyalty and protection the vassal to his lord and the lord to his vassal is still in these States the chief cementing force which holds society together. When, therefore, the Indian Government, acting through its Residents, imports into one of these States a policeman or some other low functionary of its own to be a ruler and judge over it, it inflicts upon both sovereign and people as gross an insult and humiliation as can be imagined. But for the protection of the British Resident such a fellow as this Abdul Huk would not have been permitted to enter the palace of the Nizam except in some menial capacity, as the guardian of his slippers, or the bearer of his hookah.

Abdul Huk's case, it must be remembered, is by no means a solitary one. Of late years there is hardly a native State which has not been tormented and harassed by creatures imported into it by British Residents. The Residents are entirely in the hands of these men, and they, knowing their power, abuse it in every possible way. For the wretched Prince and his people there is no escape from the intolerable affliction; for neither the Governor-General nor the India Office nor anyone else knows, or can know, aught of what is going on except what the Resident is pleased to report, and the more that the Sovereign resists the policy or the creatures of the Residents the worse become the reports made of him to Calcutta. The Sovereign, in fact, cannot show his discontent except at the peril of summary deposition for misrule, and therefore it is that we hear so often that this or that native chief has ceased to hold communications with the Resident; that he lives secluded in his palace; that he takes no interest in the affairs of his State; and so forth. In almost every such instance an independent inquiry would reveal that it is the arbitrary behaviour of the Resident that is in fault, not the character of the native prince.

Our policy should be to attach these native princes to ourselves by the utmost respect for their legitimate authority, by striving in all ways to elevate their dignity in the eyes of their subjects. For their hold upon the loyalty and obedience of their people is far stronger than we can ever attain to over the population of British India. This was shown abundantly in the great crisis of 1857. The waves of mutiny and insurrection never surmounted the barrier presented by the boundary line of an independent native State. British fugitives—men, women, and children—were safe from pursuit and the fear of sudden death as soon as they passed out of British India into the territory of a loyal native prince. In many parts of India, at that time, when British authority had ceased to exist in British India (properly so called), a loyal native State furnished the base from which we began operations for the re-establishing of our power. But in India, at the present day, there is hardly a single political agent who does not make it his particular business to reduce the authority of the prince to a nullity, to break down the administrative system which, by reason of its antiquity, has perfectly adjusted itself to the needs of the people, and substitute in its stead such fellows as Abdul Huk.—*Weekly Dispatch*, July 1.

The inquiry into what has been called the "Deccan Scandal" has been closed, but the report has not yet been issued. We shall be curious to see it when in due course it shall see the light. The committee of investigation were set to curse the administration of the company and to bring rebuke and punishment upon the concessionnaires. But if we read aright, the evidence, as it has been published in the newspapers, has exonerated these gentlemen altogether. They had a chance of selling the rights and privileges conceded to them and they sold them—on hard terms for the company. As a rule, men of business estimate the value of anything they have to sell by what it will fetch, and that is exactly the rule on which the concessionnaires acted. It may not always be an excellent and a praiseworthy rule, but it is the rule of the City.

What the Committee has brought out is that Abdul Huk, under the benign influence of the British Residency, developed into a Hyderabad nobleman of ancient family who was high and mighty enough to represent the Nizam at the Queen's Jubilee, and who has an itching palm for gold. This worthy was the inspiring genius of the whole enterprise, and he who was great enough for his mission to England in 1887 was good enough to be trusted with the prosaic business of dealing with the mining rights of the Nizam and of granting terms and fixing the responsibilities of concessionnaires.

It has also transpired that the British Residency was very lax in its oversight of the affair—always supposing that it had a right to interference—that the Nizam's Government allowed itself to be hoodwinked while it slept. Last of all, that the India Office does not consider itself the dry nurse of the Nizam. This last finding is a grand discovery which is worth all the fuss that has been made about the matter. Thus ignominiously ends an investigation that was to prove the existence of a great scandal, and bring home fraud to somebody—the accusers did not exactly know to whom.

Hyderabad-Deccan shares are about £7, and will we think go better. It may be remembered that a fortnight since we advised their purchase when they were about £6. Those who have followed our advice have cleared £1 a share—a nice little profit. Now that the inquiry is over we think they will go better.—*Evening Post*, July 2.

INQUIRE WITHIN.

I CANNOT make out what the world is about,
But we're suffering sorely from something no doubt,
For day by day
There's a solemn inquiry, preceding report,
Anent something or other of serious sort,
Be what it may.

If a shocking suspicion should chance to arise,
It is fasten'd upon the folk who surmise
It must be true;
"Inquiry! Inquiry! Inquiry!" 's the cry,
And, with eagerness worthy of any Paul Pry,
Inquire they do.

As pigs hunt for truffles with wonderful zeal,
These folk hunt for scandals—which, maybe, they feel
Are pearls of price;
But the parallel ends there, for truffles are good,
While the scandals dug up in inquisitive mood
Are—not so nice.

The works of the great Metropolitan Board
Fine field for inquiry appear to afford;
Added to which,
The pranks that the Deccan Mine people have had
With the Government agent from Hyderabad
Are likewise rich.

Of course they inquire when they're wanting to know
If of emigrant paupers the swift-growing flow
We ought to stem;
And amid the vast subjects dissected with skill,
The system of Sweating, so fruitful of ill,
Is nuts to them.

With Committees on this and Commissions on that,
Scandal-seekers by now should be getting quite fat
Upon their spoil,
Whilst dreadful disclosures so constantly soothe
And nobody tries any trouble to smoothe
By pouring oil.

Indeed, recently Parliament seems to have been
An inquisitorial sort of machine;
And 'twere no sin
Or libel that any false notion would bring,
To write on its doors—"Upon everything
Inquire within."

—*Vanity Fair*, June 30.

A Dignitary from the Deccan.—The Nizam's Prime Minister talks to a 'Star' Man.—A *Star* reporter visited the Nawab Moshin-ul-Moolk, the Nizam of Hyderabad's Prime Minister, the other morning at the Alexandra Hotel. He does not see a Nawab every day of his life, so he fell into the pardonable error of addressing him as "Your Highness." The Nawab, however, is only what the Germans would call a Translucency. The private secretary of the "dark gent from India," as the hotel waiter summed him up in a loose classification, entered when the *Star* man had made his salaam and his greeting, and explained that the Prime Minister is of the third degree of Indian nobility—"ul-Moolk"—above his title come those of "Jung" and "Doolah." The Nawab was dressed very plainly in a compound costume, in which the quiet attire of an English gentleman was combined with the easy garb of the Oriental. He wore a short, high-buttoned black coat, a deep forage cap took the place of turban, and a loose grey robe reached his patent leather shoes.

He is a short handsome man of fifty, whose black beard is tinged with grey. His placid East Indian features were occasionally agitated by a puzzled expression as he tried to walk along the zigzag path of grammatical English. The Nawab was breakfasting, but he showed no disinclination to be chatty and agreeable. Had our reporter been of a flippant turn he would have put the first question which arose, and asked the Prime Minister "how he liked London." But thinking that even an Indian Prime Minister's education might not embrace an acquaintance with the famous patentee of that famous expression, he put the question less categorically. The Nawab was very generous in his admiration of what he was pleased to call our "noble institutions." "Your fine buildings—the House of Commons, where I saw the Empress's Ministers, the Courts of Justice, and the Mosque of Westminster—all these have a constant interest for me," he said. "But what I cannot help admiring in England, is the admirable civil police and its law-abiding people. Every Englishman seems to me to have such an independent, courteous bearing, just like Mussulmans," added the Nawab, flatteringly. "The wealth of your country is shown by the loud traffic, like the roar of the ever-flowing ocean." The Nawab really looked as if his admiration was real.

"Has your experience of London comprised a visit to the theatre?"

"Yes, I have seen 'David Garrick,'" replied the Nawab, without the assistance of his interpreter. "I was much pleased. It was to me a big lesson, a study of morals."

"Do you like Italian opera and English music?"

"Amongst Mussulmans," he replied, "there is not much music. It is confined to a few professionals. Ladies, besides, do not sing in public. This last," he added, "is a little more than I can understand by the most liberal construction of the freedom of European manners. But it looks beautiful. My wonder," added the Prime Minister, "is great in examining the contents of those mighty bazaars where buying and selling"—("Or perhaps 'selling' only," interjected the secretary, with a slight twinkle)—"is carried on so quietly." From this the talk naturally drifted to the Deccan Deal.

"Ah, the Deccan Company. Well, I cannot say much about that. Of course Abdul Huk's conduct was most unsatisfactory. He has been suspended, and his concessional claim will be investigated by the Council of State of Hyderabad; more than that I cannot say. Do I think any of the money will be recovered? That, too, cannot be said till the judges have received all the evidence."—*Star*, July 6.

More Inquiry into Hyderabad Affairs.—The Indian papers, English as well as native, have still a great deal to say about Hyderabad and its affairs. We have had a Deccan mining scandal, and now, if half what is said about the matter be true, we may have a Deccan railway scandal. There appears to be good ground for inquiry, both as to the manner in which this project was placed before the Government of Hyderabad immediately after the sudden death of the Regent Salar Jung in 1883, and as to the way in which its acceptance was finally obtained. In the promotion of the Deccan railway, as in the promotion of the Deccan mining company, the moving spirit was the Nizam's enterprising "Home Secretary." But it would seem that even Abdul Huk would not have been able to carry the scheme through without the support of certain officials of the Government of India; and this support he astutely obtained. There is, of course, no desire in any quarter to injure the credit of the railway company, in which the Nizam's Government itself is a shareholder to the extent of about three-quarters of a million's worth of shares. But an inquiry starting with a definite avoidance of doing this, and yet eliciting evidence as to the measures that preceded the floating of the railway company, would serve to enlighten the British public as to what an adventurer may contrive to do in a native State under circumstances favourable to his designs. It would seem that for some reason or other there was an anxiety to carry the railway scheme through before the Nizam attained his majority. The final acceptance of the scheme by the Provisional Government was of a somewhat dramatic character—if it is true, that is, that the necessary sanction was obtained in a railway carriage as the young Nizam and his Ministers were on their way to visit the Viceroy at Calcutta. The light that is now being thrown on Hyderabad affairs by the Indian press, as well as certain parts of the evidence taken by the Select Committee, renders it possible to form some idea of what went on at the time, and it may be advisable hereafter to explain the means adopted to secure the floating of the railway company. Meantime, it may be noted that the *Pioneer*, which has taken the lead in India in clearing away the fog in which for some years past the affairs of the Nizam have been enveloped, gives some interesting particulars as to the financing of the railway when it was floated. The outcome of the calculation made by the *Pioneer* is that the promotion-money, &c., amounted to a total of £297,093 for raising funds amounting to only £1,961,307. The scheme provided that the Nizam was to pay 5 per cent. per annum on the whole of the capital raised; but it would seem that he pays nearly 6 per cent., owing to the modest little remuneration taken by the "Home Secretary" and the other promoters of the present Hyderabad State Railway. During the past few months it has been our business more than once to call attention to the financial curiosities of Hyderabad. But more remains behind. When it got noised abroad some years ago that an official of the Hyderabad State Railway had pocketed the sum of £33,000 as his commission on the sale of the State Railway to an English company, remonstrance was addressed from several quarters to the Government of India. The invariable official answer was that the Indian Government could not interfere in such a matter in a Native State. Now it incidentally appears, in a Parliamentary return recently issued, that the Nizam's "Home Secretary" did not resign his appointment in the British service till the 1st of January, 1887. What, it may be asked, was the reason that the Government of India was not able to interfere with one of its own servants whose services were up to that date openly lent to the Nizam, and whose malpractices cannot be said to have been concealed except from those, apparently, who would not see?—*St. James' Gazette*, July 7.

THE labours of the Select Committee appointed by the House of Commons to inquire into the Hyderabad-Deccan affair have at length been brought to a close, and we may now look forward to an early presentation of the report. What its precise nature will be we cannot of course foreshadow, but it is perfectly safe to predict that if it is based upon the evidence, oral and written, which was adduced at the various sittings of the Committee, no blame will or can be attached either to the company or the concessionnaires, who have throughout acted in perfectly good faith with the public, notwithstanding the exaggerated statements put forward by certain interested persons. The responsibility for any questionable acts which may have been committed rests solely upon the head of the now notorious Abdul Huk, with whom both the company and the concessionnaires treated as the accredited official representative of the Nizam's Government, as also did Her Majesty, when she conferred the distinction of C.I.E. upon this dusky (or shady) diplomat and financier.—*Financial Times*, July 12.

ANOTHER HYDERABAD SCANDAL.—There seems to be no end to the Hyderabad scandals. Even before the Special Committee presided over by Sir Henry James has had time to report on the evidence recently laid before it, public opinion in India is demanding an inquiry into the circumstances connected with the floating of the Hyderabad Railway Company. Then there is the Rumbold affair, of which we surely have not heard the last. And now we have to call attention to another story which is not a pretty one as it stands.

That well-known publication, *Stubbs's List*, in its issue for the week ending the 20th of June, contains an announcement of the bankruptcy of Messrs. William Hulbert Wathen and Edward King, trading under the name of H. Wathen and Son as wholesale tea dealers in some places and as grocers in others. In the notice appears the following items :—

SEPARATE ESTATE OF WILLIAM HULBERT WATHEN.
Creditors Unsecured.

Thomas, Miss	£1,000	0	0
Marshall, Colonel, Hyderabad, India	5,250	0	0

The explanation of the last item is this. Colonel Marshall is private secretary and confidential adviser to the Nizam. Colonel Marshall was sent by Lord Dufferin to Hyderabad with the laudable object of purifying the State and of setting the native officials an example of probity and self-devotion. Now, when Sir Salar Jung ceased to be Prime Minister, his successor, Sir Asman Jah, happened to be in this country representing the Nizam at the Jubilee ceremonies.

Colonel Marshall thus became for the time being virtually Minister of Hyderabad. In that capacity he took upon himself the responsibility of appointing Mr. Wathen, whose wife is Colonel Marshall's sister, General Agent of the State. There was no necessity for such an appointment. Mr. Joseph Rock is, and has been for twenty-five years, the trusted representative of the Hyderabad Government in England. With the appointment by Colonel Marshall of his sister's husband a new procedure was instituted. The "General Agent" was supplied with funds in advance. An order was sent to the Hyderabad Treasury to remit to Mr. Wathen £5,000, to which was added £1,000 from the Nizam's private purse, making in all £6,000. Of this amount Mr. Wathen only expended £750, and the question arises, Who is to lose the remaining £5,250. Is the loss to fall on the Hyderabad Government or on Colonel Marshall? Lord Dufferin should decide this question before he leaves India. From the extract quoted above it appears that, although Mr. Wathen was constituted State Agent and received State funds, it is Colonel Marshall and not the Hyderabad Government who is returned as the creditor for the £5,250. Perhaps it may be assumed from this fact that Colonel Marshall has already made himself responsible to the Nizam.—*St. James's Gazette*, July 16.

THAT POOR NIZAM!—ANOTHER HYDERABAD SCANDAL—COLONEL MARSHALL AND HIS BANKRUPT BROTHER-IN-LAW.—That well-known publication *Stubbs's List*, in its issue for the week ending the 30th June, contains an announcement of the bankruptcy of Messrs. William Hulbert Wathen and Edward King, trading under the name of H. Wathen and Son, as wholesale tea dealers in some places and as grocers in others. In the notice appear the following items:—

SEPARATE ESTATE OF WILLIAM HULBERT WATHEN.
Creditors Unsecured.

Thomas, Miss	£1,000	0	0
Marshall, Colonel, Hyderabad, India	5,250	0	0

The explanation of the last item is this, says the *St. James's Gazette*. Colonel Marshall is private secretary and confidential adviser to the Nizam. Colonel Marshall was sent by Lord Dufferin to Hyderabad with the laudable object of purifying the State, and of setting the native officials an example of probity and self devotion. Now, when Sir Salar Jung ceased to be Prime Minister, his successor, Sir Asman Jah, happened to be in this country representing the Nizam at the Jubilee ceremonies. Colonel Marshall thus became, for the time being, virtually Minister of Hyderabad. In that capacity he took upon himself the responsibility of appointing Mr. Wathen, whose wife is Colonel Marshall's sister, general agent of the State. There was no necessity for such an appointment. Mr. Joseph Rock is, and has been for twenty-five years, the trusted representative of the Hyderabad Government in England. With the appointment by Colonel Marshall of his sister's husband a new procedure was instituted. The "general agent" was supplied with funds in advance. An order was sent to the Hyderabad Treasury to remit to Mr. Wathen £5,000, to which was added £1,000 from the Nizam's private purse, making in all £6,000. Of this amount Mr. Wathen only expended £750, and the question arises, Who is to lose the remaining £5,250. Is the loss to fall on the Hyderabad Government or on Colonel Marshall? Lord Dufferin should decide this question before he leaves India.—*Star*, July 17.

THE HYDERABAD (DECCAN) COMPANY.—The fact that the £10 shares in this company are still unobtainable under about £7 10s., in spite of the trailing through the mud which they have had, shows clearly the unabated confidence of the shareholders in the value of their property. Nor is this at all surprising when we regard the series of reports which the directors have just forwarded to the shareholders with a view to showing the latter the position and prospects of the company. These reports have already been put in as evidence before the Parliamentary Committee, in explanation of the unforeseen difficulties which have so far delayed the operations of the company. These, however, are now overcome, and satisfactory results may be confidently looked forward to at no very distant date. One highly favourable feature in the report is the result of the gold prospecting in the Raichur Doab, by Mr. T. W. H. Hughes, Deputy Superintendent of the Geological Survey of the Government of India, whose services were lent to the company by the Indian Government.

The attention of Mr. Hughes had been early directed to the gold-bearing strata in the Raichur Doab, that is the country between the Kistna and Toongbhoodra Rivers, in the south-western portion of the Nizam's territories, not far to the west of the Great Indian Peninsular Railway. As a geologist, he held the opinion that the Mysore Reefs were continued into this tract, and the researches of the prospecting staff have amply confirmed this view. The report of Mr. J. H. Stevenson, dated so recently as April last, also shows that the existence of three bands of gold-bearing rocks have been established, covering respectively areas of 200, 70, and 280 square miles, or a total of 550 square miles. Of this area 130 square miles have been proved to be auriferous and riddled with ancient workings, which everywhere in the world are held to be the best evidence of the existence of gold in paying quantities, and which the primitive methods of the ancients were incapable of exhausting, whilst all the samples of "dump" taken from the old workings have proved to contain gold. Mr. Stephenson points out that there are two other tracts, one to the north of the Bheema River and the other further east of Lingasagur towards the line of railway, which have not yet been examined, and which are worthy of serious attention. A small portable plant of three sets of stamps, with engines and boilers, has been ordered for the prospecting work, and 20 tons of quartz are shortly expected to arrive in England to be crushed and tested.

In addition to the above, there is also a report by Messrs. Thomas and William Morgans, of Bristol and London, who, on a comparison with the present market value of the Kolar gold properties in Mysore—making full allowance for capital expended and labour already performed there—arrive at the estimate of £1,080,000 as the net value of the company's gold discoveries so far as they have gone, leaving out of the question an immense tract of auriferous ground not yet traversed.

As to the Sangareni coalfields, which are included in the concession granted to the company, Messrs. Morgans point out that their value depends greatly upon the demand, the available supply being ample, viz., 94 millions of tons. Estimating the profit at the modest sum of two shillings per ton, a sale of 400,000 tons annually would produce £40,000 net profit. Of this quantity, nearly one-half is practically assured for railways alone, according to the calculations of the Government of India. The reports furnish no figures as to the diamondiferous portions of the company's property, but these are also believed to be of great value, and machinery has been sent out to profitably develop them.

When it is seen that the territories comprised in the concession cover an area of 81,500 square miles (exceeding that of England and Scotland together) of some of the wealthiest mineral deposits in the world, there can be little doubt that the shareholders possess a veritable *El Dorado*, if money and labour be properly expended. Dealing with this subject in a recent issue, we referred to the fact that the sittings of the House of Commons Committee appointed to inquire into the affair had finally closed. We may now supplement this by adding that it was stated at the last meeting of the Committee, by counsel for the Nizam's Government, that it was not, and never had been, the intention of the Nizam's Government, no matter what the report of the Select Committee might be, to interfere in any way with the title of the company, but on the contrary, they would do all they could to protect the interests of the shareholders. This will prove anything but reassuring to the energetic "bears," who, in furtherance of their object, talked loudly of a probable rescission of the contracts.—*Financial Times*, July 17.

The Hyderabad (Deccan) Company.—The directors of the Hyderabad (Deccan) Company have forwarded to the shareholders copies of a number of reports received from India, showing the position and prospects of the company. These reports have been put in as evidence before the Parliamentary Committee. They show that unforeseen difficulties have delayed the operations of the company. These are: (1) The non-completion of the railway to the coalfields until the commencement of the current year, whereas the chief engineer of the railway had estimated that it would have been opened in April, 1887; (2) delay on the part of the manufacturers in the supply of the machinery for the diamond washing and coal mines; (3) severe outbreaks of cholera, which had absolutely driven away all the labourers. Now that these difficulties are disappearing, the monsoon has set in, which must tend to check work for the next two or three months. The most favourable feature in the reports is the result of the gold prospecting in the Raichar Doab. The existence of 550 square miles of auriferous country has been already established, of which 130 have been proved to contain old workings, from the dump of which every sample has been found to contain gold. In addition to the above-mentioned reports, and based on them, is one from Messrs. Thomas and William Morgans of Bristol and London, who, on a comparison with the present market value of the Colar gold properties in Mysore, and making full allowance for capital spent and work done there, arrive at the estimate of £1,080,000 as the value of the company's gold discoveries, so far as they have gone. As to the Singareni coalfields, they point out that its value depends on the demand, the available supply being ample, viz., nine millions of tons. Estimating the profits at 2s. per ton, a sale of 400,000 tons annually would produce £400,000 net profit. Of this quantity nearly one-half is practically assured for railways alone, according to the calculations of the Government of India. Messrs Morgans believe that a very profitable business can be carried on by the establishment of suitable ironworks at Singareni. Until diamonds are actually found, of which Messrs. Morgans believe there is every prospect, it is impossible to make any estimate of the diamondiferous portion of the company's property. The general conclusion from the reports, which certainly read as honest and *bona fide*, seems to be that, though the expectations of profitable results have proved to be over sanguine as to the time in which they could be accomplished, the property of the company must in time prove extremely valuable.—*Financial News*, July 17.

The Hyderabad (Deccan) Concession.—The report of the Select Committee on the Hyderabad (Deccan) concession is expected to be out in a few days. It is understood that two separate drafts are being written—one by the Secretary-General for Scotland and the other by the Chairman of the Committee. Other members of the Committee may contribute personal suggestions, and the whole will be boiled up into a State document, which will, at least, read plausibly. In the interests of the India Office, justice will have to be tempered with mercy, and it is possible also that a friendly hint or two may be thrown out on behalf of the poor shareholders. It is they who have most to complain of, and if any reparation could be done to them it would be more acceptable than the whitewashing of Olympian officials who, by their own confession, indulged in Jove's privilege of nodding when there was special occasion to be wide awake.

It must be admitted that the Select Committee have a very delicate and rather intricate task to perform. As a committee, they have had no direct jurisdiction over any of the parties appearing before them. Of the two transactions which formed the scandal, one took place in a semi-independent State and the other within the limits of a private association. The concession was obtained from the Nizam's Government, and whether the proceedings connected with it at Hyderabad were regular or irregular the House of Commons has no special authority to pronounce. The objectionable shares were issued through the London Stock Exchange, in accordance with its rather lax rules as to that class of business. The Select Committee can bring no influence to bear either on the London Stock Exchange or on the Nizam's Government. The most they can do is to offer recommendations, which, however, would doubtless be respectfully received in both quarters. Even the India Office is comparatively safe, unless Mr. Labouchere happens to have a majority of followers on the committee.

It would be a public misfortune if such a scandal had been raked up for nothing, and so much dirty linen washed in public without any useful result. The members of the Select Committee may be trusted to appreciate that danger, and to do what they can to avoid it. Indirect remedies are likely to be suggested in their report. The Nizam's Government can be recommended to uphold the concession in the interest of *bonâ fide* shareholders who have bought their shares at high prices. In such a case, however, it would be entitled to impose conditions, both on its own behalf and on that of the public. It might require the promoters to conform, as far as they yet can, to the essential terms of the concession, either by cancelling all the original shares left in their control, or by providing the company with funds to continue the work which it undertook. All the Hyderabad and India Office witnesses examined by the Committee agreed that the intention in giving away for nothing what were supposed to be valuable rights, was to have capital introduced into the State for the development of its resources. According to them, the raising of one million sterling was the consideration expected from the promoters for the concession. Had that proviso been clearly defined instead of being left vague, neither the British public nor the Nizam's Government would have suffered. They have now a common interest in obtaining whatever redress may be possible.

Either by a reduction of the share capital improperly issued, or by a further contribution of capital from the promoters, the company might have its financial credit restored and be put in a position to carry out its original object. Shares remaining in the hands of the promoters, or which were in their hands when the parliamentary inquiry commenced, might have their validity challenged with a fair prospect of success. Unfortunately, only a small proportion of them is in that position. The largest block is the twelve thousand and odd shares which Abdul Huk was compelled to take back from the Nizam. He has had to return the money for them, and so far the Nizam has been no loser. But the existence of such shares in hands like his is also a wrong to the Company which the Nizam has now an opportunity of correcting. It is clearly within his right to lay down conditions for the maintenance of the concession, and what is best for him will be best also for the *bonâ fide* shareholders.

The last man to deserve any consideration in the case is Abdul Huk, who was the arch offender in abusing the concession. The shares found in his possession, and which he too adroitly tried to get rid of by selling them to the Nizam, were *ab initio* dishonest. He defrauded his employer, first, by secretly accepting the shares, and, in the second place, by secretly selling them. No one will think it a hardship on him if they be absolutely cancelled, and the Nizam has that in his power. Over the English promoters he has, of course, no authority, any more than have the Select Committee which has investigated the scandal. They may be safely left, however, to the influence of public opinion. A voluntary offer of compromise on their part is not at all improbable. Already they have attempted to forestall the judgment of the Committee by publishing a series of documents proving that since the company was formed its business has been conducted both with energy and ability. Apart from the one fatal vice of creating so much paper capital; there is no fault to be found with the management. In the face of serious obstacles and many disappointments, they have had the country thoroughly prospected, not only for minerals, but for gold and diamonds. They have demonstrated the existence of a coal-field at Singareni, and have opened up mines which are yielding a regular supply of saleable coal. It may not be as yet of very high quality, but at lower depths it will improve. In gold and diamonds positive results have not, so far, been reached, though the presence of both has been proved in various places.

Apart from its financial methods, the Hyderabad-Deccan Company had a good, legitimate object. It has only to be brought back to sound financial shape in order to continue its work with a fair prospect of success. As a prospecting company with a *bonâ fide* capital of £150,000, or even £200,000, it would have been a fair speculative venture, and the shortest way to correct the errors of its infancy might be to reorganise it on these lines. With twenty or thirty thousand of the present shares wiped out and the rest written down to five or six pounds, it will be still a feasible venture. As soon as the Select Committee issue their report the directors will be wise to consult the shareholders frankly and candidly on the situation.—*Financial News*, July 18.

THE directors of the Hyderabad (Deccan) Company have forwarded to the shareholders copies of a number of reports received from India showing the position and prospects of the Company. These reports have been put in as evidence before the Parliamentary Committee, and show that unforeseen difficulties have delayed the operations of the Company. Among the difficulties encountered are the non-completion of the railway to the coalfields until the commencement of the current year, whereas the chief engineer of the railway had estimated that it would have been open in April, 1887; delay on the part of the manufacturers in the supply of the machinery for the diamond washing and coal mines; and severe outbreaks of cholera, which have absolutely driven away all the labourers. The most favourable feature in the reports is the result of the gold prospecting in the Raichur Doab. The existence of 550 square miles of auriferous country has been already established, of which 130 have been proved to contain old workings, from the "dump" of which every sample has been found to contain gold.—*Financial Chronicle*, July 18.

A PORTION of the documentary evidence supplied to the House of Commons' Select Committee appointed to inquire into the Hyderabad-Deccan affair has just been issued to the shareholders in that company in the form of reports upon their property. These reports show clearly the enormous value in the concession granted to the company, and, following so closely upon the declaration made by counsel for the Nizam's Government, that "whatever the result of the Parliamentary inquiry might be, no attempt would be made to interfere in any way with the title of the company," they will considerably reassure the minds of the shareholders. There is probably no limited liability enterprise in existence which has been so bedraggled through the mud as the Hyderabad Deccan Company, and yet, in spite of the attack upon its genuineness, and the violent attempts made—even in Parliament—to bring about an invalidation of the contracts, the £10 shares have at no time been procurable at less than about £7 per share. Indeed, it would be surprising if it were otherwise, seeing that the prospecting rights of the company extend over a total area of 81,500 square miles of country abounding in mineral wealth. The sittings of the committee having now closed, the result of its deliberations is eagerly expected, but whatever this may be, it cannot alter or lessen the value of the company's property. It might be desirable to know, however, whether Mr. Labouchere, at whose instigation the inquiry was instituted, and who throughout has posed as the "advocate for the prosecution," will take any part in voting on the report.—*Whitehall Review*, July 19.

Hyderabad (Deccan) Company.—(To the Editor of the *Financial Times*.)—Sir,—The following are verbatim though fragmentary extracts from letters I have received from a relative who resides at Secunderabad, near Hyderabad. They may interest holders of shares and debentures in the two companies. The writer is not connected with either, but he is in a position to furnish most trustworthy information of the resources of the Deccan:—

"There is little coal in the north of India. Wood is used on the railways, or English coal imported through Kurrachee or Bombay. Wood is getting scarce and expensive, and coal, after a haul of many hundreds of miles to the north of India, is equally expensive or more so. Experiments have been made in connection with burning Beloochistan petroleum in the locomotive engines of the North-Western Railways, but with what result I cannot say. Mr. ———, locomotive superintendent, who made the experiment, is now in England. . . . We have good coal in many parts of India, but none in Scinde or the north or north-west. We have coal here, and very good coal too. The mines are now being worked by the Hyderabad (Deccan) Company, formed in England about a year or so ago. The Nizam's Government, I know, will not run the company or the concessionnaires hard, and the shares should certainly be worth par of £10 . . . . because if it be admitted, that the agreement giving the concession of the mining rights contained any defects or omissions, the result (1) of carelessness or imperfect supervision of the Government of India, or (2) with the Nizam's Government, or (3) sharp practice of Huk, the official representative of the Government of the Nizam in the matter, it is unlikely that the Government will allow innocent investors to suffer. The coal alone forms a most valuable property. This is real, and the coal to the extent of 1,000 tons a day can be sold at a good thumping profit. It is the only coal on this side of India, and bound to throw English coal, coming through Bombay, out of the market here. Gold and diamonds will come. Good reliable men are working at them, and they are sanguine of success. . . . The look-out in connection with the coal and gold is good. . . . I learn that the shares of the railway company have dropped quite £10. They are as good as gold, and might be bought as a spec. if any are for sale. The guarantee has to run for about 15 years, and the interest will be surely forthcoming all the time. The position of the railway company is not affected one way or the other by the mining company. There is not the slightest ground for the drop which has occurred in the railway shares or debentures."—Yours, etc., A. T.—London, July 19.—*Financial Times*, July 20.

The Hyderabad-Deccan Concession.—The report of the Select Committee has not yet been published, but it is expected within a few days, and meantime it is awaited with considerable interest. But the professional reports of engineers and mining experts which were put in as evidence before the Parliamentary Committee, have been printed in separate form for the benefit and reassurance of shareholders. These reports are full of conclusive evidence of the superabundant wealth of the district covered by the concession, and sustain the belief that after all the so-called scandals of the business, the company will eventually succeed in winning a rich harvest of profits. Through all the difficulties of the present crisis, the Nizam's Government stands firmly by the company, and at the last meeting of the Committee, counsel on behalf of that Government distinctly stated that there would be no interference with the company in any way, but that the Government would support the directors and do all in its power to promote the welfare of the enterprise. From the first, considerable expectations have been formed of the Singareni coalfields. One of the main objects, indeed, of the concession was the development of these coalfields and the distribution of the coal throughout a large portion of the Madras Presidency, and also through a part of the Bombay Presidency. This object has been steadily kept in view, and a great deal of preliminary work has been accomplished, the further progress of the work confirming the abundance and superior quality of the coal, and furnishing proofs of the manner in which it will be appreciated in India. The calculation is of an output of 400,000 tons per annum, or a little more than 1,000 tons per diem; and it is estimated that a net profit of 2s. per ton will be realised. This will yield £40,000—no insignificant sum as the backbone of the enterprise. Mr. T. H. W. Hughes, Deputy-Superintendent of the Geological Survey of India, has made surveys on behalf of the Company, and has shown what may be done by inexpensive machinery. It appears, with shafts at work on the first seam at depths of 47 feet, 100 feet, and 67 feet respectively, that between 200 tons and 300 tons per day might be obtained from each shaft before the close of the present year. That would be a very substantial approach to the estimate of a diurnal output of 1,000 tons. The works at these shafts are now being pushed on with energy.

The Singareni Coalfields are, however, not the only coal measures in the Nizam's dominion which have been made over to the concessionaires, but Singareni is situated contiguous to the line of railway which is now under construction between the capital city of Hyderabad and the head waters of the canal system of the great river Kistna, and which will soon connect the ports of Coconada and Masulipatam with the great railway systems of India. It is, therefore, desirable first to develop the Singareni fields before extending the operations of coal winning in places more difficult of access. The railway surveys show that within a single year railway communication can be completed up to Singareni. Even now a sale of 200,000 tons of coal per annum—half of the full estimated output—is assured by the Railway Companies, who are eagerly waiting for the time when the coal shall be in the market and ready for delivery. Apart from the supply of the railways a large demand for private use is springing up, for the wood fuel to which the natives have been accustomed is becoming exhausted in some places, and the price is growing very high. The potentialities of the trade in coal winning are immense, and active operations will be quite enough to save it from disaster.

The existence of gold has been reported, and it is stated the ore has been discovered in a position which seems to imply that the Mysore Reef extends into the Hyderabad territory. The remarkable evidence of old workings strengthens this belief; but no investigations have yet been carried on by the present concessionnaires. The attention of Mr. Hughes was early directed to the gold-bearing strata in the Raichur Doab. That is the country between the Kistna and Toongbhoodra rivers, in the South-Western portion of the Nizam's territories, not far to the west of the Great Indian Peninsular Railway. As a geologist, he held the opinion that the Mysore Reefs were continued into this tract, and the researches of the prospecting staffs have amply confirmed this view. The report of Mr. J. H. Stevenson, dated in April last, also shows that the existence of three bands of gold-bearing rocks has been established, covering respectively areas of 200, 70, and 280 square miles, or a total of 550 square miles. Of this area 130 square miles have been proved to be auriferous and riddled with ancient workings, which everywhere in the world are held to be the best evidence of the existence of gold in paying quantities, and which the primitive methods of the ancients were incapable of exhausting, whilst all the samples of "dump" taken from the old workings have proved to contain gold. Mr. Stephenson points out that there are two other tracts, one to the north of the Bheema River and the other further east of Lingasagur towards the line of railway, which have not yet been examined, and which are worthy of serious attention. A small portable plant of three sets of stamps, with engines and boilers, has been ordered for the prospecting work, and twenty tons of quartz are shortly expected to arrive in England to be crushed and tested.

The reports furnish no statistical information respecting the diamond mines on the property, but it is affirmed that probably the most valuable part of the concession is the right to mine for diamonds in what is called the old Golconda Fields. This industry at one time engaged 60,000 persons, and was the source of great wealth to the rulers of the State of Golconda; but for two centuries at least no extensive operations have been carried on. The industry has, in fact, been practically abandoned, and at present the workers confine their investigations and labours to turning over the old *débris*, out of which they obtain a very small return, but get sufficient to encourage their researches. This modern experience shows that the natives who originally sought for diamonds in this historic region discarded all the smaller stones, because of the richer ones which were at that time in the mine. Now, however, powerful machinery of the modern type has been sent out, and diamond mining will henceforth be carried on under conditions of which the old workers never dreamt. The result of the spirited operations that are contemplated and are being actively prepared will restore the ancient renown of Golconda, and enrich the shareholders of the Company. According to Mr. T. H. Lowinsky, a diamond-mining expert, who, on behalf of the Company commenced his examination of the old workings in December, 1886, there is every prospect of finding diamonds in the areas upon which operations have been begun by going to lower depths than the natives uncovered for their washings in the past, and by excavating and washing the untouched diamondiferous earth between and around the old workings. The decay of the native industry in diamond mining is thus described by Mr. T. H. Lowinsky:—"As the natives never excavate virgin ground, I am of opinion that they have gone on washing the same *débris* from generation to generation. If that be correct, the ground in its virgin state must have been very rich indeed. It is hardly necessary to ask why the natives do not excavate the virgin ground; their laziness and want of energy are past all belief. I have questioned thoroughly all the natives in the district, as to the reasons of the works being stopped. The idea of the mines being worked out they think is absurd. They say that when the largest pit (No. 1) was worked a great depth, and they had gone below large rocks, the water burst into the pit, and a large number of men were drowned. Since that time the pit has never been clear of water; besides which they had no inclination to go into such risky work. This may be the reason the work has been stopped in the deeper pits, but it would not explain the cause for no work having been carried on in very shallow pits. From information gathered in the district, I think work was stopped in the shallow pit through the oppression of the rulers. Not only was every diamond over 10 carats to be the absolute property of the Nizam, but licenses had to be paid to the Crown by every man that worked, washed, dealt in, valued or sold diamonds. Many of the pits in Krishna and other districts were worked up to about eighty years ago, but since that time I can find no trace whatever of work having been done. It was about the same period that the Nizam then on the throne was severely defeated, and the whole of the country thrown into a state of chaos, and industry of every kind brought to a standstill."

The Company's staff has not yet found time for directing its attention to the copper, lead, and other valuable minerals, which it is reasonably expected occur in paying quantities in the ground covered by the concession. Among minor products—if we may call them minor—talc has been discovered, and will certainly be valuable. Garnets in large quantities are found, but whether or not their exportation would yield a good return on capital is up to the present time uncertain. The whole enterprise is full of great possibilities, and notwithstanding all the diligent attempts which have lately been made to prejudice the Company, it still holds a firm hold on the favour of investors. As the vastness of the mineral wealth of the districts in question becomes better known, and as it is now abundantly clear that the Government of the Nizam will stand by the concessionnaires, investors at home begin again to rally round the undertaking. It is a significant fact that the £10 shares, at one time driven down to less than 5, have after many fluctuations rallied, and are now firm at 6¾, though this is not the highest quotation of the week. The publication of the report brought the price at one time to 7 and upwards.—*Bullionist*, July 21.

PUBLIC interest in what has become known in certain quarters as the "Hyderabad-Deccan Scandal" is likely to be revived by the report that will shortly be presented by Mr. Labouchere's Select Committee of the House of Commons, now that the functions of the latter have practically ceased. The inquiry, which has been of an exhaustive character, will hardly be fruitful of the results anticipated; for the bulk of the evidence submitted went to show that the concessionnaires simply followed the usual practice in such cases by attempting to make a profit out of the transaction. Persons who risk large sums expect to realise proportionately large profits, and it is simply absurd to contend that because Mr. Watson and his colleagues sold the concession made to them at what they considered a fair market value they committed any breach of faith with the public, who should by this time perfectly understand such transactions. Both the concessionnaires and the company will possibly be absolved from all serious blame by the Committee, even though Mr. Labouchere should exercise the right of voting on the report.—*Admiralty and Horse Guards Gazette*, July 21.

THE HYDERABAD-DECCAN CONCESSION.—(To the Editor of the *Financial News.*)—Sir, In the voluminous report just circulated among the shareholders of this hitherto unfortunate undertaking, although the despatches received from agents and surveyors are reproduced with laudable prolixity, I have looked in vain for any intimation from the directors as to their views or anticipations regarding the actual position of the Company.

Of course, we shall be told that any such expression of opinion on their part would be premature and uncertain while the verdict of the Parliamentary Committee is yet in embryo; for which reason, it appears to me, the aforesaid budget of agents' reports might have been withheld a little longer for the purpose of adding some actual value to it.

However, it is to be hoped that so soon as the pending inquiry is completed the board will not only favour the shareholders with a clear and explicit statement of the position of the company, but also of the steps which they intend to take for the recovery of the 85,000 shares which have been so generously disposed of. The Nizam has set a good example in the way of recovering plunder; let the directors emulate it.—I am, Sir, yours, &c., A SHAREHOLDER.—*Financial News*, July 21.

IN another column we have referred at some length to the official reports recently published by the Hyderabad (Deccan) Company, which reports abundantly prove the superabundant resources of the large area conceded to the Company. The report of the Select Committee is now daily expected, and, though we do not expect from it much of practical value, yet it would be well to await its issue before the discussion of any plans for the future operations of the Company. It has been suggested by a contemporary that the nominal amount of the capital should be reduced, or that the promoters should find a further sum for working capital. The former of these proposals seems to us to be absurd and impracticable, and, as for the second, the promoters have already found £150,000, and they probably do not feel themselves under temptation or in a condition to find again an equal—or it may be a larger—sum. However, in the absence of the Select Committee's report, it does not seem profitable to discuss any proposition for reconstruction. Probably the report will bring out the fact that Abdul Huk has all along been the evil genius of the business, and that whatever of evil has been in it from the beginning to the end is traceable to his insatiable rapacity. This is the fact that the public has apprehended from the beginning, and this apprehension explains the general indifference. At no time were the wire-pullers of this sensational incident able to work up the public mind to any serious interest in the miserable squabble.—*Bullionist*, July 23.

The directors of the Hyderabad (Deccan) Company (Limited) request us to publish the subjoined summary of a number of reports which they have issued to the shareholders. Among the unforeseen difficulties which have delayed the operations of the Company they mention the following:—

"1. The non-completion of the railway to the coalfields until the commencement of the current year, whereas the chief engineer of the railway had estimated that it would have been open in April, 1887. 2. Delay on the part of the manufacturers in the supply of the machinery for the diamond washing and coal mines. 3. Severe outbreaks of cholera, which had absolutely driven away all the labourers. Now that these difficulties are disappearing the monsoon has set in, which must tend to check work for the next two or three months.

"The most favourable feature in the reports is the result of the gold prospecting in the Raichar Doab. The existence of 550 square miles of auriferous country has been already established, of which 130 have been proved to contain old workings, from the 'dump' of which every sample has been found to contain gold. In addition to the above-mentioned reports, and based on them, is one from Messrs. T. and W. Morgans, of Bristol and London, who, on a comparison with the present market value of the Kolar gold properties in Mysore, and making full allowance for capital spent and work done there, arrive at the estimate of £1,080,000 as the value of the Company's gold discoveries so far as they have gone. As to the Singareni coalfield, they point out that its value depends on the demand, the available supply being ample—viz., 94 millions of tons. Estimating the profits at the low figure of 2s. per ton, a sale of 400,000 tons annually would produce £40,000 net profit. Of this quantity nearly one-half is practically assured for railways alone, according to the calculations of the Government of India. Messrs. Morgans believe that a very profitable business can be carried on by the establishment of suitable ironworks at Singareni. Until diamonds are actually found, of which Messrs. Morgans believe there is every prospect, it is impossible to make any estimate of the diamondiferous portion of the Company's property."—*Times*, July 23.

The Hyderabad Mining Scandal.—The feature of the week has been the strange disclosures concerning the Hyderabad Deccan Company. This company was started in January, 1886, with a capital of £1,000,000, the whole of which was represented to have been subscribed and fully paid. Its object was to work a concession which had been practically given away by the Nizam, and in this very company, formed to exploit the minerals in his own territory, the Nizam is reported to have invested £125,000. It seems odd that the Nizam should not have spent his money in mining for his own benefit; but he seems to be of a very generous nature, and preferred to give away the right to dig for coal, gold, and what not, to an English Company. The concession was introduced to London by one Abdul Huk, whose sudden disgrace during the last few days have brought the whole matter prominently to light. The concessionnaires, one of whom was a Mr. W. C. Watson, who is a director of the company, started the undertaking with a modest capital of £1,000,000, keeping £850,000 in shares for themselves. So far so good!

Obviously, however, shares, however pretty they may look on paper, are not much good unless they can be turned into cash. The next thing to do, therefore, was to make a market for them. Mr. William Morris, of the Stock Exchange, was called in. It soon began to be rumoured that "Deccans" were the things to buy, certain to go to 20. About July, 1886, the City writer in *Vanity Fair* took them up, and reference to the back numbers of that journal will prove instructive if unpleasant reading to those who unluckily followed the tip. The shares, which are £10 each, went to 13 or 14, and as there was but one tap to supply them, they could be fed out quietly without any fear of a big block being suddenly forced on the market. When the bag was sufficiently emptied the excitement quickly died out, and the concessionnaires or promoters, or whatever they may like to call themselves, had realised an enormous profit. It does not seem to be known so far what Abdul Huk received as his share of the transaction, but out of 85,000 £10 shares, many of which were worked off at a premium, there would be no difficulty in making that gentleman a handsome present. The whole point of the thing is that the company was practically and is now one with, I believe, only £25,000 of real capital, which the promoters found to start it.

The money paid by the public for shares has gone into the promoters' pockets, not into the company's treasury. The company, in short, seems to be on a par with the Standard Electric Light Company, now in liquidation. In the latter concern the capital was about £90,000, "agreed to be considered fully paid." But there was no capital in the company. It was financed by Mr. Hugh A. Fergusson, who held some £80,000 in shares, which he sold as a favour to those who liked to buy them. One fine day Mr. Fergusson got tired of running his company, and it came to an end; but in the meantime his holding of shares had become reduced to £40,000 instead of £80,000 nominally. Now, although the Deccan Company has been going for two years, there has been no dividend as yet, and the question for the shareholders to discover is what actual funds the company has in hand with which to carry on the work in India. For there is no doubt that there are very rich coalfields in the Nizam's territory if nothing else. It is not the balance-sheet of profit and loss, but the capital account which requires to be looked into. Was there ever any more than £25,000 in cash at the company's disposal? And if not, how much of that sum remains now? This is an important matter for the shareholders to discover, quite apart from the other question whether their concession can be cancelled or not. I do not see myself how any fraud between Abdul Huk and the Nizam can invalidate a concession once granted by the Nizam's Government. But in the light of the circumstances under under which it was brought before the public, a searching investigation by the India Office might result in a very unpleasant state of things for the shareholders. A strong committee should at once be formed of shareholders to look into their affairs, and possibly they may find that they can obtain some redress from the original promoters, one of whom, by the way, is a brother of the *Vanity Fair* city scribe.—*Topical Times*, April 2.

In the old days of Lord Clive and the Honourable East India Company, the peninsula of Hindustan was understood to afford adventurers a fine field for *loot*; but in the year of grace, 1888, it would have been supposed that this once fertile field for plunder had been about worked out. This, however, does not appear to be the case, if the facts regarding the Hyderabad-Deccan Company are as stated in the columns of a contemporary. It has been believed for some time that this district contained various and valuable mineral resources, and it was represented to the Nizam that it would be desirable to attract English capital for their development. Accordingly, in 1885 a concession was given to Messrs. Watson and Stewart on the following terms: The concessionnaires to form a company with a capital of not less than one million pounds sterling to acquire the rights of the concessionnaires, who were bound to issue shares to the amount of £100,000, with £25,000 absolutely paid up by January 1, 1886. It is, moreover, stated that a further issue of shares is contemplated when circumstances require it. Messrs. Watson and Stewart, the concessionnaires, proceed to fulfil their bargain in the following manner: The company is brought out in July, 1886, and not only the £150,000 necessary for working the coal mines of Singareni, but the whole amount of one million sterling is issued, the above-named gentleman pocketing 85,000 shares of £10 each, which are described as fully paid, or, in plain figures, the sum of £850,000, thus realising on paper a colossal fortune, to which they do not appear to have had one shadow of right. Having succeeded in getting themselves this paper, the next part of the plan was to endeavour to turn it into hard cash, which, unless the paper be Bank of England notes, is always far more preferable. After casting about in various directions how best to accomplish this, and apparently not hitting on any other method of bringing the public in, they conceived the scheme, worthy of the palmiest days of financial enterprise, the South Sea Bubble, Law's Bank, or even the Emma Mine—to wit, by inducing the unfortunate Nizam to buy for golden British sovereigns his own shares in the concession he had granted. To accomplish this puppets were necessary, and these appear to have been found in the persons of Abdul Huk, since transformed into the Sirdar Diler-ul-Mulk, the British Resident, and the Nizam's secretary. The native worthy, who represented the Government of the Nizam at last year's Jubilee, appears to have succeeded in convincing the Sovereign of the Hyderabad State and his advisers that this would be a grand stroke of business. He obtained, therefore, authority to go to the extent of £120,000 sterling in the purchase of shares at a maximum price of £12. Accordingly, eight brokers were sent to the London Stock Exchange to compete for the concessionnaire's shares by the concessionnaire himself, and the following telegram was despatched to India:—

"Deccans firmly held by public, therefore with greatest difficulty succeeded purchasing 8,750 full paid shares at 12, 3,750 half paid *pro rata* at 7, thus by chance securing 2,500 shares more at cost £11,250, and contingent liability £18,750 in excess sanctioned amount £120,000. Market closes 12¾. Government shares now worth £9,000 more than paid.—Sirdar Diler-ul-Mulk."

The ingenious inventors of this scheme also most probably succeeded in selling a further number of shares to the British public; but, until we have inspected the register, which we propose to do next week, we cannot give precise information on the point. It is not surprising that when these facts became known there should be a heavy fall in the shares, and that the intelligent Hindoo who acted as mediator in the affair should be dismissed. The annals of company promoting contain some curiously strange histories, but we doubt if one more cunning in its construction and daring in its execution has ever been perpetrated. The unfortunate ruler of Hyderabad has parted with his concession for a term of ninety-nine years, and has presented no less a sum than £75,000 to the obliging concessionnaires into the bargain.

This is spoiling the Egyptians with a vengeance, and the matter will doubtless not be allowed to rest here. It is the duty of the Government at home to protect the interest of its dependencies. The concluding chapter and the retributive justice which we trust will overtake the guilty has yet to be written.

During the past week there has been but little speculative business on the Stock Exchange, though investments have still continued. Operators are for the moment holding aloof from the markets owing to the uncertainty of the political situation. The movement in prices in all departments has, however, been trifling, with the exception of a sensational movement in the shares of the Hyderabad-Deccan Company, to which we have referred above.—*Sunday Times*, April 2.

When the announcement was made of the Nizam's offer to the Government of India, a warning was given in the *Evening Dispatch* that some mystery lay at the bottom of it. The circumstances of the Hyderabad State and the intrigues formerly carried on by its rulers both in India and England, suggested that some sinister motive was responsible for such an extraordinary act of generosity. This seems to be now confirmed by the strange statement published prominently in the *St. James' Gazette* last night.

"Barker's Trade and Finance," April 25.—Many shareholders in the Hyderabad Deccan must be anxiously awaiting the result of what the *Times* has hinted at, namely, whether the entire promotion of the company has been a dishonest piece of finance. In an article which appeared in our issue of March the 28th, some rather crucial and, perhaps, uncomfortable questions were asked which the company did not deem necessary to answer.

Leaving alone all about the Nizam having been induced to purchase 10,000 shares at £2 premium, and whether he has been swindled or not, I should like to hear some of the questions answered about the coal. By October or November last year the company hoped, or expected, to be raising 1,000 tons of coal per diem. Are they doing this even now?

Are they raising 100 tons of coal a day? Again, why is Mr. Theodore W. Hughes-Hughes, Deputy Superintendent of the Geological Survey of the Government of India, silent? He estimated that the Singareni Coalfield contained 94,000,000 tons of good steam coal lying within 300 feet of the surface, after allowing 40 per cent. for waste. Could Mr. Hughes have been bribed by the promoters into making this estimate?

The entire change in the Company's affairs has rather fallen as a bombshell upon the public. "The ominous point about these shares is that a twelve months' patience has not improved their value . . . . if one-tenth of what has been said or inferred officially proves correct, then no fear need cross anyone's mind. Should anyone buy shares at the present price? Wait and see." It is to be hoped our readers did wait and see.

The above sentences are quoted from our article of the 28th March upon the Hyderabad Deccan Company—a company which to-day occupies considerably more attention than it did three weeks ago. It is sincerely to be hoped that the company will be able to clear itself of the charges brought against it by the *Times* and *Financial News*.—*Edinburgh Evening Despatch*, April 19.

And has it come to this? A few short months ago we were slapping ourselves on the back, and drinking our own health, on the strength of a "spontaneous" offer by the Nizam of Hyderabad to contribute sixty lakhs of rupees towards the defence of the North-West Frontier. Nay, we were so pleased by the conduct that we stood our friend Dangle a small cold gin; and now it seems the Nizam's spontaneous offer was promoted by his wicked Minister, the Sirdar Abdul Huk, who went home from England, where he had been doing the Jubileeries and told the Nizam that an English Cabinet Minister thought it would be good business for him to make such a spontaneous offer, and that the Minister would see that the offer should not be accepted. And now the whole thing is blown, and Mr. Abdul Huk is under arrest, and the loyal natives will swear, and the Russians will smile, and we shall be the sport of kings—of nasty foreign kings who love us not. Indeed, the world is full of guile, and we are sore distressed about this thing. Abdul Huk will no doubt be punished, and the Nizam has got his sixty lakhs safe under lock and key —but that cold gin is gone for ever. *Sic transit gloria mundi.—Sunday Chronicle*, April 22.

THE arrest of Abdul Huk, one of the leading officials in the State of Hyderabad, has caused much talk among Anglo-Indians here, for, from very various reasons, the Sirdar Diler Jung, as he is otherwise entitled. is well known to many of them. A friend of mine, who knows Hyderabad well, tells me that Abdul Huk, who was educated by the missionaries, and who is an exceedingly plausible personage, was the principle instrument in tempting Sir John Gorst four years ago (when, of course, the latter was out of office) to support the claim of the Peshcar or Deputy Minister of Hyderabad, to be made Chief Minister upon the death of Sir Salar Jung; Sir John being paid 50,000 rupees for his unsuccessful endeavour, which mainly consisted in drafting the claim in question. It was through this Peshcar that Abdu Huk, who was originally a police officer, had had a rapid rise in Hyderabad, land he was so trusted that he was allowed a sum of £80,000, in recognition of his success during a visit to England in financing a loan for the Nizam's State Railway. But a fall at Indian Courts is usually as rapid as the rise, and this fact Abdul Huk has now discovered for himself.—*London Correspondent of the Liverpool Echo*, April 20.

I UNDERSTAND that we are likely to have another Hyderabad scandal shortly, in which the names of two or three British officers are concerned—not quite of the magnitude of the Abdul Huk affair, but it is said to be an exceedingly bad business indeed; and from what I hear the Nizam's treasury will ultimately suffer to the extent of 50,000 rupees. It almost looks as if nothing would set things right in that State but a general clearance of all the British officials connected with the Nizam.—*Manchester Guardian*, July 21.

THE HYDERABAD DECCAN COMPANY, LIMITED.—Few joint-stock companies have had to undergo an ordeal equal to that to which the Hyderabad (Deccan) Company has been subjected. All sorts of charges have been bandied about, and the concern has been "sat upon" by Parliamentary action, and in every other kind of way. For obvious reasons, it is not our intention upon the present occasion to deal with the Parliamentary inquiry, which may be regarded as in some sense still pending, nor with any of the charges which have been made respecting the terms of the concession or the subsequent dealings with it. As financial journalists, and analysers of investments, the position from which we propose to start is just this:—Here is an English joint-stock company, comprising a large body of shareholders, and there—in India—is a property the value of which it behoves us to ascertain, the more especially as, in spite of all that has been said respecting this much-debated matter, the validity of the concession is not called into question.

Starting, then, from these premisses, we find, as the result of all the information procurable, that the concession is a most important one, and that the Company's property is of enormous intrinsic value and pregnant with huge possibilities. The information previously available on the subject has now been supplemented by a well-timed Memorandum, or pamphlet, which has just been issued "for the information of the Shareholders" by order of the Board of Directors.

The attention of the Company is at present directed chiefly to three branches of enterprise, the success of any one of which may render the future of the concern, in spite of its early troubles, one of exceptional prosperity. Those three branches are Coal, Diamonds and other precious stones, and Gold. Let us see what has been done in regard to each of these three divisions of work.

The misfortune is that, in regard to each one of them, the Company's operations were greatly crippled at a critical time by an outbreak of cholera. As to the value of the coal-fields, which are of immense extent, abundant evidence of the most authoritative character is forthcoming. For the coal fields and general prospecting, the services of T. W. H. Hughes, Deputy-Superintendent of the Geological Survey of the Government of India, were lent by that Government to the Company, and he arrived at Singareni in the middle of January, 1887. His report on the coal field, dated the 4th March, showing an available supply of 94 million tons, was furnished to the Shareholders on the 2nd May 1887. On the 21st of that month the Board urged on Mr. Furnivall, by telegram, to sink enough pits and order machinery insuring a coal output of 1,000 tons daily as soon as possible. Mr. Winter, a Director of the Company, had proceeded to India at the end of January, 1887, and, in consultation with the officers of the Company, arranged for future operations at Singareni. His Report was presented in an abridged form to the shareholders at the general meeting of the 27th July, 1887. Mr. Hughes came to England with Mr. Lowinski in July, 1887, and visited several collieries to to make himself acquainted with the most recent and improved methods of working. He engaged the necessary mining and prospecting staff, and returned to India in November, leaving in the hands of the Board a memorandum explaining the method he intended to adopt in working the Singareni coal, and the specifications of plant he would require. The Board at once set to work to supply his requirements, but here again, delay occurred in the supply of the machinery ordered. The Railway which had been expected to reach the coalfields in April 1887, was not opened for traffic until the 1st January, 1888, and, worst of all, cholera appeared in April, 1888. Owing to these causes, the underground roads and galleries made slow progress, and it was therefore impossible to open out enough working faces for a large output. A telegram of the 22nd June last states that about 60 tons a day are now being raised. This will increase as labour becomes available.

Here, then, is evidence of the existence of an amount of coal estimated at 94,000,000 of tons. Everybody knows how greatly coal is wanted in India, especially now that the railway system is being so rapidly extended. But everybody knows likewise that a good deal of time is required for the development and opening out of coal mines. In a recent letter Mr. Furnivall, the agent, writes:

"The coal is undoubtedly there, and as investigations proceed its superior quality to other coal on this side of India becomes more and more apparent and the extent of the field develops rather than diminishes. We shall succeed eventually, though real difficulties beset and are besetting those who have striven and are still striving to accomplish the wish of the Directors to raise 1,000 tons a day. I do not fear for results at the coal fields, but I cannot predict how long it will take to raise and sell the quantity named by the directors."

Next, as regards Diamond Mining. Here also there is reason to believe in the existence of great wealth. Mr. T. H. Lowinsky, a diamond mining expert, was engaged by this company, and commenced his examination of the old diamond workings in the beginning of December, 1886. An epitome of his report, dated 12th January, 1887, was circulated to the shareholders on the 18th February, 1887. Mr. Lowinsky was provided with machinery and requisites for proving and testing the diamondiferous earth and worked continuously for five months, until the monsoon in the middle of June, 1887, caused the sides of his excavations to fall in. From the experience gained in these experimental workings Mr. Lowinsky decided that more powerful machinery was required, and he arrived in England to confer with the Board on the subject of his future operations, and to get the machinery and engage the necessary staff. Orders for the machinery were placed with Messrs. Davey, Paxman, & Co., on the 9th August, 1887. Considerable delay occurred in the supply of this machinery, and it was not until the 16th November that the first instalment was sent out to India, and this did not reach the diamond field until February, 1888. The final shipment of machinery from England was not made until the 4th February, 1888. These delays involved the loss of more than half the working season. Cholera broke out in the camp on the 10th February, just as Mr. Lowinsky had collected 800 labourers, and he was unable to use his machines, which he had erected and put into complete working order, "as not a man would remain on the ground." At the beginning of May, the disease having abated, Mr. Lowinsky was able again to get together a body of labourers. The following telegram was received on the 22nd June from Mr. Furnivall:—"Visited Partyall, 9th June; excavation then 5 feet over diamond layer. Six hundred labourers. Lowinsky hoped begin washing about end of June."

We come now to the third branch of the Company's operations, namely, Gold. The attention of Mr. Hughes, it appears, had been early directed to the gold-bearing strata in the Raichur Doab, that is, the country between the Kistna and the Toongbhoodra Rivers, in the south-western portion of the Nizam's territories, not far to the west of the Great Indian Peninsula Railway. As a geologist, he held the opinion that the Mysore Reefs were continued into this tract, and rumours existed of old workings. The researches of the prospecting staff, we are assured, have amply confirmed this view. The Board asks particular attention to Mr. J. H. Stephenson's Report of April 27th, 1888. This shows that the existence of three bands of gold-bearing rock has been established, covering respectively areas of 200, 70, and 280 square miles, or a total of 550 square miles. Of this area, 130 square miles have been proved to be auriferous and riddled with ancient workings, which everywhere in the world are held to be the best evidence of the existence of gold in paying quantities which the primitive methods of the ancients were incapable of exhausting. All the samples of "dump" taken from the old workings have been proved to contain gold. Mr. Stephenson points out that there are two other tracts, one to the north of the Bheema River, and the other further east of Lingasagur towards the line of railway, which have not yet been examined, and are worthy of serious attention. A small portable plant of three sets of stamps, with engines and boilers, has been ordered for the prospecting work, and twenty tons of quartz are shortly expected to arrive in England to be crushed and tested.

Now, we ask our readers to endeavour to gauge the possibilities connected with the established existence of an auriferous area extending over no less than 550 square miles, of which, moreover, 130 square miles have been proved to be gold-bearing, and "riddled with ancient workings." We think the Directors are justified in asserting, as they assert in this Memorandum, that "no efforts have been spared to make the Company's enterprise commercially successful." It is added: "The Directors have necessarily been dependent on the reports received from India, and, although experience has shown that their expectations founded on those reports have not been fulfilled so quickly as was anticipated, and that unexpected difficulties have sprung up over which they had no control, they believe that the value of the Company's property has been satisfactorily proved."

It is further announced that, supplementing the reports from India submitted to the Parliamentary Committee, the Board has obtained from the well-known firm of Messrs. Thomas and William Morgans, of London and Bristol, a report expressing their opinion as to the demonstrated value of portions of the Company's property. This Report is so important that we reproduce it in full:—

"During the past year the Company's exploratory operations in Hyderabad have borne the fruit of gold discoveries which appear to us to be of great value and importance.

"We hope to be able to show that, added to what was previously known of the mineral resources of His Highness the Nizam's dominions, the discoveries referred to demonstrate the abundance of the mineral wealth which is at the disposal of the Company.

"The facts upon which our judgment is based are testified to in various reports, and surveys received by the Board from time to time from the Company's staff in India, which includes authorities of high standing.

"The gold discoveries referred to are delineated and described on a map forwarded, and in an exhaustive report addressed to Theo. W. Hughes Hughes, Esq., the company's general superintendent, by the prospecting superintendent, Mr. Stephenson.

"In a letter dated 1st May last, addressed to the Company's secretary, Mr. Hughes sums up the extent of the discoveries to that date in the following pregnant words: 'There are 550 square miles of auriferous rocks, of which 300 square miles are proved to be gold-bearing (the remaining area has to be proved) and 130 square miles have the evidence of extensive old workings to show that they are valuable.' We attach great weight to this passage, coming, as it does, from an eminent mining geologist, and a superintendent of the Government Geological Survey of India.

"Gold mining has proved in Mysore, as is well known to mining engineers and to others, that success is to be found through bottoming the shallow mines of the ancients whose drainage appliances were too primitive to enable them to follow the gold in depth; and if gold-mining experience in India has up to the present established one useful fact more than another, it is that the existence of old workings in gold-bearing reefs is the real criterion of value.

"The best way of getting an idea of the value of the 130 square miles of gold bearing rocks (already proved by the presence of old workings to have been mined on the outcrops and shown thereby to be commercially valuable), is to apply the standard of value of a gold-bearing property of similar character, such, for instance, as occurs in the Kolar (Mysore) district in India.

"The total area of the Kolar concession is about twenty square miles, and the present market value of the mining properties established on that concession amounts to a total sum of about £960,000.

"Allowing two-thirds of this sum as being capital in part expended in opening and equipping the mines, and in part as floating capital and capital held in reserve, the remaining one-third, or £320,000, represents the market value of the twenty square miles, in round numbers, of Kolar auriferous rocks. That is equal to an average of about £25 per acre, or £16,000 per square mile. At that rate the 130 square miles already discovered by this Company would be worth £2,080,000.

"But the subdivided areas of the Kolar concession have been sub-let to subsidiary companies by the Kolar concessionnaires, who received premiums in return, whereas the sub-letting of the blocks of the Company's discoveries will involve negotiations, labour and expenditure, and it will be necessary before the whole of the discoveries can be utilised to secure the extension of railway communication up to the gold reefs. If the very ample allowance of £1,000,000 be set aside for these outgoings, then the company's gold discoveries would still be worth £,1,080,000, according to the standard of the present market value of the properties on the Kolar concession including those at a discount as well as those at a premium.

"Considering the early stage of the operations as they stand at present, it is impossible to deal with exact figures of value, but the foregoing comparative statement is useful, as an indication of the great potential value of the extensive areas of gold-bearing rocks of the discovery of which you have been advised.

"With regard to coal, the quantity already proved to be available at Singareni, after allowing for waste and loss in working, may be safely taken to be ninety-four millions of tons, as computed by Mr. Hughes in his report of March 4, 1887.

"Mr. W. C. Furnivall, whose position as an engineer entitles him to speak with authority, says, in a communication dated March 7, 1888, to the secretary, with reference to the Singareni coal, 'Its superior quality to other kinds of coal on this side of India becomes more and more apparent, and the extent of the field develops rather than diminishes.'

"The value of this coal is largely dependent on the quantities which the markets will absorb. Works are at present being carried out at the colliery for an output of 150,000 tons per annum.

"Remembering the commanding position of the Singareni fields for the markets of Southern India, and that it has been shown by a critical examination of Indian coal traffic in a memorandum drawn up in 1884 by the Public Works Department of the Government of India that the coal mining of Singareni will begin with the advantage of assured markets for at least 183,000 tons of coal per annum, we consider it not unreasonable to assume that markets will be found without difficulty three or four years hence for 300,000 tons per annum.

"This quantity could be supplied by a moderate addition to the capital already provided for the colliery plant and works.

"After careful investigation of the facts at our disposal we are of opinion that the Singareni coal can be worked at a profit of 1 rupee 10 annas, or, say in round numbers, 2s. per ton. This would give a yearly profit of £30,000 on an output and sale of 300,000 tons of coal per annum. On a yearly output and sale of 400,000 tons the profit would be £40,000 per annum. Larger profits would be certain to be derived, provided increased markets could be obtained —which eventuality is by no means improbable. On a yearly output and sale of half a million tons the profit would be £50,000 per annum, and at that rate it would take 18 ι years to exhaust the coal already proved to be available at Singareni.

"Regarding iron making, it is well known to engineers and others who have studied the iron resources of India, that some of the iron ore deposits in the Deccan are exceptionally good. If properly worked, these ores must be extremely valuable. The failures hitherto experienced in iron making in India have to our knowledge been due in the main either to unsuitable fluxing, ill-designed or over-driven furnaces, or break-downs of novel machinery and plant. We have no hesitation in saying (based upon the reports as to its ores and limestones, and the quality of the coal) that if proper furnaces and plant be erected at Singareni, a very profitable business in iron manufacture can be carried on there, and the iron ores will acquire great value.

"Coming to the diamonds, it is impossible for anyone who has taken the trouble to inform himself on the subject to doubt for one moment the existence of diamondiferous areas in your company's concession, and according to the report received by the board from Mr. Lowinsky, there is every prospect of finding diamonds in the areas upon which the operations have been begun, by going to lower depths than the natives uncovered for their washings in the past, and by excavating and washing the untouched diamondiferous earth between and around the old workings.

"The explorations of the diamondiferous tracts have, however, not yet arrived at that state of certainty which admits of forming, as in the case of the gold and coal, any distinct idea respecting their value.

"The Company's staff has not yet found time for directing its attention to the copper, lead, and other valuable minerals which are reasonably expected to occur in paying quantities in the concession.

"Enough, however, has been said herein to show that there will be no lack of mineral resources to insure a prosperous career for the company.—We remain, &c., (Signed) "THOS. and WM. MORGANS.

"The Guildhall, Bristol; and Coleman-street, London, July 9, 1888."

It will be seen that, as regards gold, proceeding upon the value at present placed upon the Kolar concessions, Messrs. Morgans estimate the value of the Hyderabad (Deccan) Company's auriferous tract already discovered at upwards of £2,000,000. As regards coal, it is pointed out that the Company "will begin with the advantage of assured markets for at least 183,000 tons of coal per annum," and that three or four years hence markets will, it is estimated, be found without difficulty for 300,000 tons per annum—a quantity which "could be supplied by a moderate addition to the capital already provided for the colliery, plant, and works." Assuming an annual output of half a million of tons, entailing a probable profit of £50,000 per annum, Messrs. Morgans say "at that rate it would take 180 years to exhaust the coal already proved to be available at Singareni."

Without going into the further question of the development of the deposits of iron, copper, lead, and other minerals, we say that ample evidence has been adduced to justify the Shareholders in holding a very hopeful view of the ultimate future of the Company, and in retaining, moreover, a very tight hold upon their property.—*Money Market Review*, July 21.

THE draft report of the Hyderabad Deccan Committee is circulated among members on behalf of the Chairman, Sir Henry James. It is, however, no secret that it was drawn up by Mr. Robertson, the Solicitor-General for Scotland. Among an influential section of the committee having special knowledge of Indian affairs the report meets with little favour. Crucial amendments will be moved at the forthcoming meeting of the Committee.—*Observer*, July 22.

THE HYDERABAD DECCAN COMMITTEE.—It is understood that at the next meeting of the Hyderabad Deccan Committee a draft report will be submitted by the Solicitor-General for Scotland in which the whole history of the concession will be set forth. It is improbable that any opinion will be expressed on the legal aspects of the case, but exception may be taken to the allotment of so many as 85,000 shares to the concessionnaires, on the ground of injury to the State of Hyderabad. There will also probably be a question raised in the report as to the advisability of English company promoters being allowed to treat directly with native officials of State, more effective advice and assistance from the Home Government to the native rulers being suggested as the best means of ensuring satisfactory results in negotiations of this kind.—*Morning Advertiser*, July 24.

Sir Henry James has been elected Chairman of the Committee appointed to inquire into the Deccan Scandal. By the way, there are rumours of trouble at the India Office owing to the complete neglect of all its business by its present Parliamentary representatives. Lord Cross is, of course, incapable; and Sir John Gorst is indolent to an extent which nullifies entirely his undoubted capacity. His clumsy evasions, and neglect to obtain information on the grave question raised by Professor Stuart, and his action in connection with this Deccan business, are said to have brought matters to a crisis. He was not in the House on Tuesday evening, though there were some important questions to be addressed to him, and his absence is now explained by an alleged difference with the Prime Minister.—*Freeman's Journal*, May 10.

The letter which we published the other day, announcing that the Nawab Mahdi Ali, the Political and Financial Secretary of the Nizam of Hyderabad, has left for England, in order to offer evidence in the matter of the concession for mining rights in the Deccan territory, will give much satisfaction, and excite some curiosity. The suspension of the Nizam's formerly-trusted Home Secretary and Director of Railways and Public Works, Sirdar Diler-ul-Mulk, or Abdul Huk, has, we are informed, caused considerable excitement throughout India. In view of the example of enterprise which Hyderabad has set to the other Native States of the dependency, it is much to be desired that the admittedly dubious circumstances connected with his downfall should be effectually cleared up. And this is not less desirable for the credit of Hyderabad than in the interests of home financiers. The Indian papers admit that the case is still *sub judice*, and that it is therefore too early to express an opinion on its merits. In plain terms, it is a question whether the Hyderabad Government or the investing public, or both, have or have not been defrauded or deceived; and, if so, then by whom? The concession is for all mining rights in the Nizam's territories for a period of ninety-nine years, and upon the satisfactory clearing up of the mystery appears to depend not only the exploitation of the Singareni coalfields—to say nothing of possible diamond and gold deposits—but also the carrying out of the great railway scheme through the State of Hyderabad, of which we lately gave an outline, and which has for its projector the same Sirdar Diler-ul-Mulk whose operations in connection with the Mining Company are now the subject of discussion. According to the order suspending the Sirdar, it was agreed between the Nizam's Government and the Government of India that the concessionnaires who acquired the mining rights should limit the issue of the shares by the Company to be formed by them to a first issue of £150,000 out of a total nominal capital of £1,000,000, with "the specific intention that the Company should have a reserve fund in the shape of uncalled-up capital wherewith to meet either possible contingencies or to enlarge the Company's operations in other directions." Now the Nizam's Government complain that the indenture of concession contains no stipulation to this effect, and that the balance of the unsubscribed capital, representing £850,000, was transferred by the Company as fully paid-up shares to the concessionnaires in exchange for all their rights and liabilities. Subsequently, it appears, the Nizam's Government were induced to give instructions for the purchase of shares to the amount of £150,000 in order to obtain a certain amount of control over the operations of the Company. It may be asked where the Nizam's Government expected these shares—equalling in amount the whole of the "first issue"—to come from. For its part, the Nizam's Government wishes to know why, under the actual circumstances, they were compelled to pay a premium for the shares thus acquired, and why one of the concessionnaires and a Director of the Company was employed to effect the purchase. It will be seen that a dispute involving the issue of shares representing the difference between £150,000 and

£1,000,000, and the payment of a premium for shares by a Government which, we are led to infer, supposed that the available supply was only three-twentieths of the actual amount issued, presents points of considerable interest.—*Manchester Guardian*, May 11.

The Hyderabad (Deccan) Company.—Many people wonder whether the Ottoman Bank has anything to do with the Deccan business, and if so, what. It seems that amongst those who received liberal donations of the fully-paid Deccan shares, are several prominent persons connected with this bank in London, and as it is well known that Mr. Watson was, and no doubt is, a *persona grata* at this Board, it is of course only natural that he should put his friends in for the good thing. What occurs to us is that there is generally a *quid pro quo* in this world's affairs. Now, in this case the *quid* is in evidence, but where or what is the reciprocative *quo?* On the whole, this concern looks like being the champion swindle of the show.—*Fairplay*, May 11.

To the Editor of *Vanity Fair*, 2nd May, 1888.—"Sir,—I should like to know what you think now of the 'Deccan' swindle, in which you have advised your readers to invest their small savings? You ought to be ashamed of yourself; but probably you were in the swim, and made a good thing out of the fraud, and are therefore dead to any feeling or pang of remorse. I should like to see you tarred and feathered for your pains.—Yours, One of Your Dupes."

This is not exactly the kind of communication we are accustomed to receive, nor one which we can regard as consonant with that politeness which generally distinguishes those who solicit our advice. Our correspondent must be aware—because we emphatically state it every week at the head of this article—that we do not pretend to be infallible, that we advise only from week to week, and then only to the best of our lights. The position of giving "Advice Gratis" was not sought by us. It causes us an infinity of trouble week after week; and, as we have often remarked in connection therewith, if we give good advice we receive no thanks, and if we counsel that which turns out wrong, we are placed in the invidious position of the Organ Grinder's Monkey, who receives more kicks than halfpence. As to our advice, it is for all of our readers to take it, or reject it as they themselves may elect. At the same time, it is only just to ourselves to state that if both the Indian Government on this side, and the Nizam's Government on the other side, armed, as they should be, at all points with the best legal and native advice, have been misled over this affair, it is possible that the writer of "Other People's Money" may also have been mistaken. As the Company in question is now the subject of a Parliamentary inquiry it would be indecorous of us to make further comment. We reiterate our belief, however, that the Concession is perfectly valid.—*Vanity Fair*, May 11.

A tale of expensive experts is told by *Indian Engineering*. Mr. Barrington Brown, the geologist sent out by the Secretary of State for India, to report on the Ruby Mines in Upper Burmah, receives, it is stated, a salary of £200 per mensem during his engagement, which is at present for six months. He is also to have all his *bonâ fide* travelling expenses paid by the Government. It is said that Mr. Theodore Hughes, of the Indian Geological Survey, draws something like the same figure during his deputation with the Hyderabad Deccan Company. It is not stated whether Mr. Bruce Foote drew anything extra for his flying prospect of the Mysore Gold Fields.—*Invention*, May 12.

It is satisfactory to learn that the Government has consented to a Parliamentary inquiry by Commission into the whole story of the formation and floating of the Hyderabad (Deccan) Company (Limited). It is, however, not so satisfactory to have to believe that urgent necessity exists for such an inquiry. It is most unfortunate that at a time when we were congratulating ourselves upon the confidence which was being placed by all the native princes of India in the justice and honesty of purpose of British rule in that country, that a scandal should arise more serious in its aspects and more damaging in its possible results than any scandal connected with business transactions between Englishmen and Natives since the "plunderful" times of the old East India Company. We can recall to mind no scandal of this nature so grave since then. The Jervis Court-martial was a scandal pitiable and abominable enough, but it only concerned two individuals, although one of them was no less a personage than the Commander-in-Chief of India. There was no question in that case of fair or unfair dealings between Englishmen and natives. In the Hyderabad (Deccan) business, however, questions involving the good name of Englishmen for honesty and rectitude are involved. Nay, more than this, the character of the relations of the Government of India and the India Office with the Feudatory States of India is also called into question. This fact alone cannot but tend to weaken that moral influence of England in India, by which influence she more than by any strength of arms holds empire there. It is to be regretted that inquiry is necessary, but it is to be hoped that that inquiry shall be open, searching, and most exacting, and also that it shall take place without delay. It is not a matter for public concern that merely the Sirdar Diler Jung at Hyderabad should clear himself of charges made against his honour and probity, or that certain promoters, jobbers and lawyers in England should have an opportunity of explaining or disposing of "extravagant charges and illusions." The character of the Sirdar concerns Hyderabad alone, the character of Company-promoters, &c., concerns themselves chiefly and their clients, but the character of British officials concerns the country at large. The many-sided gentlemen who deal in limited liabilities in the City of London may have their own code of financial ethics; they have come into the world to make money—honestly, no doubt, if they can—but to make money, and they may gain credit for astuteness from those who envy or imitate them, for actions which are not altogether founded upon a strict following of the eighth commandment. But where the question concerns the dealings of British officials there can be no shelter from consequences under a convenient laxity of even political ethics. The truth, and the whole truth, must be brought to light. If what is being rumoured be only half true, far higher reputations than those which are being bandied about in newspapers are at stake. Painful as it may be to have the fierce glare of publicity thrown upon high places, it is better than they should stand as now in a twilight which distorts. Truth and honesty will court the light, and justice now calls for it.—*Allen's Indian Mail*, April 30.

The Resident at the Court of the Nizam during the period which led to the scandals connected with the Deccan Mines, and who is at present on leave of absence, will not return to the post. The Viceroy has telegraphed to Sir Lepel Griffin, at present in London, offering him the post of Resident, and the offer has been accepted.—*Daily News*, July 25.

Pending the publication of the report of the Select Committee on the Hyderabad-Deccan concession, shareholders in the Company cannot do better than study the reports just issued by the Directors.—*Money*, July 25.

I hear that we are likely to have another Hyderabad scandal shortly, in which the names of two or three British officers are concerned. It is not quite of the magnitude of the Abdul Huk affair, but is an exceedingly bad business indeed. Needless to say, the Nizam's treasury was the ultimate sufferer to the tune of about 50,000 rupees.—*Dundee Advertiser*, July 26.

THE Select Committee on the Deccan Mining Scandal will meet to-day, not Monday next, as has been stated. The business in Committee will be discussion of the draft report drawn up by the Solicitor-General for Scotland, and submitted on behalf of the Chairman, Sir Henry James. It is no secret that the proposed report is not received with unanimous favour by the Committee.—*Daily News*, July 26.

THE DECCAN MINING SCANDALS.—The Select Committee on the Hyderabad Mining Scandals met yesterday to consider their report. The Central News learns that the statement that two hostile draft reports have been prepared is unfounded. The statement probably had its origin in the fact that Mr. Slagg has drawn up a document containing certain suggestions which will be considered and probably incorporated in the Chairman's report. It is believed that this, after it has been considered and amended, will be the report of the whole Committee. The Committee meet again to-day.—*Daily Chronicle*, July 27.

I HEAR that Sir Salar Jung, who is exiled from Hyderabad, has been allowed to return, and is now in high favour with the Nizam. But the favour is personal, not political, as the position of Sir Asman Jah, the present Dewan, or Prime Minister, is said to be perfectly secure, not only with the Government of India, but also with the Nizam. He has quite lately received a high degree in the Order of the Indian Empire, and it is expected that he will shortly visit the Viceroy to confer with him on the affairs of the State of Hyderabad.—*Glasgow Herald*, July 27.

THE members of the Select Committee of the House of Commons appointed to inquire into the Hyderabad Mining affair, met yesterday to consider their report. Some progress was made with the introductory section, and the Committee will meet again to-day to continue their work. The statements recently published regarding an alleged indifference of opinion among the members on the question of the degree of responsibility attaching to the India Office officials, and their part in the transactions are, our London Correspondent is assured, without foundation. So far as can be ascertained, practical unanimity prevails at present in the Committee, and it is expected that there will be no necessity for a minority report. Members agree that the circumstances attending the formation of the Company, and the sale of its shares to the Nizam of Hyderabad, constitute a grave scandal, and they will indicate this opinion in very strong terms in their report. Whatever may be the upshot of the inquiry, the *bona fide* shareholders will not be made to suffer by any action which may be taken, as the Nizam's Government has specially intimated that their interests will not be lost sight of.—*Yorkshire Post*, July 17.

A CURIOUS hitch has taken place in the preparation of the report of the Select Committee appointed to inquire into the Deccan Mining scandal. In accordance with usage, this Committee was nominated with a majority of one in favour of the Government. There are four Ministerialists and three Liberals. In such circumstances it was taken for granted that matters would be made to work smoothly. The evidence being closed, the preparation of the draft report was committed to the Solicitor-General for Scotland, Sir Henry James, the Chairman, not being so fond of hard work as he was before he became an associate of the aristocracy and a companion of princes. The draft report was circulated at the end of last week, and was found—to the disappointment if not to the surprise of the minority, consisting of Mr. Labouchere, Mr. Slagg, and Mr. M'Lagan—to whitewash the India Office, acquitting them of all responsibility for the admitted scandal. Had the four Ministerialists stood together and approved the report, it must needs have been presented to Parliament with whatever corrective effect is to be derived from the minority report, a corrective which long experience has proved to be exceedingly inefficacious.

The whole situation was, however, changed when it was discovered that Sir Richard Temple was not to be influenced by Party considerations, and was determined to deal with the matter entirely upon its merits, leaving the India Office to defend itself. Sir Richard Temple is perhaps not very successful as an English politician, but few men know India better than he, and his immovable resolve to see justice done in the matter of the Deccan Scandal has done a great deal to raise him in the estimation even of the Ministerialists, whose little game he has spoiled. The Committee have now resumed their sittings and are trying to patch up a report which, whilst it will satisfy the demands of justice, shall let the India Office down as gently as possible. But the Solicitor-General for Scotland's report is already practically withdrawn.—*Sheffield Independent*, July 28.

THE Hyderabad (Deccan) Committee met again yesterday without coming to a final conclusion upon their report. There is, however, no doubt that the draft report drawn up by the Solicitor-General for Scotland, and circulated at the instance of the Chairman, Sir Henry James, will undergo serious modification. There is a strong feeling among an important section of the Committee, not exclusively Liberals, that the report originally submitted fatally minimises the responsibility of the India Office in respect of the scandal that has been made the subject of inquiry.—*Daily News*, July 28.

THE HYDERABAD (DECCAN) COMPANY.—Sir R. Lethbridge asked the First Lord of the Treasury, in view of the injurious nature of the charges and allegations that had appeared in the Indian Press, both against Government and against private individuals and officials of repute in the matter of the Hyderabad (Deccan) Company's affairs, whether he would undertake that the discussion on the report should not take place before the evidence taken before the Select Committee had been printed and circulated; and whether it was the intention of Her Majesty's Government to take that discussion in the present portion of the Session, or in the autumn Session.

Mr. W. H. Smith: The Select Committee referred to was moved for by one of the hon. members for Northampton, and I have not seen, nor am I aware that the Committee have yet presented their report. Till the report is before the Government, I am unable to say whether it will be necessary to afford an opportunity for its discussion, and I cannot, therefore, give any pledge on the subject. (Hear, hear.)—*Times*, July 28.

SIR LEPEL GRIFFIN'S acceptance of the British Residency at the Court of the Nizam has given much satisfaction to his friends, who never regarded with approval his hankering after a seat in Parliament. It is strange that the House of Commons should have such an extraordinary fascination for successful Anglo-Indians, in spite of the notorious fact that few of them ever make their mark in

English political life. Sir Lepel Griffin has taken warning by the many examples before him, and decided not to bury his reputation at Westminster. He is not exactly beloved by the large and somewhat demonstrative class from which Congress delegates are selected; but his enemies will not deny that he possesses some qualities requisite for his new position. He is as energetic as he is clever, and recent events have shown that a really vigorous man is wanted at Hyderabad. Without encroaching upon the rights of the Nizam, a powerful British Resident can effect an immense amount of good if he goes to work in the right way, and I believe that if Sir L. Griffin earnestly applies himself to the task of cleansing his Augean stable, he will be strongly supported by the best of the Hyderabad officials.—*Vanity Fair*, July 28.

There is something like a panic, I understand, at the India Office on account of the "misfortunes" of so many English officials in our great dependency, such as the arrest of Mr. Crawford, in Bombay, and the resignation of Mr. Cordery, British Resident at Hyderabad. There is, indeed, reason to believe that there will be an inquiry, probably by Royal Commission, into the whole question of the relations between our officials and the native princes of India. It has been stated that Mr. Cordery's resignation has been occasioned entirely by what are known as the Deccan Scandals. I have ground for believing, however, that Mr. Cordery was induced to resign, to some extent, because of the unpleasantness that recently arose in connection with the case of a Captain Neville, who had some time ago a rather notorious litigation with his native cook. Whether Mr. Cordery deserved the censures passed on him by a certain section of the Indian Press is another question. He is tolerably well up in life, and may have thought it advisable to cut himself adrift from the worries of a very difficult position.—London correspondent of *Glasgow Herald*, July 30.

The report of the Hyderabad (Deccan) Company (Limited) states that the balance-sheet, made up to the 30th of April, shows an expenditure to that date of £55,639, leaving a balance of cash in hand of £97,955. The Directors, it is stated, would have been glad to have been able to defer the general meeting until the Select Committee, who have been inquiring into the affairs of the Company, had presented their report to the House of Commons. The Board has, however, thought it desirable not to delay the meeting any longer. They are advised and believed that the title of the Company to its property is unassailable, and will not be attacked. In this belief, they are confirmed by the statements made to the Committee by the counsel for the Government of His Highness the Nizam. In fact, it is greatly to the interest of the Government, both as to its credit in the market and its prospective profits, directly from royalties, and indirectly from the opening up of the mineral resources of the State, that the Company should be left undisturbed to carry on its operations. His Highness's Government, in its capacity of a large shareholder in the Company, has nominated Nawab Mahdi Hassan Fathah Nawaz Jung, Bahadur who is the Chief Justice of the Hyderabad State, to be a Director in the place o Sirdar Diler-ul-Mulk, C.I.E., and he has been appointed accordingly.—*Times'* July 31.

The Directors of the Hyderabad Deccan Company have issued the balance-sheet of the Company, made up to the 30th of April, 1888. The expenditure to that date amounted to £55,638, leaving a balance of cash in hand of £97,955. The following remarks are made:—

"The Directors would have been glad to have been able to defer the general meeting until the Select Committee, who have been inquiring into the affairs of this Company, had presented their report to the House of Commons. The Board has, however, thought it desirable not to delay the meeting any longer. They are advised and believe that the title of the Company to its property is unassailable, and will not be attacked. In this belief they are confirmed by the statements made to the Committee by the counsel for the Government of his Highness the Nizam. In fact, it is greatly to the interest of the Government, both as to its credit in the market and its prospective profits—directly from royalties, and indirectly from the opening up of the mineral resources of the State—that this Company should be left undisturbed to carry on its operations." It would certainly be injustice to those who have paid for shares to cancel the concession because others had sold shares in an irregular manner. The quotation is 6½ to 7.—*Daily News*, July 31.

THE HYDERABAD (DECCAN) COMPANY.—The report of the Directors, made up to April 30, says the expenditure to that date amounted to £55,638 18s. 2d., leaving a balance of cash in hand of £97,955 1s. 4d. "The Directors would have been glad to have been able to defer the general meeting until the Select Committee, who have been inquiring into the affairs of this Company, had presented their report to the House of Commons. The Board has, however, thought it desirable not to delay the meeting any longer. They are advised and believe that the title of the Company to its property is unassailable and will not be attacked. In this belief they are confirmed by the statements made to the Committee by the counsel for the Government by H. H. the Nizam. In fact, it is greatly to the interests of the Government, both as to its credit in the market, and its prospective profits, directly from royalties, and indirectly from the opening up of the mineral resources of the State, that this Company should be left undisturbed to carry on its operations. His Highness's Government, in its capacity of a large shareholder in the Company, has nominated Nawab Mahdi Hassan, Fathah Nawaz Jung, Bahadur, who is the Chief Justice of the Hyderabad State, to be a Director of the Company in the place of Sirdar Diler-ul-Mulk, Bahadur, C.I.E., and he has been appointed accordingly. The Nawab has attended, and given the Directors his assistance and advice at their Board meetings, and the relations between the Government and the Company in all respects, including the actual working of the concession in India, are perfectly cordial and harmonious. Mr. Bazett Wetenhall Colvin was appointed a Director in lieu of the late Mr. John Stewart. The reports recently forwarded to each shareholder will have shown what has been done in prospecting and developing the Company's property, and the temporary and unforeseen difficulties which have arisen in carrying out as rapidly as had been hoped the necessary works from which dividends have to be earned. These difficulties were completely beyond the control of the Board. They are now disappearing, and the Directors feel confident that the Company possesses an extremely valuable property. They will spare no efforts in their power to make the undertaking a commercial success."—*Financial News*, July 31.

IT had been expected that the Select Committee upon the Hyderabad Deccan Scandal would have been able to conclude to-day the drafting of its report, the drafting of which is awaited with much interest, not only in political, but in City circles. But this was found impossible, and, though the Committee meets again on Wednesday, it is not certain that even then the report will be complete.—*Birmingham Weekly Post*, July 31.

THE subjoined letter refers to the forthcoming meeting of the Hyderabad (Deccan) Company. We can certainly see no reason why the meeting should not have been postponed until the report of the Select Committee could be laid before it:—

"London, July 31.

"Sir,—It seems to me, as a shareholder in the Hyderabad (Deccan) Company, that the Directors' action in summoning their general meeting for next Tuesday, only a day or two before the expected date of the issue of the report of the Select Committee of the House of Commons, is one of very doubtful propriety, and still more doubtful policy. They state in their report that they 'would have been glad to have been able' to defer their meeting until the Select Committee had reported; but they do not say why they are unable to do so. It is absolutely certain that the report of the Select Committee will be a document of life-and-death importance to the shareholders, and ought to be discussed between them and the Directors (some of whom are also concessionnaires) without a moment's unnecessary delay. If, as the Directors state in their report, the title of the Company is unassailable, and will not be attacked, then there could be no possible reason why this general meeting should not be adjourned for a few days, so as to enable the Select Committee's report and evidence to be discussed. A DECCAN SHAREHOLDER."—*Times*, August 1.

THE Select Committee on the Deccan Mining Scandal will meet again today, in order further to consider the report drafted by the Solicitor-General for Scotland at the instance of Sir Henry James, which has already undergone important modifications. The report may be expected in the course of next week.—*Daily News*, August 1.

THE DECCAN SCANDAL.—The Report of the House of Commons Committee on this subject is not yet published, but in the meantime the directors of the Deccan Company—if such an organization can be called a company—have issued an *ad interim* report of their own. It is needless to say that it is a report *pour rire*. All the fine and large talk about the capabilities of the Company, as regards the production of coal, would provoke a smile from even the brazen countenance of a Hindoo idol. The estimate given of the possible output of coal, in the first place, is very satisfactory, of course; but it would be far more so had the Company the necessary money to sink the requisite number of shafts and provide the capital required for other purposes; and if, in the second place, there were any sufficient market for the large contemplated production. Another feature of this instructive report is the importance attached to what is called the "diamondiferous" district controlled by the Company. We put the portentous adjective within inverted commas, not because we object to the regularity of its formation, for in this respect it is greatly superior to the Deccan Company, but merely because, like "Mesopotamia" to the traditional old lady, it must be such a comforting word to the unfortunate shareholders. There is not a tittle of evidence to show that a single diamond has been discovered in the Deccan district for three hundred years or more, and until the Directors can furnish some less illusory evidence of the prospects of the Company in this direction, we must decline to believe in the "diamondiferosity" of the country.—*World*, August 1.

INDIAN SCANDALS.—It is painful and humiliating to reflect that within the last few months something worse than a suspicion has been cast upon the integrity of the Queen's servants in India. The Hyderabad episode, the charges against civilians filling important posts in other parts of the country, the stories of bribery and corruption in high places, the evil reports of official violence and injustice—these accumulated scandals demand the attention of every Englishman who has a thought beyond the shop-counter and the street. No doubt there must be a certain element of corruption in every public service; it is undeniable that the Government of India to-day is pure and undefiled in comparison to what it was when nabobs returned to England "infamous for plundered provinces;" and periodical scandals, recurring in accordance with some cyclic law, apparently, must be expected. But it will not do to seek refuge in these commonplace consolations. Recent revelations do not merely affect the character of the individuals concerned, or even that of the services to which they belong. They are an affront to the whole nation, and must be strictly inquired into; and, if punishment is needed, the punishment must be severe if it is to be either just or wise.

No doubt we may yet hope that some of the charges brought against English officials in India will fall through, that some of even the strongest suspicions will be dissipated altogether, and that other charges and suspicions may turn out to be greatly exaggerated. It is widely stated, and to some extent believed, in India that Anglo-Indian officials have sometimes fallen victims to the virulence and machinations of an unscrupulous press and of private intrigue; and that the authorities at headquarters, being either misinformed or prejudiced, have punished where they ought to have protected subordinate officers. Such cases may have occurred, but it will be time to talk of them when evidence is brought forward to substantiate them; and, besides, the assured fact that such cases have occurred would hardly mend matters. Leaving the utmost margin for miscarriage of justice, for accusations that will not be proved, and for sentences to be reversed on appeal, we may well fear that an appalling residue will remain. In cases, moreover, where an official, though pronounced guilty by the local government, can afterwards clear himself before a higher court, the injury done to the prestige of the British Raj only assumes a different shape. The mere fact that such accusations can be formulated, the possibility of their being well founded, does enormous mischief: a mischief that can only be averted by immediate and manifest proof that the accusers are slanderous. But in at least three of these miserable incidents the local authorities concerned not only admit the possibility of guilt, but are convinced, it would seem, that the charges have been brought home. Three of the officials implicated are preparing, it is said, an appeal to the Secretary of State. A fourth will be indicted in a court of law. The result of the Deccan inquiry has still to be made public; and we have yet to see whether the English officials concerned are held guilty of anything beyond neglect, if of that. But this does not exhaust the list of scandals that have occurred of late in India. The names of one or two other notorious and acknowledged offenders might be given. The main features of each case are much alike; and, as we are now concerned with general effects rather than with individual transgressions, there is no need to mention names. What we have to deal with is this. Men too often rise in India to responsible and well-paid posts, while their chief qualifications—beyond the fact of their belonging to a particular branch of the service—consist sometimes in mere self-advertising cleverness, sometimes in social accomplishments and nothing more. Nor is this all. Some, at any rate, of those gentlemen who have now obtained an unenviable notoriety have been promoted from one post to another in spite of previous errors of conduct or well-known defects of character. No good purpose would be served by raking up buried scandals; but it is only fulfilling a public duty to state what in India is openly talked of. It stands to reason that better men have been passed over; and this preferment of the unworthy, this unnatural selection of the unfittest, might be expected to tarnish the reputation of any public service.

It is the more necessary to call attention to these painful matters because the evil complained of is not without a remedy. There will doubtless be a full and most careful inquiry into every case. Whatever the result, there should be a stern resolution on the part of Government, of the Indian services, and of the public, that these scandals shall not be tolerated, and that the misdemeanours of a public servant shall in future be an insuperable bar to his advancement. When an official is known to be a *mauvais sujet*, it is not enough to transfer him to some obscure station till the mark against his name has been dimmed by lapse of time. The Indian Government must take upon itself to do what public opinion in England would insist on being done. The Administration might at times lose some flashy ornaments, but its character for probity would be safe. The number of high offices filled by Englishmen is not very great. Less than eight hundred appointments are held by covenanted civilians and military officers in civil employ. Every one of these posts should be strictly reserved for men whose proved uprightness would give the lie to scandal of any kind.—*St. James's Gazette*, August 1.

HYDERABAD.—To the Editor of the *Financial Times*.—Sir,—But little heed seems to be given here to what is passing in that magnificent dependency of England, India. Here is a cutting from the *Deccan Times* of July 5:—

"It is almost with emotion that we watch the dawning of a new day upon the native princes. We learn by telegram from Hyderabad that the Nizam held a very imposing durbar at the Palace on Monday evening to confer formally upon the new Minister the customary 'Diwani Kiat.' The ceremony was most imposing, from the acclamations with which the liberated people welcomed their deliverance from the bondage of the unprincipled Triumvirate who terrorised the city by their policeman Huk. The revival of harmony between the Court and the Residency was to be celebrated yesterday by a banquet given by Mr. Howell, who will at its close have the gracious task of investing the Minister with the insignia of knighthood of the Indian Empire. Not the least of the signs of the new concord is the permission accorded to Sir Salar Jung to return to Hyderabad."

English contact is already making itself felt, through the Hyderabad (Deccan) Company. Hyderabad has a population in round figures of 200,000 souls. The near advent of a supply of moderately-priced coal has given rise to a wish to have the city lighted with gas, and already plans and estimates are being prepared. Two cotton mills and one oil mill are projected, while a new palace, which is being built for the Nizam, is to be lighted throughout by electricity. These are unmistakable signs of progress.—Yours, &c., A. T.—July 31.—*Financial Times*, August 1.

THE VALUE OF THE DECCAN CONCESSION.—On this subject, which is one of great practical importance, Mr. Watson's statements are absolutely worthless. Before the Committee he stoutly maintained that the coal mines and the gold and the diamonds would yet enable the Company to sell its property for millions, or else to work it and pay six per cent. interest on the whole amount. Mr. Watson's imagination is far more robust than his memory. He had to admit that his latest authorities as to the value of the mineral resources of the Deccan are the paid servants of the Company—"all respectable men." What of that? The coal mine alone would pay a dividend on the million sterling; 360,000 tons at a profit of two or three rupees a ton would suffice. At present, it is true, only 150 tons a week are being produced, but everything is being got ready. Well, it seems a pity to spoil such good sport as this; but as we have been able to correct the aberrations of Mr. Watson's memory in regard to a telegram offering the bagatelle of £400,000, we may venture to do the same good office about his wild arithmetic. There is absolutely no demand, actual or prospective, for an unlimited out-turn of Singareni coal, whatever may be the capital expended on underground works. The quality of the coal precludes its use in the Bombay mills: the experiment has been tried, and if it were possible to sell it at half the price which it will cost to raise and bring it by rail to Bombay it would still not pay to use it. A third of it is waste, clinker, and ashes. A certain limited amount can and will be used on the railways within very exactly defined limits, beyond which it will come into competition with the better and cheaper English coal. That settles the prospect of the Singareni mines paying interest of six per cent. on a million of capital. It is only with the most careful working that the coal mines can pay a dividend on the working capital. As for the diamondiferous soil, the new Golconda, that Mr. Watson has still the courage to discourse about, he had to confess to Mr. Labouchere that of the five diamonds found one was worth thirty shillings and the rest were worth nothing. So of the gold; there is no reason whatever to suppose that the gold-bearing strata of the Deccan are likely to be more profitable than those of Mysore and the Wynaad. There is probably some gold which may yield some return if properly worked; but there is no room for further delusion. The reconstituted Company must keep very soberly to the actualities of the case if it is ever to earn a 6 per cent. dividend on the £150,000 subscribed capital. As for the concession, it was tainted by fraud in its origin, and it is difficult to see how its validity can be upheld. It will probably be cancelled, full powers to take that course having been given under legal advice to the Nawab Mohsin-ul-Mulk when proceeding to England. The rights of innocent shareholders will, of course, be safeguarded; distinct assurances have been formally given on that point. The attempt of the concessionnaires to exonerate themselves from the imputation that they had made a corrupt bargain with the agent of the Hyderabad Government on the plea that the late Sir Salar Jung's letter (partly in pencil) gave Abdul Huk a right to appropriate a fourth of the whole capital intended for the working of the mines is nullified by the secrecy observed and the deception practised on the Nizam's Government in regard to the real holder of the shares he was led to purchase. Nothing turns on the question of the authenticity of the letter in question; it contains nothing to authorise the surreptitious dealing which was stoutly denied by the agent, who was shown that it was only as a last resource that he was prepared to base his defence upon its production. The Committee learned from a telegram the damning fact which we published long before, that even after his suspension the Sirdar positively assured Mr. Howell, the new Resident, that he had never received anything in connection with the mining concession. If the possession of the letter was a sufficient explanation of the appropriation of the fourth of the £850,000, this desperate denial would not have been persevered in to the last extremity. Mr. Watson's tardy disclosure of the fact when he saw that it was certain to be found out does not in any way rehabilitate the concessionnaires, and cannot be held to free the transaction of which the concession was the fruit from a taint of fraud fatal to its validity.—*Bombay Gazette*, quoted by the *Evening Post*, August 2.

The Hyderabad-Deccan Company's Coal.—In reply to the remarks of the *Bombay Gazette* on the Singareni coal of the Hyderabad-Deccan Company, we have received the following extracts from the official report. The first is from the administration report to the Government of India on the railways in India for 1887-1888, dated May 29, 1888, by Lieut.-Colonel L. Conway Gordon, R.E., Director-General of Railways, paragraph 12, referring to Singareni coal:—

"The quality of coal is very good, the result obtained by its use on the Nizam Guaranteed State Railway comparing very favourably with English coal burned on the Great Indian Peninsula Railway, under very similar circumstances, as regards inclinations of gradients and other conditions."

Extract from report by Mr. James E. Berkeley, locomotive superintendent of his Highness the Nizam's Guaranteed State Railways, dated June 27, 1888, to the chief engineer of these railways, on the result of twelve trial trips, each trial being carried on over 121 miles of the railway, six up and six down, using Singareni coal, under his personal directions :—

"The conditions of the trial, as regards train loads and locomotive engine power, were ordinary, and the results obtained may be taken as reliable data upon which to form an opinion of the quality of Singareni coal supplied as a locomotive engine fuel. The coal used in these trials was of different qualities and conditions, such as period of exposure to atmospheric action, also from seams of different levels and shafts; so that the coal used was of average merit, and not selected for any speciality."

The average results of his trials, he writes: "I consider, conclusively prove that we have in the Singareni coal a valuable locomotive engine fuel." He concludes: "I have previously, in my report (No. 25), dated November 15, 1887, stated that that 'coal is almost as easy to handle and to work as English, and better than any Indian coal that I am aware of, or have ascertained of from drivers and others who have had experience in working various Indian coals.' The quality of this coal and the facility of handling it is most satisfactory. It may be of interest to know that I have been using this coal (nuts) in our smith's shop; also coke made from this coal in our spring and foundry furnaces. The manufacture of the coke, without proper appliances or plant, has been consequently crude, and the results or data derived are not such as I would venture to express an opinion upon.

"It is not unlikely that a better quality of coal may be supplied from these fields when seams at lower levels are reached, so that the results now obtained may be taken as preliminary."

The Government of India in 1884 estimated that the demand for Singareni coal for railway purposes would be 183,000 tons annually. Since then many more miles of railway have been and are being constructed within the area of supply.—*Evening Post*, August 2.

THE HYDERABAD-DECCAN COMMISSION.—The Select Committee on the Hyderabad Mining concession concluded their labours yesterday, and agreed upon their report. The greater part of the document, which is of considerable length, is taken up with an historical statement of the case, commencing with the granting of the concession by the Government of Hyderabad to Mr. Watson on the 7th of January, 1886. From this statement it appears that there are now about 700 shareholders in the Company, and that of the 85,000 shares issued as fully paid-up, about 55,000 have been sold to the public. The Committee express no opinion as to the prospects of the enterprise, contenting themselves with recording the fact that 150 tons of coal a week have been raised, and that fine diamonds have been found. Lord Lawrence is absolved from all doubt in consequence of his connection with the Company, the Committee being convinced that he acted throughout in the most perfect good faith. In answer to the question of how so large a number as 85,000 out of 100,000 shares came to be vested in the concessionnaires, the Committee admit the competency of the Company to make such a grant as the price of the transfer of the concession, but express some doubt as to whether this result was contemplated by the Nizam's advisers. In conclusion, it is suggested that more effective advice and assistance might have been given to the Nizam during the transaction by the British Government; but no question is raised as to the expediency of working the goldfields, &c. The report will be laid upon the table of the House to-day.—*Morning Post*, August 4.

THE Hyderabad (Deccan) Company are to hold their meeting next Tuesday. They state in their report that they "would have been glad to have been able" to defer their meeting until the Select Committee had reported. Why they did not do so they omit to explain. It would have been the proper course to take. The report of the Select Committee is expected to be out by the end of next week, and it will be a document of life-and-death importance to the shareholders of the Deccan Company. If, as the directors profess to believe, the title of their Company is unassailable, no harm would have been done in postponing their meeting for a few days. If, on the contrary, it is assailed, an adjournment of the meeting would have enabled the Select Committee's report to be discussed by shareholders with directors.—*Stock Exchange*, August 4.

THE report of the Hyderabad (Deccan) Company states that it will be seen in the balance-sheet of the Company, made up to the 30th April, that the expenditure to that date amounted to £56,638, leaving a balance in hand of £97,955. The Directors would have been glad to have been able to defer the general meeting until the Select Committee, who have been inquiring into the affairs of this Company, had presented their report to the House of Commons. The Board has, however, thought it desirable not to delay the meeting any longer. They are advised, and believe, that the title of the Company to its property is unassailable and will not be attacked. In this belief they are confirmed by the statements made to the Committee by the Counsel for the Government of His Highness the Nizam.—*Stocks and Shares*, August 4.

THE HYDERABAD (DECCAN) COMPANY, LIMITED.—The report of the Directors has been published in anticipation of the meeting of shareholders, which has been definitely fixed for Tuesday next, the 7th inst. The Directors express themselves unwilling to postpone that meeting any longer, though they would have been glad to have been in possession of the report of the Select Committee before meeting their constituents. That was very natural, for the Select Committee was granted at a time when a popular prejudice had been created against the Company and when the hostile feeling ran very high. It was naturally expected that the Select Committee would regard itself as conducting a sort of judicial inquiry into the validity of certain allegations of impropriety. Hostile feeling, no doubt, actuated the outside parties who clamoured for the inquiry; but those who carefully read the evidence, as it were, taken day by day, and was duly reported in the public newspapers, must have been struck with the utter failure of the accusations with which the controversy started. It is not for us to anticipate the report of the Select Committee, but at any rate the Directors do not believe that it will be hostile to them; they are of opinion that, whereas the inquiry was meant to involve them in condemnation, it will, on the contrary, exonerate them from the grave charges which at one time were so freely and so inconsiderately alleged against them. The Directors venture so far as to say in their report that they are advised and believe that the title of the Company to its property is unassailable, and will not be attacked. In this belief they are confirmed by the statements made to the Select Committee by the Counsel for the Government of His Highness the Nizam. That Government holds closely to the concessionnaires and the Company they have formed, and accepts the responsibility of its arrangements with them. There can be no doubt that this is the best policy of the Nizam's Government, and it is conduct highly honourable under the circumstances.

The fact is, the negotiations with the concessionnaires were, in the first instance, begun in an intelligent desire to develop the rich and vast resources of the State, but any plans of such development must necessarily have been delegated to the representatives of European experience and capital. The task was too great for the Government, which, with all its ability in statesmanship, is unaccustomed to the organization and methods of commercial life. The

Directors of the Company have fully realised this idea, and have, in felicitous language, given expression to it in their report. They remark: "It is greatly to the interest of the Government, both as to its credit in the market and its prospective profits directly from royalties, and indirectly from the opening up of the mineral resources of the State, that the Company shall be left undisturbed to carry on its operations." His Highness's Government has taken a conclusive step in identifying itself with the welfare of the Company. In its capacity as a very large shareholder in the Company, it has nominated Nawab Mehdi Hasan Fathah Nawaz Jung, Bahadur, who is the Chief Justice of the Hyderabad State, to be a Director in the place of Salar Diler-ul-Mulk, Bahadur, C.I.E., and he has been appointed accordingly. So able a representative on the board will be an acquisition to the Government, and will amply guarantee that the interest of the State will be carefully watched and protected.

The Nawab has attended and given to the Directors his assistance and advice at the Board meetings, and the relations between the Government and the Company in all respects—including the actual working of the concesssion in India are perfectly cordial and harmonious. There can be no doubt that the attack made upon the Company was intended materially to damage it, and was to a great extent one of those unscrupulous manœuvres for which the Stock Exchange and its allies have an evil notoriety. The intention was mischief, the result has been to confirm the relations between the Government and the Company, and to render them much more cordial and intimate than before. In such improved relations is the best augury of the Company's success. It has passed through many of the difficulties incidental to the initial stage of its career, and it now enters on a more direct progress towards the realisation of the vast wealth confided to its care and management.—*Bullionist*, August 4.

The Hyderabad-Deccan Committee.—A news agency states that the Select Committee on the Hyderabad-Deccan Mining Concession concluded their labours yesterday and agreed upon their report. The greater part of the document, which is of considerable length, is taken up with an historical statement of the case. There are now about 700 shareholders in the Company, and of the 85,000 shares issued as fully-paid up, about 55,000 have been sold to the public. Lord Lawrence is absolved from all blame in consequence of his connection with the Company, the Committee being convinced that he acted throughout in the most perfect good faith. In answer to the question of how so large a number of shares out of 100,000 came to be vested in the concessionnaires, the Committee admit the competency of the Company to make such a grant as the price of the transfer of the concession, but express some doubt as to whether this result was contemplated by the Nizam's advisers. It is suggested that more effective advice and assistance might have been given to the Nizam during the transaction by the British Government. If this abstract is correct, the report is certainly very colourless.—*Pall Mall Gazette*, August 4.

The Hyderabad-Deccan Committee Report.—In the House of Commons, on August 4, after questions had been asked, Sir H. James said: I have to ask permission to make a short statement relating to a matter of public interest, and to the rules of this House. In several newspapers this morning, and especially in *The Times* newspaper, there appears a statement of the contents of the report of the Committee on the Hyderabad-Deccan Mining Company. That report has not been laid upon the table of the House, but still the paragraphs to which I have referred state with some detail what the contents of that report are. As far as I can judge, the writer who communicated the contents of these paragraphs to the newspapers, who is said to be a person connected with a Press Agency, must have obtained a copy—probably the original draft copy of the report—at a stage and time when that report had not approached completion, and indeed had scarcely been considered, and when it was merely a draft report. While I cannot, for a moment, say what that report is or may be likely to be, it is, I think, my duty to say that the statements as to the contents of that report are not only insufficient, but are misleading, fallacious, and in many respects entirely erroneous. I do not think that at this stage I ought to suggest any course that should be taken to meet the evil that is so frequently displayed, as I have not yet had an opportunity of consulting with my colleagues; but I am sure they will share with me the great regret that I feel that such a course should have been taken in regard to the report to which I am referring. (Hear, hear.) I wish to say, as distinctly and as emphatically as I can, that the statements connected with the Company are false and erroneous, because it happens that the duties of the Committee were to inquire into the affairs of a Company, the shares of which have been largely dealt with—speculatively dealt with—and I believe are still being dealt with on the Stock Exchange; and it appears to me that if the report remains uncontradicted, the result will be—it may be the intentional result—that the credulous and the unwary will suffer, and that those who do not possess those qualities will benefit. (Hear, hear.)

Mr. T. Healy asked whether the Government would avail themselves of the Newspaper Law of Libel Bill which was coming down from the Lords to insert provisions that would put a stop to such practices. (Hear, hear.)

Sir G. Campbell took the earliest opportunity of asking whether in regard to the Official Secrets Bill, the Government would take into consideration the question of dealing not only which those who stole public information, but with the receivers of that stolen information. (Hear, hear.)

Mr. T. D. Sullivan asked whether offences of this sort were not constantly being committed by *The Times* newspaper, and whether it was not the habit of that journal to get information of this kind, which was the result of thefts and forgeries. ("Hear, hear," and laughter.)

Mr. Jackson: It is not possible for me to give a direct answer to the question of the hon. member for Longford, but I at once take the opportunity of saying that these occurrences have been of late so frequent that it will be the bounden duty of the Government to consider what measures should be adopted to put a stop to them. (Hear, hear.)—*Times*, August 6.

The House of Commons devoted Saturday's sitting to Supply, and on the House assembling Sir Henry James called attention to a bogus report in the *Times* on the subject of the Hyderabad and Deccan Mining Company. It would appear from Sir Henry James's statement that the *Times* is going from forgery to theft—or something very like it. In the instance referred to, it puts forth "information" in the shape of a paragraph, which is pronounced by Sir Henry James "not only insufficient, but misleading, fallacious, and, in many respects, entirely erroneous," and he further stated that whoever supplied it must have had access to the original draft report. Mr. T. D. Sullivan pertinently asked was not the *Times* becoming notorious for obtaining so-called information by theft and forgery. Of the skill exercised in Printing House Square in the forgery line the world has already abundant evidence. This new branch of the *Times* business, filching information from important official documents, opens a wide field, and if pursued with the same amount of industry as we have seen displayed in the Forgery Department, who knows what new sources of profit it may reveal to the enterprising but unscrupulous conductors of the once-great organ. But the Government are not likely to give the substantial help to the thieves as they have given to the forgers, unless, indeed, they could steal something to be used against the Irish party.—*Cork Examiner*, August 6.

THE DECCAN MEETING.—THE CHAIRMAN MAKES A LONG STATEMENT—A POLL DEMANDED BY THE DIRECTORS. -The second ordinary general meeting of the Hyderabad (Deccan) Company, Limited, was held yesterday at Winchester House, Old Broad-street, Mr. George H. M. Batten in the chair.

Mr. L. L. Hall (the secretary) read the notice convening the meeting, and the report of the Directors was taken as read.

The Chairman said: Gentlemen, I have received letters from five shareholders, stating their opinion that this meeting should have been put off until after the Select Committee have presented their report to the House of Commons. On the other hand, complaints have been made that we have delayed too long in calling the meeting, and it has been represented to us that at the end of this week many of the shareholders will be leaving London. It is not easy, gentlemen, to satisfy the conflicting views of over 700 shareholders, but we believe we have acted in accordance with the views of the vast majority. Our financial year ended on April 30, to which date our accounts have been made up and audited. The evidence before the Committee was completed on June 22. We have waited over six weeks for the Committee's report; we had no means of knowing when it would be presented. These are the considerations which have led us, with the concurrence of the whole Board, to call this meeting for to-day, for the transaction of the ordinary business of the Company. Statements have appeared in the newspapers as to the presumed contents of the report. They have been disavowed by the right hon. the Chairman, and we cannot say what the final report will be, but we await its issue with the utmost confidence. I need not tell you that for the last three months the Directors have had a very anxious time. Our anxiety has not been, however, due to any doubts as to the validity of the title by which the Company holds its property, or to any doubts as to the real great value of that property. Any unprejudiced person, who reads the terms of the concession on which our title is based, and who has made himself acquainted with the actual facts as to how that concession was transferred to the Company, cannot fail to come to the conclusion that nothing illegal, irregular, or open on any ground to valid objection was done in the initiation of this Company. Recently a great deal of correspondence has come to light which took place anterior to the grant of the concession. This correspondence was totally unknown to the first directors of this Company, who had nothing whatever before them except the actual concession itself as finally signed and sealed by the Nizam's Government. A great part of the correspondence took place between the Government of India and the Government of the Nizam, and from it has been sought to be deduced that the Government of the Nizam meant something different from what it finally expressed in the terms of the deed granting the concession. I do not personally agree in the arguments which have been put forward with this view, and I do not see how the discussions which led to the concession can in any way vary its clearly expressed terms. Now I will read to you the first article, and the beginning of the second article, of the concession as finally approved by Her Majesty's Secretary of State for India. "The concessionnaires, or their respective executors or administrators, shall on any date within six months after the capital for the construction of the line from Warangal to Singareni is practically assured, form in London, under the Companies' Acts, 1862 to 1880, a Company limited by shares, with a capital of not less than £1,000,000, with powers to increase the capital by an issue of debentures, or otherwise, if necessary, and having for or among its objects the acquisition of the rights and liabilities of the concessionnaires under these presents, and the execution of the works herein referred to. If such a Company shall be formed before the expiration of the period fixed in Clause 1, and if before that period £150,000 of its share capital, at the least, shall have been subscribed and £75,000 shall have been actually paid-up in respect of the subscribed share capital, and if such Company shall also before the said period have adopted this concession and made itself liable to make the payments mentioned in Clause 11 hereof, and in all other respects liable upon these presents to the same extent as the concessionnaires were or would be liable, then it shall be lawful for the concessionnaires to transfer to such Company the benefit of this concession."

There is not another word in the deed which refers to the terms of transfer to a Company. The stipulations which I have read were exactly and literally carried out when the concession was transferred to this Company. You will observe that there was no limitation on the capital of the Company, except that it was to be not less than £1,000,000, and no limitation on the amount to be subscribed, except that it was to be £150,000 at the least. At the same time there was an obligation on the Company to issue more than £150,000. It had an option to issue as much more as it thought proper or necessary, and that option it still retains. You will further observe that the Company had to to be formed in a very limited time, which, in fact, would have expired in September, 1886. The final sanction of the Secretary of State was not accorded to the concession until July 27, 1886, so that there was no time to be lost. Such preparations as were possible had been made in anticipation of this sanction, and the Company was registered the next day. You will next observe that the Company had to acquire the rights of the concessionnaires, and the question at once arose at what price those rights were to be acquired. Now the concessionnaires had come to the conclusion that at that time, before the value of the concession could have been appreciated by the public, it was preferable not to ask the public to subscribe the shares, and they determined themselves to subscribe and pay up the whole of the stipulated capital of £150,000. Accordingly it was all so subscribed and allotted to eight persons, who thus formed the entire Company, and who paid in cash immediately £75,000, and later the remaining £75,000, the concessionnaires paying also the whole preliminary expenses of the formation of the Company. The Company, therefore, was a private Company, like many others, which must be familiar to you. I may mention Messrs. Glyn, Mills, Currie, and Co., Messrs. Bass and Co., Messrs. Armstrong, Mitchell, and Co. Like this Company, none of these ever issued a prospectus or offered any shares to the public or in any way held out inducements to the public to buy shares from the Company. The position was therefore this—the Company was really a partneship into which the concessionnaires brought £150,000 in cash and a concession, the value of which had to be represented by paper shares. Although the public at that time could not be supposed to know the value of the concession, all the members of the Company had before them ample materials for estimating its value. These consisted of a series of reports on the coal mines, either by officers of the Nizam's Government or of the Government of India, a very full and careful account of the mineral resources of the country officially drawn up by officers of the Nizam's Government, and a mass of information contained in a publication of the Government of India on the geology of India. A special report was also furnished to the Directors by Mr. Furnivall, M.I.C.E., an engineer of ability and eminence, formerly Assistant Secretary to the Government of India in the Public Works Department, and afterwards Chief Engineer of the Nizam's Railway, who had personally examined the country. With the information thus before them, and the fact that the concession extended over a country containing an area of over 81,000 square miles, or about that of Great Britain, abounding in valuable minerals, and being opened up by the construction of a railway, the Directors thought they were justified in acceding to the valuation put upon the concession of £850,000, all in paper shares, and it was so entered in their accounts. There was no concealment of this fact. It was stated in the agreement registered with the Registrar of Joint-Stock Companies, it was published in the newspapers, it was entered in Burdett's Official Intelligence, published early in 1887, and it was finally distinctly brought to the individual knowledge of every shareholder, each of whom was in July, 1887, furnished with a balance-sheet of the Company, in which the purchase price is set out in full. This was also communicated at the same time to the Secretary of State for India and to the Nizam's Government, who had been previously informed of it. From that time until the recent newspaper attacks commenced, a period of over nine months, not one word of comment, objection, or remonstrance was received by the Board from the Nizam's Government, the Government of India, the shareholders, or from any quarter whatever. At the time these shares were allotted to the concessionnaires I do not suppose anybody had any idea that there would be any market for them until the value of the concession had been fully demonstrated by the results of the Company's expenditure. With the sale of the shares in the market the Board had no concern whatever; their duty was confined to registering the transfers as they came in.

Gentlemen, after all that has been said and done, I maintain that £850,000 is not, to say the least, an over valuation of the property of the Company. The sole cause for the present depreciation of the shares has been the organized, violent, and unmeasured attacks made on the Company and its transactions by anonymous persons for objects best known to themselves—attacks which led to this Parliamentary inquiry, the result of which we feel very confident will ultimately not injuriously affect our position. The basis of that confidence is the proved value of our property. Our researches have shown that the Singareni coal mine is even more extensive than we had been at first led to suppose. After making every sort of reduction and allowance, the estimate of 94 million tons of good steam coal within 300 feet of the surface has been arrived at as the available supply. We are certain that there will be a very large demand for this coal. The Government of India estimated that the railways would take from us nearly 200,000 tons annually. Besides this there are many industrial purposes for which our coal will be required. If, as we hope and expect, the coal can be profitably used by the coasting steamers and those belonging to the great lines, which at present burn coal brought all the way from England and Australia, it is difficult to place a limit on the demand. (Hear, hear.) As to the actual working of the coal our operations have been delayed by causes beyond our control; but we must succeed, for the coal is there, and the greater part of the necessary machinery is there also, and it will require very little more capital expenditure and time before we begin earning a revenue, the limits to which we cannot foresee. We have already, I understand, in the course of our preliminary operations, turned out more than 4,000 tons of good steam coal, besides many thousand tons of small coal, for which we shall, no doubt, find profitable employment. Last week we received a report, drawn up by Mr. James E. Berkeley, the locomotive superintendent of H. H. the Nizam's Guaranteed State Railways, which we are now supplying with Singareni coal, on the efficiency of that coal for locomotive purposes. Mr. Berkeley made six trips up and six trips down the 121 miles of line between Secunderabad and Wadi. He took very careful observations of all particulars connected with the use of the coal, which he says was of average merit, and not selected for any speciality. The averages of his trials, he considers, conclusively prove that we have in the Singareni coal a valuable locomotive engine fuel. He also states that the coal is almost as easy to handle and to work as English, and better than any Indian coal he is aware of, or has ascertained from drivers and others who have had experience in working various Indian coals. He has been using the nuts in the smith's shop, and has also used coke made in a crude fashion from this coal in the foundry furnaces. He found that 166·02 lb. of Singareni coal were consumed per 1,000 gross ton miles—that is, that quantity drew 1,000 tons one mile. Lieut.-Colonel Conway Gordon, R.E., Director-General of Railways in India, in his administration report for 1887-88, states the quality of the Singareni coal is very good, the results obtained by its use on the Nizam's Guaranteed State Railway comparing very favourably with English coal burned on the Great Indian Peninsular Railway under very similar circumstances as regards inclinations of gradients and other conditions. Lieut.-General Conway Gordon gives 176·74 lb. as the average quantity of coal consumed on the Great Indian Peninsular Railway per 1,000 gross ton miles during the first half-year of 1887. He also states that on the Nizam's Railway in that period the average consumption of wood per 1,000 gross ton miles was 565·23 lb., costing Rs.4·48 per ton. Now, 166·02 lb. of Singareni coal, which does the same work, would, at Rs.15 per ton, be cheaper than the wood. Yesterday we received a letter from Mr. Hughes, dated July 15, in which he states that the despatches for the week ending July 7 were 560 tons. He adds that we shall reach 3,000 tons in August, and that he has already sent trial wagons to Gulbarga, Raichur, Adoni, and Bellari, and that he anticipates supplying Madras and the Colar gold mines soon. We can give "nuts" at 2 rupees or 2 rupees 8 annas per ton. So much for the Singareni coal. Turning now to gold, I think no one who has read Mr. Stephenson's report on the result of his prospecting operations in the Raichore Doab, can fail to be convinced that we have a magnificent future in this metal alone. The gold area already established by this examination is 550 square miles, of which he has found 130 square miles to be full of old workings; regarding these, there was no previous information procurable. Now, we are informed by Messrs. Morgans that the fact that the ancient miners worked these lodes is of itself *primâ facie* evidence that the percentage of gold was comparatively large; for, with their primitive methods, they were unable to work poor ore profitably. These methods also did not permit them to follow the lodes beyond a certain depth when they were met by mechanical difficulties with which they could not compete. Hence it is practically certain that the lodes were not exhausted by them, and a rich harvest is left for us. We hope before long to commence reaping it. Messrs. Morgans, the well-known firm of mining engineers of Bristol and London, have estimated the present value of our gold discoveries at over one million sterling. The reports on which my remarks are based have been sent to all the shareholders, but it is possible that some of you may not have had leisure to read them. As the opinion of Messrs. Morgans is a very important and valuable one, I will, with your permission, read you what they say about the gold properties. Before doing so, I will recall to your minds that at our last meeting Mr. Hughes, Deputy Superintendent of the Geological Survey of the Government of India, stated that the auriferous reef of Mysore ran into the territory of the Nizam. Now this is what Messrs. Morgans say:—"Gold mining has proved in Mysore, as is well known to mining engineers and to others, that success is to be found through bottoming the shallow mines of the ancients, whose drainage appliances were too primitive to enable them to follow the gold in depth; and if gold mining experience in India has up to the present established one useful fact more than another it is that the existence of old workings in gold-bearing reefs is the real criterion of value. The best way of getting an idea of the value of the 130 square miles of gold-bearing rocks (already proved by the presence of old workings to have been mined on the outcrops and shown thereby to be commercially valuable), is to apply the standard of value of a gold-bearing property of a similar character, such, for instance, as occurs in the Colar (Mysore) district in India. The total area of the Colar concession is about twenty square miles, and the present market value of the mining properties established on that concession amounts to a total sum of about £960,000. Allowing two-thirds of this sum as being capital in part expended in opening and equipping the mines, and in part as floating capital, and capital held in reserve, the remaining one-third, or £320,000 represents the market value of the twe nty square miles, in round numbers, of Colar auriferous rocks. This is equal to an average of about £25 per acre, or £16,000 per square mile. At that rate the 139 square miles already discovered by this Company would be worth £2,080,000. But the sub-divided areas of the Colar concession have been sub-let to subsidiary Companies by the Colar concessionnaires, who received premiums in return, whereas the sub-letting of the blocks of the Company's discoveries will involve negotiations, labour and expenditure, and it will be necessary before the whole of the discoveries can be utilized to secure the extension of railway communication up to the gold reefs. If the very ample allowance of £1,000,000 be set aside for these outgoings, then the Company's gold discoveries would still be worth £1,080,000, according to the standard of the present market value of the properties on the Colar concession, including those at a discount as well as those at a premium. Considering the early stage of the operations as they stand at present, it is impossible to deal with exact figures of value, but the foregoing comparative statement is useful as an indication of the great potential value of the extensive areas of gold-bearing rocks of the discovery of which you have been advised."

I will now read to you the views of Mr. Stephenson, the prospector, who has personally examined the country:—"It is quite certain that this Company would be ill-advised to try and work one tithe even of what has so far been discovered, and to utilize its resources, therefore, it will have to form subsidiary Companies either within or without its own limits. To do so, blocks of land will have to be surveyed off, and full particulars within the limits of the block given, and possibly some deep prospecting undertaken in order to show something more than mere prospective value in the shape of old workings and reefs." We are taking steps to mark out a block of about one square mile, and to have put before us all the necessary information to enable us to sell this block to a subsidiary Company. If we do so, we shall certainly be one square mile the poorer, but I hope a considerable sum of money the richer, as a first instalment of our gold profits. More than this, negotiations have been commenced with persons of undoubted financial position, whose names for the present I must withhold, for the transfer to a Company of our rights over portions of our gold-bearing properties. In a letter of July 14, from our agent, received yesterday, he states that Mr. Hughes is of opinion that it will be necessary to take up a very large tract of land, but he thinks it desirable first to obtain a thoroughly reliable analysis of the ore, and for that purpose Mr. Stephenson is now packing ore to be sent home to the Board. He adds that Mr. Hughes appears very confident that the ore will give good results. There have been recent articles in the *Statist*, which is probably known to you all as a serious, high-class, and well informed paper, calling attention to the improving prospects of the Indian gold mines in the province of Mysore, which, as I have said before, are situated in reefs which extend to the Nizam's Dominions, and are, therefore, within our concession. Now, gentlemen, I come to the diamonds. You will have seen from the reports the history of our operations under the charge of Mr. Lowinsky, a highly experienced gentleman, whose energy has commanded the praise of everyone who knows what he has gone through. That gentleman, from his examination of the old workings, was thoroughly convinced that only a small fraction of the diamondiferous soil had been worked. Unless the old workers possessed a divining-rod which infallibly pointed out to them where diamonds were, and where they were not to be found, it is impossible to conceive that they can have exhausted the fields. We find in numerous localities a series of abandoned pits covering a large area; they are of no great depth, but evidence an enormous and long-continued industry. Between these pits and around them is a vast extent of totally untouched ground, beneath which lies the diamondiferous stratum. If diamonds were found in paying quantities by the ancient workers in the portion of this stratum which they were able to reach, and we know they were so found, the probability of their being found in the untouched portions seems to be overwhelming. Then, I may be asked, Why have they not been found? The answer is simply that the diamondiferous soil has first to be uncovered and next washed. For these purposes labour and machinery are necessary. The machinery we have provided, but although ordered in August, 1887, it did not reach the diamond fields until February this year. Mr. Lowinsky, with great trouble, had collected a large body of some 800 labourers, but just as the machinery was erected and ready for work, cholera broke out, every labourer left the place, and could not be induced to return by the offer of extraordinary wages until the disease disappeared. Once more Mr. Lowinsky set to work, and again collected his gangs of coolies, but the bursting of the monsoon or periodical rains flooded his excavations and rendered further work impossible for the next two or three months. That is our present position, but there is nothing really in it which disproves the arguments on which we base our hopes of profits from the diamondiferous property. We shall continue our work next October with undiminished energy and with undiminished confidence in our ultimate success. With our machinery all ready we shall have eight or nine months in which to work continuously. With ordinary good fortune we shall have something to show for that work, which will go far to re-establish the public appreciation of this portion of our property. Mr. Lowinsky, in a letter of June 28, received yesterday, states that he has sunk a small shaft in the bottom of the working, and there is an average of 6 or 7 ft. of ground to be excavated, to uncover it; this would, under ordinary circumstances, take but a short time; but, since the rains, there has been a very great influx of water, at times so much that it has been quite impossible to keep the whole of the working clear, although pumping goes on night and day. On July 14, Mr. Lowinsky telegraphed that he could not continue the work during the rains. We have encouraging accounts of mica, but I will not speak of these, nor of lead, copper or iron, or other minerals. I will say that the existence of large quantities of superior iron ore in close proximity to the coal is an ascertained fact, and the only question is whether, with the present low prices of English iron and low freights, we are justified in sinking capital in establishing iron and steel works. Gentlemen, I think I have said enough to show the great potential value of our property, and to justify the price we have paid for it. The profit made by the concessionnaires, who were given this magnificent property, is known, and requires no effort of the mind to grasp, but the value of this unprecedented concession to the Company with which those profits have to be compared is not so easily appreciated. If it were, you may be sure we should not have heard so much of the former and so little of the latter. If now, gentlemen, you will turn to the balance-sheet you will see that out of our working capital of £750,000, we had spent up to April 30, 1888, £55,639, and that we had still in hand at that date, £94,361. Our expenditure has already provided the greater part of the machinery required for the efficient working of the coal and diamonds, and for the prospecting of gold and mica. It has paid the salaries and wages of our staff and *employés* in India, as well as our establishment in London. The money we have in hand ought to carry us on for a longer period than that which has elapsed since the formation of the Company, perhaps even to the end of 1891, when our term for prospecting ceases. At our first meeting in November, 1886, I was asked whether the Company intended to work all the properties itself. I replied that this was impossible, that our plan was to form subsidiary Companies, to whom we hoped to sell those properties after we had proved their value. These subsidiary Companies will, while paying us for the right of working the properties made over to them, provide working capital for their own operations. This is one of the means by which the Company can provide further capital for the working of the properties which it may show to be worth working. We may be quite sure that if our operations succeed, as they must succeed, in demonstrating that good returns may be expected from the employment of further capital, the necessary funds will be easily procurable.

Gentlemen, you will see from the report before you that Mr. Winter and myself resign our seats at the Board and offer ourselves for re-election. I may be permitted to say that, although the greater part of the responsibility and labour involved in carrying on the affairs of the Company has come upon me as Chairman, I have received the same fees as each other Director. Since the formation of the Company, two years ago, I have, except during a few short absences from London, daily attended at the Company's offices for the purpose of carrying on its business. Without wishing in any way to depreciate the services of the rest of the Board, I must state that the most useful of my colleagues has been Mr. Winter, who has given me the greatest assistance. If it is your pleasure to re-elect us, we shall be happy to continue to give our best attention to the affairs of the Company. The matter is entirely in your own hands, and I say for myself, and am authorised by Mr. Winter to say for him, that whatever may be your decision we shall be perfectly satisfied with it. I cannot conclude without bearing testimony to the great assistance which we have met with from the Government of His Highness the Nizam in the operations of the company. When the Government thought it proper to suspend the Sirdar Diler-ul-Dowla last April, and when articles began to appear in the newspapers attacking the Company, the Minister, Sir Busheer-ud-Dowlah (Asman Jah), the present Prime Minister, on the 21st of that month invited Mr. Furnivall, our agent, and Mr. Lowinsky, to visit him, and he received them with great courtesy and in a most cordial spirit. His Excellency stated that the wishes of His Highness's Government was to the effect that the works of the Company should be in no way hindered by the recent suspension of the Home Secretary. He promised aid to Mr. Lowinsky in every form possible, and urged him to do his utmost to discover diamonds. Mr. Furnivall, in reporting this to the board added: "I am satisfied that His Excellency the Minister and Officers of the State of Hyderabad will afford me all possible aid in carrying on the works of the Company in India, and therefore the directors need not feel anxiety on that ground." In a later letter Mr. Furnivall wrote: "I am confident of the thorough goodwill of His Excellency the Minister, Sir Asman Jah. Personally he will, I feel sure, be very much averse to doing anything which may prove prejudicial to the interests of the shareholders, and, so far as work in India is concerned, I feel certain that obstacles will not be thrown in the way." In proof of these assurances of the Prime Minister, he at once nominated Nawab Mehdi Hasan Fathah Nawaz Jung Bahadur, the Chief Justice of the Hyderabad State, to take his seat on this Board, to which he was accordingly elected. He has associated himself with us in the most friendly spirit, and he has expressed himself as much pleased with the manner in which the affairs of the Company are conducted by the Board. We have to mention with regret the death of our colleague, Mr. John Stewart, last year. Mr. B. W. Colvin was elected a Director in his place—a gentleman of high official position and experience in India, who is a Director of the East India Railway Company. If I may be permitted to conclude with a few words of what appears to me to be sound advice, I would say that our best policy is to maintain a firm, confident, and united attitude. Nothing would more please the enemies of the Company than to see a split in our camp. The results of such a split would infallibly be still further to depress the market value of our shares and obstruct our operations. The line we should take is the true one—

namely, that our property is an extremely valuable one, and our sole business is to make this fact patent to all. In conclusion, the Chairman moved that the report of the Directors and statement of accounts to April 30, 1888, be received and adopted. (Cheers.)

Mr. Hewlings seconded the motion.

Mr. Germaine moved, as an amendment: "That this meeting do adjourn until the earliest possible time after the report of the House of Commons Committee has been put into the hands of the members of the Company." He appealed to the Board not to use proxies in order to defeat the amendment.

Mr. John Edwards seconded the amendment, and protested against the adoption of the balance-sheet until the House of Commons Committee had reported.

Sir Julian Goldsmid, M.P., supported the amendment, and protested against the action of Mr. Watson (one of the Directors) in sending out applications for proxies. He thought the meeting might at least be adjourned till October, and he asked Mr. Watson to support the proposal in his own interest. (Hear, hear.)

Sir Roper Lethbridge, M.P., also supported the amendment, and said it was to be regretted that the meeting should have been held before the House of Commons Committee had reported, especially as the report would probably be printed in the course of a few days. He appealed to the directors to wait until the charges, if any, were formulated. At the same time he had every confidence in the future of the Company. (Hear, hear.)

Mr. FitzHugh supported the amendment, and expressed the hope that, as a mere matter of common sense and business the Directors would agree with it.

Mr. Watson said he need merely say that he should be very happy to meet any Committee that the shareholders chose to appoint to discuss matters with himself and his co-concessionnaires. He and the other Directors would pledge themselves to meet such a Committee in the most honourable manner. With regard to the question of proxies, he had received them from shareholders who held 25,798 shares outside the concessionnaires. Those who sent the proxies knew what they were to be used for, and in their interests he certainly intended to use them.

Mr. Arthur Baker and Mr. Forbes protested against the use of the proxies, and after some further remarks by Mr. Germaine and Sir Julian Goldsmid,

The Chairman said that there was nothing in the report which affected the questions before the House of Commons. It was merely a formal statement of their operations and expenditure, and he could see no valid reason for not passing these accounts. How could they go on working if the past expenditure was not sanctioned? Obviously he could not go on signing cheques if there was a doubt whether his acts would be ratified. It would be easy to have another meeting, which the shareholders could convene themselves if they chose.

Lord Lawrence (one of the Directors) said he thought Mr. Watson had a right to use his proxies. The fact that Mr. Watson held so large a number of proxies showed that he had the confidence of the great majority of the shareholders. He suggested that a committee of shareholders should be appointed to consult with the directors. (Hear.)

Mr. B. W. Colvin (another director) also expressed himself in favour of an adjournment.

After a scene of some confusion, during which several gentlemen were speaking at once, the amendment was put in the following words: "That this meeting do adjourn till October 15," and carried by 44 votes to 9. A poll was then demanded, and after some discussion the Chairman said he thought it would be fair to adjourn the poll for seven days. (Applause.)

In making the announcement, he said that remarks had been used with regard to independent members of the Board, and he protested that if this was meant as a reflection on himself it was undeserved, for he was perfectly independent. He held 150 shares, which he bought at 11¼, and he had never made a penny out of the Company except in the shape of Directors' fees. (Hear.)

It was subsequently arranged that the poll should be taken and other business transacted at Winchester House on Monday next, at twelve o'clock: and the meeting closed with a vote of thanks to the Chairman, moved by Sir J. Goldsmid and seconded by Sir R. Lethbridge.—*Financial News*, August 8.

AFTER these notes have gone to press the result of the Hyderabad Deccan Company's meeting will be known. Mr. Watson has been touting for proxies most indefatigably, and has a strong case for the defence. In case the concession holds good, as from the articles which have appeared in *Trade and Finance* seems likely, Mr. Watson will naturally point to those who raised all the rumpus, and ask whom it has benefited. Not the shareholders certainly, for their property did stand at over par, and has since then been thrown down to 5¼ to 5¾. The Directors have not had a happy time of it at all. First, the *Times* in an article last week severely criticises them for holding the meeting at all before the result of the Parliamentary Commission can be known, while, on the other hand, other journals have been baying them to hold it for some time, and inform the shareholders what progress has been made. In this latter particular the Board have certainly been about as remiss as any Board could possibly be. Beyond Mr. Theodore W. Hughes's high-flown estimates of invisible coal shareholders have had but little to go upon for months—even years.

THE Exchange Telegraph Company state, at a general meeting of the Hyderabad (Deccan) Company, yesterday, the Chairman moved the adoption of the report. This was met by an amendment that the meeting stand adjourned until after the publication of the report of the Select Committee. A long and excited discussion ensued, the chairman saying that not to pass the accounts would be tantamount to a vote of want of confidence. The amendment was carried by show of hands. A demand for a poll was made, and the chairman ordered the poll to be taken at once, whereupon the great body of shareholders commenced leaving the room, crying, "Thieves!" "Swindlers!" etc., and strongly denouncing the Chairman and Mr. Watson. The poll was finally adjourned for a week.—*Barker's Trade and Finance*, August 8.

IN meeting the shareholders of the Hyderabad (Deccan) Company yesterday, the Directors put a bold face on the scandals disclosed by the recent Parliamentary Inquiry. Mr. Batten, the chairman, in the course of an elaborate statement, endeavoured to convince the meeting that everything that had been done was fair and above-board, and that the shareholders had good value for their money. His argument was that the whole affair was a partnership between the concessionnaires and the shareholders, into which the former brought £150,000 and the latter £850,000, which represented the value of the concession. It mattered not, according to his view, that the concession was obtained for nothing. It was worth the amount stated, and that was sufficient for the shareholders. In order to prove the latter point, Mr. Batten dangled before the meeting a seductive list of the minerals which were to be had for the working in the Nizam's dominions. There were, he told the gathering, immense coalfields, which would supply the railways of India and the coasting steamers with coal; there were diamonds which would revive the glories of Golconda; there were gold, mica, lead, iron, copper, and other minerals in abundance. The fascinating prospect which the mere enumeration of this wealth held out appeared, however, to make little impression on the ungrateful individuals who had been admitted to a share in all these good things. They clamoured for an adjournment of the meeting until the Select Committee's report shall have been published, and they have had an opportunity of obtaining an impartial opinion on the subject. This proposal was resisted by the Directors, but eventually an amendment in favour of an adjournment was carried, amid a scene of great excitement and confusion.—*Yorkshire Post*, August 8.

Hyderabad Shareholders Meet, and Excitedly Shout "Thieves!" and "Swindlers!"—Watson Beaten.—There was a not altogether harmonious meeting of the shareholders of the Hyderabad Deccan Company at Winchester House yesterday, Mr. George H. M. Batten in the chair. The report stated that the Directors would have been glad to have been able to defer the General Meeting until the publication of the report of the Select Committee of the House of Commons, but thought it desirable not to delay the meeting. They were advised and believed that the title of the Company to its property was unassailable, and would not be attacked. The relations between the Nizam's Government and the Company were perfectly cordial. The balance-sheet, up to 30 April last, showed that there was a balance in hand of £97,955.

The Chairman, Mr. George Batten, in the course of a very long speech, defended the action of the Directors in the management of the concession. He maintained that £850,000 was not an over valuation of the property. The reports of the Singareni coalfield were most satisfactory, and reports by Mr. Stephenson showed that they had

A MAGNIFICENT FUTURE IN GOLD ALONE.

Mr. Germaine moved an amendment to the adoption of the report to the effect that the meeting stand adjourned until after the publication of the report of the Select Committee.

Sir Julian Goldsmid, M.P., strongly condemned the action of Mr. Watson in trying to secure the profits of shareholders. Mr. Watson had made an immense profit out of the concession, and it behoved him to state what he proposed to do for the benefit of the shareholders.

Sir Roper Lethbridge, M.P., and others supported the amendment.

Mr. Watson, in response to loud calls, said he would be

HAPPY TO MEET A COMMITTEE

of the shareholders of the Company and hear what they thought he ought to do—(cheers)—but he would not consent to the amendment.

The amendment, however, was put and carried by 44 to 5. A demand for a poll was handed in on behalf of Mr. Watson, and the Chairman ordered that it should be taken at once. This gave rise to a startling scene. The great body of the shareholders, crying "Shame" in an excited manner, left the room. Cries of "Thieves and swindlers," were frequent, and the Chairman and Mr. Watson were strongly denounced.

The Chairman finally announced that, after re-consideration, he had decided to adjourn the poll for seven days, an announcement which was greeted with loud cheers.—*Star*, August 8.

At the meetings of the Hyderabad (Deccan) and Metropolitan District Railway Companies yesterday, shareholders and Directors seem to have had a lively time. It is an unfortunate thing, but it appears to be the case, that House of Commons methods are spreading to the proceedings of commercial bodies. Surely dignified protest is more effective than riot, the calling of names, and utterance of offensive exclamations. At the Hyderabad meeting there occurred what the reporter modestly calls "a scene of some confusion," for several gentlemen were speaking at once. More than several gentlemen then began to cry "Shame!" and, at the suggestion of a shareholder, marched out of the room. At some one else's suggestion they presently marched in again, and then there occurred a scene not only of "some," but of "the greatest" confusion. Whoever was right and whoever was wrong, these scenes are not calculated to do the Company any good. At the Metropolitan District Railway meeting there were scenes also. Some friends of Sir Edward Watkin, who imagine that he finds insufficient occupation in managing a few other railways and advocating the most mischievous (happily likewise the most hopeless) of modern enterprises, the Channel Tunnel, want to place the District Railway also in his hands, and the majority of the shareholders do not welcome the proposition. It is certain that the District Railway ought to be a remunerative affair, being, as it is, a practical necessity to myriads of Londoners, and equally certain that it does not pay a reasonable dividend; but little good can arise from shouting at the Chairman.—*Evening Standard*, August 8.

The Hyderabad Concessionnaires.—The gentlemen who have been so fortunate as to pocket £850,000, or its equivalent, for the Hyderabad concession—or such of them as were present at the meeting of the shareholders yesterday—had rather a warm time of it. The very free expressions used by some of the more excited speakers are not usually heard in such eminently respectable City circles. The cry of "Thieves!" and "Swindlers!" would not create much commotion on the fringe of a racecourse, but to be used in the company of men who deal in their hundreds of thousands and negotiate with princes created somewhat of a sensation. By the uproar, and the interposition of the Nizam's representative, the shareholders got their way, and secured an adjournment of the meeting for a week, by which time the report of the Select Committee will have been published. That document, we believe, will not prove so colourless as the News Agency epitome of the early draft.—*Pall Mall Gazette*, August 8.

The Hyderabad (Deccan) Company.—The second ordinary annual general meeting of the Hyderabad (Deccan) Company was held yesterday at Winchester House, Old Broad Street, Mr. G. H. M. Batten, Chairman, presiding. The report stated that the expenditure up to the 30th April last amounted to £55,638, leaving a balance of cash in hand of £97,955.

The Chairman, in moving the adoption of the report, said that during the last three months the Directors had experienced a very anxious time, and he proceeded to defend their action in the management of the concessions. He said that at the time these shares were allotted to the concessionnaires he did not suppose anybody had any idea that there would be any market for them until the value of the concession had been fully demonstrated by the results of the Company's expenditure. With the sale of the shares in the market the Board had no concern whatever. Their duty was confined to registering the transfers as they came in. After all that had been said and done, he maintained that £850,000 was not, to say the least, an over-valuation of the property of the Company. (Applause and hisses).

The motion for the adoption of the report was seconded by Mr. Hewlings, a shareholder.

Mr. Germaine moved, as an amendment, "That this meeting do adjourn until the earliest possible time after the report of the House of Commons Committee has been put into the hands of the members of the Company."

Mr. John Edwards seconded the amendment.

Sir Julian Goldsmid, M.P., supported the amendment, and protested against the action of Mr. Watson (one of the Directors) in sending out applications for proxies. Mr. Watson and other concessionnaires had made a very large profit in cash out of the formation of the Company, and he thought that if Mr. Watson desired to maintain his reputation in the City he ought to say what he intended to do for the Company. He thought the meeting might at least be adjourned till October, and he asked Mr. Watson to support the proposal in his own interest. (Hear, hear.)

Sir Roper Lethbridge, M.P., also supported the amendment, and said it was to be regretted that the meeting should have been held before the House of Commons Committee had reported, especially as the report would probably be printed in the course of a few days. (Hear.) Sir Henry James's words in the House of Commons on Saturday, in denying the authenticity of the pseudo report published, were of a very startling description, and he appealed to the Directors to wait until the charges, if any, were formulated. At the same time he had every confidence in the future of the Company. (Hear.)

Mr. Watson said he need merely say that he should be very happy to meet any Committee that the shareholders chose to appoint to discuss matters with himself and his co-concessionnaires. He and the other Directors would pledge themselves to meet such a Committee in the most honourable manner.

Lord Lawrence (one of the Directors) said that he must confess that he was in favour of an adjournment – (applause) – but at the same time he thought that Mr. Watson had a right to use his proxies. If he were not satisfied that Mr. Watson and his co-concessionnaires would do what was fair and honourable he would not remain on the Board. (Hear.)

After a scene of some confusion, during which several gentlemen were speaking at once, the amendment was put in the following words :—" That this meeting do adjourn till October 15," and carried by 44 votes to 9.—A poll was demanded, and after some discussion the Chairman directed that the poll should be taken at once. The decision was hailed with loud cries of "Shame!" and at the suggestion of a Shareholder the majority of the meeting left the room, again shouting "Shame!" and shaking hats and fists at the Board. Shortly after, however, most of them returned, and after a scene of the greatest confusion, the Chairman said that on re-consideration he thought it would be fair to adjourn the poll for seven days. (Applause). In making the announcement, he said that remarks had been used with regard to "independent members" of the Board, and he protested that if this was meant as a reflection on himself it was undeserved, for he was perfectly independent. He held 150 shares, which he bought at 11¼ and he had never made a penny out of the Company except in the shape of directors' fees. (Hear.)

It was subsequently arranged that the poll should be taken and other business transacted at Winchester House on Monday next, at twelve o'clock; and the meeting closed with a vote of thanks to the Chairman, moved by Sir J. Goldsmid, and seconded by Sir R. Lethbridge.—*Standard*, August 8.

THE HYDERABAD (DECCAN).—The second ordinary annual general meeting of the Hyderabad (Deccan) Company was held yesterday at Winchester House, Old Broad Street, Mr. G. H. M. Batten, chairman, presiding. The report stated that the expenditure up to April 30th last, amounted to £55,638, leaving a balance of cash in hand of £97,955.

The Chairman gave an exhaustive account of the position and prospects of the Company. He said the Directors have had a very anxious time, though their anxiety had not been one of any doubts as to the validity of the title by which the Company holds its property, nor to any doubts as to the really great value of that property. Nothing whatever of an irregular or illegal character had taken place in the initiation of the Company, and it was the opinion of competent experts that the amount paid for the property was by no means excessive. Singareni coal mine was even more extensive than the directors had been led to suppose, for, after making every sort of reduction and allowance, the estimate of 94 million tons of good steam coal within 300 feet of the surface had been arrived at as the available supply. The Government of India estimated that the railways would take from the Company nearly 200,000 tons of coal annually. The prospects with regard to gold and diamonds were also considered to be most encouraging.

The motion for the adoption of the report was seconded by Mr. Hewlings, a shareholder.

Mr. Germaine moved an amendment to the effect that the meeting stand adjourned until after the publication of the report of the Select Committee.

This was seconded by Mr. John Edwards.

Sir Julian Goldsmid, M.P., strongly condemned the action of Mr. Watson in trying to secure the profits of shareholders. He had made an immense profit out of the concession, and it behoved Mr. Watson to state what he proposed to do for the benefit of the shareholders. He supported the amendment.

Sir Roper Lethbridge, M.P., agreed with Sir Julian Goldsmid in his appreciation of the efforts of the Chairman. It was true that Mr. Batten had been qualified by Mr. Watson, but he had always worked for the best interests of the Company. He supported the adjournment. The report of Sir Henry James's Committee would be published in a day or two, and he would urge the Directors, in their own interests to accept the amendment.

Mr. Fitz-Hugh also supported the amendment.

Mr. Watson, in response to loud calls, said he would be happy to meet a Committee of the shareholders of the Company, and hear what they thought he ought to do, but he would not consent to an adjournment.

Mr. Germaine's amendment adjourning the meeting until October 15 was put by the Chairman, and, on a show of hands was carried by 44 to 9. A demand for a poll was handed in by Mr. Clements, on behalf of Mr. Watson, and the Chairman ordered that a poll should be taken at once. This gave rise to a very startling scene, the great body of the shareholders crying "Shame!" in an excited manner left the room. Cries of "Thieves, and swindlers!" were frequent, and the Chairman and Mr. Watson were strongly denounced.

Sir Roger Lethbridge, after a few moments' conversation with the Nawab Mehdi Hasan, said that the Nizam's representative was in favour of the adjournment.

It was subsequently arranged that the poll should be taken, and other business transacted, at Winchester House on Monday next at twelve o'clock; and the meeting closed with a vote of thanks to the Chairman, moved by Sir J. Goldsmid, and seconded by Sir R. Lethbridge.—*Daily Chronicle*, August 8.

The Hyderabad (Deccan) Company (Limited).—The second annual meeting of this Company was held yesterday at Winchester House. Mr. George H. M. Batten presiding. There were present: Lord Lawrence, Nawab Bahadur (Chief Justice of the Hyderabad State), Sir Julian Goldsmid, M.P., Sir Roper Lethbridge, M.P., and other holders.

The report was taken as read.

The Chairman stated that he had received letters from five shareholders suggesting that the meeting should be put off until after the Select Committee of the House of Commons had presented their report. On the other hand, complaints had been made that too long a delay had occurred in holding the meeting. It was not easy to satisfy the conflicting views of 700 shareholders, but the Directors believed that in calling the meeting they were acting in accordance with the views of the vast majority. The financial year ended on the 30th of April, and the accounts had been made up and audited. The evidence before the Select Committee was completed on the 22nd of June. The Directors had waited six weeks for the Select Committee's report, and they had no means of knowing when it would be presented. These were the considerations which had led them, with the concurrence of the whole Board, to call that meeting for the transaction of the ordinary business of the Company. Statements had appeared as to the presumed contents of the report of the Select Committee, but these had been disavowed, and it could not be said when it would appear. The Directors awaited the issue of that report with confidence. The speaker went on to say that he need scarcely tell them that for the last three months the Directors had had a very anxious time. Their anxiety had not been, however, due to any doubts as to the validity of the title by which the Company held its property or to any doubts as the real great value of that property. Any unprejudiced person who read the terms of the concession on which the title was based, and who had made himself acquainted with the actual facts as to how that concession was transferred to the Company, could not fail to come to the conclusion that nothing illegal, irregular, or open on any ground to valid objection was done in the initiation of this Company. (A cheer.) Recently a great deal of correspondence had come to light which took place anterior to the grant of the concession. This correspondence was totally unknown to the first Directors of this Company, who had nothing whatever before them except the actual concession itself, as finally signed and sealed by the Nizam's Government. A great part of the correspondence took place between the Government of India and the Government of the Nizam, and from it had been sought to be deduced that the Government of the Nizam meant something different from what it finally expressed in the terms of the deed granting the concession. The speaker said he did not personally agree in the arguments which had been put forward with that view, and could not see how the discussions which led to the concession could in any way vary its clearly expressed terms. He then read the first article and the beginning of the second article of the concession as finally approved by Her Majesty's Secretary of State for India. "The concessionaires, or their respective executors or administrators shall on any date within six months after the capital for the construction of the line from Warangel to Singareni is practically assured, form in London, under the Companies' Acts, 1862 to 1880, a Company limited by shares, with a capital of not less than £1,000,000, with power to increase the capital by an issue of debentures, or otherwise, if necessary, and having for or among its objects the acquisition of the rights and liabilities of the concessionaires under these presents, and the execution of the works herein referred to. (2) If such a company shall be formed before the expiration of the period fixed in Clause 1, and if before that period £150,000 of its share capital, at the least, shall have been subscribed, and £75,000 shall have been actually paid-up in respect of the subscribed share capital, and if such Company shall also before the said period have adopted this concession, and made itself liable to make the payments mentioned in Clause II. hereof, and in all other respects liable upon these presents to the same extent as the concessionnaires were or would be liable, then it shall be lawful for the concessionnaires to transfer to such Company the benefit of this concession." There was not another word in the deed, the Chairman proceeded to say, which referred to the terms of transfer to a Company. The stipulations read were exactly and literally carried out when the concession was transferred to that Company. It would be observed that there was no limitation on the capital of the Company, except that it was to be "not less than" £1,000,000, and no limitation on the amount to be subscribed, except that it was to be £150,000 "at the least." At the same time there was no obligation on the Company to issue more than £150,000. It had an option to issue as much more as it thought proper or necessary, and that option it still retained. It would further be observed that the Company had to be formed in a very limited time, which in fact would have expired in September, 1886. The final sanction of the Secretary of State was not accorded to the concession until July 27, 1886, so that there was no time to be lost. Such preparations as were possible had been made in anticipation of that sanction, and the Company was registered the next day. They would next observe that the Company had to acquire the rights of the concessionnaires, and the question at once arose at what price those rights were to be acquired. Now the concessionnaires had come to the conclusion that at that time, before the value of the concession could have been appreciated by the public, it was preferable not to ask the public to subscribe the shares, and the concessionnaires determined themselves to subscribe and pay up the whole of the stipulated capital of £150,000. Accordingly it was all so subscribed and allotted to eight persons, who thus formed the entire Company, and who paid in cash immediately £75,000, and later the remaining £75,000, the concessionnaires paying also the whole preliminary expenses of the formation of the Company. The Company, therefore, was a private Company, like many others which must be familiar to them, as Messrs. Glynn, Mills, Currie, and Co., Messrs. Bass and Co., and Messrs. Armstrong, Mitchell, and Co. Like the Hyderabad Company, none of those ever issued a prospectus or offered any shares to the public, or in any way held out inducements to the public to buy shares from the Company. The position was, therefore, this—the Company was really a partnership into which the concessionnaires brought £150,000 in cash and a concession, the value of which had to be represented by paper shares. Although the public at that time could not be supposed to know the value of the concession, all the members of the company had before them ample materials for estimating its value. With the information thus before them, and the fact that the concession extended over a country containing an area of over 81,000 square miles, or about that of Great Britain, abounding in valuable minerals, and being opened up by the construction of a railway, the directors thought they were justified in acceding to the valuation put upon that concession of £850,000, all in paper shares, and it was so entered in their accounts. There was no concealment of the fact. It was stated in the agreement registered with the Registrar of Joint Stock Companies, it was published in the newspapers it was entered in "Burdett's Official Intelligence," published early in 1887, and it was finally distinctly brought to the individual knowledge of every shareholder, each of whom was in July, 1887, furnished with a balance-sheet of the Company, in which the purchase price was set out in full. That was also communicated at the same time to the Secretary of State for India and to the Nizam's Government, who had been previously informed of it. From that time until the recent newspaper attacks commenced, a period of over nine months, not one word of comment, objection, or remonstrance was received by the Board from the Nizam's Government, the Government of India, the shareholders, or from any quarter whatever. At the time those shares were allotted to the concessionnaires, the speaker, said he did not suppose anybody had any idea that there would be any market for them until the value of the concession had been fully demonstrated by the results of the Company's expenditure. With the sale of the shares in the market the Board had no concern whatever. Their duty was confined to registering the transfers as they came in. After all that had been said and done, he maintained that £850,000 was not, to say the least, an over-valuation of the property of the Company. Last week the Directors received a report, drawn up by Mr. James E. Berkeley, the Locomotive Superintendent of His Highness the Nizam's Guaranteed State Railways, which that Company was now supplying with Singareni coal, on the efficiency of that coal for locomotive purposes, Mr. Berkeley made six trips up and six trips down the 121 miles of line between Secunderabad and Wadi. The averages of his trials he considered conclusively proved that the Company had in the Singareni coal a valuable locomotive fuel, and that the coal was almost as easy to handle and to work as English. The speaker dealt in detail with the value of the coal and the prospective value of the gold, giving reports of surveys on this point, and dealt also with the belief of an experienced gentleman, Mr. Lowinsky, that a large diamondiferous soil existed. The working of that soil had been interfered with by the breaking out of cholera, and subsequently by the bursting of the monsoon. Then there were encouraging accounts of mica, and reports of the existence of superior iron ore near the coal, and the only question was whether, with the present low prices of English iron and low freights, the Company would be justified in sinking capital in establishing iron and steel works. If they would turn to the balance-sheet they would see that out of the working capital of £150,000, the Directors had spent up to the 30th of April, 1888, £55,639, and that they had still in hand at that date £94,361. The expenditure had already provided the greater part of the machinery required for the efficient working of coal and diamonds and for the prospecting of gold and mica. It had paid the salaries and wages of the staff and *employés* in India as well as the establishment in London. The money in hand ought to carry the Company on for a longer period than that which had elapsed since the formation, perhaps even to the end of 1891, when the term for prospecting ceased. At the first meeting in November, 1886, he was asked whether the Company intended to work all the properties itself. He replied that that was impossible, that the plan was to form subsidiary Companies, to whom Directors hoped to sell those properties after they had proved their value. Those subsidiary Companies would, while paying for the right of working the properties make over to them, provide working capital for their own operations. That was one of the means by which the Company could provide further capital for the working of the properties which it might show to be worth working. The shareholders might be quite sure that, if their operations succeeded, as they must succeed, in demonstrating that good returns might be expected from the employment of further capital, the necessary funds would be easily procurable. They would see from the report that Mr. Winter and himself resigned their seats at the Board and offered themselves for re-election. Although the greater part of the responsibility and labour involved in carrying on the affairs of the Company had come upon himself as Chairman, he had received the same fees as each other Director. Since the formation of the Company two years ago he had, except during a few short absences from London, daily attended at the Company's offices for the purpose of carrying on its business. Without wishing in any way to depreciate the services of the rest of the Board, he must state that the most useful of his colleagues had been Mr. Winter, who had given the greatest assistance. If it was the pleasure of the Company to re-elect them, they should be happy to continue to give their best attention to the affairs of the Company. He bore testimony to the great assistance which the Directors had met from the Government of His Highness the Nizam in the operations of the Company. The present Prime Minister, Sir Busheer-ud-Dowlah, had stated to them that the wishes of his Highness's Government were to the effect that the works of the Company should be in no way hindered by the recent suspension of the Hyderabad Home Secretary, who had nominated Nawab Mehdi Hasan Fathah Nawaz Jung Bahadur, the Chief Justice of the Hyderabad State, to take his seat on that Board, to which he was accordingly elected. The latter had associated himself with them in the most friendly spirit, and had expressed himself as much pleased with the manner in which the affairs of the Company were conducted by the Board. The Chairman had to mention with regret the death of their colleague, Mr. John Stewart, last year. Mr. B. W. Colvin was elected a Director in his place, a gentleman of high official position and experience in India, who was a Director of the East India Railway Company. He concluded by moving the adoption of the report and the statement of accounts.

Mr. Hewlings seconded the motion.

Mr. Germaine contended that the Company should wait until the report of the Select Committee of the House of Commons had been received, and he moved that the meeting should be adjourned until the 15th of October. He then commented upon the "prospective advantages" to the shareholders set forth by the Chairman, and remarked that the Company had the same promises made at the last meeting. The average shareholder had no information upon which he could form a judgment as to these "prospective advantages," and, therefore, it would be just that the Company should wait for the Select Committee's report. The report was one merely on the expenditure of money—they had spent £56,000 in doing nothing, for the Company was not in a position to earn anything.

Mr. John Edwards seconded the amendment for adjourning the meeting. He had only one object, and that was the interests of the Company, of which he was a shareholder.

Sir Julian Goldsmid, M.P., supported the amendment for the adjournment, and expressed his opinion that Mr. Watson, whose action had been before the Select Committee, would have done well not to have asked for proxies, and he would have done well, having obtained them, not to use them. Mr. Watson had made an extremely large profit, and not only extremely large, but an immediate profit on the bringing out of the Company, and the shareholders' profits were even now only prospective. If Mr. Watson wished to maintain his position in the City of London he would, in view of the position of the Company, say what he was going to do for the shareholders. Sir Julian said he had had the pleasure of knowing the Chairman for many years, and it had been suggested that he and others were qualified by Mr. Watson. Lord Lawrence was a Director who would look after the interests of the shareholders, and Lord Lawrence and independent Directors should be strengthened.

Sir Roper Lethbridge, M.P., in supporting the amendment for the adjournment, said he was sure that the Chairman would devote his best attention to the interests of the shareholders. Sir Roper also congratulated the Company on the acquisition to the Board of Lord Lawrence and the Nawab Bahadur. Though himself only a small shareholder, he was trustee for others, Sir Roper said, and he was there entirely in the interests of the Company. He thought it would be wise of the Directors to accede to the proposal for an adjournment until October; but he did not agree with all the mover of the amendment had said, for a good deal had been done for the development of the Company. The report of the Select Committee had been already laid upon the table of the House of Commons, and would be shortly ready. In it there were matters of interest to the shareholders which the Directors would have to answer, and which he had no doubt they could answer. There was, for instance, the subject, of which there was a telegram from Bombay, of litigation between the Nizam and his late Minister, and he should like to ask the representative of the Nizam if this was correct.

The Nizam's representative replied that he had no information. The Sirdar Diler-ul-Mulk Bahadur had been suspended.

Sir Roper Lethbridge, M.P., urged that there were many reasons which made it advisable for the adjournment of the meeting.

After other speeches, there were calls for "Watson."

Mr. Watson then rose and said that, in answer to Sir Julian Goldsmid, he could say that the concessionnaires, to deal with the question of what they would do for the shareholders, would be happy to meet with a Committee of the shareholders to discuss any proposition made to them, and for himself he would say they were ready to do what was right and honourable. As to proxies, he held, he was happy to say, the large number of 25,798, outside the concessionnaires' shares. He should use these against the adjournment.

Sir Julian Goldsmid, M.P., after other speeches against Mr. Watson's declaration of action, challenged the Directors to say whether they would countenance Mr. Watson's disastrous action of so using the proxies.

The Directors conferred with Mr. Watson, who also conferred with persons off the platform.

The Chairman then said that the only thing the Directors asked was that the accounts should be passed.

A shareholder said that this would be assenting to the payment of the 85,000 shares out of the 100,000 (for £1,000,000).

The Chairman said that this was assented to at the previous meeting, an adjournment would weaken the position of the Directors, as their responsibilities would be increased by the accounts not being passed.

Sir Julian Goldsmid, in the midst of much excitement, reminded the Chairman that he was there as the Chairman of the shareholders, and not as Mr. Watson's representative.

Lord Lawrence then rose, amid cheers, and gave his views in favour of the amendment, and pressed the shareholders not to get at loggerheads.

Mr. Colvin, another Director, was also in favour of adjourning; but pressed that means should be taken to carry on the affairs of the Company.

Mr. Bladon suggested that the accounts should be passed, and another meeting called.

Sir Julian Goldsmid suggested that this was a proposal on behalf of a relative of the Chairman, but withdrew and apologised for the statement when he found he was mistaken.

Ultimately a vote was taken, when the whole room, less about six or seven, voted for the amendment.

Mr. Clements, solicitor to Mr. Watson, demanded a poll, and the requisition was signed by Mr. Watson, Mr. Clements, Mr. Soliaque, and Mr. Coulter.

A demand was made on behalf of the majority of those in the room that the poll should be in seven days, and, after much discussion,

The Chairman, amid much uproar, stated that he decided that the poll should be taken at once.

Mr. Germaine then called upon the rest of the shareholders to leave the room.

An extraordinary scene then occurred. The great majority of the shareholders rose from their seats, and went out towards the door in an excited manner, shouting "Shame!" "Monstrous!" and other words. The Directors, or most of them, rose from the table, and amid the uproar, Sir Roper Lethbridge, after a conference with the Nizam's representative, declared that that gentleman was in favour of adjournment of the poll for seven days.

The Chairman then called the majority back, and announced that he had reconsidered the matter, and would grant the adjournment over several days.

Ultimately the matter was adjourned until Monday next, and thanks were voted to the Chairman, on the motion of Sir Julian Goldsmid, seconded by Sir R. Lethbridge.—*Times*, August 8.

THE REPORT OF THE HYDERABAD (DECCAN) COMMITTEE.—In the House of Commons, on August 7, Mr. Isaacson asked the Secretary to the Treasury whether he would make an application to the proprietors of *The Times* newspaper for the name of the person or persons who communicated to that paper the contents of the report of the Hyderabad (Deccan) Committee before the said report had been officially placed upon the table, in order that the Government might deal with the offenders.

Mr. Jackson: The paragraph in question appeared in other papers as well as *The Times*, and seems to have emanated from the Press Association. I do not think that it would be for the public interest that the steps which are being taken in the matter should be published.—*Times*, August 8.

IN view of the fact that the report of the Select Committee which has been investigating the affairs of the Hyderabad (Deccan) Company has only just been presented to Parliament, it was very natural that the shareholders of the Company, at their meeting to-day, should have wished to postpone passing the accounts submitted to them until the conclusions arrived at by the Committee shall have been made public. The vast majority of the shareholders present at the meeting expressed their wishes in this respect in an unmistakeable manner, but Mr. Watson and the other concessionnaires refused to allow the wishes of independent proprietors present to have effect. Unless those who have sent their proxies to Mr. Watson withdraw them before the poll, which is to take place on Monday next, the wishes of a large and independent body of the shareholders are in danger of being utterly disregarded. Mr. Watson and his colleagues will incur a heavy moral responsibility if they insist upon passing their accounts against the wishes of so many of those who bought shares upon the faith of the prospectus.

THE HYDERABAD (DECCAN) COMPANY, LIMITED.—EXCITED PROCEEDINGS.—The second ordinary general meeting of the shareholders of this Company was held yesterday in the Great Hall, Winchester House, Old Broad Street, and was numerously attended.

Mr. G. H. M. Batten occupied the chair.

The report of the Directors—which stated that the balance-sheet was made up to the 30th April, up to which date the expenditure amounted to £55,638, leaving £97,955 in hand—having been taken as read, the Chairman, in a speech of great length, moved that it be adopted. The Company, he said, was really a partnership, into which the concessionnaires brought £150,000 in cash and a concession, the value of which had to be represented by paper shares. With the information before them, and the fact that the concession extended over a country containing an area of over 81,000 square miles, abounding in valuable minerals, and being opened up by the construction of a railway, the Directors thought they were justified in acceding to the valuation put upon the concession of £850,000, all in paper shares, and it was so entered in their accounts. He maintained that £850,000 was not an over-valuation of the property of the Company, in proof of which he cited the reports on the value of the Singareni coal mine, which it was estimated would yield ninety-four million tons of good steam coal; in addition to which there was a gold area of 550 square miles, which was valued at more than a million, after deducting all outgoing; and there were also very valuable diamond fields, for the working of which machinery had already been provided.

The motion having been seconded by Mr. Hewlings, Mr. Germaine said he thought they ought not to pass this report until the shareholders had the opportunity of reading the report of the Committee of the House of Commons on the affairs of the Company which Sir Henry James brought up last night, and he moved as an amendment, "That the meeting be adjourned until the report of the House of Commons has been in the hands of the shareholders," which was seconded by Mr. J. Edwards, and supported by Sir Julian Goldsmid, M.P., who said he thought Mr. Watson, one of the concessionnaires, was ill-advised in sending out circulars asking for proxies. The shareholders had not made one penny of profit, whereas the profit made by Mr. Watson and the other concessionnaires was extremely large, and he thought they ought to hear from him what he proposed to do for the Company.

Sir R. Lethbridge, M.P., and Mr. FitzHugh followed in support of the amendment.

Mr. Watson said he should be happy to meet any Committee that the shareholders might appoint, and discuss with them any proposition they would like to make; and so far as he was concerned, and he spoke for the other concessionnaires, he would meet them in any way that was honourable and right. As regarded the amendment, he was happy to say that 25,798 shareholders, outside the concessionnaires, had sent him their proxies; they knew perfectly well what was coming before the shareholders, and therefore he should use the proxies on their behalf, and certainly should not consent to the adjournment. (Murmurs.)

Sir Julian Goldsmid appealed to the Directors, as men of honour, of respectability, and of high standing, not to use the proxies obtained by one of their colleagues for the purpose of overriding what was evidently the feeling of the meeting.

The Chairman said the proxies were Mr. Watson's, and were only sent to the office because the Articles of Association required that they should be.

Mr. Watson interposed with the observation that he had asked for the proxies and paid for them himself.

The Chairman said all the Board asked was that their accounts should be passed. In the report there was nothing that affected the questions that came before the Committee of the House of Commons.

Mr. Watson remarked that if the accounts were not passed they would have to discharge thousands of workmen.

Mr. Forbes asked if the other Directors agreed with Mr. Watson, and Lord Lawrence (a Director) said he must confess he was in favour of adjourning the meeting, and he regretted very much that Mr. Watson had taken the course he had. The concessionnaires, in his opinion, would do what was right and honourable. If he did not believe that he could not stay on the Board. Of course, Mr. Watson's having that large number of proxies showed that he had, to a large extent, the confidence of the shareholders. He suggested that a Committee of shareholders should be appointed to consult with the Directors.

Mr. Colvin, a Director, had no hesitation in saying that he was in favour of an adjournment, but at the same time hoped that no kind of hitch would occur in the carrying on of the works in consequence of any resolution passed at the meeting.

The Chairman said he regarded the amendment as a vote of want of confidence. How could he go on signing cheques if there was a doubt as to whether his acts would be ratified?

Sir J. Goldsmid, and one or two others, combatted the view that the passing of the amendment would suspend the action of the board.

The amendment was then put in this form: "That this meeting be adjourned till the 15th of October," which was carried by 41 votes to 9.

Mr. Clements demanded a poll, and suggested that it should be taken immediately and continued till six o'clock.

Sir J. Goldsmid remarked that Mr. Clements had put in his demand on behalf of Mr. Watson, and said if the Chairman decided the matter in the interests of the shareholders he would adjourn the poll for seven days.

The Chairman said that would be doing what the amendment proposed. He directed that the poll should be taken at once.

A shareholder appealed to the Chairman not to try and stifle the independent shareholders.

The Chairman replied that he had given his directions that the poll be taken at once, upon which there were loud cries of "Shame!" and Mr. Germain said if the Chairman persisted in that determination he hoped the shareholders would leave the room in a body.

This advice was loudly cheered, and at once acted upon, most of the shareholders rising and leaving the room, crying out "Shame! shame!" at the top of their voices; and while this was going on Sir R. Lethbridge called out "Here is a representative of the Nizam who is in favour of adjournment," an announcement received with cheers; and a number of the shareholders returned to the hall.

The Chairman then rose, and said on consideration he thought it fair to adjourn the poll for seven days, and he added that he had 150 shares in the Company, which he bought at £11 10s., that he had never sold one, and that he was perfectly independent. He then directed that the poll should take place on Monday next, between twelve and two, at Winchester House; and the proceedings were brought to a close by a vote of thanks to him, moved by Sir J. Goldsmid, and seconded by Sir R. Lethbridge.—*Daily News*, August 8.

HYDERABAD (DECCAN).—The second ordinary general meeting of this Company was held yesterday at Winchester House.

Mr. G. H. M. Batten (Chairman) having referred at considerable length to the present position and prospects of the Company, said that the Directors had had a very anxious time, though their anxiety had not been due to any doubts as to the validity of the title by which the Company held its property, nor to any doubts as to the value of that property. Nothing whatever of an irregular or illegal character had taken place in the initiation of the Company, and it was the opinion of competent experts that the amount paid for the property was by no means excessive. As regarded the formation of the Company, there was no limit on the capital of the Company, except that it was not to be less than £1,000,000, and no limitation on the amount to be subscribed, except that it was to be at the least £150,000. There was, however, no obligation on the Company to issue more than that amount. The Company had to acquire the rights of the concessionnaires, and the concessionnaires came to the conclusion that at that time, before the value of the concession could have been appreciated by the public, it was preferable not to ask the public to subscribe and pay up the whole of the stipulated capital of £150,000. It was accordingly subscribed and allotted to eight persons, who represented the whole Company, and who paid in cash immediately £75,000, and later the remaining £75,000. The Directors thought that they were justified in acceding to the valuation put upon the concession of £850,000, all in paper shares, and it was so entered in their accounts. There was no concealment of facts. As regarded the Singareni coal mine, that was even more extensive than the Directors had been led to suppose, for after making every sort of reduction and allowance the estimate of 84,000,000 tons of good steam coal within 300ft. of the surface had been arrived at as the available supply. There was certain to be a very large demand for this coal, and the Government of India had estimated that the railways would take from the Company nearly 200,000 tons annually. Having also referred to the prospects of the Company with regard to gold and diamond mining, he stated that the Directors had every confidence in the future success of the undertaking. He moved, in conclusion, the adoption of the report, which was seconded by Mr. Hewlings.

A discussion followed, and Mr. Germaine proposed, as an amendment, that the meeting should be adjourned until October, having regard to the fact that the Parliamentary Committee, which had been sitting to investigate the affairs of the Company, had just made its report, and it would be as well for the shareholders to be in possession of the facts of that report before adopting the accounts now presented.

Mr. Edwards seconded the resolution.

A long discussion followed, and on a show of hands the amendment was carried. A poll was demanded on behalf of Mr. Watson and other shareholders, and it was decided that the same should take place on Monday at Winchester House between the hours of twelve and two.—*Morning Post*, August 8.

THE moral which the Hyderabad Deccan Committee deduces from its survey of the gigantic swindle which its Report exposes is that the direct contact of London speculators with Native Ministers is attended with such serious risks that it ought to be discountenanced. It is the old story. The microbe of Western usury is fatal to the Eastern races. But what is new is that the Government of India should have allowed one of the most colossal frauds of modern times to be perpetrated under its nose, when, if it had done its duty, it might have saved its *protégé* from this wholesale plunder. It is a grave scandal, and one on which there will be much to say hereafter.

MR. BRADLAUGH's motion to-night for a Commission to inquire into the Administration of India comes, in one respect at least, at an opportune time. Not the most confirmed optimist can declare, on the morrow of the report upon the Deccan Scandals, that there is nothing that needs inquiring into. The British Residents at Native States are supposed to stand in some sort *in loco parentis* towards "the inferior race," but in the case of Hyderabad the most barefaced plundering went on under the very nose of the Resident, and persons not unremotely connected with the Indian Government itself shared in the plunder.—*Pall Mall Gazette*, August 9.

THE report from the Select Committee on the Hyderabad-Deccan Mining Company has reached me to-night, and after the most careful inspection it is difficult to see where the summary of it, published last Saturday, and for the issue of which Sir Henry James apparently wished to bring some unnamed person to the Bar of the House, was so very wrong. A microscopic examination reveals that one word was obviously misspelt, but that is all.—*London Correspondent of Birmingham Daily Post*, August 9.

THE Report of the Select Committee of the House of Commons on the Hyderabad Deccan Mining Company—the substance of which we publish in another column—will disappoint a good many people. This Deccan Company has been represented as a gross fraud, and it was expected by not a few that the Committee would not only expose the fraud, but also pave the way for a wholesale attack upon the British Residents at Native Courts in India, if not upon British Indian officials as a body. We were told that the whole Administration of India was utterly corrupt, and that the participation of English officers in the plunder of the Nizam was certain to be brought to light by the Committee. It became evident in the course of the inquiry that these assertions were not tenable, and now that the Report of the Committee has been made public, it will be clear to everyone that we have to do with a very ordinary kind of Company indeed. The sums of money involved are rather larger than usual, the relation of the Native Indian States to the protecting English Government of India also gives the affair a peculiar interest, but in other respects there is nothing at all remarkable in the story of the Hyderabad Deccan Company. If its history be the history of a "fraud," all we can say is that the "fraud" is of the commonest type. Certain men obtain a "concession" to develop the mineral resources of the State of Hyderabad, in Central India, and, among other privileges, were given power to raise capital for this purpose to the extent of £1,000,000. By their own estimate they consider £850,000 of this £1,000,000 the value of the concession, and the other £150,000 is the sum they apportion to the work of finding out what the mineral resources of Hyderabad are. This view of the relative "values" of the concession and the thing conceded they carry out on the London Stock Exchange in an extremely clever manner. The shares of the Company incorporated to work the concession are "put upon the market," not in the regular way, but after a fashion, for the display of which the Stock Exchange gives, in the very teeth of its rules, the most ample facility. Mr. Watson and his friends "knew the ropes," we may say, and, knowing them, understood that the best way in certain circumstances to get the support of the Stock Exchange is to set its rules at defiance. They issued no prospectus to the public, for the very good reason that such a step would have brought them under the rule which ordains that two-thirds of the share capital of a Company must be offered to and subscribed for by the public before its shares can obtain a quotation in the official list. It was never their intention at the start to give the public the chance of subscribing to this extent, and had it not been for the *Standard*, as the Committee point out, the public would have known nothing. This was well. Credulous as the investing classes are, the demands of the concessionnaires would have been too much for their credulity had they been openly made. Messrs. Watson and Co. had nothing to say about the mineral resources of Hyderabad of a definite kind, and without glowing reports there would have been no subscription. But by hiding the facts, by dealing in the shares outside Stock Exchange rules, it was not difficult to pull the market in. Vague rumours of a premium were enough. By this plan, too, the manufacture of a premium was made all the easier. The dealings were brisk, especially after it became public that "the Nizam was a buyer," and dozens of shrewd men on the Exchange lost their money almost before they knew where they were. From this point of view all was common-place, vulgar, uninteresting in the extreme, not a patch upon the great sensation of the South African Diamond Mines, hardly a worthy rival to the latest "Company to develop a rich deposit of silver ore in Mexico."

It does not, however, follow that the Committee of the House of Commons had nothing to do, or that its report is in other respects valueless. In some aspects, its labours and conclusions have the highest possible value. Among other matters, the Committee has succeeded in bringing vividly before the public eye the doings and character of Abdul Huk. This worthy is, more than Mr. William Clarence Watson, the hero of the piece. He manipulated the Nizam's Government, and in his capacity of Home Secretary, as we might say, arranged the terms of the concession to the mutual advantage of himself and the nominal concessionnaires. Thanks, apparently, to this person, the British Resident in Hyderabad was kept in ignorance of the true character of the operation in hand. It was known to nobody outside the inner ring that £850,000 out of the £1,000,000 was to go into the pockets of Abdul Huk and partners. What was presented to the British authorities was a praiseworthy scheme for the development of the coal deposits, and possible gold and diamond deposits, of the Hyderabad State. There could be no more laudable object than the increase of its riches, and it may well have occurred to the authorities at Calcutta that £1,000,000 was not too much for the enterprise, they assuming, of course, that the £1,000,000 was to go in exploitation. But it certainly could not have occurred to any person gifted with all his faculties that £150,000 out of this £1,000,000 was enough to demonstrate, still less to develop, the mineral wealth of Hyderabad. We may, therefore, assume that Abdul Huk and his confederates successfully hoodwinked the British authorities. There is no evidence whatever that these were corrupted. After the Company was floated, and in operation as a money-making engine for the promoters, questionable transactions took place, as the Committee's Report points out, between a Mr. Hughes, a Mr. Furnivall, and Mr. Watson. Both Hughes and Furnivall became interested in the Company's shares after having been appointed to make professedly independent investigations into its prospects. Mr. Hughes seems to have made a little money by transactions in these shares, and Mr. Furnivall received from Mr. Watson 500 shares "for nothing," whether to his profit or not is not shown; but the authorities at Calcutta and Hyderabad knew nothing of these transactions, and cannot be implicated in any disgrace which may attach to them. Mr. Furnivall, indeed, had ceased to be their servant. Nor is the Government of the Nizam apparently in any way to blame, except for folly. Its intentions were, to all appearance, honest throughout—so honest that the Nizam innocently invested in 10,000 shares belonging to Abdul Huk, as partner with Watson, Stewart, and Co., at a premium of twenty per cent. or so, in the belief that he was helping the Company. The money paid for these shares has, since the exposure of this Committee, been refunded by Abdul Huk to the Nizam, and by that deed alone this worthy confesses that he took part in a scheme to cheat his own Government. We may, therefore, leave him to the judgment of his misdeeds, with the passing remark that he has thoroughly exonerated the authorities in Hyderabad from all complicity in his plots. His act of restitution has even exonerated Mr. Cordery, the British Resident in Hyderabad, from everything except the charge of incompetence. From that it is impossible to set him free. Nobody with any sharpness, in matters of business, would have permitted the Government of Hyderabad to be robbed as Mr. Cordery did. His evidence was, in some respect, the most depressing episode in the whole inquiry.

With these censures, however, the judicial part of the Report now made public may be held to end. It is mainly a descriptive Report, and its condemnations are more implied than expressed. Because they are so, their effect may perhaps be more far-reaching. Nowhere is there a trace of evidence that Abdul Huk, Watson, Stewart, and their confederates desired to do any good to the State or people of Hyderabad. All that is visible is a keen eye for plunder. So much money had been made by the promotion of railways in Hyderabad, and that had whetted the appetite of the projectors for making so much more through other schemes. Hence the concession procured by Abdul Huk for working the minerals of the State—minerals the existence of which in paying quantities had never been in any way verified. This concession was secured so exclusively for the purpose of putting it on the market at a huge profit, that no objection was raised to clauses in it safeguarding the Nizam's revenues. These were rather welcomed, apparently, as serving to show the *bona fides* of the promoters. They were able to say, "whoever suffers, the interests of the State of Hyderabad are not injured." None the less is it for the shareholders a barren gift, this concession. They held a meeting two days ago, and stormed at their "Board" and at Watson—Stewart being dead. When they read this Report they will not find comfort. They have bought for £1,000,000 rights which are not, so far as any evidence has gone, worth as many pence, and unless they can compel the English members of the concession to do as Abdul Huk has done in India—refund the money—they must, we fear, be content to treat their investment as a bad debt. We doubt very much their ability to force a restitution of their money. Many of them went into the matter with their eyes open, actuated by the same spirit of gain as Watson and Co., and they must take the consequences. The Indian Government, however, must not allow any more of this kind of thing to be perpetrated. Incapacity may be pleaded as excuse for its officials this time, but the excuse will not serve again. That astute natives should be permitted to fleece English investors and others, with official countenance in Calcutta, Hyderabad, or anywhere else in India, is a thing that cannot be tolerated.—*Standard*, August 9.

THE HYDERABAD-DECCAN INQUIRY.—REPORT OF THE COMMITTEE.—The printed report was issued last evening of the Select Committee appointed to inquire into the formation and promotion of the Hyderabad-Deccan Mining Company, Limited, the circumstances under which the concession was obtained from the Government of Hyderabad, and the subsequent operations on the London Stock Exchange by persons interested in the Company. Counsel appeared during the inquiry for the Nizam of Hyderabad, Sirder Diler Jung (Abdul Huk), the Hyderabad-Deccan Company, Limited, Mr. William Clarence Watson, Mr. Henry Parkinson Sharp, and Mr. James Graham Stewart. It was elicited by the Committee that a concession, dated January 7, 1886, was granted by the Hyderabad Government to William Clarence Watson, 7, Great Winchester-street, London, and John Stewart, 26, Throgmorton-street (since deceased), conferring upon the concessionnaires the exclusive right of prospecting for minerals throughout the Nizam's territories until December 31st, 1891. During that period the concessionnaires would have the right to select fields or mines, to be held on 99 years' lease, subject to royalties, to be fixed by agreement or arbitration. An obligation to work the Singareni coal fields was attached to the concession, and it was stipulated that not later than June 30, 1888, the concessionnaires should supply 500 tons or more of good coal per week. A Limited Company was to be formed in London to work the concession, with a capital of not less than £1,000,000. In the preamble of the concession, mention was made of the previous formation of another Company for constructing a railway connecting the northern and southern frontiers of Hyderabad. In 1871, Mr. Winter, then a solicitor in Bombay, whose firm had acted professionally for the Nizam's Government in 1874, met with Abdul Huk at Hyderabad, and negotiated with him on the subject of the railway. Mr. Winter is brother-in-law to Mr. Watson, one of the concessionnaires. Abdul Huk was the accredited agent of the Nizam's Government in the negotiations regarding the railways and the mines. An understanding was arrived at involving the raising of a capital of £2,000,000, but on reference to the Viceroy it was advised that the persons connected with the scheme were not persons of sufficient financial standing to be recognised by the Nizam's

Government. Mr. Winter stated that he arranged with Abdul Huk that the latter should receive for his own use £120,000 from the railway, and an interest in the mining concession. Neither the Indian nor the British Government was informed of this arrangement. Abdul Huk subsequently came to London, and a Railroad Company was ultimately floated by Mr. Watson, who received £100,000 for his services and the cost of promotion. The Nizam agreed to give a guarantee of 5 per cent. for 20 years on the £2,000,000 capital. The draft of the mining concession, which was negotiated separately, was settled in 1883, and Abdul Huk returned to Hyderabad to obtain the approval of the Nizam's Government, and after further negotiations it was signed, with modifications, in January, 1866. The Memorandum of Association was subscribed by Messrs. Winter, Hemmerdy, Batten, Pearce, and Milne, besides the two concessionnaires. The agreement to transfer the concession to the Company was approved on August 10, 1886, when application for 15,000 shares was considered, and allotment was made. Mr. Watson, on October 3, gave Mr. Hemmerdy 1,000 fully-paid shares for "services rendered to me twenty years previously." Another agreement was approved between the Company and Mr. Watson and Mr. Stewart, whereby the Company undertook to allot the concessionnaires 85,000 shares of £10 each fully-paid. The 85,000 shares, when received by Mr. Watson and Mr. Stewart, were by them divided among the partners in the enterprise, Mr. Watson and Mr. Stewart having been appointed additional Directors in the meantime. Abdul Huk received one-fourth, but his name did not appear as transferee in the Minute Book, his proportion of shares being transferred to Mr. Winter, and then turned into share warrants to bearer, and lodged with Abdul Huk's bankers. In May, 1887, and subsequently, various transfers of shares were made by Mr. Watson to Mr. Hughes and Mr. Furnivall. About the time of the first statutory meeting, November 26, 1886, Mr. R. Stanton Evans began to sell shares for Mr. Watson on terms arranged, and from time to time transactions on the Stock Exchange were frequent. "Of the 85,000 shares issued as fully-paid, about 55,000 were sold to the public. There are now about 700 shareholders. The prices of the shares ranged during the period between September, 1886, and April, 1888, from 13¾ to 5⅞. Mr. Watson, by dealing in his fourth of the 85,000 shares and by transactions in buying and selling shares in the market, had, at the time when he gave his evidence, realised £209,300 (out of which he had paid in brokerage and commission £20,829), and he still retained 5,559 shares. Mr. Watson also gave away many shares." No application for a settlement or quotation was made to the Committee of the Stock Exchange, and no prospectus of the Company was issued. The method adopted by the sellers was apparently not to place before the public specific information, but to "stimulate interest by affording hints and glimpses of the magnitude of the enterprise." A printed memorandum regarding the Company contained a description of the scheme very favourably coloured: "It will be observed by reference to this memorandum that no statement is made in it which would convey to the public that the 85,000 shares had been passed to the concessionnaires under the circumstances mentioned above." The memorandum was headed, "Capital £1,000,000, in 100,000 shares of £10 each; 85,000 being fully-paid, and 15,000 on which £5 per share is paid. The Company have been carrying on mining operations in the Singareni coalfields to the extent of raising about 150 tons a week. They have also been prospecting for diamonds and for gold. Five diamonds have been found in some refuse. No gold has been produced." The Committee express no opinion as to the prospects of the enterprise. Reference is made to the purchase in June, 1887, on the Stock Exchange, for the Nizam's Government, of 8,750 fully-paid and 3,750 shares £5 paid. This purchase was rescinded after the Committee commenced its sittings. Abdul Huk was commissioned to purchase 10,000 shares at or under

£12 per share, and he carried out the transaction in concert with Mr. Watson. "What was done, in fact, was that Abdul Huk received the price and handed over to the Nizam so many of the shares which had fallen to himself in the distribution of the shares of the concessionnaires." Abdul Huk, in consideration of this transfer, received £131,250 of moneys belonging to the Government of Hyderabad. In July, 1887, Lord Lawrence became a Director of the Company. He did so in consequence of a request made to him by the Directors to represent the Nizam. There can be no doubt that Lord Lawrence, in all his dealings and connection with the Company, acted in perfect good faith. On the facts as above established the Committee observe: "The history of the Hyderabad Deccan Company shows that the concession has in fact proved highly lucrative to the concessionnaires. They have appropriated to themselves and dealt with £850,000 of the capital of the Company, but the question remains how the 85,000 shares out of the total of 100,000 shares have passed into the hands of the concessionnaires." The Committee consider that no such deficiency in the remuneration received by the concessionnaires for their services in promoting the Railway Company existed as to entitle them to obtain the mining concession. "The Committee desire to abstain from expressing any opinion on the legal rights or liabilities of the Nizam, the concessionnaires, the Company, or individual shareholders. But your Committee are of opinion that the concessionnaires have used the concessions for the purpose of realising great gains not intended to be conferred on them, that this has been done to the injury of the State from which they obtained the concession with the assistance of their partner, Abdul Huk." The fact that the concessionnaires were placed in a position to claim to appropriate to themselves £850,000 of the capital was the indirect effect of a set of provisions which were carefully considered with another object. Only £150,000 being necessary for application to the coalfield, no express provisions appear to have been inserted as safeguards to protect the other £850,000 of capital from being immediately dealt with. "The circumstances under which the mining concession was obtained show that serious risks to the interests of Native States attend the direct access of London speculators to Native Ministers. In the present case, the initial arrangements were made between Abdul Huk and the concessionnaires, and it was after a settled draft had been prepared under his instructions that particulars were considered by British officials. When the matter came before the Resident, the Government of India, and the Secretary for India, no one of them was aware of the circumstances relating to Abdul Huk which called for a peculiar vigilance; and apart from this it is clear that the terms of the concession were subjected to less complete review than they would have gone through had they not already been agreed upon by the accredited negotiator of the Nizam. This result is to be regretted; and it is apparent that if more effective and direct British assistance and advice had been given to the Government of Hyderabad the events that have occurred could not have taken place. It appears to your Committee that so long as the Government of India interferes with the proceedings of a Native State in business matters, such as granting an important concession, great care should be taken to fully fulfil the responsibility thus assumed, and that there will be considerable difficulty in discharging such duty by the Indian Government if the communications between the Government of the native State and speculation be allowed to be of a direct character." (Dated 6th August, 1888).—*Daily News*, August 9.

The report of the Committee on the Hyderabad Deccan Scandals is not of much public interest, and it is not of very great potency. The City people, of course, are those mostly concerned by it, and of the City people those in particular who are professionally engaged in promoting. It lays a heavy hand upon these. Unfortunately the City dwells in a wall of brass, in so far as it is invulnerable to the attacks of the moralists, while the race of investors lives so fast that it is not able to remember the philosophic counsel of its advisers for long. The report is a master-piece of literary composition, the thunderous declamation of Sir Henry being nicely pointed by the epigrams of Mr. Henry Labouchere and the saponaceous saws of Sir Richard Temple. It is a document of considerable length, but, with the exception of its doctrines, which are deserving of all praise, I am not inclined to run the risk, in the present state even of the amended law of libel, of saying anything about it.—*London Correspondent of Notts Daily Express*, August 9.

The India Office.—The India Office does not often attract the attention of the outside world. As a rule its operations have little interest save for those directly concerned in them. Its successes never attain striking dimensions, and the blame for its failures, hitherto, has been shifted without much effort on to the shoulders of some department or other in India too remote and impersonal either to feel censure or to resent it. So, while the defects of many of our public offices have been not only talked about, but to some extent removed, the rather overgrown institution over which the Secretary of State for India presides has been left till now pretty well alone. After all, people may have thought, the conditions of Indian Administration differ widely from what is needed for the public service in England. The India Office does what it is meant to do fairly well; otherwise there would be complaints from India. But these comfortable reflections will not bear much examination. As a matter of fact, complaints are very often made in India; though, of course, they are as inaudible in London as the street shouts of Delhi or Calcutta. Events, however, have come to pass within the last few months which have given rise to a public outcry in England against the India Office; and as any shortcomings or inefficiency in the India Office might, in not improbable contingencies, imperil not merely private interests, but the safety of an empire, it is as well that the present feeling of discontent should be directed into proper channels.

The functions of the India Office were not too precisely defined by General Strachey in his evidence before the Hyderabad Commission. Its main duties are to act as a connecting link between Parliament and the Indian authorities; to see that the proceedings of the Governor-General for the time being are in accordance with the policy of Her Majesty's Ministers. It supplies Parliament, through the Secretary of State, with all the information deemed requisite to a proper understanding of Indian affairs. It watches the practical application in India of principles laid down in Westminster; and since its opinions are sought by the Secretary of State on every Indian question of any moment, it can exercise a ponderable influence for good or evil on matters connected with every branch of the Administration. The India Office, moreover, manages all the home business of the Indian Government: the purchase of stores, the payment of pensions, the engagement of English officials, mostly by means of competitive examination, but to a certain extent by patronage. But the chief motive of the India Office, the reason of its existence, is to know what is done in India, and to offer an expert's opinion as to what ought to be done. As a means of reporting and registering the operations of the Indian authorities, the spacious palace of clerks in Charles Street is far from being an economical arrangement. Probably it spends a good deal more in this way than other offices in the neighbourhood; and since the cost has to be defrayed by a country with a sadly depreciated currency, the burden is a heavy one. Yet all this is a secondary evil. The real weakness of the India Office must be sought for in the constitution of the Council. It is here the mischief lies; here that reform should begin.

It need hardly be said that the Council of the Secretary of State for India numbers amongst its members men whose experience of Indian affairs is unrivalled, and whose ability and eminence in every way qualify them for the highest offices. Men like the late Sir Henry Maine, Sir Henry Rawlinson, and Sir Alfred Lyall have earned a reputation which no man can question. Some of the recent appointments to the Council, too, are unassailable. On the other hand, there is too often a tendency to regard a seat in Council as a pleasant and fitting reward to bestow on some superannuated functionary whose working days were over years ago, or whose knowledge of India is altogether out of date. Again, while mature experience is requisite in a Councillor, it is apt at the end of a decade to become almost as unserviceable as if it were immature. The true and obvious remedy is the appointment of Councillors for a short r period. Five years would be ample; and in nine cases out of ten both ethe India Office and India itself would benefit were these five years taken not from the end of an official career but from the middle.

Not that this measure alone would do away with all the evils of the present system. The fact is that the India Office is out of touch with India. This is why the scandals now becoming so painfully frequent are not discovered and stamped out long before they become dangerous and disgraceful. By an elaborate and expensive system of check and report the India Office secretes a profound statistical knowledge of India. Of personal acquaintance with the living India to-day there is far too little. It was very different in the days of the Company, when the Court of Directors knew as well what went on in India as if they had sat within sight of the masts in the Hooghly. They kept up their knowledge, too, and were careful and eager to learn the latest news and the latest opinions from every servant of the Company who might come home. Nowadays an Anglo-Indian officer, if he can help it, never goes near the India Office. It may sound trivial enough, but the weekly breakfasts at the old East India House to which any Anglo-Indian was welcome, the levées and receptions, the public dinners given to every Governor on his appointment or return, did more to keep the Directors well posted up as to the actual state of affairs in India than whole piles of nicely-tabulated statistics and formal reports. The India Office and its Council ought to know, as well as the old Court of Directors did, the personal character of every man of standing in the Service; and the knowledge would prevent that amazing selection of the wrong men for responsible posts, which, as we complained the other day, is really at the bottom of nearly all the Indian scandals one hears of.—*St. James's Gazette*, August 9.

The Select Committee appointed to inquire into the Deccan scandals have published a most unsatisfactory report. Those who remembered the good service rendered by Sir Henry James, when Chairman of a similar Committee some fourteen years ago, expected much from the present inquiry, and looked for a complete exposure of the scandalous transactions which fleeced the Nizam and State of Hyderabad to the tune of nearly a million sterling. But nothing of the kind is to be found in the report. Nobody, it seems, was very much to blame except Abdul Huk, and he has made restitution. True, the promoters pocketed fabulous sums; but, after all, they did nothing more than scores of other men on the Stock Exchange would do if they had the chance. As for the officials in India, "not one of them was aware of the circumstances relating to Abdul Huk which called for a peculiar vigilance," not even Mr. Cordery, the British Resident at Hyderabad. The

Committee do, indeed, venture to hint, in most guarded language, that if that official had been less dull or indolent he might have checkmated Watson and Co. That is all. A good many heads in India, and elsewhere, will rest easier to-night.—*Star*, August 9.

THE HYDERABAD (DECCAN) INQUIRY.—The Press Association states that the printed report of the Select Committee appointed to inquire into the formation and promotion of the Hyderabad (Deccan) Mining Company (Limited), the circumstances under which the concession was obtained from the Government of Hyderabad, and the subsequent operations on the London Stock Exchange by persons interested in the Company, was issued last evening. It was elicited by the Committee that about the time of the first statutory meeting of the Company, on November 26, 1886, Mr. R. Stanton Evans began to sell shares for Mr. W. C. Watson, one of the concessionnaires, on terms arranged, and from that time transactions on the Stock Exchange were frequent. "Of the 85,000 shares issued as fully-paid, about 55,000 were sold to the public. There are now about 700 share-holders. The prices of the shares ranged during the period between September, 1886, and April, 1888, from 13¾ to 5⅞. Mr. Watson, by dealing with his one-fourth of the 85,000 shares, and by transactions in buying and selling shares in the market, had at the time, when he gave his evidence, realised £209,300, out of which he had paid in brokerage and commissions £20,829, and he still retained 5,559 shares. Mr. Watson had also given away many shares" No application for a settlement or quotation was made to the Committee of the Stock Exchange and no prospectus of the Company was issued. The method adopted by the sellers was apparently not to place before the public specific information, but to "stimulate interest by affording hints and glimpses of the magnitude of the enterprise." A printed memorandum regarding the Company contained a description of the scheme very favourably coloured. "It will be observed, by reference to this memorandum," says the report, "that no statement is made in it which would convey to the public that the 85,000 shares had been passed to the concessionnaires under the circumstances mentioned above. The memorandum was headed, 'Capital, £1,000,000, in 100,000 shares of £10 each, 85,000 being fully-paid, and 15,000 on which £5 per share is paid.' The Company have been carrying on mining operations in the Singareni coalfields to the extent of raising about 150 tons a week. They have also been prospecting for diamonds and for gold. Five diamonds have been found in some refuse. No gold has been produced." The Committee express no opinion as to the prospects of the enterprise. Reference is made to the purchase in June, 1887, on the Stock Exchange for the Nizam's Government of 8,750 fully-paid and 3,750 shares £5 paid. This purchase was rescinded after the Committee commenced its sittings. Abdul Huk was commissioned to purchase 10,000 shares at or under £12 per share, and he carried out the transaction in concert with Mr. Watson. "What was done, in fact, was that Abdul Huk received the price and handed over to the Nizam so many of the shares which had fallen to himself in the distribution of the shares of the concessionnaires." Abdul Huk, in consideration of this transfer, received £131,250 of moneys belonging to the Government of Hyderabad. In July, 1887, Lord Lawrence became a Director of the Company. He did so in consequence of a request made to him by the Directors to represent the Nizam. There can be no doubt, the Committee say, that Lord Lawrence in all his dealings and connexions with the company acted in perfect good faith.

The report goes on to say:—

"The history of the Hyderabad (Deccan) Company shows that the concession has in fact proved highly lucrative to the concessionnaires. They have appropriated to themselves and dealt with £850,000 of the capital of the Company; but the question remains how the 85,000 shares out of the total of 100,000 shares have passed into the hands of the concessionnaires."

The Committee consider that no such deficiency in the remuneration received by the concessionnaires for their services in promoting the Railway Company existed as to entitle them to obtain the mining concession.

"The Committee desire to abstain from expressing any opinion on the legal rights or liabilities of the Nizam, the concessionnaires, the Company, or individual shareholders. But the Committee are of opinion that the concessionnaires have used the concession for the purpose of realizing great gains not intended to be conferred on them, and that this has been done to the injury of the State from which they obtained the concession, with the assistance of their partner, Abdul Huk."

The fact that the concessionnaires were placed in a position to claim to appropriate to themselves £850,000 of the capital was the indirect effect of a set of provisions which were carefully considered with another object. Only £150,000 being necessary for application to the coalfield, no express provisions appear to have been inserted as safeguards to protect the other £850,000 of capital from being immediately dealt with. The report concludes as follows:—

"The circumstances under which the mining concession was obtained show that serious risks to the interests of Native States attend the direct access of London speculators to Native Ministers. In the present case the initial arrangements were made between Abdul Huk and the concessionnaires, and it was after a settled draft had been prepared under his instructions that particulars were considered by British officials. When the matter came before the Resident, the Government of India, and the Secretary for India, not one of them was aware of the circumstances relating to Abdul Huk which called for a peculiar vigilance; and, apart from this, it is clear that the terms of the concession were subjected to less complete review than they would have gone through had they not already been agreed upon by the accredited negotiator of the Nizam. This result is to be regretted, and it is apparent that if more effective and direct British assistance and advice had been given to the Government of Hyderabad the events that have occurred could not have taken place. It appears to your Committee that so long as the Government of India interferes with the proceedings of a Native State in business matters, such as granting an important concession, great care should be taken to fully fulfil the responsibility thus assumed; and that there will be considerable difficulty in discharging such duty by the Indian Government if the communications between the Government of the Native State and speculators be allowed to be of a direct character."—*Times*, August 9.

I SEE that Mr. Watson refers, in a circular addressed to the shareholders of the Hyderabad-Deccan Mining Company, to his connection with the Nizam's Railroad Company, and that he says that this latter Company was also attacked, the effect of the attack being that the shares of the Company sank to a heavy discount, but that he stood to the Company, at a considerable personal loss, and succeeded in re-establishing its credit, it being now in a prosperous condition, and its stock at a premium of 11 per cent. My mouth is closed for the present in regard to the Mining Company, but as regards the Railroad Company, Mr. Watson seems to have made the comfortable sum of £7,000 by his own showing; the poor Nizam was forced to accept, in lieu of cash, debentures which are only valuable because he himself guarantees the interest on them; the railroad, far from being prosperous, is costing the Nizam £100,000 per annum, which he has to pay to make up the annual deficit; and the shares of the undertaking are worth, I suspect, 11 premium, because their owners are not aware that the guarantee which now provides the dividend will cease in seventeen years. Whether the railroad will ultimately pay its expenses and dividend on its shares is a matter which can only be proved by results; but I confess that, from all I can gather, this seems to me to be the most improbable.—*Truth*, August 9.

THE GNAT AND THE CAMEL IN INDIA.—It is announced this morning that the Government of India has withdrawn the charge which it had preferred against Mr. Crawford, one of the most notable members of the Anglo-Indian Civil Service, and every one will feel relieved to learn that the suspicions which led to his arrest are groundless. The case for the Government seemed sufficiently dubious to justify great reserve in dealing with the charge brought against him. The Inspector-General of Police who obtained the warrant on which Mr. Crawford was arrested did so by declaring that a native had received money in order to induce Mr. Crawford to favour certain persons, one of whom at least the said native had introduced to Mr. Crawford, but whether or not the introduction had led to the anticipated result is not stated. When the charge was first made Mr. Crawford is said to have lost his head under the influence of cerebral excitement, and attempted to escape. He was thereupon arrested, and sent for trial, bail for £7,000 being accepted for his surrender. Sixteen subordinate Native officials were suspended, and eighty more were said to be implicated. As Mr. Crawford had for thirty years held a leading place in the official hierarchy, the scandal of his arrest was almost as great as if the Dean of Westminster had been sent to the Old Bailey on a charge of peculation. The case came on for hearing on August 1, but at the request of the prosecution it was adjourned for fifteen days. Now the Government appears to have come to the conclusion that it has no case, and Mr. Crawford is discharged, let us hope without a stain upon his character.

If the Government of India had in reality nothing more to justify its proceedings against Mr. Crawford than the fact that a Native with whom he was on terms of more or less intimacy, converted that intimacy into a means of personal profit, it is difficult to frame a censure sufficiently severe of the precipitancy and violence of the action which has now been abandoned. On such a principle of action no one would be safe. There is Sir John Gorst, for instance, who last night congratulated the House of Commons that "corruption was now almost unknown in the advanced provinces," and who is generally recognised as being the Indian Office incarnate. How does he know that none of the natives, or Englishmen for the matter of that, whose acquaintance he made during the lucrative visit which he paid to the Nizam's dominions, have not exploited the honour of being on speaking terms with the Under-Secretary for India? It would not be at all impossible to conceive that some iniquitous rascal who has spent his life in bleeding the exchequer of the Nizam might make Sir John Gorst's acquaintance, and on the strength of a visiting-card, or some such flimsy evidence, palm himself off as the intimate friend of the all-powerful Minister and receive money from suitors who wished to be introduced to Sir John Gorst. That such a thing has ever happened of course no one can say, but that it might happen to-morrow, either with Sir John Gorst or Lord Cross, or any one else who has made acquaintances among creatures like Abdul Huk, is obvious. Yet how monstrous it would be to arrest Sir John Gorst on a criminal charge, and send him to Bow-street, merely because some rascal with whom he had dined made money out of the credulity of Native suitors by promising to use his influence to secure favours from Sir John! Yet, unless there is something more behind, this is what the Government of India has done with Mr. Crawford. It would be unjust in England: it is doubly unjust in India, where the credulity of the natives affords a rich field for the operations of the trader upon their innocence. One of the most familiar of the stories with which Anglo-Indians amuse their guests describes the way in which an ex-lackey of the Royal household secured for years a steady supply of guineas from a Native potentate by passing himself off as Her Majesty's Private Secretary, and promising to use his influence with the Queen in order to secure the objects which his paymaster had at heart. Sir John Gorst perhaps may remember the story, and possibly has met the rogue who palmed off the pseudo-secretary upon the Native Prince. The fraud is said to have been effected by the judicious use of the Royal notepaper to which the lackey had access. To institute criminal proceedings against Her Majesty on account of the bribes taken by the lackey would be on all fours with the prosecution of Mr. Crawford, because a native took money in order to induce Mr. Crawford to favour certain persons, unless of course there is other information in the possession of the Government which is not before the public.

We are loth to censure Governments for too great severity in dealing with officials. Certainly with Lord Cross's whitewashing of the hero of the Cambay scandal, still fresh in the memory, and while the disgraceful exploits of Mr. Kirkwood remind us of the license allowed to discredited magistrates, it goes sorely against the grain to have to condemn the Administration for the one case in which they displayed severity. But to prosecute Mr. Crawford when they take no steps to prosecute the men who "conveyed" £850,000 to their own use out of £1,000,000 sterling capital of the Hyderabad-Deccan Mining Company seems very much like straining at a gnat and swallowing a camel. The public has not heard the last of that colossal theft. If honesty has not become a principle with which the India Office has nothing to do, the Government will stick at nothing, whether in the shape of *ex post facto* legislation or anything else, which may assist them in compelling the plunderers to disgorge their ill-gotten wealth. It is nothing less than an Imperial scandal that criminal proceedings cannot be at once instituted against all concerned in this gigantic fraud.—*Pall Mall Gazette*, August 10.

The Hyderabad Deccan Company.—It is perhaps yet too early to conclude that the shareholders in the Hyderabad Deccan Mining Company are without a remedy. The law ought not to be too ready to acquiesce in the conviction that it is powerless to right men who have been so grievously wronged. How much they have been wronged is apparent on the face of the Report of the Select Committee of the House of Commons published in these columns yesterday. A few shrewd persons in the City obtained a concession for the development of the mineral resources of the State of Hyderabad in Central India. For this purpose they were empowered to raise a capital of a million sterling. They succeeded in selling their concession for £850,000 to a Company, leaving only £150,000 for the "development of the mineral resources of Hyderabad." The fully paid-up shares in which payment was made were afterwards sold in large numbers to a confiding public. Some were handed over to Abdul Huk, the worthy Minister of the Nizam, who was the friend at Court of the concessionnaires. No one knew that Abdul Huk had been recompensed in this way, and he realised thousands by the sale of his shares, partly at the expense of his own master, who had been induced to invest in them at a premium of about twenty per cent. The Company—at the time, at least, when this precious bargain was struck—was the creature of the concessionnaires, and indeed, such was their influence in its counsels, that it was hard to say where the concessionnaires ended and the Company began. The Directors who agreed to the purchase of the concession were admittedly dummies of the concessionnaires—consequently vendor and purchaser were the same. The concessionnaires were about the only shareholders at the time of the purchase, and, as their apologists seem disposed to argue, the only persons entitled to a voice in the matter. They had a perfect right, it is said, to sell to themselves what themselves chose to buy. The reply is obvious Directors are trustees of a Company, as a whole, that is, not only of the shareholders at any particular time, but of all possible future shareholders. The Company, therefore, as at present constituted, or the shareholders, might find a remedy by filing a bill in Equity. The Judge would no doubt uphold the sale, but insist upon a valuation of the property sold. It would then be shown that, when the £850,000 was paid there had been no inquiry worthy of the name as to the real value of the concession, and the proceedings might admit of other legal developments as interesting in their way as the development of the mineral resources of Hyderabad.—*Daily News*, Aug. 10.

THE report of the Deccan Committee, published to-day, has been eagerly scanned. It is very different from the colourless draft drawn up for Sir Henry James by the Solicitor-General for Scotland. But it does not go nearly as far as four members of the Committee desire in its condemnation of the supineness of the India Office, which made this gigantic scandal possible. The section of four actually formed a majority of the Committee. But they were won over to accept the compromise of censure which the Report presents. The next thing that will be heard of this remarkable case will be in the courts of law. There are seven hundred shareholders who were drawn into the net, and who, as was shown at the meeting the other day, are in a pretty lively state. It is now proposed that a Committee of the shareholders shall file a bill in equity calling in question the whole transaction. It is held, upon high legal authority consulted in the matter, that the result would be that the judge would order a valuation to be taken of the property sold at the time when the promoters fixed its value at £850,000, and received that sum. It is believed that by this process they may be made to disgorge.—*Sheffield Independent*, August 10.

THE worst phase of the Hyderabad business is the negligence which the Indian Government officials displayed in reference to the formation of the Company. The Nizam is so dependent on us that if he wishes to appoint a European groom to look after his horses he has first to obtain the sanction of the British Resident; yet in this matter in which vast interests were involved, his agents were allowed to contract obligations which enabled the concessionnaires to appropriate to themselves £850,000 of the capital of the Company without let or hindrance from the British officials at Hyderabad or Calcutta. The Select Committee in their report let these officials down very lightly with a mild censure, and with a recommendation that in future greater vigilance should be exercised in these matters. But the question is altogether too important to be dismissed in this manner, and more will certainly be heard of it. In apportioning the blame, however, it is to be hoped that Lord Ripon's responsibility will not be overlooked. It was during his tenure of office that the present scandals originated, and he cannot shelter himself under the plea of ignorance, as the whole of the circumstances under which English capitalists in association with Abdul Huk were operating at Hyderabad were brought to light in the Anglo-Indian Press at the time. Lord Ripon was implored to take action to prevent the young Nizam from being made the victim of Stock Exchange speculations; but he was too deeply engaged in devising visionary schemes of self-government for the Hindoos, and in exciting race hatred by unwarranted alteration of the law, to pay any heed to such a practical question. The little band of jobbers were permitted to pursue their course unmolested, and to wax rich on enormous commissions. If Lord Ripon had put his foot down, as he ought, and sent the speculators to the right-about, there would, in all probability, have been no cause for the assembling of the Select Committee.—*Yorkshire Post*, August 10.

The Report of the Select Committee of the House of Commons on the Hyderabad Deccan Mining Company will be found in another column. It is not, as was anticipated in some quarters, an exposure of Anglo-Indian official corruption, but an ordinary story of Company-promoting in which the financial juggling is of the commonest type. The sums of money involved are rather larger than usual, the relation of the Native Indian States to the protecting English Government of India also gives the affair a peculiar interest, but in other respects there is nothing at all remarkable in the story of the Hyderabad Deccan Company. Certain men obtain a "concession" to develop the mineral resources of the State of Hyderabad in Central India, and, among other privileges, were given power to raise capital for this purpose to the extent of £1,000,000. By their own estimate they consider £850,000 of this £1,000,000 the value of the concession, and the other £150,000 is the sum they apportion to the work of finding out what the mineral resources of Hyderabad are. Abdul Huk and Mr. William Clarence Watson figure as very smart financiers indeed, and they seem to have manipulated the Nizam's Government and the British authorities to some tune. Mr. Cordery, the British Resident in Hyderabad, is exonerated from everything but the charge of not being sufficiently wide awake, nor is the Government of the Nizam apparently in any way to blame, except for folly. Its intentions were, to all appearance, honest throughout—so honest that the Nizam innocently invested in 10,000 shares belonging to Abdul Huk, as partner with Watson, Stewart, and Co., at a premium of 20 per cent. or so, in the belief that he was helping the Company. The shareholders have bought for £1,000,000 rights which are not, so far as any evidence has gone, worth as many pence, and unless they can compel the English members of the concession to do as Abdul Huk has done in India—refund the money—they must be content to treat their investment as a doubtful debt. The Indian Government will, no doubt, take care that a job of this kind does not occur again. Astute Natives must not be permitted to fleece English investors and others, with official countenance in India.—*Home and Colonial Mail*, August 10.

The report of the Select Committee of the House of Commons which was appointed to inquire into what is known as the Deccan Scandal will not be pleasant reading for British officials in India, though the hopes that were raised in sensation-loving breasts that extensive corruption in the Indian service would be brought to light have been happily disappointed. Blundering and incompetence on the part of our officials are apparent, but there is no trace of anything worse. Very instructive, however, is the history of the Hyderabad Deccan Mining Company, Limited, as told in this report. The chief actors are William Clarence Watson, John Stewart (since deceased), and Abdul Huk, until recently one of the trusted agents of the Nizam of Hyderabad and his Government. The two former had something to do with floating a Company to take over the Nizam's State railway, on which they made £100,000 and expenses; and according to their account the Nizam, partly out of gratitude, and partly from a desire to develop his territories, conceded to them, in 1886, the whole mining rights of the State until December, 1891. During that time they were to prospect for gold and diamond mines, which, when found, they might lease from the State for ninety-nine years, subject to the payment of certain royalties to be hereafter fixed. This concession had been the subject of negotiations for three years previously, for the Nizam is under British influence, and our Government had to be consulted to see that the Native Ruler did not part recklessly with his own. Of course a Company had to be floated, and after the draft concession had been studied and altered by the Nizam's Government, by Mr. Cordery, the British Resident at Hyderabad, by the Government of India, and by the Secretary of State in Council, it was finally agreed to. In the opinion of all these persons, the Company was to have a capital of £1,000,000, of which £150,000 only was to be at first subscribed for the working of an existing coal-field and for prospecting, the rest to be subsequently called up for the development of the resources of the State. But, will it be believed, so badly was the concession drafted that the concessionnaires were enabled to pocket, and did pocket, £850,000 themselves, and the only available capital of this formidable-looking Company is merely £150,000? It seems incredible that the draft concession under which this was possible should have passed through all these official hands without its true meaning being discovered. In fact, the trick was only done by extensive bribery. Abdul Huk, whose name never appeared as a shareholder, received one-fourth of these 85,000 £10 shares; the rest were divided amongst Messrs. Watson and Stewart and their creatures, who formed the original Company and subscribed the requisite £150,000. Of course an official quotation on the Stock Exchange could not be obtained because of the rule which provides that two-thirds of the share capital must be publicly subscribed, but rumours were floated in the City of the enormous value of the shares; brokers were given "an interest" in the Company; "confidential" circulars were issued, and gradually most of these 85,000 shares were disposed of at a premium. This operation was simplified by a report that the Nizam had become an extensive shareholder. Mr. Cordery, the Resident, honestly enough advised the Nizam that it would be well for him to have an interest in the concern. Telegrams were despatched to Abdul Huk in London to purchase shares, and the Hyderabad Government was told that they could not be bought under £12 each. And then the shares that were sold to the Nizam were the very shares with which Abdul Huk had been bribed, and for which, of course, he had never paid a farthing! That astute Native has since refunded the money of which, practically, he robbed the Government, whose agent he was, and the purchase has been rescinded; but the unfortunate English shareholders are no better off, and at a recent meeting they vented their displeasure upon Mr. Watson. Nor, unless the concessionnaires can be induced to follow Abdul Huk's example, does there seem much hope for them. The Committee express the opinion that "the concessionnaires have used the concession for the purpose of realizing great gains not intended to be conferred upon them;" they comment on the fact that none of the British officials knew of the circumstance of Abdul Huk being bribed, and remark upon "the serious risks to Native States which attend the direct access of London speculators to Native Ministers;" and finally suggest that when a Native State is under the influence of the British power, communications between that State and speculators should not be of a direct character. All this means that the Indian Government and its officials have been, in plain English, careless, and that if they have any care for their reputations, they will be less trustful in future of the London speculator. —*Morning Advertiser*, August 10.

There was a particularly lively scene on Tuesday afternoon at the meeting of the Hyderabad Deccan Company. The shareholders present were largely in favour of an adjournment until after the report of the Select Committee had been presented; but some of the Directors, armed with proxies of absent men, were anxious that the report of the Directors and the accounts should be passed forthwith. The feeling of the meeting was plainly expressed by a vote of forty-four to nine in favour of adjournment. Notwithstanding this, there was an attempt to force an immediate poll. Thereupon the indignation of the meeting was loudly testified. A large body left the room in disgust, but afterwards returned to have the fight out with their opponents. In the end the Directors holding proxies found it desirable to bend to the storm, and the poll was put off for seven days. The moral power of indignation, backed by a sense of injustice, was in this case very effectively illustrated, and the system of proxies as effectively discredited.—*Tyldesley Weekly Journal*, August 10.

The report of the Deccan Committee published to-day has been eagerly scanned. It is very different from the colourless draft drawn up for Sir Henry James by the Solicitor-General for Scotland, but it does not go nearly as far as four members of the Committee desire in its condemnation of the supineness of the India Office which made this gigantic scandal possible. The section of four actually formed a majority of the Committee. But they were won over to accept the compromise of censure which the report presents. The next thing that will be heard of this remarkable case will be in the courts of law. There are 700 shareholders who were drawn into the net, and who, as was shown at the meeting the other day, are in a pretty lively state, as it is now proposed that a Committee of the shareholders shall file a bill in equity calling in question the whole transaction. It is held upon high legal authority consulted in the matter that the result would be that the judge would order a valuation to be taken of the property sold at the time when the promoters fixed its value at £850,000, and received that sum. It is believed that by this process they may be made to disgorge.—*Bradford Observer*, August 10.

The Gorst Inquiry.—A Contradiction from the India Office.—The India Office and the Nizam's Solicitors.—Having called attention the other day to the charges which the Indian papers—of all shades of opinion—were making against Sir John Gorst in connection with the affairs of Hyderabad, we wrote to Sir John Gorst in the hope that he would enable us to prove that the charges were without foundation.

In reply we have to-day received the following letter from Sir John Gorst's Secretary:—

"India Office, Whitehall, S.W., August 15, 1888.

"Sir,—Sir John Gorst desires me to acknowledge the receipt of your letter of the 14th inst., and to say that he saw it, and the articles in yesterday's *Pall Mall Gazette*, to which it refers, as he was passing through London to-day on the way to the Continent."

"Sir John Gorst desires me to say, in reply, that had your representative applied to him earlier, he could have saved you from giving currency to a number of misstatements which the *Pioneer* article contains. The charge which is insinuated against Sir John Gorst in the *Pioneer* is wholly false. Mr. Palmer, so far as Sir John Gorst is aware, had and has no connection with, or interest in, the Deccan Company; and Sir John Gorst throughout the proceedings consistently refused to have any communication in reference to the Deccan inquiry with any of the parties interested therein, with the exception of an official interview at the India Office with the Nawab Mahdi Ali.—I am, yours faithfully, Richmond Ritchie."

We have much pleasure in giving the fullest publicity to Sir John Gorst's contradiction; but at the same time it is necessary to point out that the contradiction does not go by any means so far as the original charges. Thus, in the first place, the statement of the *Pioneer*, endorsed by the *Statesman and Friend of India*, was not, so far as we understand, that Mr. Tom Palmer had any specific "connection with or interest in the Deccan Company," but that he was generally mixed up with the seamy side of affairs at Hyderabad. Further, it was stated that he is on intimate terms with Sir John Gorst, and the suggestion was that Mr. Palmer might have acted as intermediary between his friend the Under-Secretary of India and other persons who did have "connection with or interest in the Deccan Company." This "charge," whatever it may be worth, is not, our readers will see, covered by the terms of Sir John Gorst's letter.

Further it will be noticed that what Sir John Gorst contradicts is that he had "any communication in reference to the Deccan inquiry with any of the parties interested therein." This is a different thing from saying that he did not have "any communication with any of the parties interested therein." We are compelled to make this distinction by the analogy of Mr. Smith's statement with regard to his dealings with the *Times*. Mr. Smith also denied that he had "any communication in reference to the Commission with any of the parties interested therein." But that denial it subsequently appeared, was not inconsistent with the fact that he did have communications with his "old friend," Mr. Walter. An unbelieving generation has questioned whether the "old friends" confined their conversation to the state of the weather. With this precedent before the public, it is unfortunate that Sir John Gorst has has not given a less qualified denial to statements which are causing so much disquiet in India.

This feeling that there is something wrong somewhere will not be diminished, we fear, by a fact which we are able to state on unimpeachable authority. The gentleman who has hitherto been acting as Solicitor in this country for the Nizam of Hyderabad is Mr. Spencer Whitehead, of Lincoln's Inn. The conduct of the case has, however—so we are informed on independent but entirely trustworthy authority—been transferred from Mr. Whitehead's hands to those of Messrs. Freshfield. This transference has, it is said, been made at the instance of the India Office, and is not disconnected with the embarrassing nature of the evidence procured by Mr. Whitehead.—*Pall Mall Gazette*, August 11.

THE HYDERABAD DECCAN COMPANY.—The report of the Select Committee of the House of Commons which inquired into the circumstances under which this Company was formed and brought out is a very unsatisfactory document. It shows very clearly indeed how the concessionnaires and their accomplice. Abdul Huk, put immense sums of money into their pockets which were not intended for them; but it is exceedingly chary in the expression of opinion, and the only definite recommendation upon which it ventures is that as long as the Indian Government interferes with the proceedings of Native States in business matters great care should be taken fully to fulfil the responsibilities thus assumed. In other words, the Committee are of opinion that direct access to Native Ministers should not be allowed to London speculators. This may or may not be sound advice, but it certainly is not as much as the public had a right to expect from the Committee. The Committee, indeed, is careful to tell us that it abstains from expressing any opinion upon the legal rights or liability of the Nizam, the concessionnaires, the Company, or individual shareholders. But, while the Committee cannot be expected to pronounce upon the legal rights of these several parties, it surely must have formed some opinion as to the justice of the claims of the several parties against one another. Very grave suspicion has been entertained respecting the British Resident at Hyderabad and some of the higher officials both in Calcutta and in London. Surely the Committee ought to have stated in plain unmistakable language whether those officials have been guilty of anything more than negligence in the discharge of their duties. The report says that the initial proceedings were conducted between Abdul Huk and the concessionnaires, and, in fact, that a draft agreement had been drawn up between them; that in consequence of this, less attention was given to the matter by the authorities both in London and Calcutta than otherwise it would have received. Does this mean that in the opinion of the Committee the various British officials simply took for granted that the Nizam's Government was capable of taking care of itself, and did not look, therefore, very carefully into what it had done? Or does it imply any graver censure respecting any of the said officials? The public has a right to plain speaking on the matter. Again, it seems to us that the public had a right to expect from the Committee some expression of opinion as to whether the concessionnaires and Abdul Huk should be allowed to retain the £850,000 which they pocketed. The report shows that the intention was that a very large sum should be spent in the Deccan in exploring for minerals and in mining. At the same time the capital was limited to one million sterling. But of the million so created the concessionnaires and Abdul Huk were given by the Directors £850,000, leaving only £150,000 as working capital for the Company. Assuming that the Directors had power to make this bargain, do the Committee believe that the concessionnaires ought to be allowed to retain the £850,000, or is anything to be done to right the shareholders and to relieve the State of Hyderabad from the injury which the report says it will suffer in consequence of the action of the Directors and the concessionnaires?—*Statist*, August 11.

THE HYDERABAD DECCAN MINING COMPANY.—We prefer to reserve comment upon the report of the Select Committee appointed to inquire into the circumstances attending the formation of this Company until the evidence upon which it is based has been published. The Committee state "that they desire to abstain from expressing any opinion on the legal rights or liabilities of the Nizam, the concessionnaires, the Company, or individual shareholders, but that they are of opinion that the concessionnaires have used the concession for the purpose of realizing great gains not intended to be conferred on them, and this has been done to the injury of the State, from which they obtained the concession, with the assistance of their partner, Abdul Huk." This, it will be observed, reserves the question as to whether the concessionnaires have or have not acted up to the letter of the bond, however much they have acted contrary to the ideas of those by whom the agreement was drawn up, and it is to that phase of the subject that the attention of the shareholders of this Company should now be directed. We understand that in order that they may have time to consider their position, a number of shareholders intend at the adjourned meeting of the Company, fixed for Monday next, to move that another adjournment until the 15th October be made. That Mr. Watson, the concessionnaire, is strongly opposed to this course is, it seems to us, a very good reason why it should be adopted, and it is to be hoped, therefore, that shareholders will attend in sufficient numbers to prevent those whose conduct the Select Committee have so strongly reprehended, succeeding in any effort they may make to stifle inquiry.—*Economist*, August 11.

THE HYDERABAD DECCAN INQUIRY.—The shareholders who met last Tuesday appear to have wasted a good deal of indignation. The ponderous report was on the eve of making its appearance. Its importance was unnecessarily added to by the questions asked in the House of Commons as to the premature publication in the *Times* of a portion, and the meeting worked itself into a ferment in anticipation of a scathing denunciation of somebody or something on the part of the Select Committee. Now that the report is out, it may be seen by anybody who takes the trouble to wade through the voluminous document that no very dreadful discovery has been made, nor have the ordinary lines of Company business been departed from.

Briefly speaking, the history of the affair is this. The concession giving rights to select fields or mines on a ninety-nine years' lease, subject to royalties, was made in 1886. A Limited Company, with a capital of not less than £1,000,000, was to be formed in London to work the concession, which also extended to the construction of a railway in Hyderabad. Previous to the formation of this Company there existed in the Nizam's territories a somewhat limited railway system. The extension of the railways had been mooted, and this was an object approved of by the Government of India. In 1881 Mr. Winter met with Abdul Huk, and negotiated with him on the subject of the railway, and a company was ultimately floated by Mr. Watson, on an agreement that the Nizam should give a guarantee of 5 per cent. for twenty years upon the £2,000,000 which was to be paid to him for the railway, and of which he was to take a portion in the shares of the contemplated Railroad Company which was to provide the £2,000,000. The two concessions were negotiated separately, the draft of the Mining concession being settled in 1883, and signed in January, 1886. The partners in the enterprise had 85,000 shares between them, Abdul Huk receiving one-fourth. This really is the point on which the matter rests—namely, the benefit which the concessionnaires derived from the affair. The report, it is true, observes that the concern proved "highly lucrative" to the concessionnaires, but says, "It has to be admitted that concessionnaires who hand over a concession to a Company are entitled to benefit to a greater or less extent by the transaction." The Committee appear to think that the concessionnaires were sufficiently remunerated for their services in promoting the Railway Company, and were scarcely entitled to the Mining concession, but this is a matter of opinion, and hardly warranted by the facts. This, however, is the hardest thing which the Committee can find to say, and we can see no reason why the shareholders should be alarmed. What is clearly to be done is to set to work and develop the property, and now that the shareholders know the worst, the sooner they give their support to the Board the better. Nothing can be gained by further wrangling.—*Financial World*, August 11.

THE attention of the House of Commons will be called "on an early day to the report of the Select Committee on the Hyderabad (Deccan) Mining Company's affairs;" Sir Roper Lethbridge, an ex-Anglo-Indian official, has given notice that he will move a resolution regarding it. This will afford an opportunity for the public becoming acquainted in more detail than at present with one of the most extraordinary financial transactions of modern times, and one upon which the fullest light deserves to be thrown.—*Birmingham Daily Post*, August 11.

PRESSURE on our space prevents us from printing the full report of the Hyderabad Deccan Commission, but our readers will find it *in extenso* in yesterday's *Financial News*. It is only to be regretted that the Commission has made no suggestion as to the future management of the undertaking, nor any word by way of guidance to those who bought their shares *bonâ fide* in the market. Apparently they have done nothing more than bring confirmatory evidence regarding the statements and charges formulated in our columns and the *Financial News*. We should have thought that such a Committee would have suggested some remedies, or at least some cure for the evil—if the said evil existed.—*Financial Critic*, August 11.

THE WONDROUS TALE OF ABDUL HUK.—In many respects the story of the Hyderabad Deccan Mining Company, Limited, is a very ordinary business. Whoever has lived with open eye and ear in this wicked, but interesting and amusing, City of London has heard something not unlike it. There is always a mysterious benefactor living on a heap of gold somewhere, who, out of the abundance of his goodness, concedes to a casual gentleman from England the right of working that heap for so many years. The English gentleman comes back and starts a Company, capital so-and-so, in shares so many, with so much to the favoured one of the mysterious benefactor. Then, by nods and winks—by hints that great people are in it, by promises of the floods of gold which will pour out when a teacupful of money is put in—the great venture is floated. The widow and the orphan, the foolish trustee, the country clergyman who wants ten per cent. for his money, and the naval or military officer who has commuted, exist that such things may happen. The amusing part of it all is that City gentlemen, of quite appalling smartness, can be wheedled in too. The baits differ, but when the right ones are chosen and properly dangled the fish will rise. Then at the end there comes some such meeting as that held at Winchester House last Tuesday, with an "extraordinary scene," cries of "Shame!" "Monstrous!" and so forth. Somebody is out of pocket. Commonly it is not the favourite of the mysterious benefactor.

The origin of the Hyderabad (Deccan) Company had, however, certain features worth noting. The credit of our Indian Service seemed to be touched by it for one thing, and then there was an Oriental gentleman in it who is worth looking at. Abdul Huk is his name, and though we do not know what that name may imply, it sounds appropriate. Rummun Lal was not more so. This able Oriental, having the ear of the Nizam of Hyderabad, did obtain from him, and did share with certain Englishmen, a concession for working the mineral wealth of the State. It was duly approved by the British Resident. By the terms of the arrangement made by Abdul Huk, the capital of the Company to be formed for working this concession was put at a million in 100,000 shares at £10 each. Of this, £150,000 was to be spent in developing the mineral wealth of the State of Hyderabad. What was to be done with the remaining £850,000, or where it was to come from, nobody seems to have inquired in the Deccan. One would imagine that an English Resident in an Indian Court would have obtained, in the course of his experience, a tight hold of certain elementary facts of human nature. He might be supposed to have learnt by this time that business men who are also capitalists, do not, when they have a really good thing in hand, give it away. Also it should have been within his knowledge that experienced Orientals like Abdul Huk, and the old hands that were with him, do not go into any business without hope of profit. A little thinking ought to have shown our Resident—who, though he is a political, seems to have been as innocent as Colonel Newcome—that the possessors of the concession were not working out of pure love of human nature. Something was going to be done with the remaining 850,000 shares, of course. They were going to be divided between the owners of the concession, as a matter of fact. These gentlemen did not credit themselves with the possession of 85,000 shares at £10, and then proceed to develop the resources of Hyderabad with their own capital. Naturally, they sold the shares, and the Company arose. It must be a very nice thing to know an Oriental Prince who confers on you with a scratch of his pen wealth beyond the dreams of avarice. No doubt this is all very legitimate. Hyderabad has minerals worth digging up and coal also. Moreover, if you have a saleable right to work a thing worth working, you may fairly sell it. Only we do not see why a present of £850,000 should have been made to Abdul Huk and his friends out of the pockets of buyers of shares, for that is what it amounts to, and still less ought such a transaction to have been permitted by an English Resident, who is placed as guide and friend at the Court of the Nizam. Abdul Huk is indeed a master of the art of Company-promoting. Not only did he get this extraordinary concession from his Sovereign, but he persuadad him to buy shares in the Company, and absolutely sold to the candid Prince—apparently at a premium—shares of his own for which he himself had paid nothing. Abdul has since had to disgorge, and has been dismissed from office; he may think himself lucky that there is an English Resident at Hyderabad. Time was when Abdul Huks who were caught playing these tricks on Nizams passed a very evil quarter of an hour. As it is, it is lucky for some of his colleagues that they are out of Hyderabad. The common or business moral of the story is not worth repeating. People have been told to be cautious about buying shares in Companies so often, and have neglected the advice so persistently, that it is no use to repeat it. But there is a particular moral which is not so old. It is, that if our officials in India undertake to encourage Native Princes to develop the resources of their States, they should be sure that they understand business before they give the sanction of the British Government to Companies to be floated on the London market.—*Saturday Review*, August 11.

THE Hyderabad scandals are one of the numerous questions which will have to be postponed until the Autumn Session. Sir Roper Lethbridge has given notice of a motion with reference to the matter which he will propose on "an early day," and the earliest day available will be in November. If the Select Committee's Report had been presented earlier in the Session there would probably—our London Correspondent says—have been a very useful and instructive debate on the subject, as there is a strong feeling among members of all political opinions that the Government of India and the India Office come very badly out of the affair. "I believe that Sir Richard Temple and Mr. Labouchere were anxious that the censure of the officials concerned contained in the Report should have been made much stronger, but they were overruled by the other members, who thought that the negligence displayed was to some extent excusable. When the affair comes before Parliament some hard things are likely to be said, and it is not impossible that one result will be the reorganization of the Council of the Secretary of State for India, which, as at present constituted, is more ornamental than useful."—*Yorkshire Post*, August 11.

DECCAN COMPANY.—At the meeting on Tuesday an amendment, proposing adjournment till October 13, was submitted, but the poll regarding it will not be taken till Monday next, when the meeting will be resumed at Winchester House, at one o'clock. The Chairman, Mr. G. H. M. Batten, confined himself mainly to an exposition of the prospects of the Company as regards coal, gold, diamonds, mica, and other minerals. He said the property was extremely valuable, and, in his opinion, good value for the £850,000 given to the concessionnaires. The report of the Select Committee of the House of Commons, appointed to inquire into the affairs of the Company, was issued on Wednesday. It is of a negative character, reciting the history of the formation of the Company, and censuring by implication rather than by direct assertion. To expose Abdul Huk after his restitution is like blackening a sweep, and to censure the Indian Government for its ineptitude to grasp what was going on is, for all practical purposes, empty talk. The legality in point of strict law of what took place, and the intrinsic value of the property, are the two points the shareholders want to know about, and this information the report of the Select Committee does not give. One great point is left untouched—that is, whether the concession is valid; also whether the present capital will be left intact. In fact, as far as we can see, the report leaves the shareholders pretty much as they were before. Two courses, as far as we can see, remain open. Recourse to a law court or to a Committee of independent shareholders to meet Mr. Watson, as he himself suggests. We should, for many reasons, recommend the latter. There may be a good deal of more than cleverness in the inception and formation of the Company, but it must be admitted there is great scope for possibilities in an area of 81,000 square miles. If the capital in hand, £90,000, or the original working capital, £150,000, be deemed insufficient, perhaps the concessionnaires would not deem it prudent or just to exact the pound of flesh. There will be an opportunity on Monday to throw out feelers. The report of the Select Committee clears the atmosphere a good deal, and we shall await with some interest the next phase of development.—*Herapath's Railway and Commercial Journal*, August 11.

In the report of the Select Committee on the Hyderabad and Deccan scandal, there is an allusion to diamonds. The Company have turned their attention to these gems, and "five diamonds have been found in some refuse." This does not look very promising, and I don't suppose that any speculator would care to invest his money on the faith of this discovery. But in the report of the Committee, which was surreptitiously published, "five diamonds" appeared as "fine diamonds." It would be interesting to know how this curious mistake was made, and what was the effect of it in mercantile circles.—*London Correspondent of Eastern Daily Press*, August 11.

What is the Deccan Concession Worth?—Mr. Watson and other concessionnaires have always justified the payment to themselves of the enormous sum of £850,000 for the concession of the mining rights of Hyderabad, on the ground that they are of unlimited value, and that in due time the coal mines, the gold, and the diamonds will be worth millions to the Company. On this part of the case the *Bombay Gazette* says: "There is absolutely no demand, actual or prospective, for an unlimited out-turn of Singareni coal, whatever may be the capital expended on underground works. The quality of the coal precludes its use in the Bombay mills; the experiment has been tried, and if it were possible to sell it at half the price which it will cost to raise and bring it by rail to Bombay, it would still not pay to use it. A third of it is waste, clinker, and ashes. A certain limited amount can and will be used on the railways within very exactly defined limits, beyond which it will come into competition with the better and cheaper English coal. That settles the prospect of the Singareni mines paying interest of 6 per cent. on a million of capital. It is only with the most careful working that the coal mines can pay a dividend on the working capital. As for the diamondiferous soil, the new Golconda, that Mr. Watson has still the courage to discourse about, he had to confess to Mr. Labouchere that of the five diamonds found one was worth 30s., and the rest were worth nothing. So of the gold; there is no reason whatever to suppose that the gold-bearing strata of the Deccan are likely to be more profitable than those of Mysore and the Wynaad. There is probably some gold, which may yield some return if properly worked; but there is no room for further delusion. The reconstituted Company must keep very soberly to the actualities of the case if it is ever to earn a 6 per cent. dividend on the £150,000 subscribed capital."—*Norwich Mercury*, August 11.

The Hyderabad-Deccan Company.—We said last week that the Directors of this Company ought to have deferred the ordinary general meeting until the report of the James Committee is in the hands of the shareholders, and this was the opinion, very vigorously expressed, of those who were present at the meeting on Wednesday. But the directors would not assent, and, beaten by 44 to 9 on the question of adjournment to October, they demanded a poll, the result of which is to be announced on Monday.

If we are to accept the assurances of the Chairman, the title of the Company to the property is unassailable, and the property itself is of immense value. The Chairman puts the Company's gold discoveries at over a million. There must be (so he says) diamonds in paying quantities; and, as for the coal and iron, it would be difficult to calculate its value. Unfortunately, from one cause and another, there is nothing tangible as yet to show.

Why, it may be asked, if there are so many diamonds on the property have some of them not been found? Well, the diamondiferous soil has first to be uncovered, and then washed. But machinery was ordered a year ago? Yes, but it did not reach the diamond-fields until February? And since? The cholera broke out, and every labourer left the place. But the cholera has passed? Yes, but after it had disappeared the rains came and flooded the excavations, and so nothing can be done until next October, when the manager and his men will begin again with "undiminished confidence in ultimate success."

But what of the other minerals upon the property? Here, again, shareholders have to be content with what will be. "I will say," said the Chairman, at Tuesday's meeting, "that the existence of large quantities of superior iron ore in close proximity to the coal is an ascertained fact, and the only question is whether, with the present low prices of English iron and low freights, we are justified in sinking capital in establishing iron and steel works?" Iron ore is not of much use unless it can be worked at a profit, and if profitable working is to be dependent upon any material advance in the price of English iron, we are afraid that the Deccan Company will not get much in the way of profit from its iron ore.—*Stock Exchange*, August 11.

THE report of the Select Committee appointed to inquire into the Hyderabad Deccan Mining Company is scarcely pleasant reading for any of the persons interested. True, the Government of the Nizam is acquitted of any blame in the matter, unless it be on account of carelessness or folly, but Messrs. Abdul Huk, Watson and Company, scarcely come out of the matter so pleasantly. Nor are there many grains of comfort for the unfortunate shareholders who have bought the shares of the concessionnaires. Supposing that £150,000 still is available, is this sum sufficient for the working of a Company whose schemes are of such magnitude; and, allowing it to be sufficient, is there any assurance of such success as will make any return on the entire capital of the Company? The following extract from the report is of interest:—

"The history of the Hyderabad Deccan Company shows that the concession has, in fact, proved highly lucrative to the concessionnaires. They have appropriated to themselves and dealt with £850,000 of the capital of the Company, but the question remains how the 85,000 shares out of the total of 100,000 shares have passed into the hands of the concessionnaires. The Committee consider that no such deficiency in the remuneration received by the concessionnaires for their services in promoting the Railway Company existed as to entitle them to obtain the mining concession. The Committee desire to abstain from expressing any opinion on the legal rights and liabilities of the Nizam, the concessionnaires, the Company, or individual shareholders. But the Committee are of opinion that the concessionnaires have used the concession for the purpose of realizing great gains not intended to be conferred on them, and that this has been done to the injury of the State from which they obtained the concession, with the assistance of their partner, Abdul Huk."

It is understood that Abdul Huk has refunded the money paid by the Nizam for 10,000 shares. Will Messrs. Watson and Co. do likewise to the purchasers of their shares? I fear not.—*Topical Times*, August 11.

THE meeting of the Hyderabad (Deccan) Company, Limited, held on Tuesday (as reported in another column) passed off more quietly than many of the shareholders anticipated. The discussion which followed the exhaustive speech of the Chairman was conducted in the case of some of the speakers with considerable heat; but, under the circumstances, this was hardly a matter of surprise. It was proposed, in view of the report of the Parliamentary Committee, that the meeting should be adjourned until October 15th. This was carried by a show of hands, but a poll was demanded, which will be taken on Monday next.

THIS seems, under the circumstances, the best course to pursue. It will give the shareholders time to "read, mark, learn, and inwardly digest" the report of the Select Committee. This report, of which a summary appears elsewhere, will not be very pleasant reading for some, though it is a less exciting document than many expected it would be. The report will not increase the admiration of the shareholders or the public for the concessionnaires or their *modus operandi*; and some of the mud that has been stirred up and thrown will assuredly stick. But one cannot help feeling that the whole business has been elevated into a position of unnecessary importance, for its details are, after all, in some respects, quite commonplace, and in others, vulgar. If the experience proves anything like an effective lesson to English investors, it will have served at least one useful purpose. Meanwhile, the shareholders evidently mean to make the best of their property and of the situation, and in following this course they are acting wisely.—*Mining Journal*, August 11.

Hyderabad-Deccan.—So this ghastly tale is supposed to be finished, and everybody comes off with flying colours. Nobody to blame, and the only wonder that the time of a Royal Commission should have been wasted. What a farce! This is English justice—no, we beg pardon—law. English justice is a thing we are still looking for.—*Weekly Bulletin*, August 11.

The Meeting of the Hyderabad (Deccan) Company, Limited.—An excited meeting of this Company was held on Tuesday the 7th inst., according to the announcement which we made in our issue of Saturday last. No practical conclusion was reached, but the malcontents by no means scored a victory. In the course of the final discussion the Chairman (Mr. George H. M. Batten) said the only thing the Directors asked was that the accounts should be passed. This, indeed, was the object of the meeting, and whatever discussion arose outside of this matter was irrelevant. A shareholder volunteered the bold assertion that to pass the accounts would be to assent to the payment of the 85,000 shares to the concessionnaires. It is strange that shareholders should so far forget themselves as to force on the attention of a meeting of the kind questions which have already been decided. The only effect of this ill-timed observation was to give to the Chairman the opportunity to say that the payment of the 85,000 out of the 100,000 shares obtained the assent of the previous meeting, and was not, therefore, liable to further discussion.

From first to last there is no possibility of charging anything like irregularity against the concessionnaires in their dealings with the Company. The terms which bound the concessionnaires were definite and precise. They were to this effect that "their respective executors or administrators shall, on any date within six months after the capital for the construction of the line from Warangal to Singareni is practically assured, form in London, under the Companies' Acts, 1862 to 1880, a Company limited by shares, with a capital not less than £1,000,000, with powers to increase the capital by an issue of debentures, or otherwise, if necessary, and having for or among its objects the acquisition of the rights and liabilities of the concessionnaires under these presents, and the execution of the works herein referred to. If such a Company shall be formed before the expiration of the period fixed in Clause 1, and if before that period £150,000 of its share capital, at the least, shall have been subscribed and £75,000 shall have been actually paid up in respect of the subscribed share capital, and if such Company shall also before the said period have adopted this concession and made itself liable to make the payments mentioned in Clause II. hereof, and in all other respects liable upon these presents to the same extent as the concessionnaires were or would be liable, then it shall be lawful for the concessionnaires to transfer to such Company the benefit of this concession."

After this came the crucial question, on what terms should the Company acquire the rights of the concessionnaires, which had been acquired with no little difficulty and after an anxious consideration of the value of the rights and privileges involved? The value of the concession was at that time one which the public could not appreciate. They had no knowledge of the rare amount of mineral wealth that was secured to the contracting parties, and no idea of the intelligence, expense, and anxiety that had been directed to the acquisition of the concession. Consequently, it was thought desirable that no direct appeal should be made to investors generally. There was a certain amount of risk in the adventure which it might have been fairly assumed the public was not prepared to undertake. They were ignorant of the rare value of the mineral wealth conceded by the terms of the covenant with the Nizam's Government. Under these circumstances the concessionnaires came to the conclusion that at that time, before the value of the concession could have been appreciated by the public, it was preferable not to ask the public to subscribe for the shares, and they determined to subscribe and pay up the whole of the stipulated capital of £150,000 themselves. Accordingly the capital was so subscribed and allotted to eight persons, who thus formed the entire Company, and who paid in cash immediately £75,000, and later the remaining £75,000, the concessionnaires paying also the whole preliminary expenses of the formation of the Company. The Company was, in fact, a private Company, like many others with which the mercantile world is familiar—Messrs. Glyn, Mills, Currie and Co., Messrs. Bass and Co., Messrs. Armstrong, Mitchell and Co, for instance. Like this Company, none of these ever issued a prospectus or offered any shares to the public, or in any way held out inducements to the public to buy shares from the Company. The position is therefore this—the Company is really a partnership into which the concessionnaires brought £150,000 in cash and a concession, the value of which is said to be represented by paper shares.

This aspect of affairs effectually disposes of all charges of irregularity, and indeed the shareholders have of all persons the least ground for complaints. They entered into the transaction with their eyes open, and believing that they were partners in a property of exceptional value. That belief is fully justified by the disclosures which have been made since the formation of the Company. The Singareni coalfields are full of wealth of black diamonds, and the markets are ready to absorb at a profit to the Company all the produce of the many seams which run through the ground. The gold area is proved to be of immense area, and of superabounding wealth. The value of this may be estimated, if we compare it with the Colar concession, the present market value of the properties combined in that concession amounting to £960,900. The value of this property, it is said, is equal to £25 per acre, or £16,000 per square mile. At this rate the value of the gold-bearing area belonging to the Deccan Company, as already discovered, would be £2,080,000. This is no extravagant estimate, and it is an asset of the first importance to the Company. The diamondiferous wealth is still greater, and indeed this is held by many to be the chief value of the property. In numerous localities abandoned pits have been discovered, and they testify to the enormous wealth that lies beneath and around. If diamonds were found in paying quantities by the ancient workers in the portion of the stratum which they were able to reach—it is known that they were so found—the probability of their being discovered in the untouched portions seems to be overwhelming.

It is convenient for malcontents to ignore these facts, but they are facts nevertheless, and they prove, with unimpeachable testimony, the exceptionable value of the privileges and property which the Company has acquired. They have in their possession a mineral wealth which is unprecedented, and which amply justifies the price they have paid for it—and paid for it, as the Chairman observes, in paper shares. Before the next meeting shall be held we shall probably have in our possession the report of the Select Committee, but to whatever view it may incline it cannot invalidate the fact that the Hyderabad concession covers an area of ground unequalled for its splendid mineral wealth and its potentialities of exceptional dividends. The position of the Company is strong, its title cannot be invalidated, the Nizam's Government holds firmly to it as a partner in its fortunes, and behind all these are riches in coal, in gold, in diamonds, and even in minor products sufficient to yield handsome returns for more than one generation to come.

[Since these remarks were written the Report of the Special Committee has appeared, and we have commented on it in another column.]—*Bullionist*, August 11.

THE report of the Select Committee appointed to inquire into the formation and promotion of the Hyderabad (Deccan) Company, Limited, has at length made its appearance. It was published on the evening of Wednesday—the day after the meeting of the shareholders, on which we have commented in another column. The report is a singularly lame affair. Through its long string of halting sentences there is manifest a dread of saying anything positive. According to some authorities, the use of language is to disguise the thoughts. This report is a magnificent example. The Select Committee was set to work to sift to the bottom some atrocious crime, and to fix the guilt on the criminals. It has succeeded in doing nothing of the kind. It furnishes us with occasional glimpses of the concessionnaires—their family connections, their enterprises, their business aptitudes, and their emoluments. But it is discreetly silent on the accusations of fraud which were hurled at their heads a few weeks ago, when first the "Deccan Scandal" exercised the tender consciences of City men and their representatives in Parliament. From first to last the report is the record of a verdict of "Not guilty"—of a verdict in favour of the concessionnaires who were so rashly accused. The accusations were the outcome of unfriendly rivalry; the "deliverance" of the Select Committee is an absolute acquittal. Even Abdul Huk—the arch offender, as we were told—is completely whitewashed. The report is a pleasant testimony to the innocence of all the parties concerned. We find no fault in the outcome of it all. Lord Lawrence, whose perfect good faith no one for a moment doubted, is in good company. They are all honourable men. If there be any blame expressed it is not against the concessionnaires, nor against Abdul Huk, who was the Nizam's trusted Councillor and agent, and who made the initial arrangements.

Such blame, if any be, is reserved for the Indian Government and its representatives. "When the matter came before the Resident, the Government of India, and the Secretary for India, no one of them was aware of the circumstances relating to Abdul Huk which called for a peculiar vigilance, and apart from this it is clear that the terms of the concession were subjected to less complete review than they would have gone through had they not already been agreed upon by the accredited negotiator of the Nizam. The result is to be regretted, and it is apparent that if more direct and effective British assistance and advice had been given to the Government of Hyderabad, the events that have occurred would not have taken place." This seems to us like defending the value of "British assistance and advice" at the expense of British vigilance. In a word, the report exculpates those whom popular prejudice hastily charge with flagrant offences, and reserves its strictures, such as they are, for those who represent the Government of India and of Great Britain. It was for this precious report that the objectors at the meeting on Tuesday were waiting, when they postponed the passing of the report and accounts. For this certificate of character which the Select Committee has presented to the concessionnaires, promoters, and directors, they watched in great anxiety, and meanwhile raised their little tempest. What will they do now?

With reference to the recent meeting of the Hyderabad (Deccan) Company, which took place on Tuesday last at Winchester House, a report of which appears in another column, the following has been forwarded by Mr. W. C. Watson, one of the concessionnaires, to the shareholders. We consider with him, bearing in mind the small section of dissentients, that it would be unwise in the general interests of the Company to foment further discussion.

"The Hyderabad (Deccan) Company, Limited.

"7, Great Winchester Street, London, E.C.,
"8th August, 1888.

"I duly received your proxy, and beg to thank you and the other shareholders very much for the confidence in me which you thus displayed. The total number of shares held by those shareholders who sent me their proxies, or who were in the room prepared to vote with me (excluding my own), amounted to more than 37,000.

"At the general meeting yesterday a strong opposition (evidently organised beforehand) to the passing of the report and accounts of the Directors was raised by some of the shareholders who were present on the ground that they ought to wait for the report of the Committee of the House of Commons before doing anything. The number of shares held by the shareholders present in the room, excluding the concessionnaires and the board, was only about 6,500, and of those about 1,500 were held by shareholders who supported me, so that the total holding of the opposition was only about 5,000 shares out of the 100,000 of which the capital of the Company consists.

"On the resolution for the adoption of the Directors' report and accounts (of which a copy was sent to you) being proposed, an amendment that instead of doing so, the meeting should be adjourned to the 15th October, leaving everything in the meantime unsettled, was carried upon a show of hands. The opposition, notwithstanding the small number of shares which they held, insisted that only the votes of the shareholders present ought to be taken into account, to the exclusion of those shareholders who, unable to attend, had sent their proxies. If a poll had been taken of only the votes present, the opposition would have failed and the adjournment would have been rejected. I considered it my duty to demand a poll, that the real majority of the votes might be ascertained and due weight given to the proxies which you and others had sent to me, and the Chairman thereupon directed a poll to be taken on Monday next, the 13th inst., on the question of the adjournment.

"It is probable that an attempt will be made, by misleading statements, to induce you to withdraw the proxy which you have given me. I trust that you will on no account do so, but will continue the confidence in me which you have already shown. The course taken by the opposition at the meeting yesterday will, if it unfortunately prevails, lead to dispute, litigation, and injury to the Company; while union will benefit the shareholders, both in the market price of their shares and in the early payment of dividends.

"The last accounts from India, which was read by the Chairman at the meeting, gave increasing proof of the value of the Company's property, and the certainty that it will soon return an income, providing its working is not embarrassed by disputes among the shareholders themselves. In spite of all difficulties 500 tons of coal per week, which the concession bound the Company to raise, have already been exceeded, and the recent report of the Locomotive Superintendent of the Nizam's Railway, on which our coal is now used, and of Lieut.-Col. Conway Gordon, Director-General of Indian Railways, prove the value of the coal for railway purposes, and demonstrate that it can be sold at a price which will return a large profit. Further proof has been given of the value of the gold deposits, and large samples of them are now coming home for exhibition and further testing.

"This is not my first experience of having to maintain a Company against a hostile attack, which, although gentlemen of good intentions have been unfortunately led to associate themselves with it, on this, as on the former occasion, has for its ultimate source influences which are distinctly hostile to the welfare of the Company and its shareholders. I remain, your obedient servant, W. C. Watson."—*Bullionist*, August 11.

A circular has been issued to the shareholders of the Hyderabad (Deccan) Company, Limited, signed by Sir Julian Goldsmid, Sir Roper Lethbridge, Mr. R. A. Germaine, and Mr. Benjamin J. Scott. It urges the shareholders either to attend the adjourned meeting of Monday next, or to cancel the proxies they may have given to Mr. Watson. The wish is to have the meeting adjourned till the 15th of October, in order to give time for the consideration of the Report of the Parliamentary Committee just issued. A more reasonable or moderate demand, in the circumstances, could not well be made, and the shareholders will be unusually supine if they do not support it to a man.—*Standard*, August 11.

The Hyderabad (Deccan) Company.—In the House of Commons, August 10, Mr. Kelly asked the Under-Secretary of State for India whether his attention had been called to the statements made with reference to Mr. Furnivall on page 9 of the Report from the Select Committee on East India (Hyderabad-Deccan Mining Company), to the effect that Mr. Furnivall, who was recently in the employ of the Government of India, but had now retired on a pension, received from Mr. W. C. Watson 500 shares in the Hyderabad-Deccan Company "for nothing;" that he sold those shares at £11 each, and therefore realized £5,500 for them; whether Mr. Furnivall would be required to refund such sum of £5,500 to the shareholders of the Hyderabad-Deccan Company; and whether in the event of his refusing to refund such moneys the Indian Government would take steps to secure the amount being repaid to those shareholders out of the pension payable to Mr. Furnivall.

Sir J. Fergusson (for Sir J. Gorst) said the attention of the Secretary of State has been called to the statements respecting Mr. Furnivall in the Report of the Select Committee on the Hyderabad Mining Company. As, however, Mr. Furnivall had retired from the service of the Government of India before the transactions in question took place, it is not within the competence of the Secretary of State to take any action in the matter.

Mr. Kelly asked the Under-Secretary of State for India whether his attention had been called to the statements made with reference to Mr. Hughes on page 9 of the Report from the Select Committee on East India Hyderabad (Deccan) Mining Company, to the effect that Mr. Hughes, a Government official in India, one of the superintendents of the Survey, was nevertheless allowed by that Government to be employed and paid by the Hyderabad (Deccan) Company to ascertain the value of the concession obtained from the Nizam, that he received from Mr. W. C. Watson, the promoter and Director of the Company, shares of the value of £3,200, only paying £1,000 for them, and that that transaction amounted, according to the statement of Mr. Watson, to a gift by him to Mr. Hughes, who, in return was to "work and throw his whole energies into it"; and whether Mr. Hughes would be required to refund that sum of £2,200 to the shareholders of the Hyderabad (Deccan) Company.

Sir J. Fergusson (for Sir J. Gorst) said: The Secretary of State has noticed the statements to which the attention of the Government of India will at once be called. Mr. Hughes's services were lent to the Deccan Company, they arranging for his remuneration. During his employment under the Company no salary was paid him from the Indian Treasury.

A circular has been issued by Sir Julian Goldsmid, M.P., Sir Roper Lethbridge, C.I.E., M.P., and Messrs. R. A. Germaine, M.A., and Benjamin J. Scott to the proprietors of the Hyderabad (Deccan) Company, Limited, asking shareholders to attend on the 13th inst. and vote for the proposed adjournment of the meeting to the 15th of October, in order that the Report of the Select Committee of the House of Commons, which is now printed, and will shortly be in their hands, can be adequately considered.—*Times*, August 11.

The report of the Select Committee on the Hyderabad Deccan scandal is, in some respects, satisfactory. The story of the concession does not constitute so great a scandal as was at first anticipated, and the suspicion cast upon the integrity of British officials in India has not been confirmed. All who know India will recognise the supreme importance to our position and authority of maintaining the reputation possessed by British officials for spotless purity in their judicial and administrative functions. Nothing, as Sir Fitzjames Stephen well-said on a memorable occasion, does more to uphold the British Empire in Hindustan than the knowledge and conviction on the part of all our subjects there that justice is done, and that official hands are clean. "British ideas" and British practices are novel to, and alien from, "Native ideas" and practices. A magistracy and judiciary which knows no distinction of rank, of class, of caste, or of person when a question of wrong or a point of law is at issue; officials who are not to be bribed, and whose ruling motive is to do the right, not to line their pockets—these are strange and impressive phenomena in climes where justice was previously a mockery and law a mere matter of price. The venality of Native officials is accepted as a matter of course. They buy and sell even as they are bought and sold, and no one of their race thinks any the worse of them for it. With British officials it is otherwise, and the security of life and property in British India and the feudatory States is now far more due to the absolute justice with which the Imperial sway is maintained than to the bare "power of the sword." Those who periodically predict an outbreak and a rebellion—now in a British province and anon in the Native States—do not appreciate how little likely the people are to make any effort to return to the condition of robbery and oppression from which they know they are only preserved by the Imperial arm.

Nowhere is this feeling more deep-seated than among the Mohammedan races, and their almost general refusal to take part in the so-called National Congresses is due to the conviction, most strongly evinced by the Mohammedans in the Punjaub and Lower Bengal, that whatever faults there may be in the British Administration, it is a thousand times preferable to anything that could result from any travesty of Home Rule. The idea of Home Rule for India is something like a plea for "nationality" on behalf of the Continent of Europe; indeed, the racial characteristics and religious differences of the peoples of Europe are less marked and less wide than those of the peoples of India. It was, then, a very grave incident that our prestige in the greatest Mohammedan State of India should be threatened by the alleged corruption of a British public servant. The charges made were more general than precise; but, of course, the Home Rule or anti-British politicians and writers in this country did their best, by hints and insinuations, to blacken the character of our whole Indian Civil Service. The charges hinted at have not been sustained. The Select Committee do not find that the British Representative has in any, even the remotest, way benefitted by the Deccan concession. He has acted throughout in the most perfect good faith and, in the sole desire which should actuate a British Resident, to advance the interests of the State to which he was attached, and to fairly represent the providence of the Viceroy in Council. There is all the more reason to be gratified at this result in this case, coinciding as it does with the withdrawal of the charges against Mr. Crawford, because ugly stories have been afloat within the last ten years in the Madras Presidency, some of which have turned out to be only too true, and some of which remain yet to be investigated. Residents at the Court of an independent—or semi-independent—potentate, are in a more delicate position than "civilians" in the Imperial Provinces. However, the utmost that can be established against the British Resident, it would seem, is that he has not been wary enough.

The story of the Deccan concession is now tolerably well known in its main features, but some of them are bought out more clearly by the Committee. The mining concession was a sort of natural corollary of the railway scheme which was floated in 1882. Parties to that railway scheme were a Mr. C. A. Winter, of Bombay, and Abdul Huk, Head of the Home Department and Director of Railways and Mines in the Nizam's territory. Then followed the scheme for the Mining concession, and it was agreed between Mr. Winter and Abdul Huk that the latter should receive £120,000 for the railway business and one-fourth of the proceeds of the Mining concession. But neither of them told Mr. Cordery or anybody else of this arrangement. The concession conferred the exclusive right upon the concessionnaires of prospecting and mining for a term of 99 years at royalties to be fixed by mutual agreement. The leading intention was to develop the Singareni coalfields, which are reported by those who know the district to be much more valuable than the Select Committee seem to think. By the terms of the concession an output of not less than 500 tons of coal per week was to be assured by the date of the opening of the railway, but up to the present the Company seems to have only extracted about 150 tons per week. Nor is it difficult to see why. The concession was granted to Mr. W. C. Watson, a brother-in-law of the Mr. Winter, who originated both schemes. It was granted on the condition that within a given date a Company should be formed with a capital of not less than £1,000,000 to work the concession, but it was stipulated that a first subscription of £150,000 would suffice to "develop" the Singareni coalfields. The terms of the concession were submitted to Mr. Cordery and approved by him, but neither he nor any of the officials at Calcutta or in the India Office seems to have noticed that no limit was fixed to the sum for which the concessionnaires might sell their concession to the projected Company, and that no reservation was made as to the appropriation of the remaining £850,000 of share capital. As a matter of fact the concessionnaires treated that immense sum as the "value" of a concession which no one took the trouble to investigate. They took the £850,000 in paid-up shares, and they so stimulated "the market" as to run the price up to a high premium. Then they "unloaded" the bulk of their shares upon the public. Abdul Huk was the holder of a fourth of these founders' shares, and with Oriental astuteness he managed to transfer 10,000 of them to his master, the Nizam, for a sum of £131,250, drawn in cash from the coffers of the State of Hyderabad. It was alleged that in approving this purchase by the Nizam's agent, Mr. Cordery was conniving at a scheme to defraud the Nizam. But Mr. Cordery seems to have been unaware that Abdul Huk was interested in the Company, and it appeared a desirable thing for the Nizam's Government to take a part in the enterprise. The fact of the matter is, that the Nizam was induced to purchase solely in order that "the tip" might go round in London that "the Nizam was buying." On that the shares went to a premium, and the concessionnaires sold very freely. Abdul Huk has disgorged, or refunded, to the Nizam the money obtained by the sale of the 10,000 shares to his patron. But Mr. Watson seems to have cleared £209,360 (less £20,289 paid in commissions) by his sales, and to have still several thousand paid-up shares on hand. This may be "good business," and Mr. Watson claims that he was entitled to make as much profit as he could out of the concession, especially as he had rendered "good service" in floating the railway scheme. It is a delicate question, but the Committee have come to the conclusion that no one except Abdul Huk and the concessionnaires ever contemplated that these last "should appropriate £850,000 of capital, or any part of it, to themselves." A first issue of 15,000 shares was contemplated, "leaving the remainder of the capital to be issued from time to time as the development of the gold and diamond fields might require." No one acting in the interests of the Nizam seems to have addressed himself to the question, "How much the concessionnaires should receive?" And so the Company paid £850,000 for a coal mine which is yielding 150 tons per week, for a diamond field which has yielded five diamonds, and for reputedly auriferous land which has produced no gold as yet. It is a strange story of business "smartness," of successful circumventing of the lynxes of the Stock Exchange, of Oriental double-dealing and of official laxity. But, happily, it is not a story of the corruption of British officials.—*Glasgow Herald*, August 13.

In the Miscellaneous Market everything is quiet, but both Allsops and Hotchkiss are a little firmer, while Deccans have improved after yesterday's meeting, as it is now realised that the worst has been passed, the future being in favour of better prices and a return to normal conditions, the whole proceedings having ended, as so many other examples have done, in simply damaging a reputation without benefiting anybody.—*Evening News*, August 14.

"My Friend Tom Palmer."— * * * *

Turning from the threadbare subject of the *Times'* charges against Mr. Parnell, we beg respectfully to direct Lord Salisbury's attention to the charges which the Anglo-Indian press, without distinction of party, bring against Sir John Gorst. We do not print all that our Indian contemporaries say on the subject of the Under-Secretary of State for India. We merely call attention to them, and suggest that they should be disproved, or that Sir John Gorst should disappear from the Ministry. There is a curious parallel between the charges which the *Times* has brought against Mr. Parnell and those which the *Pioneer* and the *Statesman* bring against Sir John Gorst. Not even the *Times* accuses Mr. Parnell of murder, nor do our Anglo-Indian contemporaries directly accuse Sir John Gorst of corruption. The accusation in both cases is that the incriminated politician occupies relations of such intimacy with men notorious, in the one case for murder, and in the other for laxity of financial conscience, as to render him morally an accomplice. What No. 1 and Mr. Frank Byrne are said to be to Mr. Parnell, Mr. Tom Palmer is said to be to Sir John Gorst. Of course our Anglo-Indian contemporaries may be mistaken about Mr. Palmer. But they profess the most absolute certainty as to the character of this gentleman, and they refer to proofs of the misleading nature of his representations in the past with as much confidence as the *Times* refers to the evidence about the surgical knives and "the gallant little woman." If Mr. Palmer's character be such as the Anglo-Indian papers say, then is it not a grave scandal if, as they also assert, Sir John Gorst be hand-in-glove with such a man?

The *Pioneer* and the *Statesman* belong to opposite schools of politics in India. Both are leading newspapers, quite as respectable and even more deserving of notice than the *Times*, because in a despotically-governed empire like India the Press has thrown upon it the responsibility of exposing scandals which in a constitutional country would be brought out in Parliament. The accusation of complicity in the corruption which flourished at Hyderabad, which is brought against Mr. Palmer, whose influence over Sir John Gorst is said to be so great, is not one which the India Office can afford to overlook. At a time when the Indian Government has just been prosecuting Mr. Crawford because a Native tried to make money out of his friendship by introducing friends, we can hardly wonder that Anglo-Indian papers should say that the intimate of "My friend Tom Palmer" is not the proper person to be the Under-Secretary for India. For Sir John Gorst is really the Indian Government at home. Lord Cross is little better than a *roi fainéant*. It would do for our prestige in India if it were believed that the Home Government is practically in the hands of "My friend Tom Palmer." They seem to think so in Hyderabad, and if we are to have Special Commissions for investigating all charges brought by newspapers against public men, is not Sir John Gorst as fitting a subject for its exercise as Mr. Parnell?—*Pall Mall Gazette*, August 14.

"Deccan" Watson Wins.—But a Committee will Watch the Shareholders' Interests.—The Hyderabad (Deccan) Company's shareholders met again at Winchester House yesterday.

The poll on Mr. Germaine's motion that the meeting should be adjourned until October 15, was rejected by 40,636 against 5,870.

Mr. G. H. Batten, the Chairman, moved the adoption of the report and accounts. On a count of hands it was announced that 26 were for the adoption of the report and 41 against.

Mr. Clements, Mr. Watson's solicitor, demanded a poll, and said it was apparent that Mr. Watson was supported by a large majority. He hoped on the next show of hands that the motion would be carried.

Sir Julian Goldsmid, M.P., wished to know what Mr. Watson's future plans were.

Sir Roper Lethbridge, M.P., moved that a small Committee of the shareholders should be formed with a view to considering the matter. With the Chairman and the concessionnaires he thought that they might possibly that way retrieve the fortunes of the Company.

Mr. Germaine directed attention to the fact that a bye-law showed that if they approved of any action of the conduct of the Directors they could not afterwards question it. He hoped the Committee would be appointed.

Mr. Soligne contended that nothing could now be done with regard to past transactions.

It was moved that Mr. Winter should be re-elected. This motion, on a show of hands, was declared lost.

Mr. Clements demanded a poll on that question also.

On the polls the report was adopted and Mr. Winter re-elected, by a large majority.

Sir J. Goldsmid, M.P., asked the shareholders to stay, now that the meeting was over, to hear a proposition. He would propose that Mr. Arthur Fitzhugh, Mr. Benjamin Scott, and himself should be appointed on the Committee.

This motion was carried.—*Star*, August 14.

Yesterday's adjourned meeting of the Hyderabad (Deccan) Company was, in one sense, a triumph for the concessionnaires and their friends, but they won't gain much by it. The majority of the shareholders, in numbers, was conspicuously adverse to those who have lined their pockets so nicely out of the Company, and the action of men like Sir Julian Goldsmid and Sir Roper Lethbridge shows how deep is the distrust of Mr. Watson and his partners. That, under such circumstances, the Directors cling to their places is a proof how much "oak and triple brass" there is in the composition of those who cross the sea in search of concessions.—*Evening Post*, August 14.

THE HYDERABAD (DECCAN) COMPANY.—The Annual Meeting, adjourned from last Tuesday, of the Hyderabad (Deccan) Company was held at Winchester House, Old Broad Street, yesterday, Mr. G. H. Batten, Chairman, presiding.

At the previous meeting the motion for the adoption of the report was met by an amendment in favour of an adjournment until October 15, in order that the shareholders might have before them the report (since presented) of the Select Committee of the House of Commons which inquired into the circumstances attending the promotion of the Company. This amendment was carried by a large majority at the meeting, and a poll was thereupon demanded by Mr. Watson, one of the concessionnaires and a Director, who held a large number of proxies, but, yielding to urgent appeal, refrained from using them on that occasion. The poll was opened at twelve o'clock and closed at two, and half an hour later the Chairman announced the result as follows:—Present: For the amendment, shareholders representing 5,870 shares; against, 24,422. Proxies: For the amendment, none; against, 16,214. Total: For the amendment, 5.870; against, 40,636.

Mr. Germaine said that, with the permission of the Chairman, he would supplement the result of the poll; and he should like to say that those who had voted against the amendment greatly outnumbered those who had voted in favour of it.—(No.) The number of shareholders who had voted in person that day in favour of the adjournment till the 15th of October was 72—(A Voice: "How's that?" and "No")—whilst those who voted with Mr. Watson against the adjournment only numbered 14, most of these being concessionnaires. It followed, therefore, that they had failed to secure the support of the main body of the shareholders.

A Shareholder: I protest against that statement, and I wish here to state that I have had nothing whatever to do with Mr. Watson. I know many others who are in the same position.

The Chairman: I have now to put the original motion.—("No.") I say yes; and then we shall be in order.

A Shareholder: I object.

The Chairman: Well, we must keep in order and dispose of the business. Those in favour of the resolution please vote.

A Shareholder: I object, and ask that a poll be taken.—("No," and disorder.)

The Solicitor to the Company explained that that would entail much delay, and he hoped the hon. proprietor would not press for a poll.

The Shareholder said he would not press it, and the motion was then put.

Another Shareholder: We will first vote for the Chairman, and then against Mr. Watson. ("No, no.")

The Chairman then put the resolution for the adoption of the report, which was rejected by 41 to 28.

Some disorder followed, in the midst of which

Mr. Clements demanded a poll on behalf of Mr. Watson, who was, he claimed, supported by a large majority of the shareholders. ("No, no.") He hoped the proceedings would go on without any further interruption. ("Oh!" and "No.")

Mr. Edwards: I beg to say that we do not demand a poll.

Sir J. Goldsmid, M.P., thought that a great deal of unpleasantness might be avoided if Mr. Watson expressed to the shareholders some intention of his future action. He said that, in the interest of Mr. Watson, as well as in the interest of the shareholders, it was most desirable that he (Mr. Watson) should put a different face on the matter from what he did at the last meeting. He was supported by a large number of the shareholders now, but that might not always be the case.

Sir Roper Lethbridge, M.P., supported the contention of his friend Sir Julian Goldsmid in the interests of peace, and in what he believed to be the interests of the Company. He would, therefore, make a suggestion, in which he was supported by Lord Lawrence, one of the Directors, who had written him a letter in which he said, "I hope you will be a member of the Committee of the Shareholders of the Deccan Company proposed to be appointed," and his lordship concluded, "I should like to have your views on the matter, as the public have great confidence in you." He (Sir Roper) would suggest that it would be most advisable, in the interests of everyone concerned, that a Committee of shareholders be appointed to confer with the concessionnaires before any further action was taken. He believed, from the statement made by Mr. Watson at the last meeting, that he would be prepared to meet them in a fair and honourable manner. The shareholders had had an opportunity of studying the report of the House of Commons Committee, and that report was clearly in favour of the advisability of fair and honourable conference between all parties in the matter. The Committee had refused to judge the legal questions involved, but it laid down certain points which it virtually declared should be the subject of careful consideration. He was anxious that there should be no ill-feeling between the shareholders and the present Board and the concessionnaires, because it must be clear to everyone that litigation, whatever might be the result, would be emphatically injurious to the interests of the Company. He thought that the only way of avoiding litigation was that there should be some such conference as he had suggested, and he should be prepared to move the appointment of a small Committee.

Mr. Clements (solicitor for Mr. Watson) rose to address the meeting, but was greeted with loud cries of "Watson" and "Speak up for yourself, Watson."

Mr. Watson said that, in response to the appeals made to him, he would read a letter which he had addressed to the Chairman on August 10th. (Cries of "After the meeting.") Yes, after the meeting, and which was in the following terms:—

"10th August.

"Dear Mr. Batten,—You have told me of your conversation with Sir Julian Goldsmid, who wishes me to make proposals for the purpose, as I understand, of restoring the credit of the Hyderabad (Deccan) Company, and ensuring that it should obtain further capital. I cannot help saying that I am not responsible for the unfounded attacks which have damaged it in public estimation, but I take so much interest in its welfare that I have always been, and still am, desirous of assisting it in any difficulty, and I much regret that Sir Julian and other shareholders who thought I ought to take any particular course did not long ago place their views before me in a direct and formal manner. I think that a small Committee should be formed of Sir Julian and other substantial shareholders whom I could meet after the business of the General Meeting is disposed of, and discuss the matter in a business-like manner.

I should do so with a sincere desire to meet their views as far and as reasonable as possible, and I should hope that we should come to a conclusion which would be satisfactory to all the shareholders. After the business of the meeting is over I intend to have this publicly stated.

"I am, dear Mr. Batten, yours very truly,

"W. C. Watson."

Mr. Clements said that, in his opinion, it was advisable that the Committee should be appointed at some future day.—("No.") It was quite impossible for the meeting to appoint the Committee now, inasmuch as Mr. Watson evidently held a large number of proxies, and it might be considered that he had nominated the Committee.

A Shareholder protested against adopting the accounts lest it should be supposed hereafter that they had ratified the transactions in which the Directors had been engaged, and for which action might hereafter be taken to secure the restoration of their money.

Mr. Germaine urged the meeting not to pass the report then, because, according to Article 66, anything approved of by the general body of shareholders could not afterwards be objected to.

In reply to a shareholder, the Chairman said that the Nizam's Government held 3,750 shares. He added that it was true that His Highness's Government had taken action against Abdul Huk, who had restored the money paid for the shares. (Laughter.) The Government, in fact, had impounded the shares, and if they succeeded, they would get both the money and the shares. (Renewed laughter.)

After some further discussion, the Chairman put the motion for the adoption of the report, which was rejected by a large majority.

Mr. Clements then demanded a poll on behalf of Mr. Watson, and the Chairman announced that it would be taken at the close of the meeting.

Sir Julian Goldsmid said he was prepared to nominate his committee of independent shareholders. He named the following gentlemen:—Sir J. Goldsmid, M.P., Mr. Ernest Ruffer, Mr. Benjamin Scott, Mr. James Edwards, Mr. A. J. FitzHugh, and Mr. Germaine, and he asked whether Sir R. Lethbridge would also act.

Sir R. Lethbridge said he was afraid he must decline to do so.

The next business was the proposal to re-elect the retiring Directors, Mr. Batten, the Chairman, and Mr. C. A. Winter. The name of Mr. Batten was put first, and a poll was demanded. Ultimately, however, the Chairman, who said he should be extremely glad to retire, was elected by a show of hands. On Mr. Winter's name being put, Sir Julian Goldsmid proposed that Mr. Benjamin Scott should be elected instead, but it was pointed out that the nomination of a candidate for the Directorate must take place fourteen days before the meeting. Upon this Sir Julian demanded a poll, and it was arranged that this should be taken concurrently with the poll on the question of the adoption of the report.

The result of the poll was declared shortly before five o'clock, and the Chairman announced the figures as follows:—For the adoption of the report, 40,956; against, 3,913. The figures for the re-election of Mr. Charles A. Winter as director were as under: 40,706 in favour of his re-election, and 1,258 against.

The Chairman thereupon declared the report and statement of accounts to be duly carried, and Mr. C. A. Winter to be re-elected a director of the Company.

On the motion of Mr. Edwards, seconded by Mr. Passmore, a cordial vote of thanks was passed to the Chairman for his conduct in the chair, and for his past services in the interests of the Company.

The Chairman, in acknowledging the compliment, said he had endeavoured to act impartially for all the shareholders, both present and past, and he trusted that they would approve of his conduct.

The meeting then terminated.—*Morning Advertiser*, August 14.

The Hyderabad (Deccan) Company.—The adjourned ordinary general meeting of the Hyderabad (Deccan) Company, Limited, was held yesterday at Winchester House, Old Broad Street. Mr. G. H. M. Batten presided. At the meeting on the 7th inst. the adoption of the report and accounts was moved by the Chairman, when an amendment was proposed by Mr. Germaine adjourning the meeting till the 15th of October. On a show of hands the amendment was declared carried, whereupon a poll was demanded, which was taken yesterday between twelve and two o'clock, Mr. Germaine and Mr. Clements being appointed scrutineers.

Shortly before three o'clock the result of the poll was announced by Mr. Clements as follows:—Present—for the amendment, 5,870 votes; against it, 24,422 votes; proxies—for the amendment, none; against it, 16,214 votes. Total—for the amendment, 5,870 votes; against it, 40,636 votes.

The Chairman read the result again, and announced that the amendment was lost.

Mr. Germaine, supplementing this declaration, stated that, although the number of votes was greatly in favour of Mr. Watson, the number of shareholders who had voted in person in favour of the amendment was 72, while the number who had voted with Mr. Watson against the adjournment was only 14, most of them being concessionnaires.

The Chairman then put the original motion, for the adoption of the report and accounts, and announced that 26 had voted for and 41 against the resolution, which was, therefore, lost on the show of hands.

Mr. Clements thereupon demanded a poll. He maintained that the poll which had already been taken showed that Mr. Watson was supported by a large majority of the shareholders ("No, no") in the sense of the votes held by the shareholders. He (the speaker) therefore felt it his duty to demand a poll; but in the interests of peace he suggested that the report and accounts be passed ("No, no"), and that no further poll should be taken. Every one knew from what had already taken place what the result of the poll would be; and it would only add to the irritation which already existed. If, however, the meeting insisted on rejecting the report and accounts he must ask for a poll.

Sir Julian Goldsmid, M.P., thought that a good deal of unpleasantness would be avoided if he again appealed to Mr. Watson to express to the shareholders some intention with reference to his future action. In Mr. Watson's own interests, as well as in the interests of the shareholders, it was desirable that that gentleman should put a different phase upon the matter to that which he placed upon it the other day. Though Mr. Watson might for the present be supported by a majority of the votes, it did not always follow that in the future the large majority of the shareholders would support him. The result of the issue of a small circular had been that proxies representing over 7,000 shares which had been sent in in Mr. Watson's favour had been withdrawn. He thought it was undesirable that the matter should remain as it was, and he believed that arrangements might, perhaps, be made which would meet the views of the shareholders, and which, in the end, would not prejudice Mr. Watson's position in the City, or the position of his co-concessionnaires.

Sir Roper Lethbridge, M.P., desired to add a suggestion for which he was authorized to state they had the full support of Lord Lawrence. Lord Lawrence spoke to him after the last meeting on the subject, and his lordship in a letter written to him subsequently said, "I hope that you will be a member of a committee of the shareholders of the Deccan Company proposed to be appointed." Lord Lawrence had been good enough to conclude his letter as follows:—"I should like to have your views on the matter, as the public would have great confidence in you." He (the speaker), would suggest that it would be most advisable, in the interests of every one concerned, that a committee of shareholders should be appointed by those present to confer with the directors and the concessionnaires before any further action was taken. He believed it probable—especially after the statement of Mr. Watson at the last meeting, that he was prepared to meet such a committee in a fair and honourable spirit—that something might be attained from such a conference that would retrieve in every way the fortunes of the company. They had had the opportunity of studying the report of the Select Committee of the House of Commons, and the report was clearly suggestive of the advisability of a fair and honourable conference between all parties. The Select Committee had very fairly stated that it refused to judge as to the legal responsibilities of the directors on the one side, of the concessionnaires on the other, and of the shareholders on the third part; but it did lay down certain points which it clearly, or virtually, declared should be the subject of careful consideration, and also, it was implied, of conference. It was clear that litigation, whatever might be its result, whether it were in favour of the concessionnaires or in favour of the shareholders, would be emphatically injurious to the interests of the company. He thought the only possible way of avoiding litigation was to have some conference of the kind which he had suggested, and which had largely originated with Lord Lawrence, one of the directors.

Mr. Clements rose, as he stated, to express Mr. Watson's views, but there were loud cries for Mr. Watson himself to address the meeting.

Mr. Watson stated that he had written the following letter to Mr. Batten, who, he believed, had forwarded it to Sir Julian Goldsmid. The letter was dated the 10th inst.:—

"Dear Mr. Batten,—You have told me of your conversation with Sir Julian Goldsmid, who wishes me to make proposals for the purpose, as I understand, of restoring the credit of the Hyderabad (Deccan) Company, and ensuring that it shall obtain further capital. I cannot help saying that I am not responsible for the unfounded attacks which have damaged it in public estimation, but I take so much interest in its welfare that I have always been, and still am, desirous of assisting it in any difficulty; and I much regret that Sir Julian and other shareholders who thought I ought to take any particular course did not long ago place their views before me in a direct and formal manner. I think that a small committee should be formed, of Sir Julian and other substantial shareholders, whom I could meet after the business of the general meeting is disposed of and discuss the matter in a business-like manner. I should do so with a sincere desire to meet their views as far as was reasonable and possible, and I should hope that we should come to a conclusion which would be satisfactory to all the shareholders. After the business of the meeting is over I intend to have this publicly stated."

Mr. Clements stated that from the beginning of the discussion he had been of opinion that a committee should be appointed, but it was impossible for the meeting to appoint a committee. Sir Julian Goldsmid and his friends should meet together and form a small committee, and Mr. Watson and himself would be glad to meet them. The matter immediately before the meeting, however, was the adoption of the report.

A Shareholder said he desired to abstain from being in any way committed to the report. The question was, did the directors have the power to be vendors and purchasers, and did they have the power to pay £850,000 for the concession? In buying his shares he had no idea about the £850,000.

Mr. Germaine read clause 66 of the articles of association, which, he said, was a little binding on the shareholders, and if they took any step which approved of any act of the directors, they could not afterwards disagree from it. It was, therefore, not fair to the shareholders to "rush" the report through. He favoured the suggestion of Sir Roper Lethbridge as to the appointment of a small committee. There was nothing to be gained by disunion.

Mr. Soliague pointed out that the accounts passed at the first general meeting contained the reference to the 85,000 shares given to the concessionaires. (A Voice: "That was before the facts were known.")

Sir Julian Goldsmid said he did not agree that the sentiments in Mr. Watson's letter conveyed what he (the speaker) had put forward in his conversation with Mr. Batten. He was quite prepared to nominate a committee of independent shareholders, and if the proxies were not used against that nomination he did not see that there would be any difficulty as to the appointment of a committee. The article read by Mr. Germaine was only of importance if the shareholders were aware of the payment at the time they attended the meeting; but he did not consider that it would bind any future shareholder, or any shareholder who was unaware of the facts of the case. He could not agree to the passing of the report.

The Chairman intimated that the poll on the motion for the adoption of the report and accounts would take place at the close of the meeting.

Mr. F. J. Bladon then proposed the re-election, as a director, of Mr. Batten, andthe motion having been seconded,

Mr. Gutman moved an amendment to the effect that the election of directors should stand over until after the poll.

The Chairman, in answer to a remark of Sir Roper Lethbridge, stated that the Government of the Nizam was still on the register of shareholders as holding 3,750 shares; and there were also the share warrants to bearer.

After some further discussion the amendment was withdrawn, at the instance of Sir Julian Goldsmid; and Mr. Batten was then re-elected to his seat at the board.

Mr. Clipperton then proposed, and Mr. Hewlings seconded, the re-election, as a director, of Mr. C. A. Winter.

Sir Julian Goldsmid proposed an amendment appointing Mr. Benjamin Scott a director in the place of Mr. Winter.

The Chairman read clause 18 of the articles of association, which required notice to be given before the meeting of the nomination of any new director. He then put the motion, which was lost, on the show of hands, by 23 to 25.

Mr. Clements demanded a poll.

Sir Julian Goldsmid said he assumed the committee would now be appointed.

The Chairman replied that the business was concluded with the exception of taking the poll.

Mr. Burt (the solicitor) stated that the committee spoken of by Sir Julian Goldsmid would not be a committee between the board and the shareholders, but a committee between Mr. Watson and his friends and Sir Julian Goldsmid and his friends. He understood that Mr. Watson was quite ready to meet such a committee, but it could not be appointed by the meeting, as it was not before them, and it did not seem to be relevant to anything before the meeting.

Sir Julian Goldsmid, however, proposed the election, as a committee, of himself, Mr. Germaine, Mr. Benjamin Scott, Mr. Ruffer, Mr. Edwards, and Mr. Fitzhugh. He put the motion to the meeting and declared it carried.

The polls as to the adoption of the report and the re-election of Mr. Winter as a director were taken at the close of the meeting.

The Chairman declared the result as follows: For the resolutions adopting the report and accounts, Present, for the resolution, 24,742 votes; against it,

3,913 votes; proxies, for the resolution, 16,214 votes, against it, none. Total, for the resolution, 40,956 votes, against it, 3,913 votes. He therefore declared the resolution carried. For the resolution re-electing Mr. Winter, the result of the poll was as follows: Present, for the resolution, 24,492 votes, against it, 1,258 votes; proxies for the resolution. 16,214 votes, against it, none. Total for the resolution, 40,706 votes, against it, 1,258 votes. He therefore declared Mr. Winter re-elected.

On the motion of Mr. Edwards, a vote of thanks was passed to the chairman, and the meeting then separated.—*Times*, August 14.

A GOOD deal of satisfaction has been expressed in London that the tale disclosed by the Deccan Commission, bad though it was, was no worse. An impression has gone abroad that, with some restitution by the State of Hyderabad and disgorging by Abdul Huk, the disagreeable matter may be slurred over. There are other matters behind, however, which still call for explanation, and it will be wonderful if they are allowed to let sleep. There is first the strange story of the Nizam's gift of five millions, to which the *Times*' Calcutta correspondent was never tired of pointing as proof of the wonderful loyalty of the Native Princes, and which has turned out a sham. Then there is the conduct, or misconduct, of the British officials at Hyderabad. Even if not personally incriminated, they cannot be acquitted of an utter lack of judgment, proving their unfitness for similar responsible occupation elsewhere. The relations of Sir John Gorst with the Nizam's Government are also a legitimate subject of inquiry. It is true that his visit to Hyderabad was made solely in his private capacity, but circumstances which have since been disclosed invest the affair with suspicion. Sir John owes it to himself to court the fullest investigation.—*Edinburgh Evening Dispatch*, August 15.

ANOTHER debate, moreover, will take place which will not be prolonged, but will certainly be heated. It has already been stated in this column that some of the members of the Hyderabad Committee, notably Sir Richard Temple and Mr. Labouchere, are far indeed from being satisfied with the rather milk-and-watery conclusions to which the majority arrived concerning the very gross scandal which was unearthed before them. When Sir Roper Lethbridge's motion on the matter comes on for discussion, the principal interest of the public will centre in the contribution to the debate of Sir John Gorst. The transactions of 1883, in which the then legal member of "the Fourth Party" was engaged, he having been paid 75,000 rupees for advice to certain of the Hyderabad authorities, have never been fully explained; and, as they seem in some sort a prelude to later events of considerable importance, a frank account of them from one in the best position to know cannot fail to be of value.—*Birmingham Daily Post*, August 15.

THE DECCAN REPORT.—It is long since a Select Committee of the House of Commons laid upon the table a more vapid and inconsequent report than that which has sat to inquire into the formation and promotion of the Hyderabad (Deccan) Company, Limited. The speeches of counsel and the interjectory pyrotechnics in which members of the Committee indulged pointed to revelations of gigantic robbery and fraud. The report results in a complete rehabilitation of the promoters and concessionnaires. Such blame as it contains is awarded to the Indian Government and its representatives. Its strongest allegation is, that "if more direct and effective British assistance and advice had been given to the Government of Hyderabad, the events that have occurred would not have taken place." We fail to see what good the Committee has accomplished. The outcome of a palace intrigue, its only effect has been to harass the minds of shareholders, and to depreciate the value of their property. At the meeting of Monday, which had been adjourned pending the publication of the Committee's report, the shareholders showed their entire confidence in the concessionnaires in passing the accounts by the enormous vote of 40,000 shares against 3,900 shares polled by the dissentients. The prospects of the Company are stated to be excellent, the last advices reporting the finding of gold in rich deposits. It may be that the recent large of discoveries of minerals may call for the application of more capital, and if so it will probably be provided by the concessionnaires.—*Money*, August 15.

The notoriety obtained by the Parliamentary Committee appointed to inquire into the promotion of the Hyderabad Deccan Company, has naturally caused more than special interest, and an adjourned meeting was held at Winchester House on Monday. A poll took place between twelve and two o'clock, and at half-past two the adjourned meeting of the shareholders to receive a report on the result of the poll was held. The scrutineers reported that the votes given for the adjournment to October 15 were 5,870, against 24,422, and proxies 16,214; total, 40,636. It appears that although the numbers against the adjournment were vastly larger in point of number of shares, yet the number of persons who voted in the room were 72 in favour of the adjournment, and 14 against, most of the latter being concessionnaires.—*Life*, August 16.

The Deccan scandal has entered on a new phase. The scope of the inquiry into it was very much restricted by the Government. The Committee of Inquiry was granted unwillingly, and after strong pressure from the Opposition. The result of its inquiry has been to tell the public nothing more than it had already been told by Mr. Labouchere and others. The fact is confirmed that Abdul Huk and his fellow-operators with the shares made vast sums of money out of the Nizam by selling him his own concession to them; but this is all. Some of the Indian papers said from the beginning that the inquiry would thus prove abortive, and now they give reasons for their predictions. They assert that Sir John Gorst, Under-Secretary for India, and the real representative of the Indian Government in this country, got the inquiry restricted to screen friends of his own, and to prevent the exposure of transactions in which he himself was concerned. They do this in very plain terms. The effect of their statement is that Sir John Gorst was in intimate relations with men by whom the Nizam was made use of. One of them, the *Pioneer*, declares that to keep Sir John Gorst in his present position is an affront to India; and the *Friend of India* goes almost as far. It relates that Sir John Gorst went to Hyderabad on professional business in 1883. He got the appointment through a friend, a half-breed barrister, whom the Indian journals denounce. His fee, they say, was 75,000 rupees. This fee, we are told, was entered in the Treasury accounts as money "that was required for large purchases" by the young Nizam. The Prince himself declared the entry to be false, and then it was made known that through the barrister's influence the money had been paid to Sir John Gorst for advice about the Prince's approaching succession. Sir John Gorst may know nothing of these transactions. It may not be true, as the Indian newspapers assert, that he and his friend the barrister virtually "nobbled" the Deccan inquiry to save the reputations of persons in more important positions than Abdul Huk. But the charges made against him by these responsible journals need clearing up. The new doctrine of his party, and of the Government of which he is a member, is that if you are slandered and libelled your duty is to clear your character by seeking redress in a court of law. Sir

John Gorst has been "slandered" just as much as Mr. Parnell. What in the doctrine of the Tory party is good for Mr. Parnell is therefore good for him. He should bring these Indian journals to the bar of justice, or he himself should appoint a Committee to investigate the charges made against him.—*Dundee Advertiser*, August 16.

WE understand that negotiations are pending between the Nizam's Government and the concessionnaires of the Hyderabad (Deccan) Company which will result in great advantages to the Company. The latter have submitted a proposal which proves their good faith, and also the belief which they hold in the value of the property.—*Financial News*, August 7.

NOTHING more amazing has happened in finance for a considerable time than the notorious Hyderabad-Deccan swindle, as to which the Parliamentary Commission has just issued its report. All the revelations with which we have become familiar through the evidence given in the law courts fade away into nothingness when compared with this gigantic robbery. The clique which originated this swindle issued to themselves £850,000 of fully paid-up £10 shares, and managed to saddle the greater part of them on the public at high premiums, although their value is practically nothing.—*Society*, August 18.

THE result of the poll demanded on the 7th instant was declared at the meeting of the Hyderabad (Deccan) Company on Tuesday last. For the amendment, which was for an adjournment until the 15th October. Present: For the shareholders representing 5,870 shares, against 24,422. Proxies: For the amendment, none; against 16,214. Total for the amendment, 5,870, against, 40,636. The amendment having been lost, the Chairman put the original motion for the adoption of the report. After a second poll the motion was carried, and the report adopted, the voting being for: 40,956; against, 3,913 votes. Mr. Winter's re-election was also carried by 40,706 votes, against 1,258. Mr. Watson, in the course of the proceedings, intimated that he would be glad to meet a Committee of shareholders to discuss the position of affairs generally. In consequence of this intimation the undermentioned gentlemen were appointed at an informal meeting for the purpose indicated by Mr. Watson, viz., Sir Julian Goldsmid, M.P., Mr. Ernest Ruffer, Mr. Benjamin Scott, Mr. James Edwards, Mr. A. F. Fitz Hugh, and Mr. Germaine. Under the circumstances this was the best course to be adopted, and it is to be hoped that, with the full concurrence of all parties, effective measures will be framed to enable the Company quickly to realise the splendid prospects which it enjoys.—*Bullionist*, August 18.

SIR JOHN GORST, Under-Secretary for India, has denied that he had anything to do with the "nobbling" of the Deccan Commission, and though the terms of the denial are qualified and restricted, the denial ought to be accepted. The Conservative party has, however, set the example of treating all denials of charges against opposing politicians as worthless unless they are backed by the finding of a jury or a commission, and Sir John Gorst will not be surprised to find that the same justice which he and his friends meted out to Mr. Parnell is meted out to him. Of the asserted intimate relations between him and the shady people about the Nizam's Court Sir John Gorst says nothing, nor does he say anything of the 75,000 rupees paid to him for his professional services in 1883.—*Dundee Advertiser*, August 18.

Thanks to the insane people who forwarded Mr. W. C. Watson their proxies, that gentleman was enabled to have matters all his own way at the adjourned meeting of the Hyderabad Deccan shareholders on Monday. With the help of these proxies he effectually stifled all opposition, and although the majority of the shareholders present (including Sir Julian Goldsmid) were antagonistic to Mr. C. A. Winter being re-elected a Director, yet he was, with the assistance of the Vendors' votes, re-instated. Sir Julian Goldsmid, on behalf of the independent shareholders, wanted to propose Mr. Benjamin Scott for the vacancy, but a technical objection was taken to the proposition. Mr. Batten was also re-elected, so that matters still remain in their present reprehensible condition, which they are likely to do for some considerable time in spite of the thorough investigation of the Royal Commission. One good thing was accomplished, and that was the appointment of an independent shareholders' Committee to watch the proceedings of the Directors. This committee is composed of the following gentlemen:—Sir Julian Goldsmid, Mr. Ernest Ruffer, Mr. A. J. Fitz Hugh, Mr. Benjamin Scott, Mr. James Edwards, and Mr. Germaine. The Vendor, of course, did not object to the appointment of this Committee, knowing full well that the proxies at his command could always swamp any opposition, and also being fully alive to the fact that the committee would have not the slightest power to counteract the policy of the subservient Board. We cannot sympathize with the shareholders of this concern unless they shake off their apathy and "go" for Mr. W. C. Watson and the whole crew.—*Financial Critic*, August 18.

Scandals from India are becoming unpleasantly frequent. Sir John Gorst now seems to be in hot water, and will doubtless have his attention drawn to the Anglo-Indian papers which have just reached this country. According to one of them the field of investigation of the Deccan Mining Committee has been somewhat narrowed by the party obligations of some of its most influential members to do as little damage as possible to the Government in settling the terms of its report. But the apparent escape of Sir John Gorst from the pillory that had been prepared for him must have been regretted, even by those who have no natural taste for throwing dirt. "We regard the possession of such a post as Under-Secretary of State by an official of this stamp as an affront to India. The particulars of Sir John Gorst's expedition to Hyderabad, as professional adviser to the Peshkar, in a case in which his extravagantly paid professional services could not be of the slightest use to his clients, are notorious. Equally notorious is the name of Mr. Tom Palmer. Our latest private letters from home discuss in scornful terms the open alliance between her Majesty's Under-Secretary of State for India and Mr. Palmer. We hear first of Mr. Palmer calling upon the Hyderabad delegate, now in England, and the Nawab refusing to him. But there is a reception at the Foreign Office, when Sir John, meeting the Nawab in the crowd, asks him if he has seen 'his friend Tom Palmer.' Need it be added that the barrier which the discreet representative of the Hyderabad State had judiciously raised was at once removed."—*Hereford Times*, August 18.

The Deccan Scandal—as it is called—develops new features from day to day. During the week the adjourned meeting of shareholders was held to receive the declaration of the poll. The result was, the report was adopted by an overwhelming majority, and Mr. Winter was re-elected as a Director. Of equal importance was the appointment of a Committee of the principal shareholders to confer with the Directors on the state of affairs, and on the best means to be adopted to carry on the business. A great part of the available capital, £150,000, has been expended, and the balance is by no means adequate for the proper exploitation of the mineral property. In fact, what has been hitherto spent has gone in experimental operations in the coalfields, and in prospecting the gold and diamond fields. More capital is urgently required, and it is to be feared that the Nizam will not come to the rescue. As for the public in this country, it is not likely that they will subscribe more capital under the circumstances. There remains, therefore, so far as I can see, only one course open—to form subsidiary Companies, to buy concessions for working the gold, the diamond, and other mineral areas respectively. But even in this arrangement this would be the fatal fault, that the shareholders to these subsidiary Companies would individually make themselves liable to the burden of £890,000, which the original concessionnaires have secured to themselves. These concessionnaires, in fact, have killed the goose with the golden eggs, and it is difficult to see what further can be extracted from the concession. However, the best thing under the circumstances has been done in the appointment of a Committee of influential shareholders to discuss the situation in a business-like manner, and make a way for escape from the difficulties that now beset the enterprize. The undermentioned gentlemen will form the committee:—Sir J. Goldsmid, M.P., Mr. Ernest Rutter, Mr. Benjamin Scott, Mr. James Edwards, Mr. A. J. Fitz Hugh, and Mr. Germaine. Sir R. Lethbridge was also asked to act, but he excused himself by saying that he held only one share on his own account, though he represented 150 shares held by a Trust Company. The worthy knight is to be congratulated on his escape from a difficult position.

It is proper here to note that there is considerable dissatisfaction in India at the course taken by the Select Committee of the House of Commons. I wonder what the Indian people will say when they read the lame report of the Committee, to which I referred last week. The opinion in India is that the field of the investigation of the Deccan Committee was narrowed by the party obligations of some of its most influential members, to do as little damage as possible to the Government in settling the terms of the report. I have always contended that the allegations of fraud were altogether untenable, but for all that the concessionnaires over-reached themselves, and it will now be very difficult to resuscitate the strangled enterprise.—*Stock Exchange Times*, August 18.

The Hyderabad Deccan Company, Limited.—All's Well that Ends Well.—The trite observation that after a storm comes a calm is as true in company as in meteorological matters. Two stormy meetings in succession rarely happen, and it was only in accordance with the fitness of things that the meeting of the Hyderabad Deccan on Monday was as placid as its predecessor was noisy. The shareholders were then nervously excited; they have since had time to calm down and examine the position coolly, and the result, we may take it, was satisfactory, for the meeting was in a good humour, or it would not have laughed so heartily at Mr. Clements's over-fatherly attitude towards Mr. W. C. Watson.

It will be recollected that at the meeting of the 7th a poll was demanded by Mr. Watson and other shareholders on the question whether the report and accounts should be adopted, an amendment having been moved by Mr. Germaine, seconded by Mr. J. Edwards, that the meeting be adjourned to October 18th, and it was to hear the declaration of the poll that the shareholders assembled on Monday at Winchester House. The chair was taken by Mr. Batten, who fulfilled his functions admirably, both in appearance and in suavity of manner. The meeting was summoned for half-past two, but it was a quarter to three before Mr. Clements and Mr. Germaine entered the room, and, advancing to the table with a certain amount of dramatic effect, read out the following figures, which were—For the amendment, present 5,870 votes (no proxies). Against the amendment, present 24,422; proxies, 16,214. Total 40,636. The Chairman thereupon declared the amendment lost, The Chairman then put the original motion, "That the report and accounts be adopted," which, on a show of hands, was negatived by 46 to 21. Mr. Clements, on behalf of Mr. Watson, demanded a poll, at the same time protesting against the waste of time, as the result was inevitable, Mr. Watson having the majority of the shareholders with him.

Sir Julian Goldsmid, in his most funereal and lugubrious manner, implored Mr. Watson to give the meeting some intimation of his future action, so as to avoid unpleasantness.

Sir Roper Lethbridge, who was as chirpy as Sir Julian was dismal, joined in the request, and pointed out that the Report of the Committee (which Report, by the way, Sir Roper held in his hand—not "the common report of the newspapers," but printed on the official paper of the House of Commons)—was suggestive of a fair and honourable compromise between the two parties.

Mr. Clements (solicitor) rose to explain Mr. Watson's views on the matter, but there were cries for "Watson," and in response that gentleman read the following letter which he had written to Mr. Batten:—"10th Aug. Dear Mr. Batten,—You have told me of your conversation with Sir Julian Goldsmid, who wishes me to make proposals for the purpose, as I understand, of restoring the credit of the Hyderabad (Deccan) Company, and ensuring that it shall obtain further capital. I cannot help saying that I am not responsible for the unfounded attacks which have damaged it in public estimation; but I take so much interest in its welfare that I have always been and still am desirous of assisting it in any difficulty, and I much regret that Sir Julian and other shareholders who thought I ought to take any particular course did not long ago place their views before me in a direct and formal manner. I think that a small Committee should be formed of Sir Julian and other substantial shareholders, whom I could meet after the business of the General Meeting is disposed of, and discuss the matter in a business-like manner. I should do so with a sincere desire to meet their views as far as was reasonable and possible, and I should hope that we should come to a conclusion which would be satisfactory to all the shareholders. After the business of the meeting is over I intend to have this publicly stated.—I am, dear Mr. Batten, yours truly, W. C. Watson."

Mr. Clements, whose anxiety to speak was not reciprocated by the meeting, contended that the Committee could not be appointed at that meeting, but that Sir Julian Goldsmid should nominate four or five shareholders whom Mr. Watson would be glad to meet.

After some discussion, during which the speakers showed a tendency to stray away into side issues, the order of business was restored by Mr. Bladon proposing the re-election of the Chairman, Mr. G. H. Maxwell Batten, as a member of the Board. This motion was unanimously carried, but the proposition to elect Mr. C. H. Winter was negatived. A poll was then demanded, which the Chairman said would be taken at the same time as the poll on the adoption of the report.

A discussion then followed as to the terms of the appointment of Sir Julian Goldsmid's Committee, and it was during this discussion that Mr. Clements caused the hearty laugh already referred to. Mr. Clements stood gravely contemplating the merriment, and then suddenly realizing that the cause of the joke was himself, joined good-humouredly in the hilarity.

After this, acrimony was out of the question, and Mr. Burt, the Company's Solicitor, settled the point at issue by pointing out that the Committee could not be appointed by the meeting, as it was entirely a matter between Sir Julian Goldsmid and other shareholders, and Mr. Watson.

The proceedings then practically terminated, save for the declaration of the poll, and Sir Julian Goldsmid nominated himself and Mr. B. Scott, Mr. Germaine, Mr. J. Edwards, Mr. Ernest Ruffer, and Mr. T. Fitz Hugh as the Committee.

On the declaration of the poll the numbers were: For the adoption of the report, 24,742 votes (present); proxies, 16,214; total, 40,956. Against, 3,913 (present), proxies, none. For the re-election of Mr. Winter as Director—present, 24,942, proxies, 16,214, total, 40,706. Against, 1,358 present; proxies, none.

The Chairman declared both motions carried; and on the motion of Mr. Edwards, seconded by Mr. Passmore, a vote of thanks was given to him for his conduct in the chair.—*Financial World*, August 18.

THE report of the Select Committee of the House of Commons into the Deccan "scandals," is a sweeping censure on the concessionnaires, who, the the Committee declare, have used the concession to realise great gains not intended to be conferred on them, to the injury of the State from which they obtained the concession, and with the assistance of their partner, Abdul Huk. But the report will be useless unless followed by a prosecution, which, be it remarked, never follows.—*Tattler*, August 18.

COLONEL MARSHALL, OF HYDERABAD.—In the House of Commons on August 18, Mr. T. P. O'Connor asked the Under-Secretary for India whether his attention had been called to an article in the *St. James's Gazette*, of July 16 last, entitled, "Another Hyderabad Scandal," which gave a quotation from "Stubbs' List" of June 30, showing that in the bankruptcy of H. Wathen and Son, wholesale tea dealers, of Fenchurch Street, E.C., Colonel Marshall, Hyderabad, India, was put down as an unsecured creditor for £5,250 in the schedule of the separate estate of William Hulbert Wathen; whether Colonel Marshall was Private Secretary and confidential adviser to the Nizam, and William Hulbert Wathen was Colonel Marshall's brother-in-law; whether, when the Hyderabad Prime Minister was in this country representing the Nizam at the Jubilee ceremonies, Colonel Marshall became for the time being virtually Minister of Hyderabad, and in that capacity took upon himself the responsibility of appointing Mr. Wathen Agent of the Hyderabad State; whether with the appointment a new procedure was instituted, Mr. Wathen being supplied with funds in advance, and £6,000 were thereupon remitted to Mr. Wathen from the public and private funds of the Nizam, of which amount Mr. Wathen only expended £750, dealing with the whole £6,000 as an unsecured loan to himself personally, for the balance of which—namely, £5,250, as above shown—Colonel Marshall was now ranked on his separate estate as a creditor; whether the unsecured debts of the firm were put down at £26,121 and of the separate estate of Mr. Wathen at £6,250, while the net assets of the firm were quoted at £3,177, and of the separate estate as £512 only; whether the above allegations and facts were known to the India Office or to the Government of India when it was arranged that Colonel Marshall should accompany or precede the Hyderabad Minister on his visit to Simla to meet Lord Dufferin about the 19th of last month; and what steps would be taken by Her Majesty's Government, or the Government of India, in dealing with Colonel Marshall.

Sir J. Gorst: The Secretary of State has no means of knowing whether the statements in the *St. James's Gazette* are correct. The matter is one which it is the function of the Viceroy to deal with in the first instance.

Mr. T. P. O'Connor asked whether he was to understand that when such a charge was made against an officer in the position of Colonel Marshall, the Secretary of State did not consider it his duty to call attention to it.

Sir J. Gorst said that the Secretary of State was not in the habit of calling the attention of the Viceroy to paragraphs in the newspapers. ("Oh, oh.")

Mr. Kelly asked whether the Government were not sending Colonel Marshall back to Hyderabad.

Sir J. Gorst said the question was a matter which was entirely within the functions of the Viceroy, and a matter with which the Secretary of State had in the first instance no right to interfere.

Mr. T. P. O'Connor asked was he then to understand that when a serious charge was made against a public official, the fact was not considered by the Secretary of State a sufficient reason for ordering an inquiry, or suggesting such an inquiry to the Viceroy.

Sir J. Gorst said he did not think the hon. member understood the principle on which India was administered. The person responsible for the administration of India, and for the conduct of Indian officials, was the Viceroy; it was only the Viceroy who could take such a matter into consideration, and pronounce an opinion upon it; and it was not in accordance with the practice of the Government of India that the Secretary of State should interfere.—*Times*, August 19.

I HEAR that on behalf of the Nizam of Hyderabad the report of the Select Committee on the Hyderabad Deccan Mining Company has been submitted to Mr. Edward H. Pollard for his opinion on the legality of the concession. It will be remembered that the Committee, while they abstained from expressing any opinion on the legal rights or liabilities of the several parties, observed that the concessionnaires had "used the concession for the purpose of realising great gains not intended to be conferred on them, and that this has been done to the injury of the State from which they obtained the concession with the assistance of their partner, Abdul Huk."—London Correspondent of the *Manchester Guardian*, August 20.

THE HYDERABAD (DECCAN) SCANDAL.—There is a timidity—a sort of half-heartedness—in the report of the Select Committee appointed to inquire into this subject which is decidedly disappointing; sufficiently so, indeed, to provoke the feeling that as soon as it was discovered that the inquiry could not be turned into a vehicle for mud-throwing between English politicians it was abruptly closed, with the determination to get the thing through as quickly as possible and in a somewhat perfunctory manner. The net result of the inquiry is to demonstrate the patent fact that, in the matter of the Deccan concession, the Nizam and the shareholders of the Company have been most shamefully and deliberately defrauded, and to make things as pleasant as possible for the Indian officials, who, in the discharge of their duty of guiding and protecting the Nizam, have, to say the least, shown an incapacity and child-like simplicity suspiciously approaching imbecility. All the Calcutta machinery of safeguards and official routine set up for the purpose of guarding the folds of Native Princes from the outside wolves appears to have broken down or to have proved incapable of protecting the Nizam's Government from the single wolf in sheep's clothing, Abdul Huk, who ravaged in its midst. It is not even due to the vigilance of Calcutta, the Resident at Hyderabad, nor to the India Office, but to the unswerving loyalty, integrity, and single-mindedness of the Nizam's Prime Minister, Sir Asman Jah, that Abdul Huk has at last been run to earth, and his rascality exposed. For some years past this rapacious preyer on his country's interests has revelled in profitable corruption secure from interference, since, by his incessant intrigues he had set master and man—Nizam and Minister—at variance On the appointment of Sir Asman Jah, who is the brother-in-law of the Nizam, Huk again did his utmost to effect an estrangement, and he so far succeeded as to set Colonel Marshall, the Nizam's Secretary, in open and violent hostility to the Minister. Happily, however, the good relations between the Nizam and his Minister withstood the strain, and they worked together determinedly to free the State from Huk and his gang of unscrupulous confederates—and succeeded. The political aspect of this question appears to us to be this: In the past, the Residency influence has been thrown into the scale of men like Abdul Huk; the weaker the feudatory State, the better for the paramount Power. The result of this Machiavellian policy is what we now see disclosed by this Deccan scandal—a State abandoned to corruption from within and without. Certain it is that the Nizam, disgusted with such interference and pretence of "Government," retired, so to speak, into private life; but since the exposure of the system and the downfall of Abdul Huk he has become, as it were, a new man, and now mixes freely with his people. The moral of all this seems to be that wisdom—to say nothing of honesty—is not always the outcome of a multitude of counsellors; and that the Nizam and Sir Asman Jah should be allowed as free a hand as possible, with as little official interference as may be from Calcutta.—*World*, August 22.

WHO IS TOM PALMER?—I see that the question who "Mr. Tom Palmer" may be is being discussed in connection with Hyderabad affairs. Mr. Palmer is a gentleman who persuaded the late Sir Salar Jung that he had special facilities for interesting the Queen in the retrocession of the Berar Provinces, and who obtained from that Minister many thousand pounds (£5,000 per annum for several years, I believe) in consideration of his services and influence in high places. R. Loehlein, his Windsor friend, had been a valet to the late Prince Consort, and it need hardly be said that the assertions in the following letters, respecting what Her Majesty said and thought, are purely imaginative. That a man should have been able to obtain large sums of money from the Prime Minister of a great Indian State by telling him that he could exercise influence on the Queen, through a Court valet, is remarkable:—

"London, December 29, 1871.

"My dear Nawab Sahib,—I have the pleasure to acknowledge yours of the November 29. As to the railway loan, the London market is at your service whenever you may desire to enter it. The terms upon which you can do so are also with you.

"In the other matter, it was arranged that I was to be in Windsor to-day. The enclosed reached me yesterday. You will understand the cause of the delay. But I trust it will not last much longer.

"In the meantime I have great pleasure in informing you that all the assistance the India Office can render you in the way of favourable reports will be given.

"It is unnecessary to go further into this matter.

"Your anxiety is most natural, but the business is too important, and the interests at stake are too numerous, and of too great magnitude to be dealt with very speedily without prejudicing your interests. Trusting this may find you very well,

"I remain, yours very sincerely,

"T. N. PALMER."

[Enclosure.]

"Dear Palmer,—I am very sorry to tell you that the Queen goes to Sandringham on Thursday (to-morrow) for a few days, and I have to go with her. Will you postpone your visit? The Prince is, unfortunately, not so well, and causes still great anxiety.—Yours sincerely, R. Loehlein.

"December 27, 1871."

"London, August 9, 1872.

"My dear Nawab Sahib,—I had not the pleasure of hearing from you by the last mail, but I was extremely gratified yesterday evening by the receipt of your Excellency's telegram of the 8th through Remington and Co.

"I shall await the arrival of the letters referred to with particular interest.

"I saw my friend at Windsor yesterday. He was at home for the day to celebrate his eldest son's coming of age. He asked when your Excellency proposed to send in your letter. I replied in October next, and gave my reason for the delay. It is Saunders's absence. He will inform Her Majesty of your intention to develop the resources of your country by the introduction of railways to your coalfields, etc.

"This information will be particularly gratifying to Her Majesty, who takes a warm interest in the happiness and prosperity of the people of India.

"Trusting this may find you in the enjoyment of perfect health, and with every good wish,

"I remain, ever yours very sincerely,

"T. N. Palmer."

"London, October 1, 1875.

"My dear Nawab Sahib,—Mr. Gorst has sent a copy of your telegram of September 24 to Lord Salisbury. Gorst's opinion, when I dined with him, was that if we get the support we have every reason to expect, the question will be settled immediately after the papers have been asked for, by Lord Salisbury yielding to the opinions of the influential members who may express themselves in favour of restoration.

"Although your Excellency does not appreciate the services of my friend at Windsor, I must repeat the assurances he made me of September 28 of the Queen's warmest sympathy for your Excellency and the case. He told me that her Majesty took your Excellency's telegram from him, said that it was very wrong, and that she would explain the matter to the Prince of Wales, which she did. The Queen said she was glad the matter was coming before the House, and that she was certain you would regain the Provinces.

"My official friend, having lost his mother, is out of town.

"I have not seen Russell since I last wrote.

"With every good wish, yours sincerely,

"T. N. Palmer."

The following is only "a fragment," but it is so highly interesting that I think it well to give it:—

"The Nizam would remain the Nizam only in name.

"He would be powerless in the government of his country, and the Mookhar-ul-Moolkh would become a Karpurdar of the British Resident, with infinitely less influence and power than the Resident's own Meer Moonshee.

"If Your Excellency penned the words, 'How could your Government make such kind and liberal offers' in satire, I agree with you, for we have bitterly learnt that 'their tender mercies are cruel.'

"If, however, you have really thought of consenting, I would tell you in the words of Virgil, the old Roman poet, 'Fear the Greeks [here Indian Government], especially when they bring gifts.'

"Better their threats of anger than their benevolent interference in any way whatever.

"Keep them at arm's length in all your affairs.

"The more you give in to them, the more will they strive to grasp and hunger for, until not an inch of territory or a breath of authority will remain to the Nizam in his kingdom.

"My advice to you is as follows: Send your proposal in to the Government through Mr. Saunders.

"Urge him to expedite its transmission, and strive to obtain his support for it. Endeavour to see the Governor-General, and secure also his promotion of it. Insist upon its coming home to Her Majesty's Government, and then leave the matter to us.

"The Providence which has hitherto guided your honest endeavours for the welfare of your Government will lead you to success in this great work.

"With every good wish, I remain, ever yours sincerely,

"T. N. Palmer."

"Simla, April 7, 1884.

"My Dear Nawab,—I return, with thanks, the two original letters from Mr. Palmer which you sent me on February 3.

"I showed them to his Excellency the Viceroy, who has now authorized me to return them.

"I hope you are well, and do not find your work very trying. It must be heavy.—Yours sincerely, "H. M. Durand.

"Nawab Salar Jung, Bahadur."—*Truth*, August 23.

It is reported on good authority that the Government of the Nizam contemplate raising a special loan for the purpose of irrigation works in the State of Hyderabad.—*Times*, August 23.

It is announced that the Nizam proposes to raise a new loan for irrigation works in Hyderabad. He should leave the business in the hands of Mr. Watson. A man who can water Stocks so well ought to be able to irrigate a whole Indian State.—*Financial News*, August 24.

The Deccan Mining Concession.—Bad News for Mr. Watson and His Friends.—We are enabled to state on the best authority that Mr. E. H. Pollard, the counsel to whom the report of the Select Committee of the House of Commons on the Deccan Mining scandal was submitted on behalf of the Nizam's representatives, has given his unqualified opinion that the concession was obtained by unlawful means, and that the Hyderabad Government are legally entitled to have it cancelled.

We understand that the Hyderabad authorities, in conjunction with the Imperial Government, are now considering what further steps shall be taken in view of Mr. Pollard's opinion. It is to be hoped that the India Office will exercise a little more care than it did when the matter previously came before the Secretary of State's Council.—*Pall Mall Gazette*, August 24.

It appears from the Report published yesterday that the Hyderabad-Deccan Committee held several sittings before they were able to agree to their Report, and that a much more searching one, brought up by Sir Richard Temple, was only defeated by a majority of one. In this rejected Report it was very properly suggested that if there is to be control over promoters who select the Protected States for the field of their operations, it should be effective control, and that the India Office should have as little to do with it as possible. The incompetence of that department was pretty clearly indicated in the rejected Report, which altogether was a much more vigorous document than that which a narrow majority of officials substituted for it.—*Star*, August 25.

THE *Pall Mall Gazette* has attempted to throw some of the blame for the Deccan Concession on Sir John Gorst, the present Under-Secretary for India. As a matter of fact, the Deccan concession was sanctioned by the India Office when Mr. Gladstone was Prime Minister, and Lord Kimberley was at the head of the India Office.—*Vanity Fair*, August 25.

A THOUGHT-READER'S THOUGHTS.—ABDUL HUK.—The originator of the proposal (for a gift of sixty lakhs in behalf of Indian Imperial defence) appears to have been one Abdul Huk, whose name has of late been figuring in connection with certain railway and mining concessions, which are to occupy the attention of a Select Committee appointed by the House of Commons.

I do not like to throw stones at a man when he is down, but the Sirdar did not impress me favourably, and the conclusions I formed regarding him were at the time pretty well known in Hyderabad. He formed one of the deputation appointed by the Nizam to attend Her Majesty's Jubilee celebrations; and it, to me, seemed strange that a man with such a record should have obtained that coveted position.

I do not aim at being a prophet, but the day before Abdul's downfall I was lunching with an ex-Cabinet Minister, and the conversation turned upon India, and I gave my host a description of the state of affairs existing at Hyderabad, in which I included my impressions of the then all-powerful Sirdar, whose speedy downfall I ventured to predict. The next day, like a bolt from out of a clear sky, came a telegram announcing the Sirdar's suspension.

Abdul Huk, who had all the swagger and volubility of a Bengali Baboo, was a great favourite with London Society, whom he feasted with great lavishness during his recent visit. How uncomfortable some of the high and mighty folk must feel at the thought of how the money which was paid for the sumptuous repasts he provided for them was obtained. *O tempora! O mores!*

THE NIZAM AS A SUBJECT.

As a subject for thought-reading, the Nizam was not quite so good as some of the other Princes. The Maharajah of Mysore, a very intelligent man, and the Thakore of Bhaonagar (probably the most enlightened ruler in India) were two of my best subjects, with whom I experimented. He was too nervous and impetuous for any sustained concentration of thought, but I managed to do one or two very interesting experiments with him. But with Sir Salar Jung, who, when he likes to exert himself, is a man of considerable concentration of thought, I had some very remarkable successes; and he was undoubtedly the best "subject" I experimented with during my stay in India.

SIR SALAR JUNG.

Sir Salar Jung is a fairly able honest man, but he is woefully lazy, and were it not for his love of idling, he would, I have no doubt, play an important part in Indian politics. Yet Sir Salar is well-informed, and his recent visit to England served (if such a thing were possible) to strengthen his regard for us.

At present he is in the shade, but to-morrow may see him once more in power; who knows? Hyderabad is a hot-bed of intrigue; and one day one party has the upper hand, and the next day another, and so on and so on until the onlooker is bewildered as to which is which. Hyderabad Residency is considered the blue ribbon of Indian diplomacy, and the Resident there certainly has no sinecure.

MEHDI ALI.

One of the most competent and painstaking Ministers of the Nizam's is Mehdi Ali, who is, I understand, shortly to visit this country in connection with what is called the "Hyderabad-Deccan affair." He is a man not only thoroughly conversant with all matters relating to his own State, but he is well acquainted with Indian affairs generally. In so corrupt a State as Hyderabad, where it is difficult to find the one honest man, it is gratifying to know that Mehdi Ali is of undoubted probity, and that his loyalty is altogether unquestionable. In India it invariably happens that the more corrupt a Native is, the more disloyal he is; and I cannot help thinking that Abdul Huk, in spite of his numerous friends in England, would not have proved the paragon of loyalty that he was supposed to be.—*Echo*, August 30.

HOUSE OF COMMONS, SELECT COMMITTEE ON HYDERABAD AFFAIRS.

WEDNESDAY, 9th May, 1888.—Members present: Sir Henry James, Sir Richard Temple, Mr. Labouchere, Mr. Bristowe, the Solicitor-General for Scotland, Mr. M'Lagan. Sir Henry James was called to the Chair.

The Committee deliberated.

Motion made, and question proposed: "That any person or body deeming themselves interested, who wish to appear by counsel, shall make application in writing to the Clerk on or before Monday next"—The Chairman. Question put, and agreed to.

Adjourned till Wednesday next, at half-past four o'clock.

WEDNESDAY, 16th May, 1888.—Members present: Sir Henry James in the chair. Mr. Solicitor-General for Scotland, Mr. Bristowe, Sir Richard Temple, Mr. Labouchere, Mr. M'Lagan.

The following letters were read:—

"1, New Square, Lincoln's Inn, London, W.C.,
"11th May, 1888.

"SIR,—His Highness the Nizam of Hyderabad desires to be represented by Counsel at the meeting of the Select Committee on the Hyderabad Deccan Mining Concession, and I am instructed by Nawab Fathar Nawaz Jung, the Chief Justice of Hyderabad, and His Highness's Director of the Hyderabad Deccan Company, to ask if such attendance would be in accordance with the rules of the House of Commons.

"I am, etc.,
(Signed) "SPENCER WHITEHEAD."

To the Chairman of the
Select Commitee on East India (Hyderabad
Deccan Mining Company).

"17, Gresham House (Ground Floor),
"Old Broad Street, London, E.C.,
"Saturday, 12th May, 1888.

"SIR,—Referring to the announcement by the Committee, at the meeting of the 9th inst., that any of the parties interested who wished to be heard before the Committee by Counsel should communicate with you, I am instructed by Mr. William Clarence Watson, the survivor of the two original grantees of the

Concession now held by the Hyderabad Company, to submit that it would be fit that he should be heard by Counsel, who should take such part in the examination and cross-examination of the witnesses, and otherwise, as the Committee may think fit. The reason for his request is, that the conduct of the concessionnaires is the principal subject of the inquiry, and that his interests and reputation may be prejudiced if the facts are inaccurately or imperfectly presented to the Committee.

"I am, etc.,
(Signed) "G. M. Clements."

To the Clerk of the
Select Committee on East India (Hyderabad
Deccan Mining Company).

"36, Bedford Row, London, W.C.,
"12th May, 1888.

"Dear Sir,—In pursuance of the direction given by the Right Honourable and learned Chairman of the above Committee, we beg to place before the Committee our application, as Solicitors and Agents for the Sirdar Diler Jung, that he by his Counsel may be permitted to attend the inquiry and take part therein, by cross-examining witnesses and calling and examining witnesses, and tendering evidence and addressing the Committee as he may be advised.

"The Sirdar occupied the position of Home Secretary of the Government of His Highness the Nizam of Hyderabad, and was deputed to conduct certain negotiations on behalf of the Nizam in London, previous to the formation of the above-mentioned Company, and it appears from the speech of the Honourable Member for Northampton, Mr. Labouchere, in moving for the appointment of the Committee, and from other matter which has been made public in reference to the proposed inquiry, that very grave charges will be made against the Sirdar in the nature of having failed to carry out the duties cast upon him as a Minister of State.

"It is, therefore, we respectfully and urgently submit, of most vital importance to the Sirdar to have the fullest opportunity of refuting such charges, and we trust a favourable answer will be returned to this application.

"We shall add that on the 9th instant, Mr. Mowbray, the Member for the Prestwich Division of Lancashire, presented our petition to the House of Commons to the same effect as this application, which petition was at once referred by the order of the House to the Select Committee.

"We are, etc.,
(Signed) "Chester & Co."

To the Clerk of the
Select Committee on East India (Hyderabad
Deccan Mining Company).

"19, Bedford Row, London, W.C.,
"10th May, 1888.

"Sir,—Acting upon the announcement by Sir Henry James, the Chairman of the Hyderabad (Deccan) Committee, at the meeting on the 9th instant, that parties desiring to attend by counsel before the Committee should apply in writing, we are instructed by Mr. Henry Parkinson Sharp to apply for leave for him to appear and be represented by counsel before the Committee, and take such part in the inquiry into the circumstances of the granting of the concession as the Committee may think.

"Though Mr. Sharp had a considerable interest in the concession which was granted to Mr. Stewart and to Mr. Watson, his name was not mentioned therein, and owing to Mr. Stewart's death, and to the fact that Mr. Sharp personally held no communication with the parties in India, Mr. Sharp's position and interests are necessarily wholly distinct from those of any other persons interested in these matters, and it is of paramount importance to him that he should be separately represented.

"Mr. Sharp instructs us to express his desire by himself and counsel to assist the Committee in every way and to give them all the information in his possession.

"We are, etc.,
(Signed) "C. and S. HARRISON & Co."

To the Clerk of the
Select Committee on East India (Hyderabad
Deccan Mining Company).

"46, Parliament Street, Westminster, S.W.,
"12th May, 1888.

"SIR,—Acting on the intimation made on the 9th inst. by the Chairman of the East India (Hyderabad Deccan Mining Company) Committee, we are instructed by the Hyderabad (Deccan) Company to ask that the Company may be represented by counsel on the inquiry.

"Their reasons for the request are:—

"That the obtaining of the Mining Concession, which concession constitutes the principal property of the Company, and the purpose of its existence, will be under consideration and inquired into.

"That the interests of a large body of *bonâ fide* shareholders (upwards of 700 in number) who had no part in the negotiations for the concession may be affected.

"That the interests of the shareholders and their position generally are substantially different from those of the concessionnaires.

"And that the presence of counsel on the Company's behalf will, it is believed, materially assist the inquiry.

"We are, etc.,
(Signed) "BIRCHAM & Co.,
"Solicitors to the Company."

To the Clerk of the
Select Committee on East India (Hyderabad
Deccan Mining Company).

"Leadenhall House, 101, Leadenhall Street, London, E.C.,
"10th May, 1888.

"SIR,—We are acting for Mr. James Grahame Stewart, one of the executors, and the only son and residuary legatee of Mr. John Stewart, who died on the 19th July last, and to whom, jointly with Mr. William Clarence Watson, the Mining Concession, dated the 7th January, 1886, was granted by the Government of His Highness the Nizam.

"On behalf of Mr. James Grahame Stewart, we ask for permission to appear by counsel before the Select Committee, in order that the good name and interests of the late Mr. John Stewart, who cannot now defend himself, may be adequately protected.

"We are, etc.,
(Signed) "TURNER & HACON."

To the Clerk of the
Select Committee on East India (Hyderabad
Deccan Mining Company).

The Committee deliberated.

FIRST AND SECOND REPORTS FROM THE SELECT COMMITTEE ON EAST INDIA (HYDERABAD DECCAN MINING COMPANY).

Ordered, by the House of Commons, to be Printed, May 17 *and August* 6, 1888.

"*Ordered*,—[*Thursday, May* 3, 1888]:—THAT a Select Committee be appointed to inquire into the formation and promotion of the Hyderabad (Deccan) Mining Company, Limited, the circumstances under which the concession held by that Company was obtained from the Government of Hyderabad, and the subsequent operations on the London Stock Exchange by persons interested in the Company.

"Committee nominated of—Sir Henry James, Sir Richard Temple, Mr. Slagg, Mr. Solicitor-General for Scotland, Mr. M'Lagan, Mr. Bristowe, and Mr. Labouchere.

"That the Committee have power to send for persons, papers, and records.

"That three be the quorum of the Committee.

"*Ordered,—[Thursday, May* 17, 1888]: That the Select Committee on East India (Hyderabad Deccan Mining Company) have leave to hear counsel (to such extent as they shall think fit) upon the matters referred to them.

FIRST REPORT.

The Select Committee appointed to inquire into the formation and promotion of the Hyderabad Deccan Mining Company, Limited, the circumstances under which the concession held by that Company was obtained from the Government of Hyderabad, and the subsequent operations on the London Stock Exchange by persons interested in the Company, have made progress in the matter to them referred, and have come to the following resolution, which they have agreed to report to the House.

That the Committee having received applications from the Nizam of Hyderabad, the Hyderabad Deccan Mining Company, the Sirdar Diler Jung, Mr. William Clarence Watson, Mr. Henry Parkinson Sharp, and Mr. James Graham Stewart, to be represented by Council before a Committee, the Committee are of opinion that it will be advisable to allow Counsel to represent the said Applicants, for the purpose of assisting the Committee to such an extent and purposes as the Committee may from time to time direct.

17th May, 1888.

SECOND REPORT.

The Select Committee appointed to inquire into the formation and promotion of the Hyderabad (Deccan) Mining Company, Limited, the circumstances under which the concession held by that Company was obtained from the Government of Hyderabad, and the subsequent operations on the London Stock Exchange by persons interested in the Company, have made further progress in the matters to them referred, and have agreed to the following Second Report:—

Your Committee have heard evidence on the matters referred to them. An application was made at the commencement of the proceedings, by certain parties interested in the inquiry, to be represented by counsel. Leave having been obtained from the House, counsel were allowed to attend and to take part in the examination of witnesses on certain points. Counsel also addressed your Committee at the close of the evidence. The parties represented by counsel were: His Highness the Nizam, Sirdar Diler Jung (Abdul Huk), The Hyderabad Deccan Company, Limited, Mr. William Clarence Watson, Mr. Henry Parkinson Sharp, Mr. James Graham Stewart.

H. C. No. 328, Session 1887, pp. 26-33. The following facts were proved before your Committee:—On the 7th January, 1886, by an indenture of that date, a concession was granted by the Government of Hyderabad to William Clarence Watson, of 7, Great Winchester Street, London, merchant, and John Stewart, of 26, Throgmorton Street, London (who is since deceased).

Ibid. p. 32 It will be seen that the concession confers upon the concessionnaires (Clause 17) the exclusive right of prospecting or testing for minerals of all kinds throughout the territories of the Nizam, until 31st December, 1891. The concessionnaires also obtain the right to select, during that period, such mines or fields as they desire to acquire for mining operations, and to obtain from the Nizam's Government a lease or leases of such mines or fields as they may select for a term of 99 years from the date of the concession, at royalties to be fixed (Clauses 17 and 11) by mining engineers, one to be appointed by each of the parties, or, in default of agreement, by a mining engineer to be appointed by the Government of India. The fixing and determining royalties was to be based and founded on the general principle of a fair rent. Such, generally stated, are the rights applicable to minerals of all kinds, including gold, silver, or precious stones, conferred on the concessionnaires. H. C. No. 338, Session 1887, pp. 32, 28. *Ibid.* p. 28.

The concessionnaires came under obligation forthwith to work certain coalfields, called the Singareni coalfields. The indenture declared (Clause 3) that the first object of the Company was to work the coalfield at Singareni; and that the Company were to open up the mine in such a manner that they should be in a position to supply (if so required) not less than 500 tons of good coal per week by the date of the opening of the railway communication to either Hyderabad or Bezwara, or by the 30th June, 1888, at latest. By the indenture (Clause 11A) it was provided that the royalties in respect of the Singareni coal-field should be computed on quantities won, and should, if the scales were less than 100,000 British tons per annum, be fixed at eight annas per ton. Any excess over the above quantity might be charged with a higher rate of royalty up to a limit of one rupee per ton. *Ibid.* p. 26. *Ibid.* p. 28.

The two first clauses of the indenture contain the provisions relating to the formation of a Limited Company to work the concession. The first clause requires the concessionnaires to form in London a Company under the Companies' Acts 1862 to 1880. This was to be done within six months after capital had been raised for the construction of a railway to Singareni. The capital of the company was to be not less than £1,000,000 with power to increase the capital by an issue of debentures, and otherwise if necessary. *Ibid.* p. 26.

If the Company was formed within the stipulated period, and if before the expiration of that period, £150,000 of its share capital at the least was subscribed for, and £75,000 thereof actually paid-up, and if the Company adopted the concession, the concessionnaires would be entitled to transfer to the Company the benefits of the concession. On these things being done and a transfer made and notified to the Nizam's Government, the concessionnaires were to be released from their obligations under the indenture. *Ibid.* p. 26.

The preamble of the concession makes mention of the previous formation of another Company for the construction of a railway connecting the Northern and Southern frontiers of the State of Hyderabad. In order to state the circumstances under which the mining concession was obtained, it is necessary to briefly refer to the history of the formation of this Railway Company. *Ibid.* p. 26.

Previous to the formation of this Company there existed in the Nizam's territories a somewhat limited railway system. The extension of the railways had been mooted, and this was an object approved of by the Government of India. At first, the project of extending the railways was coupled with a proposal for a mining concession. This double scheme was broached by Mr. Charles Albert Winter in 1887. Mr. Winter was then a solicitor in Bombay, and his firm had acted professionally for the Nizam's Government in 1874 in regard to the old railway system. He is brother-in-law to Mr. William Clarence Watson, one of the concessionnaires; and in those matters Mr. Winter acted, if not by Mr. Watson's authority, at least in reliance on Mr. Watson's co-operation, should business transactions take place. In 1881 Mr. Winter met with Abdul Huk, thereafter Sirdar Diler Jung, at Hyderabad, and negotiated with him on the subject of the railway. Despatch, Foreign Secretary at Calcutta, to the Resident of Hyderabad 17th February, 1882. Appendix A. Q. 3681. Q. 1299. Q. 1245. Q. 1242. Q. 1241. Q. 1323. Q. 1752-4. Q. 1218 *et seq.*

Abdul Huk was at this time head of the Home Department, and Director of Railways and Mines in Hyderabad. Sir Salar Jung, the elder, was, until his death in February, 1883, the Prime Minister of Hyderabad. From beginning to end of the negotiations, regarding both the railway and the mines, Abdul Huk was the accredited agent of the Nizam's Government. He and Mr. Q. 2778-2782. Q. 1275-1309

Winter came to an understanding, of which the main features were that Mr. Winter and his friends should form a Company, to find £2,000,000 for forming extensions of the railways, 5 per cent. on this sum being guaranteed by the Nizam's Government for five years. Mr. Winter and his friends were also to receive a concession of a mining monopoly in the Deccan. The proposal was

Q. 2762. Letter of 17th February, 1882, Government of India.

ultimately referred to the Viceroy, and the Nizam's Government was informed that the persons connected with it were not of sufficient financial standing to render it advisable for that Goverment to enter into such important monetary relations with them.

Appendix A. Q. 1290. Q. 1300-8. Appendix B.

Mr. Winter stated to the Committee that he and Abdul Huk arranged that the latter should receive for his own uses "£120,000 for the railway" and also one-fourth interest in the mining concession. Abdul Huk produced to Mr. Winter a letter, dated 5th January, 1882, apparently signed by Sir Salar Jung, written "to assure you that I shall have no objection to your receiving any remuneration on the railway and mining schemes with which they may reward your services, and that I shall consider whatever you receive from them as only your due." The relation thus established between Abdul Huk and the proposed concessionnaires was not, at any period of the subsequent negotiations, disclosed by either of them to the Government either in England or India.

Abdul Huk was subsequently sent to London to endeavour to find someone ready to finance the railroad scheme, and to make some arrangement in

Q. 3683. Q. 1313.

respect to the mining concession. The two schemes were left entirely separate. After submitting the railroad proposals to Messrs. Rothschild and to Messrs, Morton, Rose, and Co., a Railroad Company was ultimately floated by Mr. Watson, on an agreement that the Nizam should give a guarantee of 5 per cent. for 20 years upon the £2,000,000 which was to be paid to him for the railway, and of which he was to take a portion in the shares of the contemplated Railroad Company which was to provide the £2,000,000. For floating this new Railroad Company Mr. Watson received £100,000, of which he stated that he expended in costs of promotion £93,000, and £83,000 was subsequently paid to Abdul Huk for his services in connection with the negotiation.

The attitude of the British Government during those negotiations of Abdul Huk is indicated in two despatches written, one by the Marquis of

Appendix C. H. C. No. 318, Session 1887, p. 9. Q. 3669.

Hartington, dated 24th May, 1882, and the other by the Earl of Kimberley, dated 5th July, 1883, on the occassion, in each instance, of Abdul Huk announcing his arrival in London on his mission. By the despatch of 24th May, 1882, Abdul Huk was informed by the Secretary of State for India that he was at full liberty to act upon the instructions of the Nizam; that the Secretary of State would be ready at any time during the progress of the negotiations to give him such advice and assistance as he might desire, and would expect to be informed of any engagements into which he might purpose to enter before their actual completion, and that the Secretary of State would recognise no liability, financial or otherwise, in relation to any Company or persons with whom Abdul Huk might negotiate, excepting so far as a specific contract might be entered into directly between the Company, the Secretary of State, and the Nizam's Govern-

Appendix D. Q. 3675.

ment, with the intention of defining such liabilities. The Government of India during the negotiations, by a despatch of 15th March, 1883, laid it down that they, as the paramount power in India, were bound to satisfy themselves in transactions of this nature: (1), that the Native Government fully realised its responsibility and obligations; (2), that every reasonable precaution had been taken to protect its interests; (3), that the European contractors distinctly understood that the Government of India disclaim all responsibility whatsoever in respect of the soundness of the basis on which their proposals may be founded and of the general success of the enterprise to which such proposals related.

Meantime the project of a mining concession proceeded separately. In 1883, Abdul Huk, having been informed by the India Office that the proposal for the mining concession put forward by Mr. Watson ought to be submitted to advisers of experience, instructed Messrs. White, Borrett and Co. to act on Q. 3698 behalf of his Government in settling the terms of a mining concession with Mr. Watson and Mr. Stewart. The draft of a concession was accordingly prepared, and, after negotiations, which lasted several months, was settled by Messrs. White, Borrett and Co., with the advice of eminent counsel (Mr., now Lord, Q. 1343. Macnaghten, and Mr. Blakesley). But Abdul Huk was informed by the India Office that it would be desirable that the project should be submitted to the H.C. No. 338, Session 1887 Nizam's Government, and that further negotiations in respect to it should take pp. 4, 33. place at Hyderabad before it was finally adopted.

Abdul Huk returned to Hyderabad with the draft of the concession. *Ibid.* p. 5. It was considered by the Nizam's Minister, Salar Jung the younger, who canvassed several points in the draft, and then submitted it as accepted by him to the Resident, by whom it was transmitted to the Government of India at Calcutta, together with the letter of Salar Jung, dated 14th January, 1885. *Ibid.* p. 20. The Government of India carefully considered the draft, and approved generally of it, but they proposed a number of alterations in various clauses. Two memoranda were forwarded to the Resident, one describing the alterations *Ibid.* p. 20. suggested, while the other explained the grounds on which they were recom- *Ibid.* p. 21. mended. The Resident was requested to recommend to the Minister of the *Ibid.* p. 20. Nizam and to the agent of the Company that the agreement should be concluded, that is, that the concession should be granted on terms embodying the suggested alterations. Such alterations, together with some further modifications, were agreed to, and the concession was signed on 7th January, 1886.

Upon the concession being signed it was forwarded to the Government of India. The fact of the execution of the concession was communicated to the Secretary of State for India by a telegram dated 29th January, 1886. On the *Ibid.* pp. 3, 4. 2nd of February, 1886, a letter was sent by the Governor-General and Council to the Secretary of State for India, in which the following sentence occurs: "We have considered, in connection with the observations in the concluding portion of the 23rd paragraph of the Despatch, No. 19, Railway, dated 21st *Ibid.* pp. 4, 5. February, 1884, from the Right Honourable the Secretary of State for India, that any liabilities which might be incurred in pursuance of this agreement, under 37 Geo. 3, c. 142, s. 28, would be removed by the formal 'consent and approbation' of the Governor-General in Council 'in writing,' but as your Lordship has suggested that the previous approval of the Secretary of State is desirable to contracts of the nature of this agreement, we would solicit that we may be favoured with this sanction by telegram." The subject of the concession was considered by the Secretary of State for India in Council, and certain conditions being imposed, they were communicated to the concessionnaires and agreed to by them. On 27th July, 1886, the sanction of the Secretary of State, conditional on such modifications, was intimated to Mr. Watson in *Ibid.* p. 36. London.

The Hyderabad-Deccan Company, Limited, was forthwith registered, its objects being to acquire and work the concession. The fifth clause of the Memorandum of Association was as follows:—

"5. The capital of the Company is £1,000,000, in 100,000 shares of £10 each. Any shares in the capital of the Company may be issued as fully, or in part, paid-up, in payment for the said concession, or any other property which the Company is authorized to acquire; and the shares of which the capital shall from time to time consist may be divided into different classes, with such preferences, priorities, restrictions, or special incidents as may from time to time be prescribed by the articles and special resolutions of the Company."

The Articles of Association contained the following articles:—

"Article 3. The Board may make and carry into effect any agreements with any Company, association, or person, whether a Director or Promoter of the Company or not, for any of the objects referred to in the Memorandum of Association, and any such person shall, notwithstanding that he is a Director or Promoter of the Company, be entitled to retain the benefit or profit of the agreement.

"Article 12. The Board shall consist of such number of Directors as a general meeting shall from time to time determine, and until and subject to such determination shall consist of any number not more than seven nor less than three.

"Article 14. The first three Directors of the Company shall be appointed by the subscribers of the Memorandum of Association of the Company. The Board may at any time before the ordinary meeting, to be held in the year 1888, appoint duly qualified persons as additional Directors, so that the total number of Directors shall not at any one time exceed seven without the authority of a general meeting. The first Directors, and any others appointed under this article (except such of them as shall in the meantime vacate their offices under any of the provisions of these presents), shall continue in office for two years from the incorporation of the Company."

The persons subscribing the Memorandum were, besides the two concessionnaires, Messrs. Winter, Hemmerdy, Batten, Pearce, and Milne. It is sufficient at present to say that those gentlemen were all friends of, or employed by, the concessionnaires.

Minutes of Hyderabad Deccan Company. On 10th August, 1886, these gentlemen met and elected as Directors Mr. Batten, Mr. Hemmerdy, and Mr. Milne. On the same day the Directors met, and the minutes of the Board record the following proceedings:—

"The agreement between the concessionnaires, the applicants for 15,000 shares of the Company, being the agreement to transfer the concession to the Company, was submitted and explained and approved. It was resolved that the common seal of the Company be affixed thereto, in accordance with the Articles of Association, when and so soon as £5 per share has been paid by the allottees of the 15,000 shares to the Company's bankers.

"The application for the 15,000 shares by the persons described in the schedule to the above-mentioned agreement was considered, and the shares numbered 1 to 15,000 inclusive were allotted as follows:—

John Stewart - - - - - - -	5,000
Henry Parkinson Sharp - - - - -	5,000
William Clarence Watson - - - - -	4,599
Charles Albert Winter - - - - - -	100
George H. M. Batten - - - - - -	100
James Hemmerdy - - - - - - -	100
John Martyn Milne - - - - - -	100
Richard Pearce - - - - - - -	1
	15,000

"Resolved,—That the National Provincial Bank of England, Limited, 112, Bishopsgate Street, E.C., be appointed the bankers of the Company.

"Resolved,—That the allottees be requested to pay forthwith to the Company's bankers £5 per share, and that allotment letters be prepared and sent to them. The Secretary submitted an agreement between the Company and Messrs. Watson and Stewart, prepared in pursuance of the before-mentioned agreement in relation to the 85,000 shares to be numbered 15,001 to 100,000, and to be allotted as fully-paid shares to them.

"Resolved,—That the same be approved, and the common seal of the Company affixed thereto after the first-named agreement has been sealed, and that the same be then duly filed with the Registrar of Joint Stock Companies."

Q. 628 Q. 629. Of these Directors, Mr. Batten originally obtained and paid for 100

of the shares with £5 paid on them. In October, 1886, Mr. Watson paid Mr. Batten £500 for those 100 shares, and at the same time transferred to
Mr. Batten 100 paid-up shares. At the time of this transfer, and since, no Q. 632, 633. Q. 486.
payment for these last-mentioned shares has been made, but Mr. Batten Q. 4121.
stated that if the Company paid a dividend he was to pay Mr. Watson for Q. 4116.
them, or to return them. Mr. Hemmerdy, on 3rd October, received from
Mr. Watson 1,000 fully paid-up shares. Dealings in the shares had Q. 4199.
previously taken place at a price of £9 per share. As accounting for this gift Mr. Watson stated: "Mr. Hemmerdy was an old friend of mine, and I
"gave these shares to him (I hoped they would be worth £10,000), for Q. 4117.
"many services he had rendered to me for twenty years previously."

Of the two agreements thus approved the former effected the transfer Appendix E.
of the concession to the Company, the allotment to the persons named of the 15,000 shares with £5 paid, and the allotment of the 85,000 fully-paid
being terms of the bargain. The other agreement between the Company Appendix F.
and Mr. Watson and Mr. Stewart set forth that it had been agreed that the concessionnaires should assign and transfer to the Company the concession, and that in exchange the Company should allot to the concessionnaires, 85,000 shares of £10 each in the Company, which shares should be deemed for all purposes to be fully paid-up. It was, therefore, thereby agreed that Company should allot to the concessionnaires or their nominees 85,000 fully paid-up shares in the Company, and that the shares should be numbered 15,001 to 100,000, inclusive, and should be accepted by the concessionnaires in full satisfaction of all claims and demands whatsoever of the concessionnaires in respect of the transfer of the concession. These agreements had been drawn by the solicitors of the Company on the instructions Q. 585, 589
of the concessionnaires.

The £5 per share on the 15,000 shares were duly paid into the Company's bank; and thereupon the two agreements were sealed, and the Q. 767.
contract as to the allotment of 85,000 fully paid-up shares was registered with the Registrar of Joint Stock Companies. These conditions having been fulfilled, the Directors (Mr. Batten, Mr. Hemmerdy, and Mr. Milne), on 19th August, 1886, proceeded to allot to Mr. Watson and Mr. Stewart the 85,000 shares as fully paid-up, and certificates were signed, sealed, and handed to the allottees.

The shares of the Company having been distributed, as mentioned above, Mr. Watson and Mr. Stewart were, on 24th August, 1886, appointed additional Directors; on the same day Mr. Milne resigned his Directorship to become Secretary. On 2nd November Mr. Henry Parkinson Sharp was elected a Director, and Mr. Hemmerdy retired from the direction on 10th November, 1886.

The 85,000 shares issued as paid-up, when received by Mr. Watson and Mr. Stewart, were by them divided among the partners in the enterprise—viz., Mr. Watson, Mr. Stewart, Abdul Huk, each a fourth; Mr. Winter, Mr. Henry Parkinson Sharp, and others participating the remaining fourth. Abdul Huk's
name does not appear as an allottee or transferee of shares in the Minute Book; Q. 1639.
but the proportion of the shares to be received by him were transferred to Mr. Q. 1651-6.
Winter; they were then turned into share warrants to bearer; and these latter were lodged with the bankers of Abdul Huk on his account. At the same time he received one-fourth share of the 15,000 shares, and at a later date he paid through Mr. Winter £5 per share upon them.

Before the allotment of shares no reports upon the value of the rights Q. 168.
conceded were received by the Directors or promoters of the Company. At a later date, and when dealings on the Stock Exchange were taking place on the shares, such reports were received from Mr. Hughes and Mr. Furnivall. Mr. Hughes is a Government official in India, being one of "the
Superintendents of the Survey," and had been employed as such in the Q. 4051.
geological examination of Hyderabad and contiguous districts. The

Q. 1052. Secretary of State for India, upon being applied to, granted permission for Mr. Hughes to be employed and paid by the Company, in order "to see really what was the value of the concession they had got from the Nizam."
Q. 1138. Before any reports were made, in May, 1877, Mr. Watson transferred to Mr. Hughes 200 fully paid-up shares and 200 shares with £5 paid on them
Q. 1139. At the then market price these 400 shares were worth £3,200. Mr. Hughes
Q. 1146. paid Mr. Watson £1,000 for them. On the 4th July Mr. Hughes re-transferred the 200 fully paid-up shares to Mr. Watson, receiving £2,390 for
Q. 1154. them. The 200 shares with £5 paid on them were retained by Mr. Hughes.
Q. 1155. Mr. Watson stated that this transaction amounted to a gift by him to Mr. Hughes, but that "it was not to make reports," "but that he (Mr. Hughes)
Q. 4156. might work and throw his whole energies into it." Reports were also received from Mr. Furnivall. This gentleman was an engineer, formerly in the employ of the Government of India, but now retired upon a pension.
Q. 2852. Mr. Watson gave Mr. Furnivall "500 shares for nothing." These shares
Q. 1175. Q. 1179. were sold by Mr. Furnivall at £11 per share, therefore realising £5,500.

It is to be observed that the share in the concession received by Abdul Huk is in accordance with the terms of the arrangement made with Mr. Winter in 1881, as above set forth.

Q. 877. Q. 2111. The shares of the Company began to change hands, but not to any considerable extent prior to the first statutory meeting of the Company on 26th November, 1886. At that time Mr. R. Stanton Evans, a gentleman
Q. 864. Q. 875-911. Q. 2117. engaged in financial operations in the City, began to sell the shares for Mr. Watson on the terms that Mr. Watson should pay to Mr. Evans 10s. on every share sold by him "over par and up to a certain premium," and the shares were freely bought and sold on
Q. 1152. the Stock Exchange from that time. Of the 85,000 shares issued as
Q. 2393. fully paid-up, about 55,000 have been sold to the public. There are now about 700 shareholders. The prices of the shares ranged, during the period between September, 1886, and April, 1888, from £13¾ to £5⅞. Mr. Watson, by dealing in his fourth of the 85,000 shares, and by transactions in buying and selling shares in the market, had, at the time when he gave his evi-
Q. 3576-3582. dence, realised £209,300 (out of which he had paid in brokerage and commissions £20,829), and he still retained 5,559 shares. Mr. Watson had also given away many shares.

It should be remarked that whilst numerous transactions in these shares took place on the Stock Exchange, no application for a settlement or quotation
Q. 3. was made to the Committee of that body, and although the evidence shows
Q. 20. that operations in the shares of Companies, for which no such application is made, frequently occur on these occasions, the rules and regulations of the Stock Exchange are entirely disregarded, and it will be observed that had a settlement been applied for and granted in the shares of this Company, the 85,000 shares allotted to the concessionnaires would have been excluded from that settlement, not being a good delivery on the Stock Exchange.

Q. 10 It will also be observed that had a quotation been applied for, it would not have been granted, as the rules and conditions of the Stock Exchange with regard to these matters had not been complied with.

Q. 2131, 2532. No prospectus of the Company was issued; and the title "Prospectus" was disclaimed before your Committee for the Memorandum, which is afterwards mentioned. The method adopted by the sellers seems to have been not to place before the public specific information, but to stimulate interest by affording hints and glimpses of the magnitude of the enterprise.
Q. 1220 At the same time, the fact that the 85,000 shares had been issued
Appendix G. as fully-paid to the concessionnaires cannot be said to have been a secret. A paragraph in the money article in the *Standard* newspaper of 13th December, 1886, drew attention to the transactions, and set out at length the agreement between the concessionnaires and the Company,

dated 17th August, 1886. Again, "Burdett's Official Intelligence," which Q. 1211.
is a publication giving particulars of Companies, in its issue of February,
1887, contained a description of the Hyderabad-Deccan Company, in which
it was stated that "The 85,000 fully-paid shares, 15,001 to 100,000, represent the price at which the concessionnaires transferred the concession to
the Company. The 15,000 shares with £5 paid (No. 1 to 15,000) were subscribed for by the concessionnaires. All the 100,000 shares have an equal
right to participate in the profits of the undertaking." The balance-sheet
of the Company issued in July, 1887, sets forth in its first entry on the
credit side, "By purchase of concession, £850,000," while on the other side
the capital is stated as £1,000,000 in 100,000 shares of £10 each, of which Q. 322, 2860.
85,000 are fully-paid and 15,000 £5 paid. This balance-sheet and the
Memorandum and Articles of Association were sent to the Nizam's Government. A printed Memorandum regarding the Company, of which Mr. Q. 2531.
Watson says he had some thirty copies printed in order to give information Appendix H.
to people asking for shares (but the statements in which obtained, perhaps,
a more extended publicity than is indicated by those numbers), contained a
description of the scheme very favourably coloured. It will be observed by
reference to this Memorandum that no statement is made in it which would
convey to the public that the 85,000 shares had been passed to the concessionnaires under the circumstances mentioned above. The Memorandum
was headed, "Capital £1,000.000 in 100,000 shares of £10 each, 85,000
being fully-paid, and 15,000 on which £5 per share is paid."

The Company have been carrying on mining operations in the Q. 115-121, 503-4.
Singareni coalfields to the extent of raising about 150 tons a week. They Q. 505.
have also been prospecting for diamonds and for gold. Five diamonds have Q. 2568, 2900. Q. 2903.
been found in some refuse. No gold has been produced, but Mr. Watson Q. 2980-1.
relies on the reports of Mr. Hughes, Mr. Furnivall, Mr. Lowinsky, and others
stating the existence of auriferous and diamondiferous strata. Your Committee express no opinion as to the prospects of the enterprise. It was
stated by Mr. Watson that no dissatisfaction with his investment has been Q. 3654, 2539
expressed by any of the shareholders, except in one instance; but beyond
this statement no evidence on the subject was brought before your Committee.

On the 3rd June, 1887, there were purchased on the Stock Exchange
for the Nizam's Government 8,750 fully-paid and 3,750 £5 paid shares of
the Company.

The importance of this transaction, as affecting the Nizam's Govern- Q. 1691.
ment, is largely abated by the fact that since your Committee began its
sittings they have been authoratively informed that the purchase has been
rescinded, by arrangement, and the money expended by the Nizam has been
refunded to His Highness. The facts attending this purchase appear to be
as follows.

The resolution of the Nizam's Government to invest in shares of the
Company was deliberately arrived at. Nawab Mahdi Ali, who gave evidence
before your Committee, and who is, and was at the time, Political and Appendix I.
Financial Secretary of the Nizam's Government, had placed before him a
Memorandum by Abdul Huk, which, while recommending the investment,
discussed very fully the objections to it that might be stated on account of
its speculative nature. The Nawab Mahdi Ali recommended the proposal, Q. 2760.
and it was sanctioned by the Nizam. The Resident, Mr. Cordery, approved
of the purchase, and Abdul Huk was ordered to purchase 10,000 shares at Q. 2761.
the most favourable terms up to £12 per share.

When the shares were bought Abdul Huk was in London, and he carried
out the purchase in concert with Mr. Watson. The documents which
record the transaction somewhat exaggerate its complexity. What was
done, in fact, was that Abdul Huk received the price, and handed over to

the Nizam so many of the shares which had fallen to himself in the distribution of the shares of the concessionnaires. The method adopted to accomplish this object was somewhat circuitous. Mr. Watson and Abdul
H.C. No. 141, Session 1888, pp. 51-60. Q. 951. Huk met in the office of the former, but their communications in respect of the purchase purport to be expressed in their letters set out in the Parliamentary Paper referred to in the margin. Mr. Watson deemed it to be necessary to consult Mr. Evans. All were agreed that the transaction, to be duly carried out must be effected by way of sale and purchase on the Stock Exchange. Mr. Evans employed and sent into the Stock
Q. 962-997. Q. 1095. Q. 1099-1100, 2193. Q. 2189. Exchange six separate brokers, with orders to buy, and at the same time employed a broker to sell at an arranged price. Each person concerned received a commission. Mr. Watson, in his evidence, said that he considered it to be desirable that the transaction should be recorded, and Mr. Evans understood the object to be that it should be known on the Stock Exchange that the Nizam's Government was buying shares, and that this would be a good thing for the Company.
Q. 1097, 1110. The shares thus purported to be bought and sold all belonged to Abdul Huk, who, in consideration for the shares thus transferred to the Nizam, received £131,250 of moneys belonging to the Government of Hyderabad.

Q. 2157. Q. 1228. It does not appear that at the time in question shares could have been obtained at a lower rate than was actually paid to Abdul Huk. The market price was about £12¾; and any large purchase of the shares would certainly have raised that price.

Q. 4161. In July, 1887, Lord Lawrence became a Director of the Company. He did so in consequence of a request made to him by the Directors to represent
Q. 4165. the Nizam. Knowing that the Nizam had purchased shares, and "thinking that the concession and the details of the whole thing had been through the
Q. 4166. Government of India and the India Office," Lord Lawrence purchased 500 shares on the Stock Exchange, paying upwards of £6,000 for them. There can be no doubt that Lord Lawrence in all his dealings and connection with the Company has acted in perfect good faith.

Your Committee, having fully considered the evidence brought before them establishing the above facts, have arrived at certain conclusions.

The history of the Hyderabad-Deccan Company shows that the concession has, in fact, proved highly lucrative to the concessionnaires; they have appropriated to themselves and dealt with £850,000 of the capital of the Company, but the question remains, how the 85,000 shares out of the total of 100,000 shares have passed into the hands of the concessionnaires.

It has to be admitted that concessionnaires who hand over a concession to a company are entitled to benefit to a greater or less extent by the transaction. In this case Mr. Watson urges that the concessionnaires were entitled to obtain from the Nizam's Government a large profit, and contends that the concession in its terms admitted of the 85,000 shares being appropriated by the concessionnaires as such profit.

The previous history of the Railway scheme is referred to in support of this view. It was suggested by Mr. Watson that in the matter of the Railway he had done the Nizam's State service, for which he had not been adequately remunerated, but, after considering the service performed by the concessionnaires in promoting the Railway Company, and the amount received by them for such services, your Committee consider that no such deficiency in remuneration exists as to entitle the concessionnaires to obtain the Mining concession.

The Committee desire to abstain from expressing any opinion on the legal rights or liabilities of the Nizam, the concessionnaires, the Company, or individual shareholders. But your Committee are of opinion that the concessionnaires have used the concession for the purpose of realising great gains not intended to be conferred on them, and that this has been done to the injury of the State from which they obtain the concession with the assistance of their partner, Abdul Huk.

It appears to your Committee that throughout the transactions which occurred before the granting of the concession no one, excepting Abdul Huk and the concessionnaires, ever contemplated that the concessionnaires should be entitled to appropriate the £850.000 of capital, or any part of it, to themselves. A first issue of 15,000 shares was contemplated, leaving the remainder of the capital to be issued from time to time, as the development of the gold and diamond fields might require. No one acting in the interests of the Nizam seems to have addressed himself to the question how much the concessionnaires should receive. Mr. Cordery's statement was, "that if it had been pointed out to the Government of India that the Q. 1241.
wording of the contract was such as to admit of such a transaction taking place, they would probably have pointed out to the Nizam's Government, and have suggested that the Nizam's legal advisers, who were responsible for drafting the contract, should look to that point."

The fact that the concessionnaires were placed in a position to claim to appropriate to themselves £850,000 of the capital of the Company was the indirect effect of a set of provisions which were carefully considered with another object.

In support of the course which has been taken, the concessionnaires rely on a clause in the concession which has throughout the negotiations stood in precisely the same terms, except as hereinafter mentioned, as when the concession was signed. It was originally settled by Messrs. White, Borrett, and Co., under the advice of eminent counsel. Under the original suggestion the first issue of capital was to amount to £500,000; such amount was afterwards altered to £150,000. This change was discussed with reference only to the amount which would be required for the immediate operations of the Company, and without any reference to the effect the change would have on the remuneration of the concessionnaires. But the concession at no time contained any direct provision as to what was or was not to be done with the balance of unissued capital. Thus, £150,000 only being necessary for application to the coalfield, and the rest of the capital not being immediately required, unfortunately no express provisions appear to have been inserted in the concession as safeguards to protect the other £850,000 of the capital from being immediately dealt with.

The concession having been framed under the above circumstances, the Directors of the Company entered into the agreement under which the £850,000 of capital was transferred to the concessionnaires. The responsibility for this transfer rests with the Directors, but it is established that no investigations Q. 510.
were made as to the value of the property so transferred, and it was contended Q. 2318. Q. 560.
on behalf of the Company, and alleged by Mr. Batten, the Chairman of the Company, that it was not the duty of anyone to inquire whether the consideration given by the concessionnaires to the Company was or was not of a value equal to the sum received by them. It may be doubtful what was the value of the rights under the concession transferred to the Company, but whatever that value may be, no steps were taken to ascertain it.

It appears to your Committee that the transfer of the 85,000 shares to the concessionnaires, under the circumstances mentioned above, has affected, and will affect, injuriously the interests of the State of Hyderabad. If 85,000 shares still remained unpaid, capital could from time to time be obtained by further issue of shares beyond "the first issue" of 15,000. Such capital so obtained would in the main be expended within the State of Hyderabad, which would necessarily be benefited by such expenditure. But the money which the Nizam and the Government of Hyderabad seem to have regarded as destined to develop the Deccan has passed into the possession of the concessionnaires and their associates. The whole of the shares having been issued, the means of obtaining capital beyond the £1,000,000, the new capital of the Company, can only be regarded as of a speculative character, dependent upon the estimation in which the enterprise may hereafter be regarded by the public, from whom the future means of working the gold and diamond fields will have to be sought.

The circumstances under which the mining concession was obtained show that serious risks to the interests of Native States attend the direct access of London speculators to Native Ministers. In the present case, the initial arrangements were made between Abdul Huk and the concessionnaires; and it was after a settled draft had been prepared under his instructions that particulars were considered by British officials. When the matter came before the Resident, the Government of India, and the Secretary for India, no one of them was aware of the circumstances relating to Abdul Huk which called for a peculiar vigilance; and, apart from this, it is clear that the terms of the concession were subjected to less complete review than they would have gone through had they not been already agreed upon by the accredited negotiator of the Nizam. This result is to be regretted; and it is apparent that if more effective and direct British assistance and advice had been given to the Government of Hyderabad the events that have occurred could not have taken place.

It appears to your Committee that so long as the Government of India interferes with the proceedings of a Native State in business matters, such as granting an important concession, great care should be taken fully to fulfil the responsibility thus assumed; and that there will be considerable difficulty in discharging such duty by the Indian Government if the communications between the Government of the Native State and speculators be allowed to be of a direct character.

August 6, 1888.

PROCEEDINGS OF THE COMMITTEE.

Friday, 1st June, 1888.—Members present: Sir Henry James in the Chair, Mr. Labouchere. Sir Richard Temple, Mr. M'Lagan, Mr. Slagg, Mr. Bristowe, Mr. Solicitor General for Scotland.

The Committee deliberated.

Question, "That the evidence of all witnesses examined before this Committee (except those who shall be exempted by special resolution) shall be taken upon oath, in accordance with the powers conferred upon Committees of the House of Commons by 34 & 35 Vict., c. 83"—(The Chairman),—put, and agreed to.

The Order of the House, 17th May, read, as follows:—

"Ordered, That the Select Committee on East India (Hyderabad Deccan Mining Company) have leave to hear counsel (to such extent as they shall think fit) upon the matters referred to them."

The Committee decided—

That the Committee propose retaining the conduct of the inquiry referred to them entirely in their own hands, but will accept the assistance of counsel when they think it necessary.

That all Witnesses, except as hereinafter mentioned, will be called and examined by the Committee.

That if the Evidence of any Witness shall affect the interests of any person or body represented by counsel, application may be made to the Committee for leave to cross-examine such Witness.

That if it be desired to call any Witness not examined by the Committee, counsel must apply for permission to call such Witness, who will be examined as the Committee may think fit.

That the extent to which counsel may address the Committee will be determined at a later stage of the inquiry.

Messrs. Pember, Q.C., and Lewis Coward appeared as counsel for the Hyderabad Deccan Company, Limited.

Mr. Myburgh appeared as counsel for Mr. Henry Parkinson Sharp.

Mr. Brown appeared as counsel for Mr. James Grahame Stewart.

Messrs. Littler, Q.C., and Cripps appeared as counsel for Mr. William Clarence Watson.

Sir Horace Davey, Q.C., and Messrs. Inverarity and Trevor White appeared as counsel for Abdul Huk.

Messrs. J. D. Mayne, Eardley Norton, and the Hon. A. Lyttleton appeared as counsel for the Nizam of Hyderabad's Government.

Mr. Francis Levien, Mr. Lauchlan L. Hall, and Mr. George H. M. Batten were sworn, and examined.

Adjourned till Tuesday next, at twelve o'clock.

Tuesday, 5th June, 1888.—Members present: Sir Henry James in the Chair, Mr. Solicitor General for Scotland, Mr. Bristowe, Mr. Labouchere, Mr. M'Lagan, Sir Richard Temple.

Mr. Lauchlan L. Hall was further examined.

Mr. R. Stanton Evans and Mr. Charles Albert Winter were sworn, and examined.

Adjourned till Friday next, at twelve o'clock.

Friday, 8th June, 1888.—Members present: Sir Henry James in the Chair, Sir Richard Temple, Mr. Labouchere, Mr. Solicitor General for Scotland, Mr. Bristowe, Mr. Slagg, Mr. M'Lagan.

Mr. William Clarence Watson was sworn, and examined.

Adjourned till Tuesday next, at twelve o'clock.

Tuesday, 12th June, 1888.—Members present: Sir Henry James in the chair, Mr. Labouchere, Sir Richard Temple, Mr. M'Lagan, Mr. Slagg, Mr. Bristowe, Mr. Solicitor General for Scotland.

Resolution of 1st June; –

"That the evidence of all Witnesses examined before this Committee (except those who shall be exempted by special Resolution) shall be taken upon oath, in accordance with the powers conferred upon Committees of the House of Commons by 34 and 35 Vict. c. 83," read.

The Committee resolved—

"That Nawab Mohsin ool Moolk Bahadoor be exempted from the foregoing Resolution, and be examined unsworn."

Nawab Mohsin ool Moolk Bahadoor, examined through an interpreter.

Mr. William Clarence Watson was further examined.

Mr. Fitzgerald, sworn and examined.

Adjourned till Friday next, at twelve o'clock.

Friday, 15th June, 1888.—Members present: Sir Henry James in the Chair, Mr. Labouchere, Sir Richard Temple, Mr. M'Lagan, Mr. Solicitor General for Scotland, Mr. Bristowe, Mr. Slagg.

Mr. John Graham Cordery and General Strachey were sworn and examined.

Adjourned till Tuesday next, at twelve o'clock.

Tuesday, 19th June, 1888.—Members present: Mr. Solicitor General for Scotland, Mr. Labouchere, Sir Richard Temple, Mr. M'Lagan, Mr. Bristowe, Mr. Slagg.

In the absence of the Chairman, Mr. Solicitor General for Scotland was called to the Chair, afterwards Sir Henry James in the Chair.

General Strachey, Mr. William Clarence Watson, and Mr. John G. Cordery, were further examined.

Sir Theodore Hope was sworn, and examined.

Nawab Mohsin ool Moolk Bahadoor was further examined.

Mr. William Morris, Mr. William Henry Bishop, Lord Lawrence (a Member of the House of Lords), and Mr. William Morgans, were sworn, and examined.
Adjourned till Friday next, at two o'clock.

FRIDAY, 22nd June, 1888.—Members present: Mr. Solicitor-General for Scotland, Mr. Bristowe, Mr. Slagg, Mr. Labouchere, Mr. M'Lagan, Sir Richard Temple.
In the absence of the Chairman, Mr. Solicitor General for Scotland was called to the Chair, afterwards Sir Henry James in the Chair.
Sir Edward Bradford was sworn and examined.
Mr. Mayne addressed the Committee on behalf of the Nizam of Hyderabad.
Sir Horace Davey addressed the Committee on behalf of Abdul Huk.
Mr. Littler addressed the Committee on behalf of Mr. Watson.
Mr. Pember addressed the Committee on behalf of the Hyderabad Deccan Company.
Adjourned till Thursday, 26th July, at a quarter past four o'clock.

THURSDAY, 26th July, 1888.—Members present: Sir Henry James in the Chair. Mr. Slagg, Sir Richard Temple, Mr. M'Lagan, Mr. Bristowe, Mr. Labouchere, Mr. Solicitor General for Scotland.
The Committee deliberated.
Adjourned till to-morrow, at a quarter past four o'clock.

FRIDAY, 27th July, 1888.—Members present: Sir Henry James in the Chair, Mr. Labouchere, Sir Richard Temple, Mr. M'Lagan, Mr. Solicitor General for Scotland, Mr. Bristowe, Mr. Slagg.
The Committee deliberated.
Adjourned till Monday next, at twelve o'clock.

MONDAY, 30th July, 1888.—Members present: Sir Henry James in the Chair, Mr. Labouchere, Sir Richard Temple, Mr. M'Lagan, Mr. Solicitor General for Scotland.
The Committee deliberated.
Adjourned till Wednesday next, at twelve o'clock.

WEDNESDAY, 1st August, 1888.—Members present: Sir Henry James in the Chair, Mr. Labouchere, Mr. M'Lagan, Mr. Bristowe, Sir Richard Temple.
The Committee deliberated.
Adjourned till Friday next, at four o'clock.

FRIDAY, 3rd August, 1888.—Members present: Sir Henry James, in the chair, Mr. Labouchere, Mr. M'Lagan, Mr. Solicitor General for Scotland, Mr. Bristowe, Sir Richard Temple.

DRAFT REPORT, proposed by the *Chairman*, read the first time, as follows:
"1. Your Committee have heard evidence on the matters referred to them. An application was made at the commencement of the proceedings, by certain parties interested in the inquiry, to be represented by counsel. Leave having been obtained from the House, counsel were allowed to attend and to take part in the examination of witnesses on certain points. Counsel also addressed your Committee at the close of the evidence. The parties represented by counsel were—His Highness the Nizam, Sirdar Diler Jung (Abdul Huk), the Hyderabad Deccan Company, Limited, Mr. William Clarence Watson, Mr. Henry Parkinson Sharp, Mr. James Graham Stewart.

H. C. No. 338, Session 1887, pp. 26-33.

"2. The following facts were proved before your Committee: On the 7th January, 1886, by an indenture of that date, a concession was granted by the Government of Hyderabad to William Clarence Watson, of 7, Great Winchester Street, London, merchant, and John Stewart of 26, Throgmorton Street, London (who is since deceased).

"3. It will be seen that the concession confers upon the concessionnaires (clause 17) the exclusive right of prospecting or testing for minerals of all kinds throughout the territories of the Nizam, until 31st December, 1891. The concessionnaires also obtain the right to select, during that period, such mines or fields as they desire to acquire for mining operations, and to obtain from the Nizam's Government a lease or leases of such mines or fields as they may select for a term of 99 years from the date of the concession, at royalties to be fixed (clauses 17 and 11) by mining engineers, one to be appointed by each of the parties, or, in default of agreement, by a mining engineer to be appointed by the Government of India. The fixing and determining royalties was to be based and founded on the general principle of a fair rent. Such, generally stated, are the rights applicable to minerals of all kinds, including gold, silver, or precious stones, conferred on the concessionnaires.

H. C. No. 338, Session 1887, p. 32.
Ibid. pp. 32, 28.
Ibid. p. 28.

"4. The concessionnaires came under obligation forthwith to work certain coal-fields, called the Singareni coal-fields. The indenture declared (clause 3) that the first object of the Company was to work the coal-field at Singareni; and that the company were to open up the mine in such a manner that they should be in a position to supply (if so required) not less than 500 tons of good coal per week by the date of the opening of the railway communication to either Hyderabad or Bezwara, or by the 30th June, 1888, at latest. By the indenture (clause 11a) it was provided that the royalties in respect of the Singareni coal-field should be computed on quantities won, and should, if the sales were less than 100,000 British tons per annum, be fixed at eight annas per ton. Any excess over the above quantity might be charged with a higher rate of royalty up to a limit of one rupee per ton.

Ibid. p. 26.
Ibid. p. 28.

"5. The two first clauses of the indenture contain the provisions relating to the formation of a limited company to work the concession. The first clause requires the concessionnaires to form in London a company under the Companies Acts, 1862 to 1880. This was to be done within six months after capital had been raised for the construction of a railway to Singareni. The capital of the Company was to be not less than £1,000,000, with power to increase the capital by an issue of debentures, and otherwise, if necessary.

Ibid. p. 26.

"6. If the Company was formed within the stipulated period, and if before the expiration of that period £150,000 of its share capital at the least was subscribed for, and £75,000 thereof actually paid up, and if the Company adopted the concession, the concessionnaires would be entitled to transfer to the Company the benefits of the concession. On these things being done, and a transfer made and notified to the Nizam's Government, the concessionnaires were to be released from their obligations under the indenture.

Ibid. p. 26

"7. The preamble of the concession makes mention of the previous formation of another Company for the construction of a railway connecting the northern and southern frontiers of the State of Hyderabad. In order to state the circumstances under which the mining concession was obtained, it is necessary briefly to refer to the history of the formation of this railway company.

Ibid. p. 26.

"8. Previous to the formation of this company there existed in the Nizam's territories a somewhat limited railway system. The extension of the railways had been mooted, and this was an object approved of by the Government of India. At first, the project of extending the railways was coupled with a proposal for a mining concession. This double scheme was broached by Mr. Charles Albert Winter in 1881. Mr. Winter was then a solicitor in Bombay, and his firm had acted professionally for the Nizam's Government in 1874 in regard to the old railway system. He is brother-in-law to Mr. William Clarence Watson, one of the concessionnaires; and in those matters Mr. Winter acted, if not by Mr. Watson's authority, at least in reliance on Mr. Watson's co-operation, should business transactions take place. In 1881 Mr. Winter met with Abdul Huk, thereafter Sirdar Diler Jung, at Hyderabad, and negotiated with him on the subject of the railway.

Despatch Foreign Secretary at Calcutta to the Resident of Hyderabad, 17th February, 1882.
Appendix A.
Q. 3681.
Q. 1290.
Q. 1245.
Q. 1242.
Q. 1241.
Q. 1323.
Q. 1752-4.
Q. 1218 et seq.

[Q. 2778-2782.] "9. Abdul Huk was at this time head of the Home Department, and Director of Railways and Mines in Hyderabad. Sir Salar Jung, the elder, was, until his death in February 1883, the Prime Minister of Hyderabad. From beginning to end of the negotiations, regarding both the railway and the mines, [Q. 1275-1300.] Abdul Huk was the accredited agent of the Nizam's Government. He and Mr. Winter came to an understanding, of which the main features were that Mr. Winter and his friends should form a company, to find £2,000,000 for forming extensions of the railways, 5 per cent. on this sum being guaranteed by [Q. 2762.] the Nizam's Government for five years. Mr. Winter and his friends were also [Letter of 17th February, 1882, Government of India Appendix A.] to receive a concession of a mining monopoly in the Deccan. The proposal was ultimately referred to the Viceroy, and the Nizam's Government was informed that the persons connected wtth it were not of sufficient financial standing to render it advisable for that Government to enter into such important monetary relations with them.

[Q. 1290.] "10. Mr. Winter stated to the Committee that he and Abdul Huk arranged that the latter should receive for his own uses '£120,000 for the railway,' and [Q. 1300-8. Appendix B.] also one-fourth interest in the mining concession. Abdul Huk produced to Mr. Winter a letter, dated 5th January, 1882, apparently signed by Sir Salar Jung, written 'to assure you that I shall have no objection to your receiving any remuneration on the railway and mining schemes, with which they may reward your service, and that I shall consider whatever you receive from them as only your due.' The relation thus established between Abdul Huk and the proposed concessionnaires was not, at any period of the subsequent negotiations, disclosed by either of them to the Government either in England or India.

"11. Abdul Huk was subsequently sent to London to endeavour to find someone ready to finance the railroad scheme, and to make some arrangement [Q. 3683.] in respect to the mining concession. The two schemes were left entirely separate. After submitting the railroad proposals to Messrs. Rothschild and [Q. 1313.] to Messrs. Morton, Rose & Co., a Railroad Company was ultimately floated by Mr. Watson, on the agreement that the Nizam should give a guarantee of 5 per cent. for 20 years upon the £2,000,000 which was to be paid to him for the railway, and of which he was to take a portion in the shares of the contemplated Railroad Company which was to provide the £2,000,000. For floating this new Railroad Company Mr. Watson received £100,000, of which he stated that he expended in costs of promotion £93,000, and £83,000 was subsequently paid to Abdul Huk for his services in connection with the negotiation.

"12. The attitude of the British Government during those negotiations of Abdul Huk is indicated in two despatches written, one by the Marquis of [Appendix C. H. C. No. 398, Sess. 1887, p. 9. Q. 3669.] Hartington, dated 24th May, 1882, and the other by the Earl of Kimberley, dated 5th July, 1883, on the occasion, in each instance, of Abdul Huk announcing his arrival in London on his mission. By the despatch of 24th May, 1882, Abdul Huk was informed by the Secretary of State for India that he was at full liberty to act upon the instructions of the Nizam; that the Secretary of State would be ready at any time during the progress of the negotiations to give him such advice and assistance as he might desire, and would expect to be informed of any engagements into which he might purpose to enter before their actual completion; and that the Secretary of State would recognise no liability, financial or otherwise, in relation to any Company or persons with whom Abdul Huk might negotiate, excepting so far as a specific contract might be entered into directly between the Company, the Secretary of State, and the Nizam's Government, with the intention of defining such liabilities. [Appendix D. Q. 3675.] The Government of India, during the negotiations, by a despatch of 15th March, 1883, laid it down that they, as the paramount power in India, were bound to satisfy themselves in transactions of this nature—(1) that the Native Government fully realised its responsibility and obligations; (2) that every reasonable precaution had been taken to protect its interests; (3) that the European contractors distinctly understood that the Government of India disclaim all responsibility whatsoever in respect of the soundness of the basis on which their proposals may be founded, and of the general success of the enterprise to which such proposals related.

"13. Meantime the project of a mining concession proceeded separately. In 1883 Abdul Huk, having been informed by the India Office that the proposal for the mining concession put forward by Mr. Watson ought to be submitted to advisers of experience, instructed Messrs. White, Borrett & Co. to act on behalf of his Government in settling the terms of a mining concession with Mr. Watson and Mr. Stewart. The draft of a concession was accordingly Q. 3608. prepared, and, after negotiations which lasted several months, was settled by Messrs. White, Borrett & Co., with the advice of eminent Counsel (Mr., now Q. 1943. Lord, Macnaghten, and Mr. Blakesley). But Abdul Huk was informed by the India Office that it would be desirable that the project should be submitted to H. C. No. 338, Session 1887, the Nizam's Government, and that further negotiations in respect to it should pp. 4, 33. take place at Hyderabad before it was finally adopted.

"14. Abdul Huk returned to Hyderabad with the draft of the concession. It was considered by the Nizam's Minister, Salar Jung the younger, who *Ibid.* p. 5. canvassed several points in the draft, and then submitted it as accepted by him *Ibid.* p. 20. to the Resident, by whom it was transmitted to the Government of India at Calcutta, together with the letter of Salar Jung, dated 14th January, 1885. The Government of India carefully considered the draft, and approved generally of it, but they proposed a number of alterations in various clauses. Two memoranda were forwarded to the Resident, one describing the alterations *Ibid.* p. 20. suggested, while the other explained the grounds on which they were recom- *Ibid.* p. 21. mended. The Resident was requested to recommend to the Minister of the *Ibid.* p. 20. Nizam and to the agent of the Company, that the agreement should be concluded; that is, that the concession should be granted on terms embodying the suggested alterations. Such alterations, together with some further modifications, were agreed to, and the concession was signed on the 7th January, 1886.

"15. Upon the concession being signed it was forwarded to the Government of India. The fact of the execution of the concession was communicated to the Secretary of State for India by a telegram dated 29th January, 1886. On *Ibid.* pp. 3, 4. the 2nd of February, 1886, a letter was sent by the Governor-General and Council to the Secretary of State for India, in which the following sentence occurs: "We have considered, in connection with the observations in the concluding portion of the 23rd paragraph of the despatch, No. 19, Railway, dated 21st *Ibid.* pp. 4, 5. February, 1884, from the Right Honourable the Secretary of State for India, that any liabilities which might be incurred in pursuance of this agreement, under 37 Geo. 3, c. 142, s. 28, would be removed by the formal 'consent and approbation' of the Governor-General in Council 'in writing,' but as your Lordship has suggested that the previous approval of the Secretary of State is desirable to contracts of the nature of this agreement, we would solicit that we may be favoured with this sanction by telegram." The subject of the concession was considered by the Secretary of State for India in Council, and certain conditions being imposed, they were communicated to the concessionnaires and agreed to by them. On 27th July, 1886, the sanction of the Secretary of State, *Ibid.* p. 36 conditional on such modifications, was intimated to Mr. Watson in London.

"16. The Hyderabad Deccan Company, Limited, was forthwith registered, its objects being to acquire and work the concession. The fifth clause of the Memorandum of Association was as follows:—

"'5. The capital of the Company is £1,000,000, in 100,000 shares of £10 each. Any shares in the capital of the Company may be issued as fully, or in part, paid up, in payment for the said concession, or any other property which the Company is authorised to acquire; and the shares of which the capital shall from time to time consist may be divided into different classes, with such preferences, priorities, restrictions, or special incidents, as may from time to time be prescribed by the Articles and Special Resolutions of the Company.'

"17. The Articles of Association contained the following Articles:—

"'Article 3. The Board may make and carry into effect any agreement with any company, association, or person, whether a Director or Promoter of the Company or not, for any of the objects referred to in the Memorandum of Association, and any such person shall, notwithstanding that he is a Director or Promoter of the Company, be entitled to retain the benefit or profit of the agreement.

"'Article 12. The Board shall consist of such number of Directors as a general meeting shall from time to time determine, and until and subject to such determination shall consist of any number not more than seven nor less than three.

"'Article 14. The first three Directors of the Company shall be appointed by the subscribers of the Memorandum of Association of the Company. The Board may at any time before the ordinary meeting to be held in the year 1888, appoint duly qualified persons as additional Directors, so that the total number of Directors shall not at any one time exceed seven without the authority of a general meeting. The first Directors, and any others appointed under this article (except such of them as shall in the meantime vacate their offices under any of the provisions of these presents), shall continue in office for two years from the incorporation of the Company.'

"18. The persons subscribing the Memorandum were, besides the two concessionnaires, Messrs. Winter, Hemmerdy, Batten, Pearce, and Milne. It is sufficient at present to say that those gentlemen were all friends of or employed by the concessionnaires.

Minutes of Hyderabad (Deccan) Company.

"19. On 10th August, 1886, these gentlemen met and elected as Directors, Mr. Batten, Mr. Hemmerdy, and Mr. Milne. On the same day the Directors met, and the minutes of the Board record the following proceedings:—

"'The Agreement between the concessionnaires, the applicants for 15,000 shares of the Company, being the agreement to transfer the concession to the Company, was submitted and explained and approved. It was resolved that the common seal of the Company be affixed thereto, in accordance with the Articles of Association, when and so soon as £5 per share has been paid by the allottees of the 15,000 shares to the Company's bankers.

"'The application for the 15,000 shares by the persons described in the schedule to the above-mentioned agreement was considered, and the shares numbered 1 to 15,000, inclusive, were allotted as follows:—

John Stewart - - - - - - -	5,000
Henry Parkinson Sharp - - - - -	5,000
William Clarence Watson - - - -	4,599
Charles Albert Winter - - - - - -	100
George H. M. Batten - - - - - -	100
James Hemmerdy - - - - - - -	100
John Martyn Milne - - - - - -	100
Richard Pearce - - - - - - -	1
	15,000

"'Resolved,—That the National Provincial Bank of England, Limited, 112, Bishopsgate Street, E.C., be appointed the bankers of the Company.

"'Resolved,—That the allottees be requested to pay forthwith to the Company's bankers £5 per share, and that allotment letters be prepared and sent to them. The secretary submitted an agreement between the Company and Messrs. Watson and Stewart, prepared in pursuance of the before-mentioned agreement in relation to the 85,000 shares to be numbered 15,001 to 100,000, and to be allotted as fully-paid shares to them.

"'Resolved,—That the same be approved, and the common seal of the

Company affixed thereto after the first-named agreement has been sealed, and
that the same be then duly filed with the Registrar of Joint Stock Companies.'

"20. Of these Directors, Mr. Batten originally obtained and paid for 100 Q. 628.
of the shares with £5 paid on them. In October, 1886, Mr. Watson paid Mr. Q. 629.
Batten £500 for those 100 shares, and at the same time transferred to Mr.
Batten 100 fully paid-up shares. At the time of this transfer, and since, no
payment for these last-mentioned shares has been made, but Mr. Batten stated Q. 632, 633.
that if the Company paid a dividend he was to pay Mr. Watson for them, or to Q. 486 Q. 4124.
return them. Mr. Hemmerdy, on 3rd October, received from Mr. Watson Q. 4116.
1,000 fully paid-up shares. Dealings in the shares had previously taken place
at the price of £9 per share. As accounting for this gift Mr. Watson stated, 'Mr.
Hemmerdy was an old friend of mine, and I gave these shares to him (I hoped Q. 4199.
they would be worth £10,000) for many services he had rendered to me for
twenty years previously.' 4117.

"21. Of the two agreements thus approved the former effected the transfer of Appendix E.
the concession to the Company, the allotment to the persons named of the 15,000
shares with £5 paid, and the allotment of the 85,000 fully-paid being terms
of the bargain. The other agreement between the Company and Mr. Watson Appendix F.
and Mr. Stewart set forth that it had been agreed that the concessionnaires
should assign and transfer to the Company the concession, and that in exchange
the Company should allot to the concessionnaires 85,000 shares of £10 each in
the Company, which shares should be deemed for all purposes to be fully paid
up. It was, therefore, thereby agreed that the Company should allot to the
concessionnaires or their nominees 85,000 fully paid-up shares in the Company,
and that the shares should be numbered 15,001 to 100,000, inclusive, and
should be accepted by the concessionnaires in full satisfaction of all claims and
demands whatsoever of the concessionnaires in respect of the transfer of the Q. 585, 589.
concession. These agreements had been drawn by the solicitors of the Company
on the instructions of the concessionnaires.

"22. The £5 per share on the 15,000 shares were duly paid into the Q. 767.
Company's bank; and thereupon the two agreements were sealed, and the contract as to the allotment of 85,000 fully paid-up shares was registered with
the Registrar of Joint Stock Companies. These conditions having been fulfilled,
the Directors (Mr. Batten, Mr. Hemmerdy, and Mr. Milne), on 19th August,
1886, proceeded to allot to Mr. Watson and Mr. Stewart the 85,000 shares as
fully paid-up, and certificates were signed, sealed, and handed to the allottees.

"23. The shares of the Company having been distributed as mentioned
above, Mr. Watson and Mr. Stewart were, on 24th August, 1886, appointed
additional directors; on the same day Mr. Milne resigned his directorship to
become Secretary. On 2nd November, Mr. Henry Parkinson Sharp was elected
a director, and Mr. Hemmerdy retired from the direction on 10th November,
1886.

"24. The 85,000 shares issued as paid-up, when received by Mr. Watson
and Mr. Stewart, were by them divided among the partners in the enterprise,
viz., Mr. Watson, Mr. Stewart, Abdul Huk, each a fourth; Mr. Winter, Mr.
Henry Parkinson Sharp, and others participating in the remaining fourth.
Abdul Huk's name does not appear as an allottee or transferee of shares in the
Minute Book; but the proportion of the shares to be received by him were Q. 1639.
transferred to Mr. Winter; they were then turned into share warrants to Q. 1651-6
bearer; and these latter were lodged with the bankers of Abdul Huk on his
account. At the same time he received one-fourth share of the 15,000 shares,
and at a later date he paid, through Mr. Winter, £5 per share upon them.

"25. Before the allotment of shares no reports upon the value of the rights Q. 168
conceded were received by the directors or promoters of the Company. At a
later date, and when dealings on the Stock Exchange were taking place on the
shares, such reports were received from Mr. Hughes and Mr. Furnivall. Mr.
Hughes is a Government official in India, being one of 'the Superintendents of

Q. 1051. the Survey,' and had been employed as such in the geological examination of
Q. 1052. Hyderabad and contiguous districts. The Secretary of State for India, upon
being applied to, granted permission for Mr. Hughes to be employed and paid
by the Company, in order 'to see really what was the value of the concession
they had got from the Nizam.' Before any reports were made in May, 1887,
Q. 4138. Mr. Watson transferred to Mr. Hughes 200 fully paid-up shares, and 200 shares
with £5 paid on them. At the then market price, these 400 shares were
Q. 4139. worth £3,200. Mr. Hughes paid Mr. Watson £1,000 for them. On 4th July
Q. 4146. Mr. Hughes re-transferred the 200 fully paid-up shares to Mr. Watson, receiving
Q. 4153. £2,390 for them. The 200 shares with £5 paid on them were retained by Mr.
Q. 4155. Hughes. Mr. Watson stated that this transaction amounted to a gift by him
to Mr. Hughes, but that "it was not (made) to make reports, but that he (Mr.
Q. 4156. Hughes) might work and throw his whole energies into it." Reports were also
Q. 2852. received from Mr. Furnivall. This gentleman was an engineer, formerly in the
Q. 4175. Q. 4179. employ of the Government of India, but now retired upon a pension. Mr.
Watson gave Mr. Furnivall '500 shares for nothing.' These shares were sold
by Mr. Furnivall at £11 per share, therefore realising £5,500.

"26. It is to be observed that the share in the concession received by Abdul Huk is in accordance with the terms of the arrangement made with Mr. Winter in 1881, as above set forth.

Q. 877. "27. The shares of the Company began to change hands, but not to
Q. 2114. any considerable extent prior to the first statutory meeting of the Company on
26th November 1886. At that time Mr. R. Stanton Evans, a gentleman engaged
Q. 863. in financial operations in the City, began to sell the shares for Mr. Watson on
Q. 875-941. Q. 2117. the terms that Mr. Watson should pay to Mr. Evans 10s. on every share sold
Q. 1152. by him 'over par and up to a certain premium,' and the shares were freely
Q. 2393. bought and sold on the Stock Exchange from that time. Of the 85,000 shares
issued as fully paid-up, about 55,000 have been sold to the public. There are
now about 700 shareholders. The prices of the shares ranged, during the
period between September 1886 and April 1888, from £13¾ to £5⅞. Mr.
Watson, by dealing in his fourth of the 85,000 shares and by transactions in
buying and selling shares in the market, had, at the time when he gave his
Q. 3576-3582. evidence, realised £209,300 (out of which he had paid in brokerage and
commissions £20,929), and he still retained 5,559 shares. Mr. Watson had
also given away many shares.

"28. It should be remarked that whilst numerous transactions in these
shares took place on the Stock Exchange, no application for a settlement or
quotation was made to the Committee of that body, and although the evidence
Q. 3. shows that operations in the shares of companies for which no such application
Q. 20. is made frequently occur on these occasions, the rules and regulations of the
Stock Exchange are entirely disregarded, and it will be observed that had a
settlement been applied for and granted in the shares of this Company, the
85,000 shares allotted to the concessionnaires would have been excluded from
Q. 10. that settlement, not being a good delivery on the Stock Exchange.

"It will also be observed that had a quotation been applied for, it would not have been granted, as the rules and conditions of the Stock Exchange with regard to these matters had not been complied with.

Q. 2131, 2532. "29. No prospectus of the Company was issued; and the title 'prospectus
was disclaimed before your Committee for the Memorandum which is afterwards
mentioned. The method adopted by the sellers seems to have been not to place
before the public specific information, but to stimulate interest by affording hints
and glimpses of the magnitude of the enterprise. At the same time the fact
Q. 1220. that the 85,000 shares had been issued as fully-paid to the concessionnaires
Appendix G. cannot be said to have been a secret. A paragraph in the money article in the
'Standard' newspaper of 13th December, 1886, drew attention to the transactions, and set out at length the agreement between the concessionnaires and the
Q. 1214. Company, dated 17th August, 1886. Again, 'Burdett's Official Intelligence,'

which is a publication giving particulars of companies, in its issue of February,
1887, contained a description of the Hyderabad-Deccan Company, in which it
was stated that 'The 85,000 fully-paid shares, 15,001 to 100,000, represent the
price at which the concessionnaires transferred the concession to the Company.
The 15,000 shares with £5 paid (No. 1 to 15,000) were subscribed for by the
concessionnaires. All the 100,000 shares have an equal right to participate in
the profits of the undertaking.' The balance-sheet of the Company issued in Q. 322, 2860
July, 1887, sets forth in its first entry on the credit side, 'By purchase of concession, £850,000,' while on the other side the capital is stated as £1,000,000 in
100,000 shares of £10 each, of which 85,000 are fully-paid and 15,000 £5 paid.
This balance-sheet and the Memorandum and Articles of Association were sent
to the Nizam's Government. A printed Memorandum regarding the Company,
of which Mr. Watson says he had some thirty copies printed in order to give
information to people asking for shares (but the statements in which obtained, Q. 2534.
perhaps, a more extended publicity than is indicated by those numbers), contained Appendix II.
a description of the scheme, very favourably coloured. It will be observed by
reference to this Memorandum that no statement is made in it which would
convey to the public that the 85,000 shares had been passed to the concessionnaires under the circumstances mentioned above. The Memorandum was
headed, 'Capital £1,000,000 in 100,000 shares of £10 each, 85,000 being fully-
paid, and 15,000 on which £5 per share is paid.'

"30. The Company have been carrying on mining operations in the Q. 115-121,
Singareni Coal Fields to the extent of raising about 150 tons a week. They 503-4. Q. 505.
have also been prospecting for diamonds and for gold. Five diamonds have Q. 2568, 2900.
been found in some refuse. No gold has been produced, but Mr. Watson Q. 2903. Q. 2980-1.
relies on the reports of Mr. Hughes, Mr. Furnivall, Mr. Lowinsky, and others,
stating the existence of auriferous and diamantiferous strata. Your Committee
express no opinion as to the prospects of the enterprise. It was stated by Mr.
Watson that no dissatisfaction with his investment has been expressed by any
of the shareholders, except in one instance, but beyond this statement no Q. 3654, 2539.
evidence on the subject was brought before your Committee.

"31. On 3rd June, 1887, there were purchased on the Stock Exchange
for the Nizam's Government, 8,750 fully-paid and 3,750 £5 paid shares of the
Company.

"32. The importance of this transaction, as affecting the Nizam's Government, Q. 1691.
is largely abated by the fact that since your Committee begun its sittings, they
have been authoritatively informed that the purchase has been rescinded by
arrangement, and the money expended by the Nizam has been refunded to His
Highness. The facts attending this purchase appear to be as follows:—

"33. The resolution of the Nizam's Government to invest in shares of the
Company was deliberately arrived at. Nawab Mahdi Ali, who gave evidence
before your Committee, and who is and was at the time, Political and Financial Appendix .
Secretary of the Nizam's Government, had placed before him a memorandum
by Abdul Huk, which, while recommending the investment, discussed very Q. 2760.
fully the objections to it that might be stated on account of its speculative
nature. The Nawab Mahdi Ali recommended the proposal, and it was Q. 2761.
sanctioned by the Nizam. The Resident, Mr. Cordery, approved of the
purchase, and Abdul Huk was ordered to purchase 10,000 shares at the most
favourable terms up to £12 per share.

"34. When the shares were bought, Abdul Huk was in London, and he
carried out the purchase in concert with Mr. Watson. The documents which
record the transaction somewhat exaggerate its complexity. What was done,
in fact, was that Abdul Huk received the price, and handed over to the Nizam
so many of the shares which had fallen to himself in the distribution of the
shares of the concessionnaires. The method adopted to accomplish this object H. C. No. 141,
was somewhat circuitous. Mr. Watson and Abdul Huk met in the office of the Session 1888, pp. 54-60
former, but their communications in respect of the purchase purport to be Q. 951.

expressed in their letters set out in the Appendix to this Report. Mr. Watson
deemed it to be necessary to consult Mr. Evans. All were agreed that the transac-
tion, to be duly carried out, must be effected by way of sale and purchase on
Q. 992-997. the Stock Exchange. Mr. Evans employed, and sent into the Stock Exchange,
Q. 1095 six separate brokers, with orders to buy, and at the same time employed a
Q. 1099-1100, 2193. broker to sell at an arranged price. Each person concerned received a com-
Q. 2189 Q. 1097, 1110. mission. Mr. Watson, in his evidence, said that he considered it to be desirable
that the transaction should be recorded, and Mr. Evans understood the object
to be that it should be known on the Stock Exchange that the Nizam's Government was buying shares, and that this would be a good thing for the Company.
The shares thus purported to be bought and sold all belonged to Abdul Huk,
who, in consideration for the shares thus transferred to the Nizam, received
£131,250 of money belonging to the Government of Hyderabad.

Q. 2157 "35. It does not appear that at the time in question shares could have
Q. 1228. been obtained at a lower rate than was actually paid to Abdul Huk. The
market price was about £12¾; and any large purchase of the shares would
certainly have raised that price.

Q. 4461. "36. In July 1887, Lord Lawrence became a Director of the Company.
Q. 4463. He did so in consequence of a request made to him by the Directors to
represent the Nizam. Knowing that the Nizam had purchased shares, and
'thinking that the concession and the details of the whole thing had been
Q. 4466. through the Government of India and the India Office,' Lord Lawrence purchased 500 shares on the Stock Exchange, paying upwards of £6,000 for them.
There can be no doubt that Lord Lawrence in all his dealings and connection
with the Company has acted in perfect good faith.

"37. Your Committee, having fully considered the evidence brought before them, establishing the above facts, have arrived at certain conclusions.

"38. The history of the Hyderabad-Deccan Company shows that the concession has, in fact, proved highly lucrative to the concessionnaires; they have appropriated to themselves and dealt with £850,000 of the capital of the Company, but the question remains how the 85,000 shares out of the total of 100,000 shares have passed into the hands of the concessionnaires.

"39. It has to be admitted that concessionnaires who hand over a concession to a company are entitled to benefit to a greater or less extent by the transaction. In this case Mr. Watson urges that the concessionnaires were entitled to obtain from the Nizam's Government a large profit, and contends that the concession in its terms admitted of the 85,000 shares being appropriated by the concessionnaires as such profit.

"40. The previous history of the railway scheme is referred to in support of this view. It was suggested by Mr. Watson that in the matter of the railway he had done the Nizam's State service for which he had not been adequately remunerated, but after considering the services performed by the concessionnaires in promoting the railway company, and the amount received by them for such services, your Committee consider that no such deficiency in remuneration existed as to entitle the concessionnaires to obtain the mining concession.

"41. The Committee desire to abstain from expressing any opinion on the legal rights or liabilities of the Nizam, the concessionnaires, the Company, or individual shareholders. But your Committee are of opinion that the concessionnaires have used the concession for the purpose of realising great gains not intended to be conferred on them, and that this has been done to the injury of the State from which they obtained the concession with the assistance of their partner, Abdul Huk.

"42. It appears to your Committee that throughout the transactions which occurred before the granting of the concession no one, excepting Abdul Huk and the concessionnaires, ever contemplated that the concessionnaires should be entitled to appropriate the £850,000 of capital, or any part of it to themselves. A first issue of 15,000 shares was contemplated, leaving the remainder of the capital to be issued from time to time, as the development of the gold and diamond fields might require. No one acting in the interests of the Nizam seems to have addressed himself to the question how much the concessionnaires should receive. Mr. Cordery's statement was, 'that if it had been pointed out to the Government of India that the working of the contract was Q. 4241. such as to admit of such a transaction taking place, they would probably have pointed out to the Nizam's Government, and have suggested that the Nizam's legal advisers, who were responsible for drafting the contract, should look to that point.'

"The fact that the concessionnaires were placed in a position to claim to appropriate to themselves £850,000 of the capital of the Company was the indirect effect of a set of provisions which were carefully considered with another object.

"43. In support of the course which has been taken the concessionnaires rely on a clause in the concession which has throughout the negotiations stood in precisely the same terms, except as hereinafter mentioned, as when the concession was signed. It was originally settled by Messrs. White, Borrett and Co., under the advice of eminent counsel. Under the original suggestion the first issue of capital was to amount to £500,000; such amount was afterwards altered to £150,000. This change was discussed with reference only to the amount which would be required for the immediate operations of the Company, and without any reference to the effect the change would have on the remuneration of the concessionnaires. But the concession at no time contained any direct provision as to what was or was not to be done with the balance of unissued capital. Thus, £150,000 only being necessary for application to the coal-field, and the rest of the capital not being immediately required, unfortunately no express provisions appear to have been inserted in the concession as safeguards to protect the other £850,000 of the capital from being immediately dealt with.

"44. The concession having been framed under the above circumstances, the Directors of the Company entered into the agreement under which the £850,000 of capital was transferred to the concessionnaires. The responsibility Q. 510. for this transfer rests with the Directors, but it is established that no investiga- Q. 2318. Q. 560. tions were made as to the value of the property so transferred, and it was contended on behalf of the Company, and alleged by Mr. Batten, the Chairman of the Company, that it was not the duty of anyone to inquire whether the consideration given by the concessionnaires to the Company was or was not of a value equal to the sum received by them. It may be doubtful what was the value of the rights under the concession transferred to the Company, but whatever that value may be, no steps were taken to ascertain it.

"45. It appears to your Committee that the transfer of the 85,000 shares to the concessionnaires under the circumstances mentioned above has affected, and will affect, injuriously the interests of the State of Hyderabad. If 85,000 shares still remained unpaid, capital could, from time to time, be obtained by further issues of shares beyond 'the first issue' of 15,000. Such capital so obtained would in the main be expended within the State of Hyderabad, which would necessarily be benefited by such expenditure. But the money which the Nizam and the Government of Hyderabad seem to have regarded as destined to develop the Deccan has passed into the possession of the concessionnaires and their associates. The whole of the shares having been issued, the means of obtaining capital beyond the £1,000,000, the now capital of the Company, can only be regarded as of a speculative character, dependent upon the estimation in which the enterprise may hereafter be regarded by the public, from whom the future means of working the gold and diamond fields will have to be sought.

"46. The circumstances under which the mining concession was obtained show that serious risks to the interests of Native States attend the direct access of London speculators to Native Ministers. In the present case, the initial arrangements were made between Abdul Huk and the concessionnaires; and it was after a settled draft had been prepared under his instructions that particulars were considered by British officials. When the matter came before the Resident, the Government of India, and the Secretary for India, no one of them was aware of the circumstances relating to Abdul Huk which called for a peculiar vigilance; and, apart from this, it is clear that the terms of the concession were subjected to less complete review than they would have gone through had they not have been already agreed upon by the accredited negotiator of the Nizam. This result is to be regretted, and it is apparent that if more effective and direct British assistance and advice had been given to the Government of Hyderabad the events that have occurred could not have taken place.

"It appears to your Committee that so long as the Government of India interferes with the proceedings of a Native State in business matters, such as granting an important concession, great care should be taken fully to fulfil the responsibility thus assumed; and that there will be considerable difficulty in discharging such duty by the Indian Government if the communications between the Government of the Native States and speculators be allowed to be of a direct character."

Question, That the Draft Report, proposed by the Chairman, be read a second time, paragraph by paragraph,—put, and agreed to.

Paragraphs 1—45, agreed to.

Paragraph 46.—Amendment proposed in line 13, after the word "place," to insert the words "Those who officially controlled this affair in England and India do not seem to have acted on a sufficiently definite view of their relations towards the Nizam as the head of a Native State. They asserted their right to interfere, but did not render their interference so effective as to afford that protection which the Nizam's Government and possible investors in this country had a right to expect. They did too much or not enough. There also appears to have been a want of consistent policy in the official proceedings, and General Strachey's evidence indicates the extreme difficulty of fixing upon any single official the responsibility for any error or omission. Such handling is to be deprecated, for it must often leave a loophole for practices like those of Mr. Watson and his associates, on which the Committee have been animadverting" (Mr. Labouchere). Question put,

That these words be there inserted.—The Committee divided:

Ayes, 2.	Noes, 2.
Mr. Labouchere.	Mr. Bristowe.
Sir Richard Temple.	Mr. Solicitor General for Scotland.

Whereupon the Chairman declared himself with the Noes.

Paragraph agreed to.

Amendment proposed, That the following new paragraph be added to the Report:—

"In conclusion, your Committee bear in mind the fact that Mr. Watson and his associates were enabled to do what has been described by your Committee in the foregoing paragraphs is due to what was virtually a defect in the agreement as settled in England. This defect was aggravated by the alterations made in India by the Government. But it existed apart from these alterations, and was not brought into existence by them. Your Committee proceed to consider briefly how far the officers of the Government in India and England are responsible for not observing and remedying this defect. There are several links in the chain of official responsibility, and at each point a failure occurred in one and the same respect. First, the British Resident at Hyderabad had an understanding of the intention of the concession, and certainly, as so understood, the intention was reasonable and just. But it was his business to see that this intention was carried out. Now, the terms of the concession-agreement received from England, as drafted under legal advice, were, as the event has shown, in one respect defective. It was hardly in the power of the Resident who had no legal advice on the spot at Hyderabad, to perceive or to rectify the defect. So far, he is excusable. But he submitted the case to the Government of India, his immediate superior, and it pertained to that Government to consult the legal advisers at its command, and to render the agreement safe in all respects. If, however, these legal advisers did not perceive the defect, perhaps the omission of the Government of India may be in some degree excused. But inasmuch as considerable attention was given to several details in the case, it is unfortunate that the flaw in the agreement escaped detection. Further, the proceedings were under the observation of the Secretary of State for India in Council. It was under advice from that Department of State that Abdul Huk instructed Messrs. White and Borrett, the solicitors, to draft the agreement. Possibly the fault in this agreement may have been due to the instructions thus received. But in this, as in other parts of the case, the India Office does not appear to have undertaken any complete responsibility, as is to be inferred from the evidence of General Strachey, a member of the Indian Council in England, and considered itself to be acting partly as a supervisor and partly as a friendly counsellor. It appears to your Committee preferable that if the British Government interferes to exercise any control, the control should be effective throughout, especially as the known fact of Governmental interference will induce investors to place confidence in the undertaking. Your Committee deem it necessary to indicate the exact steps in official responsibility throughout this case, without, however, attributing any particular blame to any officer of Government under the circumstances. But the experience of this case ought not to be lost in the future. It seems to your Committee that transactions of this nature between European speculators and any Native State in India ought from first to last be under the absolute supervision of the Government of India, to be exercised through its political residents or agents on the spot, subject, of course, to the general control of the Secretary of State in England. Thus, there will be a real security against miscarriages such as those which have happened in this case, and the official responsibility will be definitely fixed "—(Sir Richard Temple).

Question put, That the proposed New Paragraph be added to the Report.

The Committee divided:

Ayes, 2.	Noes, 2.
Sir Richard Temple.	Mr. Solicitor-General for Scotland.
Mr. Labouchere.	Mr. Bristowe.

Whereupon the Chairman declared himself with the Noes.

Question, That this Draft Report be the Report of the Committee to the House,—put, and agreed to.

Ordered, to Report, together with Minutes of Evidence, and an Appendix.

LIST OF WITNESSES.

The Report of the Select Committee of the House of Commons on the Hyderabad Deccan Mining Company has been issued to-day, and it is stated to-night, on what professes to be the best authority, that Mr. E. H. Pollard, the counsel to whom the Report was submitted on behalf of the Nizam's representatives, has declared that the concession was obtained by unlawful means, and that the Hyderabad Government are legally entitled to have it cancelled. The Hyderabad authorities are said to be now considering, in conjunction with the Imperial Government, what further steps shall be taken in view of Mr. Pollard's opinion.—*Glasgow Herald*, August 25.

It is reported, on what purports to be good authority, that the Government of the Nizam of Hyderabad contemplate raising a special loan for the purpose of irrigation works in the State of Hyderabad. It is to be hoped that the Nizam will be more fortunate in his agents in this country than he has been hitherto.—*Stock Exchange*, August 25.

Nawab Mehdi Ali, the Hyderabad noble who has spent several months in this country in connection with the Parliamentary Inquiry into the Deccan Mining Scandal, and who was one of the "lions" of the past season, leaves England on the 11th of September, and will embark for Bombay at Port Said on the 17th of October. *En route* the Nawab will make a pilgrimage to Constantinople, where he will doubtless be heartily welcomed by his co-religionists. The Chief Justice of Hyderabad, Nawab Mehdi Hasan, returns to India with the Nizam's delegate, but does not call at the Turkish capital. He will be a guest at the Cutlers' banquet, and respond on behalf of his native country to the toast—a novel toast, I believe, at that gathering—of "Our Colonial and Indian Empire."—*Manchester Guardian*, August 28.

I hear that the Government of the Nizam has, under what practically may be said to be the orders of the India Office, but which that Office is pleased to call "advice," removed the business connected with Hyderabad Deccan Mining from the eminent firm of solicitors which had it in hand before the Committee of the House of Commons, and placed it under the control of another firm. The only ground for this can be that the first firm was not sufficiently subservient to the India Office.

Should this system of interference continue, it will be necessary to ask the House of Commons to grant a Committee to inquire into the entire relations of the India Office and its officials with the Government of the Nizam. The evidence of General Strachey, who appeared before the House of Commons Committee on the Mining Scandals, was most unsatisfactory. He seemed to consider that the House of Commons was guilty of impertinence in having sought to investigate these scandals, that India is an Empire which exists solely for the benefit of the Strachey and other Anglo-Indian families, and that for the House of Commons to dare to call upon such high and mighty personages to explain their conduct was a positive crime.

By his evidence, General Strachey showed that Mr. Watson, an obscure financial agent in London; Mr. Winter, an obscure solicitor in Bombay; Mr. Parkinson Sharp, already known, not too favourably, in connection with the House of Commons Committee that sat some years ago on the Foreign Loans scandals; and Abdul Huk, an *employé* of the Nizam, whose relations with the India Office seemed to be particularly intimate, had been able to secure to themselves the modest trifle of £850,000 for a concession that cost them nothing, and was about worth what it cost them, through the negligence, incompetence, and stupidity of a Committee of the India Office, of which the

General was the leading spirit. He further admitted that Sir Richard Strachey, his brother, had been made Chairman of a Hyderabad Railway by Mr. Watson, the concession for which he had obtained with the approval of this India Office Committee, and that Mr. Batten, a brother-in-law to the Stracheys, had been made the Chairman of the Mining Company, which was the outcome of the concession.

Under these circumstances it would be well for the India Office to be exceedingly careful in its dealings with the Hyderabad scandals. Instead of doing its best during the sittings of the Mining Scandals Committee of the House of Commons to make things clear, it sought in every way—even by bullying the Nizam's representatives in England—to hush up the affair; and if it continues to pursue this course, it will only bring further discredit upon its mode of transacting business, and render a further and more searching investigation necessary.—*Truth*, August 30.

A SECOND report of the proceedings of the Select Committee of the House of Commons appointed to inquire into matters affecting the Hyderabad Deccan Mining Company, has been issued. This supplementary report, however, indicates more of the inner workings of the Select Committee itself than it serves to throw any fresh light upon the tangled skein which the Committee was appointed to unravel. It appears that the Committee held five meetings for the consideration of their report before its final adoption was decided upon. The originally drafted report was presented by the Chairman, and at the final sitting Sir Richard Temple and Mr. Labouchere proposed the addition of an important paragraph, the intention being to fix direct official responsibility for the future.

This paragraph was important. It stated that: "Mr. Watson and his associates were enabled to do what has been described by your Committee in the foregoing paragraphs, in consequence of what was virtually a defect in the agreement as settled in England. This defect was aggravated by the alterations made in India by the Government." It then pointed out that the India Office did not appear to have undertaken any complete responsibility, and concluded with the following sentences: "If the British Government interferes to exercise any control, the control should be effective throughout, especially as the known fact of Governmental interference will induce investors to place confidence in the undertaking. . . . . The experience of this case ought not to be lost in the future. It seems to your Committee that transactions of this nature between European speculators and any Native State in India ought, from first to last, to be under the absolute supervision of the Government of India, to be exercised through its political residents or agents on the spot, subject, of course, to the general control of the Secretary of State in England. Thus there will be a real security against miscarriages such as those which have happened in this case, and the official responsibility will be definitely fixed."

It seems to us a pity that this paragraph was ultimately rejected, as unfortunately was the case. There were five members of the Committee present on the occasion of its retention being moved, but on a division being taken, Sir Richard Temple and Mr. Labouchere voted for it, and the Solicitor-General for Scotland and Mr. Bristowe opposed it. Under these circumstances the Chairman gave his casting vote for its rejection, and rejected the paragraph accordingly was. It seems to us that only when some such provision is made, as was suggested in the paragraph in question, will there be anything approaching to a guarantee that the questionable proceedings which characterised the promotion of the Hyderabad Deccan Company may not be repeated with indefinite frequency.—*Mining Journal*, Sept. 1.

THE HYDERABAD-DECCAN SCANDAL.—WHAT IS TO BE ITS SEQUEL?—A consolatory feature of scandals is their wonderful facility of dying out and being forgotten. They are apt sometimes to be lost sight of before they have pointed their moral, though they may have adorned a considerable number of spicy tales. In a community overrun, as ours is, with Society papers and five-o'clock teas, they tread so fast on each other's heels as to crowd each other into the background. When the scandals affect private life that is a merciful disposition of Providence against which nothing need be said, but when they trench on public interests it may often be a disadvantage. It would, for instance, be a grave misfortune if all the outcry there has been lately about the Hyderabad-Deccan concession were to fizzle out and be looked back on only as one of the piquant incidents of the year 1888. The affair was of much greater importance than that comes to. It has been no ordinary scandal like the floating of a bogus Company, or a particularly clever rig in the Stock Market. Both these features it had, but they are accompanied with others of much greater gravity. So far as the City itself is concerned, there is nothing very peculiar about the Hyderabad-Deccan business. It differed only in degree from plants which the wily promoter attempts every day, and sometimes succeeds in when he is not well watched. As a mere financial escapade, there is not much to distinguish the Hyderabad-Deccan Company from the Mulattos Mine or Ashley's Patent Bottle Company, or a dozen other promoters' *coups* which we have to warn our readers against every week. The Watson Group merely excelled their competitors in making a grander-looking scheme, in employing more seductive decoys, and in getting away with a bigger swag than was ever heard of before.

If that were all, the scandal might willingly be permitted to go to the dust-bin of joint-stock fiascoes, but there is much more behind. Its City aspect is of small consequence compared with its political bearings. These last are so very ugly, and there has been such a suspicious anxiety to slur them over, that it is impossible to let them quietly pass. After all has been said about the wickedness of the men who made over three-quarters of a million sterling out of a concession which cost them practically nothing, that only leads to a further and more practical question—how could they have got it under the very nose of men who have hitherto been held up as models of vigilant and capable administrators? Until this happened the sharpness of our Anglo-Indian officials was a popular proverb among us. Their integrity was supposed to be beyond suspicion. The discovery that they had allowed themselves to be taken in as meekly as a country parson ever fell into the net of the circularising broker, came on us like a thunder clap. Rather than believe in such incredible innocence, cynical-minded people inclined to a still worse conclusion—that officials concerned had known too much. When a sharp watch-dog gives no warning against the housebreaker, the inference that he has been drugged is at least as probable as that he has all at once turned stupid.

This is a painful aspect of the scandal which has been touched very gingerly as yet even in private discussion, and not more than hinted at in the public Press. It is present, however, to the public mind as a subject which requires elucidation. Insinuations have been thrown out against more than one distinguished official, and suspicious circumstances have been put together in such a way as to look awkward for them. The matter is too serious both for them and for India to be left in that vague nebulous state. In order to satisfy the public suspicions, which seem reasonably well-founded, must be cleared up. Men naturally argue that if in the narrow compass of a single transaction so much laxity and carelessness, if not worse, have betrayed themselves, what might not a wider inquiry bring to light? To put it scripturally, if such things have been done in the green tree what may not have been done in the dry? The British officials who, whether in London or India, indirectly rule the tributary States, must have thousands of opportunities quite as good as the Hyderabad-Deccan concession to exercise their easy-going virtue or their unsuspecting complaisance. Residents at Courts like that of the Nizam, when honest and vigilant, must have great difficulty in keeping clear of the network of intrigue continually surrounding them. Where they have been at all inclined that way themselves, they have had the most tempting field to work in.

Consider for a moment what sort of a Court it must be in which an ex-policeman and an uneducated, unscrupulous adventurer like Abdul Huk could, in a few years, work his way to the highest offices of the State, and it will appear how great the moral danger is that has to be guarded against. If now and again the temptation has proved too strong for British virtue, what wonder? But even if every British official who has had to do with the affairs of Hyderabad-Deccan should, on investigation, prove himself immaculate, the argument remains no less strong that human nature should not be exposed to an ordeal so trying while resisted and so demoralising when yielded to. Surely some way can be found of supervising the tributary provinces of India without putting a premium on intrigue and obliquity as was done at Hyderabad. It would be bad enough had a person like Abdul Huk risen to position and power in spite of British Residents, who were supposed to be there to check abuses; but when he turns out to be a *protégé* of more than one British Resident, and to have owed his rise to their patronage more than to anything else, our responsibility becomes clear. For the vindication of our credit in India, and a reparation to the Native States which have suffered so seriously through our default, the whole system must be searched into, regardless of the susceptibilities of the India Office, and of possible consequences to the official Ring.

That there will be a sequel to the Hyderabad-Deccan scandal, and possibly a rather sensational one, cannot any longer be doubted. The Report of the Select Committee almost anticipates further action, and that may be the true explanation of the tameness and inconclusiveness charged against it. It is inconclusive in the sense in which any inquiry would be inconclusive which felt that it was only touching the hem of a great subject and could not go to the heart of it. As soon as Parliament meets again, the Hyderabad-Deccan scandal will re-appear in a much larger and more imperative form. The new demand will be for a thorough inquiry into the position and powers of British Residents at tributary Courts, and how they have been exercised. On the evidence elicited, it will have to be considered whether or not the British Residential system can be improved on. It seems to us that a better, cheaper, and more effective plan would be to put the tributary States on a similar footing to the Colonial Governments, and let them be represented in London by their own agents. This would certainly be popular with Native Ministers, as bringing them into direct relations with the Imperial Government, and throwing open to them ambitious posts of high social and political distinction. It would be with them as with Colonial politicians—Whitehall would be their Mecca.—*Statist*, September 1.

The Nizam proposes to raise a new loan for irrigation works in Hyderabad, and if the business be entrusted to the right people the money will be got easily enough, for the State is rich, the public burdens are few, and irrigation is a sound investment. More attention should be paid to the Native States, as they are really the most prosperous in India. They have all the advantages of British protection, without the drawback of having to pay stiffly for it. What they do pay is small, compared with their resources.—*Political World*, September 1.

The Value of Deccan Shares.—To the Editor of *Vanity Fair*.—Leicester Road, Loughborough, 27th August, 1888.—Sir,—When you were so strongly recommending the purchase of Deccans (they were then 13½), I unfortunately bought 200, and have held them since. For weeks I have noticed that you have not touched on Deccans in *Vanity Fair*, and this has much surprised me, as now that the Parliamentary inquiry is over, there are, I know, others besides myself who would like your opinion respecting them. If they are worthless, we might as well know the worst, whereas if there is a good chance of their improving in value, it would be folly to sacrifice them at present price, about 6.—Yours truly, HOPE.

[In reply to "Hope," it would be an act of indiscretion to sell Deccans at their present price, after all the anxiety which you have undergone during the vexatious Parliamentary inquiry. We firmly believe that, notwithstanding the attempts which have been made to injure and depreciate the property, it will turn out to be all we stated. We did not think it worth while to criticise the report of the Committee, because that report shows conclusively that, after a wearisome cross-examination and expense to various individuals, at a cost of about £40,000, nothing really practical was elucidated by the inquiry.]—*Vanity Fair*, September 1.

NAWAB MAHDI ALI ON THE PROPOSED NATIONAL CONGRESS IN INDIA.—The Central News sends the following account of an interview with the representative of the Government of the Nizam, now in Brighton, on the subject of the proposed National Congress in India:—

The Moulvi Mahdi Ali Mohsin Ool Moolk Bahadur, political and financial secretary of the Nizam's Government, now on a special mission to England, is well-known throughout India as one of the most distinguished Native officials in the peninsula. He served with high reputation for seventeen years under the Indian Government and left the service with the highest testimonials to accept an important appointment offered in Hyderabad by the late Sir Salar Jung in 1874. It is the testimony of men like Sir Richard Meade and Sir Charles Elliott that the reconstruction and reform of the revenue and fiscal service of the Nizam's dominions are mainly due to the integrity, capacity, and energy of the Moulvi Mahdi Ali. In 1885 a very remarkable letter written by him on the attitude of the Mohammedans of India towards the then threatening advance of Russia was published. This letter called forth from Sir Mackenzie Wallace, writing for the Viceroy, Lord Dufferin, a special letter of thanks, and made the name of the Moulvi Mahdi Ali familiar to all who have been watching with attention the progress of events in India during the last five years. The attention of Moulvi Mahdi Ali having been called to a letter published on Monday touching a letter written by the Maharajah of Benares in opposition to the assembling of an Indian National Congress, he was asked with whom this movement for the National Congress in India originated. "It originated," he said, "with the so-called Baboo, or educated Bengalee. The first Congress was presided over by Dadabhai Naoroji, an able man, and it was made up chiefly of Bengalees and Parsees. I paid little attention to the subject when first mooted, my time being fully occupied with the affairs of the Native State which I have the honour to serve. I first seriously considered it when the Congress met last year at Madras. For this there were two reasons. One was the interest taken in it by a distinguished public servant in India, Mr. Allan O. Hume, one of my oldest friends and instructors, who took me by the hand as a boy when I first entered the Indian Service, and to whom I owe much gratitude and affection. Mr. Hume was devoted to the idea of a Congress, and spent four months in Madras. The presiding officer of the congress also was an old personal friend of mine, a highly-educated man, Budrooddeen Tyabjee, of Bombay. He made a striking address before the Congress, which attracted wide attention, and I wrote him a friendly letter, congratulating him on its ability and its success. In reply, he wrote, asking my opinion as to the idea of a Congress itself. This was nine months ago, and I have not yet replied to his letter.

This will show you, perhaps, that I have not enthusiastically adopted the idea of a Congress. The question as to whether such a Congress is advisable has, in my judgment, first to be settled. I do not wish to be hasty in coming to a decision on that point, for I am also on most intimate terms of friendship with Sir Syed Ahmed, whom I have always supported in the great reformatory work he is doing for the benefit of my people, the Mussulmans, and Sir Syed by no means approves of a Congress. I am sure both Mr. Hume and Sir Syed Ahmed are equally honest and equally devoted to the cause of order and of progress in India; and when two such men differ so widely as to the wisdom and timeliness of the proposed National Congress, I think it right to reserve my final opinion till I can go over the whole matter with them face to face, and find out what reasons for or against the project each has to give. As at present advised, however, I will frankly say that my own predisposition is against it. I cannot think it a thing to be desired for India in general or for the Mussulmans of India in particular. I do not believe India is really ready for it. Some of the Indian populations are much in advance of others in education and training for public affairs. Many of the Bengalees in particular are, perhaps, advanced enough to deal with the grave matters which would come before a National Congress sagaciously and wisely, but certainly the people of India in general are not in that condition. Is it not better to await a further development of the education and the capacity of the Indian people before sending them to take action in such a Congress on subjects about which they cannot possibly now be well advised or well informed? I have a great respect for the educated Bengalees. I believe them, indeed, to be quite loyal to the British Government, but whether their loyalty is according to wisdom in this matter is another question. Perhaps they think the masses of the people are as enlightened as themselves, which is hardly the case. They are, I fear, in too great a hurry. They certainly know next to nothing of the less educated military class among the Mussulmans. They are not soldiers themselves, and they do not understand the military class. If they could succeed in impressing the Mussulman population with the belief that there are very great defects in the British system of governing India, what would be the result? Not to produce an intelligent desire for a reasonable reform of anything that may be wrong in the Government system, such a desire as the educated Bengalees themselves would feel. Not at all. It would only produce a sullen disposition on the part of the military class to distrust the Government, and desire to see it overthrown. This would be a bad thing in itself, and though it might do no great harm to-day or to-morrow, while all is peaceful, who can say what might happen from it were India suddenly exposed to a great war —to attack by a foreign enemy? Where you now have honest, simple loyalty to the Government among the military classes, you would then have a body of dangerous discontent, all the more dangerous because vague and not intelligent. All Mussulmans who know the history of the world and of their own religion know that the Mussulmans of India are better off to-day under the British Government than are the Mussulmans of Egypt, of Turkey, of Afghanistan, and they know that this is due to the general honesty, firmness, and justice of the British rule. I have frankly stated these views of mine to one of the ablest native friends of this Congress now in England, so I see no objection to stating them to you as you ask me for them. If the day of danger ever comes to England in India, upon whom can England reply? Not upon the timid Baboo with his clever pen, but upon the Mussulman Rajpoot or Pathan with his loyal sword. I don't think it well to be in too great a hurry to disturb the mind of my own people with questions which they are not yet fully prepared to understand.—*Morning Post*, August 16.

Hyderabad (Deccan) Company.—Mr. Editor,—In the recently-published reports of the meeting of the Hyderabad (Deccan) Company reference is made to coal, diamonds, and gold. We know there is coal there, but can anyone tell us whether the quality is good, and can the Directors assure the investing public that there is any reliable information that gold or diamonds exist in marketable quantities? For my part I would rather hold my golden sovereign than a paper diamond.—INVESTOR. August 29, 1888.—*Herapath's Journal*, September 1.

HYDERABAD DECCAN SHARES have settled down to about their value. The "scandal" has quite fizzed itself out and been already almost forgotten, and Mr. Watson can spend his profits unmolested. He has done what the Americans call a very "smart" piece of business, and legally cannot be made to give up anything that he has made.

None of the transactions can be looked on with any gentlemanly satisfaction, and are certainly nothing to be proud of, but *legally* there is not the shadow of a doubt that the concession must remain as it is. No one will ever think the same of Mr. Hughes-Hughes or of his estimates after this. He must have been very handsomely paid in one way and another.

Hundreds of mines are now quoted in the market which were promoted in the same way. The vendor sells his piece of ground to a "pal" and then comes to England and inaugurates a Company to buy it. He then has the effrontery to act as Director of the Company—for a consideration—and when some disagreeable shareholder points to the fact that he has no right to act in that capacity, being the real vendor of the piece of ground, our wily friend points to the name of his "pal" and produces everything in legal order.

How is it that one of the directors "has known the property for over twenty years," as shareholders will generally find is the case? Simply because the man who has known the "Company's property" was the original vendor of the land. His name did not appear, of course. He took good care to transfer it to Mr. Smith, so that the contract could run in the prospectus "between Mr. Smith on the one part and the Gold Mining Company on the other part," etc.

Many mines—many dozens of mining companies—are nothing more or less than legalised swindles, and the sooner the Joint Stock Companies' Act is radically reformed the better for the public.—*Barker's Trade and Finance*, September 5.

BY those who know Berar, I am told that the moral of such intrigues as that in which Mr. Tom Palmer and his friend Lochlein were engaged, is that a radical reform of the relations which at present subsist between this province and the Government of India is urgently called for. Berar was handed over to us in 1853 as security for the payment of the military contingent which the Nizam is under terms to maintain at our disposal. The arrangement, as I understand it, is that we hold the province in trust—first, for the application of the revenues in payment of the contingent; and, after that, to hand over the surplus revenue to the Nizam. The surplus was not expected to amount to much when the treaty was made, but under British administration the gross annual revenue of the province has grown from 32 to 108 lakhs, and a surplus of about 20 lakhs per annum has lately been handed over to the Nizam. The natural result is that the Hyderabad Government is perpetually hankering after the province. Hence the blackmailing of Sir Salar Jung (who was specially keen on the subject) by Tom Palmer and his friend in the manner which I described a fortnight ago.

If the matter ended here, it would not be serious. But I understand that under its present constitution Berar is wretchedly misgoverned and oppressed. To begin with, the surplus revenue handed over to the Nizam is exactly equivalent to a tribute extorted from the province. It means that twenty lakhs per annum is wrung from the population, and taken out of the country for good. It is not surprising, therefore, that the province is disastrously impoverished, in spite of the growth of its revenue under our scientific methods of tax collecting. A well-informed authority tells me that it is "the most backward province in British India in all the arts of civilization"; that there are no towns, no industries, and no private wealth; and that the population consists solely of a badly-housed and half-fed peasantry.

In the next place, it was provided in the treaty of 1853 that the province should be administered under the supreme authority of the Resident at Hyderabad. This was a concession to a whim of the then Nizam, and results, as might be expected, in chronic misgovernment. The Resident at Hyderabad knows personally nothing of Berar—possibly does not visit it during his term of office. He has no one to assist and advise him but his staff as Resident, who are drawn in the usual way from the general Political Service of India, and who know and care as little about Berar as their chief. This is obviously a most discreditable state of things all round—and for the unlucky people of Berar most disastrous. What really seems to be wanted is the abrogation of the Treaty of 1853, and the substitution of British sovereignty in Berar in fact, if not in name. Failing that, it would be better to hand the province back to the Nizam than to perpetuate the present state of things.—*Truth*, September 6.

A THOUGHT-READER'S THOUGHTS.—THE NIZAM OF HYDERABAD.—The foremost in loyalty towards the British rule is undoubtedly the Nizam of Hyderabad, the greatest of the feudatories. He is about three-and-twenty years of age, and is the son of the Nizam Afzal-ud-Daula, who so firmly stood by us during the Mutiny.

His full title, which runs as follows, takes a lot of remembering:—His Highness Sipah-Salar, Muzaffar-ul-Mumalik, Rustam-i-Dauran, Aristu-e-Zaman, Mir Mahbub Ali Khan Bahadur, Fatheh Jang, Nizam-ud-Daula, Nizam-ul-Mulk, Asaf Jah.

The founder of the present dynasty was one Chin Kilich Khan, whose father had been a favourite officer of Aurungzeb. He was an able man of conspicuous courage, and he rapidly rose in favour of the Emperor, and whilst comparatively young was made Viceroy of the Deccan. There he exercised such undisputed power that he eventually excited the jealousy of the Emperor, who gave orders for his assassination. The task of carrying out the plot was entrusted to Mobariz Khan, the local Governor of Hyderabad, who, however, failed in the attempt. The revolt he instigated was suppressed, and he himself was slain.

The Nizam, who was a humorist, if of a somewhat grim kind, wrote to the Emperor congratulating him on the successful suppression of the revolt, sending him at the same time the head of the "traitor" Mobariz.

This was in 1724, and henceforth Chin Kilich Khan, who assumed the title of Nizam-ul-Mulk conducted himself as an independent prince.

The present Nizam has none of his great ancestor's warlike qualities, but he is an intelligent young prince of some ability, with a decided will of his own.

As a boy, he was exceedingly delicate, and spent much of his time with his mother, Wadid-u-Nisa, Begam, and his grandmother, Dilwar-u-Nisa, Begam, who did their best to spoil him. He has outgrown somewhat the weakness of his youth; but he does not look particularly robust. Small in stature, he, however, bears himself with marked dignity, and gives you at once the impression that he is fully conscious of the fact that he is the First Prince in India. (The area of the Nizam's dominions, including the assigned districts of the Berars, exceeds by more than 10,000 square miles that of Great Britain, with a population of about 11,000,000.) He is passionately fond of horse-racing, and is a liberal patron of the local races.

We stayed some weeks in Hyderabad, as guests of Sir Salar Jung, the then Prime Minister, and frequently came across the Nizam, who went out of his way to show us attention.

On one occasion His Highness gave a dinner in my honour, at which all the principal nobles of his Court were present.

DINING WITH THE NIZAM.

In the East time is no object, and the dinner did not take place till fully an hour after the appointed time. The guests had arrived, but there was no host, and, pending his arrival, we wandered about the palace. Presently cries were heard in the gardens beyond, and, looking out, I saw the flickering of torches in the distance. The sounds came nearer, mingled with the sharp clatter of horses' feet. Then came a rush of servants bearing flaming torches, and, amidst a flood of light, His Highness's carriage dashed up to the entrance hall. The officials made a deep obeisance as the Nizam entered, and made way for him on all sides.

Singling me out, His Highness bade me follow him, and with much courtesy, he conducted me to the dining-hall, where he sat me on his right.

Then ensued a curious scene. Every guest before he took his seat had to catch the Nizam's eye, and to make sundry salaams; and the sight of so many hands, moving up and down like the flapping of birds' wings, was an exceedingly novel one.

I was the only European present, and amidst the flash of jewels and brilliant uniforms, my plain evening dress seemed sombre in the extreme.

A MAHARAJAH'S IDEA OF A GOOD DRINK.

At this dinner every one, including the Nizam, drank water, but by my side were placed the choicest wines; for, although Mussulmen do not, or are not supposed to, partake of strong drink, they, unlike the fanatics in this country, do not object to wine or spirit drinking in others. In fact, the native mind believes that the European requires spirits with every meal; and I have, whilst a guest of the various Native Princes, been struck with the persistency with which either brandy or whisky has been produced from the early breakfast to the late dinner. But when a native acquires a taste for spirits, he is as immoderate in its use as any Red Indian; and the favourite drink of a Maharajah of my acquaintance was an equal mixture of champagne and brandy. This Maharajah, needless to say, was not always quite the thing.

The Nizam, who speaks English fluently, conversed with considerable intelligence upon current matters, and seemed especially anxious to know something about Russia, which country I had recently visited. He ridiculed the idea of there being any native sympathy with Russia, and he assured me that he would be willing to place his army and the resources of his State at the disposal of the British Government in case India were threatened.

THE NIZAM'S LOYALTY.

"We," he said, "may not have all we want under British rule, but we are undoubtedly better off than we should be under that of Russia. England respects our religion, and allows us our liberty; but if India were to pass into the hands of Russia, we should have neither; and on religious grounds, at least, we Mussulmen would resist to the death an invasion by Russia."

His Highness was most emphatic in his manner, and I have every reason to believe that he was perfectly sincere.

THE PRIME MINISTER'S CONFIRMATION.

I took occasion the next day to speak with Sir Salar Jung upon the matter, and His Excellency, who is deeply loyal to us, assured me that the facts were as stated by His Highness, and that His Highness longed for an opportunity of proving his loyalty.

This was months before anything was heard of what has been called the Nizam's offer, and it serves to prove what, irrespective of the jugglery that has been practised in connection with the proposed subsidy, His Highness's intentions with regard to the matter really were.

The Nizam's proposal created an admirable impression throughout India, and it was followed up by substantial offers from almost all the other Native Princes.

The *Times*, in an able article on the defence of India, analyses and discusses the various offers of money and troops made by certain feudatory Princes to the Government. The total amount of money offered reaches 1,03,80,000 rupees, including Hyderabad 60,00,000 rupees, Cashmere 10,00,000 rupees, Jodhpore 10,00,000 rupees, Bhurtpore 8,00,000 rupees, Kota 6,00,000 rupees, Kapurthala 5,00,000 rupees, Nabha 4,00,000 rupees, and Maler Kotla 80,000 rupees. These Princes offer troops in addition. Of the other Princes, the ruler of Mysore expresses a wish to raise and maintain a suitable military force, trained by British officers; the ruler of Patiala offers troops whenever required; the ruler of Bhawalpore a contingent of troops and money aid, proportioned to his resources; the ruler of Tonk the services of himself, his family, his troops, and the whole resources of his State; the ruler of Alwar money and troops whenever required; the ruler of Rampore to defray the expense incurred in raising and maintaining a native infantry regiment in every war, together with all the resources of his State; the ruler of Mandi the services of himself and the resources of his State; the rulers of Suket and Mantes the like; the ruler of Loharu the services of himself, his brothers, his property, and a caravan of fifty camels; and the ruler of Chamba land for cantonments.—*Echo*, August 29.

THE Nawab Mohsin-ul-Mulk Mahdi Ali, the principal delegate of the Nawab of Hyderabad, and his secretaries, have taken up their abode at the Star and Garter Hotel, Richmond, and there are no signs of their speedy return to India. Although legal proceedings are freely spoken of with a view to annul the contract which has given rise to the recent proceedings, it is not improbable that a compromise will ultimately be agreed upon.—*World*, September 12.

MR. GLADSTONE AND THE NIZAM'S REPRESENTATIVE.—As the proceedings in the Deccan case, since its examination by Sir H. James's Committee, are now drawing to a close, the chief representative of His Highness the Nizam sent out to England by the Premier, Sir Asman Jah, is preparing to return to India. The Nawab Mohsin Ool Moolk Mahdi Ali is a well-known public servant, formerly of the Indian Government, and for some years past of the Nizam. He now fills the important post of Financial and Political Secretary of Hyderabad. As he desired to make a tour of England before returning, he accepted an invitation from Mr. Gladstone to visit Hawarden last week. Stopping on the way at Manchester, he was received there by Mr. Macneil, Mr. Dods, and other gentlemen actively connected with the affairs of that city, and visited most of its points of interest. Going on to Chester, he drove thence with Major Robertson, formerly Assistant-Resident at Hyderabad, to Hawarden Castle. They were there most courteously received by Mr. Gladstone.

The following account of the interview has been drawn up for the information of the Nizam's Government:—

Mr. Gladstone commenced by remarking that he did not ordinarily receive gentlemen at Hawarden, as while there he was glad of some relaxation and retirement, but it gave him much pleasure to make an exception in the case of a native gentleman of distinction.

He then inquired whether Mahdi Ali had made many journeys in England, and especially whether he had seen Liverpool, explaining the interest of the Mersey, and contrasting its changed appearance now and the length of docks, about six miles, with the state of things in the time of his father, mentioning that, though far larger in amount now, the shipping appeared for various reasons, less in bulk and magnitude than it was then. Mr. Gladstone mentioned that his father, in 1812, sent out one of the first merchantmen to India, called the "Kingsmill." Learning that the first and only journey Mahdi Ali had made was to visit Hawarden Castle, Mr. Gladstone gracefully acknowledged the compliment, and expressed the great pleasure it gave him to meet a delegate from His Highness the Nizam.

Mahdi Ali said he had heard much of Mr. Gladstone's name and fame, both in India and in England, and, alluding to the letter sent by Mr. Gladstone to Salar Jung on the subject of an article in a magazine written by that nobleman, said he would be much gratified to learn from his lips that he entertained favourable sentiments towards the natives of India in general, and his (Mahdi Ali's) co-religionists in particular. Mr. Gladstone then proceeded to express at some length his personal feelings towards India and its people, which were of a most friendly and sympathetic character. He said that the letter to Salar Jung might be taken to express his views and opinions, which were still unchanged and to which he had nothing to add. As regards the natives of India, he was glad to be able to think that there was in these days among all politicians a growing approximation to that feeling, which consisted in strict adherence to the notion that the presence of the English in India was only justifiable for the good of that country, and he was glad to know that all recent measures had been directed towards the fulfilment of this beneficent and enlightened policy. Mahdi Ali said he was glad to hear these sentiments from the mouth of so learned and famous a statesman, on which Mr. Gladstone replied that he personally was, to a great extent, taken up with the consideration of the mode of government in Ireland to the exclusion of other subjects, and that, as regards the internal affairs of India, the opinions of younger men who had a better opportunity than he of estimating the position of affairs would be more valuable; to which Mahdi Ali replied that the opinions of such an eminent statesman were of the greatest value. Mr. Gladstone deprecatingly said that he had entered now the last stage of his political life, having been a member of the House of Commons for more than fifty-six years, and humorously remarked that there was such a thing as being over-ripe.

When asked for his opinion upon the propriety of England's maintaining and repeating, if necessary, the policy of the Crimean War, in respect to the assistance given to Turkey, the fount of Mahomedanism, not only as tending to retain the sympathy of the Indian Mussulmans, but also as assisting to retard the advance of Russia eastwards, Mr. Gladstone said that this question was one of great magnitude, affording room for lengthy discussion, but, without attempting any detailed exposition of his views, he had no hesitation in saying that he personally entertained very friendly feelings towards Turkey. Instancing the bombardment of Alexandria, an act which had been criticised in some quarters as amounting to an attack on an outlying portion of the Turkish dominions, Mr. Gladstone added that the night before the bombardment took place, he was dining with Musurus Pasha, the Turkish Ambassador, and told him that the British Government was then paving the way for the entrance of Turkish influence into Egypt, and that Turkish troops could enter Egypt and thus free the Khedive from the unwholesome influences to which he was then subject. This suggestion was, said Mr. Gladstone, telegraphed at once by the Ambassador to Constantinople, but His Majesty the Sultan did not, unfortunately, as Mr. Gladstone thought, see fit to accept it. As regards the occupation of Egypt, Mr. Gladstone expressed himself as entertaining no doubt that the British Government were determined to clear out of the country and to keep troops there no longer than was absolutely necessary.

As regards his feelings towards the people of India, Mr. Gladstone alluded to the appointment made by him when Prime Minister of his old friend and colleague, Lord Ripon, who had done such great things in India, and also that of Lord Dufferin, who had not, perhaps, had the same opportunities as Lord Ripon of carrying out reforms, but who was doubtless anxious to follow on the same lines as his predecessor.

Mahdi Ali here remarked that, so far as his co-religionists were concerned, they recognized that the reconstitution of the old Mogul Empire was impossible, and that a Government which not only respects and encourages their religion, but had also conferred upon Mahomedans such signal temporal advantages, was in every way worthy of their support and affection, and that, should any emergency arise, the spirit of fire and devotion which formerly animated the hearts of Mahomedans in India would still be found keen and alive, enabling them to meet the common danger shoulder to shoulder with the British nation. More especially was this true in regard to the Hyderabad State, which was conspicuous in its unalterable loyalty to the British Crown. He mentioned that the late Sir Salar Jung, whose opinions he had every means of knowing, frequently told him that, recognizing what a blessing the British Government was to India, he unhesitatingly threw in his lot with them during the mutiny thirty years ago.

Mr. Gladstone replied that these welcome and valuable assurances, coming as they did to him direct from an authentic and influential source, were peculiarly gratifying.

The conversation then turned upon the offers of assistance made by native Princes of late years to the British Government, and the foremost and largest of these offers, viz.: that made by His Highness, the Nizam of Hyderabad, a principality which must be regarded as the centre from which all influential Mahomedan feeling radiates in India. Mention was also made of the intention of Sir Asman Jah, the Prime Minister, and a wealthy noble of the State, to follow the example of his master, and to place his entire resources, should they be required, at the disposal of the British Government. Mr. Gladstone said that the feeling which had prompted these offers was most praiseworthy, and that the fact of their having been made constituted one of the most remarkable incidents that had ever come under his cognizance; the remembrance of these genuine tokens of allegiance to the British Crown would, he felt sure, never die out.

On the subject of the National Congress Mr. Gladstone said he had only imperfect information, and consequently had some hesitation in discussing this subject; but, so far as he remembered, the questions involved consisted mainly of reform of the marriage laws and prohibition of early marriages, matters chiefly affecting Hindoos. Mahdi Ali explained that his co-religionists, as a body, had not yet joined the Congress movement, preferring to allow a Government which had done so much for them and their religion to proceed with its reforms without interference or pressure by political agitation, adding that there was, no doubt, an advantage in educated natives coming forward to give their opinions on points arising in the government of the country; but, on the other hand, there was some danger that the vast masses of the population of India, who were to a great extent uneducated and unable to comprehend administrative questions, would regard public animadversions upon the conduct of the Government as evidence of inefficiency and weakness, which it was highly undesirable to disseminate. Mr. Gladstone said that might be so, but he wished especially to guard against being understood to express any opinion in this matter; all that he could undertake to say was that all legitimate and reasonable efforts on the part of the people to represent their requirements and improve their position commanded his warmest sympathy.

Mr. Gladstone then took the party over the beautiful ruins of the old castle, explaining its history and antiquity, and pointing out the beauty of his park; and in the course of further conversation expressed the great pleasure it gave him to hear that His Highness the Nizam, allowing his feelings of affection and respect to break through the traditions of the past, had attended the funeral of his grandmother. He had also heard with much satisfaction of the intellectual progress among Mahomedans which modern times had witnessed, one of the signs of which might be found in the presence of about thirty young Mahomedan gentlemen at present studying at the Universities of Oxford and Cambridge. Mr. Gladstone was much interested to hear that Mahdi Ali had heard of his affection for trees and his prowess in using an axe, and presented him with a copy of his photograph taken while engaged in cutting down a tree, agreeing to accept one of the Nawab's photographs in return. Mr. Gladstone then introduced the Nawab to the various members of his family now at Hawarden Castle. At the conclusion of the interview, which was most friendly and pleasant throughout, Mr. Gladstone asked the Nawab to convey his respectful compliments and best wishes to His Highness the Nizam, repeating once more that he could never forget the generous offer of assistance to the British Government made by that Prince.

On his way back to London, the Nawab, by special invitation of His Grace the Duke of Westminster, paid a visit to Eaton Hall, where he was received with great courtesy and shown over the whole of that splendid mansion, with its magnificent outbuildings, park, and gardens.

We publish this morning an account, drawn up for the information of the Nizam's Government, of an interview at Hawarden between the Nawab Mahdi Ali, now in England as representative of the Nizam in the Deccan case, and Mr, Gladstone. The interview, we learn with pleasure, was most friendly and pleasant throughout. Compliments, it will be seen, passed freely between the two parties to it. Mahdi Ali had heard much of Mr. Gladstone's name and fame both in India and in England, and he came prepared to attach due weight to the opinions of so eminent a statesman. He will carry back to the Nizam Mr. Gladstone's assurances of the respect and good wishes which he entertains towards that distant potentate, and, indeed, towards all mankind, so wide and warm-hearted was the sympathy which Mr. Gladstone expressed for all the persons and peoples who came before him in the course of the discussion. But if Mahdi Ali came to Hawarden in quest of definite information on Mr. Gladstone's political views, he has gone back, we fear, not much wiser than he went. There were two very definite points on which he tried to sound the depths of his august entertainer's mind, but on neither of them could he succeed in eliciting the kind of answer which he wished for. On the policy of the Crimean war, and on the propriety of England's maintaining it and, if necessary, repeating it by giving armed help to Turkey, Mr. Gladstone would only say that the question was one of great magnitude, affording room for lengthy discussion. Personally, he entertains very friendly feelings towards Turkey, but how far he would be prepared to go in giving effect to them we are not very clearly told. The bombardment of Alexandria was the single instance he could allege of anything approaching a friendly act, and, since this has been termed, truly enough, an attack on an outlying portion of the Turkish dominions, it is not conclusive on the face of it. But Mr. Gladstone's deeds, like his words, must be closely looked into, if we are to discover their esoteric sense. The bombardment, we now learn, was intended to pave the way for the entrance of Turkish influence into Egypt. The Sultan, unfortunately, did not so interpret it, and he failed in consequence to take advantage of the opportunity held out to him by his unsought allies. On the cognate subject of the occupation of Egypt, Mr. Gladstone has no doubt that the Government are determined to clear out of the country, and that they will not keep troops there longer than is absolutely necessary. This is common form, and when no time is suggested at which the occupation is likely to be at an end, and no conditions are stated which would show that it had ceased to be necessary, it means simply nothing.

On the Indian National Congresses Mahdi Ali was equally unsuccessful in probing Mr. Gladstone's views. There were several difficulties in the way. Mahdi Ali has come to England as the representative of a Mahomedan State, and the Mahomedans of India have as a body kept aloof from the Congress movement. To have approved the movement would have been to condemn those who had declined to take any part in it. To have condemned it would have been out of harmony with the position which Mr. Gladstone occupies towards the whole order of malcontents, in whatever part of the world they are to be found. Mahdi Ali was a little pressing. He pointed out the dangers of the Congress movement, and the sound reasons which had induced his Indian co-religionists to proceed in a different way. Mr. Gladstone was not to be drawn. He took refuge in generalities. On the special matter before him he had no opinion to express, and he carefully guarded himself against being understood to express any. All that he could say was that all legitimate and reasonable efforts on the part of the people to represent their requirements and to improve their position commanded his warmest sympathy, but that the efforts in question were of such a kind he neither affirmed nor denied. One obstacle in the way of a more positive sentence on either side seems to have been that Mr. Gladstone's information was imperfect. If he said nothing, it was because he knew nothing. We must look at this as no more than a convenient excuse, so abundant are Mr. Gladstone's resources and so supreme is his habitual indifference to a slavish accuracy about mere matters of fact. But that it was a well-founded excuse we see no reason to doubt. All that Mr. Gladstone can remember about the Congresses is that the questions proposed at them had to do mainly with the reform of the Indian marriage laws and with the prohibition of early marriages—matters, as he remarks, chiefly affecting Hindoos. Mr. Gladstone is happy in what he remembers and in what he manages to forget. If a reform of the Hindoo marriage laws was all that the Congresses aimed at, it was quite right and quite natural that Mahdi Ali's co-religionists should keep aloof from a movement which could have no possible interest for them. But when Mahdi Ali went on to ask whether uneducated people were the best judges on administrative questions, and whether it was not dangerous to encourage them to think that they were, Mr. Gladstone's defect of memory served him in excellent stead. We do not suppose that Mahdi Ali intended his questions to be discourteous in any way to the eminent statesman whom he was addressing. But Mr. Gladstone must have heard them with some twinges of conscience, and must have been glad to think that he had started with a confession of ignorance which he could plead as an excuse for giving no definite reply to them. On his love for India, and more especially for Indian Mahomedans, he could speak without reserve. He was glad to be able to think that all people and all political parties are now approximating to him in this, and that a beneficent and enlightened policy has come to be followed in all recent measures affecting India. But, when he went on to give proof of the warmth of his feelings towards India and Indian Mahomedans, he was not more fortunate than in the proof of his love for Turkey. He had shown his love for Turkey by bombarding Alexandria. He had shown his love for Indian Mahomedans by sending over Lord Ripon as Viceroy, to carry out a policy which they had special reasons to dislike and disapprove, as tending to deprive them of their rightful share of influence in public affairs and administration. Mr. Gladstone, we know, has a warm affection for everything, even for trees, but this, he assured his visitor, he does not suffer to interfere with his prowess in using an axe. Mahdi Ali will carry back to India a photograph of Mr. Gladstone taken while he was in the act of cutting down a tree. It will be an interesting memorial of his Hawarden visit, and will bring to his mind the occasional severity of treatment with which Mr. Gladstone tempers his universal love.

Mr. Gladstone is so much taken up with the consideration of the mode of government in Ireland that he has little attention just now to bestow on anything else. His sympathies run to overflowing in every channel that offers itself, but it is on Ireland alone that his intellectual regard is fixed. The internal affairs of India he is content to leave to men younger than himself. But as a looker-on he is well pleased with the direction which things are taking. On the willingness of the Nizam and of other native chiefs to place their entire resources at the disposal of the Indian Government he expresses himself with hearty approval. On the purpose for which they may be required he says nothing. He regards the offers as prompted by the most praiseworthy feelings, and as constituting one of the most remarkable incidents that had ever come under his cognizance. This may seem, perhaps, a somewhat exaggerated statement, but Mr. Gladstone throughout the interview was in the upper region of hyperbole. Turn where he would his feelings were too strong for him and must have utterance given to them in words. If a proof of the loyal allegiance of the Nizam to the British Crown was a source to him of perennial delight, so, too, was the dutiful conduct of the same potentate in attending the funeral of his grandmother. There was a rosy tint over everything, the reflection of a beneficent mind. If Mahdi Ali has not learned much from his interview on matters about which he sought to be informed, he can hardly have failed to carry away a most pleasant impression of Mr. Gladstone's personality, and we must add, too, a very high opinion of his prudence in refusing to commit himself, and of his dexterous steering amid difficult and dangerous topics.—*Times*, September 21.

THE interview between Mr. Gladstone and the Nizam's representative was, no doubt, very gratifying to both parties; but it does not possess much public interest. Compliments were flying about with Oriental-Gladstonian prodigality. The Nawab expressed great admiration of Mr. Gladstone's character, and Mr. Gladstone declared that he felt a very keen interest in the welfare of the Indian people. This he had sufficiently proved by sending out Lord Ripon to govern them. This was conclusive. The conversation then drifted away to the Eastern Question, and Mr. Gladstone declared that he entertained a warm friendship for Turkey. In fact he goes to dinner with the Turkish Ambassador. This again was quite conclusive. After these preliminaries the two statesmen went as near to business as either of them meant to go. Mr. Gladstone explained that at the present time he was too busy with Ireland to attend seriously to Indian politics. Ireland blocked the way. The next turn is claimed by Wales and Scotland. When these three countries have each got a Home Rule of its own, then it may be India's turn. For the present India must wait.—*St. James's Gazette*, September 21.

THE theory that Mr. Gladstone is not one person but two, and that he is in reality two single gentlemen rolled into one, will gain ground after a reading of the narrative given by the Hyderabad Envoy of his visit to Hawarden. We all know what are the views of the Liberal leader upon the unspeakable Turk, whom he denounced in tones of thunder as the one great anti-human specimen of humanity. But that other Mr. Gladstone, the Gladstone-Hyde as distinguished from the Gladstone-Jekyll, seems to have been well to the front when the Hyderabad Envoy was making inquiries at Hawarden as to whether Mr. Gladstone would care to repeat the Crimean war. Of course, Mr. Gladstone would not; but he dodged the question, and then went on to tell an anecdote which the friends and supporters of the Gladstone-Jekyll will read with very mixed feelings.

Without attempting any detailed exposition of his views, Mr. Gladstone said he had no hesitation in saying that he personally entertained very friendly feelings towards Turkey, and as a proof of this he referred to what the Envoy inadvertently described as the bombardment of Alexandria. Mr. Gladstone, of course, never bombarded Alexandria, he only bombarded its forts. This, however, is by the way. He then told the following story:—

"Mr. Gladstone said that the night before the bombardment took place he was dining with Musurus Pasha, the Turkish Ambassador, and told him that the British Government was then paving the way for the entrance of Turkish influence into Egypt, and that Turkish troops could enter Egypt and thus free the Khedive from the unwholesome influences to which he was then subject. This suggestion was, said Mr. Gladstone, telegraphed at once by the Ambassador to Constantinople, but his Majesty the Sultan did not, unfortunately, as Mr. Gladstone thought, see fit to accept it."

Now of course we do not mean to say that every word of this is not strictly true. Only if instead of making this remark privately to Musurus, the Gladstone-Hyde had then publicly stated that we were bombarding Alexandria in order to establish Turkish authority over the fellaheen, he would have been out of office in twenty-four hours, and it would have served him right. But at that time the Gladstone-Jekyll alone appeared in public. It was only at Turkish dinner-tables that the Gladstone-Hyde was visible.—*Pall Mall Gazette*, September 21.

BUTTERING "THE UNSPEAKABLE."—Mawab Mohsin Ool Moolk Mahdi Ali cannot fail to carry back to India very pleasant recollections of his visit to Hawarden. Native noblemen are not insensible to the pleasures of flattery, and it must be confessed that Mr. Gladstone laid it on thick. It was not merely that he buttered his distinguished guest; he applied the same process to the whole world of Islam. Can it really be that the same eloquent lips once uttered many disparaging things about the Sultan, the great head of that faith? If our recollection serves, Mr. Gladstone formerly enunciated the proposition that the time had come to bundle the Caliph, "bag and baggage," out of Europe. We seem to remember, too, that it was a catch word among his followers to denounce the Turks as "unspeakable." The Indian Mahomedans are not Turks, it is true, but very close touch subsists between them, and this is more especially the case with the Moslim of the Deccan, the country represented by Mahdi Ali. Indeed, he reminded his host of that well-known fact by asking whether Mr. Gladstone was prepared to give assistance to Turkey against Russia should occasion arise, in pursuance of the traditional policy of England. It need scarcely be mentioned that this home thrust was skilfully put aside. Mahdi Ali cannot have studied the peculiarities of his host very closely, or he would never have asked such a question. It, nevertheless, elicited some valuable information, although quite wide of the point. We learn, for one thing, that Mr. Gladstone has always entertained the warmest regard for Turkey. It was, we suppose, Lord Beaconsfield who denounced that country and all its ways during the "atrocity" agitation; Mr. Gladstone may have dissembled his love for "the unspeakable," but it was burning in his bosom all the time. Nor does this reversal of history rest merely on his own word; most fortunately, he is able to demonstrate his long-abiding affection by proof which none will call in question. He assured Mahdi Ali that the real motive for the bombardment of Alexandria was "to pave the way for the entrance of Turkish influence into Egypt." And how was this to be done? By admitting Turkish troops into the country, thus freeing the Khedive "from the evil influences to which he was then subject." This is a somewhat startling revelation: we should not be surprised were some of Mr. Gladstone's former colleagues to affirm that they never had the slightest idea of placing Egypt under direct Turkish rule when they consented to the bombardment of Alexandria. And those "evil influences" which surrounded Tewfik Pasha—what were they? We had imagined that the young Khedive had placed himself entirely under British influence, as the only way of saving himself from dethronement by Arabi. But, of course, we defer to Mr. Gladstone's recollection: his memory is never at fault.

That is, in cases where it can be turned to profitable account for some temporary purpose. In other instances, such as that of the Indian National Congress, it is a perfect blank. Mahdi Ali not unnaturally wished to learn his host's candid opinion on the advisability of annually assembling a number of demagogic agitators in India, for the purpose of stirring up popular discontent. That may not be the professed object, but none who have read the speeches delivered on these occasions will question the truth of Mahdi Ali's view that the masses regard these "public animadversions upon the conduct of the Government as evidence of inefficiency and weakness." Under native rulers, such licence of vituperation would not have been allowed for a moment, and the populace consequently infer that the English are afraid to put it down. Mr. Gladstone admits that this danger may exist, but his remembrance of the Congresses is confined to a vague impression that the only questions they have dealt with are reform of the marriage laws and prohibition of early marriages. For the rest, he fully sympathises with "all legitimate and reasonable efforts on the part of the Indian people to represent their requirements and improve their position." So do we, for the matter of that, but what Mahdi Ali wanted to know was whether "the learned and famous statesman" whom he addressed considered organized sedition a "legitimate and reasonable" method of securing Home Rule for India. Mr. Gladstone could not be expected, of course, to answer such an inconvenient question as this at a moment when he is the chief patron of organized sedition in a much nearer part of her Majesty's dominions than Hindostan. He acted judiciously, therefore, by changing the conversation to less prickly matters, which would admit of a plentiful use of the butter-boat. But he could not resist the temptation of saying a good word for Lord Ripon, while administering a back-handed blow to Lord Dufferin. Here he made a mistake, as even "learned and famous statesmen" are wont to do, when swayed by feelings of personal affection. Lord Ripon was not regarded by the Indian Mahomedans as a friend of their community; Lord Dufferin is so regarded for very good reason. This allusion was, therefore, singularly *mal apropos* when addressed to a Mahomedan nobleman, who would naturally feel anything but grateful for "the great things which Lord Ripon did in India." The unfortunate blunder was, however, fully compensated for before the interview terminated. Delighted indeed must Mahdi Ali have felt on hearing Mr. Gladstone extol the sublime conduct of the Nizam in "attending the funeral of his grandmother." These glad tidings will, no doubt, give great joy at Hyderabad, but not so much, we feel convinced, as the photograph of Mr. Gladstone felling a tree. As it passes round the zenana, the admiration of all beholders, the houris will conclude that England must be a more wonderful country even than they had believed—wonderful in consenting to be governed for many years by a septuagenarian whose favourite amusement is destruction.—*Globe*, September 21.

THE Nawab Mahdi Ali, a confidential Minister of the Nizam of Hyderabad and the special representative of His Highness in this country in respect of the Deccan business, has just had an interview with the Sage of Hawarden. Full details of the conversation have, of course, been drawn up by the envoy for the information of his Government, and the report exhibits Mr. Gladstone in a somewhat new light. The Separatist leader apparently has a profound regard for *ensemble*, and accordingly his demeanour on this occasion was framed upon the model of the Oriental potentate of fiction. Interviewer and interviewed rivalled each other in compliment and self-deprecation, and one is led to the conclusion that had a photographer been present the world might by this time have been favoured with a picture of the ex-Prime Minister exchanging salaams with the Nawab as if "to the manner born." Orientals, and especially Britons, will, however, note with pleasure the fact that the Western statesman was more than a match for the Eastern envoy. The latter was evidently anxious to get at the opinions of his host on one or two definite matters of importance to the Indian, and especially the Mahommedan, community, but Mr. Gladstone with his wealth of words signifying nothing, his convenient lack of precise information, and his ready compliments, was a very hard nut for the Nawab to crack. Mr. Gladstone absolutely overflowed with sympathy, not only for the Nizam, but for every class and individual mentioned in the course of the conversation, not even excepting Turkey and its ruler. Of course, Ireland was forcibly introduced into the flow of talk—it is now as inseparable from Mr. Gladstone's writings and speeches as was King Charles's head from the lucubrations of Mr. Dick—by the remark that the affairs of that country will monopolise what is left of the veteran Parliamentarian's political career. It formed on this occasion, as on others, a convenient pretext for refusing to commit himself. Mahdi Ali was anxious to know his host's opinion on the propriety of England's maintaining, if necessity should arise, the policy of the Crimean War—*i.e.*, giving armed help to Turkey but Mr. Gladstone could only say that the question was one of great magnitude, affording room for lengthy discussion. Similarly, about the recent so-called National Congresses in India he was conveniently lacking in information. Even when the Nawab, representing, as he does, the largest Mahommedan native State, pressed for an expression of opinion as to the advisability of educated Hindoos animadverting in the hearing of millions of their countrymen absolutely ignorant of political or administrative question on the conduct of the Government, Mr. Gladstone fenced the inquiry with generalties. One impression left on the mind of the impartial reader of this interview is worth noting. It is the peculiar manifestation which Mr. Gladstone gives of his affection towards the objects of that affection. He is fond of trees, he told Madhi Ali, and his chief recreation is their destruction. He has unlimited respect for the Sultan, and his principal exploit during his premiership was the bombarding of an important town in that potentate's dominions. He explained to the Nawab—and this is an addition to our knowledge of these proceedings of the Gladstonian cabinet—that the attack on Alexandria was intended to pave the way for the entrance of Turkish influence into Egypt; but, unfortunately, the Porte looked upon the matter in a different light. Mr. Gladstone is brimming over with love for the Mahommedan population of India, and he exhibited it by sending out as Viceroy Lord Ripon, who did more than any other Governor-General has ever done to deprive the Mahommedans of that share of influence in the administration which rightfully belongs to them by their numbers, their wealth, their education, and their unswerving loyalty. Above all, Mr. Gladstone has an undying affection for Ireland, and this he displays by a desire— But we will leave our readers to complete the parallel for themselves.—*Morning Advertiser*, September 22.

The personal aspects of political life are not ordinarily the most tranquil. Controversial issues between one side and the other are represented by the leaders of each, and those leaders seldom appear in any other character than that of disputants. This is especially true of Mr. Gladstone, who is always foremost in the vanguard of his party. It is therefore gratifying to have Mr. Gladstone presented to us in another aspect—that of an agreeable host, a complaisant and complimentary critic, and a statesman with a humour for making everything pleasant to everybody. It is in that light that we see him in the account of his interview last week with the Nawab Mahdi Ali, who holds the responsible post of Financial and Political Secretary in the Government of the Nizam. The Nawab has been for some time in this country, in connection with the inquiry into the Deccan case by Sir Henry James's Committee. Before returning to India he desired to see something of England, and among the invitations which he accepted was one from Mr. Gladstone. He visited Mr. Gladstone at Hawarden, and an account of the conversation that occurred between the two distinguished men has been drawn up for the information of the Nizam's Government. It is first put on record that Mr. Gladstone displayed great personal interest in his guest. He asked him if he had ever been to Liverpool, and entertained him with a description of that sea-port and of its six miles of docks and vast crowds of ships. But the Nawab's first and only journey in England was that which he had taken to Hawarden. He had heard, he said, much of Mr. Gladstone's name and fame, and his chief concern was to hear from his own lips that he entertained favourable sentiments towards the people of India. Mr. Gladstone assured him that his sentiments were of that character. The account from which we quote, and the accuracy of which we should not think of questioning, states that "he proceeded to express his feelings at some length." But it would appear that his observations were somewhat general, for in replying to questions from the Nawab he found it necessary to explain that "he personally was, to a great extent, taken up with the consideration of the mode of government in Ireland to the exclusion of other subjects." It, therefore, happened that the internal affairs of India had not received much of his attention, and his opinions upon them, he modestly suggested, could not be of much value. The Nawab flatteringly dissented from this view, and a later period in the conversation returned to the subject. He was anxious to know Mr. Gladstone's ideas about the recent Indian Congress. The topic was an inconvenient one, for Mr. Gladstone was obliged to confess that his only impression about the Congress was that the questions before it had reference to the marriage laws. The Nawab was naturally better informed on the subject than his host, and he explained that his co-religionists as a body had not joined in the Congress movement, "preferring to allow a Government which had done so much for them and their religion to proceed with its reforms without interference or pressure by political agitation." Mahdi Ali could not have known that he was making a pointed home-thrust at his host, or with his overflowing courtesy he would have refrained from these observations. In the innocence of his heart he went on to say that "there was some danger that the vast masses of the population of India, who were to a great extent uneducated and unable to comprehend administrative questions, would regard public animadversions upon the conduct of the Government as evidence of inefficiency and weakness." With his thoughts preoccupied about Ireland, as he admitted they were, Mr. Gladstone could hardly fail to be conscious of the parallel suggested by this shrewd judgment. How he should reply to it without being so rude as to disagree with his amiable visitor must have exercised him not a little. "That might be so," he said, but he added that his information was so limited that he must guard himself against expressing a confident opinion. It is impossible not to regret that the want of accurate knowledge does not restrain Mr. Gladstone from expressing confident opinions on other subjects quite as important as Indian questions. If he had been equally prudent on another recent occasion when he spoke at Hawarden, he would not have exalted King Bomba to the disadvantage of Mr. Balfour, or heaped shame on his own country by declaring the pre-eminent virtues of Austria and Russia.

While there were some matters on which the Nawab was content to accept Mr. Gladstone's eloquent generalities, there were others and they were particularly awkward ones—on which he seems to have pressed him rather closely. He wanted to know Mr. Gladstone's feeling towards

Turkey, for whom, as the fount of Mahomedanism, the Nawab had a Mussulman's regard. He asked especially whether Mr. Gladstone would be willing to repeat if necessary the policy of the Crimean War. Mr. Gladstone's reply might have been recorded by himself from the closeness with which the report of it evidently follows his language. He is stated to have said that "this question was one of great magnitude, affording room for lengthy discussion, but without attempting any detailed exposition of his views he had no hesitation in saying that he personally entertained very friendly feelings towards Turkey." If, when the Nizam and the Nizam's Government have these weighty words before them, they are able to extract anything intelligible from them, they will possess a degree of skill unknown to us in England. But Mr. Gladstone did specify one proof, and a remarkable one, of the goodwill he has entertained towards Turkey. This consisted in the bombardment of Alexandria. That bombardment prepared the way, he said, for the entrance of a Turkish army into Egypt. Perhaps it is singular that the Turkish Government did not regard the circumstances in that light. To them it seemed that we were attacking their territory. In any case they did not send an army to accentuate by a forced military occupation the ruin which our cannon had already effected. Mr. Gladstone could not have descended from his generalities into particulars fraught with more danger than this reminiscence of the bombardment of Alexandria. It is an incident in British policy to be remembered with even less satisfaction than the Crimean War. The conversation happily reverted to personal topics, and it must have reached its most interesting point when the ex-Premier and the Nawab exchanged portraits. That of Mr. Gladstone, we are told, represented him in his emblematic occupation of hewing down a tree. The leave-taking was as cordial as the greeting. The Nawab will return to Hyderabad impressed with the largeness of Mr. Gladstone's sympathies for all sorts and conditions of men—the natives of India in particular (next after those of Ireland)—and the Nizam will rejoice to know that his presence at his grandmother's funeral gave especial satisfaction to the ex-Prime Minister of England.—*York Herald*, September 22.

We never know, we probably never shall know, the full mind of Mr. Gladstone. It is so happily provided with turns and corners of which no one suspected the existence, that each new revelation seems to leave us more astonished than the last. Mr. Gladstone received at Hawarden last week Mahdi Ali, the representative of the Nizam of Hyderabad. A State paper has been made for the benefit of the Nizam by his diplomatic agents. It contains some facts not mentioned in current biographies of the great statesman. Mr. Gladstone's father sent out one of the first merchantmen to India. This gave him a claim upon Indian regard. Mr. Gladstone himself sent out Lord Ripon to India, the great Viceroy who raised a discussion about the Ilbert Bill, and then did not pass it. Mr. Gladstone seems to think that that gave him a claim to the love of the Indian people. The oracle of Hawarden, being pressed as to the policy of the Crimean war, and the chances of its repetition, by a Mahometan who must have disapproved of Mr. Gladstone's policy from 1876-1880, announced "that he personally entertained very friendly feelings towards Turkey." Mahdi Ali must have been very much surprised at this confession, as much as he was subsequently to hear of Mr. Gladstone's affection for trees, and his prowess in using an axe. The conjunction of two professions would seem to imply that what Mr. Gladstone most loves he seeks to destroy. "In the course of further conversation Mr. Gladstone expressed the great pleasure it gave him to hear that his Highness the Nizam, allowing his feelings of affection and respect to break through the traditions of the past, had attended the funeral of his grandmother." There are many things in Indian life which would have been regarded worthy of formal mention in conversation of this kind; but none more striking than the exuberance of contempt which Mr. Gladstone displayed over the attendance of the Nizam at his grandmother's funeral. But Mr. Gladstone's best point was a bit of biographical history in proof of his affection for the Turks. "Instancing the bombardment of Alexandria, an act which had been criticised in some quarters as amounting to an attack on an outlying portion of the Turkish dominions, Mr. Gladstone added that the night before the bombardment took place he was dining with Musurus Pasha, the Turkish Ambassador, and told him that the British Government was then paving the way for the entrance of Turkish influence into Egypt, and that Turkish troops could enter Egypt and thus free the Khedive from the unwholesome influences to which he was then subject. The suggestion was, said Mr. Gladstone, telegraphed at once by the Ambassador to Constantinople, but his Majesty the Sultan did not, unfortunately, as Mr. Gladstone thought, see fit to accept it. As regards the occupation of Egypt, Mr. Gladstone expressed himself as entertaining no doubt that the British Government were determined to clear out of the country and to keep troops there no longer than was absolutely necessary." The story is so characteristic that it deserves emphasis. Here is a statesman who is still, apparently, of opinion that the Sovereign whose system produced the Bulgarian massacres and who at this moment is unable to pay his cooks a sovereign, whose financial necessities forced him to make a milch cow of Egypt, is a better guardian of law and order, the prosperity of the fellaheen, and the political and commercial future of the Nile Valley than Great Britain. We understand the case. Anything to get rid of responsibility! Even the restoration of the Turk to Egypt was thought better than the taking up of our own appointed task, doing the work thoroughly, and making, as Lord Rosebery said, a good job of it. But why should we trouble over a statesman whose highest delight flows forth at the attendance of an Indian Prince at the funeral of his grandmother?—*Western Morning News*, September 22.

Mr. Gladstone on India.—Mr. Gladstone has permitted his retirement at Hawarden to be invaded by a distinguished Mahomedan, the Nawab Mahdi Ali, the Financial and Political Secretary of Hyderabad, now in England as the representative of the Nizam. The substance of the conversation, which had been put in writing for the information of the Nizam, is now published, and may be turned to as affording some glimpses of Mr. Gladstone's thinking on a subject rarely treated in his public addresses. Truth to tell, the opinions actually expressed are of too general a kind to be in any wise helpful to the understanding of the Indian problem now being pressed forward. The native politician was complimentary in the extreme: and Mr. Gladstone—it goes without saying—was not to be outdone in courtesy; but friendly sentiment is one thing and a declaration of policy another. There were two points on which Mahdi Ali seemed anxious to get a positive assurance—he wished to know Mr. Gladstone's attitude to Turkey, the country regarded by Indian Mussulmans as the fount of their religion, and what Mr. Gladstone thought of the Indian National Congress. On both, Mahdi Ali received answers showing how remote the questions involved are from the daily matter of Mr. Gladstone's reflections. Perhaps Mahdi Ali has not taken lessons in the western art of interviewing, or he could hardly have failed to extract some more definite sentiment than that Mr. Gladstone personally entertains very friendly feelings for Turkey. Where these friendly feelings would carry Mr. Gladstone in the case of a Russian encroachment upon Turkey is the question Mahdi Ali was eager to have answered, and which Mr. Gladstone naturally found to be of too great magnitude for instantaneous discussion. While the public will be thankful for reticence on a matter likely to bring Britain's duty in Europe into sharp conflict with the sentiments of the Mahomedans in India, it could have been wished that Mr. Gladstone had also refrained from citing the bombardment of Alexandria as an act paving the way for the entrance of Turkish influences into Egypt. This opens a vein of reminiscence by no pleasant to these who desire to think well of the Liberal party; and it appears that even the Sultan was far from sharing the view that the bombardment was for the benefit of Turkey. It is more agreeable to find Mr. Gladstone assuring his visitor of his belief that the British troops will be cleared out of Egypt with no unnecessary delay. This accords with his general sentiment as to the moral basis of the British occupation of India. It is only justifiable so long as it is for the good of the country—a sentiment which could not fail to throw Mr. Gladstone into the ranks of those who welcome the voice of India as heard in the National Congress were his mind not loaded with the politics of Ireland. The National Congress, it is evident, will receive little encouragement from the Mahamedan portion of the Indian populations whose traditional theory of Government will be the last to succumb to doctrines based on the claim of the masses to rule. With the easy assumption of the right to govern according to his humour characteristic of the Mohamedan nearer home, Mahdi Ali is of the opinion that the system of rule now established in India will do well enough. He is satisfied that a Government so beneficent as that of Britain should be allowed to take its own course, reforming when it so minded, and standing still when changes are inconvenient, rather than obey any pressure from political agitation. Evidently Mahdi Ali has in him the elements of a choice Conservatism that must command the admiration of many of our full-grown native specimens. Mr. Gladstone's opinion of the Oriental form of a thing so familiar to him at home is left to surmise. He was careful to profess only imperfect information regarding the reform movement in India, and he seems to have entered with much more fulness and zest into an account of the history and antiquities of Hawarden for the benefit of his guest. In its way the somewhat fruitless interview is significant of the Indian problem. Here we have a native of ability and distinction coming out of the swarm of Indian life, very much contented with institutions as they are, and only anxious that Britain should do nothing to lower the prestige of his co-religionists in Europe; and, receiving him, a statesman who would be profoundly dissatisfied with these institutions if he realised their character, and were not too busy endeavouring to settle the affairs of a population amounting to about the eightieth part of that of India. After all, it is well that Conservatism is the note of the Oriental.—*Scottish Leader*, September 22.

Mr. Gladstone ought to have been a little more frank with his Mahomedan interviewer, and told him that there was not the slightest chance of this country going to war for the maintenance of the Turkish Empire. He knows that this is so better than any other man, for he has been the main instrument in convincing the public mind that this country has no real interest in the maintenance of the corrupt and feeble despotism of the Sultan. It was all very well to be courteous to the representative of the Nizam, but it should have been made clear that we have no intention of supporting European Turkey.—*Dundee Advertiser*, September 22.

The Financial and Political Secretary of Hyderabad being in this country in connection with the Deccan scandal, received an invitation from

Mr. Gladstone to visit Hawarden. Mahdi Ali accepted the invitation, and has drawn up for the information of the Nizam an account of the conversation he had with the Liberal leader on the occasion of his visit. Mr. Gladstone's references to public questions affecting India were very cautious. Mahdi Ali was anxious to obtain an expression of opinion on the subject of the National Congress, and made what looks like an attempt to draw Mr. Gladstone into a discussion on the question whether it was not disadvantageous that the uneducated masses of India should be encouraged to criticise the conduct of the Government. Mr. Gladstone, without entering into details of the Congress movement, his information with regard to which he believes to be imperfect, answered Mahdi Ali that "all legitimate and reasonable efforts on the part of the people to represent their requirements and improve their position commanded his warmest sympathy." Earlier in the conversation he reminded his guest that his appointment of Lord Ripon to the Governor-Generalship was an indication of the lines on which he would like to see the country governed, and the friends of the Congress will not infer from the published conversation that he is against them. Mahdi Ali is not for them, but he appears to have been very well pleased with his reception at Hawarden. Mr. Gladstone chatted with him pleasantly about the rise of Liverpool, remarking that his father in 1812 sent out the first merchantman from the port to India. "Explaining the interest of the Mersey, and contrasting its changed appearance now and the length of the docks (about six miles) with the state of things in the time of his father, he mentioned that though far larger in amount now, the shipping appeared, for various reasons, less in bulk and appearance than it was then." Mahdi Ali having evinced an interest in tree-felling, was presented by Mr. Gladstone with a copy of a photograph of himself in the act of cutting down a tree.—*Dundee Advertiser*, September 22.

Mr. Gladstone and the Nizam's Representative.—The Nawab Mohsin ool Moolk, Mahdi Ali, the chief representative of the Nizam in connection with the Deccan case, paid a visit to Hawarden last week before his return to India. Mr. Gladstone cordially received him, and mentioned in conversation that his father, in 1812, sent out one of the first merchantmen to India, called the Kingsmill. When asked for his opinion upon the propriety of England's maintaining and repeating, if necessary, the policy of the Crimean War, in respect to the assistance given to Turkey, the fount of Mahomedanism, not only as tending to retain the sympathy of the Indian Mussulmans, but also as assisting to retard the advance of Russia eastwards, Mr. Gladstone said that this question was one of great magnitude, affording room for lengthy discussion, but without attempting any detailed exposition of his views, he had no hesitation in saying that he personally entertained very friendly feelings towards Turkey. As regards the occupation of Egypt, Mr. Gladstone expressed himself as entertaining no doubt that the British Government were determined to clear out of the country and to keep troops there no longer than was absolutely necessary. On the subject of the National Congress Mr. Gladstone said he had only imperfect information, and consequently had some hesitation in discussing this subject; but, so far as he remembered, the questions involved consisted mainly of reform of the marriage laws and prohibition of early marriages, matters chiefly affecting Hindoos. Mahdi Ali explained that his co-religionists as a body had not yet joined the Congress movement, preferring to allow a Government which had done so much for them and their religion to proceed with its reforms without interference or pressure by political agitation, adding that there was, no doubt, an advantage in educated natives coming forward to give their opinions on points arising in the government of the country, but, on the other hand, there was some danger that the vast masses of the population of India, who were to a great extent uneducated and unable to comprehend administrative questions, would regard public animadversions upon the conduct of the Government, as evidence of inefficiency and weakness, which it was highly undesirable to disseminate.—*Scottish Leader*, September 22.

The Nawab Mohsin-ool-Moolk, Mahdi Ali, as a "Citizen of the World," and as the Political Secretary of the Nizam of Hyderabad, whose financial affairs have been engaging the attention of a Parliamentary Committee, has been paying a visit to this country. Fortune, or orders from home, brought him, in the course of his tour, to Hawarden Castle; and he has drawn up for the information of his master an account of an interview he was privileged to have with Mr. Gladstone. Usually the impressions carried away by the Oriental mind of the public men and public affairs of Western countries are more amusing than complimentary—witness the journal kept by Goldsmith's Chinaman and by the Shah of Persia. It is quite otherwise with the impressions and recollections which Mahdi Ali took away from Hawarden, for the information of his august master. The host and the guest seem to have striven each to surpass the other in the profoundness of the salaams he made to the other's fame and character, and in the interest he expressed in the other's affairs. Mr. Gladstone, indeed, gravely professed that the "consideration of the mode of government in Ireland" had lately taken up so much of his time that younger men had been enabled to form more valuable opinions regarding "the internal affairs of India." But the Nizam's representative courteously declined to listen to the idea that the ex-Premier's views on any subject could become, as Mr. Gladstone expressed it—with the recollection doubtless of a recent speech on fruit culture and jam-making in his mind—"over-ripe." Eastern impassivity, as represented by Mahdi Ali of Hyderabad, must have been sorely tried, however, on hearing from Mr. Gladstone's own lips that "personally he entertained very friendly feelings towards Turkey." No country has ever been called upon so often and under such painful circumstances to take the good wishes of its best friends on trust as Turkey. Lord Beaconsfield was the "best friend" of the Turk when he sought to "concentrate" him within half his former bulk; Mr. Gladstone, also, must have been actuated by the most friendly feelings when he used his powers with such success to kick this unhappy Turk "bag and baggage" out of Bulgaria. New light is thrown on a remarkable passage of recent Eastern history by what the ex-Premier is reported to have said about the "bombardment of Alexandria." On the night before Mr. Gladstone was dining with the Turkish Ambassador, and told him that the work the British Government were engaged in was that of "paving the way for the entrance of Turkish influence into Egypt." If Mr. Gladstone loves the Turk, how much more must he love the Egyptian, in thus preparing for him the blessing of that Ottoman control which the Bulgarian was not worthy to retain? Or must we think that the truth, the whole truth, and nothing but the truth, is not what always passes between Ministers and Ambassadors, or for that matter between ex-Ministers and emissaries from the Orient, and that the passages of conversation are so gilded with Eastern compliment, especially on repetition to headquarters, that they cease to bear any resemblance to realities? The richest fusion of Western matter-of-fact with Indian hyperbole is, however, to be found in Mr. Gladstone's compliment to the Nizam, for having so far "allowed his feelings of affection and respect to break through the traditions of the past, as to attend the funeral of his grandmother." If this is not a new "invention of the *Times*," it is an example of the very finest and rarest water of Mr. Gladstone's sense of humour.—*Edinburgh Evening Dispatch*, September 22.

A MORE harmless occupation of Mr. Gladstone has been the entertainment at Hawarden of the emissary of the Nizam. The Indian and English statesmen conversed in the most pleasant way on the neutral ground of the wealth of Liverpool and the general welfare of India. But when they touched such burning topics as the occupation of Egypt and the friendship of Turkey and the conflict between the Mussulman and Hindoo subjects of the Empress, Mr. Gladstone skilfully parried the questions of his Mahommedan interlocutor. The bombardment of the Alexandrian forts was ingeniously converted into a proof of his friendly feeling to the Sultan; and he evaded any opinion on the National Congress of India, which ought on Separatist principles to have his full sympathy, by professing to think that it was only concerned with such purely Hindoo questions as early marriages. They parted accordingly the best of friends, Mahdi Ali carrying away with him as a memorial of Hawarden a photograph of the ex-Premier engaged in cutting down a tree.—*Guardian*, September 6.

CONFIDENCES AND RECRIMINATIONS.—Last week a remarkable interview took place at Hawarden Castle. The Nawab Mohsin ool Moolk, Mahdi Ali, a high official in the service of the Nizam of Hyderabad, who has been representing his master's interests in this country before the Deccan Commission, called on Mr. Gladstone before his return to India. On either side some striking things were said. The ex-Premier, after an interchange of compliments, remarked that he was now in the last stage of his political life; he had been a member of the House of Commons for over fifty-six years, and there was such a thing as being over-ripe. The Nawab put to Mr. Gladstone the delicate question whether, if it were necessary to retain the sympathy of the Indian Mohammedans, and check the eastward advance of Russia, he was in favour of repeating the policy of the Crimean War, by assisting Turkey, the fount of Mohammedanism. It is somewhat suprising to learn that Mr. Gladstone, though he judiciously refrained from giving a direct reply, unhesitatingly declared that "he entertained very friendly feelings towards Turkey," and that the night before the bombardment of Alexandria he told Musurus Pasha, the Turkish Ambassador, at a dinner party, that the British Government was paving the way for the entrance of the Turkish influence into Egypt, and that Turkish troops could enter Egypt and free the Khedive from the unwholesome influences to which he was subject. The Sultan "unfortunately," said Mr. Gladstone, did not accept the offer. The Nawab referred in the highest terms to the "signal temporal advantages" British rule has conferred upon the people of India, and said that, should any emergency arise, the spirit of fire and devotion which formerly animated the hearts of Mohammedans in India would still be found keen and active, enabling them to meet the common danger in complete unison with the British nation. Contrasted with this pleasant intercourse is the mutual recrimination that has taken place between Mr. Gladstone and his old colleagues in the Cabinet in 1882. Mr. Gladstone, in reviewing the "Life of Mr. Forster," asserted that Mr. Parnell and the other Irish members imprisoned in 1882 were released "because of an unanimous judgment of the Cabinet that these gentlemen were not associated with crime." Lord Selborne has taken the trouble to collect the opinions of Mr. Bright, Mr. Chamberlain, Lord Hartington, Lord Northbrook, Lord Carlingford, and Lord Monk-Bretton, and none of these can recollect any such "unanimous judgment." Still, the fact remains that in announcing the release, Mr. Gladstone stated that the imprisoned Members were to be released, and likewise "all persons who are not believed to be associated with the commission of crime." Mr. Gladstone promises to substantiate his case by "conclusive documentary evidence." But surely if it was understood that the Members were believed to have been associated with the commission of crime, they would never have been released. If it was believed they were so associated, and the late Ministers consented to their release, they have no right now to assume a high moral attitude towards their ex-chief.—*Christian World*, September 27.

The Hyderabad delegate, Moulvi Mahdi Ali, who was to have returned to the East this week, has, by direction of the Nizam's Government, postponed his departure from England until the questions relating to the Deccan mining concession are in a fair way of settlement. The Nawab Mahdi Hassan, Chief Justice of Hyderabad, has also received a telegram from India instructing him to remain in this country in order to assist the State delegate in the pending negotiations.—*Manchester Guardian*, September 14.

The Nawab Mahdi Ali, who last week visited Mr. Gladstone, would place the people of this country in his debt if he would make public the estimate he formed of the great English politician when the interview was over. As a Minister of the Nizam of Hyderabad he has drawn up an account of the interview for the information of the Government of that Prince, but the Nawab has carefully refrained, so far as is known, from giving his own impressions of Mr. Gladstone or his opinions, so far as he could obtain any expression of them. Mr. Gladstone mentioned the interesting fact that his father once sent out a merchantman to India, and then added that he himself always entertained feelings of the most friendly and sympathetic nature towards India and its people. He then conveyed to Mahdi Ali the information that, much as he was interested in India, his time was so much occupied with the consideration of the government of Ireland that he had little leisure for other subjects—possibly with a latent feeling that the Government of Hyderabad might thereby be influenced in bringing about Irish Home Rule in order that Mr. Gladstone might turn his attention to India. This did not, however, seem to strike any responsive chord of hope in the breast of the Nawab, who took occasion at a later stage of the conversation to tell Mr. Gladstone that the State of Hyderabad and the Mussulmans generally looked upon the British Government in India as in every way deserving their support and affection—afraid, no doubt, that if Mr. Gladstone could settle the Irish question to his mind, he would be casting in his lot with the disaffected and the revolutionaries in India. The "wily Oriental" and the "old Parliamentary hand" do not seem to have come to anything like close quarters, but to have fenced with each other throughout, and a very pretty mock duel it was; but, as a matter of fact, the Nawab appears to have tried to convey to Mr. Gladstone his opinion that the Home Rule agitators in India were about the least desirable people to be found in that country. He delicately suggested that the people of his faith—the bravest and most loyal of the Indian races—refused to join in the movement for a National Congress, expressing confidence that the Government should be left alone to pursue reforms in its own way, and also giving utterance to the opinion that "there was some danger that the vast masses of the population of India, who were to a great extent uneducated and unable to comprehend administrative questions, would regard public animadversions upon the conduct of the Government as evidence of inefficiency and weakness, which it was highly undesirable to disseminate." To these very sensible remarks Mr. Gladstone volunteered no reply, saying that he would express no opinions on the subject—conscious that the leading party in the promotion of the National Congress are the Bengali Baboos, the noisiest, least dignified, and most disloyal of the Indian peoples; and with the recollection that they send over Lalmohun Ghose and other cheaply garrulous people to fight constituencies in the

Gladstonian interest he refrained from committing himself. Mr. Gladstone's part of the conversation was full of expressions of lovingkindness for everybody mentioned, and he tried, whenever possible, to give proofs of it. Some of these proofs were a little remarkable. Those people who did not know that Mr. Gladstone had an undying attachment to the Turk and the Turkish Government may know it now. He proved it by bombarding Alexandria—not, as some people may have thought, to put down Arabi's rebellion in the interests of the Khedive, who was supposed to guarantee European interests in Egypt, but—will it be believed?—in order to open a way for the admission of Turkish troops and the restoration of Turkish influence in that country! This will be news to some of the people who supported him in that policy. But his love for the people of India was shown in much the same way. He sent the Marquis of Ripon to rule over them.—*Yorkshire Post*, September 22.

MR. GLADSTONE IN TWO CHARACTERS.—Two interesting communications in yesterday's *Times* exhibited Mr. Gladstone to us in two, and these perhaps the most piquantly contrasted, of the numerous characters with which that versatile comedian has identified himself. The less pleasing undoubtedly of the two—a character, indeed, which contains some elements of the painful—is that in which he is presented to us by Lord Selborne. It is that of the man who will—how shall we put it most delicately?—who "will say anything"; and we will leave it to Hegelian metaphysicians to say whether "anything" can possibly include "the thing that is not." Perhaps, by the way, if "pure Being" and "pure Nothing" are really identical, as the followers of that philosophy assure us, a new mode may suggest itself of discovering the truth contained in some of Mr. Gladstone's statements. But for the present we prefer to waive the point of Transcendentalism, and confine ourselves to the neutral description of him as "a man who will say anything." He has lately said that the liberation of Mr. Parnell and his two fellow-suspects in 1882 proved the existence of "a unanimous judgment of the Cabinet" of that date that "these gentlemen were not associated with crime"; by which all the world understood that the question of their association with crime came specifically before that Cabinet, and that Mr. Gladstone was, in accordance with his Privy Councillor's oath of secrecy, simply disclosing the result of its Ministerial consideration. As this, however, did not accord with Lord Selborne's remembrance of the facts, he has consulted the recollections of Mr. Bright, Mr. Chamberlain, Lord Hartington, Lord Northbrook, Lord Carlingford, and Lord Monk Bretton, and they have with one voice replied that they are in the same case with Lord Selborne. The Cabinet of 1882 never pronounced on the question of Mr. Parnell and his two colleagues' association with crime, never considered it, never even had it propounded for consideration. The whole and sole question before them was whether Mr. Parnell, Mr. Dillon, and Mr. O'Kelly, whatever their antecedents may have been, were or were not persons who could at that time be set at liberty without danger to the public interest. Nor has this question ever been combined, mixed up, complicated, or in the remotest degree associated with or prejudiced by any other question whatever.

In the other communication to which we have referred the Mr. Gladstone "who will say anything" gives place to the Mr. Gladstone who will say everything and nothing at the same time. A more humorous colloquy—quite unintentionally so, of course, on both sides—than that which is reported between the eminent statesman and the Nawab Mohsin ool Moolk, Mahdi Ali, chief representative of the Nizam of Hyderabad, has seldom appeared even in the pages of professedly comic periodicals. The Oriental ceremoniousness of the visitor's address and the constitutional effusiveness of the host's colloquial manner combine to make the dialogue quite unique of its kind. We regret that we have not space to follow the two interlocutors through their prolonged interchange of compliments. We must even deny ourselves the pleasure of dwelling upon such gems of the conversation as Mr. Gladstone's remark—illustrated by a reference to the bombardment of Alexandria, with no doubt, the "bag and baggage" speech held in reserve as a supplementary proof—that he "personally entertained very friendly feelings towards Turkey." We can do no more than note the touching passage in which Mr. Gladstone, after pointing out the beauty of the Hawarden ruins, and explaining the history and antiquity of the Castle, "expressed the great pleasure it gave him to hear that his Highness the Nizam, allowing his feelings of affection and respect to break through the traditions of the past, had attended the funeral of his grandmother." We must content ourselves with noting generally the remarkable illustration which the instance affords of Mr. Gladstone's powers in the second of the two characters which we have mentioned. Judging from the amount of words which he expended in replying to Mahdi Ali's questions, he might be supposed to have said everything. Considered from the point of view of meaning, he said nothing. Mahdi Ali pumped him on the policy of the Crimean War, on the offers of the Native Princes to contribute to the assistance of the Government of India, on native education, on native self-government, on we know not what; and on all these subjects Mr. Gladstone answered fluently, copiously, blandly, even passionately. Yet, if Mahdi Ali goes home a wiser man on any one of them, by so much as a single gleam of additional enlightenment, he must possess powers of miraculous divination.—*Saturday Review*, September 22.

Nawab Mahdi Ali, an Indian Mohammedan gentleman who at present represents the Nizam's Government in this country, recently accepted an invitation from Mr. Gladstone to visit him at Hawarden, and has sent an interesting account of the interview to his own Government. Mr. Gladstone (says our London Correspondent) was very loquacious about his family affairs, but was characteristically vague and inaccurate when invited outside the domain of the personal. A knotty question was put to him by his visitor as to the propriety of England repeating the policy followed in the Crimean War, of upholding Turkish supremacy in the Bosphorus, not only with a view to retaining the sympathy of the Indian Mahommedans, but in order to check the progress of Russia eastward. Mr. Gladstone dexterously evaded the point thus presented to him, and dwelt in a lofty manner upon his sympathy with the Turkish Government, instancing as a proof of his good-will towards the Sultan the fact that the night prior to the bombardment of Alexandria he, in a casual way, mentioned to the Turkish Ambassador, whom he met at a dinner party, that the British Government would not object to the employment of Turkish troops to free the Khedive from "the unwholesome influences to which he was then subject." Mahdi Ali, with the proverbial courtesy of his race, does not appear to have made any reply to this extraordinary statement, but he must have thought that his host had a peculiar way of displaying his love for the Sultan. The interviewer next endeavoured to elicit Mr. Gladstone's opinions as to the operations of that singular Indian political organisation which is grandiloquently termed "The National Congress. Mr. Gladstone confessed that he was imperfectly informed on the subject, and—good, innocent man—thought that the Congress had been established for the purpose of dealing with such trifles as the marriage of infants and the prohibition of the re-marriage of widows. He had never heard, it appears, that Indian agitators, inspired mainly by the encouragement he has extended to the disloyal Irish, have inaugurated a movement having for its object the establishment of a system of Home Rule in India. - *Yorksh ire Post*, September 22.

It is reported that Colonel Marshall, the adviser and private secretary to the Nizam of Hyderabad, who is at present in Simla, will not return to his post in Hyderabad, but will probably revert to the service of the Indian Government. By the way, Mr. Cordery, the late Resident at Hyderabad, who recently reverted to the home department of the Government of India, has now resigned his post in the Bengal Civil Service, which he entered in 1855. He has earned a pension and rest by his 33 years' service.—*Manchester Guardian*, September 25.

What a quantity of mud has been stirred up, and dust raised, by all this Hyderabad Deccan scandal or inquiry. In the meantime the coal is left peacefully reclining in the bosom of the earth waiting for the disputants to settle upon something. This quarrelling cannot possibly benefit anyone except the lawyers, and the sooner it is adjusted the more chance will the shareholders have of seeing their property developed.

There are three parties in the matter—the Nizam's Government, the concessionnaires, headed by Mr. Watson, and the shareholders. The Nizam's Government are mortified at seeing what an enormous profit has been made out of what they sold. Mr. Watson is hoping and fearing about the permanent ratification of the concession; and the unfortunate shareholders are waiting for the muddy water to settle, which all this quarrelling has stirred up.

Nothing much has been proved against Mr. Watson after all, except that he has asked an exorbitant profit for what he was the possessor. This is reprehensible, certainly, but a fault not very uncommon in this city of London, where every promoter that breathes soon acquires the faculty of opening his mouth pretty widely over anything he has to dispose of to the public.

To turn to the actual business of the company, all their coal raising efforts have been paralysed by repeated outbreaks of cholera, which creates a panic among the coolies, and soon scatters them to the four winds of heaven. Of course, the Board will speak of this as an "unforeseen circumstance," which, in my opinion, it was not. All the planting districts of the Wynaad and Travancore are well aware of the labour difficulty and contract with maistries, or headmen, for a supply of coolies.

Any plan known to them should have been known and *must* have been known to the board of the Hyderabad-Deccan Company. The Chairman's and Mr. Hughes-Hughes' peurile estimate about raising 1,000 tons of coal a day mentioned nothing about the labour supply. They could, however, hardly imagine that the coal was going to raise itself.—*Trade and Finance*, October 10.

An Old New Zealander in a Storm.—An old New Zealander, in the person of Sir John Gorst, has had a good deal of pitch flung at him lately, on account of his supposed connection with the Hyderabad-Deccan scandal. The Indian newspapers generally had evidently expected to see the Under-Secretary of State for India pilloried by the Committee appointed to investigate the whole affair, and the *Pioneer* and the *Statesman* discuss the question in a very disappointed and injured strain. From their jeremiads it appears that Sir John, whilst in India, had been guilty of associating with a certain "Tom Palmer," who, to put it mildly, was not in sympathy with the official delegate of the Nizam, who went to England in connection with the inquiry into the scandal. The delegate, evidently anxious to keep out of temptation's way, refused to expose his virtue to danger, by granting the insidious Thomas a personal interview. Alas for his good resolutions! there is a reception at the Foreign Office, when Sir John, meeting the Nawab in the crowd, according to the indignant Indian *Pioneer*, asks him if he has seen "his friend Tom Palmer." Need it be added that the barrier which the discreet representative of the Hyderabad State had judiciously raised was at once removed? Later on, and through Mr. Palmer's amiable intervention, Sir John calls upon another Hyderabad official, of whom he had expressed himself unfavourably. And as the scene for the moment closes, we are told of a little dinner given by Mr. Palmer, at which Sir John Gorst and the Hyderabad delegate are the guests.

When opposition papers agree, their unanimity is wonderful, and having evidently prepared themselves for the inculpation of Sir John in the scandal, the *Statesman and Friend of India* joined with its rival in expressions of disappointment, asserting Sir John's escape from the pillory that was prepared for him, in its most grandiloquent style, to be "an affront to India." The *Statesman*, as well as being very malicious, has evidently a very long memory, and reminds its readers that it was by the recommendation of Mr. Palmer that Sir John Gorst was engaged by the old Peshkar to come to India in 1883, for a fee of 75,000 rupees. It says:—"Thomas Palmer has a very curious history, the facts of which have never yet, we believe, been told. He is a Eurasian barrister in advanced life, and, at the time of which we write, was the old Peshkar's unofficial adviser and bosom-friend. The immense fee that was paid to him by Sir John Gorst was entered by the Peshkar in the Treasury accounts as money that was required for large purchases made by the young Nizam in Bombay. The Prince declared the statement to be altogether false, as he had made no purchases whatever there, and wanted to make none. When pressed for further explanation, the Peshkar declared that the money had been paid to Sir John Gorst for advice in connection with his Highness's approaching accession! Sir John Gorst is now Under-Secretary for India, and it is stated in Hyderabad that upon the arrival of the Nizam's representatives in London, Sir John Gorst opened a correspondence with them, through his old friend and ally, Tom Palmer. Sir John Gorst himself is hardly the proper man to be Under-Secretary for India. With the India Office already compromised through General Strachey, we have the Under-Secretary himself mixed up in this very unpleasant way with the Nizam's affairs, and we certainly can express no surprise at the fear entertained by the Nizam's Council that the investigation will end in a fiasco."

The *Statesman* has for once proved a true prophet in predicting the collapse of the inquiry, but whether it is equally successful in implicating Sir John Gorst in the scandal is another matter. The will has not been wanting on its part, but the way is not quite so clear, especially in view of the following letter, which has been addressed by Sir John Gorst's Secretary to the *Pall Mall Gazette*, which, as might have been expected, from its scandal-loving tendencies, has taken up the charges of its Indian contemporaries *con amore*.

Mr. Ritchie writes: "Sir,—Sir John Gorst desires me to acknowledge the receipt of your letter of the 14th inst., and to say that he saw it, and the articles in yesterday's *Pall Mall Gazette* to which it refers, as he was passing through London to-day on the way to the continent. Sir John Gorst desires me to say, in reply, that had your representative applied to him earlier he could have saved you from giving currency to a number of misstatements which the *Pioneer* article contains. The charge which is insinuated against Sir John Gorst in the *Pioneer* is wholly false. Mr. Palmer, so far as Sir John Gorst is aware, had and has no connection with, or interest in, the Deccan Company; and Sir John Gorst, throughout the proceedings, consistently refused to have any communication in reference to the Deccan inquiry, or with any of the parties interested therein, with the exception of an official interview at the India Office with the Nawab Mahdi Ali.—Yours faithfully, RICHMOND RITCHIE."

Despite the above contradiction, the *Pall Mall* still sticks to its point, asserting that the denial does not go by any means so far as the original charges. "Thus," it continues, "in the first place, the statement of the *Pioneer*, endorsed by the *Statesman and Friend of India*, was not, so far as we understand, that Mr. Tom Palmer had any specific 'connection with or interest in the Deccan Company,' but that he was generally mixed up with the seamy side of affairs at Hyderabad. Further, it was stated that he is on intimate terms with Sir John Gorst, and the suggestion was that Mr. Palmer might have acted as intermediary between his friend, the Under-Secretary of India, and other persons who did not have 'connection with or interest in the Deccan Company.' This 'charge,' whatever it may be worth, is not, our readers will see, covered by the terms of Sir John Gorst's letter. Further, it will be noticed that what Sir John Gorst contradicts is that he had 'any communication *in reference to the Deccan inquiry* with any of the parties interested therein.' This is a different thing from saying that he did not have 'any communication with any of the parties interested therein.' We are compelled to make this distinction by the analogy of Mr. Smith's statement with regard to his dealings with the *Times*. Mr. Smith also denied that he had any communication *in reference to the Commission* with any of the parties interested therein.' But that denial, it subsequently appeared, was not inconsistent with the fact that he did have communications with his 'old friend, Mr. Walter.' An unbelieving generation has questioned whether the 'old friends' confined their conversation to the state of the weather. With this precedent before the public, it is unfortunate that Sir John Gorst has not given a less qualified denial to statements which are causing so much disquiet in India."

Probably Sir John's old friends in New Zealand will be inclined to put a more generous construction on the Under-Secretary's action than is possible for a journal which is nothing if not omniscient in its backbiting propaganda.—*Auckland Star*, October 4.

WE learn from India that Colonel Marshall has been withdrawn from the appointment which he took up two years ago as Private Secretary to the Nizam. The appointment was unprecedented. It was made on the recommendation of Lord Dufferin to enable the Nizam and Sir Salar Jung to carry on the work of administration by furnishing as an intermediary a man of tact who, it was hoped, would be able to soften the personal incompatibility which had unfortunately arisen between the youthful Sovereign and his young Minister. The new arrangement was cordially welcomed by the Nizam—indeed, was pressed by him upon Lord Dufferin on the occasion of his visit to Hyderabad. For a time the arrangement worked satisfactorily. Eventually, however, the tension between the Nizam and the Minister became so great that the latter sent in his resignation, the Private Secretary performing the part of a mutual friend in endeavouring to settle the matter in dispute.

At the moment of Sir Salar Jung's resignation, his successor in the Ministry, Sir Asman Jah, was in London, representing his Highness for the

Jubilee. Until the return of Sir Asman Jah, the Private Secretary held a unique position. After Sir Asman Jah's return, Colonel Marshall's presence became no longer necessary, but the Nizam wishing to retain him, the Viceroy consented to lend the officer's services for a further period. There was never any question of the appointment being made permanent. On this point there is evidently misapprehension. Sir Asman Jah was himself desirous that the Nizam's wish to have the advantage of Colonel Marshall's assistance in the transaction of business should be acceded to. The Viceroy, however, has written to his Highness a letter couched in very cordial terms, setting forth that the special circumstances under which the services of Colonel Marshall had been lent being now at an end, that officer will be withdrawn. The Nizam has very cordially acknowledged his obligations to Colonel Marshall for zealous services always rendered with geniality and tact. There has been no misunderstanding of any kind between the Indian authorities and the Nizam, and certainly there are no grounds for the withdrawal of Colonel Marshall detrimental to that officer's character.—*Army and Navy Gazette*, October 27.

THE affairs of the Hyderabad (Deccan) Company will be recalled to the notice of the House of Commons, on Friday, by a question to be addressed to the Government by Mr. J. R. Kelly, Conservative member for North Camberwell. The hon. gentleman proposes to ask whether negotiations are in progress with the object of altering the terms under which the Company holds its concession; whether the proposed alterations involve the abandonment by the Nizam of certain royalties which the Company have agreed to pay him; and whether the Under-Secretary for India will undertake that no alteration shall be sanctioned which is likely to be in any way detrimental to the Nizam's interests.—*Manchester Courier*, November 14.

THE DECCAN MINING COMPANY.—In the House of Commons, on November 16, Mr. Kelly asked the Under-Secretary for India whether he was aware of any negotiations now being on foot with the object of obtaining from the Nizam's Government an alteration of the terms of the contract made between that Government and Mr. Watson, such alteration being intended to include some fresh arrangement with reference to the royalties payable by the Deccan Mining Company. Whether any such negotiations could proceed without sooner or later passing through the Residency at Hyderabad: And, whether he would undertake that no alteration in the terms of the original contract should be sanctioned by the Indian Government if it were detrimental to the interests of the Nizam.

Sir John Gorst said the Secretary of State was aware that proposals with regard to the Deccan Company were now under the consideration of the Nizam's Government. The terms had not yet been submitted to the Secretary of State in Council, but of course alteration detrimental to the interests of the Nizam would be objected to.—*Evening Post*, November 16.

SIR J. GORST AND THE AFFAIRS OF HYDERABAD.—In the House of Commons, on November 16, in answer to Dr. Clark, Sir J. Gorst said: My attention has been called to an article in the *Pioneer* of Allahabad, which I understand to insinuate a charge that I have employed Mr. Palmer as an intermediary either in the affairs of Hyderabad generally or in reference to the Hyderabad Committee of this session in particular, is wholly false. It is not my intention to take any action in regard to such statements. Perhaps the House will allow me to add that in the winter of

1883-84, before I had ever held office, I acted as legal adviser to the Prime Minister and Senior Regent of Hyderabad. Since that time I have had nothing to do with the affairs of Hyderabad, except recently as Under-Secretary of State for India. In that capacity I have acted under the direction of my noble friend the Secretary of State, and through the regular officials of the India Office.—*Times*, November 16.

Sir John Gorst's answer in the House of Commons last night concerning his relations with Tom Palmer was by no means satisfactory. I believe, however, that on one point injustice has been done to Sir John Gorst. The story that he received £10,000 for going to Hyderabad is an exaggeration; he never received anything like so much, and he is still living in hopes that he may vindicate the receipt of such sum as was paid him by posing as the tribune for the injured and oppressed people of that native State.—Correspondent of *Pall Mall Gazette*, November 16.

The visit of the Nawab Mahdi Hassan, Chief Justice of Hyderabad, to this country, was not undertaken for nothing. He came over here to interview the Colonial Secretary, Lord Knutsford, with regard to the appointment of Home Secretary of Hyderabad, which had been offered to him by the Nizam. The Nawab, who has been over here for some time representing the Nizam's Government, is mainly concerned in looking into the Deccan mining scandal, concerning which he holds very pronounced opinions. His appointment as Home Secretary of Hyderabad will necessitate his throwing up the appointment of Chief Justice of that State.—*Society Herald*, November 19.

The Indian Princes.—The telegram which we published yesterday from our Special Correspondent with the Viceroy at Patiala contains an announcement which must have an important bearing on the future of India. The Viceroy has announced the decision of the Government in regard to the numerous and most gratifying offers which he has lately received from the Indian Princes and chiefs in regard to the defence of the North-Western frontier. Our loyal feudatories offered money for this purpose, but Lord Dufferin has told them that he would rather have men. He prefers, in fact, to take their gifts of good fellowship in kind, and he invites them to reorganize a portion of their levies in such a way as to make them available for co-operation with the Queen's troops for the common defence of India. The decision best accords with the dignity of the Sovereign and of the country that Lord Dufferin represents.

We could hardly pocket the cash of the chiefs, however freely offered, for a purpose of this sort, but we honour them and ourselves in asking them to make their soldiers worthy to stand side by side with our own. A present in specie would have given no stimulus to loyalty, but a union between Englishmen and natives on the field must have the happiest effect. The Government deserves the more credit for its decision, as the offers in question were of the most tempting description. One of them, that of the Nizam of Hyderabad, amounted to 40 [60] lakhs, and 40 [60] lakhs is £400,000 [£600,000.] Its value as a tribute of loyalty was enhanced by the terms in which it was made. The Nizam said that he had for some time observed that the revenue of India had shown little increase, while the expenditure had gone on steadily growing.

The growth was due solely to the heavy outlay on the improved defence of the Indian frontier, rendered necessary by the aggressive advance of

Russia in Central Asia. As "the oldest ally of the English in India," the Nizam felt it incumbent on him to show that, in this matter, the interests of all the inhabitants of India, British and native, are identical. He therefore undertook to make the Government a free gift of twenty lakhs (£200,000) yearly for two [three] years, for promoting the military defence of the North-West. He added that, when the hour of battle came with any invader of India, England could count upon his sword. The Indian Government has wisely and magnanimously converted this generous proposal into one for an exchange of presents.

While the Indian rulers will supply the men, England will furnish weapons and competent instructors, under conditions that ensure our respect for territorial sovereignty. We may thus by one stroke of policy double our force for the defence of Hindostan. This arrangement will, of course, enlarge the responsibility of each of the parties to it. The responsibilities on our side are so obvious that it is needless to refer to them in detail, but it is evident that they include a continuance of that policy of conciliation which has already had such happy results. Lord Dufferin has justified Lord Ripon. The natives—to use the term in its most comprehensive sense—who are fit to co-operate with us in arms as allies and equals are certainly fit for increased privileges of self-government.—*Daily News*, November 20.

The Indian editor is evidently a person of independent action, free from the trouble of trying to meet the regular habits and customs of his patrons. The last number of the *Decca Gazette* contains the cheerful announcement that "We are all so fatigued by the incessant labour of bringing out this paper for the last year, that the next publication will be postponed for a month, as the staff wants a holiday." London journalists will smile enviously at the prospect opened up by the last sentence.—*Echo*, November 20.

The Government of India have turned to the best possible advantage the offers of monetary contributions towards the defence of the frontier so liberally tendered by the Nizam of Hyderabad and other Indian feudatories a few months since. Instead of accepting these offers in hard cash, the Indian authorities intend to request the princes concerned to allow their armies to be reorganised under competent European supervision, so that they may be able, if necessary, to take their place in the field side by side with the Imperial troops. If no obstacles arise to prevent the carrying out of this policy, a great reform will have been carried out. At present the armies of the native States, almost without an exception, are ill-armed hordes of men without discipline or training, and entirely unfitted to meet an uncivilized, to say nothing of a civilized, foe. Nevertheless, they are maintained at enormous cost, and constitute a serious drain on the revenues of the various States. We cannot check the expenditure, but we can divert it into a proper channel, and this is what the Government of India propose to do now that the opportunity offers. When the work of reorganization is complete we shall have at our disposal a magnificent reserve to supplement our regular fighting forces in time of need.

There is splendid military material in the native armies of India, and the value of European discipline in training the rawest native levies has been shown over and over again. Quite recently, at the request of the Gaekwar, some British officers were told off to take the native army of the Baroda State in hand. They found the army little better than a mob, and it is now one of the best trained bodies of troops in the country. What has been done at Baroda may be done elsewhere. But the Government will have to be careful that in carrying out their policy they do not tread on the corns of the native princes. These potentates are extremely jealous of their prerogatives, and take especial pride in their armies, useless and ineffective as these at present are, and they would regard with extreme suspicion any attempt to alter the basis upon which the control of the forces rests.—*Yorkshire Post*, November 20.

THOSE who remember the evidence given before the Special Committee on the Hyderabad scandal by General Richard Strachey, R.E.—often confounded with his civilian brother Sir John—will hear without astonishment that in well-informed quarters he is reported to have been the principal agent in leading Viscount Cross astray in regard to the Burmah Ruby Mines. As in India, so in England, the name of Strachey seems destined to be associated with grave official errors. The break of gauge and the Budget blunder are not inadequately matched by the Deccan Mining Concession and the treatment of the Streeter Syndicate.—"Cœlum, non animum, mutant, qui trans mare currunt."—*Pall Mall Gazette*, November 21.

IT is safe to say that not a year passes in India without a more or less extensive and serious failure of crops, and this year the failure—although it cannot be considered severe, measured by the standard of Indian experience—is, nevertheless, important. In the sea-coast district of Ganjam, in Northern Madras, there were signs of impending famine during the closing week of October, and the Madras Government sent an officer with power to open relief works. A telegram forwarded to Bombay on the 31st of the month reported that heavy showers had fallen along the coast, and it was hoped that these had reached the distressed districts.

In Guzerat (Northern Bombay) there can be no doubt that actual famine exists, striking evidence of it having been presented to the eyes of the people of Bombay city, where for several days before the departure of the last mail, on the 2nd inst., large numbers of poor people from Guzerat were going about in search of alms or employment. A local subscription was being raised for the relief of the sufferers, but it does not appear that any means of assistance had been organized by the Government of the presidency. We read, too, of considerable and sometimes rather severe scarcity of food in Hyderabad, in Central India. The danger there arises not alone from the privations of the people, but from a possibly serious loss of land revenue, which the Nizam's exchequer can just now ill afford to undergo.

There are reports, too, of deficient crops on the west coast, south of Bombay, but the deficiency there is certainly not very great; and as large quantities of grain had been forwarded by rail to Calicut, anything like famine is out of the question. Considering that the summer rains have this year been unusually light in Western India, these accounts of suffering cannot be called at all alarming, and the local scarcity, though probably more widespread than that which occurs after a thoroughly good monsoon, can, it may be hoped, be effectually dealt with by the authorities. There seems to be no doubt that on the whole the rainfall, light as it has proved, has been favourably distributed.—*Manchester Guardian*, November 22.

THE DECCAN MINING COMPANY.—In the House of Commons, on November 23, Sir G. Campbell asked the Under-Secretary of State for India whether Her Majesty's Government proposed to take any action with reference to the last two paragraphs of the report of the Select Committee on the Deccan Mining Company, setting forth the evils attending the direct access of London speculators to the Ministers of Indian native States; whether, in fact, direct negotiations had since been going on between the Nizam's Ministers and the Deccan Mining Company; whether Her Majesty's Government would interfere in the matter, and avoid the difficulty pointed out by the Committee by taking their full share of responsibility; and whether, in case in that and other matters direct communications took place between native Governments and British speculators, the latter would be warned that they were to expect no assistance whatever from the British Government in enforcing their claims.

Sir J. Gorst: The report referred to has been sent to the Government of India, and until their reply has been received the Secretary of State considers it premature either to express any opinion or take any action upon it. The Secretary of State is aware, as I have already stated in reply to a question, that proposals relating to the Deccan Mining Company are now under the consideration of the Nizam's Government of Hyderabad, in consultation with the Resident. The hon. member will deduce from my reply to the first question that I cannot at present give any pledge as to the action the Secretary of State will take.—*Times*, November 23.

The Action of the Great Loan Houses.—The speculative community are now reaping what they have sown, for the extreme weakness now shown by Stock Exchange securities is a direct consequence of the eager rush after all kinds of new issues likely to command a premium which has characterised the current year. For some time past the market has been in a very sensitive and unstable condition, owing to the continuous efflux of gold, especially to the Argentine Republic, by whom the most lavish borrowings have been made in London and on the Continent, the total sum raised this year by that country, directly and indirectly, being about £40,000,000. And this week the sharp advance in the value of money, which has been so long threatened, has occurred.

The effect upon the stock markets has been very marked, for a state of exaggerated apprehension has prevailed, and speculators for the rise in all departments have shown much anxiety to reduce their commitments to small dimensions. But although much has been done, they are still nervous, being fearful not only in regard to the speculation open for the rise, but in regard to the great mass of new securities which are in the hands of speculative investors. Indeed, the position, as a whole, has been decidedly unsatisfactory, and the future has not been regarded without some apprehension even by those not given to nervous exaggeration. In these circumstances there is a strong temptation to find a scapegoat upon whom all the blame may be cast, and recently the important group of large firms by whom the market has been so industriously fed with new issues, has rather generally been picked out for this purpose. And, as usual, the general feeling on the subject has been partly right and partly wrong.

It has been wrong, because people have formed mistaken views as to what are the proper functions of these great issuing firms, which act as intermediaries between those who borrow on a large scale and the general body of investors. These firms, as we have pointed out before, transact a business which, when kept within legitimate limits, is extremely useful to the public. It consists, like most mercantile operations, in buying in bulk and retailing out in more or less small amounts, only the business is in securities instead of merchandise. In other words, they supply home investors with a variety of investments, which afford channels for the continuous accumulation of capital in this country, and they obtain these investments by ministering to the needs of borrowers, or by the support which they afford to the extension of joint stock enterprise.

In doing this, they take care that there shall be no technical flaw in their dealings with the public, that, in fact, the formal terms of their contract shall be fulfilled, and, of course, no firm of standing would identify itself with a new issue which was obviously unsound; but beyond this they do not go. It is no part of their province to inquire into the essential soundness of the securities they offer for sale, for that must be left to the judgment of each individual investor, nor should the mere fact of them acting as sponsors to any new issue be understood to imply any guarantee on their part. In fact, to put it briefly, they simply offer certain securities to the public, and if they do this in a *bonâ fide* manner, they cannot be rightly expected to go further, and undertake in regard to investors any duties of a "trust" character.

The public, however, have been accustomed to look at the matter in another light, and, as a result, we have seen investors taking up, without the slightest regard as to their real character, great masses of securities, simply because they were issued by some firm with a great name. For many investors of this stamp we are afraid there will be some day a sad awakening, just as there was some ten or twelve years ago, when Peru, and other States which had issued large loans, through firms of the highest standing, defaulted so completely, and it may also be said so hopelessly.

In a measure, however, the public have been right in reprobating the conduct of the great houses which have been inundating the market with new securities, for in too many cases they have not kept within the legitimate limits of their business. On the contrary, they have taken many measures quite outside them. For instance, it has been notorious that some of the difficulties now being experienced in the money market are due to the fact that the firms who had new loans to issue have used very strong means to keep the value of money artificially low, and have thus neutralised the natural effect which their operations would have had upon the market. Moreover, there has been a good deal of manipulation in the stock markets in order to give prices an appearance of firmness which otherwise they would have not possessed.

The object of these operations has been, of course, to attract investors and induce them to take up securities from which, if left to themselves, they would have probably stood clear. This conduct does not differ in any essential respect from the "rigging" of shady company promoters, or the market manœuvres of unscrupulous American railway magnates of the Jay Gould type. If we take, for instance, the case of the Deccan Mining Company, just investigated, in which the stock market was manipulated in order to induce the public to buy at high prices shares whose value was extremely doubtful, or if we look at some of the tricks which have been played by speculators like Mr. Gould, we shall, no doubt, find some difference in degree, but they are, nevertheless, of essentially the same kind as those which have recently flourished in high circles in London.

In such circles the old maxim, *noblesse oblige*, had once a certain binding power, for there was a jealousy of good name and credit which was more powerful than the attraction of a "fat" commission, but for some time past this has seemed to have become almost a mere tradition. It may be of little use to utter vain regrets respecting the change, but investors will do well to bear it in mind a little more closely in their future dealings, unless they want to lose money. Unfortunately, the public have short memories, or they would not have forgotten the lessons of the last decade when it was so conclusively shown that the standing of the issuing-house had nothing to do with the soundness of the securities they offered to the public.—*Economist*, November 24.

The Native Armies in India.—Those who remember certain events that happened during the Indian Mutiny, will not feel altogether hopeful about the result of appointing British instructors to the armies of the native princes. That these raw troops will be improved in drill and discipline goes without the saying. But the question presents itself as to whether it be sound policy to increase the efficiency of forces neither paid by nor under the control of the Indian Government. As they are at present, these native levies bulk largely on paper, but very few have any military value. Holkar and Scindiah can put some serviceable troops in the field, and the Nizam is also credited with a limited contingent of some fighting capacity.

It may be safely estimated, nevertheless, that out of the grand paper aggregate of more than 300,000 men, not more than a sixth deserve the name of soldiers. All the rest are the veriest riff-raff, maintained purely for show, and no more capable of taking part in a campaign against disciplined troops than so many coolies would be. But among them there is a large mass of the right sort of raw material, which only needs fashioning into shape to become an effective force. This is the experiment, then, that Lord Dufferin has set on foot once more after it had been dropped for thirty years. At the time of the Mutiny, the Gwalior army was officered as well as instructed by Englishmen, on the same system as the Company's native troops. And like them, it threw off allegiance to its ruler, took the field, and, thanks to its superior discipline, compactness and unity, proved harder to crush than any force brought against us.

No doubt, circumstances are greatly changed; not only is the European army in India twice the strength it was when the Mutiny broke out, but all the arsenals and fortified places of any importance are in its hands. Still the fact remains that we are resuscitating a system which broke down miserably at the first serious trial in 1857. The native princes may be loyal enough, but they cannot guarantee the loyalty of their troops any more than the Gwalior chief could.—*Graphic*, November 24.

Another India Office Scandal.—The India Office is earning a bad reputation for itself as a business-like department. With the memory of the Deccan scandal so fresh, it might have been thought that, for its own sake, the India Office would take good care to perpetrate or wink at no more jugglery with commercial enterprises in the East. Unfortunately, this expectation has been disappointed, and the India Office again lies under grave suspicion—such suspicion as should never attach to a British Government department, especially an office which is, in a sense, in a position of trust as regards millions of subjects of other races than ours. The India Office is just thirty years old in its present form; but it seems already to have fallen into its dotage. It pulls along wonderfully well until it stumbles across a mine or a mining concession, and then it breaks down utterly. The India Office is only mad when the wind sets in one quarter. When it blows from the direction of a mine the Department is unable to tell a hawk from a heronshaw, and generally allows the heron to become the victim of the hawk. So it was in Hyderabad, and there are similar symptoms in the case of the Burmese Ruby Mines.

Burmah is a province of the Indian Empire which requires the most careful handling. For many years before the recent war, British Burmah was about the only province which showed a surplus of income over expenditure, that surplus going to enrich the Calcutta exchequer. Common sense should dictate, then, that the enlarged province should be most carefully nursed and tended by the central authority, so as to develop the resources of a rich country, not only as a duty to the conquered inhabitants, and as a justification of the conquest, but also to help the impoverished

Indian Treasury. In course of time Lord Dufferin came to this opinion. He put it into practice when he consented to invite public tenders for the concession of the ruby mines, instead of accepting a rent which turned out to be only half of that obtainable through the medium of open competition. Lord Dufferin and his Council agreed to grant a lease for five years, at a rent of four lakhs of rupees, or £40,000, each year, to the syndicate headed by Mr. Streeter, the well-known dealer in precious stones in London. The India Office had left the decision in the hands of the Viceroy, and the agreement was come to—subject, of course, to certain conditions regarding native rights—in April, 1886.

The negotiations between the Indian and Burmese authorities regarding these conditions continued for a long period, it being impossible to ascertain and define the native rights, owing to the disturbed state of the country. After a year of negotiation the agreement was finally signed, and the syndicate took full possession of the mines. Meantime the India Office had fallen into one of its singular fits. The presumption is that an all-powerful influence had been brought to bear at Whitehall to secure the upsetting of the concession granted by the Viceroy. Whatever the cause, the India Office certainly took steps to invalidate the concession. The Viceroy's Government, seeing its good faith endangered, and conscious that the concession had been honestly obtained and honestly granted, declined to second the attempts of the India Office. On June 5, 1887, the Viceroy telegraphed on behalf of his Government: "We see no just grounds for cancelling this arrangement." Again, in a despatch six days later, the Indian Government explained to the authorities at Whitehall that the agreement between the Viceroy in Council and the concessionnaires was actually concluded, though, for the reasons already given, not formally signed, within the period during which the right to grant a concession was specifically entrusted by the India Office to the Viceroy. Lord Dufferin and his advisers have honourably adhered to their engagements throughout; the only default has been at Whitehall.

The India Office, despite the protests of Lord Dufferin that there are "no *just* grounds" for cancelling the concession, has set the Streeter agreement aside, and has invited fresh tenders. It is, perhaps, as well for Her Majesty's Government that the Marquess of Dufferin is to stay at Rome; for if he were to come home, it is improbable that a man of his frankness and capacity would hold his tongue while the India Office was perpetrating this gross injustice, and was snubbing and ignoring the action and protests of the Calcutta Government. The country believes in Lord Dufferin; but, since the Deccan revelations, it has not a scrap of confidence in the India Office. Lord Cross used to have some reputation as a man of business; but he appears to have fallen a victim to the all-devouring permanent official. The cancellation of the Streeter contract, with the consequent loss to Burmah of the rent for two years and a half, is an incident which requires full explanation and, if it be not forthcoming, we hope that the House of Commons will insist upon a Committee to sift a scandal so seriously affecting our newest Indian province, just as it forced an inquiry into the spoliation of the Nizam of Hyderabad. Parliament, surely, will not allow the country to come to the conclusion that the India Office is a willing instrument in the hands of ambitious speculators.—*Financial News*, November 29.

THE HYDERABAD SCANDAL.—In the House of Commons, on November 29, Mr. T. O'Connor asked the Under-Secretary of State for India whether he could give any further information as to the manner in which the Viceroy had dealt with certain actions of Colonel Marshall in connection with the Hyderabad scandal; whether, as stated by the *Deccan Times* of October 4, that "the Viceroy, though condemning the connection brought about by the private secretary (Colonel Marshall) between the Hyderabad Government and his relative, Mr. Wathen, has accepted Colonel Marshall's explanation of the financial position to which public attention was recently drawn;" what Colonel Marshall's explanation was; and what steps had been taken to reimburse the Nizam's Treasury of the large sum of money which had been lost to it.

Sir J. Gorst: The matters referred to in the question are, as I stated in August last, such as it is the function of the Viceroy and Government of India to deal with. No report of any such circumstances as are alluded to in the question has been made by the Government of India to the Secretary of State.—*Times*, November 30.

A few weeks ago we drew attention to some official statements respecting Indian railways: the improving financial condition of those railways, their relations to the State, the steady and rapid development of the mileage of the railway system. The engineers are now discovering, and laying stress on, a serious fault from their own particular point of observation, which must in many instances mar the usefulness of the Indian railways. It is in the diversity of the gauge. There are, indeed, multifarious gauges adopted throughout the Indian railway system; one of these examples has just been reported, and it serves to show the disadvantages of the system, which will be further felt as the system shall become extended.

The remaining forty-three miles of the Nizam's State Railway now closely approach completion. This line will connect Bonakala with Bezwada, the latter place being the terminus on the banks of the river Kistna. On the other side of that river there is the terminus of the Bellary-Kistna Railway, and within a very short time, therefore, passengers arriving by the latter railway will see just before them the commencement of a long stretch of line which only needs the bridging of the river to place them in communication with it. But although the construction of a bridge at that point is both practicable and easy, it will not be worth the while either of the Nizam or of the projectors of the Bellary-Kistna Railway to undertake the work, the Nizam's railway being of a gauge much narrower than that of the other line. Through traffic is thus denied to all the goods carried by either railway, while passengers by one or the other of them must be ferried across the river in order to continue their journey.—*Bullionist*, December 1.

Hyderabad and the National Congress.—An Indian correspondent sends us a translation of the speech referred to in our Bombay despatch. It was delivered at Hyderabad on the 12th of November by the Nawab Mahdi Ali, and gives an interesting summary of the effect upon an unusually able and upright Mussulman statesman of his observations in Europe, as well as of the feeling with which the strongest native races of India regard the scheme of a National Congress. At a banquet given at the Hyderabad Club, November 12, in honour of his return, replying to the toast of his health, the Nawab Mahdi Ali said:—

"Gentlemen,—It is not easy for me to find expression in words for my feelings this evening, nor can I fitly acknowledge the many kind and flattering expressions which have fallen from Major Gough. At all times a reception so kind as this must have been extremely gratifying to me, but on this occasion when returning to you all, my friends, from a first visit to the great world beyond the seas, I recognise that moments perhaps the happiest I have ever known are closing for me an experience of surpassing interest. And now, as I am an officer growing old in the service of his Highness the Nizam, you will doubtless wish me to tell you something of the events of the past six months—what I have seen in that world over the great waters, and what are the more striking and visible contrasts between the civilizations of the East and those of the West. One very strong impression which I wish to convey to you is this—that if you should visit Western Europe, to observe the signs of a perpetual progress, and of a rapid adaptability to modern improvements, then truly you will find all this and much more, and attractive indeed to the visitor must be that boundless prospect of growth and change. And, further, it is very good to see the wealth and the magnificence everywhere of those Western societies, and still more the energy displayed there by the wealthy classes, who devote themselves to the arts, to politics, to literature, or country pursuits, not less steadily than if hard work was a necessity to them. In this way, and in this way only, are the European aristocracies able to justify in these days the privileges of their position against the advances of the new Democracy. All these evidences of changes now taking place appear to me very important, and in this direction valuable to us are the teachings of Europe; but if, on the other hand, the results of Government and social progress are to be estimated rather by the general happiness of the people governed than by signs of wealth or the spectacle of great armies ready for the field, then indeed I should be slow to admit that Europe can teach us any lessons, for, so far from widespread happiness, there is the appearance of a poverty more pinching and of misery more distressing in a single quarter of London than could be found in all the Deccan—yes, I believe I might safely say, more than in all India. For here at least the poorest man can enjoy the sunshine, while there the richest man cannot buy happiness, when for weeks together the sun is never seen; and thus it happens, no doubt, that while many Englishmen are content to spend the best years of their lives here, not one of our race would be able to endure any long removal to England. But if in England I failed to see that life is to the poor man so good a thing as it is with us, yet I was much struck with the evidence on all sides of England's power. To get an idea of the resources of England and where her real strength lies, you must leave London and go into the great manufacturing districts of Lancashire and the North. There, indeed, you will at once find those sources of national strength which have sent England to India and to all parts of the world, and have made her what she is. My friends, we often think of our population of 250,000,000; and we marvel when we contrast it with the 30,000,000 or so who inhabit England; but the mere comparison contained in these figures is worthless. England's real power is in that wonderful machinery which I was privileged to see at Manchester and elsewhere. What are the muscles and sinews of mere men—men who require to eat and sleep, and who a little later must die, when weighed in the scales against those gigantic men of steel and iron, who need neither food nor rest, but who continue at all times and in all climates to work as the patient bond-slaves of the British nation. So you see that behind the 30,000,000 in England there is this immense reserve force of iron men, equivalent, perhaps, to 200,000,000 more, a vast fighting army, encumbered by neither women nor children. This is the real value and significance of England's wealth, which finds no true expression in the palaces and carriages of the great nobles in London, but must be looked for in her provincial cities. And now, my friends, I am able in these few minutes to tell you very little of the many strange impressions and ideas that necessarily follow after a first visit to England. During the past six months I have learned much, and some things also it was proper to unlearn; and very much, also, I have observed which brings a conviction of the advantages we possess over the European nations. It appears to me that on the Continent, and even in England, there are many symptoms which show that the masses of the people are less contented than with us, because they are less happy than here, and that there the discontent admits remedy. Here in Hyderabad, surrounded as we are on all sides by the power of the greatest nation on the globe, we are entirely secure from revolutionary troubles both from within and without; assuredly this cannot be said of any one nation in Europe to-day, no, not one. The last view I had of Europe was of the great volcano opposite the city of Naples, its top wreathed in smoke and reflecting redly the fierce fires below the surface. And when I remembered that two days later the new German Emperor, the greatest captain of Europe, was coming there to Naples, I was reminded very forcibly that there are to-day volcanic forces more active and more inevitable than those which two thousand years ago destroyed an earlier civilisation under the overflow from Vesuvius. So until Europe has herself been able to solve these great problems which are agitating her, and which threaten a widespread destruction, let us continue as now to disregard the counsels of those who would recommend us in India to embrace revolutionary theories of what is called representative government. That form of Government, even in England, affords little satisfaction to what is wisest and best in the community. It is not too much to say that in the Europe of to-day those nations whose systems of government are most modernised are the very nations whose conditions are found to be most critical, and where even the continuance of national life is most precarious. England alone, relying on the wise arrangements of her statesmen hundreds of years since dead, promises to stand safely on the threshold of a new world, and to live to witness the new order of things. When that future has declared itself, then indeed our time of re-arrangement may have come. It has not come yet. Russia is to-day agitated by a demand for a National Congress; Russia is but one nation, we in India are many distinct nations, differing in customs, in caste, and in creeds. If it is true that these developments even in Russia threaten to destroy her unity and to leave her a little later a number of disconnected States, at the mercy either of great foreign enemies or of one another—if this is so, then what would not happen to us here were we mad enough to listen to similar teaching? When the various nations of Europe—the Russians, the French, the Germans, and the English—have shown us the spectacle of a Congress in which they can all meet and legislate, then, and not till then, may Mussulmans and Sikhs, and fighting Pathans, mingle at Allahabad or Madras in peaceful assembly with Bengalis and Mahrattas. If indeed the other peoples of India are now ready for this Congress project, I make bold to say we Mohammedans are not. Before we commence to make laws for others, let us show that all is complete within our own boundaries. Have we got so much unemployed ability here, that we can send delegates to spend their lives at distant Congress centres? Who will go from here on any such errand? No, my friends, what I have this year seen of Islam elsewhere suggests to me quite other needs. Who are the chosen Ambassadors of the Sultan and the Shah to London? Rustem, the Italian, and Malcolm, the Armenian, Christians both! Is this as it should be? And where now are the Standards of Omar? or what encouragement may we derive from the position of Egypt? When I think on these things and the lessons they contain, then I recognise that here in Hyderabad alone, unshadowed by foreign encroachments, Islam may yet revive, and something of our ancient glories may be ours. And our duty is to our own nation, here around our own shrines."—*Morning Post*, December 3.

The Nawab Mahdi Ali, who has been giving his impressions of England and the English, is a tall, distinguished-looking man of about fifty. He, it will be remembered, represented the Nizam at the recent inquiry into the Hyderabad-Deccan scandal. He is one of the ablest and certainly one of the most honest, of the native Ministers. At the present moment he stands well with the Nizam. He is very fond of the English, and a warm supporter of British rule in India. But he does not understand our language. He is a strict Mahomedan, is married, and is reputed to be wealthy. Abdul Huk was his *bête noir* for a long time; and the dishing of that *chevalier d'industrie* afforded him considerable personal gratification.—*Echo*, December 4.

I HEAR that Sir Lepel Griffin has decided not to return to India, and that, therefore, that somewhat dangerous appointment, the Hyderabad Residency, which was being kept warm for him, will test the reputation of some other bold aspirant. The Hyderabad Residency has not certainly brought its occupants luck of late years, as Mr. Cordery will confess, and probably intrigue and rivalry are just as active now in the Nizam's capital as they have ever been. Sir Lepel Griffin, who appeared in the summer as a Liberal Unionist at the banquet to Lord Hartington, intends to try his fortunes in political life. His retirement from India will greatly deprive Anglo-Indian life of its vivacity, and will force the native press to seek a new theme for their denunciations. The Governor-General's agent in Central India has been a perfect godsend to the vernacular writers of late, whom he has never failed to hit back hard, and he was fast becoming the Antichrist of the voluble Bengalees. His new move will also deprive Mr. Bradlaugh of a claim to be considered member for India. For, like the Bengalee press, Mr. Bradlaugh has quite convinced himself that Sir Lepel Griffin's action towards the Bhegum of Bhopal was a summary interference with that lady's domestic happiness.—*World*, December 5.

COLONEL MARSHALL AT HYDERABAD.—In the House of Commons on Friday, December 7, Mr. T. P. O'Connor asked the Under-Secretary of State for India, with reference to Colonel Marshall's pecuniary dealings at Hyderabad, whether the subjoined was a correct quotation of the rule in force under the Government of India regarding pecuniary transactions of officials within the limits of their jurisdiction:—

"All covenanted civil servants, statutory civilians, uncovenanted officers who hold gazetted appointments, and military officers in civil employ are prohibited, under pain of dismissal, from taking loans from, or otherwise placing themselves under pecuniary obligations to, persons subject to the official authority or influence of such Government officers, or residing, possessing property, or carrying on business within the local limits for which such Government officers are appointed;" whether Colonel Marshall's alleged lending of a large sum of the Nizam's money to his own brother-in-law was an infringement of the said rule; and whether, having regard to the fact that no report on the matter had been made to the Government of India by the Secretary of State, he would call for a report and inform the House what action had been taken in the matter.

Sir J. Gorst.—The rule is correctly stated. The Secretary of State is in possession of no information or evidence in reference to the alleged loan. The Secretary of State cannot call for reports from the Government of India unless some evidence is furnished to him upon which a reference to India can be based. If such evidence is furnished, he will immediately call for a report.

Mr. T. P. O'Connor.—Am I to understand that the India Office in London is the only body in the world which is not acquainted with these notorious facts, and that the right hon. gentleman does not think there is ground for asking for a return on the subject?

Sir J. Gorst.—If any gentleman will lay before me any *primâ facie* evidence, which will justify me in making any reference to the Indian authorities, I will do so. *Times*, December 8.

H.H. THE NIZAM'S GUARANTEED STATE RAILWAYS COMPANY, LIMITED.—The seventh ordinary general meeting of the members of this Company was held on Tuesday last at Winchester House, Old Broad Street; Lieut.-General Sir Richard John Meade, K.C.S.I. and C.I.E., the Chairman, presiding.

The Secretary (Mr. W. G. Hall) read the notice convening the meeting, and the report was taken as read.

The Chairman said: The directors' report, which is in the hands of shareholders, with the audited accounts and other statements that accompany it, furnishes the usual information regarding the progress and working of the railway during the half-year ended 30th June, 1888. As regards the progress towards the completion of the line, the Warangal-Dornakul Section, with the Mineral branch, was opened to public traffic on 1st January, 1888, and thirty-two miles of the Dornakul-Frontier Section were similarly opened on 15th August last. The chief engineer reports that the remaining twenty-two miles of the Frontier Section will be opened on 15th January next, when the whole of the Company's line of 332 miles from Wadi to the Hyderabad Frontier will be open to the public. As stated in my remarks at the last general meeting, the bridging of the Wyra, and also the Cutlair rivers, in the last part of the Frontier Section, has caused unexpected delay in completing this section. Unlooked-for difficulties were experienced in laying the foundations of some of the piers of the bridges over these rivers, and heavy floods last August showed that the provision of more water-way than was previously thought sufficient was advisable. Then the works were seriously retarded by repeated visitations of cholera. Owing to these causes, and the necessity of procuring additional girders from home, the completion of the Cutlair Bridge will be delayed till after the opening of this part of the Frontier Section, but this will not interfere with the working of the line, which will be carried on without difficulty by a diversion during the dry season. As the British Section, now called the Bezwada Extension Railway, will also be completed by 15th January, the whole line (354 miles) will then be open for through traffic from Bezwada to Wadi. I may add that the board expects to hear in the course of the next few days that an arrangement has been concluded with the Government of India for the working of the Bezwada Extension Railway by the Company. As at present advised the Board have every reason to believe that the funds provided will meet the cost of the extensions from Hyderabad to the frontier. The increased charge of bridging the Wyra and Cutlair rivers will, it is hoped, be met by savings under other heads of the estimate. Turning now to the accounts, it will be seen (page 7 of the accounts) that the net outlay on capital expenditure during the half-year was £144,260. The balance-sheet (page 8) speaks for itself, and does not call for remark from me. With regard to the annuity guarantee fund account (page 9) I have to state that, on the representation of the directors of the depreciation of the rupee paper securities, and with the concurrence of H.H. the Nizam's Government, the trustees have, since the 30th June last, invested in Consols £21,500 of the amount entered in the foot-note as being at their credit, as an additional security to bring the sterling value of this fund up to the full sum of £200,000, at which the Nizam's Government is bound to maintain it in London. The sinking fund and contingent liability for interest accounts (page 9) do not require remark. The revenue account (page 10) shows fairly satisfactory results, having regard to the fact that the extensions beyond Warangal added but little to the receipts of the half-year. As the open mileage has increased, there is little use in instituting comparisons between one half-year and another, but the returns show that the railway carried nearly 60,000 more passengers in the half-year under review than in the corresponding half of 1887—giving an increase of coaching earnings of about Rs.61,000, and that, though the receipts from goods traffic were Rs.9,000 less than in the latter half-year, the falling-off was due to the earnings for the carriage of railway materials being nearly Rs.90,000 less. There was an increase in the receipts for the carriage of cotton, salt, metals, seeds, firewood, military stores, and other items, and the traffic between Warangal and Hyderabad showed an encouraging improvement. The opening of the line to Bezwada is expected by the traffic manager to be followed by an increase in the goods and coaching traffic generally, and I may mention that there being fears of scarcity at Hyderabad, a number of the leading grain merchants recently asked the agent to arrange for the running of grain trains from Bezwada to the capital, in anticipation of the formal opening of the line, and offered to fill a trainload daily if this could be done. Mr. Furnivall has applied to the consulting engineer for railways of the Madras Government, for sanction to meet this request, and has no doubt it can be arranged. The great importance of being thus able, in times of scarcity, to draw food supplies from the rich Kistna Delta, cannot but impress on the Government and people of Hyderabad the benefits which the railway will doubtless, in this and other ways, confer on the State. The working expenses during the half-year amounted to 56·42 per cent. of the gross receipts, which was considerably less than the estimate, and may be regarded, under the circumstances, as fairly satisfactory. It must, however, be borne in mind that, on the completion of the line, all general and other charges, hitherto proportionately borne by capital, will be debitable to revenue. Maintenance charges were moderate, averaging Rs.481 per mile, but may be expected to show an increase during the current half-year, as several repairs were unavoidably deferred. I explained at the last general meeting that a considerable cost would have to be incurred, under the head of maintenance, for necessary renewals of permanent-way in the Wadi-Hyderabad section, but the directors hope that the maintenance of the rest of the line, when fully consolidated, will be light, and that the average cost per mile for the whole line will not be excessive. Locomotive and carriage expenses do not call for remark. The use of coal, so far as it has gone, has somewhat diminished fuel charges. Traffic charges were larger, owing to there being a greater length of line open. General charges show a considerable increase. That under the head of Home expenditure is due to the proportion of the charge debitable to revenue having been raised during the half-year under review from one-half to two-thirds, but the expenditure has been practically the same as before. The new audit arrangements added Rs.6,000 to the cost of that department. Printing and stationery and office furniture and fittings added Rs.5,000 to the charge under those heads. The police charge was Rs.6,000 more. Special and miscellaneous expenditure shows the large and satisfactory decrease of Rs.16,000, mostly on the charge for mileage and demurrage on foreign rolling stock. The revenue account for the half-year under review shows that the gross earnings amounted to Rs.852,312—the largest sum yet obtained in any half-year—and that the working expenses were Rs.480,880, leaving net earnings amounting to Rs.371,432, which sum has been duly handed over to the Nizam's Government. The latest returns of traffic for the current half-year show that the gross receipts up to the 3rd November were about Rs.75,000 in excess of those of the corresponding half of 1887, but the open mileage being greater, no useful comparison can be made. The imperative necessity for the exercise of the most careful economy, consistent with efficiency, in working the line, is receiving full attention from the directors, and the agent and chief engineer has been requested to submit proposals for such reductions of charges in the working establishment and other respects, as he may deem practicable. As regards coal, I regret to say that the mining and other difficulties that have been experienced at the coalfields have hitherto prevented the output being sufficient for traffic supplies. The railway received and consumed nearly 3,500 tons during the half-year under review, or about one-third of its total fuel consumption. The continued delay in the development of the coal traffic is of course very disappointing, but the directors understand that it is wholly due to the difficulties that have had to be contended with, and that were either not foreseen or were under-estimated by the Mining Company's agents. There is, however, no doubt as to the quantity and quality of the coal, and that the output will increase as the mining works progress, when there will be no lack of customers for it, and the railway will reap the full profit of its carriage. The output now of coal is about 500 tons a week. There has been a considerable increase, and we think it will rapidly increase as soon as the immediate difficulties are got over. There has been a fault in the mine which has considerably retarded the output of coal. Before closing these remarks, I must mention that the Company's engagement with the agent and chief engineer, Mr. Furnivall, terminates on the 5th March next, before which date all the engineering works which Mr. Furnivall projected will have been completed. The directors desire again to express their satisfaction at the able manner in which Mr. Furnivall and the officers working under him have continued to perform their laborious and anxious duties, and to state that they consider their good services to merit special acknowledgment on this occasion. I shall be happy to answer any questions, or to give information on any point on which such may be required by any member present. I beg to move the formal resolution :—"That the Directors' report and the audited accounts made up to the 30th June, 1888, which has been circulated to the stockholders, and are now submitted to the meeting, be received and adopted." (Applause.)

Nawab Fathah Nawaz Jung Bahadur (Official Director): I second this resolution, but before that I should like to speak a few words. (Applause.) Gentlemen, when I had the pleasure of meeting you here last I never thought that an opportunity for my doing so again would occur so soon. During the interval some changes have taken place. Then I was a mere novice; now I have had some opportunity of acquiring a little experience in railway questions. Then I was on your Board simply as a director. Now there has been added the responsibility of being Home Secretary to the Government of the Nizam. (Applause.) Gentlemen, among the thousand blessings of British rule in India is the railway system. It has connected east and west, north and south; has encouraged trade, and allayed the horrors of famine to a great extent. The State of Hyderabad also—thanks to your energies—has not been left without that boon. The Chairman of our Board has just told you in detail about the progress of the railway in that country, and from him you have learned that 310 miles of railway are already open, and that the remaining 22 miles will be open very shortly. But that is not enough. My earnest desire is to see a network of lines in that State. (Applause.) It is very satisfactory that the gross earnings of the railway per train mile for this half-year, viz., Rs. 3.97, is the highest figure yet touched, and the percentage of working expenses on the gross earnings for this half-year is also less than in many previous years. That is a most satisfactory result. Great credit is due to our able chief engineer—Mr. Furnivall—and the most energetic and popular traffic superintendent—Mr. Pendlebury. My relations, as the Government Director on your Board, I am glad to say, with my colleagues have been of the most cordial and friendly character. I take this opportunity of thanking them publicly for the courtesy and kindness which they have always shown me. During the last seven or eight months, since I had the honour of working with them, no differences have occurred. The reason is this, that I have always been anxious to limit my interference to those subjects only which bear on the finances and expenses of the Company, since they affected our guarantee, and I must admit I always found my colleagues—and especially the Chairman as anxious for economy as myself. I am sure as long as I remain on the Board the same relations will always exist. I beg to second the resolution. (Cheers.)

Sir Henry Cartwright said, from what the Chairman was able to tell them as to the output of coal, it was eminently favourable, but he would like to ask, as bearing on the point, whether the 3,500 tons—or nearly that—consumed on the railway was local coal or imported coal?

The Chairman: All local coal.

After some remarks from Messrs. Austen and Wood as to matters of account, the resolution was put to the meeting and carried.

The Chairman then moved, "That interest for the half-year ending 31st December, 1888, at the rate of 5 per cent. per annum, upon the capital stock of the Company, be paid to the holders of such stock on the register at that date."

General Alexander Fraser, C.B., R.E., seconded the motion, which was carried unanimously.

Sir Henry Cartwright: I cannot help thinking, from what you were able to tell us, that we ought to be satisfied with the progress made so quietly during the half-year by the executive of the railway, and the extension that has been carried out so well in India. We have had the gratification of hearing of the steady progress of the railway, and we should express that by giving a vote of thanks to the directors for their conduct of the business, and at the same time to Mr. Furnivall and our staff in India, who appear to have devoted themselves so energetically to the work. (Applause.)

Mr. A. B. Chalmers seconded the resolution, which was carried by acclamation.

The proceedings terminated with a vote of thanks to the Chairman for his conduct in the chair.—*Bullionist*, December 8.

To the Editor.—Sir,—In the remarks on Indian railways contained in your paper of the 1st instant, there are some few misapprehensions of facts which it may be as well to correct.

The Nizam's State Railway, which is on the point of completion, does not extend to Bezwada on the Kistna river, but only to the frontier of the Nizam's territory, which is twenty-one miles short of Bezwada. These twenty-one miles are in British territory, and the line which runs through them is the property of the British Government, although it is proposed that it shall be worked by the Nizam's State Railway Company. The gauge of the whole of the Nizam's State Railway and that of the British section to Bezwada is the Indian broad gauge of 5ft. 6in., the same as that of the Great Indian Peninsular Railway, with which it forms a junction. Thus there is one uniform gauge from Bombay to Bezwada, a distance of 730 miles, and the Nizam's State Railway is in unbroken connection with the entire broad gauge system to India, extending over more than 10,000 miles of line. It is true that the line starting south from the other side of the Kistna, opposite to Bezwada, and forming a junction with the Madras Railway at Goondakul, a distance of 279 miles, is on the metre gauge. This line belongs to the British Government, and forms part of the Southern Mahratta Company's metre gauge system, extending over 1,042 miles. It will be seen that the lines on both sides of the Kistna belong to the British Government, and that the question of bridging that river is not the concern of the Nizam's State Railway Company, whose line terminates twenty-one miles from the river, but is solely that of the British Government. It has been estimated that the bridge would cost about a quarter of a million sterling. It will also be seen that the Nizam's State Railway is not "of a gauge much narrower than that of the other line," but is 2ft. 2⅝in. broader.

Although literally true, it is misleading to state that there are "multifarious gauges adopted on the Indian railway system." Out of the 15,371 miles of Indian railways open at the end of March last, all but 141 miles are on either the 5ft. 6in. gauge or the 3ft. 3⅜in. (metre) gauge. The 141 miles are small local lines, like the 2-feet gauge Festiniog Railway in Wales. How can it be said that "when the authorities of India began to introduce railways they treated them as toys?" The introduction of railways in India was chiefly due to the wisdom of Lord Dalhousie some forty years ago, and embraced a vast system of main lines throughout the country built by private enterprise on a Government guarantee of 5 per cent. interest—a most serious and bold undertaking, having an important bearing on the welfare and finances of the country. At that time the battle of the gauges was raging in England, and had not been decided. The rival gauges were respectively 7ft. 0¾in., the Great Western Railway gauge, and 4ft. 8½in., the so-called narrow gauge. Lord Dalhousie, who had had considerable experience of railway matters as President of the Board of Trade, thought that the one was too broad and the other too narrow for the probable necessities of Indian traffic, and fixed on a medium of 5ft. 6in. as the Indian gauge. After nearly twenty years' experience, the Government of India, in 1868, came to the conclusion that this was too broad and expensive a guage for adoption throughout India, and that if the demands for railway extension were to be carried out with the requisite rapidity, the finances of India would not permit of its being adopted for the State lines which it was then determined to construct. It may here be mentioned that a mile of line on the metre gauge is on the average estimated to cost from £1,000 to £1,500 less than on the broad gauge. Hence the introduction of the metre gauge. The break of gauge was an acknowledged evil, but it was thought to be a less evil than the check on further railway extension, which would, owing to financial considerations, be imposed by the continuance everywhere of the broader and more expensive gauge. It is easy to be wise after the event, and to lament that Lord Dalhousie did not foresee the 4ft. 8½in. gauge would become the uniform gauge for England, and did not fix that gauge for India. Had he done so a second and narrower gauge would probably have never been called for. As the matter now stands, about one-third of the total railway mileage now open to traffic in India is on the metre gauge, and about 1,000 miles more are under construction. The avoidance of the break of gauge is past praying for now, but its evils are easily susceptible of exaggeration. Yours faithfully, B.—*Bullionist*, December 8.

THE NIZAM'S STATE RAILWAYS.—The appearance of the Nawab Jung Bahadur, the Home Secretary of the Nizam, at the directors' table, was the feature of the meeting at Winchester House. For the rest, the aspect was military. Lieut.-General Sir Richard Meade took the chair, and his speech was couched with a conciseness which makes it sound extremely like a despatch.

The Chairman first of all dealt with the details respecting the completion of the line. The Warangal-Dornakul section with the mineral branch was opened on January 1st, 1888, and 32 miles of the Dornakul frontier section were similarly opened on August 15th last. The remaining 22 miles of the frontier section will be completed on January 15th next, when the whole of the Company's line of 332 miles from Wadi to the Hyderabad frontier will be opened to the public. Alluding to the unavoidable delays arising from floods and from the visitation of cholera, the Chairman went on to say that as the British section, now called the Bezwada Extension Railway, would also be completed by January 15th, the whole line (354 miles) would then be open for through traffic from Bezwada to Wadi. Turning to the accounts, it would be seen the net outlay in capital expenditure during the half-year was £144,260, and the trustees had, since June 30th, invested in Consols £24,500, as additional security to bring the sterling value of the fund up to the full sum of £200,000, at which the Nizam's Government is bound to maintain it in London. The returns show that the railway carried nearly 60,000 more passengers in the half-year under review than in the corresponding half of 1887—giving an increase of coaching earnings of about Rs.61,000, and that, though the receipts from goods traffic were Rs.9,000 less than in the latter half-year, the falling off was due to the earnings for the carriage of railway materials being nearly Rs.90,000 less. There was an increase in the receipts for the carriage of cotton, salt, metals, seeds, firewood, military stores, and other items, and the traffic between Warangal and Hyderabad showed an encouraging improvement, and the opening of the line to Bezwada was expected by the traffic manager to be followed by an increase in the goods and coaching traffic generally.

In going through the various items in the accounts, the Chairman pointed out that the reserve account for the half-year under review showed that the gross earnings amounted to Rs.852,312—the largest sum yet obtained in any half-year—and that the working expenses were Rs.40,879, leaving net earnings amounting to Rs. 371,432, which sum had been duly handed over to the Nizam's Government. The latest returns of traffic for the current half-year showed that the gross receipts up to November 3rd were about Rs.75,000 in excess of those of the corresponding half of 1887, but the open mileage being greater, no useful comparison could be made. The Chairman referred to the delay in the development of the coal traffic. There was, however, no doubt that the output would increase as the mining works progressed, where there would be no lack of customers for it, and the railway would reap the full profit of its carriages.

In conclusion, General Meade referred in complimentary terms to Mr. Furnivall, whose engagement terminates on March 5th next, before which time all the engineering works would be completed.

Nawab Jung Bahadur seconded the resolution in an excellent speech, well delivered and very much to the point. He referred in graceful terms to the harmony which had at all times existed between his colleagues and himself. Dwelling especially on the benefits which railways had conferred in India, he pointed out how they had been the means of averting famines and consequent distress, owing to the facilities they had afforded for the rapid carriage of food. He was confident that when the network of railways was completed, the greatest benefit would accrue to the country and profit result to the shareholders.

Some slight discussion was raised by Mr. Austin, who wanted to introduce the topic of the Hyderabad Deccan. This, however, was ruled out of order, and the proceedings terminated with the adoption of the report, and a vote of thanks to the chairman.—*Financial World*, December 8.

Parliament and the Government of India.—Two replies which have within the past ten days been made to a question put by Mr. T. P. O'Connor to the Under-Secretary of State for India seems to us to involve such serious principles as to be worth a little examination. Sir John Gorst was asked for information as to the manner in which the Viceroy had dealt with the case of Colonel Marshall and his transactions with his brother-in-law, Mr. Wathen; what explanations Colonel Marshall had offered; and what steps had been taken to reimburse the Nizam's Treasury. Doubtless the Irish member who put the question knew that Colonel Marshall had assumed the debt due by Mr. Wathen to the Nizam, but had not paid any portion of it; that, on some ground or other, the Viceroy had been led to overlook the extraordinary action of the secretary, whom he had recommended to the Nizam, in forwarding to a relative who was a merchant in groceries and teas a large sum of money to the Nizam's credit, which Mr. Wathen appears to have employed in his own business, or at all events, to have included in his current accounts, since it figured amongst his debts. Any loss to the Nizam might easily have been avoided by keeping a separate account in his agent's name at a banker's. The transaction is not one which ought to be slurred over either by the Viceroy or the India Office. Either Colonel Marshall has acted in a manner that deserves censure, or he is a much-maligned man. In either case the Government has a duty to perform. It is as much due to him as to the honour of the Government of India that a frank explanation of the mysterious circumstances under which some £5,000 or £6,000 of the Nizam's money came to be in the hands of his brother-in-law, Mr. Wathen, who was not a banker, instead of in the hands of the National Provincial Bank or of Mr. Rock, the agent of the Nizam. If the money were deposited with his brother-in-law in Colonel Marshall's name, it could only be looked upon as a loan from the Nizam to Colonel Marshall, and that would be in direct violation of a rule of the public service in India, which is now being severely pressed against a high official in Bombay. Further, Colonel Marshall is permitted to leave the State in which he occupied a very confidential position, having assumed a personal liability to the Nizam of several thousand pounds, which he has not paid, and, so far as public information goes, has given no security that he ever will pay. That we say is the position, so far as the public has any means of judging of it, and it certainly leaves something to be explained—we will say more, something which ought to be explained, for the honour of the public service in India, for Colonel Marshall's own sake, and for the clearance of the Indian Government from suspicions of favouritism which cannot but be excited by a consideration of the facts so far as they are disclosed. We do not say for a moment that they are incapable of explanation in a manner which would vindicate Colonel Marshall from a shadow of reproach. The presumption, on the contrary, is in his favour. He was liked and trusted by the Nizam; he has on leaving the post been the object of some cordial demonstrations of good-will from the official society of Hyderabad; and, above all, he has satisfied Lord Dufferin, who has permitted him to retire without a reprimand—in other words, has put an official seal on the vindication of his good faith and integrity. All that is good. To many minds it will be sufficient. But, after the publicity which has been given to the circumstances under which the Nizam's English private secretary has retired, it is not enough. At this particular juncture in India, when the probity of several important officials has been questioned, when an active agitation is being carried on by Natives among Natives challenging the fitness and the character of our Administration, such an incident ought not to be allowed to pass without a clear explanation and a satisfactory settlement. It is the duty of the Secretary of State in Council to see that the debt is adjusted. The profession of ignorance at the India Office is too absurd. In both the *St. James's Gazette* and this paper the facts have been stated, and the Indian papers have all commented on them. We gave an extract from the official record in the Bankruptcy Court. Does the Government in dealing with its servants wait for outsiders to bring specific charges before noticing statements affecting their character which appear in respectable journals? The question put in the House of Commons has called the attention of the Secretary of State to the facts, and we hold that is enough to justify inquiry. The facts are notorious; the Government is simply asked to deny or explain. The Nizam cannot be expected to press the matter. It would place him in an awkward situation, and for a mere sum of £6,000 no Indian Prince would like to risk compromising his friendly relations to the official class in India. All the more needful is it that the Government should not allow his generosity to be imposed upon.

But a principle is involved in Sir John Gorst's reply which is of wider and deeper interest than a mere question as to the conduct of an Indian official, or as to the judgment with which the Indian Government has acted in regard to that conduct. What does Sir John Gorst mean by saying that the matters referred to in the question of the Irish member "are such as it is the function of the Viceroy and Government of India to deal with?" Does he mean to say that the determination of such questions is left absolutely to the Viceroy in Council, and that under no circumstances will the Secretary of State inquire into or review the manner in which, or the grounds on which, a determination of the kind is arrived at? We should like the Under-Secretary of State to point out in the Acts relating to the Government of India anything which warrants an implication to that effect. Neither in law nor in practice can the principle be vindicated that any matter which comes properly within the jurisdiction of the Government of India cannot be controlled or reviewed by the Secretary of State. Lately, the Viceroy in Council deliberately performed an act which came unquestionably within his functions. He accepted the tender of the Streeter Syndicate for a lease of the Ruby Mines. For reasons we do not care to inquire into, the Secretary of State somewhat arbitrarily stepped in and cancelled the solemn undertaking of the Government of India. It was a grave step, and a serious reflection on the Viceroy and his advisers. It has ended in the triumph of the Streeter Syndicate, and in a considerable loss to the Indian Exchequer. Why, we may ask, when Mr. Bradlaugh was put up to interfere, did the Secretary of State not instruct Sir John Gorst to reply that the matter was such as it is the function of the Viceroy to deal with? If it be said that there is a distinction between interfering with the discipline exercised by the Indian Government over its servants and its dealings with outsiders involving an act of policy, we reply that whatever distinction there may be it does not touch the present question. Appeals are constantly being made to the Secretary of State by discontented military and civilian officials against the resolutions of the Provincial and Imperial Governments in India. They are not only received, when forwarded through the proper channels, but they are entertained and adjudicated upon. An instance is the case of Mr. Tayler, of Patna, which gave the India Office so much trouble. It is idle to pretend that the Secretary of State has no power to intervene in cases of scandal or dispute arising between the Indian Government and members of the Services; and if it is in his power to exercise such control, the responsibility of doing so rests upon him in cases where, the integrity of an official having been impugned, the action thereupon of the Indian Government appears open to criticism.

Indeed, an important constitutional and political question is involved, and in view of the demands which are being put forward in India by the National Congress, it is essential that the relations of Parliament to the Secretary of State, and of the Secretary of State to the Viceroy in Council, should be exactly and clearly understood. The Congress agitators are asking for representation, and with it the right of interpellation and of criticism as to the acts or policy of the Government. One of the grounds—perhaps the most valid ground—on which they base these demands is that there are no effective means of calling in question any proceedings of the Indian Government, however contrary they may seem to be to the interests of the Empire, however unjust to individuals, however objectionable or suspicious in the eyes of public opinion. The Government is secret, its decisions are arbitrary, the power above it is secret and arbitrary too. Parliament, which alone can call this scheme of bureaucratic mystification to account, neglects its duty, being more than sufficiently occupied with other matters. Well, the only way in which this legitimate demand for the admission of a little more daylight into the cryptical recesses of the Indian bureaucracy can be met is by increasing the activity of Parliament, and through Parliament of bringing to bear on the acts of the Indian administration that public opinion for the expression of which the system of Government in India provides no facilities. There is no grievance which

Parliament has not a right to inquire into, no policy which can be withdrawn from its revision or control. It affords all classes in India—Europeans, Hindus, and Mahomedans a means of appeal from the decisions of the Indian administration. If it refuses to exercise its powers, if it permits itself to be balked by the officials who are responsible to it for the proceedings of the bureaucracy, if it ceases to provide those remedies against injustice and mistake which it alone can in the ultimate resort afford, why then, as we have written before, the demands of the Congress become unanswerable. In the circumstances the attitude of the India Office to Parliamentary inquisitiveness is distinctly injurious. Instead of frankness, inquiries are met with reticence, if we ought not to say with evasion. There is no use in concealing the fact that the manner in which the Under-Secretary of State is instructed to reply to members who ask for information on Indian matters is creating a widespread dissatisfaction. It is almost insulting to Parliament and to honourable members to be put off with pleas of "no information," or references to the "functions" of the Viceroy, when attention is called to departmental matters, or official scandals, or acts of the Indian Government. We cannot blame Sir John Gorst, who simply reads the replies he is instructed to give, and is always careful to couch them in courteous terms and deliver them in a polite manner. But some fine day, the Under-Secretary will be met by some disappointed member with a motion for the adjournment of the House, and will pass a bad quarter of an hour, and he may rely on it that the most indignant of his critics will not be all found on the Opposition side. It is time that the India Office should recognise its position and its duties in this matter. If it is not frank in its communications to Parliament, and Parliament declines to exact the necessary candour, the entire system of Indian Government is practically indefensible. -*Homeward Mail*, December 10.

ARMIES OF INDIAN NATIVE STATES.—In the House of Commons, on December 10, Mr. Vincent asked the Under-Secretary for India whether any measures had been taken during the past few years to induce the feudatory chiefs and princes of India to reduce their armies from 350,000 men and 4,000 guns to a more reasonable number, so that a larger share of their revenues might thereby be diverted from expenses of military display to the internal development of their States; and, if so, whether the Government of India had been able to devise any means for utilizing the forces thus reduced towards the general defence of the Empire?

Sir J. Gorst.—The Secretary of State has no official information on the subject, but is aware that the question of the utilization of the armaments and military resources of the native States has engaged and is engaging the attention of the Government of India.—*Times*, December 11.

THE Nawab Mehdi Hasan, Home Secretary of Hyderabad, having brought his mission in connection with the Deccan mining scandal to a termination, leaves London to-day for the Continent *en route* to India. The Nawab will embark in the P. and O. steamer *Rome* at Brindisi on Monday. It is believed that, as representing the Nizam's Government, the Nawab has come to terms with Mr. Watson and his co-concessionaires.—*Daily News*, December 20.

DECCANS.—At the meeting of the proprietors of the Great Indian Peninsula Railway, held this afternoon, the Chairman stated that the opening of the Singareni Coal Fields, the sole property of the Deccan Company, will effect great saving to the Railway. This means revenue to the Deccan Company. These Shares are now at a heavy discount, for no reason.—*Vanity Fair*, December 22.

A FEATURE yesterday was the rise in Deccan shares, which closed firm at 6½-¾. The reason for this advance in the price of a security which has of late been sadly neglected, but of the real value of which we have never had the slightest doubt—in spite of the Parliamentary Commission—is as follows:—At the meeting of the Great Indian Peninsula Railway Company yesterday, the Chairman, in dealing with the working of expenses, said that he hoped that with the opening of the Singareni coalfield, close to Hyderabad (the property of the Deccan Company), their expenses under the head of coal would be considerably reduced, and the Company rendered indepèndent of the English coal producers. We need hardly point out the importance that this reference has to the future of the Deccan Company, which is the owner of the coalfields in question.—*Bullionist*, December 22.

THE statement made by the chairman of the Great Indian Peninsular Company at the general meeting yesterday, which was to the effect that in future they would obtain their coal supply for the South-Eastern portion of their system from the Singari coalfields, the property of the Hyderabad-Deccan Company, is one of great importance to shareholders of Deccans. Deccan shares are now about 6¾ (£10 fully-paid), and have been for a long time neglected. This break in the clouds, however, cannot but produce a smart recovery.—*Evening Post*, December 22.

QUITE an inquiry has sprung up for Hyderabad-Deccan Shares, and from this price of 6 they have risen to 7½ 7¾. Judging from the names passed yesterday of the buyers during the past few weeks, the price should remain firm. When Indian residents buy an Indian security it augurs well, but, of course, those who bought did so at 5¾ to 5⅞, and may have already sold again at 7 or 7¼.

The most culpable over-statements were made of everything connected with this Company. That which was to have been done two years ago is not done yet. Where are the thousand tons of coal per day which were to be raised at Singareni? Are they even in the earth? Mr. Theodore W. Hughes-Hughes, Deputy-Surveyor-General to the Government of India, estimated at a time when he was not himself that ninety million tons of good steam coal lay at Singareni. This was over two years ago. Has his estimate ever been confirmed?

New Year's-day is a Stock Exchange holiday, let everyone remember.—*Echo*, December 28.

OUR usually well-informed contemporary, *Vanity Fair*, in its last issue, makes the following interesting remarks upon the Deccan Company:—"Although the strictest secrecy is maintained for the present, I believe there is some foundation for the rumour that the Nawab Mehdi Hassan, before he left England on Thursday for India, concluded a satisfactory arrangement with the Concessionaires of the Deccan Mining Company. If the conditions are ratified by the Prime Minister of Hyderabad, and the minority of shareholders opposed to Mr. Watson and his friends are satisfied, the Company will escape the terrible prospect that at one time seemed inevitable—viz., a protracted and costly fight in the Law Courts. Should it turn out that the Nawab has brought about a compromise agreeable to all parties, he will have justified his recent selection for the honourable and responsible post of Home Secretary of the Nizam's dominions." This coming upon the news we gave last week regardng the Singareni Coalfields (the property of the Deccan Company) is eminently satisfactory. We think the present far from an inopportune moment to secure a few Deccans.—*Bullionist*, December 29.

Nawab Major Afsur Jung.—When the Ameer Abdurrahman, ruler of Afghanistan, in August last, made an arrangement with Lord Dufferin's Government to receive a British political Mission at Cabul for the purpose of discussing affairs, the British diplomatic agents selected were Mr. H. M. Durand, C.S.I., Secretary to the Foreign Department of the Indian Government; Mr. Mackenzie Wallace, Private Secretary to the Viceroy; and Colonel Chamberlain, the Persian interpreter to the Commander-in-Chief; accompanied by Lieutenant Manners Smith, Military Attaché to the Foreign Office; and Dr. Owen. A native Indian member of this Mission was also appointed, namely, the Nawab Major Afsur Jung, in the service of the Nizam of Hyderabad; but the Mission has for some months been put in abeyance, owing to the Ameer of Afghanistan being engaged in his war against the rebellion headed by Ishak Khan, in the provinces north of the Hindoo Khoosh mountains. In the meantime, Major Afsur Jung joined the recent expedition under command of General M'Queen to put down the hostile tribes of the Black Mountain. He is a keen and brave soldier, and did good service as commander of the Khyberee Rifles, being the first officer belonging to a Native State of India who has ever commanded troops in a British expedition. His photograph has been sent to us by Mr. W. E. Hill, of Hyderabad, in the Deccan; and we present the portrait of Major Afsur Jung as a token of that friendly feeling towards the British Indian Empire which was lately so magnanimously expressed by his Highness the Nizam in offering to contribute to the military expenses of our Government, and which is highly appreciated by its rulers.—*Illustrated London News*, December 29.

It is reported on good authority that, after all, the famous Hyderabad mining case will come before the English Law Courts. The negotiations which have been going on between the legal advisers of the Nizam in London and the concessionaires for a considerable time are understood to have come to nothing. The latter stand by their contract, and refuse to cancel or abandon any part of it. They take the position that, so far as they are concerned, everything was fair and above board; they obtained their contract from properly authorised officials of the Nizam, and with other parts of the conduct of these latter they have nothing to do. They are willing to defend their position before a court of law, and to this it seems the matter has now come. The action, no doubt, will be one by the Nizam for the compulsory cancellation of a contract or concession on the ground that it was improperly obtained.—*Glasgow Herald*, January 1.

In a recent issue, when Hyderabad-Deccans were quoted at about £6 10s. for the £10 fully paid shares, we recommended that purchase. That advice was well justified, for a rise has since taken place to £7 5s. on influential buying. The recent remarks made by the Chairman of one of the most powerful Indian railways too, regarding the Hyderabad-Deccan Company's coalfields at Singareni, has materially assisted the market, and we should not be surprised to see them at £8 a share ere long. After all, in spite of the dismal forebodings of ignorant "bears," this Company's coalfield is to prove of some use to the revenue side of the account. We are pleased to be able to give the shareholders such a hopeful account of their property, and trust to be able to verify it soon by even better news.—*Bullionist*, January 5th.

The Deccan Mining Company.—The *Deccan Times* has reason to believe that Mr. Watson, the concessionaire, will agree to the offer of the Nizam's Government that the nominal capital of the Deccan Mining Company, £1,000,000, should be reduced by £150,000; and that, from the gains made by the promoters, a further sum of £150,000 should be contributed in cash, and paid over by the concessionnaires to the Company. The Government, on its part, engages to ratify the concession obtained. Moreover, Clause II., as to the meaning of "a fair" rent, will be interpreted in a generous spirit. The right to prospect, which expires in 1891, will be prolonged for two years further. "On the whole, a settlement is come to on the lines proposed, which, while it will still leave nearly half a million to the concessionaires, will be one to redound to the credit and capacity of Sir Asman Jah's administration. It is not, of course, forgotten that after the completion of this arrangement, Abdul Huk's shares would revert enhanced in value to the State, which, it is thought, would more than reinburse the State for the outlay and expense already incurred in the case. Throughout the whole of this affair the assistance and advice of Mr. Howell, the Resident, have been invaluable."—*Homeward Mail*, January 7.

A Calcutta telegram of this morning states that Sir Lepel Griffin, now in England, has left the Indian Civil Service. For this there are two reasons at least. It is said he means to try to enter Parliament. And in India he was not latterly placed in the posts which he was understood to covet. He was made Agent to the Governor-General in Central India at a time when he would have preferred the Residency at Hyderabad.—*Echo*, January 12.

I am sorry to hear that Sir Lepel Griffin has finally decided to quit the Indian Government service.

Sir Lepel, who was born eight-and-forty years ago, is a Suffolk man. He is a son of the Rev. Henry Griffin, of Stoke. A singularly handsome man is Sir Lepel; and he doesn't look a day older than five-and-thirty. He has beautiful silver-tinged curly hair, deep violet coloured eyes, and a perfect Cupid's mouth.

Sir Lepel is without exception the ablest of the Indian "politicals." He won his spurs whilst acting as Secretary to the Government of the Punjaub, which office he held from 1871 to 1880. He was Chief Political Officer in Afghanistan in 1880-81; and it was through his instrumentality that the present Ameer was put upon the throne. In 1881 he was appointed Agent to the Governor-General in Central India, which post he resigned a short time back.

He accompanied the Maharajah Holkar on his visit to England during the Jubilee Year, and a pretty life that very arrogant young prince led him. It will be remembered that the Maharajah went suddenly off to Paris in the sulks; and certain Radical journals were careful to explain that His Highness was huffed at an alleged want of consideration of his dignity on the part of Her Majesty and the Court officials. But Sir Lepel at once wrote to a contemporary denying the allegation, explaining at the same time that the Maharajah's sudden departure was due to an entirely different cause, namely, that of "domestic disquiet;" and those who could read between the lines knew precisely what this neatly turned phrase implied.

Sir Lepel was much disappointed at not getting the Lieutenant-Governorship of the Punjaub. He, above all others, certainly ought to have been appointed to that important post.

Lord Dufferin endeavoured to make amends by offering him the Residency at Hyderabad, in succession to Mr. Cordery. His Excellency being convinced that Sir Lepel was about the only man who could put matters straight at the Court of the Nizam. It was also the devout wish of the Nawab Mahdi Ali, when he was over here a few months ago in connection with the notorious Hyderabad-Deccan scandal, that Sir Lepel would go to Hyderabad.

But after mature consideration the Viceroy's offer was declined with thanks; and Sir Lepel will now concentrate his efforts upon obtaining a seat in Parliament He is a Liberal Unionist in politics.—*Evening News*, January 16.

Hyderabad Deccan Shares rose from 5¼ to 7 a month ago, and there they stick. The proprietary is, indeed, a long-suffering and patient one, for precious little information is vouchsafed them. What with floods, cholera, and consequent want of coolies, the Company seem as far off as ever from raising the quantity of coal they estimated from Singareni. That the concession *was* a valuable one is testified by the bad feeling which exists at Hyderabad itself among the natives. They complain that the Nizam has parted with his property to the English at a low price. But shareholders justly say the Company paid too much. So they did; but a profit of £850,000 to a middle man will reconcile any apparent paradox! *Forsitan.—Echo*, January 18.

The *Statesman and Friend of India* of the 22nd ult. says:—"The *Deccan Times* has reason to believe that Mr. Watson, the concessionnaire, will agree to the offer of the Nizam's Government that the nominal capital of the Deccan Mining Company, £1,000,000, should be reduced by £150,000; and that from the gains made by the promoters, a further sum of £150,000 should be contributed in cash, and paid over by the concessionnaires to the Company. The Government, on its part, engages to ratify the concession obtained. Moreover, Clause 2, as to the meaning of 'a fair' rent, will be interpreted in a generous spirit. The right to prospect, which expires in 1891, will be prolonged for two years further. On the whole, a settlement is come to on the linies proposed, which, while it will still leave nearly half a million to the concessonnaires, will be one to redound to the credit and capacity of Sir Asman Jah's administration. It is not, of course, forgotten that after the completion of this arrangement, Abdul Huk's shares would revert enhanced in value to the State, which, it is thought, would more than reimburse the State for the outlay and expense already incurred in the case. Throughout the whole of this affair, the assistance and advice of Mr. Howell, the Resident, have been invaluable."—*Bullionist*, January 19.

To-day the Duke of Connaught pays his long-promised visit to the Nizam of Hyderabad, and His Highness is making great preparations to receive him.

The Nizam is the first native prince in India. He is a Mahomedan, but the majority of his subjects are Hindoos.

His Highness is between twenty-three and twenty-four. He is a good-looking young fellow, but his face is somewhat effeminate. He is short and slimly built, and is as jealous as a woman.

He has several palaces, and the ladies of his harem are said to be very beautiful. Alas, I was not permitted to see them!

The Duke of Connaught will have a fine time of it in Hyderabad. He will ride the Prince's elephants, shoot his black buck, drink his imported wines, and take a whiff at his hookah. There will be racing by day and illuminations by night; and His Royal Highness will go away impressed with the gorgeous hospitality of this rich and powerful young Prince.

I spent several weeks at Hyderabad, and I have never forgotten His Highness's hospitality. Hyderabad is one of the few Indian cities which have not been spoilt by the English globe-trotter, and where the discordant notes of the spouting "black man" are never heard. Life and customs in Hyderabad have changed but little during the past century; and one obtains a pretty good idea in this remnant of the Mogul Empire what India was like under the Great Moguls.

The Nizam, in spite of his effeminate look, is a plucky young fellow; and he has warlike aspirations. He—as well as his father before him—has always been loyal to the Indian Government, and it was he who first made the offer of men and money for frontier defence.

The State of Hyderabad is rich, and the Nizam has many well-trained soldiers. His Highness, if he had a free hand, would to-morrow make short work of the political agitators so dear to the Separatists in this country, whose windy harangues are causing discord in the adjoining provinces.

I am in a position to state that not only the Nizam, but nearly all--if not all—the native princes are strongly opposed to the so-called National Congress; and Lord Dufferin did well when he, instead of pandering up the "loud-mouthed greasy Babu," endeavoured to strengthen the ties between the Indian Government and the native princes and chiefs—the men who alone would stand by our side in the time of need.—*Evening News*, January 23.

The Duke of Connaught's visit to Hyderabad is noteworthy, as his Royal Highness is the first member of our Royal Family who has ever visited the picturesque capital of the Nizam. When the Prince of Wales was in India he was very anxious to see what is considered the only really Oriental city in India. But the relations between the Indian Foreign Office and the ruling powers at Hyderabad at that time were very strained, owing to the action the late Sir Salar Jung had taken in persistently agitating for the retrocession of the Berar Province. Accordingly, it was considered advisable that the Heir-Apparent should leave the city out of his programme. Most of the Prince's staff, however, found time to pay the place a visit, and were so enchanted with their reception, and all they saw, that the accounts they took back to His Royal Highness made it hard for him to resist the temptation of throwing political exigencies to the winds and following in their footsteps.—*Yorkshire Post*, January 24.

Loyalty at Hyderabad.—(From Our Correspondent.)—Calcutta, Friday.—The Duke and Duchess of Connaught have met with a grand reception at Hyderabad.

The Nizam, in proposing the Duke's health at a banquet given in his honour, said that he was proud to be able to assure him of the abiding friendship and loyalty of himself and his people to her Majesty, and of their devotion to the cause of the great Empire which God had placed under her rule.

A telegram received here from Hyderabad says:—"The loyalty of the people is at fever heat. Thousands of the Nizam's subjects line the streets all day long on the chance of catching a glimpse of the Queen's son as he passes by."—*Daily News*, January 26.

The hysterical style of newsmen's language has penetrated to India. The Duke of Connaught and his wife are visiting Hyderabad, the capital of the Deccan. And a local scribe "wires" that the loyalty of the people, who line the streets in thousands, is at "fever heat." Now, a British crowd may exhibit something like "fever heat" when it demonstrates; but as applied to a native Indian crowd, no expression could be more inappropriate. The native crowd stands stock still, in rows, as if statues; or it squats on the ground. But whether standing or squatting, it prefers to remain silent. It salaams, it claps its hands, but it never cheers.—*Echo*, January 26.

Special prominence is given to the visit of the Duke of Connaught to Hyderabad, as he is the first member of the Royal Family who has visited the Nizam's capital. When the Prince of Wales was in India, he was very anxious to see what is considered the only really Oriental city in India; but the relations between the Indian Foreign Office and the ruling powers at Hyderabad at that time were very strained, owing to the action the late Sir Salar Jung had taken in persistently agitating for the retrocession of the Berar province. Accordingly it was considered advisable that the Heir-Apparent should leave the city out of his programme. Most of the Prince's staff, however, found time to pay the place a visit, and were so enchanted with their reception and all they saw that the accounts they took back to His Royal Highness made it hard for him to resist the temptation of throwing political exigencies to the winds and following in their footsteps.—*Glasgow Evening News*, January 29.

INDIA.—The Duke and Duchess of Connaught (says the Calcutta correspondent of the *Daily News*) have met with a grand reception at Hyderabad. The Nizam, in proposing the Duke's health at a banquet given in his honour, said that he was proud to be able to assure him of the abiding friendship and loyalty of himself and his people to her Majesty, and of their devotion to the cause of the great empire which God had placed under her rule. A telegram received at Calcutta from Hyderabad says: "The loyalty of the people is at fever-heat. Thousands of the Nizam's subjects line the streets all day long, on the chance of catching a glimpse of the Queen's son as he passes by."—*Pictorial World*, January 31.

THE PRICKLY PEAR IN THE DECCAN.—To the Editor of the *Times*.—Sir,— I would not willingly say anything to wound the professional susceptibilities of so able and zealous a sanitarian as Surgeon-General Hewlett, C.I.E., has shown himself to be throughout his long service under the Government of Bombay; but it is impossible to allow his proposal for the wholesale destruction of the prickly pear in Western India, made in *The Times* of last Saturday, to pass without protest. His proposal is, indeed, a pertinent example of the evil which may be done in India through the facilities afforded, under our academical administration, to an able official, in high authority, to inflict his particular individuality, in all its length and breadth, on the people of the country, without any reference to their real necessities and interests. The Anglo-Indian "able official" nearly always has his pet subject, and preoccupies himself with it to the exclusion of all others, however important; and the positive mischief which, in a single generation, such a one may, with the most benevolent intentions, bring on millions of his fellow-creatures, is incredible, except to those who have studied the results of hobby-riding in such a widely-extended and thickly-populated country as India.

The species of Opuntian cactus included under the popular name of (West) Indian fig and the Anglo-Indian name of prickly pear are only more unhealthy in the neighbourhood of human habitations than other plants, because the close growth of their flat succulent, jointed stems, branching out in every direction from the crown of the root, makes it more difficult than with ordinary shrubs to keep the ground under them clear of decaying vegetation. But if the ground where it grows is kept clear of its own "offscourings," the prickly pear is as harmless to man as any other plant; while as a hedge between fields or a fence round farmsteads it is invaluable, being at once impenetrable and uninflammable. These, indeed, were the purposes for which it was originally introduced into the Deccan from Delhi by one of the Sirdars of the old Poona Court—such, at least, is the local tradition—and it must often have proved the salvation of isolated villages from sudden predatory attacks in the time of the anarchy immediately preceding the English occupation of the Mahratta country. Tippoo Sahib is said to have strengthened the defences of Seringapatam by surrounding the fortifications with deep plantations of prickly pear.

Its jointed, juicy, columnar stems form an excellent supplementary fodder for cattle, and it is quite conceivable that a cheap white wine might be manufactured from them in practically limitless measure. It has spread very rapidly throughout Southern India, and chiefly through the agency of birds, which eat greedily of its pyriform fruit, but are unable to digest its hard osseous seeds.

Nothing is easier than the destruction of the plant itself; the native plan in the Mahratta country being to soak the stems in water for two or three days; the solution obtained forming a good liquid manure. The difficulty in getting rid of the plant, where its extirpation is desired, is entirely due to the hardness of the seeds. But the prickly pear never grows well in rich soils, and when areas where it has spread, while they were left neglected, are once brought under cultivation, it rapidly dies out of itself, as it is unable to face the competition of more civilized plants.

It always thrives most luxuriantly on the barrenest spots, where nothing else will grow, not even a blade of grass; and herein lies the highest usefulness of the prickly pear to all the countries of the Old World into which it has spread. since the sixteenth century, from the West Indies, Florida, and the Brazils. In the course of two hundred years it has covered the barest shelves of rocks all along the desiccated southern and eastern shores of the Mediterranean, from the Atlas Mountains to Mount Sinai, and the Taurus range, and by adding *humus* to the soil restored it gradually to cultivation. On a more restricted scale it has operated in the same way in parts of the Deccan. In short, the prickly pear has proved one of the greatest blessings received by the Old World from America, to which we owe also tobacco, maize, and the potato; and as the potato has helped to bring the heath lands of Central Europe under cultivation, so the prickly pear has served to reclaim from destruction the vast tracts of once arable soil in Northern Africa and Anterior Asia, which, under Mahomedan misrule, had lain denuded and utterly waste and corroded for centuries. I fancy the prickly pear or (West) Indian fig has been prejudiced by the evil significance of the Greek name it bears, which was, however, applied by the Greeks (Theophrastus VI., 4) and Romans (Pliny XXI., 57), to *Cynara Cardunculus*, the "Cardoon"; and Athenæus (II., 83) maintains that *kaktos* is but a corruption of *kardos*. It was called Opuntia from its at one time having been supposed to be the anonymous plant described by Pliny (XXI., 64) as growing near Opus, in Locris. But we now know that the Greeks and Romans knew nothing of the Opuntian cactuses, and that they are all American species, first described by Oviedo, Matthiolus, Dodonæus, Lobelius, and others, in the sixteenth century, A.D., and by Bauhinius, Sloane, and Jacquin in the seventeenth.

There is much more, both of antiquarian and economic interest, to say of the plant, but I have probably said enough to justify me when challenged, as one of your readers, to choose between the prickly pear and Surgeon General Hewlett, in deliberately preferring the misjudged and much-misrepresented prickly pear.—Indicopleustes, January 29.—*Times*, February 2.

Manchester, 23rd January, 1889.—Dear Sir,—Being a regular subscriber to your valuable paper, and being also considerably interested in Hyderabad-Deccans, I should be glad to know your opinion if these shares are likely to go up soon, seeing there is now such a "boom" in gold, &c., shares elsewhere; or if you have any information not generally known concerning them.—A. P. M.

[We believe that the settlement of the disputes with the Government will shortly be concluded, and the announcement of this will certainly have a very good effect on the price of the shares. Reports of the Company's working are very satisfactory.]—*Vanity Fair*, February 2.

We have reason to believe that Mr. Howell, the Acting British Resident at the Court of the Nizam, has objected to the appointment by his Highness's Prime Minister of the Nawab Mehdi Hasan as Home Secretary of Hyderabad. The Nawab, who at present holds the equally responsible office of Chief Justice of the State, represented the Nizam's Government in the concluding stages of the negotiations with the Deccan mining concessionnaires, and has only recently returned to India. In his speeches and otherwise the Nawab distinguished himself while in this country by the fervour of his loyalty to the British raj. —*Daily News*, February 5.

Manchester, 5th November, 1888.

Dear Sir,—I am one of the unfortunates who invested some money in the Hyderabad Deccan Company that has been before a Committee of the House of Commons for inquiry. The report of that inquiry was simply nothing. Will you kindly in your next number, if convenient, give me some information as to how the Company stands, and your advice what to do? Can you tell me if they (shares) are being dealt in?—Yours very truly,

Sufferer No. 1.

*** We agree with "Sufferer No. 1" as to the Report of the Royal Commission on the Deccan Company. We believe that, if he have patience, he will not be sorry for his investment in the shares, which are quoted at about 6½.—*Vanity Fair*, November 10.

Although the strictest secrecy is being maintained for the present, I believe there is some foundation for the rumour that the Nawab Mehdi Hasan, before he left England on Thursday for India, concluded a satisfactory arrangement with the concessionnaires of the Deccan Mining Company. If the conditions are ratified by the Prime Minister of Hyderabad, and the minority of shareholders opposed to Mr. Watson and his friends are satisfied, the Company will escape the terrible prospect that at one time seemed inevitable—viz., a protracted and costly fight in the Law Courts. Should it turn out that the Nawab has brought about a compromise agreeable to all parties, he will have justified his recent selection for the honourable and responsible post of Home Secretary of the Nizam's Dominions.—*Vanity Fair*, December 22.

Loyalty at Fever Heat.—A Calcutta telegram to the *Daily News* says:—The Duke and Duchess of Connaught have met with a grand reception at Hyderabad. The Nizam, in proposing the Duke's health at a banquet given in his honour, said that he was proud to be able to assure him of the abiding friendship and loyalty of himself and his people to her Majesty, and of their devotion to the cause of the great Empire which God had placed under her rule. A telegram received at Calcutta from Hyderabad says:—"The loyalty of the people is at fever heat. Thousands of the Nizam's subjects line the streets all day long, on the chance of catching a glimpse of the Queen's son as he passes by."—*Pall Mall Gazette*, January 26.

The Duke of Connaught at Hyderabad.—The visit of the Duke and Duchess of Connaught, the Hereditary Grand Duke and Duchess of Oldenburg, to the Nizam, concluded at Hyderabad on Saturday. On Thursday the Royal party was entertained at a banquet in the City Palace, 300 guests being present.

The Nizam, on proposing the health of the Queen-Empress, said:—"I am proud of the opportunity of assuring the Duke of the abiding friendship and loyalty of myself and my people to Her Majesty, his august mother, and of our devotion to the cause of the great Empire which God has placed under her rule. The address presented makes a comparison between the last and the present visit of Royalty. Two hundred years ago the Great Mogul visited the Deccan, his march being accompanied everywhere by ruin and devastation. To-day, we welcome the loved and honoured son of a greater and more powerful Imperial ruler to the same country, which, thanks to her fostering protection and friendship, has in the meantime attained prosperity beyond all conception in those days." In making offers of military assistance and service the Nizam had, he said, only expressed a widespread sentiment, and he would be supported by all his subjects.

In the course of his reply the Duke said: "I am personally aware how much the Prince of Wales has regretted his inability to visit the Nizam's dominions. I am sure my beloved mother will be glad to hear of the right royal way in which I have been received."

The Duke is still slightly lame, and is unable to ride. On Friday the illustrious visitor inspected the Nizam's army, being afterwards entertained at breakfast in the historical fort of Bala Hissar, when he expressed a strong opinion of the fitness of the Hyderabad troops to take part in the defence of the Empire.—*Globe*, January 28.

The Duke of Connaught, accompanied by the Duchess and the Hereditary Grand Duke and Duchess of Oldenburg, paid a visit to Hyderabad last week, where they were accorded a brilliant and cordial welcome by the Nizam. The Royal party were entertained at a sumptuous banquet on January 24, at which the Nizam proposed the health of the Queen-Empress in most loyal terms. His Highness expressed the pleasure and pride he felt in having the opportunity of assuring the Duke of Connaught of the abiding friendship and loyalty of himself and his people to Her Majesty, and of their "devotion to the cause of the great Empire which God had placed under her rule." These be handsome words, and it is gratifying at this particular juncture to hear such warm expressions of attachment from a Prince of such intelligence and influence as the young Nizam of Hyderabad.—*Colonies and India*, January 30.

THE NIZAM OF HYDERABAD.—The Nizam has recently shown a desire to take a larger share in the administration of the State of which he is the ruler. The Minister sees the Nizam three times a week, and disposes of all important State business in direct consultation with him. Another good sign is, we are told, that the Nizam is now to be frequently met early in the morning riding or driving in the environs of Hyderabad, thus indicating his desire to abandon the recluse-like existence he led a short time ago.—*St. James's Gazette*, February 2.

MR. MORETON FREWEN, who, it will be remembered, acted as a sort of general manager for Sir Salar Jung when he was over here some eighteen months ago, attended as a delegate of the Nizam of Hyderabad the recent congress of "black men" at Allahabad; but it is not recorded that he was converted into a supporter of what Lord Ripon is pleased to call "native sentiment."

MR. FREWEN is a tall, distinguished-looking man, somewhere between thirty and forty. He is handsome, and his exquisitely-trained moustache fills me with envy every time I see him.

HE is married to a relative—a sister, I think—of Lady Randolph Churchill.

MR. FREWEN is an accomplished *littérateur*, and he edited—to put it mildly—the various articles which appeared in the *Nineteenth Century* and elsewhere signed "Salar Jung." Mr. Frewen is the author of an exceedingly able and most readable work on bi-metallism.

SIR SALAR JUNG, one of the most powerful of the Hyderabad nobles, and who was for some time the Prime Minister of the State in succession to his distinguished father, is a tall handsome man of about four-and-twenty. He is clever and honest, but he is—even for an Eastern—distressingly indolent.

HE was to have married the Nizam's sister; but, when he and His Highness quarrelled, the engagement was broken off.

SIR SALAR—physically speaking—is a very heavy man, and his weight cannot be far short of that of "Sir Roger Tichborne," in his palmy days. The revenue from his estates is enormous, and his salary as Prime Minister was (with "perks") something like £60,000 a year. His expenditure—for he keeps up great state—is said, however, to exceed his income: and, incredible though it may seem, Sir Salar was considered to be a poor man on £160,000 a year.

THE Nizam's cousin, who is at this moment Prime Minister of Hyderabad, is perhaps the richest man in the State. He is neither so able nor so distinguished looking as his predecessor, and, unlike Sir Salar Jung, he does not speak English. He has an absurd mania for mechanical musical toys. If you sit down on a chair, or open a door in his palace, it will play a tune, and his Excellency takes a childish delight in winding up his various instruments and letting them play "tunes" against each other.—*Evening News*, February 5.

THE *Daily News* has reason to believe that the Acting British Resident at the Court of the Nizam has objected to the appointment by his Highness's Prime Minister of the Nawab Mehdi Hasan as Home Secretary of Hyderabad. The Nawab, who at present holds the equally responsible office of Chief Justice of the State, represented the Nizam's Government in the concluding stages of the negotiations with the Deccan mining concessionaires, and has only recently returned to India. In his speeches and otherwise the Nawab distinguished himself while in this country by the fervour of his loyalty to the British raj.—*Birmingham Daily Post*, February 6.

THERE are rumours that the state of affairs at Hyderabad is not much improving. Some odd statements are current as to Colonel Marshall and his final settlement of accounts with the Nizam's Government. Intrigues are said to be rife, and it is reported that the Resident, Mr. Howell, is not a stranger to them. We should, however, imagine that that gentleman has before him in his predecessor's career a warning against mixing himself up with any local party. It is said that he has interfered to the extent of objecting to the appointment of Nawab Mehdi Hasan as Home Secretary. If true this seems to be rather a strange proceeding. Nawab Mehdi Hasan made a very favourable impression in England, both by his manner and his writings and speeches, which breathed a loyal spirit. He took charge of the negotiations with the concessionnaires of the Deccan Mining Company, after Nawab Mahdi Ali had left, and gave evidence in conducting them to an issue of great tact and ability. Moreover, Nawab Mehdi Hasan's probity is unchallenged. It would be rather an arbitrary interference with the discretion of the Nizam's Minister to object to this appointment, and we believe the Nizam would resent it extremely. Moreover people outside will begin to wonder from what motives the British Resident should interfere with the appointment of an official who was generally regarded in England as one of the best specimens of the Native gentleman that has visited our shores. We can only conjecture that there is some misunderstanding as to the Resident's action. He bears a high reputation, and it is not to be supposed that, in a matter of this kind, he would be acting on his own responsibility. If the Nizam is discontented with the interference, he must probably look for the origin of it beyond the Resident. Mehdi Hasan is naturally not *persona grata* to those who were mixed up in the Hyderabad scandals, and the names of all these gentlemen have not yet been published.—*Overland Mail*, February 8.

THE native Chief Justice of Hyderabad, with whose long and dreadful name we we will not trouble our readers, has recently been on a visit to this country, and he records among his impressions that English club manners "froze his blood." He noticed, he says, that "members came and went without the slightest sign of recognizing one another." "The highest mark of esteem," says this observant "black man," "conferred on rare occasions, by one member upon another with whom he is on the best of terms, is to turn his face in the opposite direction, give a minute nod, which you can scarcely perceive, it is so small, and mutter 'How d'ye do?' We often complain of the reserved character of the English people in India, but it is just the same with them at home among their own countrymen. In club life, where one should think that they would be more than friendly, they almost appear to hate each other." This Hindoo gentleman is probably not acquainted with a little poem, entitled "Etiquette," by Mr. W. S. Gilbert, which describes how

> Young Peter Gray, who tasted teas for Baker, Croop, and Co.,
> And Somers, who from Eastern shores, imported indigo,

were wrecked upon a desert island, and

> They hunted for their meals as Alexander Selkirk used,
> But they could not chat together—they had not been introduced.

They, therefore, tacitly agreed that one should take one half of the island, and the other should appropriate the remainder.

On Peter's portion oysters grew, a delicacy rare,
But oysters were a delicacy Peter could not bear;
On Somers' side was turtle, on the shingle lying thick,
Which Somers could not eat, because it always made him sick.

At last they discovered that they each knew a mutual acquaintance named Robinson, whereupon

They soon became like brothers from community of wrongs,
They wrote each other little odes and sang each other songs.

But, alas! it was discovered that the said Robinson had got into trouble for "misappropriating stock." Somers and Gray "didn't quarrel very openly" at first. "They nodded when they met, and now and then exchanged a word"; but

The word grew rare, and rarer still the nodding of the head,
And when they meet each other now they cut each other dead.

The Chief Justice of Hyderabad, if he had remained in England long enough, would have found that the bearishness of club life is only a small part of the general unsociability of the British citizen.—*Leamington Chronicle*, February 12.

A WARM tribute is due to the perspicacity of the Chief Justice of Hyderabad. He has been paying a visit to England, and on his return to his native India he has been giving an account of his experiences. Among them I find an account of life inside a Radical club—a subject with which, personally, I am wholly unacquainted. The Nawab let us into the secret of the failure of these institutions. While the Conservatives seem able to multiply their clubs in prodigious fecundity, the Radicals can only show at most one or two starvelings. The cause, we are told (and the Nawab is speaking particularly of the Northbrook Club and the National Liberal Club), is the insufferable caddishness which members exhibit in their intercourse with one another. The way in which members came and went, without the slightest sign of recognising one another, froze the Nawab's blood. The members, he says, almost appeared to hate each other. And he himself nearly came to hate them, when, having told a member of the National Liberal Club that he had been made a member of the International Club, he was answered, "I am sorry for you; there are lords and dukes there, which is horrible to me." Since reading the Chief Justice's account I have made some inquiries, and I find that Radical club life is honeycombed with petty rivalries and jealousies to an almost incredible extent. This of itself accounts for the fact that Radical clubs are invariably failures.—*Sheffield Daily Telegraph*, February 13.

A "BLACK MAN'S" IMPRESSIONS OF ENGLAND.—The *Times of India* contains an interesting account of an interview with the Nawab Mehdi Hassan, Chief Justice of Hyderabad, who has recently returned to India from England.

SCHOOLBOY POLITICIANS.—Nothing in his visit seems to have struck the Nawab more forcibly than the singularly early and widespread development of political knowledge and opinions among all classes of the English people. Boys of twelve and thirteen, sons of London working men, astonished him by the fluency with which they spoke of political parties. "What is the difference between your political parties?" he asked on visiting a board school in a poor district. "Well," said one mature politician of eleven, "we want Home Rule, and the other party obstructs it"; while another small child volunteered the further explanation that "the Liberals want progress, and the Conservatives wish things to be as they are." "Now an Indian boy of fifteen," said the Nawab in relating this incident, "is an utter fool so far as politics are concerned, and yet some people are clamouring for native self-government. The Indian people are utterly unfit for it yet. When overgrown men know even as much of politics as young children do in England, then it may be well to consider the matter. Our rich men, the big landowners and manufacturers and agriculturists, are most of them, with very few exceptions indeed, totally ignorant of the most elementary facts of Indian government. It would be nonsense to give them what these people are asking for."

Our Home Life a Beautiful Thing.—"What were your impressions of English home life?" "It is a beautiful thing. We have nothing like it in our country—this pure home life with all its tendernesses and sympathies. In our language there is no such word as 'home'; in England every heart is stirred by it. All natural passions and questions are, no doubt, common to us and to Englishmen, but in them they are more systematic, civilized, and genuine. We love each other, but we don't express it in the same warm and impressive way."

"It is this home life," continued the Nawab, "that is one of the chief sources of England's supremacy. Their children grow up in the society of educated mothers, and become intelligent and thoughtful while they are yet children. In our country, where the women for the most part have no education, this is impossible, and they grow up into men and women quite ignorant of the simplest things—things that are known in England by the children of the very poorest people. It is impossible to express to you my sense of the great influence of English women upon English life. They refine and elevate it beyond all measure: you never know where their influence will not reach. I am a firm believer in the complete freedom of women, although I recognise that complete equality with men is not possible; but Indian people know nothing of this great influence of women upon English thought and action—the greater because it is a silent influence, working by suasion, not by force."

Club Manners froze his Blood.—On one occasion he visited the Northbrook Club. "Natives are treated there," said the Nawab, "on perfectly equal terms with Europeans. It is a most useful institution for Indians." For club life generally, however, the Nawab has no great regard. "One thing about all these clubs that froze the blood in my veins was that the members came and went without the slightest sign of recognising one another. The highest mark of esteem, conferred, on rare occasions, by one member upon another with whom he is on the best terms, is to turn his face in the opposite direction, give a minute nod which you can scarcely perceive, it is so small, and mutter, 'How d'ye do?' We often complain of the reserved character of the English people in India, but it is just the same with them at home among their own countrymen. In club life, where one should think that they would be more than friendly, they almost appear to hate each other."

The aggressive Radicalism of some of the English politicians made a singularly strong impression upon the Nawab's mind. He one day visited the National Liberal Club, and incidentally mentioned to one of its members that he had been elected a member of the International Club. "I am sorry for you, then," said the gentleman addressed. "There are lords and dukes there, which is horrible to me." "I was astonished," said the Nawab, "for I think the aristocracy is the gem of every country. There is no grandeur without it." —*Pall Mall Budget*, February 14.

Nawab Hassan, Chief Justice of Hyderabad, has just returned to India after a visit to England. He is much struck, among other things, with our domestic life. "It is this home life that is one of the chief sources of England's supremacy. Their children grow up in the society of educated mothers, and become intelligent and thoughtful while they are yet children. In our country, where the women for the most part have no education, this is impossible, and they grow up into men and women quite ignorant of the simplest things—things that are known in England by the children of the very poorest people. It is impossible to express to you my sense of the great influence of English women upon English life. They refine and elevate it beyond all measure: you never know where their influence will not reach. I am a firm believer in the complete freedom of women, although I recognise that complete equality with men is not possible; but Indian people know nothing of this great influence of women upon English thought and action—the greater because it is a silent influence, working by suasion, not by force."—*Worcester Herald*, February 16.

THE Duke of Connaught's recent visit to the Nizam of Hyderabad has been followed with great interest in Indian political circles, as this is the first time that a member of the Royal Family has been received by the Sovereign of the Deccan. When the Prince of Wales was in India he was very anxious indeed to see the picturesque and ancient capital of the Nizam. But the relations between the India Office and the ruling authorities at Hyderabad were at that time on anything but a friendly footing, mainly owing to the persistent agitation which the late Sir Salar Jung, who was the Prime Minister of the day, kept up for the restoration of the Beraos Province. So it happened that, though many of the Prince's suite paid an unofficial visit to Hyderabad, His Royal Highness had to bow to the political exigencies of the time, and leave India without having seen the treasures of the finest Oriental city in the Empire.—*St. Stephen's Review*, February 16.

H.H. THE NIZAM'S GUARANTEED STATE RAILWAYS.—The Directors have received a telegram, dated 13th inst., from their agent in India, stating that the last 22 miles of the Company's own line and the Beswada Extension Railway, belonging to the Government of India, was opened for traffic on the 10th inst., thus establishing through communication with Wadi Station, the junction with the Great Indian Peninsula Railway, and the town of Beswada, on the River Kistna, and completing the Company's southern system.—*Herapaths*, February 16.

WE Britishers, as a nation, have got to be so introspective, always dissatisfied with ourselves, and picking holes in our own armour, that it is really quite encouraging to find two foreigners giving us a good character. One is the Nawab Mehdi Hassan, a Government official from Hyderabad, who has been studying the English at home and their institutions. He is particularly struck by the intelligence of our children, and the beneficial influence exercised by women in social and private life. There, ladies, will that help to heal the sore which still rankles on account of the preference shown by some of our most eligible *partis* for American brides?—*County Gentleman*, February 16.

THE BRITISH RESIDENCY AT HYDERABAD.—The Indian papers are demanding that a permanent appointment should be made to the British Residency at Hyderabad. It was known to the Government of India so far back as the 10th of November that Sir Lepel Griffin, who was to succeed Mr. Condery, would never return to duty; but no steps have been taken to fill the vacancy. Mr. Howell holds the officiating appointment; and when Sir Asman Jah visited Lord Dufferin at Simla in August he was the bearer of an autograph letter from the Nizam begging that Mr. Howell's appointment might be confirmed. The post of Resident at Hyderabad is no great catch. The man who occupies it stands on a mine, never knowing when or in what direction it may explode. For ten months of the year the heat is unbearable, and there is no hill-refuge within reach, whilst the demands upon his hospitality devour his pay.—*St. James's Gazette*, February 19.

"DEATH in the pot," is an expression which has peculiar significance in India. Owing to the almost universal use in that country of copper cooking utensils, cases are frequently recorded in which deaths occur from poisoning due to the imperfect cleaning of the vessels after use. An instance of this kind is just to hand which will excite more than ordinary interest in England owing to the close connection of the victim with our Royal Family. The deceased was none other than Dr. Keith, the surgeon on the Staff of the Duke of Connaught, and if the report speaks truly the Duke and Duchess themselves narrowly escaped meeting with his fate. It seems that Dr. Keith contracted his fatal malady at Hyderabad during the recent visit of the Royal party to that city. He lived until he returned to Poona, but on arrival there was seized with what at first were thought to be choleraic symptoms, but which were subsequently traced to copper poisoning, and he died within a few hours. Several other members of the household were affected in a similar way, but they fortunately recovered. The Duke and Duchess of Connaught were much attached to Dr. Keith, who had been with them ever since they first went to India, and His Royal Highness attended the funeral in company with the Grand Duke of Oldenburg, who was staying at Poona at the time.—*Yorkshire Post*, February 20.

THE following question was asked in Parliament last night:—

DECCAN MINING COMPANY.—Sir George Campbell (Kirkcaldy) asked the Under Secretary of State for India (Sir J. Gorst) whether anything had yet been settled as to the Deccan Mining Company. Whether, notwithstanding the report of the Committee of the House, the Nizam had been induced to continue the concessions to the company on such terms that, though they have yet discovered nothing whatever, the shares have gone up to a high figure, almost equal to the nominal value put on them by the promoters, as reported in the money article of the *Times* of 27 February: And, whether Her Majesty's Government in India or in this country have approved of the arrangements made. The First Lord of the Treasury (Mr. W. H. Smith) answered the question in Sir J. Gorst's absence. He said he was not aware of any arrangement having been come to by the Government of the Nizam with reference to the concessions. No arrangement had had the approval either of the Government of India or of the Home Government. The Secretary of State had no knowledge of the price of the company's shares.—*Stock Exchange*, March 1.

THE DECCAN MINING COMPANY.—In answer to Sir G. Campbell, Sir J. Gorst said: The Secretary of State is not aware of any arrangement having been come to by the Government of the Nizam in reference to the concession of the Deccan Company. The Secretary of State has no knowledge of the price of the company's shares. No arrangement has been submitted for the approval of Her Majesty's Government, either here or in India.—*Times*, March 2.

HYDERABAD DECCAN.—These shares touched par—£10—during the week. Some good buying is reported from Bombay; indeed, on Wednesday it was known to insiders, whose "names" were passed for shares. We are aware, of course, that this could be dodged; but there is no reason to suppose that buyers have taken the trouble to conceal their purchases.—*Citizen*, March 2.

DECCANS.—There has been quite a demand for these shares during the last few days. We know that buying orders were received from India by the mail delivered last Monday. This seems like a healthy sign.—*Weekly Bulletin*, March 2.

THE Hyderabad Deccan shares are slowly being brought back to their former high price. They are now somewhere about £10, as contrasted with £6 a short time ago. Of course, our readers know too well the intrinsic value of these shares to be led away by any interested market operations.—*Financial Critic*, March 2.

The Hyderabad Commission on Chloroform.—In a report of the recent prize distribution at the Hyderabad Medical School, which appeared in our issue of February 23rd, some remarks of Surgeon-Major Lawrie, M.B., M.R.C.S., of the Bengal Army Medical Service, are mentioned, which deserve some comment. We learn that a Commission had been appointed to investigate the action of chloroform, and that the result of the researches made upon pariah dogs was that these animals were killed from respiratory failure, and in no case did cardiac syncope occur directly. Unfortunately Mr. Lawrie contents himself with bare statements of results, adding that these results tally with his own experience, which he believes to be uniquely large. Mr. Lawrie, as a disciple of Simpson and Syme, arrives at conclusions consonant with the teaching of those great clinicians, but utterly at variance with the experience alike of experiment and practice as carried out in Europe. We should require more than the scanty statements of experiments performed upon dogs—notoriously non-susceptible to chloroform syncope—before we could accept the conclusions of the Hyderabad Commission when they appear to go in the very teeth of those at which the Commission appointed by the Royal Medical and Chirurgical Society and by the British Medical Association arrived, and, further, are opposed to the careful and painstaking experiments of such scientific observers as Snow, Claude Bernard, McKendrick, and others too numerous to mention. All those who are familiar with chloroform are well aware that syncope, when primary, as a rule supervenes in the initial stages of inhalation, while secondary syncope due to respiratory embarrassment is the result of accumulation of chloroform in the blood leading to paralysis of the medullary centres, and occurs in a late stage of the administration. The primary syncope it is rarely, if ever, possible to induce in dogs, although, unfortunately, it is this form of chloroform heart failure which does occur in human beings, and which it is almost impossible to remedy. While welcoming the attention paid to the subject by the Hyderabad Commission, we cannot but feel that, should the Commission inculcate a disregard of the heart as a factor in chloroform dangers, it will do harm and provoke a slipshod carelessness in the use of that valuable anæsthetic, which must in the long run do damage to the cause the Commission has espoused.—*Lancet*, March 2.

The shares of the Hyderabad Deccan touched par during the week. Some good buying is reported from Bombay. This fact became known when names had to be "passed" on Wednesday, and shareholders may rely upon it that all the trouble is ended —*London and Brighton*, March 3.

The Allahabad *Morning Post* has an article on the state of affairs at Hyderabad, hinting at the imminence of another crisis. We reproduce it, along with some other information which comes by this mail, without in any way vouching for the accuracy of the facts stated or the suspicions based upon them. We mentioned a mail or two ago that there appeared to be some trouble between the Resident and the Nawab Asman Jah, and that there was a rumour of opposition to Nawab Mehdi Hassan's appointment as Home Secretary. But the nature of the difficulty and the motive of Mr. Howell's interference were not disclosed. Of course, no one will take the rumours and conjectures too seriously. Mr. Howell is an experienced official, and not likely to overstep the line.—*Homeward Mail*, March 4.

To agree with Mr. Gladstone is a keen pleasure if it is a rare one. For the present he is not disposed to extend Home Rule and Annual Parliaments to the races of India. "It would be a mistake to carry the representative system of Government *per saltum* into countries where the conditions of its application would be novel and therefore quite uncertain." So he writes to the Nawab Mahdi Ali, who had pointed out the impossibility of introducing democracy into a region which included so many differences of nationality, customs, castes, and creeds. But Mr. Gladstone adds, "I have not heard that the combination of Mahommedans with Bulgarian Christians has worked ill." After this extraordinary sentence Mr. Gladstone may be forgiven for anything. Has he quite forgotten what he said about the Bulgarian atrocities and the necessity of bundling the Unspeakable Turk out of Europe, bag and baggage? Once again Mr. Gladstone's memory has failed him just at the moment when it is convenient to forget.—*St. James's Gazette*, March 4.

THE NIZAM'S GOVERNMENT AND THE HYDERABAD (DECCAN) COMPANY.—It will be within the recollection of our readers that the affairs of the Hyderabad (Deccan) Company, and the manner in which the concession upon which it was based was obtained from the Nizam's Government were made the subject of investigation by a select Parliamentary Committee last year. That Committee drew up a report, published in August, which, while it expressed regret and disapproval at certain circumstances connected with the inception of the great mining undertaking in the Deccan, did not propound any remedy for what had been done, and left the parties concerned very much to their own unaided devices to decide as to what ulterior action should be taken to establish a *modus vivendi* between the Hyderabad ruler and the Deccan Company. More than eight months have elapsed since the publication of the report, and during this period the most active negotiations have been in progress between the legal representatives of the Nizam's Government, of the company, and of the concessionnaires. These negotiations have produced a practical result in the agreement which was recently telegraphed from India, and to which the sanction of the Secretary of State is about to be given. We have been granted the privilege of perusing the whole of the legal documents relating to this unknown phase of a question which has attracted a good deal of interest in political and financial circles, and from these voluminous papers we take sufficient matter to give a brief and intelligible narrative of the negotiations since last August which has resulted in the present arrangement.

When the report of the Committee was issued on August 10 the Nizam's representative in England was the Nawab Mohsin ul Mulk, better and more conveniently known as Mahdi Ali. The report itself, while it was vague and inconclusive, and propounded no specific course of action, was worded so as to bear the construction of inciting to further litigation or legislative action on the part of the Nizam. With that document in his hands Mahdi Ali consulted the proper authorities at the India Office, and it was decided to place the Nizam's case in the hands of Messrs. Freshfields and Williams. The next step was to take the opinion of counsel, and the services of Mr. Edward Pollard, "a barrister of long experience, and pre-eminently fitted to express an opinion on the questions in dispute," were engaged. Mr. Pollard's opinion was of a very emphatic character, and it was repeated on several occasions subsequent to the date of his first opinion in August, 1888. He held that it was "within the power of the Nizam either to affirm or to disaffirm the concession." That opinion was not shared by another eminent counsel, Mr. Finlay, Q.C., M.P., who was consulted many months later, nor did it altogether commend itself at the time to the business experience and judgment of Mr. P. Williams, of Messrs. Freshfields, who wrote on August 21 as follows:—

"I am myself, I confess—but I say so with great deference—unable altogether to concur in Mr. Pollard's views, and I should have great difficulty in coming to the conclusion that the Nizam could, after the lapse of so much time, and after having accepted advantages from the concession, and after having allowed the company to spend considerable sums of money in the State upon the faith of the concession, cancel the concession. However, I have no right to set up my opinion against that of Mr. Pollard. I must say I should infinitely prefer arriving at some arrangement by compromise rather than commence proceedings, but the question is whether proceedings in the first instance are not absolutely necessary as a means to an end."

Although the line taken by the Nizam's representatives continued for many months to be one of pronounced hostility towards the concessionnaires, there is no doubt that the expression of Mr. Williams's opinion produced a great effect on the Nizam's principal advisers, who, as the negotiations developed, saw more clearly that the outcome of any litigation would be exceedingly uncertain, and that both prudence and policy dictated an amicable arrangement. In October, Mahdi Ali returned to India, and his place was taken in London by another Hyderabad notable, Mehdi Hassan, or, to give him his full title, Nawab Fatteh Nawaz Jung. Great care must be taken in distinguishing between these two officials, and the credit of the recent arrangement belongs exclusively to Mehdi Hassan and Messrs. Freshfields, acting under the instructions of the Nizam and his Prime Minister, Sir Asman Jah. Three courses alone remained for the Nizam to make his selection from. They were, in Messrs. Freshfields' own words:—

"The first is that suggested in our letter to Mr. Clements of the 22nd August —viz., to commence proceedings against Mr. Watson and others interested in the concession. This, however, would of necessity entail lengthy litigation, which might have an injurious effect not only upon the company but upon His Highness's territory, because it is not at all probable that during the period which litigation would occupy, the company would attempt to proceed with prospecting and developing the property, and thereby not only would the works of the company be brought to a standstill, but the development of the territory for several years be retarded."

The next course open to the Nizam is by exercise of his sovereign right to cancel the concession. This we could not advise His Highness to do, unless he was prepared to at once place all holders of shares in the company who may have innocently parted with their money in acquiring shares prior to the date of the resolution for the appointment of the Parliamentary Committee in precisely the same position as they were, and this indeed the Nizam, by his counsel, Mr. Mayne, stands, as it were, pledged to do. To do this the Nizam, when cancelling the concession, would have to let it be known contemporaneously that he would grant a fresh concession to a new company, in which the *bonâ fide* shareholders would be given shares to an equal proportionate amount to that which they held in the old company. . . . Mr. Clements asserts that the adoption of such a course would discredit on the English market any concession which His Highness might have given or may hereafter give, and he also stated that Mr. Watson and his friends would attack, both in the Courts of law and in Parliament, such a course. We do not agree with Mr. Clements in his estimate of what would result from such a course, nor do we consider Mr. Clements' threat to be material; but the fact that Mr. Watson has behind him some of the largest financiers who are accustomed to deal with this class of security on the Stock Exchange is worthy of consideration, and if he was made hostile to the Nizam's interests, raising any capital hereafter for the purpose of employment in His Highness's territory might be rendered more difficult. . . . Another course open to the Nizam would be to leave the company entirely alone, and not to assist it in any way in prospecting; and although this we do not advise, it is evidently what Mr. Clements feels to be a great power in the Nizam, as should this course be adopted, even if no actual obstruction were resorted to, practically, little more of the territory would be taken, and the company's operations would thereby be materially restricted. This course could lead to no ultimate result, unless it had quickly the effect of bringing pressure to bear on Mr. Watson and others interested to accede to reasonable terms, and it is in any event not a course of action which we could either advise or recommend. The only other course open to the Nizam is to continue negotiations with Mr. Clements's clients, but we must at once point out that, unless His Highness's Government are prepared to act decisively in the event of Mr. Watson refusing to act reasonably, it will be but little use attempting to do more than merely bargain for something to be given. If, on the other hand, the Nizam's Government decide to act with firmness unless reasonable concessions be made by Mr. Watson, we think negotiations could be continued with very great prospect of success. We think that there are undoubted difficulties in the way of cancelling the concession, but Mr. Pollard considers that these difficulties lie chiefly in practically working out such cancellation, and that they could all be surmounted if the Nizam's course of action be consistent and steadily pursued; but we are not sufficiently informed of the motives and grounds of action of His Highness's Government to do more than point out what can be done if desired. We understand that Mr. Watson and his associates would be prepared in any event to find £100,000 on ordinary shares, provided the Nizam will grant a further period of two years for prospecting.

The practical points involved in the controversy may be considered as fully defined and expressed in the preceding extracts from the formal letter of the firm of solicitors intrusted with the charge of the Nizam's interests in this country, and it would serve no useful purpose to enter into the details arising from their full discussion in both public and confidential letters by Mr. Clements, acting for Mr. Watson, and Messrs. Freshfields down to the end of October last year. On the 2nd of November Messrs. Freshfields drew up the heads of an agreement which has formed the basis of everything that has since been done. The points were as follows:—

"First, that Mr. Watson and his friends should provide the further sum of £150,000 paid up capital in order to put the company on a sound financial basis, and I should not object to the ordinary share capital of the company being increased to an equivalent amount in order to accomplish that object.

"Secondly, that Mr. Watson and his friends should surrender, for the purpose of being cancelled, fully paid up shares to the amount of £150,000. Mr. Watson may be advised not to concede this on the ground that any such surrender of shares forming part of the 85,000 shares would remain as evidence against him of guilty conduct. It occurs to me that this might be met, and that Mr. Watson and his friends, instead of actually surrendering and cancelling the shares, might make them deferred shares—that is to say, that they should not rank for dividend until all other shares had been paid, say, at least 5 per cent.

"Thirdly, that Abdul Huk should surrender to the Government the shares allotted to him as his proportion of the profit made by the sale of the concession.

"Fourthly, that, if the Nizam consents to an extension of the prospecting period, adequate consideration should be insisted upon, either in the shape of an allotment of share capital to the Nizam or by way of increased prospecting fees or royalties.

"Fifthly, that in consideration of the above the Government should extend the time for prospecting for two years.

"Sixthly, that the forms of leases should at once be settled.

"Seventhly, it has been suggested that the amount of the royalties should also now be settled, but in my opinion there exists an objection to this. Moreover, the concession itself, I believe, defines the basis on which the royalties are to be settled."

These propositions were finally embodied in a draft agreement, and Mehdi Hassan telegraphed to his Government asking if it approved them, and to reply immediately, as delay was injurious. On the 21st of November Major Robertson was instructed to reply as follows in the name of the Nizam's Government from Hyderabad:—

"Regret delay replying proposals due to absence Resident, who has now returned. Long telegram going to Mehdi Hassan to-morrow. Sincere desire here is to effect such compromise as may enable company to live, but after visiting mines I feel certain this is only possible by reduction present watered capital and provision extra capital for expenditure in Hyderabad. Nizam desires deal separately and immediately with Huk by suit in Bombay if necessary; his shares therefore should not form item in compromise. Do you agree? Please wire after seeing Mehdi Hassan's telegram."

A misunderstanding, which must be noted, although its practical consequences were *nil*, arose at this stage, through the Hyderabad authorities assuming that the compromise indicated was a spontaneous offer by the concessionnaires instead of being the result of mutual negotiation, and, in the opinion of their legal advisers in London, the best possible obtainable terms. At this stage of the question Mahdi Ali reappears upon the scene, with a vigorous protest against the compromise carried out under Mehdi Hassan's direction, containing much denunciation of the conduct of Messrs. Freshfields, but even he, in this supplementary memorandum of the 12th of December, 1888, has to begin by admitting that "the cancelling of the concession has come to be almost out of the question." In fact, his only remedy was a policy of indifference and inaction, leaving the company to its own unaided resources and practically restricting its sphere of activity to the Singareni coalfields. In this opinion he seems to have had the support of the late Resident at Hyderabad, Mr. Howell, who wrote:—"My advice is not to take heroic measures, not to attempt to cancel the concession by litigation, still less to cancel it by summary State edict, but simply to sit still and to refrain from co-operating with the company in any way or supporting its operations in any other respect except at Singareni." The Prime Minister preferred to await the further reference to counsel—Mr. Finlay—as to the legal position of his Prince, and when that authority gave an unfavourable opinion of his power to cancel the concession, the news that Mr. Watson, after having refused to accept the compromise, had, on the 6th of December, given his assent to it, could not have been altogether unwelcome at Hyderabad, although it led to a somewhat heated telegraphic correspondence between the Nizam's Ministers at Hyderabad and their representatives in London. The misapprehension arose, as has been explained, from its having been too hastily assumed that Mr. Watson had shown a willingness to yield all that was demanded, whereas the reverse was the case. The following telegram of the 11th of December, 1888, from Messrs. Freshfields, in explanation of the situation, will close this portion of the subject:—

"Telegram 10th received. Unfortunate misunderstanding. Telegram 25th shows difference with us based on misapprehension. This explained by ours 26th, and your subsequent silence was considered approval. Mehdi gave us Robertson's telegram 23rd. Useless submitting these more onerous terms to Watson, as had satisfied ourselves would be rejected and would entangle you in further complications, and cannot advise this risk. We advised Mehdi submit terms to Clements, based on letter 12th of October, without waiting your approval, because delay most injurious. Terms accepted after great struggle, and after threat of cancellation, and are subject your approval, and this we advise. Finlay now clear opinion Buffalo (Nizam) no legal power cancel. He strongly recommends compromise."

Mehdi Hassan's letter of December 14, describing the negotiations about the compromise, is also an interesting and important document:—

"I am sure there is some grave misunderstanding, which, if not cleared up, will place me in an awkward position, and will lead the Government into great difficulties. On my part, I consider I have achieved a great success in making Watson accept the terms, which he had totally refused. There was left no alternative for your Excellency but to cancel the concession, which would have involved the State (to use the words of Mr. Finlay) in endless litigation and complications, or to leave Watson in possession of all his spoil. In the former case the Government would have had to repay all money spent by the company in Hyderabad, and this would have crippled the finances of the State for a long time. I did, indeed, propound a scheme for the reconstruction of the company to Mr. Williams, which he thought worthy of serious consideration, but he said in his letter to me of November 30, 'This scheme of reconstruction would lead to very great difficulties, both financially and otherwise,' and in the same letter he said, with regard to the position of the case, 'The position is surrounded with difficulties, and I confess I never had a more anxious and serious case to deal with." I humbly beg to say that I saved the Government from this difficult position. I need not say more, but simply enclose a copy of Mr. Williams's letter of the 12th instant, which requires your serious attention. On the other hand, I find your Excellency led to believe, as appears from your telegram of the 10th instant, that in not offering the terms telegraphed by Major Robertson on the 23rd ultimo I committed a fault. By your telegram of October 2nd, I was desired to exercise my own discretion in this negotiation, and moreover, in withholding the one term containing the only important difference between your proposals and ours, I acted on the strong recommendation of Messrs. Freshfields and Williams, who wrote to me on November 24, 'It is perfectly useless putting forward proposals which we know will not be accepted and which we know can only lead to useless and fruitless controversy.'"

All these proceedings were taken on the express recommendation and responsibility of Messrs. Freshfields, who, when they found that the compromise was not altogether approved of at Hyderabad, wished to be relieved of their connexion with the case, and peremptorily refused to associate themselves with proceedings that were "inconsistent with all our former action." The upshot was that a final decision was put off until Mehdi Hassan's return to Hyderabad last January. The opposition to the compromise on the part of the Resident and others did not abate, and Mehdi Hassan's conduct of his Government's case in England was severely and almost bitterly impugned. In two masterly despatches of January 22 and February 9 Mehdi Hassan successfully vindicated his honour from the aspersions that had been cast upon it, but space will not allow of our quoting these interesting documents. It only remains to place on record the two official papers embodying the final decision of the Nizam's Government in the matter, and sanctioning the compromise that had been negotiated by Mehdi Hassan and Messrs. Freshfields under exceptional difficulties in London. The first is an official letter from Sir Asman Jah, the Prime Minister, to the British Resident, and dated February 12:—

"I beg to acknowledge the receipt of your letter of the 11th inst., embodying the conclusions which commended themselves to your mind as to the policy which should be adopted as regards the pending negotiation relating to the Deccan mining matter, and to express my obligation to you for so clear an expression of your views.

"I have anxiously considered the matter and have had the advantage of hearing the divergent views held by the Nawabs Muhsin ul Mulk (Mahdi Ali) and Satteh Nawaz Jung (Mehdi Hassan) expounded by those gentlemen and discussed in consultation with other officers of His Highness's Government. I have also had the advantage of able minutes dealing with the subject from different points of view. Lastly, the Nawab Intesar Jung, Revenue Secretary, has submitted to me a very able memorandum dealing with the relative advantages and disadvantages of the several courses which have been proposed by way of solution of the difficult question before us, and I may say generally that my own opinions coincide very closely with those expressed in this memorandum. I beg to enclose for reference five copies of this memorandum, and will content myself with a brief summary of my views on the different suggested courses therein dealt with, first premising that I am under none the less obligation to you for the assistance rendered by your letter, although I have arrived, in my own mind, at other conclusions.

"The first suggestion that has been made is that application should be made to the English Law Courts for a cancelment of the concession. It seems admitted on all hands, however, that this course would not only be enormously expensive, but that its results would also be very doubtful, and its adoption does not appear to be recommended by anyone in preference to a reasonable compromise.

"The next suggestion which has been put forward is that the concession should be summarily cancelled by an Act of State. I freely confess that I feel grave apprehensions regarding the adoption of such a course. Both Messrs. Finlay and Pollard prefer a reasonable compromise to the adoption of this course; and in an opinion, dated the 21st of August last, the latter gentleman has stated that if cancelment were to be the course adopted, it should be done 'promptly, and immediate action taken in respect of it in justice to others.' As nearly six months have elapsed since then, Mr. Pollard would at present probably consider that cancelment by Act of State could not now be carried out without the action of this Government being open to just and unfavourable criticism. Moreover, even if the Government has at this moment just grounds to cancel the concession, I would be most unwilling to recommend such a course to His Highness, because, first, it would be felt to be opposed to the traditions of his ancestors; and secondly, it would inevitably entail much further trouble and expense in subsequent legal and other arrangements for protecting the interests of *boná fide* shareholders in terms of the assurance to that effect already given to them.

"The third suggestion which has been suggested is that Mr. Watson's offer to furnish £150,000 as fresh working capital for the company, in exchange for an issue of deferred shares, be rejected, and that, instead thereof, our original terms, telegraphed to London on the 23rd of November last, be proposed to him. It appears to be already practically recognised that these terms would be rejected, and so to propose them at all would appear to have little or no meaning, unless we were prepared to cancel the concession on their rejection—a course which, for reasons already given, I do not feel prepared to advise. The fourth suggestion is to adhere to our proposals of the 23rd of November, and, if they are refused, then to do nothing whatever, but to let things go on as they are doing at present. I confess I do not see any sound argument in favour of continuing the present state of things, which is felt on all hands to be extremely unsatisfactory. It certainly would be very far from satisfying the company, which would be ruined, and I cannot see that any advantage would result to His Highness's Government.

"The fifth suggestion which has been made is to accept the heads of arrangement now offered by Mr. Watson, under which he has agreed to furnish £150,000 new working capital to the company in exchange for deferred shares, which should receive no dividend until 5 per cent. had been paid on all the original capital. I think this suggestion should be accepted. It appears to me, and it is also stated in the opinion of Mr. Pollard, dated the 13th of September, that the only object which we can possibly expect to secure at this last stage is to prevent the concessionnaires from realizing further plunder out of the concession. The documents before us show that in August last they only possessed in all about £150,000 of shares unsold. If we now make them pay up £150,000 hard cash and give them in exchange only deferred shares (which shares, according to my view of the future dividend-earning power of the company, must remain practically worthless) we shall have secured the above object as far as it can be attained. On the other hand, we shall by the same acts give to the company, and therefore to the *boná fide* shareholders, as good a chance of success as they can possibly expect. I trust that you will, on further consideration, agree with the conclusions here imperfectly expressed, and which you will find stated in a fuller and detailed manner in the Nawab Intesar Jung's memorandum, and that you may feel yourself able to join with me in recommending the conclusions at which I have arrived to the favourable consideration of the Government of India as being conducive to the welfare of the *boná fide* shareholders in the company, and consistent with the credit of the State and the honour and dignity of His Highness the Nizam.

"As Messrs. Watson and His Highness's Government have been limited to four months' time for bringing the negotiations to a final conclusion, and as a great portion of this time has already elapsed, it is necessary that this question should be settled with as little delay as possible. Should the Government of India agree with my views, or should they, on the other hand, propose any modifications or any alternative course of action, His Highness's Government, I need not say, will act upon the advice so proffered and proceed in accordance therewith. "I am, my dear Mr. Howell, yours very sincerely,

"ASMAN JAH."

The second document is the draft of a letter from the Minister to Messrs. Freshfields and Williams:—

"Dear Sirs,—The arrival in India of the Nawab Mehdi Hassan, with all the documents up to date in connexion with the negotiations between the Government of His Highness the Nizam and the concessionnaires who founded the Hyderabad Deccan Company (Limited) has afforded His Highness's Government the opportunity of a full consideration of those matters.

"His Highness's Government has, after such consideration, arrived at the conclusion that a compromise may properly be effected on the general basis of the provisional heads of arrangement modified in accordance with the suggestions made by Mr. Pollard in reviewing the same, and with such further modifications as you, in your discretion, may think necessary or proper to introduce in the interests of His Highness the Nizam.

"The main terms are those dealing with the provision of £150,000 on deferred shares, and granting two years' extension of the term of prospecting monopoly to the company. These terms His Highness's Government is prepared to accept.

"The other terms are of lesser importance, and also meet with the general approval of the Government, and it is unnecessary to say more as to these save that it is left to your discretion to introduce such additional terms and modifications as Mr. Pollard suggested, or as may commend themselves to your experienced minds.

"The second head of arrangement, however, which treats of the leases and royalties, is so vague that it appears to His Highness's Government that it would be better that it should not be included as a term of the agreement; but His Highness's Government will give its assurance that, as occasion arises, the leases and royalties will be settled with due regard to the interests of the company.

"You are therefore requested to endeavour to have this term excluded, if possible, but you will understand that full discretion is given to you to effect the best possible arrangement on this as on the other matters in question.

"With these expressions of opinion and assent, His Highness's Government feels that it can safely leave the matter in your hands to effect such definite settlement as may to you under the circumstances seem fitting. I have lastly the pleasure of expressing to you the high appreciation which His Highness's Government has of the services so ably rendered by you in carrying on the tedious and difficult negotiations in this matter."—*Times*, June 17.

www.ingramcontent.com/pod-product-compliance
Lightning Source LLC
Chambersburg PA
CBHW022020110726
47901CB00006B/1605

* 9 7 8 3 3 3 7 4 0 3 6 3 8 *